# SHAKE OFF THE DUST

# SHAKE OFF THE DUST

## A Novel of
## Ministry—Romance—Mystery

### Howard Kishpaugh

VANTAGE PRESS
New York

All rights reserved. No part of the 3.5 Sony floppy disk version nor the hard copy manuscript of this novel, *Shake off the Dust*, may be reproduced or transmitted in any other form or by any other means, electronic or mechanical, including photocopy, recording or any information storage and retrieval system now known or invented, without the expressed written permission of the author and/or publisher except in the case of brief quotations embodied in critical articles or reviews written for inclusion in a magazine, newspaper, or broadcast.

*Shake off the Dust*, an original novel, is a work of fiction by Howard Kishpaugh and the product of the author's imagination. He acknowledges that some characters of the novel have been modeled after real people whose names have been changed to protect their privacy. Any recognizable resemblance of actual incidents, locales, events, or persons living or dead is both serendipitous and ancillary.

### FIRST EDITION

All rights reserved, including the right of
reproduction in whole or in part in any form.

Copyright © 1999 by Howard Kishpaugh

Published by Vantage Press, Inc.
516 West 34th Street, New York, New York 10001

Manufactured in the United States of America
ISBN: 0-533-12791-2

Library of Congress Catalog Card No.: 98-90397

0 9 8 7 6 5 4 3 2

# To:

### Carolyn Louise Kishpaugh

My forgiving and loving "preacher's" wife, adoring mother and grandmom to our progenies, without whose understanding and patience I would not have been able to write a postcard, grocery list, church bulletin, nor homily, let alone a novel.

### Irma and Bill Kishpaugh

My Mom and Dad, already years in heaven, who gave my five siblings and me our birthright, loved, inspired, edified disciplined, and "challenged" us as long as they lived.

### John "Jack" Stewart Kishpaugh, Sr.

My hero, champion, exemplar, friend, quadriplegic, and farcical younger sibling brother—founder and director emeritus of the CENTER FOR COMPUTER ASSISTANCE FOR THE DISABLED, INC. (C-CAD), based in Dallas, Texas—whose life of sacrifice, compassion for, benevolence, and dedication to "the halt, the blind, and the lame" and whose lifelong maxim, "The difficult takes a little time; the impossible, a little longer," have been an inspiration and a fountainhead of hope for the discouraged and for me!

### Romeo Castelli

Carpenter, gourmet, and the finest friend a priest could have. He also dwells in heaven!

### My children, grandchildren, siblings, relatives, parishioners of all my missions and parishes, folk of every institution and community, bishops, clergy and laity, friends, nemeses, and indigenous folk!

Those superlative children of God of every race, color, creed, and nationality around this world whom He allowed me the privilege to know and serve in the church and community in forty-three years of ministry in Mississippi, Hawaii, East Africa, Pennsylvania, and the world at large. They frequently, if judiciously, "challenged" my mind, heart, and soul, and always, if subtly, filled my life with love and seldom gave me an excuse to "shake off the dust" and travel on. God bless them and theirs forever.

. . . into whatever city or town ye enter, enquire who in it is worthy; and there abide till ye go thence. And when ye come into a house, salute it. And if the house be worthy in it, let your peace come upon it; but if it is not worthy, let your peace return to you. And whosoever shall not receive you, or hear your words, when ye depart out of that house or city, **SHAKE OFF THE DUST** from your feet.

—St. Matthew 10:12–14 (King James Version)

# Foreword
# by
# The Rev. Fr. Thomas K. Yoshida

*Shake Off the Dust,* a pastoral novel, is not written just from the mind and hands of the author, but from the heart of one who has intensely loved Life and God. It flows from his gratitude for the rich experiences and manifold blessings that both have granted him over his years as layman and priest. He claims that it is no autobiography nor biography, but it is, in many ways, the "criteria" of the man I know. I am humbled and honored to write the Foreword to his "novel" novel.

I met Canon Kishpaugh thirty-five years ago when he was priest in charge of St. Stephen's Church, Wahiawa, Oahu, Hawaii. We worked closely as Episcopal priests in my native state for ten years, and though time, vocation, and distances have separated us through the latter years of our active and retirement labor in the Lord's vineyard, we have remained close supporters of one another's ministries even to this very day.

Father Sud (as many of us know him) has a dedication and devotion to the sacred Priesthood that has both challenged and inspired me. His commitment to God and Church, his energetic, strong, and uncompromisingly strong spiritual insights and pastoral care of the people placed in his charge, have been standards I have attempted to emulate in my own pastoral and academic vocation as a priest. I count him as not only a clergy colleague and a fellow sojourner in the Faith, but as a longtime cherished friend and "brother" in every sense of the word.

The richness of this pastoral writing, embracing as it does ministry, mystery, and romance, touches not only on the human frailty of sin, forgiveness, renewal, the love between a man and a woman, the relationship between a minister and his people, but even more than that, *Shake Off the Dust* is a testimony to how the simple and difficult realities of life in this world are healed and transformed by the power of God's and our Neighbor's continuing love. The mystery factor of the book is unique, mixed as it is with its romance and wholesome sexuality, artfully expressed in the spiritual and humorous arena where they belong. I must not, here, venture any further into those enticing venues of reader curiosity, lest I accidentally give away their conundrums.

Let me just underscore that *Shake Off the Dust* enters the daily life of an individual's struggle for understanding and acceptance. By its inner spiritual tone, the novel provides an abiding sense of hope in what seems very often for many of us, to be hopelessness and a sojourn in futility in our society and world. As Father Dus struggles with his own life and vocation, he reaches out to the people in his charge to proclaim the glory of God, the teaching of His Church, and His unconditional love for them. Dus does this with humility, understanding, and compassion, while trying at the same time to control his own angry vernacular, doubts, pain, frustration, passion, and sensuality, so common to us all. And, as those around him are challenged, touched, healed, and transformed through his ministry and love, so is he challenged, touched, healed, and transformed by their simplicity of soul, stalwart hearts, if sometimes enigmatic and suspicious, friendships. In the end, Dus, his family, friends, and the people under his care, are awakened to the age old reality that even though human life nor love is always understandable, harmonious, nor fair, God and His love are always there and always good!

*Shake Off the Dust* allows the reader to enter in and embrace the author's inner fire, passion, and love for God and people, as I know him. For me, this novel by Canon Kishpaugh is a blessed and renewed opportunity to reconnect with the heart and spirit of my longtime "brother in Christ" and be lifted up to new heights of awareness of, compassion, and love for God's creation. It stimulates my mind, enriches my heart, heals and transforms my spirits, daring me to again and again accept God's, family's, friends', colleagues' love, and the love of all people in every place and every time. It reminds me again, that with the abiding gift of the Holy Spirit, we can all, no matter the tyranny of adversity in and frailty of our own lives, we can reach out to others in hope and love, not only to touch them, but by grace, heal and transform them, and that Jesus does kiss us warty swamp frogs back into princes, princesses, and lovers.

In writing this Foreword, it is my final hope that *Shake Off the Dust* will be for others as it has been for me, an instrument of teaching that enriches and blesses the reader with a cosmic reality of God's pastoral mandate for us to love Him and one another and be inspired to live in "peace and concord," and respond to His even higher calling to become "Peacemakers!"

> —Aloha, Mahalo and Pax,
> The Rev. Thomas K. Yoshida, M. Div.
> May 4, 1998, The 4th Sunday of Easter
> Honolulu, Hawaii

# Preface

The novel *Shake Off the Dust* is about sin, redemption, renewal, pastoral ministry, and romance. It is not a biography! It is a fictional story about an Episcopal priest, whose persona and ventures are developed from real-life folk and events. In writing this story about real life I wrestled with some of the more difficult paradoxes that any religious writer encounters when writing in contemporary times. Especially delicate for a clergyperson of any religious persuasion, be he "liberal" or "conservative," is the question of how much, if any, "earthy" language, "definitive" sexuality, or "spiritual" message should be embodied in a story about man's relationship with God, his failure and redemption.

Swearing: Almost every person in the world on occasion uses "bad" language. Folk who don't are a rarity to be commended. I believe theirs is the better way! I use "earthy" language in this novel to emphasize the reality of anger, frustration, and even crudity that is, sadly, common to the human soul. To have contrition, forgiveness, penance, and amendment of life, the reality of sin, whether it is in language or another dimension of human failure, must be depicted. It appears in this novel in both serious and humorous, if isolated, settings, with the apologies by the author, a clergyman, with definitive human frailties, who is not guiltless of occasional outbursts of unseemly vernacular. Neither the nature of the human beast nor my "barnyard," "marine," "proletarian" gusto justifies or excuses it. I continue to believe while "earthy" language appears sometimes to be a fitting rejoinder for human anger and frustration, it cannot make God happy. It is one of the most obvious signs not only of one's boorishness but also of humankind's poverty of vocabulary and its inability to articulate the English language. Of my own failure in this I recall one of my wise late father's dictums, that "ignorance is only seconded by one's unwillingness to learn."

Sexuality: There are billions of books and magazines in bookstores and libraries that contain vulgar and explicit sexual content. They are read and unblushingly passed around by otherwise decent, if sometimes unctuous, churchgoing, God-fearing folk of every religious stripe. The preponderance of that material is prurient in nature, having nothing to do with the

Sacrament of Holy Marriage and the God-given gift of conjugal sexual consummation and fulfillment. Little of it has to do with the nature of "love" in its purest form, though much of it is vended under that appellation and illusion. There are also thousands of explicit "instructive sexual manuals for married couples" marketed with "Christian" imprimatur and "God's blessing" in "Christian bookstores," with hosts of biblical quotes, emphasizing the value, emotion, and beauty of nuptial intercourse and commending the patience, consideration, and respect that a wife and husband in love must exhibit to each other in that powerful and necessary aspect of marriage if their marriages are to be happy and lasting. These works are helpful, of course, but even more sexually descriptive and pictorial in sexual content than most secular publications.

My remorseless intent in this writing, as a priest who has been called upon many times to counsel marriages, is to put sexuality openly within the Sacrament of Marriage, where it belongs, as good and blessed by God. The few forthright sexual discussions, innuendoes, and guileless sexual experiences found in this writing will not titillate those with prurient interest and expectations. They are but a reflection of the author's belief in the ageless biblical doctrine and historical Judeo/Christian moral theology about love and marriage. I have for years longed to put into a "novel" novel, in contrast to other texts, a vivid expression of sex as a Christian sacramental consummation between a spiritually committed couple, husband and wife, to wit: that sexual intercourse between them is a beautiful, necessary outward and physical sacramental sign of the inward and spiritual grace that makes them one in union with God and each other. To that end, the poignant sex in my novel is meant to convey the true meaning of the mutuality, beauty, gentility, respect, patience, tenderness, love, and, yes, even fun that are paramount to a husband and wife "making love" and that it is truly a beautiful gift given of God to humankind for the bonding of male and female and for the procreation of the human species. It is that intrinsic natural, deep, essential, physical need and consequence of love that attracts, joins, and binds man and woman together as one after they have made vows to one another before God and witnesses to be husband and wife "until death do us part!" It is the fervent prayer of this author that neither God nor friend will judge it otherwise and that it will be helpful to many husbands and wives who look for openness, joy, fulfillment, and fun in their nuptial sexuality. If readers are looking for vulgar references to body parts and titillating sexual episodes in this writing, they will be sadly disappointed. As a man married to a loving, fun, and forbearing wife of forty-six years and a priest confessor and counselor, I know intimately of the difficulties, joys, and vagaries of sex between a man and woman. I know it to be the most powerful, enigmatic, divisive, yet fulfilling and lovely human emotion that exists in marriage. It has tragic consequences if it is not used for loving union and/or procreation, and it is the most beautiful of God-given experiences that a husband and his wife can know, if it is. It is true good people make bad mistakes with their sexuality and many marriages have failed. Blessed are those who have not made mistakes, and blessed are those who have and been forgiven by God and each other. As to mistake and failures, it is not for me, a sinful man, to judge others. I leave that commission to a merciful and understanding God. I do hope, however, that failed marriages will be renewed through penance and forgiveness into a bond of peace and beautiful oneness. As a pastor, I pray that marriage will always be a lifelong sacramental union between wives and husband and that sexual intercourse, a God-created gift of life, will soon be popularized in both fiction and real life as the sacramental means by which all marriages of men and woman are consummated and "the two are made ONE!" The dehumanizing and despiritualizing of humankind, whether they be women, men, or children, as sexual objects is an abomination before God and decent people and, if not abrogated, will eventually destroy a civil society!

The mix of the homilies with romance and mystery in this novel is intended to reflect the main character's vocation and duty as a priest and to edify in simple fashion the significant days in the Christian Calendar and how they relate to the birth, life, ministry, death, and resurrection of Jesus Christ. They are in no way meant to reflect on any religion's expression that differs with the Christian tradition. The rest of the message and/or lesson found here is to suggest how we might live in contrition, forgiveness, and amendment of life, resolve the conflicts and mysteries that divide us as human beings, and do the will of God (however that is perceived by spiritual people) so we might live in love, peace, and harmony with him and each other as his children. If there are good lessons and helpful messages to be learned from this novel, they are the gifts of God, history, religious doctrine, moral casuistry, time, and the witness of heroic, unselfish people who were willing to die in the arenas of history to bring to humanity, justice, and truth. The less than satisfactory lessons/messages are wholly the blame of the author. I leave it to God to pass judgment on the difference.

If in any way in this writing I have offended the decency of my friends, family, honest critics, or any of any particular race, creed, nationality, or color, I confess my sin and refer you only to God, who is already aware of my flagrant follies. He knows that this writing was never intended to dishonor him or anyone of good conscience. To that end, I hope my readers will enjoy, weep, laugh, and go away from this endeavor believing that God loves them and that I do, too! In one of my most cherished New Testament lines, Jesus says, "In as much as ye have done it unto the least of these, my brothers, ye have done it unto me." I hope in some measure I have done that in *Shake Off the Dust*!

# Prologue

It has been a cold, harsh winter, but spring had now come to the mountain. Though it was still chilly with patches of snow laying on a warming earth, the weather was bright and invigorating, and it seemed an excellent day to work on a building project. A middle-aged man, clad in a stained and faded Penn State sweatshirt, shabby jeans, and muddy boots, sat at the controls of a Caterpillar backhoe, cautiously maneuvering its shovel bucket deep inside a trench he was excavating. The extended hydraulic leveling plates on the powerful machine assured him that he could proceed with the project along the damp hillside, with maximum safety. He was not a heavy-equipment operator by trade, but he handled the machinery with ease and confidence. Clawing at the hard ground inside the trench with the steel teeth of the shovel, he filled the bucket, raised it out of the channel, and deposited the loose dirt along its edge. He had been doing that maneuver for hours, intent on building an outside septic system to accommodate future plumbing facilities for the log cabin located along the rim of the forest, several yards above the area where he was working.

Suddenly, something ominous in the ditch seized his attention. He quickly raised the bucket, rested it beside the trench, turned off the machine's engine, jumped into the trench, and pawed frantically at the loose soil. In just moments, he exposed something wrapped in old, decaying kitchen table oilcloth. He removed the fabric to discover a human cadaver lying rigidly supine, its skeletal hands, folded as if in prayer, resting flat upon its midsection. To the machine operator, who had seen many human body burials, the cadaver resembled a dead person whose body had been neatly prepared by a meticulous mortician for a funeral wake, without the benefit of a coffin. An old rusty shotgun lay beside the corpse. The digger did not touch it.

The corpse's skinless skull, with its deep hollow eyes, protruding stained teeth, and traces of wispy gray hair, stared forlornly up at the perplexed digger. A disintegrating red-and-black checked jacket, remnants of patched denim overalls, and rotten boots partially clothed the skeleton.

"What the heck is this?" the digger muttered, as he lifted his tattered Marine Corps baseball cap from his head and wiped the sweat from his face.

"I wonder why this creature is buried here like this, while all those other dead people are supposed to be buried in boxes over there in the church cemetery. This wasn't any proper burial! Something's wrong here!"

Convinced that his immediate duty was to stop his digging and report his find to the local sheriff, the digger climbed out of the ditch and moved toward his Jeep. A rifle discharged. He heard and felt a bullet whistle very close to his behind and ricochet off the steep plate of the Caterpillar. Without a thought, he dove front first into the open trench, landing atop the half-clad cadaver. Opening his eyes, he scowled into its hollow eye sockets and large teeth, just inches from his face. It appeared to be laughing at him. He did not know why he said it, but his sense of reverence for the departed, mixed with the indignity of his dilemma, forced an impromptu response. "I'm sorry, friend, to be crowding you in your repose," he apologized to the grinning skull, "but our meeting like this is not all that damned amusing!"

Then out of total frustration and anger, the Reverend Dus Byrd Habak, the former dean of St. Andrew's Cathedral, bellowed, "Mare's marbles!"—a synonym the Episcopal priest often used for "horse manure" when he was angry, since refining his barnyard and Marine Corps vocabulary. "Good God. Now some loony, gun toting mountain yokel is out there thinking, 'Dat preacha isa fr'aking grav' robbin' parvert, en I'ma gonna tetch 'im a goldarn lezzon!' He caught me digging here and is going to put me in a grave up here, too!

"Lord," he prayed, greatly discomfited by the sensation of the cold skeleton against him, "I know that you're tired of enduring my profanity and, honest, I've tried to do better, but this corn whisky mission field the bishop sent me into has gotten to be a war zone, and I've had enough of that 'horse manure!' I was willing to come up to these hills, do mission work for you, 'turn my other cheek,' and all that zealous stuff, but it wasn't part of the deal that this 'shepherd' had to turn his other paleface heinie cheek so some pissed-off 'sheep' could bruise it again! I'm not a wimp, Lord," the annoyed cleric continued to entreat, "but this pasture has more wolves than sheep! These deranged ridge-running muttons need a gunnery sergeant with a pit bull to herd them, for God's sake! I know you and our friend Ollikut are weary of my obnoxious backsliding, but if this plight I've been in ever since I came to these hills isn't soon resolved, I'm shaking the dust off this sorely maimed ass, running off this mountain, and taking up some less menacing holy work like selling Bibles to pulpit pounders!"

That impious and churlish caveat, for which he was soon repentant and for which he heard no Godly response, was made by Father Habak the first Tuesday after Easter in the month of April. This story begins in middle autumn of the previous year.

# SHAKE OFF THE DUST

# 1

The Very Reverend Dus Byrd Habak had moved fairly rapidly up the ecclesiastical ladder. A tenure in the mission field, the rectorship of a large parish, then the call to be the dean of St. Andrew's Cathedral, all inside of ten years, had been almost meteoric in the generally slow ascendancy of parochial priests in the Church of England, the "mother" of the Anglican communion, of which the U.S. Episcopal Church was a prominent daughter member. Dean Habak had also been elected or appointed a member and/or chairman of a few national and diocesan committees, departments, and various ecumenical councils and community public service boards. Once a reserved farm lad, a less than "gung-ho" Marine Corps veteran, an unrenowned high school and college football player, and the proprietor of a small engineering firm, Dean Habak never quite understood why he had advanced in the priesthood as he had, nor why he had deserved the recognition accorded him in the church and the secular community. He saw himself as an unimpressive, if convicted, hard worker and intrepid man; he hoped the accolades had come because of his love for God and his people, and not because of his long friendship with the bishop of the diocese of the Shenandoah.

He and his family had enjoyed the "ministry" and been happy most of the time, considering the social and financial limitations of the vocation. The years had been mostly good for him and his wife, Virginia, and their teenage children, Dustin and Ellen, and he had not, until recently, had any cause for serious complaint about clergy life. They had had the usual complaints and ups and downs characteristic of all families, but, in general, he felt he had given his best as a priest and had been treated fairly by his parishioners, in return. He believed he had been adequately paid for his ministerial services, and had never complained to his vestries nor bishop about his stipend, allowances, and housing. He knew from the beginning when he went off to seminary that the priesthood would be a sacrificial commitment like many service-oriented vocations were, and that "God would provide." Of course, there were times when he and Ginnie wished they'd had a better cash flow to cover some little extravagances, but that longing was shared by most of the parents he knew; he was content with the old adage that quipped, "If wishes were horses, beggars would ride." They had always had enough resources for yearly vacations, birthdays, and holiday celebrations. In fact, his parishioners through the years had cared for their well-being and were generally appreciative of his pastoral efforts.

Up until Ginnie's and Dusty's violent deaths, his ministry, family, and friends had made his life both bounteously and spiritually rewarding, filling him with a joy that was inexplicable. He had known very good days and reveled in them. But now he believed that with two of his treasured family dead and gone, he and Ellen alone, nothing could ever again fill up his life. Months of grief, despair, bitterness, and depression since their deaths had consumed his whole being, and the only joy he knew now resulted from the brief memories. His disposition had radically changed, and he now reflected on his life and vocation with acrimony and regret. He had allowed his physical and mental poise to deteriorate, smoking and drinking more than he ever allowed himself in years. His self-pity had all but destroyed his usually keen ability to handle his duties. He was, by his own estimation and descriptive analysis of himself, a "certified twenty-karat dipstick," if not a clergy bum

• • •

Today, Dean Habak sat ashamed and disconsolate in his bishop's office, convinced that his years of ministry had been a monumental and tragic waste of his life, and now they were all over. His superior, the Right Reverend Peter Mueller, D.D., had reluctantly ordered him in for a "boss-to-employee" no-nonsense talk about the facts of clergy life. Dus could not help being painfully aware of his bishop's deep, southern, scolding voice. The senior cleric was admonishing his priest and friend in a room with splendid acoustics, and there was no doubt that the dejected Father Habak could hear precisely what the dignified and articulate primate was saying to him.

"You've got to get out of this breast-beating, self-pitying mood you're in, Dus," Bishop Mueller rebuked him. "I'm beginning to lose my patience with the cathedral people bitching to me about the lousy quality of services, administration, and pastoral care you are giving them. They sincerely believe they have given you enough time to get over your grief and get on with what cathedral deans are supposed to do for a living. They tell me that they have been patient, sympathetic, and understanding about your loss and pain, but they now feel you just don't give a tinker's hoot about them anymore. It's hard for me to believe that of you, Dus, but they tell me that your anguish over Ginnie and Dusty has made you insensitive to their needs, and that you spend all your time mucking around in self-pity, reflecting negatively on them as a spiritual force in this city and diocese."

These words did not come easy to this prominent and personable man who loved Dus Habak almost as a son and had been his good friend for many years. Indeed, Dus had become the dean of St. Andrew's Cathedral because of the bishop's urging. He had had great confidence in this priest, who had served him, the church, and the community so well in recent years.

"God Almighty, Dus, what has happened?" he interrogated. "You know how I feel about you! When I ordained you, it was one of my proudest moments. I thought you would do a great job for the church, and you have up until now. Where, in the name of all that is holy, are you allowing your sorrow to take you?"

Dus slouched in a chair in front of the bishop's desk, his head bowed in stony silence, nervously paring his fingernails. He knew that he had disappointed the good man who had convinced him to give up his engineering business, go to seminary, and become a priest, and who had guided his ministry through both good and bad times. A tear rolled down his cheek. He said nothing.

"We've all had our troubles, Father," the bishop continued. "You knew from the beginning that you couldn't count on priestly immunity from the personal tragedy that afflicts all people. And you know that no one who knew Ginnie and Dusty agonized more than I did when they were killed. I wept and shook my fist at God like a spoiled brat, and I have hated the dreadful plight you are in. I adored your family like it was my very own. But one must go on with life. A person can't forget, but a priest can't allow himself the luxury of wallowing at the trough of grief. What happened would be a horrendous thing for the most stalwart of men, but how many sermons have you preached about death and how Christians must overcome the terrible tragedies that happen to them in life? How many times have you told parishioners that their faith, time, good memories, and the love of God, family, and friends would heal their wounds and fill up the voids left in their lives when their loved ones dies?

"My heart aches for you, Brother, but I am now telling you as your friend and, whether you like it or not, your boss that you have to get off your self-pitying butt, stand up like a man, and be the priest that God, I, and everyone else knows you to be. You won't like me saying this, Father Habak, but neither Ginnie nor Dusty would like your whimping out on Ellen's nor your life."

Dus rose out of his chair like a catapult, his face on fire, eyes burning, neck veins protruding against his stiff collar, his knuckles white. "Why you self-righteous, pompous bas . . . !" he cried.

"Don't say nor think about doing it, son! I am still your bishop. Sit down before you do something you'll regret. You're twenty years younger and twenty pounds heavier than I am, but if it will get that debilitating grief out of your soul, I am tempted to allow you to stomp the crap out of me. But, know, the only thing you'll accomplish by doing that is hating yourself and making me the bloodiest bishop in the Anglican church!"

Dus retreated to his chair, sweat rolling down his face and tears welling in his eyes. He had been a muscular six-foot, 210-pound, forty-year-old man a few months ago, but now he felt like a mere shadow. He didn't know what to say. Everything his superior had just said was true. He had known for some time he was no longer a good priest. He expected that the cathedral people would sooner or later lower the boom on him for failing to come to grips with his life, after sporting platitudes to other people about how they should conduct theirs. He apologized. "I'm sorry, Bishop. I don't know why I did that. God knows, I would never hurt you."

"I know, Dus, and it's OK. I am sorry I said that about Ginnie and Dusty. You're right! I guess I haven't graduated from my army days. I can still be a jackass too! Would you like to take a break from this stuff for a minute and have some coffee or soda?"

"No thanks, sir. What I need is something to quench the thirst in my soul."

"Look, Dus, you and I have been through a lifetime of stuff. You're a vet with battle holes in your gut, a gridiron beast, and a businessman. You know about life! And me? I'm just a worn-out Army padre with colonel's chickens and an old basketball jock hanging in my memoir case to remind me of the glory days. It has not always been easy for us in this vocation that some people think is an easy racket! But very few of us have had to endure what you have, with Ginnie and Dusty dying the way they did and Ellen left without her mother and brother! My heart aches for you, Dus, but you and I both have an obligation to go on with our lives and do the work that God called us to do. And only the tough, recalcitrant, caring shepherds like us are going to make it better for the sheep God has called you and me to protect from the predatory wolves in this bad world. You can't leave it, no matter the ache in your heart and soul at the moment. Be ticked off at me all you want, son, but I am not going to give you a chaplain's chit to get out of God's army!"

"What do you want me to do, Boss?" Dus queried, not able to envision his future. At the moment, he just wanted to get out of the bishop's office, the cathedral, and the city. He really wanted out of life, but he knew that was stupid, with his obligation to his much-alive daughter. Ellen was a student at the priory school and in the safekeeping of the sisters there; nevertheless, he had to think of her future. She would have none without him!

The bishop did not hesitate. Dus had surmised, when the bishop called him in, that the pragmatic administrator already had a short-term solution to Dus' long-term problems. "The cathedral folk are not merciless people, Dus. They don't want you hurt any more than you have been. They are eager to have us resolve your and their problem. I suggested to them that you submit your resignation for reasons that will reflect on neither you nor them. They agreed to accept it with deep regret, pay you the remaining stipend left on your contract, and give you a testimonial dinner with a generous gift of appreciation."

Yeah, I bet they will, Dus thought, seething inside himself, then regretting the sarcasm the moment it crossed his mind. My God, my cynicism has been so ugly of late, he admitted. Actually, the congregation of St. Andrews had, in fact, been very good to him during his tenure with them, and they were especially kind and solicitous when Ginnie and Dusty died. No one could have asked for a more sympathetic group of parishioners. It was not their fault that their kindnesses and sympathy had not been adequate enough to comfort him. He simply allowed that there are just some things that folk can't do for a person crushed and defeated by bitterness and heartache, no matter how hard they try.

"Canon Burkey has an idea," Bishop Mueller offered, "that I think might help you to get your life in order and still do some good work for the church and diocese."

"What idea?" Dus carped, hearing Ed Burkey's name.

"About eighty miles or so southeast of here, maybe twenty-five miles west of Staunton, there's a small village up in the Appalachians, nestled in a valley between the Cutty and Blue Mountains along Cedar Creek, called

Joshuatown. The Episcopal Church has never made a mission effort in that area, but Ed Burkey says there are about three hundred families scattered up and down the valley that don't seem to be committed to the Presbyterians and Baptists, the only other denominations in town. Ed thinks some of those folk might be open to our kind of ministry."

Burkey the Turkey, our dauntless diocesan evangelist and assistant to the bishop, Dus grumbled to himself. What would that big bore canon and zealot for the impossible know about mountain mission work? He bit his cynical lip. Actually, Canon Burkey had a good record of developing missions throughout the church, in spite of his being, in Dus' judgment, an ecclesiastical nerd and ethereal pain in the tail. "What kind of place is it, and what would I have to start with?" Dus grumbled.

"It has a few stores, a school, bank, county courthouse, town hall, sheriff, nearby lumber mill, coal operation, and state forest and recreational park. Ed says it also has a well-equipped health clinic that the local folk built a few years ago with some federal HEW funds. A volunteer M.D. goes up there from Staunton every other weekend or so to take care of the basic medical needs of the local folk. Staunton is a city of about a hundred thousand people, not far from the university, which would be more accessible than here, for your larger needs."

Dus sighed. I'm being sent off to the "boondocks," he groused to himself, so I can't do any further damage to the holy church in my present state of mind? Mare's marbles! "What church and living facilities would I have?" he asked.

"Ed says there's a power line that goes the distance of the valley, so there is electricity for those who can afford to use it. I have never been up there, myself, but he claims there's a livable cabin right next to a small unused church building on the Blue Mountain side that the people said they would loan to us without cost. It is pretty pristine and rugged, among some good, individualistic, hard-working, if economically strapped folk, but if you can get something off the ground and going for the diocese, we will talk about acquisition, renovation, and expansion, later. How about it, Dus? Will you take a shot at it for me?"

Dus really didn't feel up to making decisions right now—neither for the church nor for himself. He had always tried to please his bishop, by going places and doing everything he had been asked. He supposed that he would do it again. It was a wise prelate and caring friend who spoke to him now, asking for his help. And, Dus believed, his bishop was really trying to rejuvenate his wounded and angry priest. He knew the kind, former chaplain loved him as a soldier and wanted him to be reclaimed for himself, Elly, and the church. "I'll go, Bishop," he said. "When would you like me to start?"

"I'll tell the sisters at the priory school to allow Elly a few days' vacation so you both can go off on a little outing together. Get through the resignation thing at the cathedral first, then move your furniture into the diocesan storerooms until you feel you need it. You won't need a lot up there, for now. Sell your Olds and I will provide you with a new Jeep that will be more adequate for the terrain. The diocese will provide car allowance, pension, insurance, will pay for all of Elly's expenses at the priory, and will give you an adequate stipend. And don't get that sacrificial look on your face. You're worth it and you will earn it. Keep me informed of your needs and I'll get them to you."

"OK, Bishop. I'll go up there, but keep Ed Burkey off my back. I don't want him overseeing my therapy. I report only to you. I'll resign from the cathedral this week, get my stuff out, spend a few days with Elly, and be up in Joshuatown in a couple weeks."

"Thanks so much, Dus," the bishop said with deep sincerity. "In spite of your differences with Ed, he is a good missionary. But I know he's not your type, so you'll report directly to me. This move will be good for you—maybe rewarding—but it's not your therapy. It will be good for the diocese, too! All that being said, I'm not going to con you, Dus. It's going to be a challenge!"

Father Habak's forehead burned as he pondered that statement. Cynicism poured into his veins again like liquid acid. "I'd like to respond to that, Bishop, without your taking offense."

The bishop felt the acrimony. "Go ahead and vent, Dus, if it will cleanse your soul, I know you're hurting, but keep it civil. I'm your friend, but if you have a mind to direct hostility at me, forget it! You are not to take advantage of our friendship nor heap abuse on me!"

"I am not angry at you, but you use the word 'challenge' as though it is some kind of combat ribbon and honor badge a priest should bust his gut to wear on his chest! No offense, but I've had it up to my Kraut ass with challenges, with 'hallowed' words and pious platitudes about how rewarding this 'Lord's work' vocation is!"

"Be careful of what you're saying and how you're saying it, Father!"

"Yeah, well, Bishop, I'm sick to death of hearing people saying what a beautiful, challenging sojourn it is, being a priest, saving people's souls. Challenge! This vocation is defeat after defeat. It's a shitty war where a priest struggles every day and night with the devil within his own soul. It's frustration, disappointment, and pain inside your heart, while smiling at people on the outside. People's souls, Bishop! Let God save them! It's his church, not mine! Why should I make the effort anymore? It's hard enough for me to save my own soul in a world that has butchered my wife and son, thrown cold water on the love I have had for God's people, and reduced me to a zero of a man.

"To hell with a world of religious hypocrites who praise the priest with one side of the mouth while joking about him with the other side. Send me into the wilderness in sackcloth and ashes if you think it will make me a better priest, Bishop, but don't give me a lot of ethereal dung about 'challenges.' Life itself is nothing, as I have seen and known it, but a damn challenge."

Dus stopped. He was breathing hard, with tears streaming down his face. He wiped them away with the back of his hand. Bishop Mueller looked with empathy and love at his longtime friend. He hated to see him like this, but knew that he needed this catharsis. He also understood. How often had he felt the same way through the years, knowing the pain and frustration of the vocation? But this priest has had his wife and son snatched from him in the prime of his life, and is aching in his heart and soul like a wounded soldier who just lost his best comrade. The bishop knew his priest well. He knew the man had relished and loved the priesthood, attacked and cleaned up sin in people's lives with the passion of a herdsman cleaning out a stable full of manure, repaired human souls like a mechanic renewing a beloved old car. He knew it was the deep pain in Dus' heart that now accentuated the sporadic difficult times of his ministry. He let Dus continue to vent, listening compassionately to his frustrated cleric. "Go on Dus; get it out of your soul. I understand."

"How can you understand what I feel about losing Ginnie and Dusty? Alright, boss man, I'll go into those mountains because I don't know what else to do, nor how to be anything other than a priest. But don't try to make me feel good by mouthing pontifical gibberish about all the good I am going to do for mother church. You're not talking to a breast-beating monk, whose cincture is knotted up in poverty and chastity. You're talking here to an Episcopal priest who has loved and bedded down a good wife and procreated two beautiful kids. You're talking to a man who has enjoyed worthless material and ecclesiastical success, and unearned accolades, who celebrated the mass at a marble altar. A fatuous patron of the arts and museums, who luxuriated in complimentary perks, including a country club membership and first-class seats on airplanes, given because I wear a clerical collar and pontificate eloquently from a marble pulpit, at hotel podiums, and at civic forums. And now that clerical wizard is losing his pulpit, altar, forums, and free perks because none of them, not you, nor God, can bring back his wife and son from the dead!"

The bishop sat rigidly, his patience beginning to wane. "Easy, Dus! Vent if you must, but you are getting very close to being accusatory and uncivil with me!"

Hurt and acrimony kept exuding from Father Dus Habak, and he spoke as if he had not heard the warning his bishop had spoken. "Challenges, Bishop? I've been challenged every damn day since you sent me to missions where the only 'amens' I got for my prayers were from the bats in the belfry and the pigs under the chancel floor, while the pigeons pooped on my head from the rood screen! Where poor folk wore blankets to church because there was no heat, and acolytes fainted and bloodied their heads on the altar because they were weak from hunger! Now you want me to go back to that for rehabilitation. I've been there and done that! And in your cathedral I've been maligned and praised, called everything from a son of a bitch to a saint. I've preached the gospel, tended the sick, the well, the rich, the poor, depraved and famous, equally. I've been ridiculed, threatened, and voted down because I didn't agree with the body politics, whether in church or state. I've listened to laity and clergy argue about 'high and low church' and didn't give a twit about a 'deep and convicted church' that Christ might have felt at home in! And I wept when folk denied their tithe to God or left his church because of my recalcitrant convictions, stupid mistakes and judgments, and words and deeds that offended them. But I have loved them! I have loved the church, her saints, sinners, and my vocation with a passion. I cried when they hurt, and felt their pain until my heart was so filled up it almost bled at the altar when I said prayers for them. I spent hours trying to mend their broken marriages and lives, and tried to get them to love God and each other. I have administered the sacraments to drunks, ingrates, and prostitutes. I've walked the corridors of hospitals, old folk's homes, and jails in the wee hours of the night until the stench of pain, death, and deprivation of body and spirit made me sick enough to throw up in my car on the way home!

"I neglected my wife and son for this illustrious, convoluted, misunderstood, denominational bastion of liberal politics, social engineering, theological confusion, and clerical anarchy, and now they are dead and gone, wiped out of my life by a drunken creep who couldn't see goose shit on his glasses, let alone Ginnie's car coming down the street. Please don't offer me 'challenges,' Bishop. Just send me where you want me to go without a lot of pious platitudes about the honor of the sojourn!" Dus stopped, sobbing in his hands.

The bishop, if he would have been any other kind of person, would have been crushed and furious by Dus' combative and cynical vendetta against the church. Now, he only looked with compassion on Dus, tears in his own eyes, understanding the depth of agony in his soul. How often have I had all those feelings, he asked himself, and never could verbalize them as this sorely wounded priest, husband, and father has? He let Dus rest for several minutes, then spoke softly to his weeping and sweating friend. "Are you finished venting your heart and soul, my brother in Christ?"

Dus sat silent for several minutes and then looked at his bishop, with red eyes, a wet smudged face, and an exhausted countenance. "Yes, Bishop, and I am so sorry! I did not mean to hurt you with my foppish conceit and stupid anger. I've never had a better friend than you! In reality, I've had a good ministry, and the people have been good to my family through the years! I'm ashamed that I've failed you, grieved, and felt sorry for myself. I know I have let you and the church down."

"You have not failed anyone but yourself, Dus. You needed to get the venom out of your heart and soul, and I'm the best and only one who ought to hear it. It's over now, Father. I love you and I know you'll recover from all this anguish, to be a fine priest again. You'll do well out there in the mountain. And, please Dus, never think I'm asking you to go up there for a lot of self-imposed discipline and therapy. I want you to go because God and I expect you to build up the church and shepherd the people in that place, for him! And if some of those good folk don't understand nor receive you when you knock on the doors of their houses, hearts, and souls, do as the Lord said—just 'shake off the dust' from your feet and go on to the next house. You are not to go up there to grab folk out of the back pew of other denominations. If there are still some folk there not yet committed to God or his church, you're going to get some of them for him, sooner or later, with your love, patience, and ministry. And I know when you have them in the pasture and sheepfold pen, you'll shepherd them well!"

He rose from his desk, went around it, and took Dus' hand. Dus stood up and the two priests hugged each other. "Let's pray, Dus," the bishop suggested, and the friends both bowed their heads and prayed. Then, as Dus stood silent, the bishop made a sign of the cross on his own and on Dus' forehead. "God forgive us, and bless you, Dus, in the name of the Father, Son, and Holy Ghost! Now get out of this ecclesiastical war room and go take that mountain for God and me," a sniffing Colonel Mueller commanded the former P.F.C. "And while you're at it, Marine, clean up your fox hole language. It's downright gruesome when you're angry, and not fitting for a man who has always said he hates cussing! It's not fitting that anyone should use bad language, but it is most unbecoming of a priest. Work on it, Father!"

"Yes sir, Colonel." Father Habak smiled, saluted, turned, and left the bishop's office, feeling a little more like a better man.

# 2

Father Habak arrived at his new mission late one cold night in middle October. He had no idea, when he drove up through Joshuatown, whether there would be anyone to meet him. The bishop hadn't said, and he hadn't cared. He just wanted to find the vicarage, get some sleep, and get on with life. He easily found the rustic old house about three miles up the valley from town and settled in for the night. There had been no parish "welcome wagon" to greet him.

As he looked out the window the next morning, the word "challenge" turned his reflections back to the conversation he had with his bishop weeks before. It had not been the best of experiences. He had acted like an egotistical whimpering jackass in front of a gracious man who truly wanted to help him, but it had been a healing discussion for him, and it provided him with an opportunity to recover and start life afresh. Realistically, he expected to continue to hurt deeply over the events of the past several months for some time, and his immediate reaction to annoyances was not likely to dissipate quickly in this place, where he considered himself to have been exiled. He lit up a cigarette and peered out through a frost-covered window of the musty cabin that would be his home for the distant future. "Mare's marbles," he groused. "Why did it have to snow again?"

From where he stood, he could see down the long valley and up to the crest line of the Cutty Mountains. Three cedar trees, standing alone, jutted up from a barren patch of ground at the very top of the ridge. He wondered how those stalwart evergreens ever managed to take root, grow, and survive in that lonely, harsh place. What possible quirk of nature, he asked himself, could have deposited those seeds so high on that mountaintop, enabling their small shoots to resist the severe cold and howling winds that roared over those peaks and swept down the slopes to the valley below? Then again, what, he asked himself, trying to conjure up an analogy, quirk of nature deposited the likes of me in this godforsaken place? He knew, and supposed God had a purpose for those trees as he must have had for him. Maybe there's an obscure symbol in those trees standing strong against the harsh elements up there on that isolated barren pinnacle. I wish I knew the secret of their strength and stamina, and could appropriate it for myself. "The Lord works in mysterious ways" was not a theological platitude wasted on Father Habak. He knew that reality when God grabbed him, a farm-boy senior in the local high school, by the scruff of the neck and sent him off to war, college, and seminary. He had had a lot of bizarre things happen to him on his sojourn in the "Lord's vineyard," and it never ceased to amaze him that God enabled him to do them. That was a mystery to him, not to be taken lightly.

He turned from the window and stood at the hearth. He kicked spitefully at a simmering log, making sparks fly and flames come alive. That tempered him. Gazing into the fire, he reflected that life has always been full of mystery. Man's inclination to stare into a fire was a mystery. Since the beginning of time, he ruminated, people have kicked, poked at, and talked to burning logs, looking into flames, contemplating life, meditating on things material and spiritual, planning a myriad of benefits for, if not ruthless mayhem against, humankind. There's a magnetism about a fire that draws a man into it, he mused. The Neanderthals, Romans, Greeks, Europeans, Asians, and primitive and civilized people of every era, nationality, creed, and color have always mysteriously gazed into a fire. What is it about a burning fire other than its light and warmth that reaches out to human beings, in some way, allaying their fears, calming their spirit, stimulating their thoughts, and helping to resolve problems? Even when one is very alone, as I am now, he meditated, a log fire seems to alleviate isolation. I guess as long as we have a log fire and the occasion to look into it, we will think about life and turn our backs to its warmth. Yeah, he thought, that's a mystery!

Sunlight edged over the mountain to the east and beamed through the window. Dus recalled how he had always relished the early mornings when no unwelcome noises interrupted his thoughts or his tranquillity. He had always loved the chirping and crowing of early birds, the soft sounds of awakening animals in the barn, and the hushed falling of rain and snow. He stared out the window again and ogled the mountain. He was impressed with its great size, majesty, and natural beauty, thinking that if it could talk, it could tell wondrous compelling stories about God's handiwork—about his giving new life to vegetation and animals in the spring; providing food from the earth in the summer; turning green into brilliant, beautiful multicolors in the autumn; and dispatching snow that would eventually melt into water flowing into the valley to refresh the earth.

Reality awakened him. So this is my new parish, he sighed. It was as far as his eyes could see, over hill and dale and beyond, and down to Joshuatown. Why do people live in a place like this?—broken-down shacks with no plumbing nor electricity, outhouses, kerosene lamps, wood stoves, and hundreds of yards between neighbors, who have to depend on their truck patches and timeworn villages like Joshuatown for the staples of life. Why would his bishop be inspired to send a priest into a place like this? Well, he has, Father Habak, he groaned to himself, and you know the answer to that question. So quit bitching and get your priestly butt out there on that frozen "sawdust trail."

He dressed, went to the outhouse, pumped water from the well, made some coffee, and inspected his new abode. Not bad, he thought, even if small and rustic. There was plenty of wood for the fireplace and a drum of kerosene for the stove. Bread, along with canned, jarred, and dried goods were stashed in the larder. Butter, milk, and some fresh vegetables and fruit were stored in an old coldbox chilled with a huge block of ice. The living room had a lot of space, with adequate furniture. The loft bedroom was cozy, with a dresser, closet, and a bed with a comfortable mattress, made up for him with clean linens and blankets when he had arrived last night. He had gone to bed early after making a fire, eating a can of peaches, and praying to God, before drifting off to sleep, to forgive him for his cynicism, anger, and failures, and to take away his painful memories of Ginnie's and Dusty's deaths and help him to forget—especially to forget, because forgetting was the hardest part of his life right now. But now he had to get on with life. He had to admit, for all his complaining about Canon Burkey, he had, with the assistance of some kind local folk, made things pretty good for himself at the cabin. He had slept well and was ready to work.

But where do I start? he asked himself. I doubt these mountain people ever heard of the Episcopal Church, and wouldn't understand it if they did. It's hard enough to explain it to Episcopalians, for God's sake. What do people really know about any church, except that it gives them comfort when they need it? We zealous, pompous clergy, ladened with our own sins, think people love to hear about sin, about how God created the earth, about how he loves them, and about how he sent Jesus to tell them how they could better get along with him and each other. But so what? They know as much about that stuff as we do. How do you get people to believe that going to church is good for them—good for them to learn a lot of stuff that seems illogical to them? How does one get these poor isolated folk in these back woods to believe that God is putting an Episcopal Church here in these back woods to save them, when they have survived for generations without pompous, academic, long-winded clergy telling them how to do it? How does a smoking, drinking, screwed-up, cantankerous, black-suited, white-collared pulpit pounder like me, with my record of doubt and faithlessness, convince them that God and Episcopalians care for them in a place like this? How do I teach Christian doctrine to people who have their own doctrine of survival and have done that pretty well? How do I talk Christian discipline to people who, if they did not have exceptional discipline of their own, would not last six months in this place? Where do I start? Dear Christ, how do I start?

A lot of questions Dus couldn't begin to answer. Of course, he could not. He had little energy nor the will to start. As hard as he had asked God last night to help him forget, he could not help thinking about Ginnie, Dusty, and Elly. Those recurring memories did not encourage him for his work in this place. He began to reminisce. No one could have asked for a better family than his. Ginnie, in fear and trepidation, had become a clergy wife and been a good one. Dusty, at fourteen, was husky, a good athlete, and was just beginning to be outwardly proud that Dus was his dad. Elly, who was the spitting image of her mother, had soft brunette hair, and a pretty face with a smile that could knock the grouch off a man's face in seconds. She was not yet the beauty her mother was, but when either one of them passed by a person, smiled, and hugged, the whole world seemed a better place. Father Habak used to refer to this wife and children as St. Virginia, St. Dustin, and St. Ellen because they just seemed to have that kind of quality. He often thought of them as a "holy trinity," and even if Ginnie vied not to be on any altar guild or sing in parish choirs, she did Trojan work at parish rummage sales and bazaars, took good care of him and the kids, and said "grace" at every sumptuous meal she put on the rectory table. Dusty was always in a snapshot with a smudged face and dirty "sneaks," in a football uniform, or an altar boy cassock. Elly, well, she was tenaciously unholy a lot of times, but as sweet as St. Angelica. No man could have gotten more joy from a family. Yes, the Lord had blessed him with them, but why, oh why, did he take them away from him so soon? God Almighty! Well, it happened, he thought, and that's it. I lost 'em, 'cept Elly; I lost my cathedral and my self-respect, and here I am in a mountain with no place to go but up. If I'm to do that here, Lord, you'd better reach down, grab hold of me, and start lifting.

Father Habak did not hear the crunch of snow outside the cabin, but the knocking on the door interrupted his cranky thoughts. He responded by yelling, "Who is it?"

"Whadda ya mean, 'who's it?'" a brusque voice yelled. "Open da dang door en fine out. Ain't ya dat preacha fella dat moved in har dat's spose ta be frienly wid folk? Ya betta git 'bout it rit now, 'cause I'm colder den a muskrat's tail!"

Wouldn't you know, Dus grimaced. His very first "challenge" had arrived early in the day! Considering how he had just evaluated the makeup of his parish, the tone of the person outside his door did nothing to enhance the image. "Just a second, friend, while I put on a shirt," he answered.

"Hell's hollow, preacha, if dat's who ya is," responded the voice. "While ya putting on yer closs, ma finga's gonna friz ta da door hanle. Hurry yerself up afor I think ya ain't awantin no callers."

"I'm coming!" Dus called. His shirt was not buttoned, his fly was still unzipped, and he had no idea where his clerical collar was. So what? he beefed. That's not the town mayor showing up for a courtesy call.

"Come in," he said, opening the door.

There, standing before him was the biggest, barrel-chested, bewhiskered behemoth of a man the likes of which Dus had seldom seen. He stood at six feet six, 250 pounds of solid muscle, and was armed to the teeth with a shotgun, axe, and knife. He was dressed in oily brown hunting togs and black hightop boots, and was wearing the greatest of Santa Claus smiles. A small, frozen dead rabbit was slung over his shoulder. "I'm Ox Conley, Preacha," he laughed, moving through the door and over to the fire, "en I come ta welcome ya ta da valley en bring ya some vittles. My missus, Nancy, tol' me ta git rit up har en see iffen you's OK wid settlin' down en has nuff food. She en da younguns wal be up later ta make ya ta home."

"Thank you, Mr. Conley," Dus said, offering his hand. "I'm Father Habak, and I am the new Episcopal priest assigned to this church. I'm glad to meet someone from the village."

"Ain't from da village, Mista, en I donna know nuffin 'bout priests, fadders, ner pisco whatchamacallits. My Nancy tol' me a new preacha was up har, en dat I was ta git up har en see if ya was all rit. I donna go ta church en I donna ned no sarmuns, butta I like ta say ''ello' ta any fella wat passes ma way, er me, his! I'ma God-fearin man, Preacha, en dat man upstars en I git along jist fine. I donna bother him none, en he donna bother me."

I can believe that, thought Dus. God created this land and this hulk of a man, and hasn't bothered much with it nor him, since. But Father Habak couldn't think that was so bad. Maybe it's good for all of us to think that way. Why bother God? Why not just take life as it comes, do your work, and set yourself against its hurts and disappointments by being carefree and unsophisticated? Maybe he is right, mused Dus. Just meet another man where he is and don't waste time on trivia. The giant had probably gotten along fine with God in his life without knowing theology and liturgy, and without listening to sermons. It was hard for a man like Dus with his education and experience to appreciate that, but he could understand it. Life had certainly gotten too complicated. "Tell me, Mr. Conley," he broke in, "do all the people in the mountain feel like you do about the church?"

"Ya donna need ta call me mista, Preacha. Ma name's Ox. Dats what I been called eva since I was a tyke. I donna speak fer otha folk bout der religion, butta I donna reckon a lotta folk noth a town go ta many prayer meetin's. We ain't a too chuchified up har in dese hills, if ya knows watta I mean. My Nancy takes our younguns a cuppa time when a preacha comes har now en agin ta have chuch, butta I neva seen no sense in comin' up har ta talk ta da man upstairs. Ken do dat jist as well at my house, en while I'ma workin' en huntin'! No regalar preacha eva bothad me wid it. Ya gonna botha me wid preaching, Preacha?"

Dus pondered that for a moment before he asked, "You want a cup of coffee? There's some on the stove. I have some milk and sugar, and it will warm you up a bit. Maybe you can spare a minute to tell me about the valley and mountains. I'd like to learn about the place and folk. You seem to be a fellow to ask."

"Coffee be good, Preacha. Donna need nuffin' in it 'cause I likes it black en strong. I 'ave time ta sit fer a spell. I'm ma own boss, hunt en cut fer a livin'. Folk 'round har donna grow much meat, en mos' can't pay da price of watta dey sell at the stores in Jtown. We likes wile meat, anyhow, en I supply mos' of it for da folk up har. I 'ave a huntin' and fishin' license from da county, so I ken hunt and fish alla time. I git deer, rabbit, squarl, en bird, en once en agin, a bar. Bar meat taste kin'a strong en it stink a bit. Folk donna like it much, but the skins er good fer winner togs, rugs en da house, en fer sellin' down en Jtown at Jed Hudson's store. I don't use no traps, ner nothin'. I kills 'em clean with my gun, Parson, en I neva hurt ner let en animal ta suffa fer a sacond, 'cause I loves en respects 'em. But folk gotta eat, en dat's what I do fer ma livin', besides cuttin' cedar en otha trees."

"How do you find and move the wood, Ox?"

"I 'ave a pick-up truck, a chain saw, an axe ta cut wid. I cut down da trees, cleans da limbs off, en cuts dem inta lengths fer da mill. Some I hauls dem ta da house ta cut watta da folk need fer logs. I splits dem widda wedge," he said, as he moved from the fire and threw the rabbit that had been hanging on his back into the sink. He took off his jacket, sat down at the table, and wrapped his huge hands around his coffee cup. "Brung dat ribbit fer ya, Preacha. Shot it on ma way up har en thunk maybe ya'd wan' some meat. Does ya know 'ow ta skin en gut it?"

Dus looked at the rabbit. It's not what I am used to, he thought, but if I am going to live here, I had better take what's offered and make friends with this giant. I can't imagine myself out there in those mountains stalking deer and rabbits for my sustenance. "Thanks, Ox, I'll manage it. I guess until I get settled, I'll have to eat at one of the local restaurants. I guess I'll be doing a lot of that while living up here alone."

"Suit yerself, Preacha. I'ma jist being neighborly. Bessie Clayton, what owns da café in town, isa fine woman, en 'as da best eatin' place ta git good vittles. She's a good cook. She en Nan be'n close frien's since dey was tykes. A man needs a good woman ta cook fer em. Don't ya 'ave no wife ta take car' of ya, Preacha?"

"No, I don't, Ox."

"Too bad. A young fella like ya otta 'ave a good wife ta cook fer em en 'ave younguns."

"Yes, I know," Dus frowned, wiping his nose and eyes. "I'm not all that young, but my life is another story."

"Wal, I donna mean ta be pryin', Son! Wadda ya say yer name 'tis? Dus Byrd Habak! Wadda kina name is dat?"

"Some Pennsylvania Dutch and English. Habak is a German name. My father called me Dus after some ancestor. Byrd was my grandfather's name on my mother's side." Dus wondered what his parents would think of his being up in this mountain. They were cultured suburban people and had great hopes for their son, an engineer turned priest. Their daughter was a successful physician married to a physician. No, he mused, they would not be happy about the events that had befallen their son. It is just as well they hadn't lived to see his downfall. It would have broken their hearts.

"Wadda es all des fadder stuff, mista, dat ya keeps callin' yerself?"

"Oh, it's just a custom in my church. I'm called father 'cause I'm sort of the head of a church family like you're the father of your family, and so church folk call me father. Do you understand?" It was a dumb question, he thought. Of course Ox didn't understand. Why should he? It's not necessary for the man's salvation. If this guy is going to think anything of me, to ever call me father, I am going to have to spend a lot of time doing the right thing around him and earn his respect.

"Nup, Preacha, I donna understand," Ox broke in, "en it donna make no diff'rence ta me nohow. Call yerself watta ya want, en I jist call ya Dus. Wadda ya wan' ta ask me 'bout da folk en place har?"

"I'd appreciate if you could tell me something about the valley, the mountains, Joshuatown, and a little about this church and cabin." Dus thought it would be best to get information about he area from the folk who lived here, and Ox sounded like he might know more history about this place than anyone.

"Des valley was settled 'bout hundert-fifty yars ago," Ox began, shifting his coffee cup and lifting his boots onto another chair. "Someone thunk dat da ceda' trees har would be good busnuss. Lodda folk, en da ole days, usta make chests en closets outa da ceda' wood ta keep da bugs oudda der closs."

Dus remembered that his mother had cedar chests and cedar-lined closets to keep out the moths for that very reason.

"En folk 'round har," continued Ox, "usta split da ceda' logs en use 'em on der roofs. Dey b'lieved a ceda' roof would last fereva, 'cause termites wonna eat ceda' wood en da wetha donna wear on it too much. Anyways, dat's why folk settled har and built Jtown. Some ole man by da name a Joshua Baum brung mules, wagons, saws, en axes up har en starta cuttin'. Den da lumberjacks moved in en brung der folk. Dat's how my folk git har. Been har eva since. Things on'y was good fer 'bout hundert yars, 'cause da mo' ceda' dey cut, da less dey had. Ceda' donna grow fast, en it jist played out. Da slope timber was jist too high up en too hard ta git. Not much work could be done in da winnertime, anyways, so folk jist give it up en left da valley. My en Nancy's kin stayed on wid some otha folk en har we is. We donna know nuffin erse. We still haul ceda' for a li'l bit a money ta live on. Big companies wid a lotta newfangled machines come up har ta cut, butta we wouldn't let 'em in. Des is our land, en we wanna dem trees fer us. We on'y cut wadda we needs ta make a li'l livin' outta 'em. Thar's a mill dat cuts otha timber fer lumber, south a town. Thar's a coal mine dat opened yars ago down thar too, owned by da same folk, en es purty good fer jobs en fer da town. The houses in dese hills en Jtown will last fereva 'cause dey is made a ceda'."

"That's interesting, Ox. Is the church and this cabin made out of cedar too?" Dus asked. He wanted to know about the beginning of the church here.

"Yeah, I guess dey are, butta like I told ya, Precha, we neva 'ave been much for church 'round har. Them dat ken read, read da Bible en git tagether 'bout it, butta da man upstairs has taken passable care a usins, true da bad en da good times, butta like ever' livin' thung, folk git sick en die. Ya gotta put 'em in da ground en say propa words ova dem. I give da town da land up har fer buryin' grounds en folk put der daid kin up har fer yars in ceda' boxes. Thadda why ya 'ave a graveyard ova der by da church. We hadda put 'em on da hill 'cause da spring wash woulda be floatin' coffins all ova da place. Get lotta snow up har en da melt drains off ta da valley. Donna wanna 'ave our kin laid ta rest en den 'ave 'em floatin' by us down Ceda' Crik."

Dus was a bit amused by that. Practicalities, he thought. That's what a lot of religion is about. When you bury someone, you don't want his coffin rising up out of the ground and floating away. It's a lot to ask folk to trudge up here for a funeral carrying a heavy coffin, but, by God, once you get it up here and in the ground, it's going to stay there. You don't have to keep reburying it. Dus thought about his burial liturgy and wondered what kind of funeral these people had. He bet they didn't use a prayer book. They probably said some prayers, full of anguish and wailing, off the top of their heads. I can imagine grief doesn't last too long around this hard place. To live in a country like this, you'd have to be hard and not wallow in self-pity. Anyway, he thought, people who die are better off. No suffering, no remorse, no penance, nor contrition. Just gone—that's all. I wish I could be like these people and put it behind me. "Death, where is thy sting? Oh, grave, where is thy victory?" asks Saint Paul, he muttered. Well, Ginnie and Dusty feel no sting now. He heard Ox's voice droning on.

"'Bout twenty-five some y'ars ago, some preacha named Bunsun came up da valley en ask me iffen he could buy a piece a my land ta build a place ta live. He warnt choosy, en I figgered graveyards en preachas to tagether en it'd be nice ta'ave someone keep da graves. Da land next ta da graves was mine too, en I told 'im dat I'd give 'im da land iffen he'd say da pray's en bury folk w'en dey died, en also keep da graves tidied. He agreed! Me en a buncha fellas offered to take lumba up ta 'im en help git his house started, butta he did wanna no help. He was good widda hammer and saw hisself, en done all da work. In no time, he was livin' in it. He neva did say war he come from ner why he wanna be up har fer."

Dus understood that. Maybe if the preacher's life had been anything like his, he would not have wanted to tell other people about himself. But, he couldn't help wondering what possessed a man to build a vicarage by himself and live way out in the hills. Maybe he, too, was running away from life, or, perhaps, reentering it.

"We neva did know much 'bout 'im," Ox said. "He neva 'sociated much wid us. We'd see 'im now en ag'in goin' ta town ta buy vittles en stuff. Keeped ta hisself. One day I seen 'em buyin' lumba down at da mill, en da first thung I knowd, der was a chu'ch builden next ta da graves. Done build it by hisself, fer as I know. Neva ran inta anyone wadda helped 'im. Iffen he'd a hollad, some a us folk woulda give 'im a hand. En, mista, dat is a well-built builden. Got good footin's en roof. It's all ceda', en der ain'ta been a storm on da slope dat has been able ta brung it down ner weaken it."

"Did he ever have any kind of church services in it? I mean, like prayer meetings?"

"Non dat I seen nor knowd 'bout."

"You mean a minister came up on this mountain, built this house and the church, stayed to himself, and did nothing but tend the graveyard? How did you know he was a minister?"

"Well, he done built a chu'ch en had prayers ova our dead at buryin's, but not lotta folk died when he was 'round. He shur made da graveyard look purty. I'd come by des way sometimes when I was trackin' critters, en da graves always look clean. I'd come by da chu'ch house ta nosey, say 'hello,' en try ta know 'im, but he'd have nuffin ta do wid me, en I seldom seen 'im. He was a loner en a strange one."

"What happened to him?"

"Dat's a secret 'round des pawts, en it's no good ta ask. I tells ya straight. 'bout tree yars after he come har en done des buildens, he up en went fer good. He took his pickup en jist drives off da mountain, en we ain't seen 'im since. Me en Nancy is 'bout fifty now. We was jes startin' wid da younguns when he come, so it's bout twenty-some yars ago." Ox seemed uncomfortable talking about the disappearance of the minister. "I donna wanna talk ta much 'bout it. I say he jist went away wid no 'good-byes' ner nuthin, en we neva seen 'im ag'in."

Peculiar, Dus thought. A minister with apparent means comes up to this remote hill, builds a house and a church, takes care of the graves, prays over the dead, and disappears. No Sunday services, no nothing!

Ox shifted his bulk and reached for the coffee pot. He poured some more of the black liquid into his cup and leaned back. It seemed to Dus that Ox was enjoying the exchange of conversation until he started to talk about the preacher going away, but still, he played the part of the well-informed village patriarch. Maybe he was.

"Eva so offen, since den, some preachas comes up har ta ask me iffen dey ken have prayer meetin's. Dey ask me 'cause, like I say, I owns da land en I know da folk har like da graves tended. I always says 'yes,' butta I donna know between da way da difant chu'ch does things. Nancy and some otha woman folk now en ag'in take da younguns up har ta pray en lissen to a talk by da preachas dat come, butta none a dem stays mo den a Sunday er two, den some one erse comes. I guess ya is da next one, eh Dus?"

"Not exactly, Ox. I plan to stay for a while."

"Ya do, Preacha? Ya plannin' ta tend da graves too?"

Dus began to like the man, and reasoned he'd need a friend like Ox in this place. He also knew he'd better not push him on religious issues. "I'll tend the graves and will be doing a lot of other things too."

Ox was surprised and said, "Der was a man wid a black shart en a white colla' turned back ta front up har a cuppa months ago lookin' 'round en askin' iffen his church folk cou'd use dis place. Iffen folk wanna use da buildens fer prayin', I'ma pleased to have 'em. His name was sumpthun like Becky. Like I told 'im, da land belongs ta da man upstairs en we be glad ta have someone keeps up da buildens en ten' da graves. I donna know who da man was. Said he heard it was har, en would like ta borry da buildens fer prayer meetin's, en send a man up ta tend it. I guess yer dat man, ain't cha, Dus?"

Dus pondered those words. It figures. Old reach-out-for-God Burkey worked this deal. Guess he saw another opportunity, a cheap one at that, to add another star to his mission crown and unburden the bishop with the likes of one misfit cleric. After all, the diocese has to evangelize. The people up here have a nice building, they ought to have a minister, and Dus needs to be somewhere to do his priesthood. Kill two birds with one stone! Right! "I guess I am, Ox," he admitted. He was irritated and showed it. He got up from the table and walked over to the hearth. He didn't know what else to ask Ox at this point. He was fairly certain Ox was not going to be a pillar of his new congregation if such were to be had, given Ox's indifference to churchly things. Oh well, it's God's church, Dus thought, and he is going to have to use what was available to him, including Ox and me. "I'm going to be here for quite some time, Ox," Dus continued. "I don't want you thinking me something I'm not. I know you don't understand about me being an Episcopal priest and that I'm going to be doing some things for the man upstairs, as you call him, but I'll appreciate your friendship while I'm here, and I am grateful for the time you have given me this morning and for the rabbit. The information is helpful. I want to thank you, your family, and the folk here for keeping this place up. It's clean, there's food in the cupboard, and the bed was fresh."

Ox looked puzzled, but answered him as directly as he was able. "Now en den I come by har en look at things. Otha folk come up har ta see da graves. We all keep a bit a food er somethun har in case some gits caught in a storm en needs shelta. Might have ta stay trew da night some time. Da women walk ova des way sometime, en mos' anyone is free ta come en go. We neva locks da doors en nobody steals nuffin in des parts. Fact is—did ya notice—da keys are rusted in da locks." After saying that, he got up and reached for his coat and gear. "Gotta git goin'," he said. "Da mornin's movin' on, en der's a six-point buck ova on da Cutty I'm anxious ta meet up wid. I wanna git 'im afore he sniffs the air. No tellin' 'bout war a buck will take off to when he gits doe smell on his nose. Nancy is lookin' fer some fresh meat fer da weekend 'cause da widda en er boy are gonna be wid us ag'in. I declah, Preacha, I donna even gits it kilt afore my good wife is already givin' it away. She's like dat, my ole Nancy, en der is no kinda fine woman alive like her. I wanna ya ta meet her soon. Anyway, ya enjoy da rabbit. Betta git it skinned en gutted en put in da kittle. I'll bring ya some meat from time ta time. Butta I unnerstand ya all be lonely en wanna git some a Bessie's good food in yer belly. En thar will be company fer ya at her eatery, too." He put on his jacket and moved to the door, picking up his gun and axe, and pulled it open. A sharp cold breeze blew by him as he said, "Dus, jist wanna leave ya wid des advice. I learnt jawin' wid ya, ya be a toler'ble good fella. It was good ta sit. Us folk donna 'have nuffin ag'in' strangers as long as dey's fr'en'ly en tends ta thar own bus'ness. We donna meddle wid one anotha en we donna cotten ta dem what does. We figga des place belongs ta anyone dat want ta tend da graves, say da prayers, en have prayer meetin's. Ya be welcome ta stop by our place en share our vittles. Nancy makes good coffee en apple dumplin's en would wanna ya ta share 'em wid us. Butta I want ya ta know dat we live as we like har. We is good folk en does as it says in da good book, even though we got ups en downs. I know what preachas do sometimes in der eagerness, en we don't wan' dat har. Donna need talk about hell, fire, damnation, en dat stuff. We done lasted in des parts fer a long spell, en we gonna keep on a doin' it. We donna want no change, en iffen dat be yar plan, 'tis best dat ya jist moves on now lest ya have a hard time wid us. Do ya git my meanin', Dus?"

Dus relapsed into his worst under-the-breath sarcasm. "Do I git yo' meanin', did ya ask, yo big Ox? Oscoss, I gits yo' meanin'. Wal, as da Lord says, I gus I betta jist git off my arse, shack off da dust from ma feets, en gits to da next house dat'll 'ave me."

Ox never heard him. He just closed the door and left. No good-byes, no handshake, no nothing. He moved down the hill a short way, turn around, smiled, waved, and then struck out in the snow toward the ridge in the east. Ox's words echoed in the cabin, and Dus felt he had blown a great beginning. Well, how do you like that, Reverend Habak? he said to himself again. The bishop has handed you a "challenge," and that man traipsing up that hill is the essence of it. He will be your friend as long as you don't bother him with the job you were put here to do. You aren't going to fool that mountain man. He knows you're here to sell some kind of religion, and he has just said, "Stick it, Preacha!"

Holy God, where does a priest start in a place where the first soul you meet is an affable giant who could be your friend, but who just left you with a not-too-subtle hint not to bother him nor his friends with the gospel around his bailiwick? So, God, it's your church, and I'm your hired hand. If you have a spirit working in me, it had better get out of the sack, because I am about to chicken out right now, go get Elly, take off, and get an engineering job far from the bishop and old Ox! Jeez, Ginnie, why did you have to die and leave me to this? Please, Ginnie, come back to me! I need you!

Dus picked up the coffee cups on the table and took them to the sink. He looked out the window and saw a whisper of wind starting to blow snow around the corner of the church. It was about eight o'clock, and he thought that he ought to get going on Burkey's mission to convert the mountain to the Lord.

There was no water left and, as he had found out in the night, there was no plumbing in the cabin. He would have to go to the water pump again—a stone's throw from the cabin's back door to the stark outhouse. Nothing like having the necessary facilities separated, he thought. Ginnie would have hated this. She'd have gone through all sorts of hell for Dus, but walking through drifts up to her buns to go wee wee would have been a little much for her dignity. He got tickled thinking about it. I'd bet dollars to doughnuts she'd think the holes, the half moon cut in the door, and the old Sears catalog and a bucket of lime would be quaint, but she'd sure hate sitting there doing what comes naturally with a twenty-mile-an-hour gale whipping around through the lower section, freezing her tootsy, while shivering like a puppy, and then having to pump water into a bucket to bring into the house to heat her bath. No, Ginnie would not have liked roughing it. She had hated camping. She was an inn and restaurant vacationer.

Damn the nostalgia! This is no retreat! This is where I live now! What the heck! I've got a good vehicle, a roof over my head, food in the cupboard, a well with water in it, a toilet of sorts, a bed, a strong back, and an income. He pushed open the back door, tramped down the snow to the pump, raised enough water to take a sponge bath, to shave, and to clean up the rabbit. Back in the house, he heated the water. The air had invigorated him and he quickly finished a quick bath. He took what was left of the hot water, soaked his face, and shaved. A tarnished mirror hung over the sink and he used it. Dus was not a chance taker with a razor. He wanted to see what he was doing. A razor needs guidance.

I'll draw blood, he thought, and he did. He knicked a small blemish on his upper lip and the blood oozed out. The accident forced his mind far afield. He thought of all the emergency rooms, hospitals, tubes, and plasma bottles. Seems like I have always been where it was spilling all over the damn place. Car wrecks, war, bullet wounds, bloody noses, kids picking scabs. The terrible blood in Ginnie's car. He shivered. Then there was the blood of church martyrs, and the blood of patriots shed in the arenas of history and on battlefields all over the world. Jeez, always blood. It's precious, of course, but not so much so that I can't afford to lose a little shaving. It makes this sacrifice in this wilderness more authentic. A very fine sacrificial beginning.

Dus wiped his face and stuck a piece of toilet paper on his wounded lip. Wouldn't the folks at the cathedral love to see this face in the marble pulpit with toilet paper stuck to it? He smiled, went to the table, and looked down at the rabbit. Preparing it for consumption was not the kind of thing he relished, but if he was ever going to make points with Ox, he had better accept his gift and eat it. Sure as the devil, that giant would ask someday how he liked it.

He did the gory chore as best as he knew how. Not bad, he thought, admiring himself. He might just invite old Ox over to share it with him. It is said, he mused, that "the way to a man's heart is through his stomach." Maybe my rabbit stew will incite old Ox the hunter, like Peter the fisherman, into doing some kind of mountain discipleship. He doubted that as he cleaned up the mess, stashed the rabbit in the icebox, put on his collar, boots, and parka, and stepped out of his new vicarage into the cold air of his new parish. He wasn't sure in what direction he was going, but he went paraphrasing John the Baptist. "Prepare ye the way of the Lord!" The voice of a rejuvenated priest crying in the wilderness! He was clothed in a girdle of black clericals around his loins, a white collar around his neck, and the fragrance of a skinned rabbit on his body, saying, "Repent, ye generation of mountain hunters, coal miners, and cedar choppers. The Kingdom of God is at hand!

"Jeez," he repented, "if the bishop would hear that kind of impiety, he'd have my head served up on a platter by Canon Burkey!"

# 3

Father Habak strolled all morning through the fresh snow. Having decided to leave the Jeep, which he named "Iodine," for its healing effect, at home, he ambled about his parish locale on foot, enjoying the sunny, if cold, day. He wore warm boots and a jacket. The snow was not deep, and he easily made his way up through the forest on the Cutty Mountain. He had noticed several cabins up the trail billowing smoke from their chimneys. He wondered, as he walked, what reaction he would get if he stopped at one or two of them to inquire of the families. Maybe he could feign weariness, he mused, or the need for a drink of water as an introductory opener. He had never had a problem making pastoral calls before, but he was convinced this was going to be a more difficult venture. After listening to Ox's skepticism, he wasn't sure how the indigenous folk of these hills would receive him. Well, did not the Lord say to the apostles, "Enter into a house, and if they don't receive you, shake off the dust from your shoes and go on?" It was not in his plans, anyway, to knock on any doors that day, so why agonize about it? he asked himself. Today he was just going to get the lay of the land and enjoy his walk and the scenery.

 He was now up near the area where he had spotted the three lonely cedar trees early in the morning. The trail was not for sissies, he allowed, stopping to catch his breath. A wet fallen knotted log offered him some respite. He had no sooner taken a gulp of water from his canteen, when he heard a crack and a bullet whistled by his head and thudded into a stump across from where he was seated. He knew it was a high-caliber rifle bullet. He had recognized the sounds that were so familiar to him in the Marine Corps. "My God. What was that?" he groaned, as he pitched his body to the ground and lay on his back behind the log. He couldn't see anyone moving and vied not to raise his head, lest he chance losing it. "Mare's marbles," he groaned. "What in the devil do I do now?" He hardly finished asking that question, when he heard the resounding din of another shot and felt the thud of a .30 caliber slug burying itself into the other side of the log. He rolled on his stomach and tried to crawl toward the larger diameter of the protecting timber.

Can you believe this? he muttered. First day on the job and some damn loony is trying to shoot my ass off. He lay there and quietly tried to think what he might do if the rifleman came closer. He waited. There were no more sounds, and no one appeared to be walking around in the woods. He thought it was better to quietly play dead, and if someone looked over the log, he would just kick him in the face and run like hell. No one came. There was no sound except that of the wind and the birds. As he slid his hand down along his backside to pull his hunting knife out of its sheath, he felt a severe pain along the underside of his buttocks cheek. He touched it and felt a wetness on his hand. He drew his hand close to his face and saw blood.

"Damn it!" he swore, wondering if a bullet had creased his behind. He quietly remained there for another few minutes, and then carefully raised his head to peer across the top of the log. His eyes narrowed as he scanned the forest, cautiously surveying the whole area. Not seeing anybody, he pushed himself up, leaned his back against the log, and checked the wound. He could not see because of its placement, but it appeared to be a fairly deep perforation in the skin, with blood oozing through his pants. There was no sign that it was a bullet wound—something his experience would have ascertained—so he looked to the snow-covered ground in search of a cause. He noticed a broken sapling stump protruding about six inches through the snow, its tip covered with blood. He conjectured that when he fell to the ground, the sharp, hard stick punctured his bottom. It was not too bad, he convinced himself, and he'd dress it with some iodine and Band-Aids when he returned to the cabin. Still, Dus mussed about who would take a shot at him—and why—on his first day in the mountain. He sure as hell would find an answer to that, but now he was going home, watching his rear end while going down the trail.

He reached the cabin in the late afternoon and found that all was well there. No one had disturbed his place, and he was glad of that. No telling what a person who was out to shoot you had in mind, he thought. Glad he didn't come up here to rob or burn my house. I gotta find out what's going on here, he pondered, and he began to think about the lone, vanished preacher Ox had told him about. The remembrance of that did not help. Besides, it was ridiculous. Why would he think about something that happened a quarter of a century ago when he was a teenager on a farm in Pennsylvania?

\*　　\*　　\*

The next day seemed to have come fast. He slept fairly well through the night after a good supper of rabbit stew, a bath, and a cigarette by the fire, but the long walk and the shooting episode of the pervious day had tired him, and the wound on his bottom hurt. He had taken a better look at it with a mirror when he arrived home, and it appeared all right. It hadn't been too uncomfortable for him during the night, and he reassured himself it would be OK. He noted that Nancy Conley and the boys must not have come to the cabin as Ox had predicted, but he would not have been there to greet them, anyway. He spent the whole of the day at the church and the vicarage preparing for a service on Sunday. He had a lot of questions on his mind. I wonder what it's going to be like to start over here with a new ministry. Would anyone show up for worship? What would he do if people did? Of course, he was a priest; he would do what priests do, and would do the liturgy, preach the gospel, and celebrate the Eucharist. He cleaned the church, sweeping, dusting, wiping the window, and shoveling a path from the road to the front door. The building was in good enough condition for doing services. There was a lectern where he could read Bible lessons and preach, and an old table that would serve as an altar. True to his word, Bishop Mueller had sent up a box with all the Communion appointments he would need for services, including a Bible, missal, linens, chalice, *paton*, wine and bread for the Eucharist, and a lot of prayer books. He would have liked to have had some hymn singing, but he didn't have the talent for leading singing; he never had. There was an old reed pump organ sitting along the wall. He thought that maybe someday he could get it working and find someone with some piano talent to play it. Dus had wished many times that his mother had been more persistent in making him learn to play the piano, like she had for his talented sister. Mom had tried, but playing with his buddies at school and in the barn was what he wanted to do instead, so she had given up in frustration. Dumb! he said of himself. How I wish now that I would have learned from that grand and talented lady who played like a concert pianist. I wonder why we dense boys waste our young lives on the mundane? No matter, now.

Strange thoughts possessed him. He wondered if the person with the gun would show up anonymously in the congregation on Sunday. He spent nearly the whole day thinking about a lot of possible perils, so he had not ventured out again. Not a soul came to visit him, and the pain in his rear end had increased so much that he had no heart to do any pastoral calling on complete strangers, no matter the Lord's admonition. He would try to do that on the next day after church when he had met some folk and felt better.

Saturday morning came and he had a fever. He took some aspirin, ate a can of chicken soup, and tried to get himself going. He lazily and feverishly worked on a sermon. Noontime came and he felt sicker, with a stabbing pain moving down his hip. He now believed it would be sensible, given his growing pain and fever, to seek some medical attention at the town clinic, if it were open and had a nurse available. After all, it would not do for him to be grimacing and limping about, with a pain in his rear end, on his first day in the pulpit. He didn't think the bishop nor any righteous soul venturing into a pew in the morning expecting the gospel to be preached would understand. Canon Burkey would have a good laugh at Dus' expense. Dus did not feel he would enjoy the humor of it.

One hour later he was sitting in the waiting room of the Joshuatown Health Clinic, wondering who would treat his bottom. Damned embarrassing. The room was empty of patients, so he assumed he would soon get attention. He took out a cigarette, lit it, took a deep puff, and coughed. Smoking was a bad habit he had given up several years ago, but had taken up again after Ginnie's death. He had decided he didn't care what was said about lung cancer. It helped his depression, tasted good, and helped his pain. God, he lamented, my habits are rotten, my thoughts, terrible, and my language, deplorable. Ginnie would hate what I have become. I should really be ashamed. Think I'll get out of here, go home, and settle down at the fire with a stiff Jack Daniel's. That oughta take the pain away. Jack Daniel's took away a lot of his pain of late—more than he needed!

"Hi, I'm Karol Marson," a female voiced echoed through the room and interrupted his self-pity. "What can I do for you?"

Father Habak stood up to respond to the woman whose soft, slightly accented voice had greeted him. Her stature forced his immediate appraisal. A white medical frock did not altogether hide her well-configured body. Long, soft, dark-brown hair cascaded over her shoulders, framing her beautiful tanned face with blue-green eyes, keen cheekbones, straight nose, attractive mouth with full lips, and a smile that Dus fancied could captive the most recalcitrant of grouchy people. He was almost speechless as he stood to introduce himself. He managed, anyway.

"Oh, hello, Ms. Marson," he stuttered. "I'm, er, Father Dus Habak and, ah, I've got a little wound on my bottom and a bit of a fever that needs some attention. It's not serious. I can come back some other time if the doctor is busy with someone else."

"I know who you are, Father Habak. A friend told me an Episcopal priest had arrived on the mountains. Besides, the black shirt and round collar give you away."

"If you're the doctor's nurse, explain to him that I won't take much of his time. I'd just like to get a little medication, if I could."

Karol smiled at him. "I guess I should have introduced myself more professionally, Father. I'm not a nurse, and, as you may have noted, I am not a him. I am Dr. Karolina Marson and I am the physician in charge of this clinic."

# 4

Ollikut Karolina Thunder Rolling In The Mountain Christianson Marson, M.D., had long, dark-brown hair, a smooth tanned complexion, and, at thirty-six, was trim and pretty, even though barely detectable crow's feet around the corners of her blue-green eyes were beginning to annoy her. "Made it half past three score and ten," she'd proudly told her mirror, "and I look fine. Muscle tone good, and not too much belly nor butt, but I wish I were at my old thirty-five, twenty-five, thirty-five inches. I guess I'll have to settle for a shift here and there!"

Weight, as for most women her age, was hard to hold where she wanted it, but she tried to keep her five-foot, five-inch frame between 125 and 135 pounds. Shawn, her fourteen-year-old son, assured her she looked OK, and bragged about his good-looking mom to his friends—all of whom loved her for being "cool," and for her laughter, friendliness, and fun-loving ways.

Karol, as her friends called her, was born in Joseph, Oregon. Her dad, Lech Christianson, a U.S. forest ranger in the Wallowa National Forest, had married her mom after, he joked, "he had rescued the pretty maiden from the dusty looms of the Pendleton woolen mills." Her mother, a full-blooded Nez Perce Indian, originally from the reservation in Waha, Idaho, was one of several Indian women who believed they were direct blood descendants of the almost legendary Nez Perce chief, "Thunder Rolling in the Mountain" Joseph. She had no written genealogical evidence to substantiate that claim, but that did not prevent her from having that illustrious Native American name included on her daughter's baptismal certificate. It was, nonetheless, from that lovely statuesque Indian woman that Karol had inherited her gorgeous figure, skin, hair, and capacity for compassion for others. Her father, a proud Scandinavian, had endowed Karol with her beautiful blue eyes, smile, strength, muscles, feistiness, and charming inclination to jest.

She graduated from nursing school at Eastern Oregon State College at LaGrande, and took a job as a floor nurse at LaGrande County Hospital. Shortly thereafter, she was introduced to Douglas Marson, a helicopter pilot for the U.S. Forestry Service, by her father, who worked with him in the U.S. Forest Service and believed Doug to have the moral, industrious qualities of a prospective son-in-law, and encouraged Karol to date him. Karol did, and found him to be a kind and loving man. They dated nearly six months; though Karol was not deeply in love with him, she was very fond of him and came to believe, as did her mother, that her father was right about Douglas Marson's potential as a good husband and father .They later married.

One year later, she gave birth to Shawn, a robust and strong boy, who grew to love the forest, lakes, and animals, and to walk in his (presumed) great-great-grandfather's moccasins. Five years after Shawn's birth, Doug Marson's helicopter was sucked into a whirlwind forest fire at Hell's Canyon and crashed. Doug died in the fire, and it was days before his body was recovered. His death devastated Karol. Picking up the pieces was hard for her. After a time, feeling suffocated by well-meaning friends and family, she came to believe she had to start over with her life, elsewhere.

She and Shawn moved out east, where she took a nursing job at the University Hospital in Virginia. While she was there, several of her physician friends convinced her that she had fine medical talents and should become a physician. She invested the life insurance money from Doug's death in medical school. It was difficult. The studies were hard, and providing for a son took a lot of effort and time, but he had been very supportive, and she graduated near the top of her class. After finishing her studies and residency in general surgery, she went to Staunton, where she established a private practice and joined the staff of the Staunton Memorial Hospital. She had been well-received by the people and did distinguished work in her medical practice. She was now very happy. Vocation and time had healed a lot of the wounds that had accompanied Doug's death.

Karol and Shawn had sorely missed the mountains and rivers of Oregon, so they were happy to be living in the Shenandoah Valley in the Appalachian Mountains. She and Shawn would often drive west up into the Cutty and Blue, canoe on Cedar Creek in the summer, and hike deer trails in the winter. She had learned to love the country folk there and they reminded her of the people back home. Her mom and dad had come east to visit her on a few occasions, and they, with Shawn, appreciated the people in the mountains who had befriended their daughter. They felt at peace with her new life and believed their grandson would mature very well where Karol had settled. They were proud of her in her new profession and rejoiced that she had found happiness in the forest environment, having overcome the tragedy of Doug's death. Her dad took Shawn into the mountains on camping trips while Karol and her mom cooked pheasant and traded old Indian anecdotes.

It was during her hikes into the Cutty and Blue that she discovered Joshuatown. It was a small and quaint sort of county seat village that was good for her nostalgia and spirits. When she had gotten to know the people there, she learned about the health clinic that had been financed by the federal government and built by the home folk. It was well-equipped, and she had asked Nancy Conley, who had befriended her after they met on the road one day, if any doctor was coming in to staff the clinic and help the people with their medical needs.

"Naw, Docta Marson, der ain't," Mrs. Conley had said to her. "De guvament helped ta build it en helped us ta put funature in it, butta nobody been usin' it. No doctas, I guess, wanna ta come dis fur from Staunton ta work, so we go down der when we needs medicine an git ourselves fixed up."

"How do you think people would feel about my coming up here to the clinic, say, once or twice a month to take care of their and the children's medical needs?"

"I b'lieve they'd think dat woulda be jist fine. Ya would do dat fer us, Docta?" Nancy had smiled and asked appreciatively.

"Well, I could talk to my bosses at the hospital and the government HEW people, and see what time I could give it. Are you sure the folk here will accept a woman doctor to tend to their medical needs?"

"Wah, iffen dey don't, de's a bunch a ninnies, dat's fer sure. Donna a worry none 'bout dat. Ox en me will help a bit started en spread da word we gonna have a docta up har ta take care a usins. Folk'll be tickled pink. My Jenny en er hubby, Cyrus, sure wo'ld like ta have someone look at my gran'baby so dey donna have ta run all da way down ta Staunton fer checkups. I donna care what da men says. Dey donna know nuffin 'bout sickness, en care lit'le iffen dey dies. It's us woman folk wadda has ta bear da burdens a der o'nery ways en take care of 'em en da chillun, en we would sure like ya ta come up 'ere."

"Thank you, Nancy, but I don't want to impose myself on anyone nor cause any trouble with the families."

"Hog snouts," Nancy cussed. "Ya ain't gonna do no sech thing. A leave it ta us women en we'd be a mighty proud en grateful if ya could tend us. Lotta times we get r'ally sick from da cold en dampness en kent git a docta up har. Den ya know, my ole Ox gits hisself all bunged up by somethun er anutha, and he donna pay no mind ta it, and it gits worrisome sore. We gotta lotta folk watta get skinned up, has ailments, en needs medicine. Butta ya knows, we ain't rich folk en couldn't pay ya much fer carin' fer us."

Karol admired and respected the beautiful mountain lady. Nancy Conley was the salt of the earth. She was born and raised in these mountains and was all heart. Married to Ox, whose real name was Oxford, she had given birth to one pretty daughter and two handsome sons, and raised them in a healthy and reliable manner. Nancy and Karol had quickly become bosom friends. She smiled a response to Nancy. "Don't worry about paying me, Nancy; that won't be any problem. I'd be grateful, though, if folk would give me a hand at the clinic now and then if I have to work long weekends. There is no motel here, and I was wondering if there would be someone who might board and room Shawn and me when we come. I'd pay them."

"No pay necesory, dear. Ita be no problum wid help 'cause we 'ave lotta strong backs en en'le hands ta help a at da clinic. Sheriff Kirsh's wife, Patty, who be a teacher at da school, also be a nurse, en she'd sho be glad ta help atta da clinic. Ox en me be glad ta shar' our vittles en a room fer ya en Shawny. Ya'd be a welcome angel a mercy, ya would, Docta!"

"Thank you. I'd do my best for all of you. We've come to love these hills and you folk have been so kind to us. Your family is a blessing to us, Nancy. We've missed our home in Oregon with all the good memories, but have found so much peace, love, and happiness here. I'm glad I made the move. It's been good for Shawn. He finds the animals, trails, and streams much the same. I think that he will enjoy coming up here with me on my clinic days, and while I'm working, he'll like roaming around. Maybe he can go on the trails with Ox and your boys sometimes."

That seemed a long time ago. She had been coming up to the clinic for three years, loving every moment of it. The people had received her with open arms and trusted her beyond her expectations. She could hardly believe the joy she found there. Shawn was in seventh heaven. He loved the Conleys and their kids, and had become especially great friends with Ox. Ox had taught him to track and hunt, and Shawn was slowly acquiring the forest expertise of his Indian ancestors. Unfortunately, Doug's parents had died before Karol had met Doug, so having only one grandfather, Shawn had become close to his mother's father, Lech. They had spent a lot of time together in the mountains in Oregon. This new life was natural for Shawn, and he was always in a bad mood when they had to return to Staunton. School and girls were OK, but in the mountains there were Ox, the trees, and the animals. Being there had eased Karol's concern for Shawn. Yes, this place and people had been good for them, and she was grateful that they had opened their hearts to them. Shawn laughed a lot these days, and so did she.

"Oh, this Saturday morning is so bright and beautiful," Karol said to herself. It was the second day of a three-day holiday weekend. She had quit work early Thursday afternoon at the hospital so that she and Shawn could pack and get an early start for the mountain. They had gotten up at six o'clock Friday morning, driven up the mountain, and gone directly to the clinic, where Ox met them in his pickup and hauled Shawn away with him. Friday had been busy with patients, but she had rested and eaten well at the Conleys. So here she was now again at her work, ready for a day of tending to and loving people. Gosh, she wondered to herself, how can anyone be so lucky? "Doug," she said, talking to the wall, "I wish you could be here with us. You'd love this place as you did Oregon." She had just seen her last patient when she walked into her waiting room late in the day, surprised that there was anyone else waiting for her. It was then that she introduced herself to Father Dus Habak.

\* \* \*

Father Habak reacted to Dr. Marson's introductory allusion to her profession and duties with a somewhat red face and stammered, "Ah, ah er, er, I didn't know there was a woman doc here at the clinic. I'm surprised!"

"Don't be surprised. I am a female doc, Father, and some folk around here think I'm a pretty good one. I'm probably as good a physician as some women will be priests, when the holy church gets around to ordaining them priests."

Mare's marbles, Dus sighed within. Wouldn't you know! Right from the start of my ministry up in these sticks, I have to meet up with a crazy lunatic with a .03 rifle, and now a smart aleck feminist medic. Jeez, all I wanted here was something for the pain in my butt. Here, I've run into a worse one! He spoke to her sheepishly. "It's OK, Doctor. I just have a scratch on my, er, ah, thigh that needs a little attention. And in case you misunderstood me, I was not reflecting on your gender as a physician. I have a very nice sister who's an incredibly good M.D.!"

"Well, good for your sister. That's very encouraging! Forget what I said about priests, Father! I was just kidding. I'm an Episcopalian too—not the best, to be sure, but I know the ladies are giving you males the hives talking about being priests. Wouldn't care to be one, myself, and I'm not sure yet that I am ready to have one listen to my hair-raising confessions, but I wish them luck. Maybe they will bring some joy to the vocation. You guy types are sort of somber with your piety. Makes us normal folk a bit itchy. Anyway, that's another story. Right now I am here to fix your—what did you say?—thigh. Come into my examination room and let me take a look at you. And, please, Father, field strip that cigarette and put it in the waste can. I don't like those putrid killer weeds stinking up my clinic."

Dus did as she had asked, and reticently followed her through the door into a well-lighted, sanitized, white-walled room with an examination table, desk, chair, myriad cabinets, and glistening surgical instruments.

"Drop your pants, Father, and let me take a look at your wound."

"Madam, I am not dropping my pants in front of any woman."

"I am sorry, Father, that my gender compromises your modesty, but you are going to have to take off your pants if I am to look at your wound. I have seen and operated around hundreds of male genitals. I have yet to be shocked by them. Amused, maybe, but never shocked. Now, please, will you let me check that cut or whatever it is? Believe me, I won't take advantage of you. My hands never rove where they ought not to. Trust me."

"You'll have to excuse me, Doctor. I guess my Pennsylvania Dutch reserve runs through my veins pretty thickly. I've had a lot of nurses working on my body, but I am still a little bit self-conscious about exposing myself around women. And then, too, I am an old-fashioned priest with old-fashioned notions about privacy."

"Oh, fiddle dee dee! Then you will have to excuse me, too, Father, because I'm a Nez Perce Indian and Scandinavian medicine woman, and my heritage and profession don't allow me to give a twit about men's privates when it comes to taking care of their wounds. I am a very competent surgeon who's really good with a knife, and hatchet, if I need it; you don't need to fear I will cut away anything I shouldn't. I shall be happy to have you cover whatever it is you don't want me to see with this," she laughed, throwing him a hospital gown, "so you won't have to blush as I check out your heinie."

Dus could not help but chuckle inside while listening to the pretty, smiling, up-front, to-the-point medic. He had already judged her as a royal pain-in-the-butt feminist, but he could no longer fight off her infectious demeanor. He loosed his belt and lowered his pants to his knees.

"All the way down and off, Father, and then up on the table so I can have a good look."

He took off his boots and pants, adjusted his briefs, and arranged himself on the examination table with the sheet partially around his hips; he turned his wounded cheek upward, so his privates were suitably veiled.

"Turn over on your stomach and pull your shorts down, Father. That wound is not on your thigh. It's on your heinie cheek."

He smiled at her reference, and pulled his briefs down over his thighs, baring his whole buttocks to the woman doctor. He was embarrassed, but he vowed he wouldn't show it. He maneuvered his body to protect his modesty as best he could.

"How in the heck did you do that, Father?" Karol asked him as she eyed the wound, pulled on some rubber gloves, and began to probe it with her hands. "Pretty nice buns for a clergyman. Guess it will be interesting for you guys to see what women's buns do for vestments—not to mention their boobs."

"You're pretty earthy, doctor, with your feminist aberrations. I hope that is an ecclesiastical phenomenon that will never see the light of day," Dus groused. She punished his chauvinism by pressing a little harder on the wound. "Ouch—that hurt!" he yelled, as he felt a stabbing pain go up his thigh.

"Serves you right! Ya ought not push my 'equality' button, Preacher, when I have the upper hand with your bare derriere. Now tell me about this."

"I fell on a sharp stump sticking out of the ground while I was hiking up on the Cutty Mountain on Thursday, and it punctured my pants. I thought it was OK last night, but this morning when I got out of bed, it was pretty painful. I think I have a little fever with it, too."

"I'm not surprised. Good heavens, Father. Do you know that you have a zillion germs in that puncture and it's badly infected? You can't see it very well, but you have some red streaking down your heinie and hip. Did you put anything on this mess?"

"Iodine and Band-Aids. It didn't seem so bad that it needed a lot of medical attention."

"Why didn't you come down here yesterday and have me fix it?"

"I said I didn't think it was that bad. I have no time to waste on scratches."

"Waste your time on scratches, huh," Karol replied angrily. "You men and your bravado! I know that it's not nice to call a priest a dummy, but that's what you are when you talk like that. You have a bad infection that's going to have to be swabbed out, salted down with sulfa, and bound up. Furthermore, you're gonna have to get a tetanus shot in that shiny clerical heinie and take a ton of antibiotics."

"Whatever you say, Doctor," Dus replied sheepishly. "Do what you have to do and let me be on my way. I have a lot of things to do before tomorrow, and I need some time tonight to do them."

"Be still and I'll be done in a jiffy," Karol admonished him as she skillfully went to work on his buttocks. He winced as she washed the wound with an antiseptic and applied an anesthetic spray to the area. She then proceeded to take a silver probe and dig into the wound to drain it. Yellow pus and pinkish blood flowed freely, and she dabbed it with medicated pads. Dus lay there, his elbow and hand holding up his head, as he tried to peer down at her work. She was gentle and careful. She showed an expertise that he appreciated, and he now felt comfortable with what she was doing. She let the wound bleed dark red blood, swabbed it away, and then applied some white powder he assumed was sulfa. "OK," she finally said, "I have to put a bandage on it and then we'll be done."

Her hands deftly applied the pad with adhesive tape. "That ought to do it for a while, Padre. That thing will have to drain tonight and then I'll change the bandage tomorrow. Now hold on while I stick your other heinie cheek with a needle. This is going to sting a bit. Think a big, brave priest can handle that?"

Why does a pretty woman have to be such a smart aleck? Dus complained to himself as he gritted his teeth, and felt Dr. Marson push a needle into his other bottom cheek. He vowed he would not yell out, and he didn't.

"There you go! All done, Mr. Clergy fellow! No sweat, no tears, and you have your privates and modesty all intact. I assume there will be no malpractice suits. You can pull up your pants and take your leave. Come back tomorrow. I'll be here till late afternoon. And, listen Rev, please give up those cancer sticks. It's a bad habit that will eventually kill you. Honest."

Dus knew she was right about his smoking, but didn't appreciate the lecture. He got up, pulled up his pants, pulled on his boots, and turned to face his new attending physician. "Thank you, Doctor, for fixing me up. How much do I owe you for your services?"

"On the house, Father! Call it 'professional courtesy.' Just say a prayer for me and mine sometime."

"Oh, no, Doc, I don't take clergy discounts. I can afford your fees."

"Gosh, Preacher, you sure are formal for a mountain mission man. OK, then. Five bucks will cover it. That's what I charge everyone unless they have no money at all, and then, like you preachers have to do sometimes, I take my payments in chicken wings, greens, and grits."

Dus, no longer amused by her banter, took out his wallet, gave the doctor a ten-dollar bill, and said, "Keep the change and buy your own grits."

She frowned at his sarcasm, but thanked him. "You know, Father, if I thought your sermons would be as eloquent as your paleface heinie and as pugnacious as your demeanor, I might just wander up to your service tomorrow morning and see what you have to offer a backslider like me. It isn't often that I get to check out the things of a priest's flesh before I check out the things of his spirit. Good-bye! I hope I didn't offend your modesty with my medical care, nor your sensitivities with my jesting. A little banter is good for folk. Helps them to enjoy their work. It wouldn't hurt you to loosen up a bit and laugh a little, too. By the way, that's very interesting kind of heinie wound. How did you really get it?"

He glared at her. "Why do you ask, when I have already told you?"

"Tripped and fell on a sapling stump, you said. Uh-huh! Well, see you around, Rev."

He frowned. "Good-bye, Doc. Oh yes—you asked me to pray for you and 'mine.' Who is 'mine'?

"My son, Shawn, my only child, a fine lad of twelve years. He is out in the mountains right now with Ox Conley, whom you have already met."

"Well, I'll pray for you both," Dus grumbled as he turned, left the clinic, and got into his jeep. She waved good-bye, smiling at him from the clinic door. He unsmilingly waved back and drove away, asking himself why she had questioned him about the nature of his wound. She had not believed him. He didn't know whether or not he liked the woman, as pretty and smart as she might be, with her weird humor, admonitions, and innuendoes. He didn't give a mare's marble whether she came to his church or not. As a matter of fact, when he thought about his church service on the morrow, how he would perform, who and how many people would be there, Father Habak didn't give a mare's marble about that, either. He felt miserable from the pain in his bottom, furious about getting shot at, and thoroughly disgruntled about his first days of "shaking off the dust" in the Appalachian Mountains.

As for Dr. Marson, she returned to her medical chores wondering if the new priest on the mountain would ever be fun to know. It didn't seem so, but then she never knew any clergy who were. She confessed to a prejudice that they were often pompous, judgmental, without joy, and generally akin to Father Habak's malady—a pain in the heinie. Anyway, she reasoned, I'm here to fix his sore behind, not his crabby character. I'm here to make these happy mountain folk well, not to make that crabby paleface person fun to be around. "But, oh my, oh my, Ollikut," she giggled, "would he be an exciting and fun challenge for an Indian medicine woman?"

# 5

Father Habak stood at the front of his new church looking at a scattered congregation of about twenty men, women, and children. He was genuinely surprised there were that many people there, given the disturbing fact that he had not announced to anyone, save Dr. Marson, when he would be starting Sunday services nor at what time they would be held. It was akin to a miracle, he thought, as he pondered that faux pas, that folk had come from their warm homes through the cold, to sit in a cold church, to hear the word of God preached by a minister they didn't even know. He could only presume that the Holy Spirit was doing his job, even if Father Habak wasn't starting out well in his. If that was true, he was duly impressed with the Holy Spirit and with these hill people who sat there. "Good morning," he said, somewhat cautiously and forcing a smile.

"Good morning, Preacher," they all responded with one accord.

He introduced himself. "I am Father Dus Habak, the new minister you might have heard was coming to have worship services at this church. I welcome and thank you for coming out on this cold morning to worship the Lord here with me. Many of you have known this building and parsonage for many years, and have known ministers to come for a while and then leave. I've heard some came just for one Sunday service or so and didn't return, and I'll understand if you think that's what I'm going to do and won't be long amongst you. But I want to stay with you for a long time, and I pray that once you get to know me as a friend and neighbor, you'll want me to stay to preach and minister to you. I don't know how much you know about the Episcopal Church that I represent, but that doesn't matter now. I'm just going to preach the gospel, talk with you about Jesus, have the Lord's Supper, pray with you, and be your pastor if you have a need to talk to one. Is there anyone who'd like to say something before services?"

He waited for a response. The people sat in their pews, some smiling serenely, others nodding, but none offering to speak. Their subdued but genuine interest gave him heart. He was vested in a white alb, a stringy cincture girding his waist, and a green stole hanging around his neck. He asked them to open the prayer books he had placed on their seats, and showed them the pages where they were to find the Holy Communion service. He began the service with opening prayers, read an Old Testament lesson, the Twenty-third Psalm that he thought would be familiar to them, and the gospel narrative about Jesus' "Sermon on the Mount." Then, the former chastened and disillusioned Dean Dus Habak leaned against the lectern, propped up his left arm, gestured with his right, and started his revived ministry in the Blue and Cutty Mountains by preaching his first sermon.

"Jesus loved the hills and the valleys of his country, and the folk who lived in them. From reading your Bibles, you know that. He was a poor and simple holy man, who did not spend much time of his ministry in large and pretty buildings, preaching to folk. Most of the time, he walked around the hills and valleys just talking to people like you, about God's love for them. He preached very often in mountains, not as big as these, perhaps, simply teaching people how to live and deal with life both in the good and bad times. He taught them, too, as he does us, how to live life to please God their creator, and why it is important to love and treat one another with respect and consideration."

Dus was not feeling very confident as he felt his verbal way with this little band of listeners. He used no sermon notes, trying to speak to them from his heart, in a vernacular they could understand. He smiled, pleased to see attentive faces, among whom was Dr. Mason, with a lad he presumed was the son she had alluded to at the clinic. So, he mused, the lady had taken time away from her work to come to worship. That pleased him, and he felt less annoyed with the feisty medic. He continued on with his homily not wholly without her in mind.

"Perhaps those of us who live in the mountains or in the valleys between them can better understand the meaning of a lot of Jesus' messages when he preached. We might think of life itself as often being mountain and valley experiences. As I walked up and down these beautiful hills the last few days, I tried to think about what God might want of my ministry to those of you who know these high and low places so well. I try to think how life was for Jesus in his time, as it is for us now, and how it must have been full of mountaintop and low-valley experiences for him, too. He had his ups and downs, so to speak," Dus explained, "and it was not only his body that experienced the high and low times of his journey, but his heart and soul, his thoughts and emotions. We human beings are very much like that—feeling very high with joy in our hearts; happiness with our families, friends, and relatives; confident with who we are and what we are doing; often feeling very close to heaven. We sniff the pure air, feel the cool and warm wind in our faces, feel fresh and good, and want to sing praises to God, never wanting to come off of our mountains of joy. That's what we call a 'mountaintop experience.' But the reality of life, as Jesus taught us and as was certainly true of himself, is that we have to go back down into the valleys of our lives and deal with the common things, the sometimes darker side of life. We have to live with stresses and uncertainties, as well as the joy, of everyday life. We have to live with pain that comes with the low times—far away, it seems, from the joy of the high times. We do very often live in the shadows of death, as well as in the presence of God, as the Psalmist says, but because of God's promises, and the mountains, there in their strength and majesty to lift us up and sustain us, we need not fear any evil. We know that we can overcome the bad times in our lives, use them as lessons, and find joy in being alive."

Father Habak was now feeling fairly good about his homiletic efforts, and went on. "On the mount, Jesus spoke to downcast folk who were in pain and confusion, yet thirsted and hungered after righteousness. He knew their pain and sin as he does ours, but yet he called them 'merciful, pure in heart, and peacemakers.' They were folk like us; he promised they would overcome the bad things in their lives, be made fresh by the love and forgiveness of God, and 'be the salt of the earth and the light of the world.' And, I want to assure you, he knows that you folk in these hills are already the salt of the earth and light of the world. I believe that, too, and I think it will be a joy for me to live among you, learn from you, and be your neighbor.

"Well, that's all I have to say this morning. I thank you for allowing me to visit with you. God bless you all, and if there is anything you need of me, don't hesitate to ask. Please tell your friends that I am the new minister here and that I'd like to meet them. Tell them to just stop me along the road and talk with me if they'd like. I know I'm a stranger among you, but I'm pretty friendly and would like to be a good neighbor. Remember that Jesus said to 'love the Lord your God with all your heart, and your neighbor as yourself.' One of the ways we show our love for God is to worship him, and break bread together as neighbors in Holy Communion in his church on his Sabbath. One of the ways we love our neighbors as ourselves is to be kind, pleasant, and helpful to one another here. Thank you again. I will be at the door after the services to meet you. Please tell me your names and if there is anything I can do for you this week."

Dus finished the liturgy, pausing from time to time to help people with the pages of the prayer book and inviting them to come forward and receive Communion. They all did, except the very little children. Some made faces when they received the wine. That was OK with him. God wouldn't care, and neither did he. He closed the service with a blessing and retreated to the back of the church to meet the people. He was not sure how he had done, but he already felt a kinship with those few people who had made the effort to be there for his first try with his new ministry.

"Good mornan, Parson," a sweet, handsome, middle-aged lady said to Dus, while extending her hand. "I'm Nancy Conley, en dese are my boys, Jason en Luke. Ya alr'ady met my man, Ox. He donna go to chu'ch, en my daughta, Jenny, da Mrs. Cyrus Gruber is home wid our three-yar-old gran'baby. Her hubby's aworkin' in da woods wid Ox. 'Tis nice ta have ya har at da chu'ch and our town. I sho enjo'd yer message en da wo'ship sarvice. A bit diffant from watta we heard before, but real nice. Ox said he stopped ta jaw wid ya Friday en though he wonna say it ta ya, Parson, he enjo'd da prattle wid ya. He hoped ya enjo'd da rabbit he brung ya and that ya got set'led in all right. Would like ya ta come ta our house fer some vittles wid us. We'd be pleased ta have ya. Jist country cookin'. Da nice lady docta wadda stay wid us en her boy is gonna be thar, too, so ya kin visit wid dem, too. Nice ta see dem in chu'ch. She told me she fixed up yer pain, yestaday. She's a good doc ena nice lady, she is. Wall, ya jist come on later affer ya is done har en we'll have some eats tagetha. Bye now."

"Bye, Mrs. Conley, and thank you," Dus said. "It was nice to meet you, and I'll come by as soon as I close up the church."

A few other ladies and children greeted him. Among them was a Mrs. Bokempt, with a sickly looking son and daughter with her, and a Mrs. Hudson and a Mrs. Clayton, who walked together. Mrs. Hudson said that she and her husband, Jed, owned a general store in town and would always be glad to help him. Mrs. Clayton said she had an "eatin' place" and would be glad to keep him full and healthy. They said they were there because their friend Nancy Conley said they ought to hear the new preacher and support his efforts. He liked Nancy and those two women immediately.

Then a grumpy old man by the name of Mr. Riggans shook his hand, told him the church was too cold and his sermon too long. But, though he didn't agree with everything Dus said, it would do for now, and he would try him again sometime. Better than what preachers usually talk about. Dus took that as a compliment and met a few more adults and young people who mumbled shy greetings. Then, last in line, came the lady physician and her young charge.

"Good morning, Father Habak. It's nice to be here. You came to see how a female surgeon does her medical thing, so I have come here to see how a male priest does God's thing," she grinned.

Lord, Dus breathed, doesn't this feminist Indian sawbones ever stop shooting her quippy arrows?" "Thank you for coming, madam. Did I say anything worth listening to?"

She ignored the sarcasm. "As a matter of fact, I liked how you handled the mountain and valley analogy. Very good. True and close to my heart, since we come from the Oregon mountains." She introduced her son. "Shawn, this is Father Habak. Father, this is my son, Shawn."

"Hi, Father," the handsome and husky lad, who looked a lot like his mother, said. "I like the Communion service. I was an altar boy at the Episcopal Church when we lived near the university."

"Glad to meet you, Shawn. Maybe you would like to serve for me at the Communion sometime, when you and your mother are here in the mountain."

"Sure. I'll help you every Sunday if Mom says it's OK. How about it, Mom?"

"We'll talk about it, Shawn. It was nice of you to ask him, Father. Tell me—how's your heinie this morning? You handled the service as though there were no ill effects. I must have fixed it pretty good."

Dus frowned and looked around to see if anyone had overheard her. No one had. The woman has no couth, for crying out loud. "It's fine, Dr. Marson. I thank you for your ministry to my behind."

"You're welcome. My pleasure. Don't forget your appointment to change the bandages this afternoon. Nancy Conley tells me we'll be having dinner at her house together a little later. Be nice to get acquainted with you on a more social level."

"It was nice of her to include me. I will be down as soon as I finish here. I'll see you there."

"Good. And bring an empty stomach. Nancy'll have venison, mashed potatoes and gravy, red cabbage, stewed tomatoes, corn on the cob, and two or three different fruit cobblers. She knows from experience that the way to a man's heart is through his stomach. You can tell that she learned that from her hubby, Ox. How about you, Parson? Is the way to your heart through your stomach, or through that clerical armor you seem to wear?"

"I will see you at dinner, Doctor Marson," he answered, discernibly frustrated with her quips. Pushing Shawn out of hearing distance, he added, "In the meantime, while you are driving down to the Conleys, you might meditate on the things you heard today, not from me, but from the Bible, which talks about loving your neighbor a smidgen, and maybe you'll find a way that you and I can communicate without barbs. Thanks again for coming to my worship service. There will be no charge."

Dr. Marson gazed at him with eyes that began to well up in tears. "Yes, I heard, and it sounded good. I'll see you at dinner. Bring your appetite and your manners, neighbor," she whimpered, turning quickly and pushing Shawn in front of her down the path. She stopped and waved back at him, now smiling. Going up the church aisle to clean up and put away the service appointments, he felt guilty. I know she didn't mean to make me mad, he berated himself, but why does she keep saying things to put me down? Must not like clergy, or maybe it's her way of dealing with life. She's a doctor, for God's sake. She sees a lot of pain, people hurting and dying. Shawn seems to be alone with her. Nice, affable kid. Cheerful and friendly. Must take after his dad, whoever he is. She never mentioned a husband. Probably teased him to death.

He put the damper on the stove, and took off his vestments and hung them in the sacristy closet, noticing an old, wrinkled mildewed cassock and surplice hanging there. They were short and must have fit a shorter person than himself. He thought about the old pastor Ox was telling him about, but then shrugged his shoulders and went to the vicarage. There were mixed feelings in his heart, and he looked up to the sky and asked, "How did I do today, Lord, with the bishop's 'challenge,' aside from blowing my pastoral duties with the feisty doc?" If God answered Dus, he didn't hear.

\* \* \*

Eight people sat in woven rope ladder-back chairs around a rough hand-hewed plank table, draped in a red-and-white checkered tablecloth. Dishes and glasses, food and drink covered the table. Ox Conley sat at one end; at the other end, his wife, the mother of his children, sat. All held hands and bowed their heads.

"Lo'd we jist gives ya thanks," Ox intoned, "fer des day a rest, fer our family, fer dese frien's who have come har ta shar' our vittles, for our neigbas, en des food lovingly prepared fer us by my good wife, Nan. Bless all da folks what donna have much en des world, and help us ta help iffen we ken.

Keep me, ole Ox, strong, so I ken hunt en bring meat home fer my family and da neigbas. We thank ya, too, Lo'd, fer Docta Marson comin' up ta mountain in da clinic en bringin' medicine ta help da sick folk. En, oh yeah, Lo'd, we thanks ya, too, fer our new frien', da preacher har, who says he will tend da graves and say da prawrs at da chu'ch. Amen."

"Amen," the group added, raising their heads and reaching for the food. They stopped to watch Ox sternly directing the food to first be passed to Nancy, who sat gracefully smiling like an honored matriarch.

Dr. Marson smiled, too, not at Ox, but at Father Habak. "How do you feel the prayer saying and the grave tending is going, Father?" she asked.

"Fine, Doctor. Did you not see when you visited our church this morning?"

Dr. Marson gave a pretty grin and said, "Yes I did, Padre. You are off to a good start, it seems. Don't you think that Nancy's food and drink look good, too?"

"I do, indeed," he answered. Then, turning to Nancy, "Thank you for asking me to come, Mrs. Conley. It all looks great, and I'm ready to feast upon it!"

"I'm glad, 'cause men sholy needs thar food. Now, Parson, my name's Nancy, en dat's jist watta ya must call me. Der's always a plenty a food on our table fer folks, en we enjo' sharin' it en havin' company. Nice to have ya har, some as Karol and Shawny. Anyway, Ox wanna ya ta try his newly smoked venison."

"Sho did, Preacha," Ox agreed. "My Nancy is da best cook in dese parts, fer as I knows, en she'll sholy fill a man's belly in a hurry. No use yer cookin' up thar by yerself when we have all des food down 'ere. How'd ya like da rabbit?"

"Did fine fixing it, and it tasted good. Thanks for bringing it to me. I'm not used to cooking for myself yet, but I'll learn. Course there is Mrs. Clayton's restaurant, too, and I'll try that."

"Bessie's my best frien', en ya'll like her en her cookin' fer sure. We learnt ta cook together as we was growing up as younguns," Nancy said, pleased that Dus knew of her friend's place.

"She ain't as good as ya is, Nan; ain't thatta so, Doc?" Ox lauded his wife.

"Ya'll er full of stuff," Nancy blushed.

"Ya is da best, darlin'," Ox kept insisting. "Now, Dus, jist let us knows when ya needs some meat, en I'll git it fer ya. Dey have aplenty a bought veg'ables down at Jed's stow ta buy. Butta most folk har have gardens in da spring en can da stuff en put it up in der cold cellars. We have lots a apples, par, en cherry trees har fer da fruit, en dey gits pickled and jarred, too. En I tell ya, Dus, der is more asparagus en rhubarb 'round here dan ya ken eva kill wid a sickle. Da stuff grows thistles en multiples faster den a field a ribbits. Lots a greens, too. Collard en dandelion, iffen ya likes dem. Nancy makes them all good, en I'm a tellin' ya, once ya eat her cookin', ya will neva say 'no' again to her invite. Sos ya better quit a talkin' en dig in ta dem vittles a hers."

Dus watched with amazement as everyone "dug in" and ate. He could not help but think that this is the way that family ought to be—decent and loving rural folk at peace on a Sunday afternoon, enjoying food provided by their own hard-working hands, sharing it with neighbors. It really had been a good day, give or take a few moments, and being here with these people around this table is so pleasant and rewarding. There was great big Ox sitting there virtually shoveling in the food that his beloved wife had prepared, enjoying her and his children, and proud to share his family and board with visitors. It's fun being here. There is a contentment among these people I somehow missed during my high-minded, sophisticated cathedral work. There I was, studying, lecturing, going to meetings and conventions, being a theologian, motivator, teacher, administrator, counselor, and, oh, yeah, of course, a biblical scholar and social activist. And what for? Guess that is what the holy church expects us priests to be. Well, I did it, and what good did it do for anybody? I neglected Ginnie and Dusty, and now they are gone. I wish they were here sitting around this table with Elly and me, breaking bread with these fine souls, smiling, talking, and enjoying life. Oh, I miss them so.

He ate heartily, tasting everything, and listened to Ox, Nancy, and Dr. Marson conversing, while the children, the young married people, and their baby interrupted now and then with their vocal offerings.

"Have ya hadda nuf, Parson?" Nancy asked, interrupting Dus' thoughts. "Hope ya saved some tummy room fer some of my homemade cherry pie en apple dumplin's."

"Oh, yes, fine, Nancy," Dus stuttered, returning to the conversation. "The food was very good. It's been a long time since I have had venison, and you make it so tasty. Thank you so much. I will have some cherry cobbler with a bit more coffee, but I think I'll wait until later until after the children have finished and gone out to play. I'm full, and I should take a respite. I'm in no hurry to go, unless Dr. Marson wants to get down to the clinic soon to see her patients and tend to my wound."

"No hurty at all," Karol broke in. "I've plenty of time to patch you up, Padre. Just sit, drink, and be merry. As old Omar Khayyam once wrote, 'For tomorrow we die.'"

"Whadda ya say, little lady?" Ox asked.

"Oh, nothing much, Ox. I was just funning the preacher."

Seems to me you enjoy funning the Preacher a lot, sawbones, Dus inwardly mumbled, glaring at Karol. Why do you want to take this joy I am feeling away from me with your bantering? "It's OK, Ox. The doctor is just joking with me about something she read in a book one time. She's just trying to tell me I ought to relax and enjoy all this good food and friendship today, 'cause we never know what is going to happen tomorrow. Of course, if she is not a very good medicine woman, I may not live to enjoy tomorrow. I'm just kidding, Ox. That's a joke, too."

Karol stopped grinning. "Well, you got your revenge there, Father."

"Well, I dunna always unnernstand such talk," Ox said, "butta donna ya worry none, Dus. Docta Marson is a good docta, en she'll take good care a ya. Ya'll sholy live ta tomorry. By da way, how 'bout tellin' me mo' 'bout how ya got dat wound?"

"It was nothing. I tripped and fell while up on the Cutty, and a tree stump poked through my pants not my backside. It got infected, but Dr. Marson cleaned it up very nicely and it's fine now. She wants me to come down to the clinic this afternoon to swab it with some antiseptic and put a clean bandage on it."

"I think more than that happened up there on Friday, Ox. Father Habak is not telling us everything," Karol interjected. "Isn't that true, Father?"

Before Dus could answer, Ox raised his voice to the children. 'Now ya younguns, git en clean up da dishes fer yer motha and en skidaddle so we grounups ken talk ova pie en coffee!"

What's the matter with that woman? Dus mumbled to himself again. Now Ox is going to ask me a lot of questions about that shooting. Damn her nosy Sherlock Holmes hide. Why can't she just stick to her medicine and keep out of other people's business? "Well, Ox, Nancy, and you, too, Doc, you might as well kn—"

"Hold on, Dus. Ya tell us nuffin ya donna wanna say, butta I need ta tell ya, I already knowd ya was up on da Cutty near da barren ceda' stand, en dat ya was ina some kin'a trouble."

"Wadda ya know, Ox?" Nancy asked. "'cause ya dint tell me ya knowd anythung 'cept wadda I told ya the doc sayed."

"I know dat, Nancy, but I dinna wanna say nuffin lest ya worry yer pretty face off. Dis is menfolk busnus, en I donna like talkin' 'bout it 'roun' da womenfolk, so iffen ya got somthun ta do, ya ken go en do it."

"Ox Conley, I ain't no squirt of a mealy mouf shiverin' bride wid my knees a rattlin' 'cause my man is in da woods with da bears en snow. I ain't never scarit 'bout you, en I ain't scarit wadda happened ta the parson up thar, neitha. We lady folk wanna har too, but I only speak fer myself, en iffen da doctor donna wanna har it, she ken say so herself. But I wanna har it, en I spect she do, too."

"That's right, Ox!" Karol agreed. "I knew when Father came into my office and told me what happened up there, there was more to it than he was telling. I want to know the whole story, too."

"No doubt," Dus frowned.

"Wal," Ox continued, "I was lookin' for dat big stag up near da barrens late en da af'ernoon on Friday, when I come on ta some boot tracks. Were big, like mine. I followed dem fer a time en den dey stopped. It lo'ked like a fella stood fer a time der. I seen some glove marks in da snow 'round thar, den it lo'ked like he backtracked en wenna on down da hill. I thunk ta foller him, butta I noticed a splintered tree stump en otha boot tracks. Dang if I di'n't nearly trip ova des log wid da snow all matted down, wid blood down its side, en on a samplin' stump stickin' outta da groun'. It lo'ked ta me like some rifle slugs done tore up da log and da groun'. Coul'n't fine no slug, butta da hole in da log lo'ked ta me like an ole 30.06 Star Gauge Springfield bullet done it. Cou'se, it coulda been a sixteen-gauge shotgun slug, too. Anways, da fella behin' thatta log what was bleedin' was you, weren't it, Dus? Might well tell da truf, 'cause da minute Nancy tol' me da story dat da doc tol' her 'bout yer leg, I had my head a thinkin', en I done put da two tales tagetha. Ain't watta I said true, Dus?"

Dus cleared his throat and decided to tell the events that took place on the Cutty. "I just didn't think it was important enough to make a big deal out of my first day on the mountain. I admit it frightened me at first, but then I understood the nature of the wound and dismissed it all as maybe an accident or a mistake. I was hoping no one would hear about it. I didn't want anyone to worry about me nor be a nuisance. I thought Doctor Marson, as a professional person, would respect my privacy and not mention to anyone what I told her."

"You wait just one darned second, Father . . . " an angry Karol trailed off.

Nancy's voice interrupted her. "Now, Dus, it was Ox dat a found out watta happened, so ya shan't git yer back up at our doc. She jist cares 'bout folk, en she wannta it ta go well wid ya."

"Mare's marbles," Dus murmured, trying to look penitent and forgiving. "I'm sorry, Doctor. I guess as one who hears a lot of private information, as I am sure yo do, I am a little sensitive about confidential things. I did not mean to reflect on you."

Yes, you did, you pompous cleric, Karol steamed within herself. Deciding, however, not to fight with him in front of the Conleys, she responded with milder pique. "It's all right, Father; we all get a little tense, and I don't blame you for being scared, considering your experience. If it had been me, I would have screamed my head off till every critter in the forest ran away, and then I would have run down the mountain like a bat out of hell. I admire your composure and self-confidence, but you ought not take lightly that your head could have been blown away by some nut."

"That's true. Has Ox told you about the minister who built the vicarage and the church? Interesting story! After the shooting up there, I kept thinking that there might be some connection. But then that was twenty-some years ago, so I suppose that has nothing to do with it."

"No, he didn't. What story, Ox?" Karol asked.

Ox repeated the story with considerable embellishment.

"Oh, shaw, Ox, thatta ole yarn has been 'round about fer yars," Nancy admonished her husband. "Ida donna know a soul watta talks 'bout it anymo', en ya ought not ta be tellin' it. I ken tell ya though, da man was strong en quiet, seyd nice prawers, en took go'd care a da graves lika we ask 'im to. Ox en me jist married en had Jenny 'bout dat time when dat preacha come en left wid nary a good-bye affer havin' done all dat work en buildin' up dat. It's a good, strong place, it is. Dinna ya notice, Karol?"

"The church is beautiful," Karol said admiringly, "and it looks like loving hands built it. I haven't seen anything but the outside of the vicarage, but it looks like it was built well, too."

"It is very adequate and comfortable for a single man. Wouldn't do for women folk," Dus assured her.

"Like I seyd," Ox continued, "da preacha was a good capenta, en he stayed ta hisself. Di'n't botter none a yas, en I donna 'member he had any regular prawer meetin's. I do knows da Nancy ner none of her frien's wenna up thar much. Ain't dat so, Nan?"

"Wal, I woulda gone more iffen he hadda 'em. Butta he jist built da house en church en stayed ta hisself. We'd see his pickup wid loads a stuff goin' up en down ta da church. Den sometimes we'd hear da organ, en it were purty music watta he played. Butta he was a strange pawson, en we ain't da nosy type. Ox give him da land, en den he stayed outta it. Up har, we donna botha otha folks' privacy, lest we is asked. Sometimes he'd walk ta town en down ta da lumber yard en coal pits. En sometimes he picked up stuff wid his truck. Der some folk in Joshuatown watta 'members him, butta none of us like ta talk much 'bout him."

"I found some old clergy vestments in the church closet," Dus said. "They were in pretty good shape, except for mildew and age. They didn't look like they had been worn much. He must have been from some organized denomination if he wore vestments."

"Wadder vestments?" Ox asked.

"Those are clothes that ministers wear when they have worship services in the church," Karol offered.

She might have let me answer that, Dus bristled, but he dismissed the thought, thinking it better to keep peace and pry a little more out of the Conley's collective memories. "Do you remember if he wore a black shirt and a white collar like I have on now?" he asked.

"Naw, I don't, Dus. He jist had on ov'alls, boots, good jacket, en hat. He hadda nice cut wiskas, en he talked good. 'Twas an edjicated man. He was 'bout middle age, like ya is, I reckon, en he had sorta a limp. But none a usins got ta knowd him too well, en so Nan seys that ain't much ta tell. She donna like gossip."

"Well, we will have to let it stop there for now," Karol insisted, "because it's nearly two o'clock and the sign on the clinic says that I will be back at three. I have to get the parson down there first and bandage his wound before others show up. Thanks for the wonderful meal, Nancy. I appreciate all that you do for Shawn and me. Tell the boy I'll be back for him a bit after six to head home for school tomorrow. You coming, Father Habak?"

"Yes. I'll follow you down in my car. Thanks again, folk," Dus said, turning to the Conleys. "It was a super meal. Don't worry about the shooting. It was nothing but an accident. The rifleman may not even know about it. Well, I'd better not keep the lady waiting."

"So long, Fadder. Glad ya could come!"

"Yah, we sho enjo'd ya," Nancy added. "Wish ya could stay longer, Karol."

"Wish so, too, Nancy," Karol replied, "but I have surgery tomorrow and Shawn has school. Maybe someone will cover for me and I can spend Thanksgiving with you. Don't make supper for me tonight. I'm beginning to look like a fat cow. Let's go, Preacher!"

*You're a royal pain in the rear, Doctor,* Dus mused, ogling the figure she was demeaning, *but you sure don't look like a fat cow!*

\* \* \*

Dus, on his stomach on the examination table at the clinic, gritted his teeth as Dr. Marson probed his wound for any further infection. There was none, so she swabbed it with iodine, applied a fresh bandage, and ordered him to put his pants back on. "Looks good, Father. The infection is nearly gone, and it will heal with no scar. Keep that bandage on it for a while so bugs won't get in it again. Wow—what a day. I got to hear the preacher preach, share luscious food with him, hear his mysterious shooting tale, and see his paleface heinie, all in one day. I'm a lucky lady! Aren't the Conleys nice people?"

"Yes, they are, Doctor," Dus answered, trying to hide his annoyance with her. He dressed quickly and started to leave. "Thank you for your care, and have a good trip back to Staunton. Say good-bye to Shawn. He's a nice lad. Oh, yes," he groused. "Since you don't take fees from clergy, I'll donate this to my educational fund. It will help me pay for a course in humor and banter. If I made your day a lucky one, I am happy for you. Preaching, eating, telling tales, and showing my lily-white heinie to women are what I do best. But, as for my heinie, Doctor, it is what it is. I assume as an Indian, your heinie is not quite as paleface, but then I didn't get a chance to compare. Glad you enjoyed the day! See you around the campgrounds."

Karol was startled, and her face showed real hurt. Dus didn't care! He turned and went out the door, shutting it hard. He was angry and tired of the silly banter that had gone on all day between them. He was anxious to get up the valley with his Jeep and try to visit some people. He climbed in the automobile and started the engine.

"Turn off that engine and get out of the car, Father Habak!" a very upset Dr. Marson screamed at him through the window. "And quit acting like a spoiled teenager, for crying out loud!" Tears welled in her eyes and rolled over her high cheekbones. She was strikingly beautiful in spite of her despair, Dus thought, but clearly devastated as she shivered in the cool air and choked out some more words. He rolled down the window to listen to what she was trying to say to him. "Please come back into the clinic," she wailed. "You're a priest, for God's sake! Come on. There's no one else there yet, and we have some time to talk. Will you please quit being so peeved at me every time I open my mouth? I seem to antagonize you with everything I say. Please—let's talk. We should listen to one another. You're hurting and we both seem to be carrying chips on our shoulders that may not have anything to do with today. You and I are supposed to be healers, not warriors!"

Dus begrudgingly turned off the car engine, got out, and walked with her to the clinic.

"Sit here in this chair," Karol directed him, "and take the frown off of your face. Smile a little; tell me I'm a pain in the buns if that will help your mood, then forgive me as priests are supposed to do, so we can start afresh and be friends."

"Look, Doctor Marson, there is no point in this discussion. I am sorry if I hurt your feelings. I am just not in the mood these days to listen to your constant smartcracks about my vocation and my clergy persona. You seem to have an unending supply of them, for whatever reason. But you have not let up on them since we met. You embarrassed me with the Conleys. Just know that I am trying to find a new direction for my life and do some decent work for the church at the same time. I am finding that hard enough up here in this wilderness without a lot of nasty witticism about it from a woman I don't even know. Some creep up here tried to shoot off my behind my first day here, and you think it's a big joke. My rear end hurts, Doctor, but not nearly as much as your not taking me seriously as either a priest or a person, when you don't know me from Adam."

"Yeah, I know," a penitent Karol apologized. "I guess I have been acting pretty tacky toward you, but what I perceive as your priestly pomposity gets my banter juices going. I'm sorry. My experience with you clergy types hasn't been all that rewarding, but that is no excuse for my being rude to you. We should talk and get rid of these ghosts hanging around us. I have skeletons of my own, Father, that I suppose make me a bit flippant, when I ought to be more understanding and compassionate. I should watch my tongue, especially with people who are not used to me. You would hardly believe it now, Father, but I am a good listener. Are you?"

"I used to have a fairly good reputation for that. If you'll lighten up on the banter and quips, I'll be glad to listen to whatever you have to say. That's what the pastoral ministry is all about, but I have never been able to contend very well with people who wisecrack about life as if it were some sort of a funny game."

"Is that what you think I do?"

"It just doesn't seem to me that you take people very seriously."

"I'm really sorry that is your perception of me. But maybe you'll see me a little differently when I quit responding to what I perceive is your clerical air. Anyway, why don't you tell me about you—what you're about, your family, where you've been, and where you're going. I'm a physician, Father, and I'm interested in your wounds, no matter their character. It's the nature of the beast!"

"I have no reason to cry on your shoulder. I'm just a recycled Episcopal priest with a mission church to get started on this mountain. I'm a single father with a thirteen-year-old daughter—a tough age for a girl with no mother, for whom I have to find a new life. I don't have much time to do that for her because she is growing up fast. She's in the Sister's Priory School at the Diocesan Center, and when I get settled I hope to bring her up here with me. It has been less than a week since I have seen her, but I miss her terribly. That's about it. So now I must get on with the job of ministering and parenting. Nothing else matters."

"Is that all you're going to tell me? Are you afraid to tell me what is eating out your heart and soul? Do you not want to expose your feelings because I'm a female doctor?"

"Look, lady, you asked me to tell you, and I have. What else do you want of me? Are you some kind of 'shrink' who wants to delve into my screwed-up psyche?"

"I'm no 'shrink.' I'm just trying to be a friend you can talk to. We pros don't have a lot of those around. Now quit being so piqued at me and tell me about you and your daughter. What's her name, and what about her mother?"

"Why? Why should I talk about my family with someone I don't know? There are just some things in a man's life that he doesn't want to talk about, and are not anyone else's business. I'm just trying to put my former life behind me and forge ahead for Elly's sake. I'm trying to do it in a priest's way because I don't know any other way to do it."

"Is that your daughter's name—Elly?"

"Yes. It's really Ellen, and she is a beautiful and wonderful girl like her mother was."

"Her mother was? Is your wife dead, Father? Or are you divorced?"

The question stung and sent Dus into a terrible temper tantrum. He lashed out at Karol. "Yes. She's dead, goddamn it!" he swore, spitting out the foul words like venom and not caring whether it was a woman, a bishop, or another Marine grunt. "And so is my son. Killed in a car crash because some drunken son of a bitch filled up his brains with a jug of whiskey, drove his car into my car, and killed my family. You wanted to hear, wise Doctor, so now that you have all that sick information, analyze it and stick it in your 'self-pitying priest' file. But it happened, didn't it? And it matters to no one, because I'm supposed to be a sacrificial priest who works for God, who is supposed to know why such things happen. Well, maybe he, the holy church I've worked my wounded butt off for, and you, smart medicine woman, can tell me why my wife and kid lay bleeding to death in a car, and I couldn't, God couldn't, and a doctor couldn't keep them alive for Ellen and me, who need them so much. Shit! Maybe I deserved it, but my wife, son, and daughter didn't deserve it!"

Dus was crying and shaking. Acrimony flowed out of him like a river broken through a dam, as it had weeks ago when he was with the bishop. He could not control his weeping, and he continuously rubbed his shirt sleeve over his face and eyes. It did no good. He could not stop the tears. Karol sat staring at him. She was weeping, too, wishing she could do something to comfort him. She moved toward him to put a hand on his arm, but he pushed it angrily away and she retreated to her chair. She pulled some tissues from a box, wiped her eyes, and offered him some. Again, he slapped away her hand and the box flew across the room. She did not know what to do or say anymore but knew she had to try. I don't know why, but it hurts to watch a grown man cry, she thought. It is so much easier for us women. "Oh, God, Father Habak! I'm really sorry," she sniffed.

"Sorry! Shit! You wanted to know all this mucky slop, didn't you? Well, now you know," Dus moaned, looking into her face with red eyes and a smeared face. "Does it make you feel good to know that I am nothing now but a grown-up whimpering priest? Does it please you to know how bitter and vulnerable a fellow professional is? To hear my stinking gutter language I haven't used in years and hate with a passion? Would you like to know, too, that sometimes I wish the drunken bastard was still alive so I could beat the hell out of him over and over again for killing my wife and son? Do you know that I would like to get as drunk as he was so I wouldn't feel this agony? Do you really want to know that I am a priest who is furious with God because he asked me to neglect my family and allowed them to be killed, and now I won't see them anymore except in my nightmares? Does it please you to see a priest cry, Physician?"

"No, but I think it's OK for a priest to be angry and weep like anyone else. If there is a God, I am sure he is big enough to handle your anger, understand your pain, and know the reason for your rancor. If it makes any difference, I understand, too. You have a right to feel hurt, to vent, and to have your broken heart tended to and healed."

"Ah, stop the psychotherapy with me. I may not be acting like it right now, but I am a grown-up boy. I know the score. I've seen and listened to a lot of pain in my life, and seen a lot of blood, sweat, and tears, and have witnessed a lot of people die. I've prayed over them, held their hands and heads, and buried them. It's what life is about in your profession and mine, isn't it? As you quoted Khayyam, 'We're here and gone tomorrow.' A man loves hard, and those whom he loves and pours his being into are snatched from him. God could care less. Nobody cares unless it happens to him. That's the truth about life, isn't it, Doc?"

"I don't know a lot about what God thinks, but I don't think so. That wasn't what you were talking about in your very appropriate sermon this morning. There are mountains and valleys in everyone's life."

"Come on, Doctor. You know very well we preachers tell people what we have to, whether we believe it or not."

"That may be true about a lot of people, Father, but this morning you really believed in your heart and soul what you were saying to those people up there, and they were listening to you and believing every word you spoke. I understand why you are feeling the way you do right now. I can't discuss with you what makes life tick. I'm no theologian. It's too big a spiritual and medical subject to deal with here, when both of us are mad at each other and feel so lousy."

Dus was beginning to feel the lady did care. He sniffed some more and blew his nose. He was still too choked up to talk coherently, but he tried. "I'm sorry I let my emotions get out of control. I guess my tears have been too long in coming. I have been acting like a baby, and I am sorry I spilled my guts all over you. I miss my wife and son so much I can hardly stand it. And I don't know what to do about Elly. I've been sent up into these mountains by my bishop because I screwed up my ministry with my grief and self-pity. I know I'm here because it's a solution for saving my priesthood, a way to get my life going again and practice my trade. How about that angle? So what do you think the Conleys and the other folk up here in these woods will think and say when they find out they are just therapeutic gimmicks for a fallen preacher? How many more weird clergy are they going to have to endure at that church? Do you have any idea how I feel, Doctor?"

"Yes, I know how you feel, and the people here are not going to be privy to the things that have hurt you. But these people would care, if they did know."

"How do you know how I feel? Well, maybe you do. I guess you have seen a lot of pain, trauma, and misery in people's lives in your work. But do you really know what those people feel down deep in their hearts and souls?"

"Yes, I really do know how they feel, Father."

"How can you? Ministering to pain, whether it is physical or spiritual, is not living inside a person where it exists. You have to live it to feel it."

"I have lived it, my friend. I am sorry about what happened to your wife and son. That was a dreadful thing, but I know in my heart that your ministry here and Elly will fill up those voids in your life, and you will find some peace and happiness again. I also know that my platitudes and experiences won't help you at this point in time."

"What about you? You said you knew how I felt."

"There is no need for you to listen to my life story. As a priest, you don't bother a parishioner with your own troubles when they are in pain. Physicians don't either. I'm a long way from the bad days in my life, and I have found my happiness with Shawn and my work. I feel good about my life now, and have put the unhappy part behind me."

"Everyone carries burdens, Doctor. I can tell you have had them, too. You said you would talk, too, so talk. We are a bit different than parishioners and patients, but maybe we professionals need to help each other, so we can help others a little bit better."

"OK, Father, but don't interrupt me till I am finished. I'll make it short and simple. Just in case you have conjured up in your mind some mistaken notions about my being a single woman with a naughty past, I was no silly teenage Indian girl with hot pants who got pregnant in the back seat of a reservation roadster. Nor am I a wild and fancy-free divorcee. Shawn is no 'bastard,' nor is he a 'mistake' child of a marriage gone wrong. I had a good husband named Doug Marson, who, in our marriage, sired and blessed me with a much-wanted boy we both adored. I was a nurse in an Oregon hospital and he was a forest ranger helicopter pilot."

She went on to tell Dus about Doug's sudden death, her move to the university, her attendance at medical school, and how she came to be at the clinic. "I went through a hell of my own, very much what you are experiencing right now. I lost a lot of faith in God, too, and I have been something of a spiritual pygmy ever since. But I have stayed with the church for Shawn's sake and because Doug would have wanted me to. I have come to terms with my grief, to serve humanity as best I know how with my skills, and to take care of Shawn. He and my work are my life, and have filled up the voids since Doug's death. I've come here to the clinic because I love the mountains, and have found in them a way to identify with my native roots and heritage without going home to Oregon and the reservation. But more than that, I feel I am doing something good in helping these people who have a real need and not many resources to pay for health care. There are still a lot of Indian ways and lore in me that help me deal with the darker side of life. I have made my peace with the Great Spirit, and I try to find joy in everything. I have learned to laugh a lot and not take life too seriously, except when I am at the operating table or in a hospital room with a patient. And yes, I know that my banter and jesting is probably a way of covering up the bogeyman within my soul, but I also know that I am not a mean-spirited woman. I don't deliberately hurt people. I am aware that sometimes I do— you being a case in point. I am sorry that I have done that to you and that you have misunderstood my persona. I will try harder with you because you are a different sort of person. But I am what I am, Father, and I cannot deal with things in this life with any other character tools than those available to me. That's the bare bones of my being. You hurt and I hurt and all God's people hurt. Now, while I don't know your bishop's full motive for sending you up here, I suspect he is a very kind and wise shepherd who loves you and has offered you a new chance to rid yourself of the monkey on your back, to get your life in order, and give you renewal for your vocation as a priest. These people are not therapy for you, Father Habak. Your bishop knows you have been a good priest, and you will shepherd them well. I'm no psychologist, but I wish that I would have had a wise and gracious person like him in my life when I was so hurt and confused, who would have cared about me and directed my life. I can love and respect your bishop without ever having met him, for doing that for you. It gives me hope for the church. And, even now, seeing you, as a priest, opening yourself up as a hurting human being, like the rest of us poor frail people, gives me a world of hope for the church."

Dus was listening to Karol very attentively, trying to think of something empathetic to say to her. He had been selfish in thinking about his own problems and pain, he lamented, and not even thinking of what she might have endured in her life. "Doctor Marson, I am really sorry I have been such a selfish and pompous dip. I am ashamed that I have treated to you as I have. I hope that one day you will forgive me. You have been kind in tending my wound, listening to my venting, and putting up with my sarcasm. I have been so full of self-pity and bitterness that I haven't thought much about others. I have learned a few good lessons during these last moments, it seems, from a very kind and intelligent person, who may be helping me to become a better man and priest. Thank you for being patient with me and for sharing your story. Maybe we can talk again sometime about the good things in our lives. I need all the friends I can get, and you seem to be that kind of person, if you can tolerate me."

"I'd like that, but I tolerate flies and mosquitoes, Father—not people. People I love, and I rejoice when they become better people. Isn't that what God and conversion is all about? Didn't you say that God loves the sinner, if not the sin, and wants us to be better? I hope he doesn't just tolerate us. Anyway, no need to worry about what's been between us anymore. We can both try to do better. Now you—you get out of here, 'cause there are some patients walking up to the door to my office, and they will need my attention. See you around. Have a good week." Tears welled in her eyes again. She dabbed her face with a tissue. "Gee whiz, Padre, look at me! I wasn't going to cry anymore. Tell me," she sniffed, "are you familiar with that part of the Roman Catholic mass where the priest asks the people to 'pass the peace' to one another? I have a good Roman Catholic priest friend, a visiting chaplain at Staunton General, who tries to explain all the changes made in their new liturgy. I'm not all that gung-ho about the changes. I argue with him, but his church is entitled to do as it wants."

"Yes, I know about 'passing the peace,' and our church Liturgical Commission is attempting to put it in our experimental liturgy, too. The idea doesn't exactly turn me on right now, but why did you argue with him about it?"

"I told him that I would start passing the peace at church services when some of the snooty people who are forced to pass the peace in church would start being nice and would start talking to the people at church socials and those outside the church door. Ignoring your neighbors, whether they are black, red, white, yellow, or chartreuse, and refusing to bid them 'good day' when they speak to you are not very Christian-like. You know we Indians have always passed the peace pipe with our neighbors. But all that aside, I brought it up, Father, because I don't have a peace pipe to pass to you. So I have to pass the peace in the only way I know how." With that, she reached out, put her arms around his neck, and sobbed on his shoulder. He held her gently, not knowing what else to do. No more words were said. They just embraced, with heads on each other's shoulders, until they heard footsteps and voices in the waiting room. They released each other.

Dus smiled and said, "Peace, Dr. Marson," left her office by the back door, and walked to his jeep. Karol hurried to the door, opened it, and yelled to Dus as he climbed into the auto, "Peace, Father Habak! That was an awful thing that happened to you up there on the Cutty. You could have been killed. Not everyone is nice in these hills, so be careful. Be wary and please give your paleface heinie a chance to heal."

He smiled back at her, threw his arms in the air, and drove away, thinking to himself, Thank you Lord! I feel better, thanks to that baffling, if pretty, lady! The "baffling, if pretty, lady" went back inside the clinic, looked in the mirror, washed the tear streaks from her tired face, opened the door to the waiting room, and smiled at a young mother who said, "Good afternoon, Doctor Marson. Ise hopes 'tis all right fer usins ta come see ya on a Sunday. Bobby's got somethun in his eye, en it hurts 'im bad."

"Of course it's all right. That's why the clinic is open. You and your mommy come into my office, Bobby, and let me see what we can do to fix that sore. It won't hurt. Maybe a lollipop will help. Would you like one?"

"Yeahzum," Bobby answered.

Karol sniffed, wiped her eyes again, knelt, and smoothed out the child's hair. She took his hand and gently led him through the door to her office. Life seemed very good again.

# 6

Three days had passed since Father Habak's first Sunday service and what had turned out to be a "catharsis" encounter with Dr. Marson. He spent that time either walking and driving over the valleys and hills of his new parish, though he had not yet ventured into Joshuatown. He wasn't sure why he hadn't. He guessed that he had been so captivated by the terrain stretching around the church, that he just hadn't gotten around to visiting the village. He hadn't met too many people, either, but that would come with time. He had a feeling he would be in his new parish confines for a long duration, and would have plenty of time for everything and anybody.

The weather today was briskly cold, but dry, and while the sky had been a bit hazy, the sun came through now and then, keeping the mountains bright. The shooting had mysteriously drawn him back up near the clump of cedar trees on the barren. The incident had not made him afraid. If anything, it had made him more curious. He was now sitting on a rock scanning the Blue Mountains and the valley, clear down to Joshuatown and beyond. He could see the picturesque little cabin home and church nestled on the hillside, and decided he would be content with his new assignment. He would let the shooting pass as an anomaly and would enjoy his present bliss.

His mind was full of the events of the few days since he had arrived in Joshuatown. He thought about Elly and wondered how things were going for her. He must call her soon. Maybe someone down in the village had a phone he could borrow. Or maybe he could drive down to the priory school soon and see her. Thanksgiving Day was approaching, and he thought, too, she might enjoy coming up to the mountain and spending the holidays with him. He wasn't a very good cook, but after the Thanksgiving Day service he planned at the church, he would take Elly to a really nice restaurant on the way back to the priory school. She would like that, he thought to himself. It will be good to see her and have her hugs and kisses. She's such a neat kid, and has brought so much joy into my life. I hope she misses me as I miss her.

Dus also assumed that Dr. Marson and Shawn had gotten safely back to Staunton. He had no fear that she had not. She appeared to be a very self-reliant and sufficient woman, and guessed her Native American heritage enabled her to cope with any kind of weather while driving, or any kind of situation, for that matter. He wondered whether women like her ever really needed anyone to help them to get along with life. Interesting, pugnacious person, but hard to stay angry with. And he had to admit, while she had challenged his sensitivity and ticked him off with her combativeness, she appeared, underneath all her audaciousness, to be a compassionate, loving, and capable physician. Well, he mused, his buttock wound was better, and so was his spirit, after she compelled him to unload a lot of debilitating and painful baggage he was carrying in his heart and soul. Dus was repentant about both his initial attitude and his earthy language toward her. No wonder she thinks clergy are a bunch of brats. I guess we are, a lot of times. Gee, she lost her husband in a fiery crash? Must have been terrible for her and the lad! No wonder she's cynical about God! Darned if she hasn't come through like a trooper, though, and made a new life for herself! Yeah, a tough gal! going through medical school, too, at the same time. You have to admire a person who could do something like that, with a son to take care of, while studying a difficult subject like medicine. Gosh, Dus noted, as he continued to muse over what he now knew of Doctor Marson. Well, maybe I'll see her again and we can share some good experiences, too. I'm sure Nancy Conley can tell me when she is coming back up to the clinic again.

His sore bottom was beginning to ache from sitting on the hard log. Stretching and plodding on, he thought he would heed her advice about taking care of his wound, wanting no more of her medical attention to that area of his anatomy. He remembered that she kept calling it a "heinie," and he smiled. Well, that's what it is, and I'd better get it moving in this parish of mine, if I am ever going to please God and the bishop, and keep this job so I can raise Elly the right way.

He traced his tracks back down the hill through pine, cedar, and hemlock stands. He enjoyed and appreciated what he saw and heard along the way. Rabbits were hopping here and there, chickadees and cardinals chirping away, and now and then he'd hear the bounding of a deer. He'd like to see an elder buck with a giant rack of antlers, to see for himself if the old ones were as big and noble as he had seen in *National Geographic*. How could one shoot anything as beautiful as a deer? he wondered to himself. Well, he sure wasn't going to ask that question around Ox Conley, who made part of his living that way and who the good Father Habek needed as a friend in these parts.

He looked from side to side and behind him along the path, wondering if there were any of those bears that Ox had spoken about around his trail. He smiled irreverently when he speculated that, while a prayer would be just the thing at a prayer meeting, it wouldn't be worth a hoot at a bear meeting. He just finished contemplating that thought, when he was jerked straight up by one of the most bloodcurdling noises he had heard since he was at war. It was more than a growl. It was a thunderous roar that echoed across the hills and down the valley. "Oh my God," he groaned aloud, "a bear!" He had known a lot of fear in his life, but he was now shaking and sweating in the cold of the day. The animal did not seem to be close by, but where was it? It did not matter. It was only important to Dus to guess the direction from which the roar had come, and to run like hell in the opposite direction and find cover. He heard it roar again, and he raced through the snow as fast as he could and made for higher ground. Passing by a patch of leafless dogwood, he noticed a dark shaded area to his left that appeared to be a large hole in the side of a limestone outcropping. It was a cave aperture, partially covered with the bare branches of small trees and an undergrowth of bushes. Without hesitating, he brushed the growth aside, entered the opening and ran a dozen or so feet, stopped to catch his breath, and scrutinized the terrain he had just covered.

With no sign of an animal of any sort following him, he breathed a sigh of relief. He quickly remembered, however, that he had read somewhere that a bear could smell a man two miles away, run as fast as a horse, and climb trees like a squirrel. Whether that was true or not didn't matter to him, either. He believed it, and felt no safe haven in the cave. But it did provide a restful reprieve and gave him time to decide what action to take to save his perspiring and shaking hide.

"Mare's marbles," he muttered. Elly, your old daddy is going to be clawed and gnawed to death by a wild beast, and you're going to be an orphan if I don't get out of these woods soon. He no sooner had that morbid thought, when it occurred to him that bears sleep in caves and that he might be standing near one of their bedrooms. "I can't stay here. What if a bear wakes up?" he said to himself, peering over the cave opening, and deciding to risk walking slowly and obliquely along the ridge and gradually down the mountain to the valley and town.

Just as he made that decision and found the courage to do it, another roar echoed through the wind, and he changed his mind. He had his sheath knife with him, but no flashlight, so he knew he would not go farther into the cave without being able to see what was in there. He sat and waited, with chills running up and down his back. Believing his hours were numbered, he did, out of sheer desperation, what he seldom had the natural ability to do—say an efficacious prayer right off the top of his head, even if he had thought a few seconds earlier it wouldn't have been worth a hoot.

"Lord," he started, with simple sincerity, "you know I have been a slob of a priest and a self-pitying dolt, of late. I lost my direction in life when you took Ginnie and Dusty away from me. I have not been very nice to you or anyone since. I've given Bishop Mueller and the church a ton of grief. You surely owe me nothing, and I have no business asking you to get me out of this mess. I never believed in foxhole promises and conversions, and I sure don't intend to burden you with one now, but if I am to be done in by some wild beast, please take good care of Elly. I know you love her even more than I do, but please have her know I loved her as I did her mom and brother. Bring her up strong and safe, with good memories of us. That's about it, Lord, but while you're handing out favors to the unrighteous, fill this unworthy servant's legs with fire, lungs with air, and heart with courage, 'cause I am going to run this body you gave me off this mountain like a bat out of hell. Amen."

Dus took a deep breath, scanned the area for a few seconds, and shot down through the forest like a bullet, with snow flying behind him, not looking back, sideways, up, nor down. His way was fairly clear, save a few fallen logs that he easily vaulted. He zigzagged through trees and bushes, sliding and stumbling, not losing his footing. He stopped for a moment behind a tree to take a breath and to listen for anything following. Hearing no bears or any animal, he still scooted again down the mountain as fast as his legs could take him. His continuing prayer was understandably incoherent, but he gasped out words like, "Oh, Lord, don't let that bear know where I am," and "Damn it, Lord. How'd you let me get into a mess like this?" By his own admission, Dus was good at assigning blame to God for many of his self-inflicted screwups. It was probably serendipitous then, without warning, that God allowed a low-hanging branch to brush his head, knocking him off his feet and causing him to fall headlong on his face and stomach down the trail. With snow sluicing down his jacketfront and cascading over his hair and back, the former dean of St. Andrew's Cathedral crashed into a pine tree and slid to a stop.

He sprawled there, brushing snow from his face and rubbing his eyes. He heard an aminous noise, like a big animal was walking behind him, and mumbled another petition to his "culpable God." Terrible thoughts crossed his mind as his eyes darted about, watching as best he could without moving his head. "Don't let that awful beast get me, Lord! I hate the idea of being eaten here in the snow." I feel all right, he admitted to himself. Nothing hurts, so I guess I'm OK. He thought he'd get up and start running again. As he began to stir, he heard crunching snow and a familiar voice.

"Whacha ya layin' thar in da snow fer, Preacha?" Ox Conley called to him. "Dija run in ta a bar er sumthun dat scairt ya so dat ya come a slippin' en sliding' like a playful beaver down da hill?" he asked as he came out of the brush, reached down with a gloved hand, and pulled Dus to his feet.

"Gosh, am I glad to see you, Ox!" Dus smiled gratefully, dusting the snow off his pants and coat, genuinely happy to have the big man there looking over him, even if he was laughing at his crisis.

"Ya looks like ya been runnin' hard, Dus. Wadda ya seen up thar?"

"You know these hills and animals around here, Ox, and I don't. I must admit they scare me. The mountains are nice, but I can't say that I am comfortable with the wild beasts running around them!"

"Nuffin ta be scair 'bout, Dus. Da crittas donna botha folk what donna botha dem. Only thing dangros dat ken hurt ya is a big cat or a bar, en dey usually run away when dey hears ya. Jest donna wanna corna dem in her dens when dey can't move away. An ya neva wanna mess wid der kitties nor der dubs, 'cause a mama ken get mighty nasty wid folk what gits near da little critters."

"Heard a bear roar up there, Ox, and it frightened me. I'm not used to being in the forest with bears. I ran up the hill into a cave up there near that bunch of barren trees."

"I heard da bar, too, butta she's harmless. Jist callin' a frien'. Cave! What fer cave?"

"I don't know. It was just there below an outcropping of rock, and I ran in it to hide from the bear. It looks deep, but I didn't have a flashlight, so I couldn't see much. I was afraid that maybe it was a den of some sort, and that maybe a mama bear was asleep in there with her cubs. Then I just prayed, looked around, and took off running as fast as I could."

"Well, ya looks all right. But, I mus' tell ya, Son, I be'n huntin' crittas and cuttin' timba 'round da Cutty en Blue mos' every week a my life, en I know every rock hangin's en sech, butta I donna know 'bout no cave up by dat cedar' clump!"

"I wouldn't tell you I was in a cave, Ox, if I hadn't been. I'm telling you the truth. There's a cave up there. I don't know how deep, how big, nothing about it, but there is a cave. I was in it, and I ran out of when I got scared."

Ox scratched his head in disbelief and wondered if his newfound friend had knocked his head on a tree limb. "Dus, I donna think ders a cave ta be up thar. Maybe ya cracked yer head a mite en jist dreamed it a lit'le."

"No, Ox, I didn't dream anything. I was in a cave—at least the entrance to one—and I know I could find it if I went back up there. I can't now because it's getting too late, I'm wet, tired, my bones ache, I don't want to meet any bears, and I want to get down to my hut."

Ox's demeanor seemed to change a bit, and his grin turned into a scowl. "Youse a city man, Dus, en ya oughten ta roam 'round des hills on yer own 'mong da crittas. Not least till ya git some meat on yer bones en learn da trails. Iffen ya found a cave up thar, I'll be dinged, butta I do b'lieve it might be yer 'magination, when yo hit yer head on somethin'."

Dus did not understand even his own fascination with the cave, nor did he understand Ox's steadfast denial that it existed. "Let it go for now, Ox. Let's go on down and get some hot coffee. Are you going home now? May I walk down with you?"

"Sure, butta I gotta stop on da way down en pick up some squirrel en ribbit I shot. I gotta git 'em home ta Nancy ta fix. Thanks fer da invite. I'll come by someday soon en have some coffee wid ya en we'll prattle ag'in."

They walked down through the forest, stopping off to pick up the dead animals. Ox talked most of the time, instructing Dus on the rules of the wild. They arrived below Dus' cabin near sunset, and he veered up the path toward it, saying good-bye to Ox.

"Salong, Dus, en have a good night. Meant wadda I seyd. Ya got lotta work tendin' dem graves, seein' folk, en havin' prawer meetin's, Son. Maybe ya oughta jist stick ta dat en not git lost in da woods no mo'. Jist leave da trails, da bars, en da huntin' ta me. Iffen ya like, I'll take ya out sometime en see if ya can't l'arn ta shoot en git a bird or a rabbit fer eatin', en even a buck."

Dus was sure now he would never discuss "animal rights" with Ox. "Thanks! I'd like that. Maybe we can find that cave together and see what's in it."

Ox shrugged his shoulders. "I ain't gonna go in no cave, Preacha, in da winna time when der could be b'ars in it. Anyway, su't yerself, butta donna git in ta no mess widda b'ars! Bye, now!"

"Bye! Say 'hello' to Nancy!" Dus hollered, as he walked up to his cabin, looking forward to sitting by the fire with a bowl of hot soup and thinking about the events of the past week. He thought about the cave on the Cutty and about Dr. Marson. He wondered when she would be returning to the clinic. He wanted to ask the Indian lady to teach him something about "tracking," and if she would be interested in helping him scout around the inside of that mysterious cave. Who needs Ox, who didn't believe him, he pondered to himself, when I can get a real live Indian, who knows about such things, to help me? Life at the moment seemed better for Father Habak, in spite of the critters in the mountains.

# 7

Dus was pleased that the diocese had provided him with a good vehicle. The bishop had been right when he said that his Olds wouldn't be good on the rough roads around the Joshuatown environs. Most people around the area had pickup trucks and, though many of them were beat-up junkers, they worked. The mountaineers were born mechanics and had a way of not only fixing their trucks, but talking to them like they were people. Treated them that way, too, by giving them names. Ox called his "Betsy." The oldest of them shined even on muddy days. Dus had always felt that his rich parishioners at the cathedral looked upon their big expensive "pickups" as status symbols. If you did not have one, you just weren't a part of the social set. His own family had had several old banged-up pickups on the farm that were strictly utilitarian. He had learned to drive on them. Here in the mountain, they were not only utilitarian, but the only means of transportation for many people. He laughed to think that his new and imprudently expensive Jeep may not have an equal standing in these hills. But it was all he had, and it worked very well. The four-wheel drive got him every place.

He picked this day to finally drive to town, stopping at the Conleys' to see if there was anything he could bring them from the store.

"Naw, thank ya kinely, Parson," Nancy said. "We have all da staples we needs right now. Ox's out wid da truck cuttin' some wood. He'll be a takin' a load down on da morrow, en iffen we needs somethun, he'll git it then. Cyrus is a helpin' him, en Jenny is har wid da gran'baby helpin' me ta make some deer jerky. Go by da Hudson stow en say 'hello' ta Jed en Helen fer me. Tell em I owes dem a pie anna Ox'll be bringin' it down thar sometime soon."

"OK, Nancy, I'll tell them. Thanks again for the good dinner last Sunday."

"Ya sho welcome! Wadda ya gonna do down in da village, Parson?"

"Oh, just look around a bit, meet some folk, and see if someone has a telephone so I can call my daughter, Elly, at school. I've been lonesome to talk to her, and want to make plans for the holidays with her."

"Das nice. Jed Hudson has one of dem telephon's at da stow far shur.

He be glad ta loan it ta ya. Sorry we donna have 'em dis far up. Be handy! Der's one at da clinic too, butta dat's closed when Dr. Marson ain't thar. Sho lookin' ferward ta meetin' yo' little girl. By da way, we know 'bout yo' wife en son from da doctor, and we's real sorry. Some folk has it bad, sometimes. Guess ya knowd da doctor had somethun bad happen ta'er hubby, too. I keeps ya'all in my prawers en hopes far ya to fine peace from da Lo'd."

"Thank you, Nancy. It'll be OK. You'll like Elly, and she'll like you. Well, I'd better get going. Bye!"

Dus drove down the wet gravel road into the village of Joshuatown. He looked harder at the stores and places he had not observed when he had first arrived, nor when he had visited the clinic. He first noted the HUDSON & SON COMPANY store on the main street. Next to it on one side was Shoney's barbershop, and on the other, the old-fashioned restaurant called "Bessie's Café," which Ox and Nancy had told him about. Across the street from that was the Joshuatown Merchant Bank. There were many big and small structures scattered here and there, many of which were located on the square that circled the county courthouse.

A saw mill and coal mine south of town, with their noise and dust emitting everywhere, reassured the local gentry that their biggest industries were running well. Paved asphalt streets and concrete sidewalks, with oak trees between them and the curbs, made the village appear well-kept. There were folk milling around giving no particular notice to him, though some nodded their heads in greeting.

Dus parked the Jeep and walked into the HUDSON & SON COMPANY store. It was a huge, long, narrow, one-story, almost cavernous building, dimly lighted, but stacked to the ceiling with furniture, hardware, clothing, staples, sundries, and foodstuffs. It boggled his mind. He had seen country stores when he was a youth, but didn't realize that such places still existed and were so huge. A few people in the store were actually shopping, while others seemed to be passing the time of day with cronies.

"Hello," a big man said, offering his hand to Dus in friendship. "I'm Jed Hudson. You must be Father Habak, the new minister at the church up on the Blue that I've been hearing about from my wife, Helen. You met her there last Sunday. Are things going well for you up there?"

"How do you do, Mr. Hudson," Dus responded to the friendly greeting. "Yes, I met Mrs. Hudson at church. Nice lady. I'm just fine, thanks. I'm getting settled pretty well. Are you the father Hudson, or the son Hudson?"

"Just call me Jed, Father. As a matter of fact, I'm the great-grandson

Hudson. This place has been a family operation for over a hundred years. There was my great-granddad, then my granddad after him, then my dad, and now me. All of us been doing business in this building right down through the years here in Joshuatown. What can I do for you?"

"I just came down to visit and to get acquainted with the village and townsfolk. No special reason other than that. Heard about your store, wanted to get some sundries, visit the bank, and make a telephone call to my daughter. I don't have a phone at the church."

"You're sure welcome to use mine. I hope you enjoy your work and stay here. If I can help you any, please yell. Nancy and Ox Conley and Helen say you're A-OK. A friend of theirs is certainly a friend of mine. I hear you're an ex-gyrene. I'm an old World War Two swabby, myself."

"Navy's a good outfit to have served in," Dus allowed, trying to avoid any discussion of war tales. "Nancy told me to tell you she is sending a pie down for you and Mrs. Hudson."

"Bless that good lady's heart! She and Ox are old, old friends of ours. She's sweet, and just doing that for us 'cause we sent some old furniture up to put in the parsonage. She shouldn't do that."

"Well, she insisted. I thank you for what you sent up, too, because I'm the one who's using it. I appreciate everything that all the folk around here have done for me to make my stay pleasant."

"That's OK, Father. Let me check on a customer. The phone is at the end of the counter; just help yourself. Dial zero for long distance, and the operator will put you through. The call is on the house."

Dus thanked the storekeeper, went to the telephone, and dialed. He spoke to the operator, who put him through to Sister Monica at the priory school. "Sister, this is Father Habak. How are you? . . . Yes, I am very well and doing just fine, thank you. . . . Yes, Sister, I am glad to hear that. Yes. . . . Yes. . . . No. . . . Yes, that will be fine. Sister! . . . Sister! I have to talk to Elly. Can you locate her for me? . . . Yes, thank you. I am calling long distance, so tell the secretary to hurry, please."

Dus waited for what seemed an eternity, then a smile broke across his face and he spoke into the phone. "Elly! . . . How are you, sweetheart? . . . Ah, that's good. I'm fine, too. . . . Yes, I want to hear all about it, honey. I have missed you so much, too. . . . Yes, baby, and that is one of the reasons I am calling. . . . . Yes. . . . Yes. . . . We can work out all of that. You're going to love it up here! . . . Elly! . . . Thanksgiving is only two weeks away, and I am going to come down and get you. . . . Ah, darling, no trouble, I want to see you so bad.... We'll have fun here for a few days, and then maybe go to a nice restaurant for dinner.... I'm glad, darling.... Yes! How about some shopping for some clothes, too. Elly, are you crying?... Yes, I miss them, too.... I'm lonely, too.... I am so sorry, sweetheart.... Yes, the sisters are nice, and I am glad they are taking good care of you.... No.... Really, I am doing all right now, but I'll be doing better when I can hug you.... Yes, you may, but be careful and get to bed early.... That's a good girl. Thank the bishop and Mrs. Mueller for me.... Hey, young stuff, no boys for now. We'll talk about that someday.... Be good, sweetheart. I love you so much, and can hardly wait to see you.... Thank you. We will make out OK.... Wipe your eyes, babe.... Keep plugging at school.... The sisters say you're doing very well. I'm proud of you. Yes.... Good-bye, sweetheart."

Dus hung the receiver on the hook and choked back a tear. He walked back to the store counter. "Thanks for the use of the telephone, Mr. Hudson. I appreciate it. Could you let me have some iodine and a box of Band-Aids?"

As Mr. Hudson went to get his order, Dus felt people staring at him. He shrugged and allowed that it was normal for people in a small town to stare at a stranger. Mr. Hudson returned with the first aid accouterments. Dus paid him.

"Nice to meet you, Father. Come back again and we'll chat sometime. Call me Jed. Maybe I can help introduce you around town to some folk, if you'd like," he offered.

"Thank you," Dus replied. "I hear the best place in town to eat is Bessie's Café. Ox said the food there is pretty good."

"Ox and I are a bit prejudiced, but we both think Bessie cooks the best food in town. You're going to love both Bessie and her cuisine. She, Ox, Nancy Conley, and I grew up together, and everyone will tell you she's one of the sweetest gals in all of Virginia. Go over to her place and meet her, and taste her food. Tell her I sent you. She'd love to take care of your appetite. She and her workers do catering work, too. Of course, as a preacher, you know better than I do that potluck food brought in by the local folk for a social gathering is also very good. That's the kind Bessie makes."

"Sounds good, Jed! Thanks again," he said, leaving the HUDSON & SON COMPANY store to cross the street to the local bank.

Mr. Raymond Brush, manager of the Joshuatown Merchants Bank, was short and rotund. Dus' judgments about some businessmen on first meeting were not exactly Christianly inspired. He thought the little banker's round face had beady eyes, and that his mustachioed mouth leered like a raccoon. He was most solicitous when he met Dus, saying he would be happy to have Dus' checking and savings account at his establishment. He added that Dus should know that his bank, however, was only a subsidiary bank of the Richmond National Bank, and the services here were somewhat limited. Dus told Mr. Brush that that was OK, since he would not be doing much banking in Joshuatown. But he would need a place to deposit his salary and write some checks for his and Elly's needs.

"We are always happy to do business with new customers, Father Habak," Mr. Brush said, pursing his lips. "We try hard to please everyone."

"I'm sure you do, Mr. Brush, but I won't have a need for a lot of banking services."

"That's all right. We're glad for any kind of business. I hear you're trying to start a little action up at the old church again. One of your 'piscapal' clergy was up here a few months ago talking to Ox Conley and a few folk about having worship services up there on the Blue. Guess you're the preacher who's going to do it, eh? I'm a Universalist, myself. When the spirit is willing, I go to church down in Staunton."

"I wouldn't characterize my work here as a 'little action,' Mr. Brush. My diocese is starting an Episcopal mission up there with the church, and you're correct—I'm the new priest in charge."

"Call it what you will, Rev. Preachers have tried before, and there haven't been a lot of takers. Some preacher, when I was a fresh young teller here in town, tried to start a church up there. He just up and left after he built the church and parsonage. Guess he got discouraged. Anyway, preachers have come and gone through the years with that place, but nothing ever seems to come of their efforts, and they move on. You think you can really do something for the Lord this time? Churchgoing folk here are pretty committed to their own brand of religion and are hard to change."

Dus was annoyed with the line of conversation that Mr. Brush was pursuing, and decided he had enough of the banker's disparaging church history lesson.

"I'm going to try, Mr. Brush," he stewed. "I don't expect to convert many Universalists and other committed Christians, but I won't be leaving here anytime soon. I'm going to stay, have services, and try to provide some pastoral care for the folk who want them. By the way, could you direct me to the sheriff's office?"

"Sure, Rev. Right across the street on the first floor of the courthouse. Good luck!"

"Thank you," Dus grumbled. He left the bank, walked across the street into the courthouse, and immediately found a room with a sign that read, "Sheriff." He entered and introduced himself to a man working at a desk. "Good morning. I'm Father Dus Habak. I'd like to talk to the sheriff."

"Good morning, Father. I'm Sheriff Scott Kirsh, your friendly law officer in this fair county. Welcome to Joshuatown. As you see, my office is small, and not overstaffed. What can I do for you?"

Scott Kirsh was a medium-built, comely, wiry, middle-aged chap, with the looks of a young Gary Cooper without the Texas drawl. He didn't sound nor look like the sort of local lawman you'd expect to find in Joshuatown. He appeared to Dus to have the demeanor of a city policeman.

Dus answered him. "Good to meet you, Sheriff Kirsh. I would like to get a permit for a gun."

"Good to know you, Father Habak, and nice to have you in our county. Hope you are getting nicely settled. I'll give you a license for your gun, but if you don't mind me asking, what in the world would a priest want with a gun? We are not the kind of people up here on the mountain, Padre, for whom your sermons wouldn't be just as effective with," the Sheriff kidded him.

Dus was not all that pleased with the lawman's humor, and showed it. "Oh, I already own a gun, handle it well, and might need it in the woods sometime to protect myself from nasty bears and polecats. Actually, I guess I just want to be sure I am obeying the law in the county by getting a license. Can you oblige me?"

"Sure can," the officer answered, and quickly took care of the registration. The meeting was soon finished, and Dus did not loiter. "Nice to meet you, Sheriff! Thank you for your help."

"You're welcome, Father. Come around when you have a little more time to talk, and we will get better acquainted. Take care with the bears, and if you run into any polecats that have four legs, shoot 'em. Leave the two-legged ones to me," he scowled, no longer pretending to be funny.

"Sometime, Sheriff. And don't worry about me. Good-bye," he answered, leaving hastily, thinking there might not be anyone on the mountain who is going to take a priest seriously.

Scott Kirsh scratched his head. Don't worry about you, eh, Preacher? When you get to know me, you will find I worry about everyone, especially clergy with guns. Oh well, most of us cops are as bizarre as priests. I'll have to talk to the guy someday about our mutual eccentricities, and find out, of course, why he needs a gun. Maybe he has a wife like Patty who understands us weirdos!

# 8

John K. Stewart, Sr. was a muscular, pigeon-breasted man with arms like a lumberjack. J.K., as he was called by his friends, and Professor Stewart, by everyone else, was built the way he was because he exercised regularly with weight machines in the Penn State University gym. He also swam 500 meters twice every week in the campus pool, with his own version of the "Australian Crawl," accounting for the peculiar way he flipped and flopped through the water.

J.K. had his feet missing at the ankle of both legs, courtesy of the North Korean army at a cold and bloody battlefield called "Pork Chop Hill." It was just one of those messy and brutal things that happen to some guys in war. J.K. was mad about it at first, and a Purple Heart and Silver Star had not kept him from being "pissed off" that he had been maimed for life. But he had gotten back alive, unlike a lot of his buddies, and had come to terms with being called a "disabled vet"—even though he was, from most people's criteria of a man, not only a very "able vet," but also a brilliant electronic engineer, teacher, and, especially, a source of inspiration and hope for the discouraged, be they physically impaired or as healthy as hogs at a trough.

Before his combat wounds, he had made over 200 jumps as an Eighty-second Airborne Ranger without a scratch, only to have stepped on a land mine leading a platoon of "Dogface" grunts up a muddy slope. Being a buck sergeant had not been worth the money nor the pain, and certainly the thought of having left two feet in Korea in a screwed-up war that the politicians said wasn't a war had not done much to placate him during his rehabilitation period.

He hadn't liked "rehab" therapy much, but he learned to get ambulatory in just a matter of weeks, was soon doing some tricky wheelchair maneuvers called "wheelies," and even participated in long-distance wheelchair race competitions and "wheelie" basketball games. Eventually, he was fit with a prosthesis. That was harder for him, and he was more frustrated with learning to walk with artificial legs than with anything else. Often, as not, he would just stand them up against a wall someplace and go on outings in his wheelchair. But the docs, nurses, and the "rehab" therapists had really encouraged him, and he was pleased when they told him that "he tried harder, did better, and accomplished more in a shorter time than anyone else they knew, with his prosthetic walking."

And he did! In a short time, he was walking with what appeared to be only a minor limp, and he was very proud of himself. He had no intention of being called, by the antimilitary types, "a sick, lame, and lazy vet, living on public largess because he had served his country!" Somewhere, in the years that followed, he married a beautiful gal named Julie, had three children, received a master's degree in electronic engineering at Penn State University, and was now a computer professor in that subject at his alma mater. He and his family lived next door to the university campus, where they had an active social life, good schools, a Catholic church, and excellent opportunities to enjoy college sports. He and Julie were, among other things, avid spelunkers.

Yesterday, J.K. had driven his Ford van, especially equipped for his disability, down from Penn State to Staunton, where he frequently did computer consulting work for Staunton Memorial Hospital. He liked driving the van because he could lock his wheelchair with a hydraulic draw-down floor hook right up at the steering wheel, and, with specially constructed extensions, could operate the brakes with his hands better than with his stilted legs. Electronic side doors with a hydraulic wheelchair lift enabled him to get aboard and promptly on his way.

J.K. never wasted any time. He was always in a hurry and never let the dust settle under his stumps, so to speak. He carried his plastic legs on a hook on the back of his wheelchair. When he needed them for any reason, he just reached over his shoulder, clamped them on his leg stumps, and went about his walking business.

It suited his purposes today to "wheel" through the hospital corridors until he got to the computer center, where he could use his legs. It just took too long for him to walk places. Besides, he wanted some breakfast in the hospital cafeteria.

"Well, look who this old range buffalo almost wiped out," he said to Dr. Karol Marson, whose foot his wheels just missed in the corridor near the hospital cafeteria. "I'm sorry, pretty Injun Princess! How ya been?"

"Hey, watch it, Sarge; you nearly ran me down with that 'Peterbuilt' of yours," she laughed, bending down and planting a kiss on his balding head. "When did you get in?"

"Drove down yesterday and holed up at the Holiday. Thought I'd get an early start on upgrading some of the modems by coming in and getting some chow at the cafeteria. How about having some with me?"

"Already had some with Shawn at home, but I'll have some coffee. I'll give you a push so you don't cripple some prima donna resident who'll sue the hide off you for ruining his trade. How are Julie and the kids?"

"They're great! Julie's into church stuff and the kids are happy in school, sports, and socials. Cold as a witch's tail up in those Nittany Lion hills. Whatta you been doing around this sanitized health spa?"

Dr. Marson's and J.K.'s friendship had started a year ago when Staunton Memorial hired him, on the recommendation of a computer manufacturer, as a consultant to update their computer systems. He'd visited there several times and met Karol when she had taken an interest in his disability. She was fascinated with his energy, his never-ceasing happy demeanor, and the way he encouraged other disabled people to try hard and become viable human beings. He was not only a good example for them but he also had conned the hospital out of a classroom where he could teach many disabled folk how to use computers and be fully employed. He even taught quadriplegics how to operate them by clamping a mouth stick in their teeth, sliding "floppy disks" in place, and pounding out letters on a keyboard. Karol estimated that J.K., in a very short time, had inspired at least fifty handicapped men and women to go on and be expert computer operators and programmers.

He had changed their lives. She admired his ability to overcome his own adversity and empower others with self-worth. She wished she could be as empowering to people the way J.K. was. She loved him dearly as a friend.

"You really look good, J.K.," she went on. "You look like you've been keeping up your weight lifting and swimming."

"Yeah, Doc. Julie thinks I spend too much time at it, but moving the chair and using those wooden legs is tough work, and I need the muscles. I like swimming time for pure thinking and cleaning off the body and brain dirt."

"I admire your discipline, J.K. I need a little of that, myself. Getting kinda fat around the middle just standing around poking and cutting on folk. Mornings here, then afternoons at the office don't give me much time for the exercise I need to do to keep the pounds off. Shawn and I hike in the hills, though, when we go up to the clinic. That helps a bit."

"Well, you look awfully good and pretty to me, darlin'! How are things going up there? Do you feel good about your work with the clinic?"

"I try to get up there a couple times a month. It's lots of work, but the people are wonderful. They've been so good to us. Shawn likes to go there, too. Neither of us has ever gotten away from our Indian roots. Mountains are just natural to us."

"Tell me, Injun Lady, you got any big brave on the string around this place? A pretty squaw like you sure shouldn't be dancing around campfire grounds fancy-free. Loosen up, get some social life. Get those tom-toms working, honey, and let the good guys know you're ready to leave the teepee for a pony ride in the moonlight!"

"You're sweet, pegleg paleface, even if your Indian imageries are pretty tacky, but my love life is none of your business," Karol winked. "What, with this place, the office, the clinic, Shawn, and keeping the 'teepee' clean, I don't have much time for the moonlight stuff. Really not too interested, to be honest with you, J.K.! Couple of guys have asked me out for dinner, but you know what some of them have on their minds. I'm just not into that stuff nor involvements. Guess I'm just busy and still have too many memories."

"Tell you what, Medicine Woman, if I didn't have Julie and those three girls I love so much, I'd sure give you a run around this reservation."

"You think those wooden legs of yours could run fast enough around the teepee to catch a young squaw like me, you old swayed-back hay burner?"

"Now that's a nasty thing to say to a cripple. By God, woman, you wouldn't believe how I can make these sticks work when I'm motivated. All I need to do is switch the 'woodies' to the 'wheelies,' and nobody can outrun me. You ever sit in the lap of a guy going 'sixty' in a wheelchair? It's pretty fun and sexy! Ask Julie! But, all kidding aside, Karol, a beautiful lady like you should not be living and talking like a nun. You have so much life in you to give to a good guy. You deserve good things, and you need to put the bad things behind you. You know what I'm saying?"

"Thanks, J.K. You're very kind, and I know what you mean. You'll be the first to know if I ever catch an eagle! If he is anything like you, it won't make a hoot if he has one, two, or three legs; he'd be a blessing to my life. You're something else. All that brawn, brains, and compassion. Julie is a lucky gal."

"She's a smart, but fibbing, Irish lass who keeps me thinking she's lucky, I love her for it. I'm the lucky one. Anyway, I cherish your friendship, and I just want a lot of happiness for you and Shawn. I do hope the right guy comes along someday for both of you."

"By the way, while we're talking guys, I ran into a fellow up the mountain a piece, who graduated from that great PSU place you're always bragging about. I wonder if you might have known him."

"Thirty thousand students on that campus, darlin'. Not very likely. What's his name?"

"A guy by the name of Habak."

"I knew a Dus Habak! That's not a common name. That would be a real coincidence if it's the same guy. He was a teenage Marine BAR-carrying grunt who got a Chinese bullet hole in his gut in Korea, and came into Tripler Military Hospital in Honolulu the same time the medics were patching my stumps. He never talked much about himself. We talked a few times about what we might do after the wounds healed. He was interested in being an engineer, and I was thinking some kind of electronics at the time. We were there for a few weeks before being sent statewide for a discharge. Believe it or not, a few years later we ran into each other at Beaver Stadium at Penn State as students. He was a walk-on recruit and a pretty fair wide receiver on the Nittany Lion football team. He was studying mechanical engineering. I was interested in UNIVAC in those days, and what was developing in the computer field. We had a beer or two on occasion, and once in awhile crossed tracks in classes. I graduated before he did, and we lost contact. Friendly guy with a good outlook on life. Had a pretty solid spiritual side to him, too caused, I think, by the Korean thing. I remember he went to the hospital and campus chapels a lot. We'd talk religion sometimes. I was Catholic and he was sort of inclined that way, but I never knew what denomination he was. I'll be darned. How did you run into him?"

"Gosh, J.K., what you're telling me is an incredible coincidence. If the Dus Habak I met is the same one you're talking about, he is Father Dus Habak, priest of all outdoors up in the Cutty and Blue Mountains and Joshuatown!"

"Now, honey, it ain't nice for an Injun to tell a fib to a U.S. of A. buck sarge. It can't be! It just can't be! Dus went on to be an engineer in a big company someplace, from what I read in the alumni news a long time ago."

"Well, he isn't that now. I know. I have met him, talked to him, listened to his sermon, and fixed another hole in his body just last week!"

"Another hole?"

"Wasn't serious. He'll be OK."

"Well, it's a small world and anything can happen. Boy, I sure would like to see him. How far is it up there?"

"About twenty-five miles. I go up there a lot to the clinic. Takes about an hour. Not a bad drive, but gets a bit tough in the winter."

"Maybe I'll just try to get up there this weekend if I can get caught up with my work here. Can hardly believe this. Would be good to see old Dus. Holy smokes. A priest! Sure would be nice to touch base with him and reminisce. I'll be goldarned! Dus—a priest, by God. I'm not surprised, really. He seemed the kind."

"He's not a Roman Catholic like you, J.K. He's an Episcopal priest, big, strong, younger than you, and not bad looking. He's a terribly intense guy, though, with a lot of hard-core convictions. I want to caution you, without going into detail, he's carrying some wounds other than war ones. I don't know him very well, and he seems like an OK guy when he isn't uptight. It's not for me to say, but he's had some rough times lately, and an old friend like you can help him with them."

"Yeah, maybe a reunion with old Buck Sarge J.K. will do him some good. I'll take my chances. Thanks for the info. That's good news. Thank ya, honey. Well, I'd better get down to those ornery, blinking, squeaky, electronic wonders. Thanks for the time."

"Thanks for the coffee. Will I see you around the hospital for a few days?"

"Sure will, honey! By the way, speaking about these legs of mine, did you know I have them working so good now, I can hike? It would be slow, but maybe you, Shawn, Julie, the girls, and I could go hiking around your mountains sometime. Julie and I have become spelunkers. It ain't easy with wooden legs clamped on to these stumps, but we do it a lot around Pennsylvania and New York, and we really love it. Julie's really patient with my gimping around. Gosh, the things you find in caves! Bones, stalagmites, streams, and things."

"What in the world, J.K., are spelunkers?"

"We go in caves, darlin'. Haven't you ever heard of spelunking? It's crawling around in, and exploring caves and stuff."

Karol smiled. "You mean to tell me that you, Julie, and the kids go crawling around and exploring caves at vacation time?"

"Sure do, sugar. Want to go along with us sometime and do a little spelunking?"

"Well, I'll be darned. Sure, J.K. I'd love to! Are there bats, snakes, and slimy crawling things in caves?"

"Sometimes."

"Then I wouldn't love it. Thanks, anyway, spelunker! This hospital cavern here is spooky enough for me. See you around it. If you get up there, let me know how your old friend is doing. Tell him I said 'Hi'. And, J.K., be patient with him. Unlike you, he can be a pain in the derriere."

"Shame on you, Doc. That's no way to talk about a wounded vet, especially a Marine."

"Vet, Marine, dogface, engineers, clergy, whatever—you're good guys, but, yes, from time to time, under all your sweetness and bravado, you can be a pain in the rear as well as the heart!"

"My—such talk from a lady. Did you run into a pesky intern this morning who pulled your chain?"

"Nope. Just an uptight preacher last week who could, if he tried, be an effective pastor to a lot of good people who are in need of a lot of love and shepherding."

"Hmmn! Sounds like an Indian princess ran into a warrior in the forest who has some potential, but who ain't gonna be much of a brave until he runs her gauntlet and kills a few ghosts in his closet!"

"Go to work, old goat, before you become a pain in the butt, too," Dr. Marson scolded her friend while bending down and giving him a kiss on the cheek.

# 9

"And so my friends," Father Habak intoned, ending his Sunday sermon, "when we celebrate Thanksgiving Day this week and enjoy the delicious foodstuff that God has blessed us with, let's remember the hardships the Pilgrims who came to this country so long ago endured, so we can today worship God free of governments telling us how to do it. Those Pilgrims and the colonials, though not without some political sin of their own, fought the great war against state control and abuses, and gave us a fine country worth sacrificing for. Let's remember also, how God has provided us, as he did them, with sustenance from fertile fields where we can harvest his gifts, enjoy the fruits of our own labor, and have enough to share with our neighbors who don't have as much of this world's goods as we do. That's why we celebrate Thanksgiving. It is meant for us to take a holiday, to thank God for all his blessings bestowed on our country and the world, and to enjoy with friends and family. God bless you all. Have a nice holiday. Thank you for your kindness to me and for supporting my ministry here. You have been good to me. I hope you will get to meet my little girl, Ellen, who is coming up to the mountain to spend Thanksgiving with me."

Father Habak finished the rest of the worship service, gave the final blessing, and walked down the aisle to greet the people. He was baffled by a familiar face in the congregation. He knew the man from somewhere, but was not sure where. In a few more minutes, he would be called to remembrance. Again, he greeted an increasing number of folk who had come to worship. He counted about thirty people in the congregation, and that made him happy. It only takes a few more people each Sunday, he thought, to make one feel that he is accomplishing something. Nancy Conley was again among the first to leave the pews and to greet Dus. She quietly invited him and Elly to Thanksgiving dinner at her house. He thanked her, and said Elly would like to do that. Nancy smiled and went on. He greeted the other folk; then there was only one person left standing and waiting to introduce himself to Dus.

"Father Habak, I am, perhaps, a ghost from your past. I am Professor

J.K. Stewart of Penn State University and an old cellmate of yours at Tripler Hospital."

"My gosh, Sarge Stewart," he smiled, vigorously shaking his old hospital- and collegemate's hand. "It's good to see you! What in the name of all that is holy are you doing in these mountains?"

"Dus Habak, you old gyrene, this is a real pleasure seeing you here, doing this. A mutual friend down in Staunton told me you were the priest up here at this little church. I can't believe it! It has been so long! You, a priest? Gosh, this is so great! There is so much to talk about!"

"Who'd you see in Staunton who's supposed to know me, Sarge?" Dus queried, knowing very well who J.K. had been talking to.

"Oh, some pretty doctor at Staunton General Memorial Hospital by the name of Karol Marson, who comes up to the clinic here and recently patched up your old, hard tail. She's a good friend of mine."

"I'll be darned. What a coincidence. Yeah, she did do that for me. That is as well as I know her, but how do you know her? Wait! Don't answer that now. Let me clean up here a bit, and we'll go over to my cabin. I'll break open some beans and stuff, and we'll have some coffee and talk. Gosh, it is good to see you, J.K.!"

J.K. waited by the church stove while Dus cleaned up the altar and put away his vestments. Dus soon joined him, dampened the fire, and the two old GI buddies walked to the cabin. There was a low fire already burning in the hearth, and Dus kicked it alive, adding another log and blowing it with the bellows. It was warm, and J.K. put his back up to it for warmth. Dus thought he looked healthy after so many years, considering what he had been through. Age had not weathered him much.

"Nice place you have here, Father. Cozy, though a little rough and rustic for a mod engineer guy, as I remember you. How did you get here?"

"Come on, Sarge, call me Dus. You don't want to hear all that history," Dus hedged. "I want to know all about you. What have you been doing since I last saw you up at Happy Valley? I haven't seen an alumni newspaper in years."

J.K. related his teaching experience. He told Dus about his return to his alma mater as a professor in computer science, his marriage and children, and how he happened to know Dr. Marson at Staunton Hospital.

"Mighty interesting! How are those wooden legs of yours working?"

J.K. hit his artificial leg with the log poker. "Well, they're here and still working good. I do a lot with them, but when I am in a hurry, I use my wheelchair when I'm on the ground and in my van. Now, are you going to get us some chow, or do I treat you to lunch at the local eatery?"

Dus bustled about, opening cans of vegetables, breaking out the coffeepot and condiments, and started warming up a large piece of cold venison.

"You like venison?" he asked. "It's a heck of a lot better than your dogface K rations!"

"Love it! Have to! Julie makes me eat everything she puts on my plate as an example for our girls, so I've acquired a taste for most foods. I stop at broccoli. Don't want those green, smelly clumps even close to me!"

"Don't worry. I don't have any. Got some canned corn. I'll have this stuff ready in a minute. Keep talking. I want to hear about Julie and everything you're doing."

J.K. and Dus ate heartily, drank coffee, and talked into the afternoon. It was getting late and finally J.K. said, "Dus, I'm not leaving here until you tell me about your life. Now, come on. I've told you about mine."

"OK, J.K., but I'll make it very short, and then let's put it behind us."

Dus told J.K. about his engineering business, his time at the seminary, his work in the church, and the auto wreck in which Ginnie and Dusty had been killed. Then, he reticently added the story of his breakdown and his new priestly assignment on the mountain.

"Good Lordy, Dus. I'm terribly sorry about all the stuff that's happened to you. I just didn't know. You've been through a lot!"

"Didn't Doctor Marson tell you any of this?" Dus asked, somewhat skeptically.

"She said she didn't know you real well, but that you seemed to be an OK sort who had some tough times. She didn't go into any details, except about fixing you up. She said it was not her business to comment on your private life. Did she do a good job on your rear? You heal up OK?"

"It's fine. Just a little wound that got infected. That experience reminded me of the days when those Army nurses at Tripler Hospital in Hawaii were always sticking our bods with needles. Anyway, Dr. Marson came to church one Sunday, and we had dinner together at a parishioner's house. She's a smart girl. She told me she is part Nez Perce Indian from Oregon, who went through a lot of difficult times of her own, and came out here to the East to put her life back together. But why am I telling you all this? I guess you know more about her than I do."

"She's really a nice lady, Dus, and I admire her for what she has accomplished in spite of her tragedy. She's overcome a lot. She has a reputation for being a fine surgeon and is highly respected at the hospital. She's getting very good on the computer, too."

"That's good. And what do you do with your spare time, J.K.?"

"Oh, I work out at the college gym and swim a lot to exercise my legs. But Julie and I are spelunkers, and we hike around a lot of hills up in Pennsylvania looking into caves. We're pretty good at it now. We've had a few years of it, and we have found some fascinating things in caves."

Dus' eyes widened. His ears seemed to bend, and he moved closer to J.K. "You are? You do? You're a caver, a real son of a gun caver with those wooden legs of yours? I'll be darned! So you really know about caves?"

"Sure do, Padre. Julie and I are no experts, but we're pretty good at going through caves, and these legs of mine work well enough for me to crawl most anywhere. Courage, a big heart, a warm coat, old pants, good climbing boots, a rope, a flashlight, and lots of nosy desire are all one needs for caving. Our girls like spelunking, too!"

Dus Habak's mind was traveling a mile a minute remembering his experience with the bear forcing him into the cave up on the Cutty. His old acquaintance's spelunking expertise was conjuring up some ideas.

"That's really something, J.K.! What a neat avocation. So you, Julie, and the kids do all that climbing around, and you do OK with your gimpy legs?"

"Sure do. You have to know, now, I'm not talking about caverns or anything big and deep. We have been to the commercial caverns and take those tours, you understand, but I'm talking about the kind of shallow caves that are natural to the local mountains. We just look around old rock outcrops, dry water flow holes on the side of the hills, and even the old places that Native American cliff dwellers once used for housing. We don't discover them. We just hike around places where we know there might be one, and then we find all sorts of things. Some of the caves go pretty far inside of the hills and have stalagmites, bones, and stuff. Sometimes we even take bedrolls and lunches and camp in them. They're all over these Appalachian Mountain trails that you know go clear from Maine to Georgia. I hear there are lots of caves down in this country and farther south into Tennessee in the Blue Mountains. One can take spelunking courses in college these days. I've attended several seminars where geologists teach folk all about spelunking."

Dus' interest heightened. "Have you thought about looking around this area for caves?"

"No, but it might be fun doing that with you, if you have the knack and desire."

"How about tomorrow?" Dus asked.

"Are you crazy, man? You just don't crawl around caves in the wintertime. It's too cold and icy. Pardon me for the quip, but you could break a leg, and I don't have too many of them to spare. Caving is a spring, summer, and autumn sport, my friend. One doesn't go poking his nose into caves this time of year—at least I don't, and I'm not going to tomorrow nor ever. Anyway, spelunking takes preparation."

"Wait a minute. Let me tell you about something that happened to me before you say 'no,'" Dus responded. He told J.K. about his experience of running into a cave while trying to escape from what he believed was a bear. He related how his friend, Ox Conley, who knew these mountains well and tracked and hunted animals all his life in them, thought Dus was imagining things when he told Ox about the cave. "But I was in that cave, J.K., hiding from a bear. You won't believe it, but I was more scared than I was in Korea. I peed my pants like a little kid. I stayed in there for some time before I hightailed it down the hill and ran into Ox. I'm telling you the truth. That cave is up there! I want to go back and find it."

"Why?"

"Just out of curiosity. Maybe because I was in that cave, and Ox, who knows these hills better than I know my own hand, denies its existence. He appears to be hiding something that he doesn't want me to know about."

"Holy Moses," J.K. grunted. "You went into a cave in the beginning of winter after hearing a bear roar? Are you some sort of a nut? Do you have any idea about where bears hibernate and keep their cubs in the wintertime? I don't know much about bears, but we have thousands of them up in the Pennsylvania mountains where I live, and I am never going to go around a cave in the wintertime when I know that is where bears live. I don't mess with bears, gyrene, and you're as nutty as a fruitcake if you do. No spelunking in the snow for me, either. I just can't run fast enough from critters. Sorry, pal. Just not interested, period, Father Habak."

Dus was now convinced J.K. would not go up in the cave with him anytime soon. But he did want to pick J.K.'s mind about caves. "I guess it was pretty stupid of me to go into a cave during hibernation time. I must admit that it frightened me! Tell me, J.K., why would a bear be roaming around this late in the fall?"

"I told you I'm not an expert on bears, but it could have been an old poppa bear who had not gotten enough food to get the layer of fat that his body needs to make a good sleep through the winter. Maybe, too, he felt sorry for himself because he missed a lot of mama bear's cuddling to take care of his love life. I don't know. I just think it isn't very smart to go around where bears live in the winter. They don't bother people much any other time if you don't surprise them nor mess with their cubs."

"Ox said that, too. He thought it might just be a bear looking for a friend or for her cubs. But I sure wonder about that cave he denied existed. I sure have a craving to look into that mystery some more."

"What for? You ought to heed your friend's warning."

Dus told J.K. about the shooting, how he had gotten his wound, and the story he had heard about the old pastor who built the church and disappeared. He admitted that it was in the back of his mind that the shooter had taken a shot from the cave, even though he had found tracks and tramped snow only behind a tree.

"Laddy, you're something else! The bishop sends you out here to preach the gospel and take care of people's spiritual welfare, and you have already, inside a month, gotten yourself shot at, wounded, and pursued by a bear on the sniff. Then you went into its den, and you have a mystery on your hands. I'll tell you, this old boy ain't afraid of much, but I have had enough war scares and scars, and I'd have thought you would have, too. Better cool it until spring, and don't mess with the bears, gyrene. Anyway, I gotta get back to Staunton and finish some work there. I have to be in State College by Tuesday night 'cause Julie is counting on me to carve the turkey on Thanksgiving Day. Might interest you to know that I have built a little computer program on how to carve up a turkey just the right way so it will last a few days and make everyone happy with his selection of parts and shades of meat. Might try doing one on how to carve up a deer to get maximum venison meat out of it. I'll send you a copy of it."

"I'd like that, J.K., and I will wait until spring for my caving expedition. Maybe when you make a trip down to Staunton, you can bring Julie with you, and you both can teach me something about spelunking."

"I'd like that. Our girls are out of school for Easter break, and maybe they would come, too. We could have some fun after the thaw, when the buds are blooming and the critters are up and about and not caring about spelunkers. Maybe you could have your girl up from school and they could all get acquainted. Our girls are a little older, but Elly sounds like the kind of kid who would get along well with them. Maybe they could convince her she ought to someday look into her paw's alma mater for her college education."

"That sounds interesting, but college is a long time away for her. In the meantime, I'll look forward to spring with your family. I'll find out from the sisters at the priory about Elly's spring break."

"Be fun! Well, I'd better get down the mountain. It was awfully nice to see you, Dus. Good sermon today, and I like your version of the mass. Not much different than ours. Guess you noticed I don't kneel too good with these knees, and no offense, but you know our Catholic bishops still don't want us to take Communion in other denominations. I don't agree with that, but I try to behave. One day, my friend, all this denominational division will end, and we will all be breaking bread together at the same Communion rail. Thanks for the food and hospitality. Really is a cozy cabin."

Dus retrieved J.K.'s parka for him, put on his own, and offered to help the sarge down to his van.

"Thanks, Dus, but I can manage fine. You might like to see how I use my computerized lift to get in and out of my van with my wheelchair. I took a trip one time down to Dallas, Texas, to a foundation to learn about how to computerize my lifestyle. It is a great place for disabled folk to adjust to life by using computers."

They walked down the hill a bit, and as they approached the vehicle, J.K. pushed a button on a little remote-control box attached to his crutch and automatically opened the side door. A lift extended out and lowered to the ground. He walked on it, raised it, sat down in his wheelchair, maneuvered it to the front of the steering wheel, and pushed a switch. A steel hook came up out of the floor, snagged a bar on the undercarriage of the wheelchair, and clamped it solidly to the van's chassis. He shut the door, rolled down the window, and smiled at Dus.

"Ain't it neat the way all this stuff works? Course I only do that when I'm in the wheelchair. Well, so long, caver. Stay out of trouble until I get back. By the way, that pretty Indian doc told me to say 'Hi' to you. She seemed a little reticent to talk about you very much. She seemed to like you, too, but acted a bit like your pain in the behind she fixed up made you something of a pain in hers. Any reason for that? Well, none of my business!" Then J.K. embellished the truth a little with, "She also allowed that under the right kind of conditions, like the absence of bats, bears, and snakes, and the companionship of a less quarrelsome and congenial godly type, she might consider going spelunking with us. Even if I have tried to direct her soul in a more enlightened direction, she is a stubborn Episcopalian! But then you knew that, didn't you? Well, Semper Fi, Father, see you around!"

He drove away grinning and waving. Dus smiled and waved back at his friend. Then, for some reason, not apparent to the nearby chickadees, rabbits, and deer, he raised his arms to heaven and yelled, "All right!"

# 10

"It's good to see you," Bishop Mueller said, greeting Dus at his office door and throwing his arms around him. "I've really missed you around here. How are you getting along up there with your cool, wild, and woolly frontier mission? Come on, lad, sit down, and tell me about yourself. What're you up to these days?"

Father Habak was glad to see his old friend. It had not been all that long since he last saw him, but his bishop was an exceptionally spiritual man, cross-fertilized nicely with a bit of Dus' kind of farm earthiness. Dus always felt close to the old chaplain and had missed him. The animosity and hurt he had felt at their last meeting had dissipated, and he was genuinely glad to be talking to his solicitous boss about his life on the mountain.

"Doing good, Bishop. Just drove down to get Elly, to take her back with me for Thanksgiving break. Thought she'd enjoy coming home to Dad for the holiday."

"That's fine, Dus. I knew you were coming because I saw Elly a few days ago over at the priory. I had a meeting with the sisters, inquired about her, and then I talked to her. The sisters said she was doing very well in school, and she did, too, and she is excited about your spending some time together. And, Father, I am glad you not only came to get her but sneaked in to see your spiritual advisor."

That bit of a pastoral irony was well-noted by Dus, who now was embarrassed that he had not sought an appointment with him, his bishop. Canon Burkey had often told the diocesan clergy not to just walk into the bishop's office to see him without talking to his secretary, first. He could have called the bishop from Hosea's Auto Repair and let him know he was in town and he was repentant. "I should have called you, Bishop, but the telephone service up there isn't too good. Like you warned me, it's a bit back woodsy with not a lot of utilities nor facilities. I'd like to talk to you about fixing some of those problems when you have some time."

"I always have time for you, Dus. It's the day before Thanksgiving, and I'm all caught up with my work. I have an hour or so before I have to pick up some goodies for the family dinner tomorrow, so tell me about yourself, and anything else you have on your mind."

Dus spoke very positively about his new ministry, the people, how the mission was developing, the visit from his old friend from Penn State, and the continuing history and geography lessons he was getting from Ox and other folk about Joshuatown and its environs. He made no point in mentioning the mystery of the missing pastor, but thought the bishop would enjoy hearing about the odd circumstances involved in meeting the woman physician at the clinic. He avoided any reference to the shooting incident that led to their introduction. He tried not to embellish the incident; without delving into the more emotional aspects of his meeting with Dr. Marson, he put a humorous slant to the tale for his jocular primate.

Bishop Mueller chuckled. "You mean, Father Habak, that your first meeting with the lady necessitated your dropping your pants and baring your privates to a lady? Are you really sure this is something you want to be confessing to your bishop?" he bantered. "All this time, I thought I was sending you up there to build a church, preach the gospel, pastor the people, and get your life in order. Shame on you!"

Dus laughed, too. The incident did seem a bit peculiar the way he told it, but it was good to laugh with his friend. "Well, Bishop, as you know, I'm kind of a private person, and my relationship with the lady, because of the circumstances, did not start off very well. But don't worry; it was purely platonic and medicinal. A woman doctor, especially that one, would be the last of my 'concupiscent' interests, if I had them."

"Well, well, has my country parson taken up 1611 King James biblical jargon? I knew what that word meant, Dus, long before our vaunted prayer book gurus decided that it was too big a word for God and the common folk to understand. Tell me, do you have some hang-ups about women physicians as well as clergy? Your prejudices about women being ordained priests are well-known. Women physicians have been a reality for the better part of this century, and you might as well know the time is coming for their ordination as priests, whether we like it or not. It's going to happen, just as sure as God made little green apples."

"Ah, Bishop, I don't want to get on the dreary subject of women professionals. My sister is a pediatrician, and an excellent physician. It's just that the lady doctor felt compelled, right off the bat, to argue the correlation. I have what I feel is a genuine historical and theological problem with women being priests that has nothing at all to do with their worthiness and capabilities. Perhaps God will prove me wrong someday, and the vindictive ladies will throw wood on the fire when I am burned at the stake for my heresy. Are you going to support their ordination to the priesthood when it comes up on a final vote at General Convention?"

"Not me! I share your theology and I may be at that stake with you, but we are going to lose that issue the next time around, believe me. You know what the priory sisters said to me when I told them that if ordination of women to the priesthood ever happened in my diocese, it would be over my dead body?"

"No. What?"

" 'We can easily arrange for that, Bishop.' Disrespectful feminist smart alec!"

Dus chuckled. "Seems to me you opened yourself up to that, but it wasn't a very nice thing to say to a bishop. Well, the heck with it. I'm sure that the women who are into equality to that degree don't give a twit about what you and I think about it. I expect I am rather expendable when it comes to that issue. Anyway, I have too much to do these days to think about it. I'm just trying to do a few things in the mountain for the Lord and Elly. I don't need angry women priests nor doctors giving me apoplexy."

"That's right! You'll be busy enough up there in the sticks. What are you doing for Thanksgiving?"

"A nice mountain family by the name of Conley, who has befriended me, invited Elly and me to join them for dinner. I hear the lady medic and her son will be up to the clinic over the holidays, too, and will be joining us. I'm looking forward to having a nice family meal. Maybe I'll get to appreciate her a little better over the holiday."

"That'll be nice for you and Ellen. Watch your manners with the lady, and don't wreck your day with controversial subjects. You said something about a problem with the facilities up there?"

Dus would have liked to have had more time to go into some detail with the bishop with his idea about modernizing the vicarage, but there was none now. He made his request short and to the point. "I think things are going well enough to be thinkin of the possibilities for a long-term ministry there, Bishop. I'm planning to stay for a while, if you'll let me. I'd like you to think beyond my therapy and support a ministry for the long term. I like it up there, and I feel I'm making progress. I want you to put up some diocesan money so I can put in some plumbing facilities for Elly, and get a generator or hook into the valley electrical system. I can do a lot of that work myself if I have the means. I also want to ask Dr. Marson if she would rent me some office space at the clinic so I could latch into her telephone system and keep in contact with you and Elly."

"You're moving awfully fast, aren't you, Father? Well, I am glad for your zeal. Let me think about what you have proposed, and I promise I'll get back to you soon. Why do you want the clinic space? And do you think the doctor will let you have it, given your bad start with her?"

"Maybe, maybe not. But there is a lot of extra space she isn't using, and she is not there very often. It would give me more privacy for talking with folk who want some pastoral counseling. She might give me the space if I show her the need. She doesn't appear to have all that much admiration for us clergy types, but she is a charitable sort and likes doing ministry to people. I'd appreciate your thinking about it. Have a nice Thanksgiving."

The bishop looked at his watch, got up, put on his coat and hat, and ushered Dus out of his office. The meeting was over. That was fine with Dus, 'cause he wanted to get on his way, too. As they walked out of the building and onto the street, the bishop said, "Thanks for dropping by and bringing me up to date on your work. Glad things are going well for you. I keep you in my prayers, and I am always here if you need me."

"Thank you, and I'll appreciate your thinking about my request. I have to go over to Hosea's Repair and Body Shop, get my Jeep, and pick up Elly. I want to get her up the mountain tonight before the bad weather sets in."

"You having trouble with the new jeep, already?" the bishop inquired, frowning.

Dus could have bitten his tongue for mentioning the jeep. "No. It'll be all right. Brakes were slipping a little coming down the mountain, and I took it right over to Hosea's shop to check them out. Mountain roads are tough on brakes."

"I'll bet. Well, Hosea is a good mechanic. What was his diagnosis?"

"He said some fluid had leaked out of the brake line, and that he could fix it in a jiffy."

"Good! You don't want bad brakes coming down a mountain. Tell him to send the bill to the diocese. Blessings, Dus. Come see me soon. Have a nice holiday with Elly."

Dus thanked the bishop, wished him happy holidays, said "good-bye," and walked toward Hosea's auto shop, unrepentant that he had fibbed to his bishop.

To put it into the vernacular, what Hosea had said to Dus about the jeep, after apologizing to the priest for his language, was, "Some asshole beat da living hell out a da goddamn hydraulic line, buggered up da connector nut, en nearly all da freakin' brake fluid laked out a da cylinder! If all a it hadda laked out, Fadder, dem brakes shurly woulda neva wo'ked when ya was comin' down da mountain des mornin', and you'd be a deader den a possum a crossin' da road. You'd be a laying o'er a cliff er in a canyon somewhar! Holy shit, Fadder!"

Dus had wanted to say, "Holy shit," too, but his white collar, black shirt, and suit would only allow him to say, "Holy mare's marbles!"

# 11

"I have really missed you, Daddy," Ellen Habak said to her father, who was peering out the windshield of the jeep, trying to concentrate on his driving through what had developed into a heavy snowstorm.

"I've missed you, too, honey, and I'll be glad to get you up to Joshuatown and snuggled into the cabin, where we can talk about school and make some plans for our future together. I'd like to hear some of your ideas about that."

Both Dus and his daughter were fastened into their seat belts as the car skittishly climbed the mountain road toward their destination. Elly was at ease in her seat, and it was apparent that even as the weather grew progressively worse, she had great confidence in her father's ability to get them home safely. She wanted to talk, and Dus tried to be responsive, though his mind and eyes were set upon the road and snow beating against his windshield.

"I've really been doing good with studies at school, Daddy," Elly said, "and the sisters and Bishop Mueller have been nice to me. I have good marks and a lot of friends, but I miss you, Mom, and Dusty so much, and I get awfully lonely for all of you."

"I know, sweetheart," Dus replied. He didn't have to take his eyes off the road to know Elly was shedding tears. The sniffing was obvious, and her voice was unsteady. Dus wished they could wait until they were home to carry on with the building emotional discussion.

"We'll talk about that when we get to the cabin, have a nice meal, and sit by the fire. You can talk about whatever you want to, and I'll listen real good. How about that?"

"Why did God let Mommy and Dusty get killed, Daddy?"

Dus gripped the steering wheel so hard he thought it might crack. The windshield wipers were rocking in cadence with the heartbeat he felt in his chest. Snow was coming down faster and was beginning to cake on the glass. It was dark, and the visibility decreased. Dus feared if Ellen continued with the conversation on a subject he was trying to avoid, he would have to stop the car and they would be marooned on the mountain. Though he tried not to, he raised his voice. "Elly, please. I must concentrate on getting us home through this storm. I said that we would talk about everything when I have you safe and sound, including your mother's and brother's deaths, if that's what you want to talk about, but I can't do it now. I'm sorry, honey."

Ellen was noticeably hurt. "I'm sorry, too, Daddy. I didn't mean to make you mad at me. It's just that I've been so lonely and needed to talk to you about what has happened to our family. I won't bother you anymore." She withdrew from Dus, leaned her head against the cold window, slouched down, and quietly sobbed. Dus felt lousy and castigated himself with all sorts of epithets. But he said no more to his daughter and concentrated on the road. In a few minutes, Ellen was sound asleep. He released her seat belt and gently laid her head on his lap. While adjusting his seat belt to accommodate them both, he stroked her hair and asked, "Yeah, Lord, how about answering her question for me, too. Why, God, why?"

They arrived home in a moderate storm, but the jeep had performed well up the mountain and through the village, and now they were safe. Ellen had slept most of the way, and he was glad of that. He rustled her awake. "Wake up, sweetheart. We're here. Let's get in the house, build a fire, get cozy, and have a good supper."

"Gee, Dad, I didn't mean to fall asleep on you and be bad company. Guess I was tired," she said, having forgotten his earlier exasperation with her.

"That's OK, sweetheart. Just take my hand and I'll lead you through the snow to the house. I'll come back for your bag later."

They went to the door and walked into a warm room with a blazing fire, lanterns lighted, and an aroma of pine all about the house. A sign made from several pieces of taped-together cardboard and thumbtacked to the hearth mantle read, "Welcome Home, Elly!"

Ellen jumped up, threw her arms around Dus' neck, and pelted him with kisses. "What a nice sign. It's a beautiful house, Dad! I love it. Thank you for bringing me home! It's going to be a wonderful Thanksgiving."

Dus smiled, both at his daughter and at the greeting sign. "I'm glad that you like it, honey. I was afraid it would be a little too rugged for you after what you have been used to. We'll be doing something in the future to make it a bit more modern and comfortable, but in the meantime, when you are not at school, this will be your home."

Elly moved to the hearth and stoked the fire. As she stood there, Dus' eyes clouded with moisture, and he wondered who had cleaned the house, made the fire, lighted the lanterns, and made the welcome sign. He realized then, in this mountain where his heart had hung heavy the last several weeks, the hill folk, upon whom he had looked at somewhat skeptically, had reached out in love in their simple ways, offered their friendship and care, and invited him and his daughter to be a part of their lives. He smiled, wiped his eyes, and watched Elly put another log on the fire. The scene was beautiful. She turned and smiled at him. It was the first happiness he had known in a very long time.

"Let me help you with supper, Daddy," she offered.

"Well, cookie, what do ya have for supper tonight for your old worn-out mountain Papa?"

"You're not an old papa. You're just tired from driving and worrying about your teenage kid."

"That's right. So what would you like to eat? We have most everything a kid likes, including hamburgers, hot dogs, baked beans, fries, chips, pickles, salad, and some nice venison."

"What's venison?" Elly scowled.

"Deer meat."

"Deer meat? You mean the kind of meat like Bambi and Rudolph are made of?"

"Well, not quite, but it is deer, and that's what a lot of mountain folk eat, like the rest of us eat cows, pigs, and stuff. Want some?"

"No way! I'm not ready to munch on a Bambi nor a Rudolph. How about just the hot dogs, fries, beans, and salad?"

"Fine. I'm hungry, too. But let's save tummy space for a big Thanksgiving meal after church tomorrow with some friends we have here."

"Who are they?"

"They're some nice people who have looked after me and want to be your friends, too. They have kids about your age and are very nice. You'll like them. Mrs. Conley, the mom, is a wonderful cook and will fill us with lots of goodies. But for tonight, it is doggies and beans."

Suddenly Ellen, looking forlorn, changed the subject. "I don't like to interrupt the dinner preparation, Pop, but your little daughter hasn't been to the bathroom since we left the priory, and I have to piddle pretty bad. Where's the bathroom in this place? Upstairs?"

Dus smiled and wondered how he was going to tell his daughter about the facility that was to service her nature call in the wild. Honesty would have to do! "Ah, ah, Elly, do you remember when we went to the national parks on camping trips and you had to go to the bathroom?"

"Yeah, Dad, but couldn't we wait awhile for the travel lesson? I really gotta go!"

"I know, and that is what I am trying to explain to you. Remember where you and your mother went to the bathroom and she complained so much about the facilities?"

"Yeah. You mean one of those little brown buildings called 'outhouses,' with the door hook and the big wooden holes we had to sit on? Are you going to tell me we have one of those kind of bathrooms here?"

"Yep!"

"No way, Jose. You're surely kidding your modern daughter!"

"I wish I were, honey, but I am not. I told you it was rugged up here in these hills. Not only that, but that little house is out in the snow. We also have to pump our water out there, bring it in here, heat it on a stove, take sponge baths in a tub, and do our cooking on a kerosene stove."

"Gosh. It is rugged here, isn't it? Well, a certain fact of life right now, pioneer Pop, is that your daughter has to go wee wee real bad, so show me how to get to that weird thingamajig." She giggled, putting on her coat.

"You want me to go with you?"

"I'm thirteen years old, and it's time my father should know that fathers aren't supposed to go to the potty with their daughters anymore. I can handle it; believe me."

"Good. Take the lantern with you. It is only a few yards through the snow, and there are no wolves out there."

"Wolves? What about wolves?" she asked, reconsidering her need.

Dus felt dumb saying that. "I was just kidding. There are no wolves in this area of the country. It's OK to go to the bathroom out there. Trust me. I go there all the time."

"All right. I trust you, but I bet I'm going to have a cold bottom sitting on a dumb wooden toilet hole in the wintertime. I'll yell if I need you to come and unfreeze my little fanny."

"I'll be there if the need arises, camper, but you'll be fine. Just think of how you always liked to go camping and try to enjoy. Things will be much better come next summer. Just remember, young lady, that you at least have all the modern facilities at your school, and I have to use what we have here all the time. So enjoy!"

"I get your meaning, Dad, but enjoy? You're weird, Dad," she laughed, taking the lantern and going out the door. "Brrr! It really is cold. Come if I yell!"

Dus laughed, too, but hurriedly put on his coat and followed her at a distance to make sure that she would be OK. After a few minutes, the outhouse door opened, and Elly passed him in the snow, heading for the cabin. Keeping the lantern, she yelled to him through the howling wind, "You're next, old man. It's freezing in there. You guys are lucky you don't have to sit down on those holes and have the wind swirling around your behind."

"Well, sometimes we do, smarty pants. Now get inside and make your old man some vittles. Be there in a sec!"

It was a good evening for Dus and Elly. They ate, cleaned up the dishes, and relaxed by the fire. They talked and laughed, watching the flames, and renewed their family bonding. Life was healing and getting better, Dus mused. I just have to work harder and be a good priest to the people here, and a good father to this precious gift I have in this girl.

Elly took her father's hand, held it tight, and said, "Daddy, it is time for us to talk about Mom and Dusty. You promised. I need to know some answers so I can put it all behind me and go on with my life. And so you can go on with yours. I know that you still think of me as a little girl and don't think I understand things. Well, maybe I am and don't, but I am not going to bed tonight until we talk about Mom and Dusty. You're all I have now, and I'm all you have. I don't want to be alone with questions about them. Please, Daddy?"

Dus steeled himself and prayed he would say the right thing to the precious child who was his to nourish and care for by himself for a very long time to come. "Honey, it was just a very bad accident. God did not want it to happen. No one wanted it to happen. It's the price we pay for carelessness, for owning powerful cars with frail human beings driving them, passing one another, going too fast, not wearing seat belts, and not watching out for the other person. You are young, but you know that things like that happen all the time, every day on the streets and highways. Well, it happened to us. Your Mom went to pick up Dusty from his ball game. On the way home, a man driving a pickup truck went through a stop sign very fast and hit our car broadside. The doctors and nurses at the hospital tried very hard to save your mom and brother, but they both died within an hour. You were still at school with your activities. They were dead, honey, long before you even got home. I would have waited a long time to tell you all this, but you wanted to know now."

"Yes, I do, Dad."

"The driver of the truck was killed, too. The doctors said that your mom, Dusty, and the man never knew what hit them, and they did not suffer. It was just a bad, terrible, senseless thing, and there is nothing we can do about it. It does not help to blame anyone, to be angry, nor try to escape life. I was very angry at the time and thought about suing the man's family, but I knew, too, that they had lost a husband and father, and it was not their fault. They had no money, anyway, and certainly needed no further pain in their lives. I can't put a price on your mother's and brother's lives, anyway. We had insurance, and with that and my income, we can do OK with our needs. But, darling, like a friendly doctor told me, we have to let time, good memories, God's love, and your love for me and mine for you fill up the voids in our hearts left by the accident. We must believe that God is taking care of them until we see them again in heaven."

Elly cried out, "I don't care if they are with God in heaven. I want them here with you and me, now. We need them, Daddy, more than God needs them!"

"I know that, darling, but that's not possible. I don't have all the answers for you. Your mother was my wife, your brother, my son, and I love and miss them just as you do. But they are gone, Elly, and I can't bring them back. This is the way of life and death for all living creatures. It happens to animals, trees, flowers, and human beings. Our bodies are fragile, and sometimes they are so frail that they don't survive some of the buffeting they get in this life. We are all going to die someday—some folk earlier than others, but we are all going to die and go to heaven. Your mom and brother just went earlier, and we have to learn to accept that. You will and I will in time, baby."

Ellen's face tightened up. It was a pretty face and had the features of her mother. Tears began to flow down her cheeks and she blurted out angry words. "Lots of girls at school say some bad words when they feel bad about things. You taught Dusty and me never to swear, and I have tried not to, but I have said some very nasty things to God."

"Like what, Elly?"

"Like, 'God, if you love and care so damn much about people, why did you take my mom and brother from me and Daddy?' I told him, 'Daddy worked hard for you all the time, telling everyone how great you are, and then you allow this to happen to us. Why did you let them die so we don't have them anymore?'"

"I have had the same feelings and have sworn, too, honey. We ought not swear, but God understands that we are hurt and are angry about Mom and Dusty dying. I think he is big enough to handle our frustration and anger. God did not invent automobiles and make them powerful and dangerous. He did not make us careless and selfish. We are just human beings who make a lot of mistakes, and this was a very big one in our lives. It happened, and the only thing God can do for us now is help us to be more careful with our lives, mend our wounds, heal our pain, and show us again how to find happiness in our memories and in helping each other in this life. He did not do this to us, darling, but I have accused him, too, and used worse words than you have. I have been madder than you about this, and I am sure that God knows that we still love him even when we are angry. I hope so, don't you? God's not God if he won't forgive us and doesn't understand the anger we feel when our hearts and souls are in terrible pain," Dus lectured, trying not only to convince his daughter, but himself, as well.

Ellen was listening intently to her father. "I don't know much about religion, except what I learned from you, Mom, Sunday school, and the sisters. I don't want to be angry with God or anyone, but I miss Mommy, Daddy, and not having her hurts so much. When will the hurt go away? When will I feel good, have all those good memories, and not be mad at God? I look at all of our pictures with Dusty, Mom, you, and me in them, and I just cry and cry," Ellen sobbed, breaking Dus' heart.

He took her in his arms, smoothed out her hair, and wiped her tears. "Soon, honey, soon. As soon as you grow older, happy times and wonderful people will come into your life and fill up your heart and mind with beautiful thoughts and things. You won't forget your mom and brother, but their absence will not hurt so much anymore. You have to believe that, and so does your old man."

"What is going to fill up your life, Dad, besides your work and me?"

"Well, you and work will keep me very busy, and there are a lot of wonderful people around. I hope to meet a lot of them. You will, one day, have your own life to think about. I will have to find things to do. But your mom will always be near me, Elly, as she will always be near you. You will always feel her presence and love as you grow up and become a beautiful lady like she was."

"Is that true? Do people keep on loving you when they go to heaven?"

"Yes, they do, sweetheart. Their presence, just like Jesus', is always felt if you cherish them and keep them in your heart, even though you can't see or touch them. That's the way it is with God's love."

Ellen sniffed and wiped her eyes. "I guess I'd better try harder to understand God a little better, just as I had to understand Mom when she got mad at me. She did things I didn't like, too. So do you, Daddy."

"So do you, camper, and so did Dusty, and you are sure right about me. We all make mistakes; we all get mad, and we are forgiven when we try to do better. That's the way God works, and now that we are so smart about God and everything, why don't you put on your nightie and go to bed? You feel better now?"

"Yeah, I do, Dad, Why is it so wrong to swear? It just seems to come out naturally when you feel mad and hurt about things. Some of my friends use bad language even when they are laughing and talking."

"I know, honey, and sometimes I say some bad words I shouldn't, but it is a very bad habit people get into. It's not natural. It's not the way people usually converse. God doesn't want us to swear and use dirty words. I, too, swear at things. Swearing is a poverty of vocabulary. Anger and hurt are not an excuse. I'm always confessing my bad words."

"Do priests sin and have to confess, Dad?"

"Do we ever! We are just frail human beings like everyone else, honey, and we make a lot of mistakes. I have made many, especially since your mom and brother died. I have been very angry about that, and I should know better. God is more likely to forgive little girls than he is me."

"I thought God forgives everyone, even priests."

"Oh, I hope so, darling. I hope so!"

"Well, I'll pray for him to forgive you and help you correct your vocabulary. Then you don't have to worry. It'll work. My prayers are good. You wait and see!"

He hugged her, tears came, and Dus thought about the meaning of "Out of the mouths of babes" and "Unless you become like these little ones, you cannot enter into the Kingdom of God." He stammered, "Sure they will, Elly. Thank you for being my little girl and setting me right."

"It's all going to be OK, Daddy. Well, where do I sleep?"

"Up in the loft. It's a big room with a soft bed and a cozy quilt to keep you warm. I'll run out to the jeep and get your bag." He did that, and then admonished her to get to bed. Elly scrubbed her teeth, gave her daddy a big hug and kiss, and ran up to the loft. She stopped, looked over the rail, and said, "Thank you for talking to me about Mom and Dusty. I'll think about the things you said, and will talk to God more than I have. I'm glad that he understands about my getting mad, and I'm going to try hard not to cuss anymore. And, Dad, this really is a neat house and place to come home to. Thanks for that, too. And I really don't mind the outhouse. It's fun! I love it, the house, and you!"

"You're welcome, darling, and I love you, too. Rest well up there and have good dreams. Big day for us tomorrow, full of fun and good things to eat and do. Good night!"

"Oh, Dad, are there bears around here?"

Dus frowned, "Why do you ask, Elly?"

"Because the sisters at the priory told me there were big old black bears that live up here in the mountains."

"They aren't so big, and they won't hurt a sweet girl like you, Goldilocks. Besides, your old man is here to protect you and I'll fight 'em to the death for you!"

"I know you would, but I don't want you to die for me or anyone. I don't want to lose you, too."

Dus' eyes filled up again. "Don't worry about that, honey. You and I are going to live a long life together. There is not a beast in the world that can lick your daddy, nor that wouldn't love you if it met you."

"That's comforting to know. Oh, by the way, if I have to tinkle again, what do I do if there are bears around and I can't hold out until tomorrow?"

Dus murmured to himself, "Darn those sisters. It's not enough that they scare us clergy with their threats of burning us at the stake, but they have to scare little kids with dumb talk about bears." "You hold it for now," he told her, "but if you really have to go, wake me up, and I'll go with you and chase away the bears. Come summer, you won't have to worry about that anymore. I'm going to build this house strong and beautiful, and when the bears come to visit you, you can invite them in for dinner and have a blanket party."

"Oh, you're really daffy, mountain man, but I do love you. Good night!"

"Good night, sweetheart. I love you, too." Dus gazed into the fire. He had told his daughter the truth. He had strong hands, muscles, and good skills, and would make a nice place for her. He'd rent a backhoe someplace and dig a septic system for a nice bathroom. He loved that little girl, and would work his hands to the bone to give her a good life. They were going to have a fine house and a good life together in this place when school was out, and he knew that Ginnie would be pleased with his efforts.

"Yes, honey. I will make you a comfortable house, with a warm bathroom, and I won't ever allow anything to frighten you."

There was no answer from her. He could hear her deep breathing, and I knew she was sound asleep, not worrying anymore about bears, cold potties, nor heaven. "I'll make her a good home, Ginnie, and take good care of her for you. I promise! And you take care of Dusty for us until we get there with you," Dus said to the dying embers in the hearth. He fell asleep in his chair there, finally believing, after many months of experiencing a terrible spiritual drought, that the things that he told Ellen about God, his love, Ginnie, and Dusty were true. He fell asleep also believing in himself again.

# 12

It was near dusk at the Conley house on Thanksgiving Day. Ox, Nancy, Karol, and Dus were sitting around the fire musing about how good the day and how sumptuous and tasty the meal, served by the ladies, had been. Wild turkey with cornmeal stuffing, flour gravy, yams, corn, stewed tomatoes, cranberry sauce, mince and pumpkin pie, and lots of hot cinnamon cider and coffee to drink.

All the children had finished, put on their winter togs, and were up on the hill sliding in the snow. Jenny and Cyrus had taken the baby on a sled to visit their friends down the road. The dishes had all been washed and put away, and there were "ohs and ahs" about the quantity and the quality of food everyone had eaten.

"I'm stuffed," Karol said. "I should not have eaten so much, but it was so good, Nancy."

"Ah, ya needs some fat on ya, missy," Ox answered for his wife. "Ya gits too skinny en a place lak des, da cold a git ta ya, en ya'll git da croops er somethun, butta yer shur right. It was a good meal. Thank ya, Nan. Ya done good fer us."

"Y'all welcome, indeed," Nancy said, "butta ya needs ta thank Karol har too, 'cause she brung da pies, cooked da yams en tamatas, en basted da turkey. Corse, ol' Ox brung in da bird. Wadda ya think, Dus?"

Dus had been thinking a lot as he ate, watched, and listened to the people around the table and now around the fire. His mind had wandered here and there about the whole day. He had been pleased beyond expectation with the Thanksgiving service. Though the snow had been fairly deep, about forty people had trudged up the path to the church, listened attentively to his sermon about thanking God for daily bread, and had participated in the Communion. He had a chance afterward to introduce Elly to all the people who had come, and was awfully proud of her friendliness, her happy demeanor, and courtesy. She was a joy, and everyone was pleasant to her. Nancy had complimented Dus about what a pretty and smart girl she was, as did Karol and the other ladies. The men were impressed that she had spoken to them with respect, a pretty smile, and a vigorous handshake.

Shawn introduced himself and immediately asked her if she'd like to go sled riding after dinner with the Conley kids. He also asked her if her school was any fun with no boys in it. Elly told him that it was just fine without boys in classes, but they did have parties and stuff where they were allowed by the sisters to invite boys. But she was still pretty young for that. Her dad didn't let her date yet. Dus had allowed her to go ahead with Karol, Shawn, and the Conleys to their house, while he closed the church and locked the cabin. He arrived there soon after.

"Wampum for your thoughts, Padre," Karol said to Dus.

"Just thinking what a nice day it has been with Ellen here and with all of you. I appreciate the way you have welcomed her and taken us in on this holiday."

"'Tis shurly our pleasure, Parson," Nancy said. "She's a mighty purty en spunky li'l sweet'art. Yer lucky ta have a nice youngun lak 'er."

Karol broke in with, "You're right about that, Nancy. She's a darling girl. Looks like Shawn is a bit smitten with her, too."

"I'm blessed to have her," Dus responded. "It has not been easy for her at school with her mother and brother gone. She asked a lot of questions last night, and coughed up a lot of things that she needed to say. We caught up on our lives and vowed a fresh start together. She likes the cabin, except for the outside johnny and the basin bath, and thinks she'll be happy there. She wants a place to come home to and says it will be fine. I plan to put in some inside plumbing and electricity this spring, and fix up the place to make it more livable for us as a family. I talked to my bishop about renovations, and he says there might be diocesan funds available for the project."

"Who's gonna do dat kina work, Dus?" Ox asked.

"I am!"

"Ya know jow ta do dat kina carpenry en otha stuff?"

"Sure! I have known how since I was a kid on the farm. I did a lot of plumbing and electrical work in my job before I went off to be a preacher, Ox."

"Wa'll swanee! Ken I help ya? Donna know 'bout piping en 'lectric, but I ken carry, dig, carpen'ry, en do what's needful in thatta way."

"Thanks. I'll appreciate your help. It shouldn't be too hard. Just need to get a gasoline generator, hook up some electric lines to the house and church, and get a pump for the water in the well, some pipe and fittings, a toilet, and wash sink for the bathroom and kitchen. I can make a shower very easily. I'll rent a backhoe and dig a trench and cesspool. I'll need some wire, and then we'll have plenty of electricity for our needs. With your help and the right tools, it won't take more than a couple of months to do it all. I have a friend up in Pennsylvania who can do anything with tools, who might come down to help."

"What's yo' frien'd name, Dus, what ken help ya?"

"Lou Casalano. We've known each other since we were in the third grade. Great man and craftsman!"

"Sounds like a big job to me," Karol added. "I guess I can help, too. I'm pretty strong, and know how to do some building. I'd like to see that little girl have some comforts if she's going to live up there with you."

"We ain't use ta dem kina comforts up har, Doc," Ox broke in sourly. "Wadda ya need all dat stuff fer?"

"Ah, mine yer own busnus, mountain man," Nancy scolded her husband. "Jist 'cause we ain't neva had need a dem things, Ox, it donna mean udder folk don't. Da parson en da youngun en da doctor is use' ta dem whar dey come from, en it's all right iffen dey wanna dem. We's use' ta da udder way, ahselfs, but dey's nice at da clinic, ta be sho. Modern comforts, I hear tell, is mo' healthy fer folk. Might be a good idea ta be thinkin' 'bout dem fer our younguns and grandkiddies too, as dey come along."

"What you said is true, Nancy," Karol agreed. "One of the most important things for good health is sanitation, and the more modern facilities we have, the better to keep people clean and healthy. I could not have the clinic operate without running water, electricity, and waste disposal. The federal government wouldn't have allowed you folk to build it, nor me to keep it open, if we did not provide those things in it."

"Wah, young Doc, I'm en ol' man what donna know much 'bout sech things, so iffen Nan seys it be OK, 'tis OK. Nan knows she en da tikers ken have anything dey wanna have iffen we has da means ta git 'em. Maybe me en Dus ken git tagatha en do 'em har fer Nan too, someday."

"Git on wid yer nonsense, Ox," Nan chided. "Thar's mo' important things fer ya to do 'bout har. Ya help da preacha, da doc, en da li'l girl Elly, first. They's da ones what needs dem da most, en we ken look ta our needs some otha time."

"While we are on the subject of the clinic, Doctor Marson," Dus said, turning to Karol, "I was wondering if you and I could talk about a mutual business arrangement. Could I come down to the clinic and talk to you about some business possibilities, sometime?"

"Business?" Karol chortled. "Now what sort of business would a priest have up here in these mountains, with all you have to do, running over these hills and valleys, preaching the gospel, spreading the word and shepherding the sheep. What kind of business, Father?"

Mare's marbles, Dus cursed to himself. Isn't this woman ever going to get off my back with her sarcasm? I thought we had an understanding not to do that to one another. Can't ask one darned question without her making a joke about me. Just when I thought we were beginning to respect one another.

"Forget it," Dus said, testily. "It was a bad idea that wouldn't have worked, anyway."

"What was it, Father?"

"Nothing, really. Nothing important. Now, if you'll all excuse me, I'm going up the hill to see where the kids are. It's time I took Ellen home. Thank you so much for the nice dinner, Nancy. Elly will be in to express her appreciation. Bye, now!" He put on his coat and left abruptly, closing the door hard behind him.

"Ut-oh," Nancy muttered. "I t'ink da parson is a bit miffed 'bout somethun."

Ox added, "Donna ya worry 'bout 'im none, Nan. He's jist got some chaff roun' his neck."

"He'll be all right," interjected Karol. "He wanted to ask me something and I kidded with him. I might have said something that irritated him. I joke too much for my own good. I'll go after him and make it right. Don't either one of you worry about him. He has a lot on his mind these days. I'll go fix it with him."

Karol put on her togs and went out the door. She saw Dus climbing the hill toward the children, and started trudging up the hill after him, slipping and sliding all the way, and then finally fell headlong down in the snow. She yelled up the hill at him.

"Hey, Father Dus, come back down here. I've fallen down and can't get up. How about giving me a hand?"

"Give yourself a hand!" he yelled down at her. "You said you were strong and could do anything. Maybe that mighty wit of yours can help you figure out the dilemma you're in and help you get out of it!"

Karol ignored the slight. "Ah, come on, Father!" she yelled at him. "Don't be a sourpuss. I'm sorry you're nettled. I didn't mean my answer to your questions to sound like I was ridiculing you."

"Sure you did!" Dus yelled.

"OK, then I don't deserve a hand, but come down anyway for a minute and we'll talk about that business of yours. If you quit being peevish about so much and want to be friendly, I'll let you have the extra room at the clinic for some church office space."

Father Habak's face lit up. He was not sure that he understood exactly what she had said, but hoped that he had heard what he wanted to hear. He trudged back down the hill to where she sprawled in the snow. "Are you OK?" he asked.

"Oh, I'm fine. Hurt feelin's, maybe. I just wanted you to talk to me. How about sitting with me for a moment?"

Dus sat down beside her, not unaware of her lovely wet face, gorgeous long, damp hair, and beautifully formed body, tightly fitted into a snow-flecked, leather-thonged doeskin jacket, skirt, and boots. Yes, he said to himself, she is an Indian princess, in spite of her clowning around so much. "Did I hear you say something about the clinic and office space?" he stammered.

"Yes, I did, but before I talk about that, I want to tell you that was a damned rude exit you made on the Conleys' back there. Whatever your grievance with me, you have no right to treat them that way. They like you very much, and have been good to you. You owe them an apology."

Dus saw her face change and felt the pique that came with the words out of her pretty mouth. He lowered his face in repentance. "I'm sorry. You are right! You made me mad again, and I reacted stupidly. I'll go back and apologize to Nancy and Ox. But, gee, Doctor, why do you always make a quip every time I open my mouth?"

"I apologize, too, Padre. I'm just as obtuse as you are, sometimes, but we'll talk about that later. What I yelled up to you about was an offer to loan you some space at the clinic for a parish office until you get better settled at the church."

"How did you know I wanted to ask you about that?"

"I didn't; honest Injun. Maybe it was women's intuition. I've been thinking for awhile that maybe the mission and you would need some space to do some parish business closer to town and to have a telephone available for Elly, the bishop, and stuff. I had planned to ask you when I saw you this weekend. There's plenty of room."

"That would be great, but isn't that a government-funded project? Wouldn't it be a violation of the laws governing separation of church and state?"

"Fiddle on the government. The clinic is to help folk with their problems no matter how they are manifested, and you help them with problems, don't you? Anyway, what the g-men don't know won't hurt 'em! Who's gonna tell? Let me worry about that. I'll smile at the politicians and tell them they're messing with an Indian and a poor folk's project. We Indians have a lot of clout these days. American Indian concerns are the 'in thing!' No g-man wants to offend Indians and doctors doing good works. Like my good ol' great-grandpappy, Chief Joseph, used to say of U.S. Government, 'May the coyotes pee on his moccasins!'"

"Did he really say that?"

"I don't know, and I don't even know if he's my great-grandfather, but it sounds like something he would say to the U.S. Government. If you know his history, you'd know he gave 'em fits."

"I'll be a monkey's uncle," Dus laughed, scratching his head.

"Well, you act like it, sometimes, Father. But that isn't a very nice thing for a priest to say about himself, even if I have thought it, myself. When a priest acts like a monkey, it gets one to thinking that there is a lot to evolution!"

"Talk about monkeys—Lordy." Dus smiled, feigning exasperation. "What in the world am I going to do with a smart alec Indian woman?"

"Well, like clergy have vowed to do, you might begin by being a little patient with and forgiving of sinners like me. You might also be a good Samaritan and help me out of the snow because my heinie is getting wet."

Dus pulled her up by her hand, and, while staring at her wet, brown, pretty face, asked, "Are you really a granddaughter of Chief Joseph?"

"That's what my mom tells me, Parson. A great-granddaughter. Do you know about him?"

"I have read about him. It is said that he was one of the most peace-loving of the great Indian chiefs."

"So he was. A bit too peaceful with you 'white eyes' for my liking, but then I am a bit prejudiced. I inherited part of my name from him."

"You're kidding!"

"No, I'm not."

"What part?"

"Thunder Rolling in the Mountain."

Dus laughed. "His name—your name—is 'Thunder Rolling in the Mountain?'"

"Don't laugh, Preacher. You can get scalped making fun of Indians. It was appropriate for him, and it is appropriate for me. You may find that out someday when you get to know me."

"I think I know that already! What's the rest of your name?"

"None of your business. I don't know you well enough to tell that appalling secret. Now, please scream at our kids to get in the house so we can settle down in front of the Conley's fireplace, warm my wet heinie, get some hot cider into my cold gizzard, and calm your spirit. And don't forget the apology, paleface."

He yelled to the children to follow them, and they walked to the house. Karol put her arm through his, allowing him to steady her down the slope. He glanced at her wet and smiling face. All of a sudden, he felt very warm. He relaxed his arm where she held it, and said to a spirit somewhere in the open space of snow and beautiful scenery, "I'm sorry, Ginnie. I'm trying hard not to notice, but isn't she the prettiest Indian you ever saw, even if she is the most ornery woman I ever met?"

# 13

Christmas was just two weeks away. Dus had taken Elly back to the priory school in Ox's pickup. After dropping her off, he went by the diocesan office and discussed with the bishop the office arrangements at the clinic, as well as future plumbing and electrical conveniences at the vicarage. Bishop Mueller had assured him that funds would be available for those needs. As promised, Karol provided space at the clinic, having avoided "church and state" conflicts by telling no one about the arrangement. Dus had returned to the clinic with Ox's truck full of furniture, including an office desk with swivel chair, a couple of stuffed chairs, coffee table, lamp table, bookshelves, and some religious wall paintings that had been stored at the Diocesan Center. He had also bought a multiline telephone, and snaked a line through the walls and attacked it to Doctor Marson's office line. With it, he installed a two-way cutoff circuit so they both could have telephone privacy. He had tested the circuitry by calling both the bishop and Elly. It worked fine.

His new office had a door to the clinic waiting room and one directly to the outside on the far side of the building. Karol and Nancy had put up some pretty cottage curtains at the windows, and Ox had constructed stacked brick and plank shelves for his books. The floor was a bit too clinical for him, so he decided to find a used carpet someplace. He was very pleased with his new quarters, believed they would be an asset to his ministry, and was grateful to Doctor Marson for making it all possible. He had found her to be a helpful person, generous with her time and effort. He certainly admired much about her, but continued to ask himself how long it would take him to penetrate her mysterious irascibility.

He looked forward to the Christmas season with his small flock and daughter, and he hoped the doctor and her son would come to the mountain, too. He had prevailed upon her to help build a life-sized Nativity crèche outside the church. She agreed. She and some artistic friends at the hospital would cut and paint all the needed Nativity figures on some three-quarter inch plywood down in Staunton, if Dus and the folks on the mountain would build the stable, and mount the figures when she brought them up to the church. He had asked Jed Hudson if he could look around for some oil "tiki"-like torches to put around the crèche so it could be lighted up and seen from afar. Jed had no trouble doing that. Helen Hudson had acquired some during a trip to Hawaii and brought them back with her.

"By gosh," Dus had said to Nancy and Ox, "when we get it up and lighted, people from all over this mountain are going to see it, come see the baby Jesus, and see what Christmas is about."

"Wal see 'bout dat, Dus, boy," Ox grunted.

"Hush yo' mouf, husband," Nancy admonished, then turned to Dus. "En donna listen ta 'im. Folk'll come en enjo' it! Ya'll see! Ol' sweet Ox neva seen sech a thung, en he donna think it'll be nice. Ya'll lak it when it's done, wonna ya, Ox?"

"Whateva she sey, Pawson; she nearly right mos' a da time. She'll always make me eat crow. Ya go ah'ad, en I'll sees fer myself if it's purty."

\* \* \*

Dus spent the last two weeks when he was away from the office walking and driving around the mountain, and visiting people, both near and far. They were generally hospitable and friendly, some a bit suspicious of him, but none hostile. A few invited him to have coffee or tea, while others shared a full meal with him. The mountaineers were economically poor in contrast to most of the people he had associated with in his life, but they were rich in spirit, proud, hardworking folk; while their houses were modest in size, with few creature comforts, they were well-built and immaculately clean. He never waved to a person while passing on the way who did not appear to be taking care of his home or shed. Mountain language was something of a problem for Father Habak, but he was learning to decipher the colloquialisms, and began to pick up some, himself. People laughed at his mannerisms and the funny way he talked, but he knew it was in good fun, and Nancy had told him not to pay attention to it.

"Da folk har er good folk, Pawson," she had said, "en effin ya eva gits in tro'ble, ya'd not have betta frien's in da whole wide world. Dr. Marson ken teach ya somethun 'bout dat. She has lea'nt dat fer shur."

He had walked down to Joshuatown a few times, just to get acquainted with the business people and village folk, some of whom sat around smoking pipes and "jawing" at Bessie's Café. He had eaten there often, and became well-acquainted with Nancy's friend, Bessie Clayton, the widow, and their other friends, Jed and Helen Hudson. Father Habak had judged Bessie to be close to fifty years old. She was still an attractive and cheerful lady, who might have been very beguiling to men in her youth. Dus liked her and her restaurant—good coffee, breakfast, and friendly people with whom he never had to instigate a conversation. It came to him in friendship and laughter. He'd reminded himself, often, as he walked around the village and mountain, that he had been missing a lot of life up until now.

He stopped over at HUDSON & SON COMPANY and had some friendly chats with Jed, then bought a few tools and necessities. He banked at Merchants Bank and did the best he could to manage Mr. Raymond Brush's unappreciated and not-very-funny humor. "How's the Lord's work going, Rev? Got some of the people saying 'Alleluia' yet?" the banker needled from time to time. "Can't get much done working only one day a week, can ya? Ha, ha!"

"No, I can't, Mr. Brush. That's why I have to work seven. I wish I had banker's hours," Dus said, trying to outwit the pompous man. Stick it, money changer, he had thought to himself. That's the oldest clergy joke in the world, and no one believes nor tells it anymore, not even Universalists, except, ha, ha, dipsticks like you. He could tell that he and the banker were not going to be friends. Dus' sensitivity never allowed him to enjoy demeaning jokes about his priestly vocation, especially from bankers with banker's hours.

Sheriff Scott Kirsh, with whom Father Habak had become more friendly over the past weeks, was sitting in Simon Shoney's barber shop, getting his hair trimmed, when Dus walked in for the same reason. "Morning, Father Habak. How are things going? Getting settled in the clinic and up at the church?" the sheriff asked pleasantly.

"Fine. Is Si doing a good job on your head?"

"I tries ta do a good job, Pawson. Anyways, I'm da only barba what's in town," Si laughed. "Butta how ken anyone do anythung wid a skimpy head a 'air lak dis wid nuffin butta wisps a weeds en sidebons?"

"Quit complaining, Si," the Sheriff scolded. "You already got too much money for the little work you do on my head. By the way, Father Habak, would you mind coming over to my office when Si gets done with you? Like to talk to you about some things," Sheriff Kirsh asked.

"Sure, Scott; be along in about half an hour." Then, to the barber, he said, "Just a trim today, Si."

Twenty minutes later, Dus was sitting in front of Scott Kirsh's desk.

The policeman's face was a bit grim, and Dus wondered what was on his mind. He soon found out.

"Father Habak, I've enjoyed our short acquaintance. As a matter of fact, even though my family and I are Catholic and go down to Staunton for mass, my wife, Patty, whom you have not yet met, and I are thinking we might like to come with the youngsters up to one of your masses."

"Be glad to have you. Our faiths aren't that much apart."

"Yeah, I know that. I was familiar with the Episcopal Church in Toledo, Ohio, through many friends. Anyway, it seems that in just a couple of months, you've made yourself pretty well-known, and folk here say nice things about you. Even though they don't much understand the clergy clothes you wear, they know you're a minister, and seem to like you."

"That's nice to hear, Scott."

"There are, however, Father, some rumors floating around about some of your activities that I want to ask you about."

"What kind of rumors, Scott?" Dus asked in surprise. "I can't imagine anything that I have done that would attract much attention. I just do my work of having services and visiting folk."

"That's good, and I'm not sure of the content of the rumors. I don't put a lot of stock in hearsay, but I'd feel better if I could put them to rest. Think you could help me?"

"Sure! How?"

"First, let me tell you a little about my background, and then you might understand why I ask."

"Sure, Scott; I'd like to know you better, anyhow."

"Guess you noticed, by the way I talk, I'm not from around here. Patty and I are from Toledo, where I was a member of the city police force. I spent five years on patrol and six more in the detective division. As a matter of fact, I have a degree in criminology from Ohio State. You know that college, don't you?"

"I remember very well beating the tail off of your alma mater in football a few times, Scott. I'm a Penn State graduate, and had some nice successes playing your alma mater."

"Ah, ha," he smiled. "That's interesting! I remember it being the other way around, but we'll talk about the football stuff later. Anyway, I wanted Patty and the children away from the stress of life with a city cop, so when I heard about this sheriff job opening up here, I applied for it and got it, as you can see. As county sheriff around these hills, I keep pretty busy. Besides covering a fairly large territory, I teach a course in investigations down at the policy academy in Staunton a few days a month. Between that and Patty teaching school here in Joshuatown, we do OK financially. Patty also has a practical nurse certification and helps Dr. Marson at the clinic on some of the weekends that she is there. They are also good friends. I assume that you have not run into Patty at the clinic."

"No, I haven't, Scott, but I'd like to. Of course, I know Dr. Marson."

"Well, everyone around knows you have moved into an office at the clinic. Hope that will be helpful to your work. Maybe you'll meet Patty there, but we'd like you to come around to the house and break some bread with us sometime soon."

"Love to, Sheriff. But that's not why you asked me to come by the office, is it?"

"Well, Father, I guess my detective experience makes me a bit nosy when I hear rumors about things happening to people. Added to that is the fact that you asked me for a gun permit soon after you came here."

"Come on, Scott, you're beating around the bush. What are you getting at?"

"How come you got shot in the butt up on the Cutty and didn't tell me about it when you visited me here and asked for your permit?"

Dus was annoyed with that question. Someone—Ox or Karol—snitched, he thought to himself. Goshdarn their big mouths. There's nothing private on this mountain. "Where did you hear that story, Sheriff?"

"It wasn't from a birdie, and it doesn't matter where I heard it, Father. Is it true or isn't it?"

"I did not get shot in the butt. It was no big deal. I was walking around the Cutty, when I thought I heard a rifle shot. When I ducked behind a log, I fell on a stump, and it punctured my tail end. I had a bad reaction at first, but then I figured it wasn't important. Just someone shooting in the woods. Didn't see any need to bother you or anyone with it."

"Wasn't important, eh?" Scott responded, rather miffed. "Then why the hell, if you'll excuse my language, Father, did you buy a gun?"

"I didn't buy a gun, Scott. I only asked for a permit, if you will remember. I own an old .38 pistol I brought home with me from the service. I don't shoot it, but as a law-abiding citizen, I register it every place I live. Maybe I'll get a shotgun and do some rabbit and bird hunting."

"You don't need a permit for a shotgun in this county!"

"I know, and it's OK. Believe me! Nothing serious happened to me up there on the Cutty. There is nowhere safer than these hills. Whatever the rumors were, you don't need to pay any attention to them. Folk like to talk a lot, anywhere one goes, especially about new people around a town."

"People like to shoot a lot, too, Father. Why do you think a policeman like me is here? You can't believe I moved all the way down here to direct traffic and set radar traps in Joshuatown?"

"Come on, Scott, you don't have to get sarcastic. I supposed that you were here to protect folk from the evils of crime and keep the peace."

"That's right. Did anything happen after that incident that would have given you cause to wonder if you might be a target for someone's anger?"

"None," Dus lied to the detective. He was not going to tell him of his conversation with the auto repairman and the brake incident. He knew it might cause him trouble later if anything else happened, and he wanted no further issue made of it. And he would certainly tell Ox and Dr. Marson to stow their loose lips.

"Well, I guess I have to believe a priest. But hear me, Father Habak, and remember what I am telling you, please. If anything like that happens again, I'd better hear about it from you, and not from other people, pronto. And I do mean right away! Do you hear me, my friend?"

"Yes, Sheriff, I hear you. You don't have to raise your voice at me. I'm not a child. I'll tell you if I feel threatened."

"Didn't mean to scold you, Father, but while you may think this is a nice place, there are some meanies here, like everywhere else on earth, with prejudices, psycho problems, hard hearts, and secrets. Some people have secrets, as you well know, and don't want priests and cops finding out about them. Sometimes they send some pretty harsh messages to tell us to butt out of their lives. These mountain folk are a bit different than us Yankees. They protect each other, related or not, like family. Most of them are decent and honest folk with no malice in them. But some can be meaner than city street creeps when they get their dander up and feel threatened. Just remember that no one, not anyone, in these mountains fires a rifle by mistake. Remember that, OK?"

"Sure will, Scott, and thanks. I'll tell you anything you have to know, if ever I feel the need."

"Then we understand one another. So I'll be seeing you around, Father. I was serious about you having some dinner with us sometime. You'll like Patty and will enjoy her food, though it's not as good as Bessie Clayton's."

"Thanks. I will. So long," Dus said, as he started to leave.

"Take care! Oh, by the way, Father Habak," Sheriff Kirsh shouted after him, "there's some old-time moonshiners cooking up 110-proof 'white lightnin' in homemade whiskey stills all over these mountains. Corn juice that'll drill a hole in your gizzard if you guzzle it straight up. It's a federal offense to brew or sell it, and it's dangerous stuff that can kill you. So are the moonies who make it. They don't like 'revnooers,' cops, nor other nosy folk. Some of those coils are in the tree thickets and caves. If you ever see smoke rising out of either of 'em, you get your tail out of there, quick. It won't be a sweet, innocent black bear after you, Father, but some irate 'moonie' ready to buckshot the hell out of your teetotaling butt. Won't be just a little hole Dr. Marson and Patty'll be patching up next time, but your backside from your hip to your knees. They'll be picking buckshot out of you for a week, if in fact we don't have to bury you in that neat graveyard you keep up there. You hear me?"

"Mare's marbles!" Dus cussed. "I hear you, Scott! See you around," and he shut the door behind him.

But that was last week. Right now he was thinking about Christmas, and could hardly wait for the joy that holy season brought to people. He hadn't known joy for a long time. Now he felt, the sheriff's warnings aside, in this place, at this special time, things are about to happen that will bring meaning to my life. Snow, lights, stars, images, worship, and the gaiety of people, meshed together, will wipe away bad memories.

"Gosh," he said, thinking about Scott Kirsh's words of caution, "moonshiners wanting to shoot at me just for traipsing around in the woods? I'd better forget about that cave and keep my parish visiting a bit lower down on that Cutty hill. I wonder if the 'moonies' would know how to beat up on car brake cylinders, too?"

# 14

It was a beautiful, crispy moonlit evening, three days before Christmas, when Karol Marson drove up to the vicarage with Ox's pickup full of neatly jigsawed life-sized plywood cutouts of animals and people, destined to occupy the rugged, thatched lean-to full of straw that Dus and Cyrus had built to represent a Nativity stable. Dus waved and smiled as he approached the truck to help her unload the goods she had brought. "Hi," he greeted her. "What do you have there for our crêche?"

"Signed, sealed, and delivered, as requested, Father Habak," responded the weary, yet attractive, lady physician. "One each: Mary, Joseph, baby Jesus, donkey and star. Five each: sheep and shepherds. Three each: wise men and camels, and twenty tiki torches to light up the mountain, some of which I got from hospital friends and others from Helen Hudson. How's that for a surgeon, whose mastery at cutting up plywood is not quite as good as that when cutting up people? Take 'em off the truck easy. Do you have some stakes and stuff to keep 'em upright?"

"Sure do, Doc. Gosh, they're great! Exactly what I wanted! Where'd you get the material and the help?"

"Had a lot of paint and junk for making signs in the hospital maintenance shop. Recruited some of my nurse and medic buddies to paint and cut in their spare time. Told 'em that it was for a worthy cause, like a mission offering for a poor old preacher and church out in the Appalachians. They really enjoyed doing it, and send you Christmas wishes."

"Well, you told 'em right. I am a poor ol' preacher!"

"No you're not, Father Habak, at least not in the important things of life. I don't know about your bank account, but you do have a lot of good qualities under that brooding Kraut veneer of yours. Especially when you aren't uptight about getting shot in the heinie by moonshiners, chased all over the mountain by bears, hiding in caves, and being scared that a gabby Indian princess is going to tease you into an early grave."

Dus scowled just enough so as not to be cantankerous on an otherwise joyful night. He scratched his head, wondering how the woman had so much data on his doings. "I know you know about my heinie and my fetishes, Indian Princess, but what snitch enlightened you about my activities? Do you have an informant sending you smoke signals about my madcap capers here on the mountain? Moonshiners, caves, and bears? My, you sure have a colorful imagination about my mostly tranquil and prayerful existence. I now have only the spirit of Christmas on my mind."

"I can't read your mind, Parson, but you are too nice, in spite of your idiosyncrasies and disavowals, to be chewed up by a bear or shot by a gun crackpot, so be careful."

"And what about being teased into an early grave by a gabby Indian princess?"

"It's best you watch out for her, too," she laughed, "but given the bears and the shooters, you're better off with the gabby Indian!"

"Well, she may be gabby, but it was really nice of her and her friends to help us with this crêche. It'll make Christmas a lot brighter up here. Give me their names, and I'll write them some 'thank you' notes."

"That's not necessary. They were glad to do it. I'll take some pictures for them. Let's get the stuff set up now. Neat stable you made, farmer lad. I see that you have had some experience with stables."

"I forked a lot of manure out of them in my life, and that, my dear, is one of the reasons I am an engineer and a priest rather than a farmer. But then, the priesthood has its share of mare's marbles, too! Actually, the crêche required little acumen. Cyrus and I put it together in no time."

"You and your 'mare's marbles.' I'm going to speak to you about that sometime. Anyway, this looks a lot like the pony shelters they had on our reservation. Can't help it, but seeing all this makes me a bit homesick," Karol confessed, a sadness developing in her face. "Did you know that the Nez Perce had the best-bred horses in the whole United States? Specialized in Appaloosas. Ol' Meriwether Lewis of the Lewis and Clark expedition in the northwest made that claim. Their guide, a Shoshoni woman named Sacagawea, told 'em that all the neighboring tribes and trappers wanted Nez Perce horses, 'cause they were the best riding stock between the Mississippi and the Pacific."

"Hmmm! I didn't know that. That's interesting. We only had mules for work; Tennessee and Pinto for riding. I'm sorry all this makes you feel sad. The crêche is meant to bring joy, but I guess Christmas away from home causes most everyone some homesickness. Stirs up a lot of good and bad memories, some of which we ought to put behind us."

"That's true," she sniffed.

"Anyway, this is Elly's and my home now, and it is where our Christmastime will be for some time to come. We're glad, too, that the mountain is going to be your and Shawn's home for this Christmas, and that you'll be at the clinic for a few days. It will make a better Christmas for the folk here. They love and need you, you know."

"That's sweet of you to say. I love the place and the people, too, Father. It's made a lot of difference in Shawn's and my life. It has brought contentment and solace to a couple of aching hearts, and it has made me feel I make a helpful contribution to others' lives."

"I'm sure you do and have, Doctor, here and down there at the hospital. Our mutual gimpy friend, J.K., says you do a super job there. I guess he might have told you he came to visit with me for a few hours a couple of Sundays ago. He is one of the good guys in this world. We had a nice nostalgic talk and shared some memories. He and his wife are going to come down in the spring to do some spelunking. He really admires and likes you.

"We are good friends. He's a great computer guy and super family man. He's overcome a great deal. He said to wish you a merry Christmas. Interesting story about you two. I'll have to hear more about your relationship sometime, if you think it is any of my business."

"War stories are the pits," Dus said, "but spelunking is an interesting activity. It's about caves. You know?"

"Yes, I know, and J.K. has invited me on one of those outings. But I'm not interested in caves and stuff. I don't like what's in them?"

"You don't? I thought Indians would be interested in caves," Dus said, a bit disappointed.

"Some are and some aren't. I'm not! I'm into clean, warm wigwams with no crawly things, neither beast nor men," she quipped. "So when is Elly coming up for Christmas?"

Dus decided he would not pursue the subject of caves, bats, and men, so he answered her question about Elly. "The sisters are going to drive her up to town about noon tomorrow. That's nice of the old girls. I'll pick her up at Bessie's and bring her here."

"I can bring her up. I shut the clinic for an hour at noon and have the time. How about my taking Shawn and her to lunch at Bessie's as long as she is there? She'll be hungry, and so will he."

"Thanks. That will be good! Well, let's get on with our Nativity work and see how it looks."

Karol and Dus worked nearly two hours pounding in stakes to hold the wood figures erect, and stood Joseph and Mary in the rear of the lean-to, looking over a crude manger. Then they strewed some hay around the ground. The star was mounted on the roof, and they staggered the other figures as aesthetically as they deemed proper around the outside of the shelter. Dus filled the tiki torches with kerosene and placed them around the perimeter of the crèche. Karol lighted them with a burning candle. Immediately, the sky seemed to light up in auras of red, green, and orange. She lifted up her head to the sky and began to weep. Great tears rolled down her cold cheeks, running into the creviced corners of her mouth. "It's very beautiful and moving," she sniffed, wiping her nose and eyes with the cuff of her leather coat.

"It's gorgeous! All I had hoped it would be, thanks to you, Dr. Marson," Dus agreed. "The people will love it!"

"Come," Karol said, taking his hand in hers and pulling him down the path. "Let's walk down to the road and see what it looks like from there."

Arriving at the road, still holding hands, they looked upward to the church and vicarage, both aglow from flickering candles Dus had lighted in the windows earlier. The Nativity crèche, with the torches ablaze, appeared hauntingly alive. The ice-crusted snow across the edge of the hill mirrored the figures and the flames of the torches, their multicolors reflecting from Karol's wet eyes and face.

"You're right, Doctor," Dus spoke quietly, turning from the scene and looking at her. "It is beautiful, and its beauty is not only reflected in the sky and snow, but in your face. You feel what you see, don't you?"

"I'm not sure, Father, what I feel, but all that imagery there brings peace to my being right now. The serenity of it conjures memories of Christian Christmas Nativity stories mixed with tales that the old Indian grannies told about the love the Great Spirit had for his people, and who manifested that love through the birds in the air, the animals, and the great trees of the forests. I see, up there, not only the imagery of God sending love to the people on earth through the infant Jesus, but through that gorgeous sky, the tall splendid trees, and, yes, Father, even through those wooden sheep, the donkey, and the camels. I believe, if the Great Spirit I know as an Indian and the God I know as a Christian are the same, then it must be that he makes himself known to us through all of creation. There is nothing of God for me, unless that is true. I am afraid, my priestly friend, that the white people have made God into their own image instead of seeing all people of every race made in his image. Do you believe that?"

"I think that's true, in a way," Dus responded, "and you express it beautifully. Sometime I would like to sit and talk to you about Indian lore and the gifts of God, but at the moment, whatever is good, whatever is God, whatever is holy and gifted, I see it all, right now, reflected in the face of a beautiful Indian woman. There is no denying that."

Pulling her hand from his and looking right into his grinning face, Karol said, "Thank you. You are very sweet to say that. But enough of that blarney. It's just a middle-aged Danish squaw, I am, getting old, fat, and wrinkled by the weather and sun, happy, however, to be here savoring the fantasy up there by the church and what I feel standing here, warm and at peace, with a preacher man, who says the right things at the right times, except when I say the wrong things at the wrong times."

"You say the right things most of the time. I'm the one who needs an attitude change, and times like this help. I'm working on it, Doctor."

"Well, don't work on it so hard, lest you lose the good stuff within you. By the way, Father Habak, in spite of my wrinkles and comeliness, I am not so venerable that you need to keep calling me 'doctor.' You asked me my name before. If you must know, my baptized moniker is Ollikut Karolina Thunder Rolling in the Mountain Christianson Marson. As I told you before, 'Thunder Rolling in the Mountain' was Chief Joseph's tribal name before he was baptized a Christian. He was a chief, and if I am his great-granddaughter—and that is a big if—I am a princess. Now that you know all this stuff, you must treat my royal blue, I mean red, blood with respect. My mom's ancestors made the chief's name their last name. Now, white eyes, you can call me by any name you want, but if you ever call me Ollikut or Ollie, I'll cut your gizzard out and feed it to the bears."

"OK, Karol," Dus agreed. "What does Ollikut mean?"

"I'm not telling you, 'cause the first thing you'll do is blab it all around, and I'll never live it down around here nor at the hospital."

"I'm a priest, not a blabbermouth snitch who tells people's secrets to other people, like some folk I know."

"Well, maybe you aren't, but 'white eyes' always make fun of us Indians because our names are taken from nature. Anyway, I am still mad at my mom for naming me Ollikut. Part of her apparition about her forefathers was that she had a great-uncle Ollikut, little brother to great-granddad Joseph, who was killed in the great northern Nez Perce War in 1877. My grandmother told her what a great warrior Uncle Ollie was, so for some odd reason, Mommy, who had no sons, had to stick her only daughter with that weird moniker. Karolina was Dad's Scandinavian grandmother's name, and I like it. Except for 'Ollie,' I like my Indian name, though it's a bit long and it's kinda hard to write the initials every time I write a check."

"You'll have to tell me about the Nez Perce people sometime. I've read about Chief Joseph and the great battle trek to Canada, but I don't know that part of American history too well. Sounds fascinating!"

"Not now, Father. It's getting cold, and I'd better get down to the Conleys and see what Shawn's up to."

"OK. Karol, it's OK to call me Dus, but, if you don't mind, until I get better established around here, I'd like a little formality around the parish."

"Fine with me, Dus, but isn't that a bit stuffy?"

"Let's just say, for the time being, that's the way I want to keep it. It's a custom of the church that I want to maintain while I am building up the chuch here. And I'll show you respect by calling you 'doctor' around other folk."

"I guess that's OK, if you want it that way. And while we're at it, scrub the 'squaw,' and all that Injun stuff, because I'm a professional too, you know. Where did the name 'Dus' come from?"

"Don't know. Something out of Sweden or Germany, I guess. My parents never told me, and I never asked. I just live with what was given me. Come on—what's Ollikut mean?"

"OK, but if you laugh, I'll take your paleface hair. It's a Nez Perce name that means 'frog'—one of those ugly, green, bulgy-eyed, wide-mouthed, wart-skinned, croaking, log-sitting, fat-assed amphibians whose legs people eat for supper, and high school kids skin in science class. Now tell me, Parson, do I look like a frog? Here I am, supposedly a beautiful Indian princess, for crying out loud. I'm supposed to be the one who kisses ugly frogs and turns them into princes. You're snickering, aren't you, Father? I can see it in your face!"

It was all Dus could do to hold back his laughter. "No, I'm not. It's a very interesting story!"

"Yep, Mom really did a number on me and fouled up the sweet Aesop fable just because she had this goofy admiration for a great-uncle who got his heinie shot off on Bear Paw Mountain. Look at this face and body, Father, not that I don't have humility, and tell me if you see a silly, repulsive 'frog' in 'em? And don't you dare even smile!"

"No, Karol," Dus answered her, trying to stifle a guffaw. "The only thing I see is the lovely face of a beautiful princess, who I wish would kiss this ugly frog and change him into a prince."

Karol looked up at Dus and planted her lips hard on his cheek, and whispered, "You are already a prince! More than that, you have become a good friend. That means so much more. Thank you for tonight. We did a good job on that project, and I think the Great Spirit is pleased. Now, Dus, I really do have to go. Good night."

"If you need to use the facilities, Karol, I can only offer the outhouse."

"I didn't mean I had to go in that way. Not on your life, Father. This is rather a personal subject, but if you must know, I graduated from the 'two hole' reservation plumbing systems a long time ago, never to return again. I'll go behind the bushes before I'll freeze my 'tootsie' one more time in an outhouse."

"Well, what do you do at the Conleys'?"

"If it is any of your pastoral business, Preacher, they don't know it, but I use the clinic plumbing before I go up to their house. But if anything arises in the night, so to speak, I hide a pee pot under my bed. But, as I said, I'm not talking natural necessity here. I just gotta go for Shawn and a lot of reasons I can't talk about now," she said, wiping an eye. She turned and walked down the hill to Ox's pickup. Dus watched her ascend and get into the truck.

"Good night, Princess," he called to her. "Thank you for all your help on the crèche."

She smiled at him through the truck window as she passed him going down the hill. He waved back, put his hand on his cheek, and said out loud to the sky, "That middle-aged Ollikut gets prettier every time I see her, and, I believe, tonight I got a little more princely!"

Dus walked up to the church and vicarage, enjoying the reflection of the lights and the candles in the windows, and feeling very happy and lighthearted. He went over to the crèche and looked very closely at the figures. He rubbed one gently with his hand. He smiled. He thought about Christmas love. But, if it had to be told, it was not just about spiritual love he was thinking about. He looked up into the dazzling starlit and moonlit sky and said, "I'm sorry, Ginnie, but I am so lonely tonight."

# 15

Christmas for Father Dus Habak had been a beautiful and joyful time. It had healed many wounds in his heart and chased away many goblins in his soul. He was ecstatic. The Christmas service brought out many worshipers whom he had not seen before, and the lighted crêche had brought mountain and valley folk from miles away to visit it. A few would come by, some would stand, some would kneel and pray, and others would just sit in the snow and gaze.

Often, during the holy season, Dus, at night, would turn down the lanterns in the vicarage so he wouldn't be seen, look out the window and see folk standing at the Nativity scene, and hear them humming and vocalizing old familiar Christmas carols. How wonderful, he thought, that these nice people, with their mountain colloquial customs and language, so far removed from mainstream America, know so well the meaning, the music, and the words of Christmas. God surely has his ways of transfiguring and transcending, all the boundaries, all the cultures, sending the mysterious and marvelous message of love and truth to all his people, everywhere. Dus had wished that he could play the old reed organ in the church, or a guitar, or even a harmonica, just to accompany them and provide some music for their voices. But he knew they did not need him. They were melodious, in rhythm and in tune. From time to time, he would just go out and sing the carols with them, sometimes as many as fifty and sixty voices at one time. He had watched their faces. There were old and young people, worn and fresh faces, some dressed in new clothes, some in old clothes, all clean and neat, some in boots and some in mountain gear, always with their heads uncovered, as though paying courteous homage to the God who was revealing himself through wooden images and reflective fire. Dus had wept a few times. Especially did he weep when he saw Ox standing in the distance behind the crowd with his old weather-beaten hat in his hands, looking up toward the crêche and wiping his nose on his sleeve; another time, when he saw Elly singing loudly with tears in her eyes while holding Shawn Marson's hand. Karol, dressed in white doeskin with a rabbit-fur band across her forehead and around the back of her long, flowing hair, stood behind the two youngsters, her arms and hands firmly cuddling them both. He knew how much Elly missed her mother and how difficult the months had been for her. He had feared there might be a great cloud over their Christmas this year. But now he saw hope and joy for his beloved daughter, and he silently thanked God, Dr. Marson, and the people in this mountain for that.

He reflected on his Christmas sermon, not remembering all that he had said. He recalled that he chose not to say much because there were more people outside enjoying the crèche than came into the service. He had felt a sort of redundancy to his words because the Holy Spirit had already brought the people up to the hill to the images already telling the Christmas story. He hadn't needed many words to make it any more powerful. He felt the people, whatever their practice of religion, already understood that God, out of love for all mankind, in every place, came to them in the flesh out of a poor family very much like themselves; that the angels sang, the shepherds worshipped, and even rich kings were humbled by a baby who was born in a stable not unlike the ones where they keep their mules, cows, and goats. No, their own knowledge of the story, reinterpreted by the silhouettes and shadows of wooden images made almost alive to them by the glowing torches, had brought them to their knees in worship, and brought songs to their voices, smiles to their faces, and tears to their eyes. It had done the same thing to Dus. God had worked his Christmas miracle again on the side of the Blue Mountain on Christmas Eve. And while Father Habak did a Christmas service and offered the Communion to everyone who walked into the church from the crèche, he knew that it had not been him who made Christmas a new experience for those dear mountain folk, but the Person who had offered them the gift of his own body and blood the very first time in another place at another time.

Christmas Day, too, had been joyful and happy, with presents exchanged, food eaten, and hot cider, toasting Jesus and the spirit of the holiday. The Conley home again was the center of love and friendship for Dus and Ellen. How would he, Dus wondered, ever repay those good folk and Dr. Marson for the renewal of his life? He had come to believe that the spirit of Christmas seemed to just mysterious change the demeanor of everyone, whether a believer or not, making him happy and friendly, making it almost impossible to be downcast and grumpy, no matter the problems that beset the rich and poor, the mountain and city folk, alike. Oh, it was great holiday. Thank you, Lord, he prayed, for being patient with me, for opening up my eyes again to the beauty of this earth and the people you put upon it!

Elly had stayed through New Year's Day. She and Dus had a wonderful time fixing up the cabin, cleaning here and painting there, arranging curtains and furniture, laughing and joking, walking and running through the hills, waving to people, and chasing the rabbits and tracking deer. They had laughed a lot together, and made fun, over and over again, about the outhouse.

They had eaten several times with the Conleys, and a couple of times Shawn and Karol joined them at Bessie's for some "normal" lunch. Elly had found a pal in Shawn and they had become friends, even if the battle of the sexes was an ongoing war in their young lives. But, then, there was an interesting look in their eyes when they were together that Dus thought he would worry about sometime in the future. Let them have their fun now.

Elly had said that she enjoyed the mountain and being with her father, but she had not complained when she had to go back to school. She had friends there, too. Dus felt the loss of her after she left, but he knew it had to be and that he must do his work where he was now. She would be back in the spring and summer months, and they would have a lot of time together. By then, maybe the plumbing and electric would be installed. I just have to do that, he noted to himself, for Elly.

He had received a beautiful Christmas card from J.K. and Julie Stewart, with a note that they might come South during spring break from Penn State with the kids and do some early spelunking, and they wondered if Dus and Elly could abide them for a week or so in the area. They said that Julie and the kids would enjoy meeting them and visiting the mountain, but they would be no trouble, as they were borrowing a motor home from a friend. So, they said, they would not be imposing themselves on Dus' crowded digs. He was overjoyed with the prospect that his old friend was going to bring his family to visit, and thought that the sleeping and eating problems would be minimal. He had returned J.K.'s phone call about the coming adventure and assured him that they were welcome. The board and room would work out. Julie insisted, and Dus conceded, that the kids were to sleep in the camper, while the adults slept in the cabin. Those who could not abide the rugged facilities at the cabin could just use the johnny and shower in the motor home. "If you're going to rough it, you gotta do it right. That is what camping is all about," Julie had reiterated.

But, conscious of J.K.'s warning about bears, Dus wondered what kind of insanity would have them snooping into caves about the time when mama bears and their new cubs would be coming out of them. He mentioned that little paradox to J.K. when they talked on the phone. "Did I understand you were a college professor, Dr. Stewart?" Dus had asked. "Are you sure you haven't lost your marbles, along with your feet—that you want to bring your wife and kids into a mountain full of bears and snoop around in their dens during cubbing season? I thought you were the one last fall who decided I was the dumb one for suggesting we go up to that cave then."

"Hey, gyrene, spring's the best time. The bears are gone from the caves, out foraging, eating and training cubs. The caves are still wet from melted snow, and streams are flowing inside. Bears won't bother us. What happened to that courage of yours? It'll be fun! I'll ask the doc at Staunton if she'd like to join us up there for a few days. Julie's looking forward to meeting you. Told her about my visit with you. She loves to have an excuse to get away from this campus and get some peaceful exercise."

Dus had enjoyed his conversation with J.K. and looked forward to their visit in the spring. So he's going to ask Karol, too? Yep, it had been a good holiday. Dus felt good. It had been a long drought. A little girl, some kind mountain folk, an old friend, and a perplexing, beautiful Indian woman were new waters quenching the thirst in his soul. Yes, God has been good. Just wish some folk didn't want to hurt other folk. But I'm going to find the answer to that, too. I don't know when, nor how, nor who will help, but I'm going to find out who and why somebody around here doesn't like me.

\* \* \*

It was now a bright, cold Saturday morning, well into February. Dus was at his desk in his newly decorated office at the clinic, where his mind was forced from reminiscing about the Christmas past to his typewriter, where he had been making some sermon notes and an order of service for the coming Sunday worship. Dr. Marson had returned to the clinic from Staunton on Friday evening and was, at the moment, at work with her patients in her section of the building. Shawn was spending the day with the Conleys, helping Ox stack wood and skating on the creek with the Conley kids. They planned to be here until Sunday evening, then they were going to head back to their Staunton home for a two-week stint at the hospital and school. Noon was approaching, and hunger was tempting Dus to head down to Bessie's for lunch. There was a knock on his inside door.

"Come in," Dus called to the visitor.

Karol walked in. "Hi. You busy?"

"Hi! No, just sitting here thinking about what God wants this shepherd to say to his sheep on Sunday that they don't already know. Not having thought up any new ideas that would stir their souls and keep them awake, I thought maybe I would, for a moment, ignore the things of the Spirit and look to the things of the flesh, leave this place, and feed my growling stomach. Or would you, mighty physician, have a cure for my growling stomach, other than chewing chalky antacid balls?"

"Well, I am not sure, Preacher, after that convoluted homiletic answer to my question. But since I have both an empty stomach and office, and no one coming in for an hour, do you wanna go down to Bessie's and get some decent homegrown medicine for our tummies? I only had coffee and juice for breakfast."

"You're a mind reader as well as a sawbones. Sure! Grab your coat and let's go. I'll treat."

"OK." She went to her office, returned bundled up, and they walked down the street to Bessie's.

"Hi, Doctor Marson; Hi, Father Habak," Bessie greeted them. "Got hot chicken noodle soup on da stove ta warm yer bones. Take a seat ova der by da furplace war it be warm. One a da gals willa be wid ya in a second to take yer orda."

Dus and Karol sat down at a table at a window by the street. A waitress took their order. "Bessie is such a sweetheart, isn't she?" Karol said.

"Yes, she is."

"She looks good for her years. Nancy told me that she had a pretty rough life years ago, what with her husband getting killed and starting up this restaurant. She must have really loved the guy. She never married again. People around this mountain sure do admire and love her. She's homegrown, you know."

"Yes, Ox told me that he, Nancy, Bessie, and Jed Hudson all grew up together here, and the four of them have been friends since they were children. She's very sweet, but behind all those smiles, there's a kind of melancholy."

"Who knows what burdens folk around here have borne? It's a hard place. Wouldn't it be interesting to just sit around and listen to people like them tell about their lives? Bet they have wonderful stories to tell."

"Yeah. I had a long talk with Ox when I first came here, and he sure is a fascinating fellow. But, then too, I'd like to hear about life on the reservation. Bet that's fascinating, as well."

"Not very," she smiled. They sipped hot tea as they waited for their lunch. To Karol, Dus' mind seemed very far away. "Two bits for your thoughts, Father Dus."

"Oh, I was just thinking about Ox, Nancy, Jed, Bessie, and all kinds of people here in the mountain. I was also reflecting on how beautiful Christmas was for Ellen and me this year. The services were good, and it was so nice to see the people coming up to see the crêche. It was wonderful to see Ellen so happy after what she's been through. What a gift you, Shawn, and the Conleys have given to us by being friends."

"Those feelings are mutual, Father, and thank you for all the words of wisdom and guidance you gave us through the season. And, you are right—the Conleys are the kindest folk in this world. I know no better."

"Yeah, that's another thing that made my Christmas—Ox sneaking up to the crêche with hat in hand, sniffing and wiping his nose, hiding in the shadows so I couldn't see him. Jed, too! Those two old mountaineers! I guess I'll never get them in church."

"Yes, I saw them. Ox is a man with a heart of gold, and deep within, there's grand softness and kindness. He's strong, with sand and grit, but he has a reverence for life and people, and a mountain of spirituality that may very well surpass our own. He talks tough and hard, but those children and Nancy love him beyond measure. Outward displays of affection may not be his thing, but he idolizes that woman and adores the children she gave him."

"You're right, Karol. God's getting to him."

"Don't get zealous now, Parson! What's happening is that God is getting to you. That blessed man, Dus, had God, love, and righteousness in his heart and soul a long time before you and I came to this mountain. So does Jed Hudson."

Dus was taken aback by that observation, and it showed in his face. Karol, sensing Dus had misunderstood her remark and took it other than she had intended, moved to cool his changing mood.

"I'm sorry. I didn't mean that to sound the way it came out. I just meant to say that Ox was aware of . . . " The waitress interrupted her words and his mood with a welcome delivery of their lunch.

"Forget it," Dus mumbled. "I get too easily irritated. I am trying to do better. Nothing is worth ruining a good lunch and visit with a quarrel. As I said, Christmas was just beautiful, so is the day, and so are you."

Karol smiled a little, looked down at her soup, and sipped a spoonful while munching on her sandwich. Neither she nor Dus spoke for several minutes. Dus wondered if he had said the wrong thing again. Karol knew she had, and was trying to be penitent. Dus sheepishly glanced alternately at her and the window. His expression sudden changed, and he spoke to her. "Well, you have heard happy news. Now do you want to hear some bad news?"

"Not particularly, but go ahead and tell me."

"Our friendly banker just came up the street and is coming in the door. Now that is just what we needed for dessert. I wonder what little clergy quip he will have for me today."

"Don't know the gentlemen very well, personally. I don't do any banking here, but I know of him. What did he do to you that is making your stomach growl again?"

"First off, he's not a gentleman, and second, his manner and sarcasm really annoy me. He could spoil a good day for a mockingbird. I hope he doesn't pass by here. I would prefer he share his witticisms and churlish gab with someone else, at least during lunch."

No sooner had Dus uttered those brusque words to Karol, when Mr. Brush edged up to their table and slapped Dus on the back. He grinned at Karol. "Well now, what do we have here today at Bessie's? Science and religion meeting on common ground. Nothing like breaking bread to bring folk with diverse philosophies together. How are you, Rev? I have met the attractive and noted Dr. Marson before, but in case you do not remember, madam, I am Raymond Brush of the Joshuatown Bank, and I'm happy to see you once again. I am afraid, with our weekend obligations, our paths do not cross often enough."

He reached over and took Karol's hand in his, held it tightly, and bent his lips to it. Karol pulled it from him and said, "Good to see you again, Mr. Brush. You're right. I am only on the mountain on weekends. Living in Staunton, as I do, I haven't had a need to visit your bank."

"But, of course, dear lady. I have seen you around the village, and what I have seen and heard about you, I like. I'm not looking for business, madam. Just wanted to greet you and the reverend. It makes a Universalist's heart rejoice to see opposing professional persuasions like religion and science talking things over and sharing cosmic insights. The world is surely a better place for such openness."

"Oh, the 'Scopes Monkey Trial' was a long time ago, Mr. Brush. Science and religion have been speaking quite agreeably to one another for years without losing anything of their truths. Just some folk haven't gotten the word yet," Karol answered, with noticeable relish.

Two points for you, Ollikut Marson, Dus smiled. But he still bristled! The man was rubbing Dus the wrong way, and he was not hiding his distaste for the banker. "That's true, Mr. Brush, and if you have a real need to know, the lady physician and I were just sitting here weighing the quintessence of soup and sandwich. She has been mentally anatomizing their components—the bone and flesh of the chicken, in particular, and assaying the nutritional value of tuna on rye. I have, in turn, been postulating the theological implications of nourishing the body, as well as the mind and soul, all at the same time. Bessie has provided both the laboratory and the gastronomical delights for our investigation and analysis, as well as for our own private, and I do mean, private, studies and conversations. We have not yet arrived at any scientific and spiritual conclusions, nor the monetary significance of soup and sandwich in this professional meeting of the minds, but since you are here, maybe your expertise with the 'bottom line' will help us to explore that venue when we receive the bill from Bessie. Maybe your accounting acumen and my theological expertise will come into play in addressing both what Bessie shall receive in payment for her food and what tithe the waitress should receive for her goodly services. I shall beckon you from yonder table for assistance at that time."

Mr. Brush flushed, and so did Karol. Her face grew pink, but as she covered her face with her napkin, the crow's feet around her eyes stretched, giving away a hidden smile.

"Well, you got me that time, Rev. I guess you're saying with all that hyperbole that your conversation is private. I am sorry if I intruded, but it is nice to see folk on opposite sides of philosophy, especially of the opposite sex, get together. I'll tell Bessie to put your bill on my tab."

"Thanks, but I am treating Doctor Marson today, Mr. Brush. Appreciate the offer!"

"Well, another time, perhaps. You two must join me for lunch someday. I'd like to talk philosophy too, you know. Nice to meet you again, Doctor. Come see us at the bank, anytime. Always glad to see a pretty face. Glad to see a rascal, too, eh, Rev," he said, nudging Dus' shoulder. "Bye-bye!" He left and joined some friends at a table out of hearing distance.

"Pompous old goat," Dus grumbled, "couldn't resist the temptation of making something out of our having lunch together. Did you see that lecherous eye he gave you?"

Karol was laughing so hard in her napkin that she could no longer hide it. Tears were coming down her cheeks and her breasts were shaking. She could only look down as she tried desperately to get her laughter under control.

Dus stared at her and whispered, "Glad you think all that was so humorous, Ollikut. You know that jackass just did that to embarrass me in front of you and other people, don't you? How can you think it so amusing?"

Karol eased her laughter into a smile. She wiped moisture from her cheeks with her hanky, and, looking admiringly at Dus, she said in a low voice, "I wasn't laughing at it or at Mr. Brush. I was laughing at you. You really cracked me up with that protracted research dialectic about our lunch. Talk about a put-down. How were you ever able to come up with that rejoinder so fast? I can't believe you said what you did to him. It was neither friendly nor nice, but it was hilarious, and, I must say, appropriate. Shame on us."

"He had no business coming into a public place and making fun of a priest and physician getting together for lunch. Pompous money changer. I'd love to throw a guy like that out of the temple."

"Ya want me to take his scalp, too, partner? After all, he did offer to buy our lunch and take us out to eat sometime," Karol continued to snicker.

"Jeez, Karol, how can you think it's so funny, when you're being put down by some garish clown in front of others?"

"Now don't get your dander up at me, Parson. I just think what you said to that fatuous and silly old man was hilarious. Scientific and theological investigation of chicken soup, sandwich, and bill! I would not have thought of that retort in a thousand years. Darn, I wish I'd had a tape recorder. The guys and gals in surgery would collapse in hysterics if they could hear that. Too bad you couldn't hear yourself." She began to chuckle again, holding her hand over her mouth. Her eyes smiled at him. He looked at those pretty eyes all welled up with liquid, and began to laugh, himself. Both priest and doctor began to giggle so openly that they drew the attention of everyone at lunch. They did not seem to care about that, nor that Mr. Brush was no longer smiling.

She was the first to regain control. "Tell me, Father, did I detect a little jealousy in you when that old man gave me the eye and tried to kiss my hand? If I did, and you were, I'm flattered."

"I am not a possessive person, Karol. I just don't like old leering wolves like him sniffing around women like they were bitches in heat," Dus grumbled.

"Why, Father, what kind of talk is that coming from a priest? Hey, I know wolves, and the real ones are Indians' good friends. Don't insult 'em! Did anyone ever tell you, white eyes, that you are really funny when you're incensed, and very attractive when you smile? You are also very intelligent. You missed your calling as a stand-up comic."

"Mare's marbles, Ollie," Dus responded. "You're just doing a hatchet job on me!"

"Father, I warned you about the 'Ollie' name, and you promised! Knock it off! No, I'm not kidding you. You are a witty person, Dus. You feel deeply about things, and when you're not too sensitive about mundane little stuff and righteously indignant about important things, you are a nice man to be around. And, so, Sir Theologian, with that little piece of psychology, I'd better get back to my suffering folk. Thanks for the lunch and conversation. And remember, Father, speaking of suffering, are you not supposed to 'suffer fools gladly?'"

"I guess! I'll pay the bill and I'll walk you back. I have a few more things at the office to finish up, and then I am off to the hills to see some shut-ins."

"How was da vittles, Fadder?" Bessie asked as she rang up the charges.

"Great again, Bessie."

"Das good! What in tarnation was ya two gigglin' 'bout so as da whole place was watchin' ya?"

"Father Habak was telling jokes," Karol added.

"Musta be'n a good one."

"It was a bad one, Bessie," Dus smiled.

"How come a preacha is tellin' bad jokes?"

Dus answered her. "Well, Bessie, the joke walked in, stopped at our table, and finally left us in peace."

Bessie scratched her head, not understanding.

"Pay him no mind, Bessie! Come on, Father, you need to get out of here and clean up your act. You're a priest, you know," Karol said, yanking on his sleeve.

"OK. Let's walk," Dus grumbled.

They walked through the cold air and up the street to the clinic. Dus opened the door to his office, and Karol opened hers, to find several patients in the waiting room. She shut the door briefly and called to Dus, "Thanks again for the lunch and the fun, Padre. By the way, I think Nancy and Ox want you to have dinner again with us after church tomorrow. She'll ask you when she's there. I need to work here till about four o'clock. After that, Shawn and I have to get back to Staunton. See you! Have a good evening."

Karol was about to open her door again, when she called to Dus, "Oh, Father Dus, I was wondering if you might be able to spare me a few minutes of personal time in your office after work tomorrow. I know your Sunday afternoons are your relaxing time, but I would really appreciate it if you'd allow me to talk to you about something really important. I have an honest-to-goodness problem that needs some priestly counsel. I do need to talk, and it is best I talk with you, I think."

"Sure, Kara, I'll have plenty of time. Anything I can do to help you with now?"

"No, but it is important. It is something I need to talk to my priest about. You are my priest, aren't you, Father Habak?"

"Of course, Kara. You know if I can help you, I'd be glad to try."

"Thank you, Father. You're sweet! By the way, you just now called me 'Kara.' Any reason for that?"

"No. It just came out and seemed right, somehow. I'm sorry if I shouldn't have. Sounds better than Ollikut!"

"Sure does! Don't be sorry. I just never had anyone call me 'Kara' before in my whole life. It's nice. I like it. Thank you for that, too. It makes me feel more special in your little kingdom, Father."

She turned, entered the door, and closed it. She did not hear Dus reply to her. He had said, "You are, Kara; you are very special in God's Kingdom, and in mine, as small as it is."

Dus went into his office, reflecting what might occur on the morrow and smiling about the events of the day. Recalling his visit to Bessie's with Karol, he mumbled to himself, "Don't you ever leer at that lady or hold her hand like that again, Mr. Raymond Brush, or I'll stomp the living mare's marbles out of you!" He then repented, "Gee, there I go again. Excuse me again, Lord!"

# 16

Dus looked out over the lectern at the forty-seven people who had come to worship in the small church. He was well into ten minutes of his homily and about to finish. He had become a no-frills preacher, and did not feel called to theologize with the mountain folk anymore. "Tell it the way it is," the bishop had admonished him, and that is what he was doing these days. These folk were of the earth, and they understood plenty without laying *Roget's Thesaurus* on them. He had taken the bishop's advice to heart.

"Christmas is past now, and we have enjoyed again the story of how much God loved us by sending his Son to show us in person about that love. These last few Sundays we've been saying that those Magi, or wise men, the Bible says traveled a long way from the Orient, were the way God chose to introduce Jesus to other folk, rather than just his own folk, the Jews. This season of Epiphany reminds us that God intended Jesus to be shared with all people, everywhere, for all time, in the whole world—North, South, East, West, in Asia, Africa, Europe, North and South America, and all the natives in the islands of all the great oceans."

Dus paused. People were listening. He would finish now. "That's why I have come to this mountain. Just to share Jesus with you folk here. I'm nobody other than that. I'm the same as you; I just have a different kind of work. Jesus loved everyone, and he wants everyone to know God, wants us to know how much God cares for us, wants us to enjoy life, wants us to care for each other in sickness and health, and wants us to be friends. I don't bring God's swift sword, nor his condemnation. I come just to let you know how much he loves you and wants you in his Kingdom here on earth and eventually in his heaven. Epiphany means 'light.' He came to light up our world with truth and love. Amen!"

He turned from the people, said a quiet prayer, and went on with the Eucharist. The liturgy ended about twenty minutes later. And then he went, as had become his habit, to the back of the church to greet the people.

They filed past him with their usual polite and gracious greetings, shaking his hand. More men were there than usual. Young Shawn had done good work as an altar boy this morning. Dus was pleased. Of course,

Shawn's mother was beaming. "What did you think of your assistant, Father Habak?" Karol asked as she greeted him.

"He did great, and I told him so in the sacristy. I appreciate your allowing him to help. He'll be here in a minute after he hangs up his things."

"He wanted to serve. He likes you, and being up there makes him feel important. Rather do that, I suspect, than fuss and squirm in the pew during the sermon. How do you like acolytes with dirty sneakers and mud-colored shoelaces? Goes well with a red cassock and white cotta, don't you think?"

"Goes fine! Where did he get those vestments? They look brand-new. What a nice surprise to see him dressed like that."

"Oh, Mama did a little cutting on some cloth she picked up at Kmart last week, and put them on a sewing machine. Not bad, huh? I am rather good at cutting and sewing cloth. Keeps me in practice for surgery."

Dus chortled. He was beginning to like her banter. "They're great! I'll come to you when I need some of mine fixed. Thanks for doing them for him."

"That's OK; you can pay me back this afternoon with some sound counseling. Don't forget. There are things on my mind that I've been praying about for some time. I did a lot here this morning, too. I hope, Father, you can help me make some decisions about my life. Things are happening very rapidly to Shawn and me, and I do need direction."

"Sounds somewhat ominous," Dus said, wondering if she had been offered another position at another hospital and would be leaving Staunton. She was a capable woman, and would be in demand at some big hospital or university medical center. That thought didn't make him happy, but he offered her his time. "I'll be glad to help in any way I am able, Karol."

She smiled and thanked him. "See you at dinner. Bye! Come on, Shawn."

"Thanks for your help, Shawn."

"OK, Father. I enjoyed it. See you later!"

"Nice lad," Nancy Conley said as she shook Dus' hand. "En dunna nice job fer ya up thar. Thank ya ag'in fer da wards en da Communion, Father Dus. Ox wou'd lak ya ta come 'ave some vittles ag'in wid usin', iffen ya wal. Ox'll be cuttin' en choppin' some wood afta he naps. Jenny be helpin' me clean up de dishes, en Cyrus, he'll be taken da chilruns out slidin' in da snow. Doctor Marson seys she 'as ta go back ta da clinic. Ya ken nap too, if ya wanna, des aftanoon."

"I'll be down for lunch, Nancy. Thank you. Then, I guess I'll walk around and visit with some folk. I hear Mrs. Bokempt is ailing. Maybe I'll take her some prayers and the Communion."

"Thadda be nice. Donna know what's da madder wid Myra. She be'n down fer a week or so wid somethun. She donna lak to botha Dr. Marson, en she's kinda privy, ya know. Maybe I'll jest tell Karol en she ken send up some medicine ta 'er. My soup might make 'er feel bedda, too. Ya ken take it long wid ya when ya go up, Dus."

"I'll do that, and then after I see her, I'll let Dr. Marson know. Thanks, Nancy! I'll be down soon."

\* \* \*

Dinner with the Conleys was again excellent, and the conversation, lively. Ox pontificated about the work ethic and how heads of the family should keep their noses to the grindstone—or, in his case, the chopping block—and take care of their families. Government shouldn't have to take care of them. He confirmed that philosophy by excusing himself for a nap, saying that following that respite, he'd get his chain saw, and cut and split some of the timber in a big pile in the back yard.

Nancy and Jenny did the dishwashing chores, Cyrus took Shawn and the children off for fun in the snow, and Karol, after reminding Dus of their forthcoming meeting, went on down to her office. He went off to visit the ailing Myra Bokempt, carrying along his Communion set and Nancy's soup.

It was quarter to four before he got back to his office to meet Karol. She would report Mrs. Bokempt's severe cough to her. Maybe she'd send up some remedy. He waited for her knock on the door. It came soon. He entered, dressed in a smudged white clinical coat.

"Hi, Father; what kind of an afternoon did you have?" she asked, slouching in a chair, trying unsuccessfully to smile through strands of hair that had fallen over her face, a couple of which stuck to the corner of her mouth. Dus could see she had had a busy afternoon. She looked like she had much on her mind and in her heart. Her body showed weariness and concern.

"OK. I think, however, you might send me up to Mrs. Bokempt with some flu medicine. She does look pretty sick."

"I'll ask Patty to go up with some antibiotics. Myra probably ought to have a shot."

"Thank you. Tell me, what's with the 'Father' stuff?"

"I guess because I need you as a priest right now, Father Habak. This morning and afternoon have been rewarding. Church was good, and I feel I really helped a lot of people this afternoon. Everybody except myself. I am a total mess, in a mess, and I've been in a mess for a few weeks. Right now, I long for the reservation just to hide in. My soul, my mind, and my body are sorely afraid, and all three crave for answers. I'm scared, just plain scared—frightened of all the ramifications of what I want to talk to you about. I haven't got a lot of courage when it comes to confession, and I don't know where to look for the courage to tell you what I need to."

Dus was slightly confused by this woman who, to him, seemed to be the epitome of strength and confidence. "Nothing can be that bad, Karol. There are answers to everything. I'll be glad to listen. Maybe I can help."

"I am counting on that. I hope you don't think I am just another giddy woman, because you're the only one I know who can help me. Well, maybe God can, too."

"Of course he will. I will too, if I can, Karol."

"What happened to the 'Kara' name since yesterday? I really liked that."

"That just came out yesterday. It just seemed right at the time. Please, if you're in some kind of trouble, tell me, and we will see if we can't resolve it together, OK?"

"Gosh, I hope so, Father Dus. It's been a long time since Doug died. He was a good man, and I had a lot of affection for him. My parents sort of arranged our marriage, and I think I was deeply in love with him. His death was devastating to Shawn and me. We have missed him a lot. Our marriage was fine. He honored me, and was an excellent father. But we only knew one another for six years when he was killed. The time has passed, and now I am a little ashamed to say that he is just a nice memory. I want it to be a good memory for Shawn because Doug was his father and loved his son deeply. He loved me, too, but I have been somewhat guilt-stricken lately about not having given Doug's memory more wifely affection and devotion."

"I think I understand that can happen to a lot of folk, Kara. I am sure that you were a good and faithful wife in your marriage, and that you pleased him."

"I was, Father, and he was faithful, too. I hope I pleased him. He always said I did."

"Then why are you telling me this, now? Time resolves a lot of things, and we should not look back on those times that were not always what they should have been. No one ever has loved and cared enough in marriage, that they could not have done better. Especially me. I really neglected my wife, and too often saw her as little more than a sweet and sacrificial support system."

"I know that. I have seen a lot of that among the doctors and nurses at the hospital. It's a dilemma, to be sure. But, Father Dus, my problem is wholly different."

"How, Kara?"

"I don't like to say this, but recently I have been thinking that maybe I might not have been in love as I should have been—not in the real deep sense—with Doug. I have a lot of guilt about that."

"I am sure you were in love with your husband, Kara. Why would you think otherwise?"

"Because if I had been, I think my memory of him would not have allowed me to fall in love with another man, and, Father Dus, I don't know what to do about it."

Dus' face clouded and his heart felt like it had skipped a beat. His mouth twitched as he absorbed her words. It was the last thing he expected, indeed, or wanted to hear from this lady. He was not, however, very shocked—selfishly disappointed, perhaps. He really admired the pretty and intelligent woman and knew in his heart that one day the right man would come along and offer her love, protection, and a good life. She deserved that, and Dus hoped that man would be a good man. Inwardly, he had hoped it would not be so soon. She had made him happy the last months with her friendship and support of his ministry, and he would surely miss her. The fun in the snow and the assembling of the crêche at Christmas had drawn them closer, and he had developed a real fondness for her. A sadness and a pain grew within him, and he stuttered a little as he encouraged her to go on with her confession. "That's wonderful, Karol," he fibbed. "You should be happy if he is the right man, not sad. It has nothing to do with your memory of Doug. He loved you and you loved him, but years pass and life has changed for you."

"I'm not sad. I believe this new man in my life is right for me, but it is far more complex than my memory of Doug and just being in love again."

"How does this man feel about you?" Dus asked, wishing he did not have to deal with the problem.

"I'm in love with him, but I don't know how he feels about me. I have not talked to him about it yet. I think he cares for me, but I'm scared to talk to him about it."

"Why haven't you talked to him? You have to do that, and soon."

Karol twisted her handkerchief. She smiled a little, but started to weep. "Because, Father, he's a priest."

Again, Dus felt his heart skip another beat. How could something like this happen to her or to me? he wondered to himself. Mare's marbles! "Good God, Karol. You mean to tell me after all this time I have known you, there's a priest down in Staunton you've been seeing and fallen in love with? Why didn't you tell me? You never even said anything about a church there. I guess I just assumed because you and Shawn were worshipping here, ah, I didn't think about . . . Ah, is he, ah, this priest, is he a Roman Catholic, or, ah, an Episcopal chaplain of some sort at the hospital?"

She propped her chin on her palms, her slender finger reaching up to her cheek. She looked up at Dus, tears running down her face. Dus felt compassion for her. He could not miss the anxiety in her lovely face, but still there seemed to be a touch of serenity there, too. He wished she could be relieved of her pain and he, of his bewilderment. Maybe I deserve the anguish, he said to himself, but she doesn't. Oh, God, he petitioned, please help this good woman at this crucial moment in her life, and help me, too, in my own confusion and pain, to help her by saying the right thing to her. "Try to tell me about him, Karol."

Looking at him and trying to smile through her tears, she sniffed, "Well, there is a very fine Roman Catholic priest at the hospital, and we have become very close."

Jeez, Dus muttered in his head. Not one of those damnable romance problems. Why does it have to be me who has to listen to this?

Karol continued, "He and I have talked about what has happened, and he thought it would be prudent for me to talk to an Episcopal priest. I have told him about you, and he said I ought to talk to you. This is all so very difficult, and you aren't making it easier."

"I'm sorry. I don't mean to make this difficult, Karol, but this is not easy for me, either. I have strong feelings about you."

"I know that, and that is why it is so hard. But anyway, what must be done, must be done," she announced courageously. "May Ginnie, Doug, and Dusty up in heaven, and Ellen, Shawn, and you down here have mercy on my soul, but I am not in love with any Catholic priest. I am hopelessly in love with my mountain priest, Father Dus Habak."

Her mouth broadened to a wide grin, teeth showing through red lips, face flushed, her brown skin glistening, and eyes shining. She was beautiful in her awkward distress. Dus sat still trying to find some semblance of composure. He could not believe his ears! He could not speak. He just gazed at her for minutes. He then pushed his swivel chair away from the desk and rolled in it across the floor to her chair. He placed his forefinger under her chin and lifted her face up to the level of his own. His eyes smiled into hers. He gently brushed the hair back from her face and pushed the long, brown, wet strands behind her ears. He took his handkerchief from his pocket and wiped the perspiration from her forehead, and the tears from her eyes and cheeks. Then he put his hands around her waist and drew her up to his body. Putting his face within inches of her own, he said, "Everybody will forgive you and love you, Kara. Now before I leave this dream world and fathom just a smidgen of what you are telling me, will you please kiss the naive frog right now and turn him into a prince, so he's worthy of a princess?"

She smiled and said nothing. Flinging her arms around his neck, she pressed her lips to his. They embraced for a long time, trembling a little, but stood holding each other as though welded together. Finally, he pushed her inches away, breathed deeply, and said, almost embarrassingly, "I love you, Karolina Marson, and I have for a very long, cold winter. You're so beautiful, good, and decent. I wanted to hold and kiss you and tell you I loved you for weeks."

"Then why didn't you, you coward? How could you put me through this frustration and terror? Do you have any idea what I have been going through trying to find the resolve to confront you with this admission, having to go through a lot of preparation for what's amounted to a confession of sin? I thought clergy were men of courage. Where was that Marine Corps gumption you jocks brag about?"

"I was afraid you would reject my love if I told you of it. Even now, it's hard to believe that you should love me. Do you really know what you have just said to me? If it's true, you honor me beyond measure."

"True? Honor? Why in the name of all that is holy do you think I am standing here trembling like a bird, panting like a puppy, and weeping like a teenager? Can't you come up with some more enthusiastic words about this earthshaking milestone in your life, than 'truth' and 'honor'?"

"I guess they are a bit innocuous given the occasion, but it serves you right with that long, convoluted spin you gave me about being in love with a priest. You planned all along to do this and scare the bajeebees out of me.

My gosh, Ollikut, my heart was breaking apart. That was not very nice of you to lead me on like that."

"I know, darling, but that's what you get for not telling me you loved me before this. Men are supposed to make the first overture."

"What do I know about such things? You're right, so I forgive you and I love you. I know that you would not have known it, my being the clumsy dolt that I am. I think I have been in love with you since that Sunday when you walked into my church, the day after you chewed me out, dug into my body, and stuck that needle in my rump. Yes, I'm sure it was that day, even though you were a king-sized royal pain at the time. They say love happens that way."

They embraced and kissed again. He explored her face, eyes, brows, mouth, and nose with his eyes and lips. "Did you know, Indian Princess, that you have a small pinpoint scar on the side of your nose?"

She pushed him away, laughing. "I can't believe you. By heavens, Preacher Man, I'm gonna cut off your ears. Here I'm talking love, smooching with a priest like a sultry concubine, and you're talking about my infirmities. If you gotta know about such things at an inopportune time like this, yes, I do have a scar on my nose and on other places on my body you might discover someday if you love me enough. For gosh sakes, I'm a Nez Perce Indian."

"I know that. What about it?"

"It means 'pierced nose' in French. Don't ya know we're into things like scars and marks on our anatomies? All of us Indian ladies had our noses perforated when we were born so we could look pretty with ornaments for you braves when we grew up. Woulda been tough for you if I'd been a Ubangi bride with one of those disks in my lips. If you have to know, my mom was into that sort of thing, but my dad would have none of it, so it all healed up and went unnoticed till a certain 'white eye' clergyman nosed around my nose and had to comment. Dad did allow pierced earlobes, though, as I guess you noticed. Now, if you are done with the history questions, how about just holding and kissing your ol' scarface for a few more minutes before we have to go? Whisper sweet things in my ear, and tell me all this stewing I did these last seventy-six hours was worth it. I love you, Dus, and I don't know what to do with all that is in my heart right now."

Dus kissed her again and lowered her into the chair. He took her hands in his and said quietly, "Kara, I love you; I wanted to tell you at Christmas when we were putting up the crèche, but I had so many thoughts then. I was afraid my feelings for you just stemmed from loneliness, too short a time after meeting you. I was scared you'd think I was taking advantage of you at a sentimental and emotional time. Then, it has not been all that long since Ginnie died, and I have had guilt about that, too. I'm sorry. I love you so much, and the joy in my heart right now is more than I can comprehend. I don't know why you love me, but I am just overwhelmed knowing you do. I'm so filled up, I hardly know what to say."

"Well, darling, I told you, I had a problem, but, as you said, 'it can't be all bad.' It is good, isn't it, Dus? I was scared, too. I don't know what this little Indian girl would've done had you treated me as a lovesick puppy and sent me off to the creek for a cold bath. I don't know where we go from here. I understand about Ginnie, and I care. I talked to God about that, too, and we will resolve those feelings we both have another time. For now, while I am gone from this place, I am going to savor your words, arms, and lips; make no plans; be happy; and just thank the Lord for giving me the courage to tell you. I'm going to thank him, too, darling, for letting you love me. Is that OK for now? Of course, we're going to have to tell Elly and Shawn about this soon. Ginnie and Doug are important to them, too, and we have to be patient with that."

"Yes, I know, Kara; we'll do that as soon as it is appropriate. Can't wait too long, because teenagers are smart, and they will notice soon. I hope both of them will be happy for us, even if some adjustments have to be made for . . ."

Just when Dus was about to continue, they heard a pounding on the outside of the waiting room door, accompanied by a screaming voice they both recognized.

"Docta Marson, Docta Marson, help, please help. Open the door, please open the door." The pounding increased.

"My God, Dus, that's Jenny Gruber!"

They rushed through the waiting room and opened the door. Jenny stood there shaking, blood covering her blouse and jeans. "Docta, Fadder, please come quick to our truck out front. Mama's der wid Papa, en he's a hurt real bad!"

"Let's go, Jenny! Come on, Dus! What happened?" Karol asked, dragging Dus by the hand out the door. They found Nancy sitting in the bed of the pickup truck holding Ox's head in her arms. Ox was moaning. "Aw, I wen' and done it des time, Doc, en it do hurt bad."

"Shush, ya ol' mule, en rest some," Nancy chided her husband, with tears running down her face. "Karol is a gonna fix ya all up, en ya gonna be all good ag'in ina no time. I knows yer hurtin', hubby, but we's all gonna take good care a ya, ain't we Karol?" Then, turning to Dus, she asked, "Would ya help me ta lif' ol' Ox up, Fadder, en tak 'im inta Docta Marson's office?"

It had grown dark, and neither Karol nor Dus could see what he was doing very well. Karol was reticent to disturb Ox's body too much until she could ascertain the extent of his injuries. "Just a second, Father; before you move him, I want to turn him over. I need to see where his injury is before we move him. Can you tell me what happened, Nancy?" she asked the pale lady while looking at the horrendous blood mess on Ox's leg.

Nancy tried to explain. "I donna ritly knows how he done it, butta I erd 'im yell out in da yard, en I run out whar he be'n cuttin' wood wid da chan saw en axe. He was on da groun' wida ter'ble lot a blood a comin' outta his leg. I yells ta Jenny to brung a belt er a rope ta stop da bleedin' en fix 'im up a liddle so as we ken brung 'im har to have ya tak' a look a see at it. Den Jenny git da truck en we brung 'im har."

Karol gave quick orders. "Grab his shoulder under the arms, Father. Nancy, you and Jenny hold up his thighs. I'll hold his bad leg, and let's take him into my examination room right away." Ox was heavy, but somehow people seem to have a lot of strength in a crisis.

"I'ma so sorry ta bodda ya like dis, Karol, butta I knows ya wal fix me up in a hary," Ox apologized, groaning as they picked him up out of the truck bed and carried him gently into the clinic.

"Put him on the table and let me take a look at that thing," Karol ordered.

Laying on the table, Ox bit his lip while Nancy held one hand and Jenny held the other. While Dus held Ox's injured leg, Karol deftly removed his boot and cut away his overall pants, exposing the massive wound to the light. "Gosh, my friend, you really did a bad job on your leg! You did the right thing, Nancy, with that tight belt on his knee. Pull it tight, Father, and keep stemming the blood flow. I'll get a medical tourniquet, and darling ..., I mean, Father..." She blushed, realizing the slip of her tongue when Nancy smiled up at her. "We will put that on, and you loosen and tighten it when I tell you."

She gave Ox a tetanus shot and something to help him with the pain, then worked skillfully with the wound. Washing it gently with an antiseptic, and checking it thoroughly, she said, "I won't lie to you, Ox; it is very bad. We are going to have to get you to the hospital. Tell me how you did this."

"I was cuttin' some oak in da yard wid da cha'n saw. I donna knows why, butt da saw wen' into somethun real hard, en 'fore I could stop it, da cha'n come off en ripped roun' my leg. I enna down on da groun' en yelled fer Nancy, en she en Jenny come, toke da cha'n from my leg, belted it up, en brung me har in da pickup, as ya saw. How bad is it, Doc? Oh, wadda did I have ta go en do dis ta maself? I'm so sorry, Nan."

"Hush, my good hubby. Yo' goin' ta be alrite. Ain't he, Karol?"

"That chain was very sharp, Ox, and it went through the muscle, tendon, artery, and nearly through your shinbone. It needs surgery right away if we are going to save it. We'll load you in the back of Father's jeep and take you down to Staunton Memorial. Father Dus, Nancy, and I will steady and give him some plasma while on the way. Jenny, you take my car keys and go get Cyrus, and ask him to drive with Shawn to our home in Staunton. Have him drop you off here on the way down, and you can take your dad's truck back to your house. Take care of the baby and your brothers, and keep them away from that bloody scene in the back yard."

Ox complained that he was a lot of trouble to everyone. Nancy scolded him again and tried to keep him quiet. Karol was afraid he would go into shock. They covered him with blankets and carried him to the jeep. Karol stripped a mattress from one of the clinic tables and laid it on the back floor of the car. She gathered up a flashlight, some plasma, and her medical bag, and joined them at the back of the jeep. While Jenny sped off, Nancy and Dus gently maneuvered Ox through the back gate and made him as comfortable as they could. While Nancy held Ox's head and mopped his brow, Karol hung the plasma bag on the car clothes hook and inserted an intravenous needle into his arm. Dus started the car, switched on the headlights and interior lights so Karol could see, and then carefully moved the converted ambulance through town and down the mountain to Staunton.

"Ya'l be alrite, hubby," Nancy told Ox between sniffles. "Donna ya worry yerself none, now. I'ma ri't har wid ya, en Karol and Dus gonna see dat you gits good car'. Ya jist rest real go'd now while I talks wid da Lo'd a liddle 'bout gitten ya well. Trust da Lo'd, Oxford. He gonna fix us alrit'. Ain't he, Fadder Dus?"

Dus nodded his head and Ox said, "It sho do hurt. Kent rememba wenna I eva done somethun so bad ta myself, butta I'ma gonna be lively soon, en take car' a ya en da younguns. Donna ya worry none. Ya knows, Dus boy, I jist kent figya how dat spike got inta dat piece a oak widout me knowin' 'bout it. It donna seem lak it war thar when I cut it down."

Dus reached up and adjusted the rearview mirror so he could see the people in the back. He especially wanted to see Karol's face. Her somber face looked up at his, stared into it with weary eyes, and she shook her head. She tried to smile, but she was biting her lip. Fear had engulfed that beautiful face that he loved so much, and he knew that Ox was in very bad shape.

\* \* \*

It was now late in the evening. Dus was sitting on a sofa in the waiting room adjacent to the operating room at Staunton Memorial Hospital, with Nancy Conley asleep on his shoulder. He did not move, fearing that he would awaken her. They had prayed together for quite some time before she drifted off. She now breathed softly as though she knew God would take care of everything. He sipped a cup of cold coffee, but his eyes were glued to the doors that read, "Surgery Suites. Authorized Personnel Only." He could only wonder what was taking place inside those doors. He thought about Karol and about their time together earlier at the clinic, and how drastically things had changed since he first went to the mountain. My, how he had come to love that woman and admire her for what she was doing for the people there and for Ox through those ominous doors. He knew that she would use her very best skills to help the Conleys, whom she loved as if they were her own family. It would be tough because they were very special people to her, but she would do her very best even with complete strangers.

Dr. Champion, the chief orthopedic surgeon, was doing the main surgery and Karol was assisting him. Dus knew their work would take several hours because Ox's injury was so severe. Inside the doors, they finished their work, the nurses cleaned up the instruments, and they moved Ox to the litter that would carry him to the recovery room. He was deeply anesthetized and did not move. Orthopedic equipment was rigged and his leg, swathed in bandages, was lifted into a sling-and-pulley contraption with weights hanging at the end of the litter. "He'll be all right, Karol," Dr. Champion assured her. "That was a hell of a nasty thing he did to himself, and I am very sorry. But he looks like a man who will heal fast and be able to get on with his life in a few months. He does have a lot of therapy ahead of him. Do you want me to talk to his wife? I'll be glad to do that, if you want, but I don't want to preempt you, knowing they are good friends of yours."

"No, Clark, I'll talk to her. Thank you for all you've done. Want you to meet Nancy and Father Habak sometime, but you go home to the wife and kids now. It's late. Get some supper and sleep." She reached up and kissed him on the cheek.

"Well now, that's nice compensation for my minor assistance. By the way, Doctor Marson, that was fine surgery you did in there, too. You're a pro, Karol, and, by the way, my help was 'professional courtesy.' A friend of yours is a friend of mine. There will be no bill from me. Good night and good luck to your friends."

"That's very kind of you, Chief. Thanks so much. I wish I would have been a better pro in there tonight." She bade him good night and went to the locker room to remove her surgical gown and wash up. Then she walked through the waiting room to meet with Dus and Nancy. Dus looked at her weary face.

"Is she asleep?" Karol whispered to Dus. Dus nodded his head. Nancy did not move, appearing totally exhausted. "Put her head on a pillow, darling, and please come with me for a moment before we wake her up," Karol said to Dus.

He laid Nancy's head on a pillow, and followed through a door off of the lounge. "How did it go, sweetheart? Will Ox be OK?"

"Yes, he will live and be OK, darling," she said, then threw her arms around his neck and sobbed uncontrollably against his shoulder.

"What's the matter, Kara? Please tell me."

"Oh Dus," she cried, "we had to amputate his leg below the calf."

"Good God. Why, sweetheart?"

"We just couldn't fix it. We tried! God, we tried, but everything was torn up and cut through—the bone, the tendons, the nerves, the muscles, everything, Dus. All was gone; his foot was hanging by a thread of flesh. I knew it at the clinic. We couldn't sew anything; we couldn't splint anything. We tried, but nothing we did would work. It's gone, Dus; his left ankle and foot are gone. We had to take it off at the shin, make a flap, and sew it up. Damn those chain saws to hell. We have had a lot of bad cuts from those things here." She wept harder. "I tried, Father Dus; I really tried. You know I adore that man. We just couldn't make anything work to save his foot. Ox is going to hate me. He trusted me so much that I would fix him up good. So did you; so did Nancy. I let you all down."

"Stop that nonsense, Karolina Marson," Dus admonished her. "Stop that kind of silly talk, right now. You didn't let anyone down. Ox and Nancy will know that you did your very best, and I know it, too. I could see too, at the clinic, it was going to be touch-and-go on saving that leg. So could

Nancy. He is alive, and he will be all right. That's what is important. Tough days ahead for them, yes, but he'll make do. They are tough, resilient people, the salt of the earth, and they will adjust. We'll help them, honey. But, God, I get disgusted with the rotten things that happen to good people!"

"I do too," Karol sniffed, wiping her eyes, "but now we have to go and wake up Nancy and let her know the bad news. I'm going to take her home to my house and have her stay with Shawn and me while Ox goes through this hospital and then therapy. Thanks for being here for us, Father Dus. I don't know what we'd do without your strong arms and shoulders."

They went back to the waiting room and found Nancy sitting up and rubbing the sleep from her eyes. She looked at them questioningly. "How's my man a doin'?"

"He's sleeping now and doing fine, Nancy, and he is going to be healthy again."

"Thank da Lod. He erd my prawers. How's his leg?"

Karol looked at Dus. So did Nancy. They both sat down on each side of her and held her hands. "We have bad news about his leg, Nancy," Dus told her.

"Didja ya have ta toke it off, Karol?"

"Yes, we did, Nancy. We did our best to save it, but it was too far gone. I am so sorry."

"Now, hush, chile. I knowed it war gone from da firs' moment I seen it, en I knows ya done what yer war able fer Ox. He ain't gonna take kinely ta losin' a leg, butta nobody en nothung is a gonna get da ol' mule down. Ya wait en see fer yourself," Nancy sniffed pitifully, with huge tears in her eyes. "Ken I see 'im soon? I needs ta be thar wid 'im when he finds hisen leg gone."

"You can see him as soon as they make him comfortable in the critical care unit, but he will be asleep for a long time. Then you must come home with me, and I'll bring you back tomorrow when he wakes up."

"Thank ya, kinely, dear. I preciates all ya done fer 'im. Truly I does. I knowd ya done yer best. En thank ya too, Fadder, fer da ride down en da sof shouda. Me en Ox will be alrit'. Donna ya two worry none 'bout usins."

While Dus waited, Karol took Nancy in to see Ox, then returned in a few minutes. "He looks peaceful, and he is going to be fine. Tomorrow will be hard for him, as will the next couple of weeks, but he'll manage. I'm sure Nancy and the kids will be very good for him once they get used to his impairment. Then, of course, we've got old J.K. Stewart to give Ox some good ideas about artificial legs. That man is a master picker-upper with disabled folk. Look what he's done with no legs!"

"I love you, Dr. Marson. You did great with Ox. I'm so proud of you!"

She turned and placed her head against his. "Thank you, darling. I'm so tired and I am so torn in half with love and pain, joy and sorrow, I feel like I'm on an emotional roller coaster."

He hugged her and wiped her eyes. "You'll be OK. You have been greatly tested these last twelve hours, what with dealing with our love and doing good for Ox. Now you and Nancy go home to your house and get some sleep. I'll drop you off and take Cyrus up the mountain with me. I'll tell him about everything that has happened, along the way."

"You can't drive up there tonight, darling. Why don't you and Cyrus just bed down in my spare room?"

"No. Cyrus has his work and family, and Jenny will be worried and will want to know about Ox."

They arrived at Karol's house in minutes. Cyrus was up waiting for them and inquired about Ox. They told him, and he was comforting to Nancy. He said "good night," pecked the two ladies on the cheek, and went out the door. "Good night, Nancy; good night, Doctor," Dus followed. "I pray all will be better in the morning. Give my best to Ox tomorrow and tell him I'll be down to see him?"

"Good-bye, Parson. Ya gonna jist walk outta har widout a hug ner kiss?" Nancy said, as she flung her arms around his waist, and looked up to his face with closed eyes and puckered lips. Dus accommodated her by lifting her up and kissing her gently. "Good night, Nancy. God bless you. Try not to worry."

"What about me, Parson?" Karol complained. "Don't I get hugged and kissed, too?"

"Yeah, Father Dus, ain't ya gonna kiss dis sweet girl good night?" Nancy scolded. "How dare ya go off en not kiss 'er? I'm gonna go into a da kitchen while ya two seys 'good night' like ya mean it. Donna ya knows dat ol' Ox en me knowd 'bout ya moonin' at one anotha fer a cow's age? Now git to it, younguns!"

She went into the kitchen. Dus gave Karol a long and breathless kiss. "I love you, Ollikut. See you soon. Take care of her."

As he went out the door, he heard her call, "Hey, Parson, you and I might be slow about love and stuff, but Nancy is not. I love you, Preacher!" He threw her a kiss and drove off with Cyrus, who was saying, "Jeepers,

Fadder, dat's a terr'ble thung what happen'd to Papa. Jenny's gonna be hurt 'bout it."

"Yeah, it was, Cyrus. Tell me, did you ever know Ox to be that careless?"

"Nah, he was born ta saw, knives, en axes. He got scars aplenty, but he don't make no mistakes wid tools."

"I don't think it was an accident. Somebody drove that spike into that log he was cutting."

"Da hell, ya sey! Pawson, I ain't a usually a cussin' man, but if I finds da man dat done dat to Jenny's pa, I'm gonna skin da bloody hide off da ass a dat son abish."

"You and me together, Son, and then I believe the doc will sew him up with no painkillers."

"Yer ri't 'bout dat, Pawson. I knows she loves 'im, too," Cyrus smiled.

Their need to talk of revenge now satiated, the two men settled back while the jeep climbed the mountain. Dus raged inside thinking that someone deliberately hurt Ox Conley, the most innocent and kindest of men to everyone he knew. "Mare's marbles on the guy who hurt him! No, horseshit and damn him to hell," he muttered under his breath. He felt better, even if he had a smidgen of guilt about his language. He knew Cyrus would understand, and he hoped God would, too."

# 17

Event-filled weeks went by. Dus was not able to get back to the hospital in Staunton for several days after they had taken Ox there. Karol had telephoned several times to bring him up to date on Ox's healing progress. And, of course, to tell him how madly in love she was with him. Nancy, Karol had said, was doing fine under the circumstances, and would return to the mountain as soon as Ox started therapy and tried on a prosthesis.

Dus reassured Karol that Jenny and Cyrus were taking good care of the house and children, and did not need to have Nancy back home anytime soon. He had checked on them every day, and had meals with them. The Conley home was relatively calm.

"I have missed you so much, Kara," Dus had heartfully expressed to her during one of their conversations, "and so do your patients up here. They need you, too."

"I know, darling, but I need to be here with Nancy and Ox during this transition. Besides, the hospital is overloaded with cases, and I can't slip away now. Won't you try to come down one day, at least, and have a talk with Ox? Nancy and I are having a very difficult time with him. He's not taking the loss of his foot very well."

"Don't blame him. I wouldn't, either. But I'll be down soon. Besides, I can't stand to be away from you anymore since I learned your poorly kept secret."

"What secret?"

"That big secret you had about loving me. You know, the one that Ox and Nancy had known about for a 'coon's age."

"And what about you, quiet one? Some fearless man you turned out to be. You were panting after me all this time, and had no heart to say anything about it. You oughta be ashamed of what you put me through, and when you knew you were in love with me all the time. I thought the guy was supposed to make the first step in a romantic relationship, like on his knees and stuff like that."

"Didn't women want equal rights with men?"

"I didn't know equality meant a gal had to be the first to speak to a man about love."

"If you hadn't been panting after me so much, yourself, you might have given me a chance. I'm not arguing with you. I am just happy you did. I can't help it if clergy aren't as cheeky as docs."

"To use your favorite expression, paleface, 'Mare's marbles.' We gals have to be cheeky these days to make it in the big world of medicine."

"That's true, and you know what people say about us clergy."

"I have heard a lot of things, but what?"

"If we weren't cowards, we wouldn't choose the ministry to hide from real life!"

"Phooey! I wouldn't have your job for a million dollars!"

"Sometimes, I wouldn't, either, if I knew how to do anything else. But, on the other hand, this job got the prettiest lady redskin physician East of the Mississippi to fall in love with me."

"Hey, what did I tell you about those tacky Indian expressions? I'm going to have to get you to a sensitivity training course. But I forgive you, 'cause it's nice to be thought of as the prettiest Indian East of the Mississippi."

"Guess I could always go back to engineering and tinker with engines and stuff."

"Why don't you just stay in the priesthood, say prayers and things, and tinker with me?"

"Karol, for crying out loud! Don't say things like that on the telephone!"

"Why not?"

"Because it isn't nice for ladies to talk like that. Anyway, you should know, I don't believe in doing that stuff before marriage."

"What stuff?"

"You know very well what stuff."

"Oh yes! Well, I don't either, moralist. Anyway, I said, 'tinker,' not 'start up the engine.'"

"I'm learning a lot about you. You're pretty basic about things, aren't you?"

"Well, Preacher, once a boy and a girl say they love one another, aren't they supposed to think about what comes next? You'd be surprised how much we surgeon types can teach you theologians about tinkering! Anyway, how about getting down here to see your buddy, Ox, and hug your baby,

Kara? I don't like being away from you anymore, and Nancy does need your help with Ox's fussing."

"OK, Tinkerer, I'll be down on Wednesday. Love ya."

Dus got to the hospital to see his friend two days later. Ox and Dus had had some pretty cranky things to say to one another at their bedside meeting. Ox was sorely angry about losing his foot and didn't mind telling.

"Well, it wasn't my fault!" Dus yelled at him. "Why the devil are you screaming at me? You're the one who lopped it off with that stupid saw!"

"'Cause yer da onny one I ken yell at. Ain'ta 'lowed ta yell at Karol, ner Nancy, ner da nurse ladies, ner da docs. Who in da thunda ken I yell at, effen I kent yell at ya? Ter'ble 'ting ta take a man's foot off 'im. 'Ow'm I gonna hunt, en fish, en cut ceda, en stuff, wid no damn foot, Dus? Ain't ri't; jist ain't ri't. Ya know'd yerself, thatta spike shoud'n't a be'n der. Gonna fine out, Son; gonna fine out!"

"We'll find out in due time, Ox, but first we gotta get you well, up, and walking again."

"Hell's fire! Nancy en Karol be'n talkin' 'bout me w'aring a peg leg, Dus. Now how da ya speck me ta wear one a dem 'tings?"

"Listen, old man, quit your shouting and pay attention to me for a minute."

"Now, Preacha, das no way ta be talkin' wid a man dat's feelin' po'ly, wid nuffin butta stump en hurtin' lik' a bobkitty wid porkypin's in his snout. Ain't ya 'ave no mercy on yer fr'en'? Yo spose ta be a pastor wid a kind heart."

"I know what I'm supposed to be, and I care about you, you big buffalo, but you have to calm down and face what is. We all feel bad about your foot, but it's gone, and we're all going to have to start all over again with your problem of walking. You're going to get a new foot. They have 'em these days that you just strap on your stump, and in a few months you'll be walking like you always did, and maybe even better, 'cause your toes won't freeze up anymore from the cold. Karol and I have a friend who has two artificial legs. He's going to be down here one of these days to show you how to use just one of them. He even crawls around in caves with his."

"I 'ates ta say dis, Preacha, butta I b'lieve yer full a bear pee. Man wid no legs walkin' 'round caves? Ya jest tryin' ta char me up er somthun, ain'tcha?"

"God's honest truth, Ox! You ask Karol. Name's J.K. Stewart. He and I were in the war together. Had both legs blown away, and he comes down to this very hospital and does some work here. Knows Karol well, and he's been to the mountain to see me."

"Now ain't dat a wild kitty's tokey, Dus? Who'da a believ'd dat? Wal, I'll take alla da help I ken git. Sho will."

"It's going to take time, Ox, but it'll work. Ya got Nancy, Jenny, Cyrus, your kids, and all those friends of yours on the mountain. They're all going to help because they care about you. I promise. You're going to be as good as new. Just won't feel a lot in your toes."

"Iffen ya en Nancy en da good Doc say so, Fadder, den I know it's da truf. When's yer wooden-legged frien' gonna git har? I needs ta git stauted soon 'cause Nancy en ma kids need me ta work."

"Soon, Ox, soon. Just be patient and quit hollering at folk. They all love you, and will take care of you."

"Dey sho does, Dus; yeah, dey sho does. Thank ya fer remindin' me a dat. Ya be'n a good frien'." He shook Dus' hand profusely as Dus left. Little drops of water rolled down his cheeks and into the beard of the big crippled man. He wiped them in case Dus should look back and see them.

Late in the afternoon, Dus dropped by to see Nancy and Karol. He told him of his conversation with Ox, and they then felt better about his progress. Karol had already talked by phone with J.K. Stewart about Ox's situation and, of course, he said he'd be glad to do anything he could to help Ox with the new prosthesis he would be needing. He'd be down to the hospital in a few weeks to check the computers, anyway, and would be glad to be encouraging to Ox, and perhaps give Ox's therapist some ideas and help.

Karol was glad to see Dus. Dus was very glad to see her. After discreetly excusing themselves, the two lovers assayed their new love with arms and lips. Then Dus went back to the mountain, believing Ox would be fine and that God had made his life a lot happier. It occurred to him, too, that if that were true, beautiful Thunder Rolling in the Mountain was prayerfully telling God that if he wanted Dus to be a better priest, Dus would need a lot of help from her. In spite of her so-called "church backsliding," Dus was confident that the Indian princess had considerable influence with the Great Spirit.

\* \* \*

That was Wednesday of last week. Thursday morning, Dus strolled down to see his newfound friend, Scott Kirsh, the sheriff. "How are you, Father Habak?" Scott inquired.

"I'm fine, Scott. How's your family?"

"They are all well. Sure was a shame about Ox, wasn't it?"

"Yeah. Did you hear they had to amputate his left foot at the shin, and that he will need a prosthesis?"

"I heard that from Jenny. Folk around here are very fond of and depend on him for a lot of things. Some of them are pretty upset about it, too. Jed and Helen Hudson and Bessie Clayton have heard the rumors, and they don't think it was an accident. They know him to be very careful and skilled with a saw and axe. My wife, Patty, is pretty much beside herself, too, and really feels sorry for Nancy and the kids. She wonders what they will do without him being healthy."

"We're all upset. But Dr. Marson believes that if anyone can overcome adversity like that and use an artificial leg, Ox Conley can and will. He'll be impatient for a while until he masters it, and then he will do all the things he used to do, with a few limitations."

"It was a pretty nasty injury from what I hear around the village."

"Very few things happen around here without you hearing about them, right, Sheriff?"

"Well, my business is to keep my eyes and ears open. I did go up to the Conley house to snoop around in Ox's backyard. When people get injured that badly and are transported out of town to a hospital in a big hurry without me knowing about it, Father, it gets my nose up a bit. The nature of my trade, I suspect."

"I suspect that you suspect a lot of things, Scott. What did you find with your snooping?"

"My, you're feisty! Jenny and Cyrus showed me the spot where Ox cut into himself. It is interesting how a skilled logger like Ox would allow a thing like that to happen. Cyrus said that Ox was wondering how his chain saw would cut into a railroad spike, when it wasn't there when he cut the tree down up in the woods. Don't you think that's interesting? But then, you have some suspicions about that, too, don't you?"

"Sure do. Can you warm my bones a bit with some coffee? Do you have a problem with heat in this office?"

"Just saving taxpayers' money. I do have coffee in the Silex. Help yourself. But, what's up with you, Dus, other than Ox's accident? Somebody take another shot at you?"

"Scott, do you think that shooting at me somehow fits together with Ox's injury?"

"I don't know. That rifle shot that came close to you last fall could have been an accident. I've been thinking about it, but you are so stingy with information, I don't have a clue. Why you? Why Ox? Maybe there are some nasty folk who don't like nosy preachers, but Ox has been around these hills forever. Most beloved guy around. A real patriarch. I don't know a soul who would want to hurt Ox, nor who isn't indebted to him for his kindness and help. I hate to think about what could have happened to him if that chain had gone up around his head. He could have been hamburger."

"I know. I've used them often. Dangerous things, and if you aren't very careful, you can get into some real trouble. Then you do have suspicions?"

"That's about all I have. The 'why' and 'whodunit' stuff, I don't have a clue. But, gosh, all that blood in the snow and leaves up there. Ox must have bled like a stuck pig. He's lucky to be alive!"

"It was pretty gory, but Dr. Marson and her orthopedic surgeon friend did a nice piece of surgery on him. It was good that she was here when it happened."

"Yeah, she is good, and a real sweetheart. Patty loves her as a friend, too. She was sorry not to have been able to help, but we didn't know about it at the time. When is the doctor due back?"

"Not sure. Nancy Conley is staying with her in Staunton until Ox goes to therapy, and then Dr. Marson will bring Nancy home on one of her clinic weekends."

"Always nice to see her and you, Father. What else is new in your life? We sure did enjoy Christmas. Loved the crèche and the carol singing. Course we did go to Christmas mass at our church, but we thought what you did up there on the hill was very special. Christmas does a lot for the spirit of man. My work sometimes makes a cynic out of me. Here it is, just a few weeks from Christmas, and one of the best people I know gets chopped up by some nasty neighbor. Tell me, Padre, what's the matter with us human beings?"

"Wish I knew, Sheriff, but it is your and my job to help God and society straighten them out, isn't it? I try my best, and I know the folk around here think you do a great job, Scott. I do, too. Joshuatown has been a peaceful place up until now. Well, I'd better get on with my chores. I want to call my bishop about Ox. I guess some people around here will want to hear about Ox. Thanks for the coffee. Let me know when your nose begins to itch for motives." With that, Dus walked out.

    Sheriff Kirsh sat back in his swivel chair, picked up his telephone, dialed, and then spoke into the mouthpiece. "Hey, Charlie, you old railroad dick. Scott here! . . . Yeah, I'm good. . . . Uh-huh, my wife and the kids are fine, too. . . . Yours? . . . Good! Say, Charlie, what kind of a hammer or sledge would it take to drive a railroad spike into a piece of oak? . . . No, not into a tie. Into an oak tree. Something heavy, you say? . . . Heavy ball peen? Sledge? Backside of an axe? . . . You mean you couldn't split oak very well with a railroad spike? . . . Could you drive it in far enough not to be seen? . . . You doubt it? . . . No, it's not important at the moment. . . . Let you know if I need more info from you! Love to Bev and the kids . . . Thanks, Charlie! Bye!" Sheriff Kirsh hung up the phone, scratched his head in bewilderment, and whistled. He said to himself, "Don't know Father Habak, but I'm thinking at the moment that Ox's accident didn't have much to do with your shooting caper. But you never can tell."

# 18

It was a very cold, snowy morning, and Dus had opened up the church for an Ash Wednesday service. He had preached a sermon on the previous Sunday about the meaning of Lent. He had explained that each year the church took six weeks before Easter to commemorate the time that Jesus spent in the desert preparing for his ministry. It was for Jesus, Dus had told his little congregation, a time of fasting, prayer, and resisting the temptations of the world, the flesh, and the devil. Historically, Christian people used this solemn period to reflect on that period of Jesus' life by fasting, praying, reflecting on being better Christians, and preparing for the time and events surrounding Christ's entry into Jerusalem on Palm Sunday, his Institution of the Eucharist at his Last Supper with his apostles, his crucifixion on Good Friday, and his resurrection on Easter morning. He had also told them that the first day of Lent was called "Ash Wednesday" because it was a custom in the Episcopal and Catholic Churches to impose on Christians' foreheads the ashes of palm leaves as a sign of humility and penance. Needless to say, Dus had encouraged the folk to come with him to church on that day to receive the ashes and the Holy Communion, and start a good Lent.

Given the cold and snowy weather and the fact that going to midweek services was an oddity for people who never heard of such a thing, who probably would not take the time from their chores and busy lives to come, Dus did not expect very many people would be there. His expectations were more than fulfilled. No one showed up. He was disappointed, but smiled and allowed that one sermon would not develop people's habits a whole lot. So he just said the Ash Wednesday prayers by himself, smudged his own forehead with ashes, closed up the church, then slipped and slid in his Jeep down to his office.

He had just managed to get the heat on and settled in his chair, when the telephone rang. "Hello. Father Habak here. What can I do for you?" he asked.

"You can come down here and give me some hugs, stranger," Karol scolded from the other end of the line.

"Oh, hi, Kara," he said. "How are you? I was just going to call you."

"'Bout time! I've really been missing you. It's been three weeks since our little talk about who loves who, and time's a wastin'. I'm not getting any younger, and I'm not happy anymore about the time and distance between us. Carving on bodies keeps me busy, but I do miss you, and I have lots to tell you. First, I want to tell you I love you."

"You do?"

"Of course. Didn't we agree on that?"

"Oh, that's right. I think I do remember something about that," Dus kidded.

"Come on, Parson, be nice! Whatcha been doing?"

"Well, I tried to have an Ash Wednesday service, but no one came!"

"I'm sorry, but maybe folk don't understand about such things yet. I found out you have to give them time with medicine and stuff, too. Did you smudge yourself with ashes?"

"Yes. Did you get smudged?"

"Nope. Shawn and I are going over to the Episcopal Church here to get that done."

"Good girl! I'm proud of you!"

"I've been trying harder, darling, because of you. But I've needed to get straight with God on a lot of things. What else have you been doing without me?"

"I've been trying to think of something to give up for Lent."

"That's very pious. And what have you decided to give up for Lent?"

"Guess!"

"Your favorite foods—Brussels sprouts, rutabaga, and broccoli?"

"Always those, but they're not the main thing."

"What, then?"

"You! I've decided to give up Ollikut for Lent. That's why I haven't called."

"That's good. I hate that name!"

"Not the name; the person."

"What? Are you a religious fanatic, or what? Look, Father, I know about Lent, and my morals are just as good as yours. I don't think the Lord would exact that kind of discipline when we have just fallen in love. That wouldn't be fair! I shouldn't have to tell a priest that Lent's about love, too, so figure out something else for your penance. We just got started. I'm not always sure about what God wants of his people, but I am sure he doesn't care if we hug during Lent."

"If you will quit trying to teach me about what God wants, I'll tell you something maybe you'll want to hear."

"OK. What?"

"I do love you and miss you, but your job is there and mine is here, so I don't expect this distance between here and Staunton to be too easy for us. Perhaps this will be a good Lenten discipline for us. When do you think you'll get back up here?"

"That's one of the things I want to tell you. Nancy wants to go home now that Ox is in rehab. I thought I would bring her up Friday and spend the weekend at the clinic. If you're a good boy, I might take some time off to walk and talk with the clergy, and learn more about Lent."

"We'd better be careful about where we talk and walk. Ole' Banker Brush will be adding to his theories about mixing theology and science. He might be looking for some stuff for his small talk."

"Well, as old Gramps Joseph would say, 'May the coyote pee on his moccasins!' Who cares what that old geezer says or thinks? If I want to kiss my priest, I'll do it wherever I want to, even if it's in the lobby of the Joshuatown National Bank during Lent."

"Shame on you, Doctor. What about your Hippocratic compassion?"

"If I recall, righteous one, you're the cleric who taught me to dislike the leering old rogue."

"So I did," Dus smiled into the phone. "I think now that this priest has a lady in his life, he'd better clean up his judgment of folk and stop influencing nice people to say bad things. That will be another one of my Lenten disciplines."

"I like the way you are. That's why I fell in love with you. You're supposed to protect me from lecherous old coots like old Brush Face."

"What I mean, honey, is that I haven't been so good about my criticisms of people, nor the quality of my language, for a long time. I've run out of excuses for my behavior, and, after all, a clergyman should set an example. I'm hoping Lent will help me to clean up my act."

"I know, darling, but don't get so 'Kingdom-bound' with me that you aren't fun. I don't want you to be a human being without frailties, unlike the rest of us mortals. Do you think God wants you to be so straightlaced and inflexible that we can't have fun, talk naturally, and respond to situations with a little righteous indignation? You, 'white eyes,' have a lot to learn about the Great Spirit's personality from us Indians. You and I are mountain people, now, darling. God expects us to be a little bit earthy. I don't like vulgarity, swearing, and dirty mouths, either, and I sure don't support women being the subject of filthy jokes, but I think even God smiles at some of the funny things in life. I grew up on a reservation and you grew up on a farm, and some sayings and colloquialisms are just part of life. Do you think God is all that uptight about our little cuss words, even during Lent?"

"I just think that my language has gotten too spicy. I have been angry, sarcastic, and ready to pounce on people about trivial things. I need to be more patient with people who offend me. My vocation expects that of me, and Lent reminds me of it."

"Well, darling, I don't have time to preach you a sermon between surgery this morning, but I think God is going to expect you to love folk, take care of them, preach the gospel, administer the sacraments, be who you are, and make some mistakes. Mistakes are made by folk. That's why I'm a surgeon and you're a priest—to help fix people up, whether it be in body or soul. I think he wants us to walk with Jesus and imitate him the best we know how and bring folk to him, but I don't think he wants you to be a Bible-thumping religious freak and zealot."

"Wow. Have you thought about being a preacher?"

"No, smarty pants, but all my preaching to you aside, I am sure there is one thing God doesn't want of you and me."

"What's that?"

"He doesn't want us giving up each other for Lent."

"How do you know that?"

"Because he told me so."

"When did you last talk to him?"

"Just a few minutes ago, before I called you."

"Oh. And what did he say?"

"He said, 'You're welcome!'"

"Why did he say that?"

"Because in my prayers this morning, I thanked him for working it out for me to love you and for you to love me. And he said, 'You're welcome!'"

"Interesting conversation! Are you trying to teach a minister about Lent, Sister Karolina?"

"Oh, darling, I don't want to fight with you. Just don't get weird on me. I fell in love with Father Habak, not Saint Benedict! You're a very good man and priest. Don't become someone else. God loves you and wants you in the mountains with those people. He wants you to be part of them. I do, too. I think he also wants you someday to be a part of me, and I, of you. Think on that during Lent! Talk to God about things as I do. And don't you dare suggest to him that I'm wrong! Anyway, I love you and miss you so much. I just want to be close to you, to listen to you, and to have you listen to me. I have a lot of things to say, too, you know. Me pretty smart Indian Princess, 'Kemo Sabe.' "

"You are, indeed, and I thank you for your insights. But, Princess, I do want to be more patient and understanding of folk. I want to be done with the bad things in my life, and be more positive about things and people. Anyway, you know what I mean."

"I do, Dus, and you will be. Anyway, I gotta go. I have a hernia to patch. Tell Jenny and the kids I'll be up Friday afternoon with Nancy and Shawn. Oh, by the way, I'm bringing you an anniversary present."

"Whose anniversary?"

"Ours. It will be five months ago Saturday that you pulled down your pants for me and I fell in love with your heinie."

"Kara!"

"What?"

"Don't you have a fragment of decorum in you, at least for Lent?"

"Sure, but it was your heinie that first attracted me to you."

"Lord, what am I going to do with you?"

"Hmm! Well, if the Lord leads us someday to nuptial bliss, maybe you're going to see my heinie."

"Kara, for crying out loud, you're talking to your priest, and this is Ash Wednesday."

"I know it is, so forgive me! Anyway, for now, you should start remembering anniversaries, birthdays, and things, because I'm really into presents, parties, and stuff."

"What's the present you have for me?"

"It won't be a surprise if I tell you now, but I'll give you a clue. It's something that'll help you and me to do our detective work."

"What are you talking about, Kara?" Dus asked, his voice sounding a bit testy.

"Look, Dus, you don't fool me a bit, wanting to nose around caves and asking J.K. and me about them. And don't raise your voice at me. I don't like being yelled at, especially during Lent."

"I'm sorry, sweetheart, but I don't want you involved with what might be some bad stuff. This is Scott Kirsh's and my business."

"It's my business now, too, darling."

"The hell it is!"

"You're cussing on Ash Wednesday, Father."

"I'm sorry, but you have to stay out of this, Kara."

"Sorry, Dus. I'm already in, so quit yelling."

"We'll talk about this on Friday when you get here."

"OK. You're going to like my present."

"I won't if it's part of your getting into dangerous trouble. People have gotten hurt, Kara, and I don't want you getting hurt, too."

"That's the point. We're going to find out about who took a shot at you and hurt Ox. Somebody hurt people I love, and he made one big grievous mistake when he made this Indian mad!"

"Kara, please don't..."

Karol interrupted him, "Good-bye, darling. Gotta run. See you Friday! You'll love your present. Love you!"

She hung up. Dus sat there with a buzzing telephone in his hand. "Mare's marbles!" he said, then added, "Karol's right. That mild expletive word just doesn't do it for some situations." He thought of his youth on the farm, and remembered even the most religious of farmers didn't say "manure." "Gee, that Indian beauty is going to drive me batty with her talk, but my, how I love her. Thank you for her, Lord, and please don't let her get hurt on my account," he prayed. Lent was not going to be easy for Father Habak, who just fell in love with a holy terror.

# 19

Karol and Nancy were to come Friday afternoon. Dus spent the morning in town, eating with the townsfolk, and eating at Bessie's. He was gradually learning about Appalachia, its folklore, and its way of life. Sometimes it appeared to him that "Li'l Abner of Dog Patch," the cartoon character in the newspaper comics of his youth, became alive there. Rural farm life in Pennsylvania, even as close as he lived to the Appalachian Mountains, seemed so dissimilar to the life he experienced here. It was a different world, he mused. These provincial, resourceful, hill people seemed to Dus to be more of a reflection of their environment than were the people back home. I really missed something in my pastoral studies about the nature of people who live in mountains, he thought to himself. They have been often characterized as lazy, unkempt, and illiterate, but they are hardworking, industrious, and smart, with their apparel reflecting the kind of work in which they engage and the social life they enjoy. The woods, the animals, hills, valleys, weather, minerals, and vegetation, really do have an impact on the lives of people here more than I ever experienced anywhere else. Those natural components almost decree a way of sociology that enables people to cope with every facet of life, from the womb to the tomb. It's incredible. I suppose that is true of American Indians, too. If it is, it's no wonder that Karol loves it here.

He had been daydreaming. Bessie interrupted his thought. "Did ya have a good lunch, Pawson?"

"Great again, Bessie. And how is the fairest lady chef in town?"

"Jist fine, jist fine, en thank ya fer dem nice words. By da way, I'll bea all slicked up en lookin' purty fer da Grange Dance Sadderday night. Think ya might come en have a twirl wid me?"

"I'll see, Bessie. I didn't know there was a dance. If I can come, I'd be honored to dance with you. I'll bet, though, I'll have to compete with Jed and the other men to twirl you. I'm not a very good dancer."

"Den we'll teach ya. Da Virginy Reel, squar' dancin', en foot stompin', Fadder, is easy. Yo'll like it, ya will. On de job trainin', as dey say. Ain't hard et all. Me en Mister Clayton use ta dance all da time fer he passed away. It's da one big thung I missed after he died. But ya sure right 'bout Jed. He en me use ta dance up a sto'm tagether when we was young en in da school. He's still good at it, too. Come en jern da crowd. 'Tis sorta a town social."

"You and Jed are pretty close, aren't you, Bessie? He is a nice person."

"Yeah we is! Me en Jed goes back a long time, ta when we jest youn-guns. We's bes' frien's for our lifetime. I was in love wid 'im somethun fierce, puppy love, ya knows, en den da war come en he wenna way ta da Navy. Den Mr. Lee Clayton come 'long en we fell in love, and dat was dat. Den Jed married Helen. She be a good woman fer 'im, and we's all frien's. Jed en Helen woulda cut dere arms offen fer me, ena I'd do da same fer dem. Butta yer right. Der bea lotta men what wonna dance wid me. I'm purty good, and I'd sho like a go wid you, Parson, if you allowed ta dance. Some folk donna think that dancin' is ri't and sho donna wanna see a preacher do it. Butta da Lo'd din't care if King David danced in da Bible, didn't he Pawson?"

Dus grinned and imagined a wispy white haloed and winged impish-looking character appearing on his shoulder, whispering in his ear, "Remember it's Lent, Father." "Remember what Kara said about having fun," another tiny, red-bearded, fork-carrying imp seemed to whisper from his left shoulder. He ignored them both. "King David did dance, Bessie, among other things!"

"Why donna ya bring da purty young doctor wid ya fer a pardner. Butta ya still gotta save me a whirl too, ya know. Come en enjo' yerselfs," Bessie insisted.

"Good ideal. Do you think she'd come with the likes of me, if I asked her?"

"I thinks so! I knows I would if I were young en purty like her!"

"You're pretty and a doll, sweet lady. Maybe I will. Thank you, and have a good day." Dus had left the restaurant, smiling and wondering if Indian women liked to square dance.

Now it was late afternoon at his office, and he heard a knock on the outside door. Couldn't be Karol, he told himself. She'd come in from her office. He went to the door and opened it. He was greeted by a big dog standing there, with a huge choke chain around its bull-like neck, attached to a chain leash leading to a pretty, smiling, parka-covered woman.

"Happy anniversary," Karol laughed. "Here's your present. Her name is Tooter. She's eight-five pounds of Labrador and German shepherd, and like me, she's gonna love you. And you are going to love her, too. Kiss me before she kisses you, because she has the biggest slobbermouth in Christendom."

Dus backed away from the dog, then allowed both of them to enter and pass right by him. He closed the door and nabbed Karol, leash and all, from the back, and kissed her soundly while Tooter sat on the floor, panting and wagging a stump of a tail. Finally, Dus released Karl. She threw her parka on a chair and quipped, "Gee, that was nice, darling. Much better than Tooter's smooches. But that's all I've had of late. Well, what do you think?"

"I think you're beautiful; your mouth is sweeter than wine, and I love you. I don't know about the dog yet. Seems to have nice legs and heinie!"

"You're impossible, but it's so good to be here," she said, putting her arms around him. He kissed her again.

"I have missed you, Kara. Talking on the telephone is OK, but I want you here, near me, so I can touch you and look at you."

"You have three days to do that. I have Monday off. I doubled up and took extra rounds for friends these last three weeks." She called to the dog. "Come here, Tooter, and meet your new master." The dog came over and sat down, looking up at Karol and Dus, anxiously waiting for a pat on the head. Dus obliged her.

"Ah, nice pup. Why was she named Tooter?"

She smiled. "You will learn why in time!"

"You say she's a sleuth dog? What's that mean?"

"Oh, I don't know. She belonged to a nurse who transferred somewhere. She wanted her to have a good home, and I thought she would go well with you and the cabin. She needs male companionship."

"Frankly, my dear, I had something else in mind as for female companionship."

"Oh, really. Maybe we'll talk about that someday. Tooter's one year old, trained in obedience school, and goes to the door when she wants to do her nature-call business, and believe me, you will know when she has to go."

"Does she count, walk on her back legs, roll over, and say 'Please,' too?"

"No, and I'm glad. I don't care for animals that do tricks. I like dogs that act like dogs and not like people."

"Think she will want to put up with the likes of me?"

"If I can, she can," Karol laughed.

Dus threw a couch pillow at her. "You're a troublemaker. You know that?"

"Yeah, I know. Anyway, Tooter is a great hunting dog. She loves the woods and the water, but she won't leave you unless you give her permission. She won't run after birds nor animals unless you give her commands. Better than that, she's been trained to sniff out things. Guess that's the shepherd in her. She should go well with a good shepherd like you, Pastor!"

"Thank you. She'll be good company. Elly will love her. You're sure you and Shawn don't want to keep her in Staunton?"

"Nope; she's too big for our house. Anyway, she needs a place like this with woods to run in. She really will be good company for you, darling."

"You're sweet. I really do appreciate your giving her to me. Maybe you and I can take a walk with her sometime."

"You're welcome, Padre. We'll walk soon, but right now I gotta take care of some folk who are coming in to the clinic. Maybe we can bundle up and hit the trail after supper tonight for a little while. She loves to romp."

"Good! How's Ox?" Dus inquired.

"He's doing OK," Karol replied. "He'll be all right. It is going to take some time at rehab for him to adjust to the prosthesis. He'll have to change his working habits a bit, but that will be up to him, Nancy, and the family. That was a terrible thing. He has no insurance and not the greatest of incomes to cover expenses. Dr. Champion and the hospital gave him a break, but you and I will have to talk about his expenses sometime."

"I'll help all I can. I have some resources."

"I know you will, darling. I can help, too. I do have to go now. See you later!"

"If you're going to leave me with this slobbering dog, how about a good-bye kiss?"

Karol and Dus embraced again, so lovingly, but she had to break away. "Wow, Parson! Let go, or I'm going to have to take a cold Lenten shower. Bye; see you tonight."

Karol went through the door, and Dus knelt down and said to Tooter, "You don't know this yet, big dog, but that gal is going to be your mistress someday, because your master is going to make her his wife someday. Count on it!"

He put on his coat, took Tooter's leash in his hand, and they both went out the door and climbed into the jeep. They spent the afternoon walking together through the woods. Tooter was playful and enjoyed running in the snow. Her ears perked up when she heard chickadees chirping, and she scanned for rabbits, but none appeared. She was a frisky dog and Dus liked her. They became fast friends. Even though Dus was still a stranger, she responded to his commands. Karol was right. She was well-trained and stayed within sight, returning to Dus every now and then after a romp. She liked the snow, and given her breed, Dus believed she would like the lakes and streams, too.

Dus tried to avoid thinking about what Karol said to him about Tooter being a sleuth dog. He did not want Karol involved in the mysterious things happening in his life, but he was determined to pursue them. He was going to find out about who tried to shoot him. He was incensed about Ox's near-fatal injury, and fought off his thoughts about reprisal. He would, he vowed, find out who did that to his friend. And then he thought that maybe none of this would have happened had he not come here. Stow the guilt trip. It is what it is, and if this black dog can help, so much the better, he thought. I'll need all the help I can get, but I can see now, I'm going to have to do that when Karol is not around. She'll get too involved in this thing, and I'll be spending all my time worrying about her getting shot, too.

He and Tooter returned to the cabin for a rest and to make some supper. She can eat scraps for now, he believed, but he'd have to get her on some dog chow. Can't afford a wolf her size on real food. I'd have to get a loan from Mr. Brush of Joshuatown National to be able to afford her. Then he looked at Tooter's big white teeth and smiled some more. "How'd you like to go to town, Tooter, and talk with Banker Brush about food?" Tooter just lay by the fire, yawned, tooted, and smiled, too. Dus then understood why his new present was named "Tooter." "Gol dern it, you foul hound," he complained, "that's awful! Being an old farmer, I don't mind the smell so much, but it burns my eyes." Tooter just smiled again!

*   *   *

Tooter and Dus arrived at the Conleys' just minutes after they had finished supper. Nancy, Karol, and Jenny were washing and drying dishes, while Cyrus and the children were talking about their father. Dus could tell there was a more lofty spirit in the family; tensions relaxed, and everyone was talking more positively about Ox's accident. They had planned how to help him cope with the changes, and how to get him on his new foot and out doing what he did best as a provider, husband, and father. This is a family, Dus thought to himself, that is really together. They love and help one another, and their pride shows. Humble folk indeed, hardworking, poor in the goods of the world, but rich in family values. Anger and resentment were not part of their lives, and together they accepted the difficulties of life as well as the blessings. The children imaged their mother's softness of tone and manner, and their father's hardness of work and resolve to provide and sustain. Ox will do well at home with all this love, with or without a leg, and it will not be long before he will be out taking care of his friends and family again. The whole family greeted Dus.

"Good ta see ya, Fadder," Nancy welcomed him to the kitchen. "Have ye 'ad suppa? We's got lo's left ova en plenty a goodies ta spar.'"

"No thanks, Nancy. Tooter and I already had supper. Good to see you back home. We really missed you. Did you leave Ox in good hands?"

"He'll be a fittin' soon en come home in a liddle w'ile! He seys hello ta ya. Da dog bea nice present, ain't she? She rode up wid us ta safter, en I enjo'd 'er. She gonna be nice company fer ya. Karol sure was hopin' ya'd be suprised."

"She's was a great surprise, and Karol was nice to bring her to me."

"See, Karol, didn't I tell ya he'd like 'er? Ox'll like 'er, too. Ken't ya jist see da tree of dem paradin' 'round da mountain? Whar's she now, Dus?"

"Yeah, war's she? We wanna ta meet en play wid her, Fadder," a chorus of young voices, including Shawn's, seemed to holler at him, all at one time.

"She's in the jeep right now. Didn't think I should bring her in the house. She's been running and has gotten wet from the snow. She's dirty and doesn't smell good," Dus said, fearing she might toot in Nancy's house.

Nancy was adamant, "Oh, fiddle, Preacha. She ain't gonna hurt des house none. Bring 'er in en let da chillun git acquainted wid 'er. Dey ken play a li'l while Karol en me does up da dishes."

Karol turned around from the sink. "Hi, Preacher. Are you going to say 'Good evening' to your evening date?"

Dus blushed and replied, "Gosh, I'm sorry, Doctor. I got so involved here with Nancy and the kids. I missed you. How are you this evening?"

He moved toward her. Karol smiled and winked, but shook her head slightly. Dus got the signal, stopped, and smiled back at her.

"I'm just fine. Glad you and Tooter had a good afternoon. Why don't you go out and get her and let the children play with her for a few minutes, while I freshen up and put on some walking gear."

Dus went out to the Jeep and returned with Tooter.

"Oh boy, what a neat pup!" one of the children said.

"Yeah," said another, and all began to pet Tooter, who enjoyed the attention. Nancy smiled at her children and the dog. It was good to see the worry off of her face.

"I'm ready to go, Father," Karol said, looking ravishing in her earmuffs, long hair, doeskin jacket, and boots.

"Can we keep Tooter here while you're gone, Father?" Shawn asked.

"Sorry, Shawn, but I think your mom thinks we ought to take a walk with the dog so I can get better acquainted with her. That OK with you?"

"Sure. You and Mom have a good time with her."

"Be back in a couple of hours, Nancy," Karol promised.

"Good night, Nancy; good night, kids," Dus said. "Come on hound; let's go."

Tooter got up and followed Dus and Karol out the door into a crisp, full-moon lighted evening. She pranced and begged her human friends to get on with their trek.

"Which way, Parson? This is your parish. Or do you just want to follow Tooter and see where she takes us?" Karol asked.

"Let's follow the dog." He took Karol's hand and commanded Tooter to move on. She did, and they moved over to the path along the creek and headed north. They walked for a long time, talking, laughing, stopping to hug and kiss, with Tooter ignoring them, but staying close. After a while, they came upon a huge log, brushed it off, and sat down for a rest.

"Whew! I'm getting a mite tired. Let's sit for a while before we start back," Karol breathed.

"Fine with me. I was tired way back there, but didn't want to let you think I couldn't keep up. Been a long day for this old codger. You young females are going to wear me out."

She laughed and pulled Dus down beside her in the snow, leaning her back against the log. She took Dus' hand and held it tightly. He reached over with his lips and kissed her on the cheek. "Going to get our bottoms wet and catch cold if we sit like this too long," he said.

"I don't care, darling. I just want to be here with you in the moonlight, looking at that magnificent sky up there and the beautiful trees, and dreaming about a time and place for us. Look at that mutt lying there staring at us. Just no privacy even in the big forest, is there?"

"Well, she's not gonna tell anybody, is she? Or can she, among her many talents, talk and gossip?"

"Who would she talk to who doesn't already know about us? Dus, don't you think we are getting pretty obvious to others about what we feel toward each other?"

"Yeah, I guess so, but I don't really care. I love you, and I can't help it if it shows. Have you said anything to Shawn yet about us?"

"Won't have to. He knows me pretty well, and it won't be long before he will be asking questions."

"Like what?"

"Well, like, 'How come your face lights up when you're around Father Habak, Mom? And 'Why do you talk about the mountain and the church up there so much, Mom?' and 'I think you got a thing for the priest, Mom.' You know how kids are! They're not dumb, and Shawn is pretty close to me. Sometimes I think he can read me like a book. He's also growing up, and knows about the birds and bees."

"Is that bad?"

"No, it's not, darling, but what are we going to do about all this stuff that is happening to us? All of a sudden, when I'm working and I start thinking of you, I want to be here instead of at the hospital. All of a sudden, I am so lonely when I'm down there and you are up here. Shawn can see that. But he likes to come here, too, and, I guess you know, he likes you and does have eyes for Elly."

"Yeah. I have seen that look on his face and her face, too. But they're just kids finding their way. 'Like father, like daughter,' as the saying goes. Better watch out for your baby, Mama; my little gal may be a chip off the old block."

"How so, love?"

"Well, I think our kids are smarter about what boys and girls do when they are in love than I was, when I was their age, and I grew up on a farm where you learn a lot from the animals."

"You would never make me believe you were all that dumb and naive about such things, even if you were a bit more Kingdombound on your 'Pennsylvania Dutch' farm than the rest of us mortals."

"Who, me? Dumb? Why, Ollikut, I was so naive about sex that when my dad told me about the birds and the bees, my first dates were with a sparrow and two hornets. Why, honey, my love affairs were so platonic, I invited the girls up to the hayloft for a drink of ginger ale!"

Karol laughed. "You're so silly. I can hardly believe anything you say. Seriously, Dus, what are we going to do about our lives, now that we are in love? We are going to have to talk about it and do some planning."

"Yeah, we will," Dus agreed. "You know, I sit here in the midst of all this wonder, looking at you, listening to you, and thinking, how can God or anyone make it any better? Thinking, this is enough for now, so why complicate it with plans? The last few weeks, I have not thought much about anything but you. I asked God why it is that after all I have been through—doubting him, being angry—such a person like you should come into my life in these mountains, where I thought I was destined to die of boredom and loneliness. It's simply unbelievable. I didn't like you much when I first met you, and within hours, I was head over heels in love with you. I feel like old man Scrooge on Christmas morning; like Tooter, when she dances in the snow; like the birds and rabbits that scurry around in happiness. I'm giddy and silly, and I love you and life, and I don't hardly even know what I am talking about right now."

"Keep talking, darling. I like it." She cuddled closer into him.

"I don't know what to do about us and our future. I guess we just have to take a day or a weekend at a time. You have to be sure, sweetheart. You have Shawn and your medicine. You have worked hard to become what you are. I admire and respect you for that, and I would never ask you to give it up. I am honored that a beautiful, intelligent woman like you would find me in this place and discover she loves me. I've asked God how that can be. He doesn't seem to answer. Then I think of Ginnie. We haven't been parted all that long, and I still have feelings for her. I don't want to dishonor her memory because I love you. I just don't know what to say about us, Kara, other than I thank you and God for your love, and I pray that he will show us a way to fulfill it, to use it for our separate ministries, and share it with the family and friends we love. It is not fair for me to talk about marriage with you, yet. We have to first talk to our hearts, our minds, and our souls. I'll wait as long as I must to resolve everything we have to. We need to do a lot of talking, we have to know, and we have to be sure. Right now, I am just unhappy every time you leave this mountain and me behind. You know what I mean, don't you?"

"I know exactly what you mean, darling, and I wanted to hear all of that. It was very difficult for me to tell you I was in love with you. I didn't want to fall in love with anyone. I didn't want any of this to happen for all the reasons you just mentioned. I thought about it for weeks. I hoped maybe you felt affection toward me and would say something to me. I knew at Christmastime something big was happening between us, but I was afraid that the season, the crèche, and the beauty of that night were pushing my heart beyond my mind. It was too short a time. I scarcely knew you. I have been a pretty lonely woman the past several years, and I have to be very careful about that emotional and physical thing called 'need.' I'm a woman. I have the feelings of a woman, so don't ever believe that because I am a professional, I don't like being a woman. I am more woman than I am physician, darling. Being both is very good for me. You are a man, as well as a priest, and they, too, are very good. But it is not just the priest in you that makes me love you. I love you because you are a man with very special qualities, the priesthood being only one of them. I didn't seek to fall in love with you, and I know the hazards of love. Both of us have been through emotional hells and back. I lost my husband tragically, and you lost your wife. It's been longer for me, but I understand about Ginnie. That takes a lot of time, and there is no need for us to forget those whom we loved. But heaven now shows its face to two people, a man and a woman, in a different time and a different place, and I believe that God allows for that. He certainly has allowed it before many thousands of times, and for many thousands of people in love."

Dus stared at her pretty face and into her eyes. He was enchanted by her words. She continued. "Men and women fall in love, darling, not widows and widowers, not physicians and priests. Those labels are just what we are after God takes our loved ones away from us. Our vocations are what we do for a living, and that certainly adds special dimensions to our lives and love. Time, I believe, will resolve the inevitable conflicts of our lost spouses and our given professions, if our love is real. Our love, like all love, will be sorely tested. But right now, without trying to be gurus and sages and all-knowing, let's just enjoy what we have, as you say, a weekend at a time, and let God and time weave a course for us, knowing there are going to be bumps and shakes along the way. There'll be questions that will need answering, and loneliness and necessity that are going to want to be satiated. I love you, Dus Habak, so much that it scares me. My beloved departed husband notwithstanding, I'm not sure that I ever loved any man as much as I do you. I don't know why I feel that way. I don't understand it. That's a difficult thing to say—an awesome feeling at my age—and I have been as pure as the driven snow since his death. I didn't have to tell you that, but I wanted you to know."

Dus was surprised that she said that, but it made it easier for him to continue in her mode. "I wouldn't have asked about your relationships with other men, Kara. I love you, and I'm only as interested in as much of your life as you want to share. Owning up about your past is not a condition of my love. I simply see you as a very beautiful, vivacious, caring, and giving woman. I don't know now whether marriage would be the best thing for either one of us. I am not asking you to make that commitment now. You have Shawn and your vocation. I have my work here. I cannot change that for you or Elly. I just thank God for your love and for allowing you to come up on this mountain to help these good people who need you. We have them and our love in common, and that may have to be good enough for now. I miss you when you're gone, but there is a telephone, and that is my lifeline to you when you're not here. Someday, as you say, God will weave a blanket for our lives, then he will tell us when we may lie down on it together. We'll just have to wait and discern his intention for us."

"Thank you, dear heart. This conversation has been worth a wet heinie."

"It seems to me, Doc, that you're really into heinies. Are they your specialty? You're a surgeon who never seems to mention any other part of the anatomy. How come?"

"Someday, if our love draws us into something bigger and the occasion presents itself, maybe I will. Anyway, a heinie is one of the anatomical things that one can refer to without offending folk. Would you like me to talk about those other things now, Father?"

"Forget it; this is no classroom. We'd better be getting back. Look at that dog looking at us, just waiting for us to do something. Suppose she wants us to get up and get going."

"Well, she won't move until we do. I guess you're right; we'd better move. Nancy will worry."

They got up from where they were sitting, kissed each other again, and started down the trail. Tooter leaped up and headed out in front of them. She seemed to know the way back. Dus and Karol held hands as they trekked back to the Conley house.

"Kara," Dus said as they walked, "I really need to ask you something."

"What is it, Dus?"

"Please don't get involved with my accident and Ox's injury. I don't want you to get hurt. Please! We don't know what's going on, and this is work for the police. Sheriff Kirsh has already talked to me, and he's investigating. It's best we don't add problems to his work. I know you love Ox and me, but while these mountains are beautiful, there are some things that aren't so beautiful. I'm pleading with you, honey."

"Are you going to get out, too?"

"That's different!"

"How's it different?"

"Because none of this stuff started until I came up here and asked questions about the old minister. I think my sniffing around has taken me into places where I am not wanted."

"Like the caves you and J.K. are going to visit in the spring?"

"Well, ah, ah . . . "

"Well, ah, ah, nothing. I know you're going sleuthing when I'm not around. I can see those chauvinistic wheels turning around in that scheming head of yours. I want you to know I was raised in the mountains; I know 'em back and forth, up and down, and sideways. I can track better than you, Scott Kirsh, peg-leg Stewart, and even that grinning Tooter over there. If you machos think you're going to cast me aside, forget it. Look, Dus, I promise I won't do anything on my own. I can't be up here often, anyway, but when I am, I want to be a part. I have a vested interest in you and the Conleys. Can't you see I love you all? You can't just cut me out! Damn it, you're starting to make me cry and cuss again during Lent, after being so sweet to me up there in the moonlight." She sniffed and looked at him. "Besides, I'm a grown-up woman, and you have no right to chase me out of the woods like some little scared bunny."

"Gosh, Kara, won't you listen to me about this at all?"

"Yes, I'll listen to you because I know you love and care about me. I am not out for revenge. I just want to find out, too, who tried to hurt you and Ox. Both of you were nearly killed!"

"OK. We'll play it as we see it. But stay close to me and promise you won't do anything on your own. Will you promise me that?"

"I promise. Honest Injun. I'll do nothing on my own. And don't worry about my going into caves. I won't do that. I hate dark, wet places and bats. If I get any information, I'll bring it right to you. I just want to help. Speaking of which, you might want to know about something interesting that happened to us in the car when we were coming up the mountain road this afternoon."

Dus was taken aback and showed it. "What?" he asked, glaring at her.

"Now don't get upset. It was nothing bad, but was kind of interesting. Gosh, you get so tense!"

"I get tense when I think you might get hurt."

"Some men stopped us. They told us to wait until they cleared away a tree that had fallen across the road. It only held us up for a moment. I didn't recognize any of them, but they knew me, and asked how things were at the clinic. They talked like local men, who I supposed worked for the state or county highway department. But they didn't have any construction helmets nor safety vests on, and the truck was just a pickup, not an identifiable government vehicle."

"What did they do or say other than that, that made it so interesting?"

"They just pushed the tree off the road to the side and let me pass. The only thing that seemed funny to me was that they laid the tree over the entrance to a wide trail. The tree looked like it had been cut, instead of having fallen down on its own. I don't know. They just smiled at me, wished me a good day, and told me to be careful on the mountain."

"Hmm. Is that all?"

"Yeah. Shawn thought it was fun, and Tooter barked at the men. They glared at him. Anyway, it was nothing important, and I am here with you, safe and sound."

"That's the way I want it."

They proceeded down the trail. As they drew closer to the lights at the Conley house, Dus stopped in front of Karol, put his hands on her shoulders, held her at arm's length, and looked into her face.

"You are a beautiful lady. I want to stop here for a moment and tell you something very important."

"Sounds like it. Thought we resolved things up on the hill."

"It's not about danger and sleuthing."

"What's it about?" She looked at him anxiously.

"It's another dimension about our talk up there at the log in the snow, concerning the future. It's a subject that needs to be discussed between us, Kara, but one that's awkward for a cornball cleric like me. I'm a private sort of man, and I'm not the most open person when it comes to talking about personal things. I am not sure, either, if this is the right time to talk about what's on my mind."

"What might that be?" she asked, somewhat bewildered.

"I am a religious man, Karol. You know that, but I am a man, and I want you to know that I have very strong feelings about you."

"I know that, darling. What are you trying to say?"

"It's about sex."

"It sounds like an important subject for a middle-aged cleric and medic, boy and girl, in love, to talk about. Go ahead, Father. I'm a grown-up girl, in case you hadn't noticed, and I am not easily shocked by that subject matter."

"I'm serious, honey. It has to do with your saying that you were 'as pure as the driven snow.' It's none of my business about whatever feelings you have had toward men nor what you did with them, but I assumed by that statement you meant that you have not slept with any man since your husband died. Is that true?"

"It is exactly what I meant, darling, and it is important to me that you know and believe that."

"I believe it, but your past male relationships make no difference to me."

"You said that, but I have had none."

"You have not asked, but I want you to know that I have not had any alliances with any other woman. There has not been any woman in my bed, other than Ginnie, in my lifetime. She was loyal to me, and I, to her. She is a wonderful memory, but I believe she would understand and approve of a new life for me. I love you now, Kara, more than I can understand or explain, and I want a new life with you. Do you believe that?"

"Yes, Dus, I believe you. I have not asked you for a confession about your previous life, nor would I pry into such things, any more than you would." She hesitated, then smiled, "But I'm not sure I would have bet my bank account, which ain't much, that an old Marine, even if he is a priest, was all that chaste."

"Most Marines are as moral as clergy, Kara, and we clergy are not, as some very fine women know, all that pure-minded and good."

"Now, Father Habak, are you going to wreck my image of clergy? Shame on you! Anyway, why this confession?"

"Because I want to tell you something that may already disappoint you about me."

She appeared a little tense, but kidded him. "Well, I hope it's nothing that I'd have to complain to your bishop about. If it's going to annoy me, wait another time. I'm just too happy tonight to have it ruined."

"I think you might want to hear it. It's important for me to tell you now."

"All right, darling. What is it?"

"When we were sitting up there in the snow, discussing love, you were very captivating and alluring. You are everything a man can imagine a woman to be. I hope God will forgive me if he must, Princess, but you were so sensual, so beautiful, I wanted to make love to you right up there in the snow. If you'd have given me any encouragement, even a little, I think I would have. Now, that desire goes against everything I believe in, but it's important to me that you understand that my priesthood does not inhibit my desire for you. I think I am a decent, moral man, Kara, but I am not a celibate monk."

Karol smiled at him and responded by edging closer to him. "I know that, and I respect your honesty. I am glad you feel that way. Don't be shocked if I tell you I wanted you to make love to me up there. I do right now. My heart is full, my loins are warm, and my need, almost overpowering. My body wants you. I'm a woman who hungers physically for her man. I understand your need, too. I am very vulnerable, Dus. Very. But I want to thank you for not trying nor encouraging me, because I would have submitted eagerly. You were good, better than me, but I want our sexual consummation to wait until we are married, for lots of reasons."

"Do you really want to talk about this? You know that you don't have to now. But we are adults, and are certainly not naive. It might be good for us to understand our feelings from the onset."

"Yes, I want to talk about it, because if we believe this love is for always and that someday we will marry, I want our consummation to be at a very special time and place. I'm an old-fashioned woman when it comes to loving. Do you mind that?"

Dus listened to her intently. He smiled and said, "No, of course not. I love you for being who you are and feeling the way you do. I respect you tremendously, Karol."

"It's important to me 'cause we both know what love leads to eventually, and I surely don't want you thinking I have a lot of weird hang-ups about sex. I don't. I am a very open person about nature and things, as you probably suspect."

"I know you are, and I would never think you were weird about sex. Funny, maybe, but not weird. I want to know how you feel about everything."

Karol continued, "What we have now, sweetheart, is precious and good, and someday, if marriage is right for us, it will be consummated. But I don't want to just have 'sex' with you because our hormones have been in limbo for a spell, and now want to run amok. I want us to be completely committed to one another before those carnal grenades detonate and blow us into a delirium we might regret. I know that sounds curious coming from an emancipated and earthy woman like myself, but when we make love, Dus, I don't want it to be a roll in the snow nor whoopee in a teepee. I want it to be total in its most complete, authentic, and lasting way."

Taking advantage of Dus' opening of the subject, Karol adamantly continued, "I'm no prude, Dus, but I have no truck with Hollywood melodramas of sexual romps by lusting men and women in the most disgusting environs at hand with breathless orgasms they call love. I hate pornography, Dus, especially the 'F' word and every connotation attached to it that dirty-mouthed moral pygmies use for the most beautiful experiences that can happen between a wife and her husband. My femininity is more than 'breasts and vagina.' I'm a person who, by God's design, happens to be a woman. I want to be treated as a woman, cuddled, pampered, and whispered to by the man who loves me. As you know, I am not a spiritual dynamo, but I really and truly want your masculinity and my femininity to be gently and meaningfully meshed in marriage, fulfilling and glorious for both of us. I want love in all its totality and dimension engraved on our minds, souls, and, especially, on our bodies. I hope you don't think that's silly, because that is the way it has to be with me. You wanted me to be honest with you, darling, and that is the way I feel about sex. That is why I have waited. That is why I want to be a celibate, if not pure, virgin for you."

"I don't think it's silly. I suspected you'd feel that way, given what you've told me of your celibacy since your husband died. I'm sure, with your beauty and personality, a lot of men have approached you with lots on their mind."

"I guess it's hard for you to believe, since you perceive me as somewhat earthy, but, even if my faith has not yet developed to the standard that God might like, I do want his approval of our consummated love. I want it decent, good, and right for us, and for him. You're a priest. You know what I mean, don't you?"

"Of course I do. I admire your openness. I respect your feelings, and I could not have expressed my own feelings any better. I want God to approve of our love. I just wanted you to understand that, up there at that log, I felt very ardently drawn to you. You are a very seductive woman, and I am passionately in love with you."

"I'm grateful you love me that way. I would be so disappointed if you did not. But I need reassurance, darling, that this thing we feel is not just piled-up, unused, and unrelieved hormones creeping around looking for a temporary nest to play in. I don't want you to be my sexual playmate, nor I, your concubine. If it's love, someday we will experience it in all its magnitude." She was very quiet for a moment, then she smiled at him. "Dus?"

"Yes, Kara?"

She grinned sheepishly. "Do you think Tooter thought we were going to make whoopee up there, and would have just sat there watching us do it? She looked like she was smiling."

"She seems to always smile, but maybe she does that when she toots. How would I know what Tooter was thinking? She'll have her own day when she's old enough. I don't imagine we will have to teach her much. Anyway, I don't care what that hound thinks. She's nice, but I only know what I was thinking and feeling about you."

"Could you put that into so many understandable and nontheological words for this little girl, teacher?"

"I was thinking what a handsome woman you are—not just physically, but through and through, and what a great privilege it will be to marry you and consummate our marriage. Love has a great desire to be welded, Kara. That isn't sex; that's sacrament."

"Wadda ya mean, theologian?"

"A sacrament is like a symbol. It's an outward and visible expression, a sign, if you will, of inward things, feelings, and thoughts. God is like that. We don't see him. Jesus is the outward visible expression of who he is."

"You're getting doctrinal. Make it simple for this medic!"

"Just trying to say, sweetheart, that love between a woman and a man is an inward emotion that is manifested outwardly. That's why we kiss, hug, and express our feelings in physical ways, and in audible words."

"Sounds pretty neat to me."

"That's what sexual intercourse is. It is the ultimate outward physical expression of a man and woman's inner love for one another. That is why God provided it, why it's so beautiful and good, why it's to be respected, and why it is the means of procreation. God gave it to us to enjoy, to be blessed by it, and not to use it selfishly. That's why I love you for saying what you did."

"You know what, theologian?"

"What?"

"In spite of all that good doctrine, and inwardly and outwardly beautiful stuff, if you had tried up there in the snow to show me your inner love outwardly, I doubt if I would have resisted it. I would have welcomed you into the depth of my being. I love you that much. Thank you for not testing nor tempting me. It will be a sacrament for us someday; I promise."

Dus just looked at her. "Well, you're a tempting and bewitching Indian princess, with your fetching face, hair, eyes, body, mind, and soul, and I can hardly wait until the time when you will share it all with me."

"Thank you. All the best and worst I am and have, with all my Ollikut bumps, scars, and warts, from the top of my head down to the tip of my toes and everything in between, will be fully shared with you someday. I promise you will not be disappointed. I should not tell a priest this, especially during Lent, but there's an old Nez Perce squaw adage that goes, 'When I'm good, I'm really good, but when I'm bad, I'm very, very good.' You will find me that way when we marry."

"You big fibber! That's no Nez Perce adage!"

"Well, it should be. It's true of this Nez Perce, I can hardly wait to test that theory. Will you help me with the experiment someday?"

"I'd like to," he said, blushing and embracing her.

She sniffed and wiped her eyes with her sleeve.

"Kara," Dus asked, "will you go with me to the square dance down in the village tomorrow night? Bessie asked us."

"I'd love to. I'll need a dress."

"Jed Hudson has some pretty country dresses down at his store. Why don't we go in there at lunchtime tomorrow and ask Helen to help us find something in your size."

"Sounds like fun. Didn't know you knew how to square dance."

"Remember, I was raised on a farm. Can you dance?"

"I had more than my share of dance dates in college. Gave up whooping around the campfire long ago. Anyway, square dancing will be a good dance for you and me, Preacher."

"Why's that?"

"Keep the gossip down around town."

"How so?"

"Well," Karol giggled, "dancing can get pretty amorous, but people don't get too close in square dancing. We won't get so close that the towns folk'll notice and talk about us. We gotta watch it. And Dus . . ."

"What?"

"Thank you for not giving me up for Lent."

"I had no intention of doing that. But I'm not so sure I ought to wed you."

"And why would you not?"

"Because, Ollikut, I'm not sure I want a wife with a hole in her nose."

"Why not? You can put a ring and a chain in it to keep your wife from going astray!"

"Better than the other way around. Ollikut, I'm not really sure I'm going to be able to handle an Indian wife."

"Sure you will. You're strong and witty, and it's too late to turn me away. 'Tis true I'll surely be a lot in your hands, but it's in your hands where I surely want to be."

They both laughed, held each other closer than they ever had before, and smothered each other with arms and kisses. Karol, her eyes and cheeks wet against Dus' face, whispered passionately in his ear, "I do love you, Father, and someday when we are wed, I want you to make love to me someplace like up there by that log, somewhere under beautiful trees and the sky."

Dus pushed her gently away, looked solemnly into her beautiful, wet face, and said, "Kara, I want you now, but the things you said are right. I know what you want for us. And I am honor bound by your words."

Karol relaxed, pulled back from him, and smiled. "Wow! This night has been a test! Thank you for loving me that much." Turning away from him and starting to run down the hill, she challenged him. "Race you down to the house!"

She ran down the hill and he raced after her down the path. He caught her as they both slid to a stop at the Conley's front door. Tooter and Nancy were waiting for them. Nancy, holding a lantern, smiled lovingly at them and asked them to come in and have some hot cider in front of the fireplace. She looked like Cupid. Karol and Dus blushed and gave her a hug. Nancy took a white hanky from her apron pocket, reached up, and wiped lipstick off of Dus' mouth. "Ya had a li'l smudge of somethun on yer lip, Pawson, dat da chilun ain't old enuf ta see," she laughed.

Dus blushed again. Karol giggled like a little girl. Her happiness was contagious. Nancy and Dus giggled with her. Tooter smiled and tooted.

# 20

Louis Casalano was a first-generation Italian American, a master carpenter, and Dus' childhood friend. They had grown up together and graduated in the same class in high school. They'd lost contact with each other through Dus' college and early priesthood years, but had rekindled their friendship during the visits when Dus went home from time to time to visit his parents. It was a joy for Dus to be able to attend family and high school reunions with "Lou," as he was known to his friends. Lou had married his high school sweetheart, Teresa Sarafani, after a tour in the Navy. They had raised three fine children.

Lou was a longtime fan of the Chicago Bears of the NFL. The only time he and Dus would argue was when the Bears played the Washington Redskins, Dus' lifelong favorite NFL team. Lou was a master carpenter and a foreman for a local construction company. He was also an excellent cook. When the construction business slacked off in the wintertime, he supplemented his income by cooking in local restaurants. He and Terry were not economically rich people, but through frugality and Terry's sporadic work in a local factory, they enjoyed a fine home and social life, and a wealth of friends and family. Their generosity to others was much admired and appreciated. They were a happy twosome, and Dus loved to get away and visit with them.

Lou and his family were active Roman Catholics, and generous supporters of the church in time, talent, and tithe. He and Dus used to have long discussions about the church and the changes in traditions and liturgy that neither were fond of in their similar, if not totally identical, liturgical doctrine. Lou liked to kid Dus that Episcopalians were, like some Milwaukee beers with less calories, "light Catholics." But the differences never divided them as friends, and they both would fret, "Why can't our bishops and like-minded reformers quit messing around with the holy church? Why do they feel compelled to fool around with a staunch institution like the church? If it ain't broke in, why fix it?" Lou would growl, "Church ought to be a stable haven for people in an unstable world, instead of being blown around like a reed by the modern winds of change. If the church is as unstable as the world, how can it offer peace and comfort to people whose lives are all screwed up?" Dus agreed with his carpenter friend.

Dus respected craftsmen and mechanics. He had a high regard for their spiritual insights and practical solutions to problems. Dus thought the Carpenter of Nazareth and his Italian carpenter friend had a lot in common. They both loved God, manifested his goodness, and both loved humanity. Lou and Terry had been a great strength to him when Ginnie and Dusty died. He loved them very much. Now he talked on the phone with his old friend. "Tonti saluti, Amico. How are you?"

"Hey, Father. How are you?"

"I'm good, Lou. Staying out of trouble. You doing OK with that cancer stuff?"

"I'm pretty good now. I have my ups and downs, but I'll make it, Paesano. How are things in the mountain? Not chasing the girls up there around the ridges, are you? Terry worries about you. Thinks you ought to get a lady in your life. She likes the Episcopal idea that priests can be married. I'd better not get ushered into the Kingdom too soon, or she might be chasing you all over that mountain herself!"

"Not to worry. I'm already taken."

"You're kidding, Amico. Got a gal, huh?"

"I think I do. Real nice lady, like Terry. She's not Italian American, but a Scandinavian, and a real American Indian beauty who says she loves this ol' Kraut. How about that? Sure want you two to meet her soon. You'd approve! She's a lady surgeon at the hospital in Staunton, and comes up here on weekends to volunteer her skills in the local government clinic. I met her last fall, and love just seemed to bloom."

"Sounds great. How does Elly like her?"

"Likes her, but doesn't know about our being in love yet. Her name is Karolina, and she's a widow with a teenage son Elly's age. He and Elly are good friends, too."

"Sounds good, buddy. Terry and I are happy for you. Hope you'll bring her up sometime and introduce her. Think she'll like Italian cuisine?"

"Sure she will, as long as Terry makes it, Paesano!"

"She will. Can hardly wait!"

"You sure you're doing OK, Lou? I worry about you and pray a lot for you. Hope you're taking care of yourself."

"I'm doing fine, Amico. Damn stuff gives me fits sometimes, but I'm a tough ol' buzzard. I trust the Lord, and I'm blessed with a good family, friends, priests, and doctors. Can't ask for more when fighting this debilitating stuff. Just keep praying, Father, and come see me. I miss you."

"Miss you, too. Monsignor Leon looking after you? Tell him I said, 'Hi.' Been missing him, too."

"Yeah, he's great, and we see lots of one another. He brings me Communion when I'm down. He's asked about you."

"You keeping a good Lent?"

"Sure. You know me—every morning to mass before work, and rosary every night. Just a habit from my altar boy days. Remember when you used to go to church with me when we were kids? You didn't know what the priest was saying in Latin."

"You didn't, either! They were great days, weren't they, Lou? I miss 'em."

"Me, too. Hey, Father, I know you didn't call me just to say 'Hi.' You have something on your mind other than my good health, don't you?"

"Shame on you for questioning my good intentions."

"I know you, Paesano. You're always into something. Jeez, do you remember some of the things we did? Remember the time we dug up all that concrete, put it into the dumpster, and covered it up with leaves, and the township garbage truck pretty nearly flipped over when the hydraulics tried to lift it? Boy, the troubles you used to get me into. Come on, Father. I can smell a plan of yours even two hundred miles away."

"Whatcha doing after Easter?"

"I knew I smelled one of your projects coming up. Terry and I are going to take a three-week vacation. We've earned it."

"How would you and Terry like to vacation with me?"

"She loves you, friend, but she's going to be mad as hell at you if you're planning a lot of work for me. She's selfish about my health."

"Is she around there?"

"Course she's here. Can hardly wait to talk to you. But you'd better be careful about mentioning things that she thinks will wear me out."

"Put her on."

"Just a sec."

"Hi, Father," a soft, gentle female voice said over the telephone. "How are you? I could hear you cooking up something with Lou. What are you up to?"

"Hi. How's the Sophia Loren of the Casalano clan?"

"Sweet-talker! I love it, but I know you are going to con me into something, aren't you?"

"Now, darlin', would I do that?"

"Yes, you old white-collared seducer."

"Terry, is Lou in the room?"

"No, he's gone to the bathroom."

"How's he doing? Be honest with me, dear heart."

"He's good and bad, Father Dus," Teresa said quietly into the phone, "but he is a fighter, and is in good spirits. I guess I take it harder than he does. He believes he will win this fight. You know he has been struggling with this ever since he had his operation seven years ago. It's been disappointing. The doctors thought they had it all then, but it metastasized and spread pretty badly. He's been through some rough chemotherapy sessions. Sometimes I get frightened that he is not going to make it. He really has great faith in God and medicine. He's still strong, though, and works hard at the construction company, where he is top foreman now. I don't know how he does it with the pain and all."

"He's always been tough and uncomplaining about the heavy work he has been doing all his life, Terry. Look what he did in the Navy!"

"I know, Father, but I love him so much, and I don't want to lose him. Pray for him and for me. I think it would be nice for him to come down there with you, if that is what you're asking. He is so stoic about all this. I think he needs to talk with someone he trusts, and to whom he can vent his feelings. You'd be good for him. I'll be glad to see him get away from here for a while. Whatever you're going to do, take good care of him, OK? He's coming back now, and I don't want him to hear me talking about that."

She raised her voice and said, "So tell me about this lovely Indian lady I overheard Lou alluding to on the phone. You've finally fallen in love? Tell me about Elly. I want to know what lovely gal is stealing my second-best boyfriend, and who's stealing my goddaughter."

"Elly's fine. I'll bring Karol by someday, and you can put your seal of approval on her, yourself. You'll love her, believe me!"

"If she makes you and Elly happy, Father, we're happy for you and can hardly wait to meet her. Love to Elly. Whatever you and Lou work out with his visit there is OK with me as long as you both take care. If you can take this old Pop off this old Mama's hands for a while, it'll be a blessed relief. I can use the rest. Well, he's standing here making me nervous, chomping on his pipe, wanting to talk to you some more. Love you, Father Dus. Thanks for calling. Arriverderci, Amico! Here's Lou again."

Lou came back on. "Had some luck with the Mama, eh, Amico?"

"She allowed whatever we decided to do."

"What do you want to do?"

"I'd like you to come down here for a couple of weeks after Easter and help me do some carpentry and masonry, and put some plumbing in my cabin. I need a bathroom, a kitchen renovation, and a septic system for Elly."

"Yo think you're going to do all that in a couple of weeks?"

"Sure. Why not?"

"You're crazy in the head! I know something about working time."

"We'll work fast. You don't want Elly, Shawn, and my new lady love sitting in a cold outhouse when nature calls, or having to pump water out of a well when they want to bathe, do you?"

"Well, I guess if you're talking necessity, I can give you a hand."

"How many days will you give me?"

"Tell you what. I'll take the three weeks' vacation. Give you two of them, and Terry, the other one. She won't want to come down there if all I am going to do is work. She'll come another time when you're not living like a stinking bear hunter in the wilderness. She likes comforts. She'll want to meet your lady later on and tell her all about your peculiar ways. Mine too, probably. You know how women like to exchange privy information on men. Anyway, Father, you get the materials up there, and I'll bring my tools down in my truck. Hope you have electricity!"

"No, not yet."

"The hell, you say! My tools are all electric. I don't whittle and hone anymore, Dus. I guess I'd better bring my portable generator, too."

"That'll be great, Lou. I'll have the ditch and septic hole dug before you get here, and all the material in place. We'll use PVC and copper pipe. When the power people get some electric lines up here from the road, I'm gonna light up my house and church, and have an electric pump in that old well. I can wire this place myself in the meantime. Just need you to help with the bathroom and kitchen carpentry construction. Sure appreciate your willingness to come!"

"How can I turn down a begging priest, Paesano? Never have found a way to keep you guys from picking my pockets and my talents. I'll see you in the spring. Keep me informed about the progress and when you want me there. I'll look forward to it. Give me something positive to think about. Don't worry about Terry. She likes me to stay busy. Anyway, she thinks you're good for me. Want you to know, old friend, you are. Thank you for asking me to come. It will be fun to do something together again after all these years. Hope you are doing a good Lent. We all need it. Have a happy Easter! Love you, Amico! Ciao!"

"I'm trying. It's harder for me. I get into more trouble than you do with the Lord. Happy Easter to you and Terry, and your family, too. Arriverderci, Lou! Love you. Take good care of yourself, and, please, if you don't feel up to it, don't come. You know I would not want you to go down."

"I'll be there, Father. Keep me in your prayers, and say hello to your sweetheart."

Dus could detect a little quivering and sniffing in Lou's voice. "Of course! Take care! Ciao, again," Dus said, and hung up the telephone. Tears welled up in his eyes. "Gosh, I cry a lot these days," he confessed out loud. "So much happiness and so much pain all at the same time. Here's Kara, that beautiful, vivacious, fine lady, given to me almost as some kind of unmatched gift, who has stirred my soul to a happiness nearly unimaginable, which makes me weep, but then the thought that my lifelong, good, and generous buddy is in such pain and maybe going to die breaks my heart and makes me weep, too. It seems there are no answers to all of this. Karol's right when she says it's OK for men to cry. Karol shouldn't have had to be the one to remind me that even Jesus wept for his friend, too." Imagine such a thing, Dus thought, recalling the scripture. The shortest sentence in the whole Bible, he remembered, simply says, "Jesus wept." That is a comfort. How good it is to feel deeply for others, Dus admitted to himself. It's just plain nuts not to cry when you love so much. He wiped his eyes with his shirtsleeve and said, "Thank you, Lord, for Karol, Lou, and Terry. You've been very good to me, and I'm sorry I have been such an ingrate. Will you forgive me?"

He was startled when he imagined he heard a female voice from heaven that sounded a lot like Kara's say, "Yeah." He smiled and said, "Oh, no."

# 21

Lent, as a penitential season, except for his own discipline of prayer, fasting, and reading, was not taking up a lot of Dus' time. The week preceding Palm Sunday had been pretty routine for him. He had walked and driven all over the mountain, visiting, counseling, and praying with people. He took Tooter on some hikes and rides, and made plans for the vicarage renovation.

Today, he sat at his desk in his office writing notes for a homily and fantasizing about his beloved Kara in all her glorious dimensions. The morning had been full of telephone calls. Kara, who had devised a before-lunch, telephone time frame for them to talk, had not yet called. Dus had not seen her since the weekend of the village dance, and missed her more than he anticipated. The dance had occasioned an even greater intimacy between them. He smiled and reminisced about that fun-filled village party.

As he promised her, Dus had taken Karol at noon before the dance to Jed Hudson's store for a new dress appropriate for square dancing. Helen Hudson, enjoying the opportunity, helped Karol pick out a pretty, puff-sleeved, red-and-white polka-dotted button-down peasant blouse, with a full, calf-length flowing red corduroy skirt. It was perfect for her. While she was trying it on and Helen was tucking and sizing it for her, Dus and Jed talked.

"Well, Father Dus, you can be very honored that you have been invited to the dance by Bessie Clayton, the queen of the ball, as I and many gentlemen would say. She is a lovely lady, and the best dancer on the mountain. She has broken many a heart, including mine. We who grew up with that lovely lady and who remember her from our youth knew her as the prettiest and most vivacious girl in town."

"She's a handsome woman even to this very day, Jed," Dus agreed.

"She is, indeed, and there is many a bachelor and widower whose hearts were broken, wanting her to marry them. She is a wonderful cook, and does well with her added catering service."

"How did Bessie's husband die?"

"He just disappeared. Never found his body. Bessie was devastated. We all were. There was a short hunt around the mountain. Bessie didn't blame anyone for his vanishing, but she grieved for years. It was an embarrassment to her, so the word got out that he fell down a mine shaft. Finally, with the help of the community and all of us who loved her, she pulled herself together, and she's been fine ever since. She had done very well with her restaurant, and does considerable charity work. She sponsors a day-care center for mothers around town who have to work outside their homes. She wanted children, but she has none of her own, God bless her. She loves them, and they adore her. She would have been a natural mother. In a way, I think, the center fills up her motherly instincts by enabling her to do things for the children around this town. She has many a birthday party for them. But, her life aside, Father, I don't know how good a dancer you are, but you are in for a real treat when you dance with her. You'll not get many dances, mind you, because all the men will be wanting to take her for a whirl. Including me! But then, look at that lovely doctor there, looking at us in that pretty getup. You won't want to leave her alone too much at the dance, either. I'd sure be pleased to dance with her, too."

Karol had smiled at Jed. "Be happy to oblige, Jed, if Helen doesn't mind."

"I don't mind. He dances till he wears me out. I'm glad to get the break," Helen had agreed. She had nicely fulfilled the assignment of getting Karol ready for the big Joshuatown social occasion.

The dance had been so much fun with her, Dus fantasized. He and Karol had met a lot of nice folk and, true to her word, Bessie had cut in on Karol and stolen Dus away as her partner for the Virginia Reel, which had left Dus so exhausted that he could hardly find the energy to dance with Nancy Conley, Helen Hudson, nor Patty Kirsh.

"Wow!" he had exclaimed to Karol afterward. "These people, old and young, have tremendous stamina to dance as they do." He had "do-si-doed, left and right, and grand circled" with Karol all evening, twirling her about, catching her hand and waist and maneuvering her in and out, puffing and sighing, believing he would surely have a heart attack. Karol seemed inexhaustible, laughing continuously. Her joy, as Bessie's, was contagious, and the people laughed with her. The village folk had noticed Karol and Dus' affection for one another, as Karol had predicted, and seemed to approve. Who would not approve of her? She loved them, healed their wounds, and was gentle, kind, and friendly to everyone she met. What a tireless, exuberant, and vivacious girl she was, he thought. Plain fun, and a joy to be with at such a social affair. He felt honored to have been her partner for that evening. She was exquisite in her new dress, and cute in her red-and-white bobby socks tucked into scuffed blue-and-white saddle shoes, most appropriate for the occasion. She was greatly appreciated by ogling village men. With her long, dark, straight hair pulled back in braided pigtails tied with red-and-white bows, she reminded Dus of a teenager on her first date. Had one not known, it would have been hard for him to believe she was a skilled surgeon, with a teenage child of her own. It was hard for even Dus to believe that a woman of such beauty, talent, and intellect, who garnered so much respect and so many accolades from these simple mountain people, would want to give her love to him. Fantastic, he said to himself. And though I am hardly deserving, I accept her as a great gift from God.

The phone rang again, interrupting his thoughts. Sheriff Kirsh, who started calling Dus by his first name as their mutual camaraderie developed over the months, spoke. "Hi, Dus. How are you?"

"I'm fine, Scott. How's the family?"

"All good, but we'll all be glad when winter is over. Patty and the kids have house fever; they're tired of soaked clothes, sniffles, and gloomy days. Want to tell you that we sure did enjoy seeing you and the doc at the dance. Lots of fun, wasn't it? Good-looking couple, I must say! Ought to arrest the two of you for overexposure and stealing all the attention. She sure is a beauty, and a nice person. Patty loves her. My wife is pretty perceptive, and she thinks you two have something going on between you, the way you look at and hold each other. Is there something between you two, Father?"

"Well, now, Sheriff, I don't know that how Dr. Marson and I dance together, nor our alliance, is the business of the long arm of the law," Dus laughed, "but you might find out if you should catch us buzzing in my jeep in a 'No Parking Zone' some night. She's a beauty, as you say. Wouldn't mind at all if she thought I had been a pretty good date and asked me out again."

"Who? Karol or Bessie? Talk about a dancing beauty. Boy, oh boy, that Bessie, for her years, is something else! Did I understand you to say that Karol asked you to the dance?"

"Of course. What do you think?"

"I think you are fibbing through your teeth to the police, and you asked her to go to the dance."

"Caught me, Sheriff. So I did. Do you blame me?"

"Oh, I don't blame you, but why would a classy girl like her want to go out with a dour preacher who's bent on getting himself in trouble?"

"You aren't very nice this morning. Did Patty burn your toast and eggs, or give you cold coffee or something? And, by the way, not to let it pass, Karol nudged me a few times at the dance to take note of you and Patty. Talk about a beautiful girl with a so-so guy. You're lucky, trooper, I'd say. You two were drawing a bit of attention, yourselves."

"Yeah, she's a great gal, wife, and mother. God has been good to me. I am a blessed man, Dus, and I know it.

"Indeed, you are. What's on your mind, Scott?"

"Just wondering if you've been snooping around the mountains or into caves lately. Have you seen or heard anything we can talk about? I keep thinking about Ox getting hurt. I don't like it. How's he doing?"

"He's doing well. Karol called me yesterday to tell me that professor friend of ours from Penn State, who wears a prosthesis on both legs, himself, was down recently and spent a lot of time with Ox, teaching him how to handle crutches and how to walk with his artificial leg. She thinks he will be in good enough shape to come home before Easter. That will do his family's spirits a lot of good."

"Be good to see the fine man around town again," Scott said. "People in these parts are very fond of him."

"Well, there is someone who isn't, Sheriff, and I want you to find him."

"You don't know that yet, Dus. That's still pure conjecture. We'll find out in due time if there is someone involved. Remember my admonition. I don't want to find out you've been doing things I warned you not to do. And I repeat, I don't want to hear about our doctor friend being involved, either. You understand what I am saying, Father?"

"What makes you think she is or wants to be?"

"Patty knows how much Karol is hurting over Ox. They both had a little female crying spell together over that bad business. Karol is an angry Indian lady, and she could get into things she ought not to. I want you to keep her from doing that."

"Don't worry, Scott. Karol isn't involved. I do, however, want to pass on to you something she told me."

"What's that?"

"Did you hear about the dog she gave me?"

"Yeah, Patty told me about it. I understand she's a bit unbearable at times."

"She is, but no matter. When Karol, Shawn, and the dog were coming up the mountain, there was a crew of men working on the highway removing a tree. She had to stop and wait for them to push it and the debris across the road. She didn't recognize them, but she said they seemed to know her. They were amiable and wished her a good day."

"That was nice, so why is that so strange?"

"It's not, but Tooter didn't like their looks, and snarled at them. Karol said they glared at Tooter."

"I'd glare at her, too, if she snarled at me."

"Karol also thought it was strange that they were piling all that tree debris in front of the entrance to a road. She said the tree looked like it had been cut down by an axe, and had not fallen by itself."

"Observant, lady. Did she say whether there was a state or county truck around, or if the men were wearing hard hats?"

"She noticed that they had no identifiable clothes or vehicles that would indicate they were any sort of state or county workers."

"I'll check it out, but don't you two get paranoid about everything you hear and see. She wasn't upset, was she?"

"No, just interested."

"Good. Tell her we said 'Hi.' Have you seen any smoke spirals up in the Cutty recently?"

"Saw some a couple of days ago. I guess there are some hunters camping up there. They must get cold up there in weather like this. Why do you ask?"

"Hunters, eh? It's not hunting season. They are 'moonshine' producers, with their coils brewing and tubs cooking. You stay away from them, Father, lest you get your tail end wounded again. I don't want to see you get hurt. Please remember what I told you about those kind of people. The Feds from Treasury, popularly known among the mountain folk as the 'revnooers,' work with me on keeping the 'moonies' in check. They're our problem, not yours. Let the law handle things in these parts."

"I will, Scott, but let me know if you sniff out anything about Ox's accident. I'll not give you cause to be angry with me. I love Ox, too, but no way will I let Karol get hurt."

"OK, Dus, and thanks. I appreciate that and trust you. It'll come together one day. Take care of yourself. Come on down to Bessie's and have some chili with me sometime. She makes the best in Virginia. So long!"

"So long, Scott, and keep warm. Love to Patty. Guess I'll see her in the clinic when Karol gets back," Dus said, as he hung up the telephone and immediately dialed Bishop Mueller's office.

"Good morning, the Episcopal Diocese. May I help you?" the nice voice of the diocesan receptionist said.

"Yes, Katie. This is Father Habak. I wonder if I might speak to the bishop. It's important."

"Hi, Father! How are things in the mountains these days? Nice to hear your voice. I'll patch you over to the bishop's secretary. Bye!"

Bishop Mueller answered the phone, himself. It cheered Dus to have direct access to the kind, gentle voice that said, "Hello, Dus. How are you? I haven't heard from you for a while. Been missing you. Mrs. Mueller asked about you just the other day."

"Hello, Bishop. Well, it's Lent, and I have been trying to stay out of trouble."

"I should hope so. What can I do for you? Are you getting along with the folk up there? Are you being nice to the lady physician? And how's Mr. Conley? Sorry about that, Dus. I know he and his family have become good friends of yours. We keep him in our prayers. And Dus, on the q.t., if they need a little help with the medical bills, I can help with my discretionary fund."

"Thanks. I appreciate that. The mission is doing OK with more and more folk coming to services and Bible class. I've gotten to know lots of people, and they are a good bunch. Ox is doing very well and might get home before Easter. It's been a bummer for him and his family, but light is beginning to shine. He has lots of friends who care for them and who will help them. The lady doctor is fine, too. I got off on a wrong start with her, as you know, but we have a good relationship now, since I have my office here. I have come to know her as a good person, and a competent doctor, who is much beloved by the people. You would not believe the amount of care she gives them in the few short days she is here. She's a good friend to everyone."

"How friendly is she with you?"

"I think she is beginning to like me a lot better. At least she acts like it. Why?"

"You said you have developed a good relationship with her. I was wondering how good."

"I don't mean to be disrespectful, your Grace, but just a few minutes ago I just told a nosy county sheriff that he had no business snooping into my relationship with Dr. Marson. I would not want to say that to my bishop. There must be some privy things that don't need to be reported to either lawmen or bishops."

"Son, if you're that edgy about me asking, there must be something happening with you. I wasn't born yesterday, Father. I'm not nosing, and you don't have to tell me anything privy, but don't forget that I talk to my little surrogate granddaughter under my charge, and she has told me some interesting things about her daddy and a certain Dr. Marson."

"Why, the little gossiper. I'll have to remind her it is not nice to be talking about private family matters. How much did she tell you?"

"Just that the doctor's interest in her dad may not be all that medical nor platonic, and that you and the lady hike a lot, hold hands, and look 'dreamy-eyed' at each other."

"I'll tan her fanny for that kind of talk."

"You'll do no such thing. I'm on her side. She seems to approve, and apparently has come to like Doctor Marson pretty much. I am glad if you're building some kind of a friendly relationship with a lady friend, Dus. I want you to have happiness in your life, and if there is a lady who gives you some of that, I already like her. Let me know how things develop. Maybe you should bring her around to meet me sometime. I'd like that."

"We haven't developed our relationship enough to make plans, but we do get along, and it's fun for both of us. She is a widow with a child, and we have some things in common. You'd like her. Your kind of woman. The Conleys and the doctor are friends, too, and have helped us to come to terms with our differences. Elly and Shawn, her son, get along, too, and that makes it nice. I'll bring her by to meet you one day. She's threatened to talk to you about my shameful ways, anyway."

"Good. I'm glad there is someone keeping you on the straight and narrow up there in the wilderness, out of my control. On the other hand, from what Elly tells me, maybe Dr. Marson is the one I ought to keep tabs on if she's leading my priest astray."

Dus laughed. "Don't worry, Bishop. She says she is as pure as the driven sn—" Dus stammered, regretting the words the second he said them.

"Are you there, Dus? Are you there? What's happened to the line?"

"It's OK, Bishop. I'm here. I should not have said that. Please don't ever repeat that I said that. She's an Indian, and would not like it that I said that. She's a very old-fashioned kind of gal with old-fashioned scruples, and wouldn't like me joking about privy things with anyone. Not even bishops."

"Don't worry, Dus. I don't repeat things. Glad to have a scrupulous person watching over my shepherd as he tends the sheep. All kidding aside, I am happy for you, and if there ever comes a time for you two to talk to me about your future, feel free. Do you feel comfortable about the time between Ginnie's death and your feelings about Doctor Marson?"

"Not entirely, but we have talked about that. Love has a way of blossoming that makes one enjoy the freshness of it, putting past times and events into perspective. I feel very deeply about Ginnie, and Karol's love does not negate the life and love we had. There is no way to get Ginnie's approval, but I believe that God will let me know somehow. I want to do the right thing, but love 'is a many splendored thing.' Karol and I want to do the right thing, and we won't move into a permanent relationship until we are sure of the past and the well-being of the children. What do you think?"

"I think you are adults, and you are being sensible. I say go for it. As far as I knew her, I think Ginnie would feel OK about you and Dr. Marson. But you are like a son to me, Dus, and I want you to be happy. I'll love whoever you love."

"Thanks, Bishop. I'll let you know as things develop, if they do. In the meantime, I called to ask you a big favor."

"Is it about the plumbing and electrical renovations at the rectory?"

"Yes."

"I've been working on it, as I promised, Dus."

"Thanks, Bishop. What do you have for me?"

"I'll tell you what I've done so far, Dus, and you can handle it from here on. I've found some money to help you with the project, but over and above that, there is a member of St. Chads on the Diocesan Finance Committee who owns a wholesale plumbing and electrical supply business here in the city. He sells directly to contractors. I spoke privately about your needs up there, and he wants to help. You can have all the small plumbing and electrical supplies you need, for free. He'll give the big stuff to the diocese at his cost. He said if you would make up a list of the material and call it into his warehouse manager, he'll load it on a truck and send it up there. How's that?"

"Terrific, Bishop. I appreciate it. Tell the gentleman I'm grateful. I'll call in the list right away. I'd like to start after Easter."

"Boy, you don't waste time, do you? I also had a talk with a Catholic layman at our ecumenical board meeting. He is a vice president of Ace Coal Mining Company, which has one of their strip operations at Bear Creek, south of Joshuatown. You know the place?"

"Sure do! Know a man who works there. It's just out of town. What about it?"

"Well, he said that if you're good at running equipment, he has a front-end loader with a backhoe that, according to his foreman, will be idle for a while. If you think you can handle it, you're welcome to use it as long as you need to. I told him you had experience with such equipment. Isn't that right?"

"Sure is, Bishop. I learned to use heavy equipment long ago. Tell that man he is an angel in disguise."

"He's far from being an angel, but I told him we'd appreciate anything his company could do to help. He said his foremen would load it on a cat carrier and haul it up for you. You get in touch with a Mr. Foley at the Bear Creek operation as soon as you can, and he'll take care of you. Good luck, Dus."

"Thanks for all your help. I do need to make a home for Elly with a few modern facilities."

"Just for Elly, eh? We'll see," Bishop Mueller laughed. "You're welcome, Dus. Before I go, do you have time to listen to a clergy story?"

"Sure!"

"Harvey Kendle, a bishop friend of mine, who was consecrated the same year as I was and sits next to me in the House of Bishops, talks a lot on the phone, discussing issues, clergy, and such. I was telling him about one of my priests wanting to build something in the mountain, and about the equipment you are going to use."

"What about it?"

"He said he had a priest, who shall remain nameless, whose congregation was building a parish house in some plantation town. This priest, like you, boasted that he was an expert with hydraulic digging equipment. So, one day, after the construction workers went home, he borrowed their backhoe without permission, mind you, to dig up some big bushes he didn't like around the front of the rectory. You know what the braggart did?"

"What?" Dus asked, beginning to think the story might not be so funny.

"First, he dug up and severed a water line that blew a geyser like Old Faithful. Excited by that fiasco, he whirled the hoe around and knocked the whole corner off the rectory living room. His wife, who had been reading on the couch, got up, looked out the new portal in her house, and calmly said to her wet, trembling, and embarrassed clergy husband, 'Dear, if you did not like the front door as it was, why didn't you speak to the vestry? Other than the fact that you have now made a carpeted Jacuzzi out of our living room, destroyed a bookcase full of my best classics, and sent your children into hysteria, you damn near killed your long-suffering wife. If you want to get rid of me, please go through the proper legal channels, but in the meantime, for the love of God, get the devil off that steam shovel before I have you arrested for wife and child abuse, desecration of church property, unlawful waste of the water supply of the city and county, and operating a deadly weapon without a license or union card!' Harvey said the poor priest had a miserable time explaining that faux pas to the vestry, the Borough Council, the city and county, to his bishop, and to the Executive Committee of the Diocese. Hurt and humiliated, he vowed never to lift a hammer or saw for the good of the church again, anywhere. He was furious at his wife, the vestry, and his bishop. Harvey said he built a nice parish house, though, and had a good ministry there, but has since left his diocese and doesn't know where he is, nor whether his wife still loves him."

Dus, listening to his bishop, guffawing and laughing to himself, managed to stutter, "The poor guy! That's awful, but it is funny. I suspect that the moral of that tale is that you don't want to hear that same disturbing story coming out of the Blue Mountains about me. Do I have that right, your Lordship?"

"You've got it right, Father," the bishop admonished. "And I don't want to hear about your getting hurt, either. You have a reputation for being accident-prone, even if you are a good mechanic. Well, God bless you, Dus. Keep me informed, and give my best to your lady friend. Hope things work out for you both, if that's the direction you're going. Say 'hello' to the folk up there. I'd like to visit the mission one day soon. Have a good Holy Week and a glorious Easter."

"Would love to have you visit, Bishop. Good-bye, and thanks for everything. I'll let you know how things go. Love to Mrs. Mueller, and have a nice Easter, yourself."

It was five after twelve noon, and no sooner had he hung up the telephone, when it rang again. He knew who it was and sheepishly said, "Good afternoon. This is the Joshuatown health clinic and Habak's pool room. Eight ball speaking. To which department would you like me to direct your questions?"

"Listen, smarty Preacher," said a miffed Karol. "I've been ringing you for fifteen minutes and got nothing but busy signals. I'm a busy girl, and need some food before I go back to surgery, so I don't have a lot of time to waste on gabby priests."

"Is that you, Doctor Marson? I would not have recognized your voice had you not talked of being busy and wanting food. What can the holy church do to administer to one of the lost sheep of Staunton Memorial?"

"You sure were on the phone a long time. Any of my business who you were commiserating with?"

"No, and watch your attitude. This is still Lent, you know."

"I'm sorry, darling. I know your conversations are privy. I was just kidding. Just called to tell you I love you, miss you, and won't be able to get up there until Holy Thursday. I can stay through Easter Monday, then. I have only a few minutes to talk now before I go back to surgery. I really don't need to eat. Got plenty of pounds of Nancy's cooking on me. You'll be calling me a fat squaw, if I'm not careful."

"I'll call you nothing but 'beautiful.' I love you, too, Kara, and miss you a lot. It's good to hear your voice. If you need to know, I was talking to my boss."

"How is the good bishop? Is he pleased with your ministry?"

"Didn't say, but he's made arrangements for the stuff I need for the plumbing and electrical work at the vicarage. I'm grateful for that."

"That's wonderful, Dus. When will you start?"

"After Easter. Hope to have it done by the time Elly gets back for summer vacation. She needs some comforts."

"That'll be nice. I want you to know, I think I might need them up there in the future, too!"

"That sounds encouraging, but I thought you liked the old-fashioned, rugged Indian life of holes in the outhouse and the behind-the-bush bathroom style. But now that I know different, it'll make the project even more urgent. I have a longtime friend, who is a great carpenter, coming to help me. You'll like Lou Casalano and his wife, Teresa, and they'll love you. I told them all about you. Anyway, we think we can do it in a couple of weeks."

"I'd like to meet them. Well, don't hurt yourselves nor work too hard. I don't want to have to sew either of you up in the clinic."

"To change the subject, there is a sheriff here who told me we made a handsome-looking couple at the square dance, and who wanted to know if we had anything going on between us. He said Patty and he noticed we were kind of chummy and googly-eyed."

"Sweet guy, old Scott. What did you tell him?"

"That it was not any of the law's business."

Karol laughed over the telephone and said, "That's telling off the law, partner. I don't know whether he was right about me, but I thought you were a pretty cute wheeler and trotter. It was fun, wasn't it? Didn't I tell you people would guess, if we looked amorous?"

"I wasn't amorous, but could have been. You were so incredibly pretty in your buttons and bows. I was really proud that folk knew you were my date."

"Wow, Father. You know just the right things to say to a country gal. Thank you! I have a feeling that's not all the sheriff talked to you about. Anything more?"

"Yes. He reminded me to keep my nose and your nose out of the business of the law. We are not to snoop around the mountains this time of the year. More especially, he mentioned he did not want you involved in the thing with Ox and me. He said that if there was anything to it, it was his job to take care of it, not yours, nor mine."

"Oh, poo on the law. The law had better start doing something about it soon. What did you tell Scott about my involvement?"

"I told him you weren't involved, and you're not."

"I'm not going to argue with you, darling. I love you too much, and I can't get mad at a policeman who thinks I'm pretty. Thanks for telling me all that nice stuff."

"You're welcome, Ollikut."

"Please, Dus, I asked you not to call me that."

"Just thought you needed some humbling for the next missive I'm sending you."

"What are you talking about?"

"The bishop knows about us, too!"

"Why, you gabby preacher! I thought we decided we were going to wait before we opened up our hearts to the public."

"Well, you didn't mind folk ogling us at the dance!"

"That's different. They're sorta kinfolk, now. The bishop doesn't need to know every aspect of your life, does he?"

"That's what I told him. Anyway, Kara, it was not I who told him about us. It was Elly."

Karol laughed. "You're kidding. What did she tell him?"

"Something like she saw us going hiking, holding hands, and snuggling together, and that I had 'dreamy eyes' ever since I met you."

"She's cute. So she's been noticing us. I wonder if Shawn has, too. Do you have 'dreamy eyes' since you met me, Father? I haven't noticed."

"Probably! I can't help myself."

"Neither can I," she giggled. "And what were the bishop's thoughts about those trivial snippets of our budding love life?"

"He did say, and this should please you, that Elly really likes you a lot, that she found a friend in Shawn, and that she is happy to see her daddy happy. The bishop said he is happy for her daddy, too. I talked to him about the fact that we are taking it all very slowly, discerning what is right for the kids, and contemplating our attachments of the past. He wants us to be sure we have given Ginnie and your husband thoughtful consideration, but thinks this is the right move if we are content with it and in love. He wished us God's blessings on any decision we make about our lives. He invited me to bring you to visit him. He loves me, and he's been like a father to me. He's going to love you."

"Thank you, darling. He sounds nice, and I do want to meet him. Did you tell him some nice things about me?"

"Well, he did ask me if there had been a recurrence of our first meeting."

"Like what?"

"I think he wanted to be sure that you were not working on my heinie anymore."

"Dus Habak, for crying out loud! Is there nothing sacred with you?" she screamed through the phone. "Why didn't you tell him the whole truth about that episode?"

"I love to keep bishops and Indian women on edge," he kidded. "I did tell him the truth. It's just his way of teasing me. Anyway, I told him that he was not to worry, because, and I'd better tell you this before he does, you had assured me you were 'as pure as the driven snow.'"

"You told him that?" Karol chided him. "Are you clergy a bunch of gossipers? I thought you 'holier-than-thou' chaps were supposed to keep confidences. Darned if I'm going to say personal things to you anymore, blabbermouth."

"Don't get so huffy, Injun. I was just trying to impress him with your virtue. He said that he was glad I knew someone with scruples and morals to keep me from going astray. He also wondered if you might be leading his priest astray. Anyway, that's all the hot gossip out of the diocesan office."

"I should think so! Anyway, before I lead you astray today, I have to go back to work. I love you. Fun talking. I'll call tomorrow about the same time, and will let you know about Ox's trip home and my plans. And Dus?"

"Yes, honey?"

"In case you didn't know, I was only kidding. I love your bishop already. Sounds like a good friend and father in God. Maybe he will become a surrogate father to me someday. Tell him I want to meet him soon. He's probably anxious to meet someone 'as pure as the driven snow,' since he sees so few of those types at clergy conferences. Thanks for loving me, 'dreamy eyes.' Dream about me. Want to tell you just one more thing before I go."

"What is it, sweetheart?"

"Lent has really helped me with my spiritual life. I have to confess, I have been reading the Bible and prayer book for a while. I really feel like I'm getting to know God better than I did for a long time. I haven't said this to anyone, but I really think God and I are beginning to communicate a lot more than we used to. I think he does love me, and I love him. Anyway, Father Habak, God and I are going to talk a little more on Palm Sunday and during Holy Week about all this stuff I'm feeling these days. I've been talking to him about you. He knows I love you and that you love me, but he seems to be holding out with answers for our future. Says to be patient. I said I would be, but not for long. I probably shouldn't talk to him like that."

"Interesting conversations you're having, honey. I'm happy about you two getting together. Of course he loves you. He always has. Why would he not love a gorgeous creature of his own making, like you? So do I. How can either one of us help ourselves? You're such a neat, beautiful, and giving person, if irascible sometimes. And, if I can handle the way you talk to me, I'm sure God is big enough to handle your bantering with him."

"Thank you, my love. I adore you, even if I am irascible. Bye!"

"Bye, Kara. I love you. Take care, and come back to me soon!" Dus sort of shouted to her as they both hung up the phone. His heart sang, and he bowed his head. "Lord, you have been so good to me today." And, quoting a part of an old litany, he said, "'Lord, I am not worthy to come under thy roof, but say the word only and my soul shall be healed.'"

He put on his coat and walked out into the cold. He thought he would take Tooter and walk about the valley, and visit with people along the way. It is a very cold day, he thought, but talking to the bishop and Kara makes me feel so warm, I hardly feel it.

He walked down to the post office to see if a package of palm leaves had arrived for his Palm Sunday church service. They had come, and it made him feel even warmer to know that his life and ministry were going well. Then he looked up in the Cutty Mountains and saw smoke spirals. He thought about what Scott had told him about the moonshiners, and decided the smoke spirals would not ruin his day. He vowed nothing would ruin his day—not as long as he had a lady "as pure as the driven snow." And God and the bishop loved her, and wanted her to make him happy.

# 22

Palm Sunday arrived. During the Eucharist, Dus had a short liturgy of Blessing the Palms, and then he distributed them to the people in the congregation.

"Christians do this," he explained, "because it is the beginning of Holy Week and the day Jesus rode into Jerusalem. Many people believed he was the Messiah, the true messenger of God, and they threw palm leaves before him as a way of honoring him. The palm leaves we have here this morning are a simple way of reminding us of that event. We must remember, however, that in this week before Easter, Jesus was not only hailed by some of the people as 'King,' but later was called a blasphemer and a liar; many people saw him as a great danger to Rome and their own concept of God, and wanted him out of the way. It was in this week that he ate his Last Supper with his friends. It was an important gathering, when he likened the bread and wine to his own body and blood and asked them to have many of these kinds of suppers after his death to remember him. That is what the Eucharist is. It is the Last Supper, done over and over again, to remind us that Christ sacrificed his body and blood for us. When we bless this bread and wine, it mysteriously becomes his body and blood. When we eat the bread and drink from the cup, we believe that he is mysteriously present with us, and spiritually nourishes our body, souls, and minds. Of course, there is a lot of other theological stuff about this, but for now, just understand that every time I call you to worship here and we have Holy Communion, it is Jesus' Last Supper with his disciples and his sacrifice on the cross we are remembering."

Dus paused to see if he was making any impact with his little group of worshipers. The people's faces had not changed, but he sensed they understood what he was saying, at least a little bit.

"I was hoping, that at about five-thirty Thursday afternoon, even if it is a bit cold, you might bring some friends and come here before your regular supper to worship with me and join in the recalling of Jesus' Last Supper. There will no preaching this time—just some Bible lessons, prayers, and the Lord's bread and wine. It will be just a simple celebration of his breaking bread with his friends the night before he died. I wondered, then, if you might come again on Friday night before supper to pray and to talk about Jesus' death on the cross and why he did that for us. We all love Easter, and we should, because it is a glorious and hopeful day when we celebrate Jesus' overcoming death and promising us eternal life. But it is equally important that we be reminded that before Easter, Jesus suffered for us and died for us. It is good for us to recall Good Friday, as well as Easter. Easter was not for free. Christ had to die to make it possible, so we mustn't ignore the day he died. So that's why I plan to have services here this week for our prayers and worship. If you can make the effort to come, I know God will be pleased. It will be meaningful to you, too. You'll find it a blessing and a good experience because Eucharist means 'Thanksgiving.' It is the sacrament that shows our appreciation for the sacrifice Jesus made. In it, we offer up ourselves, with all that we have and all that we are, in gratitude. That is bound to make him and us happier. Thank you all so much for coming today. Take the palms home with you and hang them someplace in your house to remind you how much God loves you. It is just a little symbol, like a picture or a nicely designed quilt. I'd like to end with this note. If you cannot be here for service on Good Friday, visualize our Lord on the cross in your prayers. The cross is a very great Christian symbol because it not only reminds us of what the sins of people did and do to God, but especially what God was willing to do for us in forgiveness. Good Friday is as simple as that. Just meditate on that simplicity this week as you prepare for the great Easter celebration."

    He went on with the Communion, finished the service, and greeted the people at the door. They were friendly and kind, and said that they appreciated his message and understood a little more about why the church had Communion, but no one made a commitment for Thursday and Friday services. Some said they would see him "next Sunday," which was not a good omen for his Holy Week schedule. That did not discourage him. He had come to believe that only the Lord can persuade folk to worship, whatever the occasion. There were a lot of things that Dus was leaving to the Lord. These people simply would allow themselves to be shepherded, but not herded like sheep and cattle. Jesus was a shepherd who led and folded the sheep, and hoped they would follow. He never sent dogs out to nip at their back legs if they didn't. I have to keep on remembering that, he told himself, as he turned off the church stove and shut the door. I might just be learning more from God from these folk than I am teaching them. Somehow, I'm beginning to feel the bishop sent me here to learn some things about God and people, as well as to teach them. Well, we will see what will happen this week. Anyway, Elly and Kara will be here, Ox will be coming home, and it will be a good week no matter what happens with church attendance. I shall leave that in God's hands.

Then he knelt with one knee in the snow and prayed, "Lord, I tried, and I do want it to be a good week in our little mission here. I hope they will come and remember this was an important week for you. But I have to trust that your Holy Spirit will move their hearts. They are good hearts, Lord, as you well know, and I have come to love them, too. If you could make me as guileless as they are, maybe I wouldn't feel I had to try so hard. Well, it's your church, and not mine. They are your people, and you know better what's good for them than I do. I don't mean to tell you what to do and impose my ideas on you, nor them, but I ask you to take good care of them, and keep them safe, steadfast, and in love with one another. And please, Lord, help them to know I'm not picking on them when I tell them that worshipping you in your church is a good thing for them. Amen."

Dus imagined he heard a voice from heaven saying, "Now donna ya wor'y none, Dus, boy. I'll take car' of 'em. Ya jest do yer job, en I'll do mine! Jest stay outta tr'uble wid da law, and know I blessed ya wid bootiful Karol." The voice startled him. It sounded like a hierarchical admonition of Bishop Mueller mixed with the mountain colloquial chiding of an Ox Conley, if not a Doctor Marson. "Gosh," he said out loud, "this place is getting to me."

And the voice said, "Wal, 'tis 'bout time!"

# 23

It was now Easter Monday evening. Father Habak was sitting in front of the fire, with Tooter sleeping at his feet. He basked in the remembrance of the past months. He had once believed that when Ginnie and Dusty died, his life was nearly over, and that when the bishop brought him into his office and decided to send him to the mountain, he thought he was being sent into exile. He had been wrong about both, as he had been wrong about so many things the past two years since that awful tragedy in his and Elly's life. The ache, the pain, the self-doubts, and the humiliation had all but disappeared, and now, as he sat contemplating the last four days of Holy Week and Easter, he had known joy that was inconceivable to him several months ago.

Karol had arrived on Thursday afternoon, bringing Ox home from the hospital with her. It had been a wonderful reunion at the Conley house. Ox had walked hesitantly with his crutches on his new artificial leg from Karol's car to greet his family waiting for him at the front door. They had welcomed him with hugs, tears, kisses, and laughter that embarrassed the big man. Dus had arranged to be there when they arrived, but after shaking Ox's hand and hugging his neck, he and Karol stood hand in hand watching the happy family reunion. Tears flowed from everyone's eyes. Dus and Karol could not speak for several minutes, nor give each other any attention until the Conleys had closed the door to their home. They had discreetly said "No, no" to Ox's and Nancy's invitation to sup with them and the children, thinking it would be better for the family to be alone and just enjoy the homecoming.

Besides, Karol and Dus were a bit anxious for a greeting of their own, and that included a walk to the cabin, a sloppy kiss from Tooter, hot coffee, lots of hugs and kisses, and talk and banter in front of the roaring fireplace.

Karol had spent most of the daylight hours in the clinic, except on Easter Day, when they both spent time with the Conleys and with one another. Elly had not come home for Easter, having vied to spend it in the home of a girlfriend. She'd be home for summer vacation.

Dus had been pleased with the turnout of folk for Maundy Thursday and Good Friday services. They were not a big crowd, but the people were learning the liturgy, even though they had long known and revered the story.

They kneeled, and sat and stood in reverence, listening, praying, and offering up their worship. They were a quiet gathering of souls, after which they silently left the church both evenings to go home, perhaps meditating on the meaning of the events that brought them to worship. Dus was not thrilled, just thankful to God and to them. It gave new meaning to his efforts as a priest, and a new cleansing of his soul. It was amazing to him how God uses his people to humble a priest's persona, and shows him a light at the end of a tunnel that is brilliant not only with the face of a smiling Jesus, but with the faces of rugged saints who have joined their Lord, with a happy countenance of their own. It was sort of a spiritual affirmation that the simple ways in which simple people worship God in Christ are good enough with each step of the sojourn to penance, forgiveness, redemption, and, finally, resurrection. It reminded him, too, that he was no longer a dean nor "cardinal rector," but a missionary—a less-complex and humbled priest, who was called to teach and did that the best he could among these good folk—and also a student, learning from God and other folk a dimension of religion and life he had never known before. It was wonderful! The cross on which Jesus hung meant more to him this weekend than it ever had.

He was elated about the overflow of people on Easter. Karol, who had never indicated any talent for playing an instrument, volunteered to play the old reed organ for the service. She did wondrously well, considering the condition of the old music maker. Her feet pumped away on the pedals while her hands glided expertly up and down the keys, with the congregation boisterously singing old Easter hymns. Shawn served as altar boy, and the little church was filled with strong voices in song and soft meditative voices in prayer. There was no elaborate story for Dus to tell on Easter Day to these mountain people, whose knowledge of God he had so greatly underestimated. Their joy was testimony enough to their understanding of the Resurrection of Jesus Christ and the fulfillment of his promises to humankind. If liturgy, vestments, symbols, and sacraments were confusing and strange to them, the Bible and the hymns were not, and they knew well the message of the season. Dus led the services, indeed, but the people, unknowingly, preached the sermon in smiles, song, and devotion.

Halfway through the singing of "Jesus Christ Is Risen Today, Alleluia," with Karol playing and pumping the organ with all her might, and the congregation singing at the top of their lungs, Ox Conley limped up the aisle, with Nancy and their children in tow, and sat down in the front row, the only empty seats left in the church.

Karol, glancing at Dus with a big smile on her face and tears running down her cheeks, missed a few chords, but immediately recovered and played on with one hand, the other wiping her face with Kleenex. Dus, who had lost contact with the hymn when he saw Ox, just stood there watching the big man crowd his family into the pew, pick up a hymnal, and start singing. He grinned at Dus through his whiskers, and gave him a wink that made Dus turn away and shed tears as prolific as Karol's. He could not remember at that moment when he had been happier. Thank you, Lord, he prayed as all the others in the congregation sang on with gusto, with every eye peeled on Ox Conley. Over on the other side of the aisle from the Conleys, standing between Bessie Clayton and Helen Hudson, and singing at the top of his bass voice, was Jed Hudson. He beamed at Dus when Ox walked in. Any other man would have bragged about the capture of those two big men, but Dus just looked up, smiled, and said, "Thank you, Lord, for bringing Jed and Ox here this Resurrection Day to celebrate Easter with their neighbors and me."

The days had been so beautiful and rewarding. Karol and Dus had taken meals with the Conleys, lunched at Bessie's, took opportunities to talk at the clinic, and walked together on the trails with Tooter. She told of her work at the hospital, and he related his plans for renovating the vicarage. He wanted to please her, and she reassured him that she knew when he and Lou finished it, would be beautiful.

True to their word, the companies that had promised the bishop supplies and equipment had come through. A backhoe and piles of material by the side of the cabin sat undisturbed, waiting to be put to use. Karol had been fascinated with the material, and by Dus and Lou's ability to put it all together and make it work. He told her that it was something like orthopedic surgery—but a lot easier, less technical, and certainly less rewarding. But Karol allowed that having a sink, tub, running water, and, certainly, an inside toilet was quite commendable to society. She sincerely believed that Dus' technical offering would be more permanent than hers, and she would rather have a broken ankle than sit in a cold outhouse when nature called.

She had returned that afternoon to Staunton. He hated to see her leave, and felt a little pity creeping up in his soul. But then he remembered that God had been very good to him, and he had no business complaining about anything. He was sure in his own mind and heart that he and Karol would someday make a home together here, and that she would not be going away from him all the time. He had to be patient as the extraordinary expectations for the future loomed ahead of him. But tomorrow, he mused, as he gazed at the red coals in the fireplace, I am going to crank up that machine, and dig a ditch and a septic system. Lou will be here soon, and we are going to make a house fit for a queen named Ollikut; a little princess named Elly; a prince named Shawn; an odorous, lovable beast named Tooter; and for a recalcitrant priest named Dus. I hope it will be a good day for working, but no matter, cold or warm, snow or sun, I'm going to break ground tomorrow for my family and start a new era in this place. Nothing, he convinced himself, could go wrong as he initiated his vicarage renovation project on the morrow.

## 24

It had been a cold, harsh winter, but spring had now come to the mountain. Though it was still chilly, with patches of snow on the warming earth, the weather was bright and invigorating, and it was an excellent day to work on a building project. Dus, clad in a stained and faded Penn State sweatshirt, shabby jeans, and muddy boots, sat at the controls of the borrowed Caterpillar backhoe, cautiously maneuvering its shovel bucket deep inside a trench he was excavating. The extended hydraulic leveling plates of the powerful machine assured him that he could proceed with his project along the wet hillside with maximum safety. Clawing at the hard soil inside the trench with the teeth of the shovel, he filled the bucket with soil, raised it out of the channel, and deposited the loose dirt along its edge. He maneuvered the shovel back into the cut to retrieve more dirt. He worked as hard and as fast as he could to finish the septic system that would accommodate his cabin vicarage.

Suddenly, something ominous in the ditch seized his attention. He quickly raised the bucket, rested it beside the trench, turned off the engine, jumped into the trench, and pawed frantically at the loose soil. In just moments, he exposed something wrapped in an old, decaying kitchen oilcloth. He removed the fabric to discover a human cadaver lying rigidly supine, its skeletal hands folded as if in prayer, resting flat upon its midsection. To Dus, who had seen many human bodies buried in his lifetime, the cadaver resembled a dead person whose body had been neatly prepared by a meticulous mortician for a funeral wake, without the benefit of a coffin. There was an old rusty shotgun beside the body. Dus didn't touch it.

The corpse's skinless skull, with its deep hollow eyes, protruding stained teeth, and traces of wispy gray hair, stared forlornly up at the perplexed digger. A disintegrating red-and-black checked jacket, remnants of patched denim overalls, and rotten boots partially clothed the skeleton.

"What the heck is this?" Dus muttered, as he lifted his tattered Marine Corps baseball cap from his head and wiped the sweat from his brow. "I wonder why this creature is buried here like this, while all those other dead people are supposed to be buried in boxes over there in the church cemetery. This wasn't any proper burial! Something's wrong here!"

Convinced that his immediate duty was to stop his digging and report his find to Scott Kirsh, Dus climbed out of the ditch and moved toward his Jeep. A rifle discharged. He heard and felt a bullet whistle very close to his behind and ricochet off the steel plate of the Caterpillar. Without a thought, he dove front first into the open trench, landing atop the half-clad cadaver. Opening his eyes, he scowled into its hollow eye sockets and large teeth, just inches from his face. It appeared to be laughing at him. He did not know why he said it, but his sense of reverence for the departed, mixed with the indignity of his dilemma, forced an impromptu response. "I'm sorry, friend, to be crowding you in your respose," he apologized to the grinning white skull, "but our meeting like this is not all that damned amusing!"

Then out of frustration and anger, Father Habak bellowed, "Mare's marbles! Good God. Now some loony, gun toting mountain yokel is out there thinking, 'Dat preacha is a fr'aking grav' robbin' parvart, en I'ma gonna tetch 'im a goldarn lezzon!' He caught me digging here and is going to put me in a grave, too!

"Lord," he prayed, greatly discomfited by the sensation of the cold skeleton against him, "I know that you're tired of enduring my profanity and, honest, I've tried to do better, but this corn whisky mission field the bishop sent me into has gotten to be a war zone, and I have had enough of that 'horse turd!' I was willing to come up to these hills and do mission work for you, 'turn my other cheek,' and all that zealous stuff, but it was not part of the deal that this 'shepherd' had to turn his other heinie cheek so some pissed-off 'sheep' could bruise it again! I'm not a wimp, Lord," the annoyed cleric continued to entreat, "but this pasture has more wolves than sheep in it! These deranged ridge-running mutton chops need a gunny sergeant with a pit bull to herd them, for God's sake! Now Lord, I know you and our friend Ollikut are weary of my obnoxious backsliding, but if this plight I've been in ever since I came to these hills isn't soon resolved, I'm shaking the dust off this sorely maimed ass, running off this mountain, and taking up some less menacing holy work like selling Bibles to pulpit pounders!"

His impiety and anger troubled Dus, even in the midst of his dilemma. It was only last evening when his heart and soul were swollen with the joy that Holy Week and Easter had brought him, and with the spiritual goodness he had felt in the mountain folk. Now one, or maybe even two, were trying to blow his head off. "Well, you bozo up there shooting, I can't think of that disappointment while you're up there aiming at my behind. The hell with you. I'm getting out of here. So you'd better take your best damned shot, 'cause when I get to my cabin, I'm going to get my own gun, and you and I are going to have a little war!"

With that caveat and threat, Dus waited no longer in the ditch. He moved off of the skeleton and crawled inside the trench up to the edge of the cabin. He peered cautiously over the edge to see if he could see the assailant. He saw nobody, and no further shots were fired. He quickly climbed out of the trench and ducked around to the rear of the cabin. Three more bullets chopped up snow and pine needles around his shoes.

He knew he had to get into the house for protection. He ran to the back door, opened it, dove through, rolled on the floor, kicked the door shut, and belly crawled military style across the room to his dresser. Another bullet crashed through a back window, shattering the glass and thudding into the wood. Dus reached up and pulled out the top dresser drawer until it fell to the floor, spilling out socks, handkerchiefs, bullets, and his Marine Corps .38 revolver. He put it in his hand, rapidly loaded it, crawled back to the window, and cautiously peered up toward the clump of pines on the Blue. He now knew from which direction the firing was coming, and decided he was not going to passively stay there and get murdered in a church vicarage. "Priest or not, I'm not going to have Elly be an orphan, nor Kara a widow again before she's even my wife, and I am certainly not going to be the first clergy martyr buried on the side of this hill," he avowed.

He broke out the window and fired his pistol up into the tops of the pine trees. Another bullet thudded through the roof into a heavy timber in the loft. "Whoever he is, he's a lousy shot, or he can't see me," he grumbled, firing his pistol up above the clump again. "Jeez, I hope I don't hit him. Even if he is a 'moonie,' I don't want a killing on my conscience!"

A frightened buck raced off across the back of the church. That started Tooter barking. Dus hoped she would stay out of the line of fire, but then he thought her barking might drive the shooter away. He wanted the assailant to know that he was armed, had a dog, and that he was not going to just sit there and be assassinated. No further shots came. He waited. He peered out the window again. He saw and heard nothing more. He crawled across the floor again and reloaded his pistol. Tooter came over and licked his face.

He slapped her fanny. "Move away from here, Tooter, and lie down at the fireplace. Go! Get out of here, now!" Tooter dropped her head and tail and slunk away, looking hurt. "Lordy, dog, don't you understand I just don't want you to get hurt?" he apologized to her.

Dus sat on the floor below the window for almost an hour, trying to convince himself that the shooter had been scared away by Dus' pistol fire and Tooter's barking, and had taken off through the woods. He was not sure if it was safe to move about the house, but he stood up, anyway, and walked over to the fireplace to pet Tooter on the head. "Sorry, girl, but I just didn't want you dead." Tooter, happy again, licked his face and gave him her doggie smile. "Listen, I am going to put my coat on, and you and I are going to fly through that door, get in the Jeep, and scoot down the valley to get Sheriff Kirsh. You understand?"

Tooter panted and pranced, sensing they were going for a ride. Dus put on his coat, and put Tooter's choke chain and leash around her neck and yelled, "OK, dog, follow me. Don't look right nor left, nor sniff for a critter before we get in the Jeep and out of here."

With that, Dus opened the door, slammed it shut after he and Tooter cleared it, and ran to the Jeep with Tooter behind him. He opened the door, jumped in, and the dog jumped in after him. No rifle shots followed him. Nonetheless, he jammed the car in gear and raced down the hill, with snow and dirty flying from his rear wheels. "I ought not to leave that corpse behind, but I gotta get out of here and get Scott," he breathed, as he settled into driving. Tooter panted happily, wagged her tail, and tooted, nearly bringing water to Dus' eyes. "Good heaven's, dog, could you not have done that outside?" Tooter smiled and looked out the windshield.

Within ten minutes, Dus was screaming to a stop in front of the county sheriff's office. Leaving Tooter in the car, he opened Scott Kirsh's office door, breathing hard. He flopped in one of the chairs, while the sheriff sat staring at him. "Well, Father Habak, to what do I owe this feverish entry into my private domain? It would appear that you've been working up a sweat. What have you been up to?"

"Scott, you're not going to believe this."

"Believe what, Dus?"

"I was digging the trench for my septic system, and I dug into a skeleton. I was coming to tell you, when some nut in the woods up behind my house started shooting at me. I thought I was in another war. He shot six or seven rounds at me, and I had to fire back at him with my .38."

"You're kidding!"

"Do I look like I'm kidding?"

"Come on; tell me about it while we go up there. You ride with me,"

Scott said as he fastened on his gun holster and put on a leather jacket.

"Can't! Tooter's in the jeep!"

"The heck with Tooter. The dog can stay there. Crank down the windows a bit so he can breathe some fresh air, and let's go!"

Scott sped up the hill as Dus explained to him about finding the body and shotgun while digging the trench, and how the rifle fire started nearly as soon as he made the discovery. "Somebody's been watching you, Dus. You found a corpse that wasn't supposed to be found. I told you there are a bunch of nuts around these woods."

"All I was doing was digging a cesspool!"

"Did you get to see anyone, or did you just hear the bullets?"

"Hear, for crying out loud? The dipstick sent bullets licking at my boots, blowing out windows, and putting holes in my house. I didn't see him, but I know he was firing from the woods above the cabin."

"Is that the direction where you aimed your handgun?"

"Of course!"

"Do you think you hit him, seeing as how he didn't return your fire a second time?"

"I hope not, but I don't know. I sure don't want to kill anyone. I have enough troubles with God!"

"Did you have a feeling he was trying to hit you or just scare you?"

"Scott, I'm telling you, he fired at me. He didn't hit me, but he sure scared me."

"What did you make of the body you found?"

"Have no opinion. That's why I was coming down to get you. Not much left to it. It looks like an elderly man, but I guess anyone buried a long time would look old. I haven't any expertise in that sort of thing. I couldn't tell how long it had been covered up. Just took the canvas and debris off its face and body, then the bullets came, and I pitched in on top of him. It wasn't fun sharing the space with it. You're the expert on such things. You tell me."

They arrived at the cabin in a very short time. Scott pulled out his revolver and cautiously approached the door, gazing left and right, and up and down the hill. He took particular care to watch the corners of the cabin and the church, in case someone emerged shooting. He believed he was safe, and beckoned Dus to come to the cabin. Dus had left his pistol in the house. *That was stupid,* he admonished himself. *I might very well have added to his arsenal.* Dus opened the door and Scott cautiously entered. Dus followed him. He looked around the interior of the cabin and then through the broken window. "You say those shots came out of that pine clump up there on the Blue?"

"Yep!"

"I'll be damned!"

"Well, it doesn't exactly make me happy, Scott."

"I'll bet not. Me neither." He went around the house looking for bullets embedded in the wood. He found none. He walked up around the pine clump above the cabin. He found matted grass and, happily, no body nor blood.

"Well, what do you think?" Dus asked, anxiously.

"I think you found something out there that someone was afraid you'd find when you came up here last fall. I don't know for sure, but let's go out there and see what you dug up."

Dus and Scott went to the ditch and peered down into it. The skeleton, as Dus had found it, had not been disturbed. It grinned upward at them. The shotgun still rested beside the bones.

"That is weird," Scott allowed. "Let's get in there and get it out. You take its feet and I'll take its arms, and let's see if we can lift it out of here and get it into the pickup. We have to get this cadaver to the coroner and have some forensics done on it. Put the gun in the cab."

"You think we ought to move it before we get the law on it, Scott?"

"Have you forgotten, Father, that I am the law?" Scott growled at him.

"I didn't mean it that way. I thought forensic people had to see it in place and all that."

"You read too many detective stories. This thing has been in that grave for years. There's no evidence of foul play yet, and my responsibility at the moment is to get it out and bring it someplace to be examined. Then I want to look around here and up in that clump of pines a little more thoroughly. I was pleased to know, and you should be, too, that you did not leave any bodies or blood around up there. But there's something the matter, for sure."

"Where are you going to take the skeleton to have it examined?"

"The county coroner isn't at the courthouse. He has an office down at Cedar Bluff, and I guess we can store it at a funeral home down there if we have to. There is nothing left to embalm, but the coroner would know the state laws regarding the disposal of skeletons."

"Think Karol could help with this?"

The sheriff glared at Dus. "Come on. You don't want her involved in this mess, do you? You're gonna have to tell her everything, you know. She's a neat gal, but nosy as hell when it comes to your and Ox's situation. I really don't need a female assistant detective crawling on my back."

"I was just thinking, since this business is just between you and me right now, we can move the body down to the clinic and get her to come up and take a look. She's no coroner, but she has the credentials to give us some ideas about the cause and, perhaps, the time of death."

"What are you talking about? Hospital physicians don't go into coroners' digs and check bodies. After people are dead, they don't mess with them. Anyway, this could be a criminal case. Buried bodies found outside of a cemetery are the business of the county coroner, and not to tell him about it is an obstruction of justice. They'd have my badge and your butt, and we'd both be in the pokey. It's against the law to dig up graves."

"Couldn't we just call down to Staunton, get her up here tonight, and then take it down to Cedar Bluff in the morning? I really do think Karol could be really helpful."

"No. She'd be too subjective, will get too personally involved, will want to go on a manhunt with me, and all that malarkey. It's bad enough you're involved. 'Scuse my language, my friend, but no. Hell no. No Doctor Marson for now. Now let's get that skeleton into my truck and head down to Cedar Bluff. You want to go with me?"

"Sure. Do you mind?"

"Yeah, I mind, but I have a feeling if I don't let you, my life is going to be made miserable, for your not knowing the answers firsthand. Then that nosy Indian woman of yours will compound that misery a hundredfold."

"Fine. Maybe we could call her and have her meet us at Cedar Bluff. She could stand by and interpret the coroner's medical report for us."

"Yeah, he'd love that. He'd love having an uninvited hospital female doctor peering over his shoulder. I don't think that would be a good idea."

"Look, Scott, before we do this, let's think about it a little bit. She may be a big help."

"Look, Parson, I'm the law and I gotta keep the law."

"Is it unlawful to have another doctor looking at a body with a coroner?"

"I guess not, but you know how Karol will stick her nose in and say something. I want to tell you again, hospital docs don't do that. She probably won't want to."

"I know that Patty will know about it from you, and then Karol will learn about it from her at the clinic, and we'll both wish we were hiding from her in the pokey. She's going to be mad. She is one smart lady, Sheriff, and she's not going to take it lightly if we don't include her. We don't need to tell her about the shooting."

"You're right, I guess. I'm not going to be able to keep this from Patty. I try to keep most of my work from her, but she's the only one I have to talk to about it. She can smell a lie, a cover, a story a mile away. When she finds out, Karol will find out."

"OK, then we will call Karol from the office, tell her the truth from the start, ask her to come right up to Cedar Bluff, and we will meet her there."

"Won't she be working, doing surgery or something?"

"Better if she is. Then she can't come. At least we would have told her and given her the opportunity."

"It's against my better judgment, but OK. I just hope it isn't going to cause problems. Anyway, for now, we are to be the only ones in town to know about this. You hear me, Father?"

"I hear you, Sheriff," Dus replied, and jumped down into the ditch.

Sheriff Kirsh followed him, and together they easily lifted the corpse from the ditch; it was fairly light. They easily carried it to the bed of the sheriff's pickup, where they set it down, still covered in the oilcloth. Having finished that, they climbed into the truck and proceeded to town. "You want to leave your Jeep at my office?" he asked Dus. "We can go right on through town and down the mountain to Cedar Bluff without anyone in the village noticing us. It's about fifteen miles down there."

"Stop at the clinic office so I can call Karol." What time is it? Dus wondered. He glanced at his watch. "It's near noon, and she'll be eating lunch. She usually calls me about now, but she also knows I was going to work up at the cabin. Maybe I can get her in the lunch room. Pull around to the back of the clinic so no one will see us."

"You're full of all sorts of intriguing ideas, aren't you, Hawkshaw?"

"Didn't you say you'd just as soon no one in town saw us and ask questions?"

"So I did; so I did."

Scott and Dus arrived behind the clinic a few minutes after noon. Dus went into his office and put in a call to Karol at the hospital in Staunton. After a few frustrating queries about her whereabouts and lost minutes, Karol spoke on the phone. "Yes, this is Doctor Marson. What can I do for you?"

"You can shed your white coat and marry me, woman!"

"Well now, Preacher, that's the best offer I've had all day. When?"

"In about an hour."

"Where?"

"At the coroner's office at Cedar Bluff."

"What did you say? Is Spring Fever getting to you? What are you talking about?"

"Karol, I gotta hurry. If you can steal away from that shop and drive up to the coroner's office at Cedar Bluff right now, Scott and I will meet you there. Can you come?"

"Gee, lover, I don't know. We types here don't often go into coroners' digs. They don't like us fooling around their sanctums. What's up?"

"We have a skeleton, Karol. Scott and I thought you could help, and thought you would want to be in on this."

"Sure I do, darling. Wow! A body," she said. "Can you tell me more?"

"Not now, sweetheart. You'll see when you get there. It's about fifteen miles from here, and about the same for you. See you there in about thirty minutes. If you can't come, we'll understand, but it would be nice to see you."

"You too, darling. I've nothing scheduled but office work this afternoon. I can dump that. Wouldn't miss this for the world. I'll grab the rest of my sandwich and get out of here. See you. I love you."

"Love you, Kara. Good-bye."

"Oh, Dus, I don't care where we are married, but I don't want any dead bodies around. I only want live bodies, like just two. Yours and mine."

"Good-bye, wicked woman." Dus smiled and cut her off.

In a matter of minutes, Scott and Dus were on their way through town and down the mountainside. "She coming?" Scott asked, his tone displaying a kind of hope that she would not be.

"Yep, she is coming, and is looking forward to it."

"Damn her brown hide. She's a great woman and I'm glad you two found each other, but this thing may get serious. I really don't want you nice people to get hurt. I sincerely mean that. You just don't know how things can develop. You're lucky to be alive. I wish you'd let me handle this alone. I can tell you to back off, Dus."

"Scott, I know you're sincere and care, and I sure don't want Karol hurt, but you have to know we are already involved, and there is no turning back. If we don't let her in on this, she is going out on her own. I know that. I tried with her. Her intrinsic, native curiosity and her love for Ox and me just won't let it go. Believe me, you, I, and she will be better off if we let her in on this to the extent that we can watch out for her. Honest, friend. She'll be off on her own if we don't, and then she will get hurt. She is powerfully persuasive and smart. She knows what she is doing in the mountains, but her zeal might lead her into the wrong places without you and me. So let's play it cool and keep her on a tight chain. She has knowledge that we don't have that we can use. Make her mad by cutting her out, and we are up a creek without a paddle."

"OK. You win! I'll never tell you, 'I told you so,' but I'll be tempted. How is our *corpus delicti* doing back there in the truck bed?"

"It's not moving much, but the canvas is flapping and some bony fingers look like they are tapping out the Morse Code."

"Maybe it's trying to tell us something," Scott laughed.

"It really is going to be interesting to find out what the coroner has to say, isn't it?"

"Well, don't be too surprised if there is no mystery. Might be just another body from the church cemetery."

"Didn't see any grave marker or coffin, did you? Doesn't that tell you something?" Dus conjectured.

"Yeah," Scott grinned. "Maybe those fingers back there in the truck bed are tapping out a message telling us who he was at one time."

"You mean like the skeleton might be saying, 'Ain't this is a sorry way to be treating an old, faithful priest who built a fine church for God and his people on this beautiful mountain?'"

"Don't be thinking a lot of nonsense about that old preacher, Dus. Surely you aren't superstitious?"

"No, but if I were him, I'd be thinking that! You know what I would be saying if I were him?"

"No. What?"

"Mare's marbles!"

"Yeah, you would, Father, but you don't want to know what I'd be saying!"

\*   \*   \*

R.F. Underpine, M.D., coroner for the city and county of Cedar Bluff, was a man of uncertain demeanor. He was a reputable physician, but had the manner of a leering mortician slinking around the bowels of death. His gapped teeth plunged out of his upper jaw at an angle of thirty degrees, suggesting that it was not altogether coincidental that his friends called him "Buck." His balding head had wisps of gray hair standing straight up that matched his steely eyes. He was tall and slender with a gray mustache and goatee, both of which were stained by cigarette smoke and coffee. His face was sallow, but his nose was a bulbous red—probably, Dus thought, due to his imbibing on something other than coffee. His mouth was thin-lined, and his frown, which sent deep wrinkles out from his bushy brows, reminded Dus of Dr. Seuss' "Grinch." He wore a blood-splattered tattletale gray medical jacket over a gray sweatsuit. It was apparent that the man liked the color gray. Perhaps he was living out his personality.

"Well, what do we have here, Scott?" he queried through a toothy grin. "Looks like you have found the remains of King Tut. Somebody cream the poor bugger?"

"Don't know, Buck. We brought him here to find that out from you."

"Who're your friends?"

"Oh, yes. I'm sorry. Doctor Underpine, this is Doctor Marson and Father Habak. We are friends who have a mutual interest in this corpse, whoever he or she is. Dr. Marson is a surgeon at Staunton Memorial, and Father Habak is the priest in charge of the Episcopal mission at Joshuatown. He was digging around his cabin this morning and uncovered this skeleton, which appears to have the build of a man. He contacted me and we brought him to you, since it's your job to investigate this sort of thing."

"It looks to me like you could use the expertise of an anthropologist or, better still, a taxidermist. What's your interest in this, Dr. Marson?" he scowled. "Why would a beautiful lady surgeon from a pristine, sanitized mecca of medicine like Staunton Memorial be coming to a dungeon of mire and rot, rife with dead flesh and bones, and the cold slabs and boxes of a coroner's butcher shop?"

Karol seethed under her skin, but held her temper in check. She found the man insulting and distasteful, but managed a smile through gorgeous lips. Mare's marbles, she thought to herself. "Where did this mule's tootsie posing as a physician come from?" She looked to Dus and Scott for approval for that under-the-breath retort. Scott grimaced and shook his head. She pouted.

Oh boy, Scott thought. I knew this was going to happen if she came here. Dus grinned and gave Karol a permissive nod. He knew she was going to respond with her curious kind of candor. "Give it to the old goat, honey," he silently mouthed to Karol.

"Well, ta tells ya straight out, Dr. Underpit, I works da govament clinic up der in Jtown as well as da Staunton Memorial, I does, en everthung bad what happens thar ta folk, I sees as my busness. Now, that boney molting cadever just alaying der, daid as a doornail, is from my liddle ol' acre, and I aims ta know what done 'im in and what ya lernt 'bout 'im!"

Oh, Lordy, Scott thought. You've met your match, Bucko!

"The name's Underpine, Doctor, and you can cut the sarcasm with me. I'm not into witticisms. I simply wanted to know why you'd come up from Staunton with the sheriff, the priest, and this corpse into this bleak den of iniquity."

"Sorry, Doctor, but what comes around goes around, and you have no cause to put me down nor Staunton Memorial. It's a darned good hospital with fine docs, as you well know. You respect it and me, and I'll respect you and what you do here. I've always had esteem for pathologists, and I came here not to offend you, but to learn from you. You have no cause to offend me."

"Don't get touchy, Doctor. I just don't like outside hospital gurus peering over my shoulder. It's shitty business that we do here, if you'll excuse the vulgarity, and not much fun for the fainthearted. You gals and boys at Memorial get a lot of accolades for healing the sick and wounded, but when you don't and they bite the dust, I gotta cut 'em up and find out what did them in. Just remember, if it were not for this butcher shop, neither the law nor you hospital types would find out very much about what causes folk to croak. Now if you can stand this mess and have a strong constitution, you're welcome to be our guest in this body shop."

"Look, Doctor Underpine, every physician chooses his or her specialty. I assume you are here because you choose to be. I'm not here to judge your work nor advise you how to do it. We are a small-knit community up there at Joshuatown, and nearly everything bad that happens there becomes the business of the sheriff, the priest, and the physician. That's so everyone works together and there will be nothing to fracture that loving community. Now the sheriff and the pastor asked me, as a courtesy, to come up here to learn about this dead guy from you, so we can help the community with this distressing event should they come to know about it. The sheriff, you, and I all represent the law, and Father Habak represents compassion, a much-needed commodity in every community these days."

Oh Lordy, I knew that Injun medic would lower the boom on ol' Buck,

Sheriff Kirsh mused. She has grit, that's for sure! That will teach that bucktoothed sawbones to mess with a woman. Talk about "fools walking in where angels fear to tread." He spoke to calm the atmosphere. "OK, Docs, let's have a truce here. You've both made your points. Dr. Marson does have a responsibility on the mountain, Buck, so let's get on with it. Strip the old codger down and give us a rudimentary picture of what he is all about."

"OK, you guys, give me a hand yanking these rags and boots off of 'im, and my guys will tag 'im. If Dr. Marson wants to give me a hand with the examination, it'll free up some of my people to do some fresh stuff. We have a lot of it here. God, there are a lot of homicides these days."

The boots and clothing were removed, and the naked cadaver looked cold and alone, stripped of all human dignity. Buck and Karol skillfully twisted and turned the body, head, and members. They examined the skull, neck, vertebrae, rib cage, and pelvis with more than routine interest. Dr. Underpine scratched his head. "No bullet holes nor knife wounds in the skull nor in the bones. The guy's been dead too long and has been just bones for too long to tell if there were any puncture wounds in the flesh, muscles, or gizzard. No bones appear to be broken, except for a crack in the neck vertebrae. He could have been hung or it could have been caused by some serious injury in his life. Could have been shot, strangled, or stabbed, but there's no evidence of that. I don't think the very top forensic people in the state would find any more than we have found here. Wadda ya think, Dr. Marson? Got any different ideas?"

She appeared happy that Dr. Underpine deferred to her. She decided to be nice to him. "Nope. Don't see any more than you see, Dr. Underpine. You're the expert in these things; I'm not. I agree with your assessment. As you say, just too long a time."

Diplomat, Dus thought. She's got a way, that's for sure, when she's not provoked. She'll have old snaggletooth slobbering in his beard.

"When do you think he died?" Scott asked.

"Can't be real sure. We can send him over to the lab at the med school at Charlottesville and ask them to take a look at him, if you think it is all that important. I just don't know the weather conditions, the ground configuration, the water runoff, the depth of the grave, nor how much stone and clay there is up there to give a good estimate. From what I see here, it might be anywhere from twenty to thirty years since he died. Don't seem to be any odor to him. Can't tell you much about him, except he is stone dead, and that's not from old age. I suspect he was about forty-five or so when he was ushered into the Kingdom, so to speak. Could there be a church record of his burial in the church cemetery?"

"None that we know of, even for those who have gravestones with names and dates on them," Dus offered. "I didn't find him in the cemetery. I dug him up near the vicarage with a backhoe, just the way you see him now."

"Hmm," pondered Buck. "No box? No canvas?"

"That oilcloth canvas-type thing we brought him in here with was covering him when Father Dus found him. There is a saga around that area, verified by many folk," Scott interjected, "that a middle-aged, perhaps strong and hearty, preacher came there many years ago and built the church and the vicarage by himself. He must have been some sort of a recluse, and didn't talk much with people. Apparently, got most of his materials out of town in an old pickup he had. He didn't have many services, but buried and had prayers for the dead, and kept the cemetery neat and trim. One day, they say, he just up and left with nary a word to anyone. There's only a few people still alive who saw his face, and they don't seem to remember any of his characteristics. I doubt if anyone up there could identify this body."

"Think this could be him, Scott?"

"Gee, I don't know, Buck."

"I found some old vestments in the closet in the church," Dus told them. "Those would seem to indicate he was a member or a minister from some liturgical denomination like Episcopalian, Lutheran, or Roman Catholic."

"Could," Buck allowed. "Have you checked with those denominations to find out if they ever sent some clergy out there for missionary work?"

"We just found him today," Scott said, "but I'll look into that. He might have been on his own, a maverick of sorts, doing his own religious thing. Maybe he'd been defrocked from some church and wanted to have his own private ministry. And then, maybe he was just a good guy who wanted to do some good for people. Who knows?"

"Well, that's your business. Preachers look pretty much like everyone else when they've been carcasses for a quarter of a century. One thing we know for sure, he didn't climb in a grave and pull the ground over top of himself! It's up to you, Sheriff. I am persuaded there is nothing here that would merit a homicide report. Too many years have passed, and there are too many fresh bodies here for me to work on to spend much time on this one. I'm not even going to acknowledge you even brought him here. I have nothing else to offer. If I were you, I'd just take him back to that graveyard up there and give him a decent burial. Anyway, I have to get back to work. Nice to meet you, Dr. Marson, and you, too, Father. Nice to see you again, Scott. Good hunting. I'll get someone to put this stiff in a body bag and put him in your truck."

"Thank you for your help," all three of the observers seemed to say at the same time.

"Take care. See you around the mountain. I am sorry I was snippy, Doctor Marson. You're a nice lady." He smiled through his gaped, protruding teeth, then turned and sluffed off, sniffing his nose and looking dour.

"What now, detectives?" Scott inquired of Karol and Dus.

"You tell us, lawman."

"I'm taking this guy back; you have a nice burial for him, Dus, and put him under again. I'm going to tell no one in Jtown; I want to be done with this whole mess. I have some other related things to think about."

"Like what?" Karol asked.

"You might as well tell her, Dus," Scott said. "She's going to find out, anyway, but I am telling you, Karol," he forewarned her, "I am not going to have you 'hawkshawing' around. I'm going to tell Patty the same thing. I don't want to hear anything from anyone in town about any of this. Do you hear me?"

"What the devil is he talking about, Dus?" Karol asked very irritably.

"Don't get so upset," Dus hedged. "It's no big deal. Someone just took some potshots at me about the time I found this body."

"Shot at you? Oh, my God, Dus, are you hurt?"

"No, he's not hurt," Scott interjected, "but he's making light of this, and it's not funny. Some son of a buck emptied a rifle at him around and in his cabin up there. Your buddy here unloaded his .38 on the guy up in a pine clump, but apparently didn't hit him. I'm not sure what caliber it was, 'cause I haven't looked too closely up there yet. Dus wasn't hurt, Karol, but I am going to find out about all of this, and you two are going to butt out. This is serious cop business, and I'm the cop. Ain't that right, Parson?"

Karol was incensed. "The heck it's right! I'm not bugging out of anything, paleface lawman. I want to know what is going on up there, because I care about this loony guy and Ox, in case you didn't know. I'm not sitting around on my red heinie watching them get killed. You hear me, Scott?"

"How could I not, for God's sake? You're talking so damned loud. Look, Karol, this is my work, and I won't have anyone—not you, nor Dus—interfering with the law. You can help when I ask, but that is the way it is going to be, or you two are going to mess up a nice friendship. You got that, Doc? How about you, Father?"

"Yes, Scott; we understand," Dus replied.

"OK, Scott; I promise," Karol conceded, her pique somewhat abated. "But, please, let me help in some way. Where was Tooter during all this rumpus?"

"Oh, gosh, she's still sitting in my Jeep at Scott's office," Dus said. "She was with me at the cabin, but didn't get hurt. She's probably wailing and bringing the whole town down to see the inhuman way her master is treating her. We gotta get back, Scott."

"Wait just a minute, you two," Karol interjected. "Tooter can handle her own problems for a little longer. Hope she pees on your seat. What about the dead guy? What about me? You asked me to come up here, and now you're just gonna leave me here in this pile of mare's marbles, stewing in fear and frustration? What do you want me to do?"

"Nothing now," Scott advised.

"I think it would be a good idea to take the cadaver up to the university and let those folk study it. They might find some clues as to why some fiend thinks Dus ought not be snooping around the ol' preacher's digs."

"Calm down, Karol, and please listen to me," Scott said almost angrily. "I'm going to tell you one more time—it's done with. I'm taking the body back to the graveyard, and we are going to bury it. If you and Dus want to ponder all this for a while, I'll go up and take care of Tooter and the jeep. You can bring him up when the Spirit moves you, but I'm going to take care of this before the townspeople and Banker Brush start gossiping. Now that's settled, isn't it?"

"Yes, Scott," Karol relinquished. Turning to Dus, she asked, "Would you like to stay down in Staunton with Shawn and me tonight, so we can talk about some things? I'll drive you up to Joshuatown tomorrow afternoon."

"I'd better not, Karol. I ought to help Scott. I also have some expensive rental equipment sitting around up there, and have a lot to do with the septic system before Lou gets down to help me. Be best if I get back tonight."

"Please, darl . . . ," she pleaded tentatively, looking at Scott, her words trailing off into silence.

"It's OK, Karol," Scott smiled. "You don't have to cover up anymore. Patty and I guessed about you two lovebirds long ago. The whole town knows now, after watching you mooning at one another at the dance. We think it's great. Why don't you go with her, Dus? You could use a bit of cleaning up, a nice night, and some calming spirit after what you've been through today. Patty and the kids will enjoy Tooter. I'll move the jeep up to your house. You two get some peace and shake off the bogeyman. Calm him down, Karol; and Dus, please knock some sense into that squaw. I don't want either one of you to get hurt."

"I'm no squaw, you insensitive Dick Tracy, and I'll take care of him. You go home to Patty and have her teach you some manners!"

"I can't go with you, honey. Look at me—sweaty, filthy T-shirt, jeans, and muddy boots. I can't go to your place looking like this. What will your neighbors and Shawn say?"

"The heck with the neighbors! Shawn will like seeing you out of your clericals for a change. You are a bit stinky, but I have soap and a shower at my house. I'll throw those clothes in the washer. We can buy a few necessities for you on the way down, if you want. Easy as pie. I'll have you looking like a real human being in no time. Add to that a little wine and a home-cooked meal. Sounds kinda romantic and amorous, doesn't it, Parson?"

"Good heavens, Karol. Do you have to say that in front of Scott, in this creepy place?"

"Scott doesn't care, and the bag of bones lying there is already smiling."

"Yeah, I love it," Scott laughed. "Sounds like a fine idea to me. Could use a nice evening like that, myself, after this bizarre day. Think I'll run on home and suggest some of your fine ideas to Patty. Come on, guys, let's get out of this gloomy place. I'm sorry, Karol, about my reference. You know I love ya even if you are a hardheaded sawbones. Please don't tell Patty."

"You're forgiven, Scotto, but you'd better be good, or I'll tell. Say 'Hi' to Patty!"

A couple of men from the coroner's lab bagged the body, took it outside, and placed it in Scott's pickup. He climbed in his truck, and they bid each other "good-bye."

As he took off up the mountain, Dus and Karol climbed in her car and started down the mountain. "Did you hear what he said about Patty?" Dus laughed.

"Yeah," Karol giggled, with one hand on the steering wheel, the other on Dus' knee. "He's just in love with his wife. After a hard day on the trail, and after hearing all those good ideas of mine for you, he's going back up the hill to a nice home life."

"It sounds good. I hope he does. I love you."

"'Bout time you said that. You haven't told me that since Sunday."

"Kara, how bad do I smell?"

"Not all that bad. Why?"

"Then pull this crate off the road. I haven't kissed you since Sunday. Lent is over, you know."

"Noo, noo! Sorry! You can lean over and give me a peck on the neck, but you're not going to get me all hot and bothered while I'm driving down this mountain!"

"Guess I'll have to settle for that," he said, snuggling up to her neck and kissing it. "I'll sure be happy to shower off the mud. What a heck of a day it's been!"

"I know it has been for you, sweetheart, but it's good to see you looking like a mountain man. Butta, now, donna ya worry none, ma love, it'll git betta fer ya, fer sure. Ya ken count on it." She laughed, taking his hand in hers. "T'will git bedda en bedda, indeed, as da night gits older. I promise ya dat! Ya jist wait en see watta I has in stow fer ya at my house!"

## 25

Karol and Dus, after stopping at a mall in Staunton to pick up some clothing and sundries for Dus, arrived at her stone-and-wood rancher in late afternoon. Shawn heard them pull into the driveway, and greeted them at the door. "Hi, Mom; hi, Father Habak," he said, hugging his mother and shaking Dus' hand. "What are you doing here, Father? It's nice to see you."

"Hi, Shawn. Your mother and I had some business up at Cedar Bluff today that we have to discuss tonight, so she invited me to stay overnight. Is that OK with you?"

"Sure is! How come you have all that dirt all over you? You're a mess, Father. What happened to you today? When I come home looking like that, Mom sends me to the shower right away."

"And that's where Father is going, too, Shawn. We'll tell you about his day later. What have you been up to? You have your homework done?"

"Yep. I have to go to baseball practice at school at six-thirty. Bill Smith's dad is going to pick me up. Bill wanted me to stay over tonight at his place and help him with his math. I told him I'd ask you. But I don't think I ought to go if Father is going to be here. I'd like to talk to him."

"I think Father will understand if you keep your date with Bill. You may stay with him, but give me a call before you go to bed. Please tell the Smiths I appreciate their hospitality. And, remember, we don't discuss our private affairs with neighbors. Father will tell you about some of the things that happened today till the Smiths pick you up, but there's to be no discussion of any of this outside the house. Now, both of you sit and talk at the kitchen table while I get you something to eat."

"Don't want to be too full for practice, Mom. Soup will be plenty. We'll snack at Bill's after practice."

Dus talked to Shawn as he ate. He explained about the events of the day, but left out the shooting encounter. Shawn asked questions and Dus answered, with Karol keeping a close ear on the conversation. Soon, Bill Smith's dad honked from outside. Shawn gathered up a duffel bag, hugged and kissed his mom, and said good night to Dus.

"See you, Father!" He then went to the priest and wrapped his arms around his neck. "I like you, Father. Thank you for being Mom's and my friend. Say 'Hi' to Elly for me. She's a neat person, and I like her, too."

"She thinks you're pretty neat, yourself, Shawn. Have a fun night, and come up the mountain soon to see me."

"I will! Bye, Mom. Have a nice night. See you tomorrow afternoon after school. Be good!"

"Bye, honey. I'll be good. You be good!" she called as he opened and closed the door. Karol smiled at him as he went out waving.

"Smarty-pants, telling his mom to be good! Ha! I adore that boy. Have you noticed how fond he has become of you?"

"Yes, and I'm grateful for that. He's a fine lad, and you're as blessed with him as I am with Elly. We're glad he likes us. And she is very fond of you two. That's good! Makes it easier to plan our future, doesn't it?"

"Sure does, darling. Sure does!" She giggled a little and added, "Tell you the truth, I'm not exactly unhappy about his staying over tonight with Bill. Makes it a bit more romantic not having a teenager hovering over our conversation and stuff."

"What stuff! You just told him you'd be good."

"Don't let your imagination carry you away, Parson, or I'll be sending you off to a cold shower instead of a hot one. Now, how about making a fire in the hearth, then off for your bath? The guest bedroom and bathroom are right down the hallway, next to mine. I want to get out of this medical gear and clean up, too. Throw your duds in the hall, and I'll put them in the washer. Won't take long. Then I'll wrestle up some crabcakes, fries, and salad. That sound good?"

"Sure does! I'm dying for a bath, and I'm hungry!"

Dus busied himself making a fire while Karol worked in the kitchen. He looked around the living room of the modest, one-floor structure. He had not been aware of it the night he had driven Kara and Nancy there the night of Ox's accident. *It is pretty,* he thought to himself. *Compact and utilitarian for a widow with a growing son.*

Soft hands from behind him encircled his waist, and a warm breath at the back of his neck said, "How do you like my teepee, handsome brave?"

Dus turned, looked into her face, and held her hands. "It's very attractive and homey, Princess; it says a lot about who you are and where you're from. I'm happy you have it. What a joy it would be to build a house for you."

"That's sweet, Dus. Thank you! I know you're going to make that mountain vicarage cozy and beautiful with your big, talented hands. Anyway, I have the crabcakes and fries thawing. You get a bath. I'll do your clothes and get pretty, and maybe we'll enjoy this room later on, OK?"

They went their separate ways. Dus took a bath, shaved, and dressed himself in the casual clothes and loafers he had purchased at the store. Karol threw his dirty clothes in the washing machine and then went to shower and refresh herself. They both returned to the living room at the same time, about an hour later.

She was dressed in a loose cotton calico pinafore, with her long, dark hair tied with two bows, falling down on both sides of her shoulders and over her bosoms. She was beautiful, and Dus wasted no time in appreciating her. He put his arms around her and kissed her with intense passion. They withdrew, sighing breathlessly. Kara spoke, "Wow! Preacher, that was not exactly a spiritual smooch. That was a marrying kind of smooch. We'd better watch out. This house is an awfully romantic place, and I have a feeling you're feeling romantic tonight. Is there some reason for that?"

"Well, maybe a little bit."

"Come on, fibber, your face is flushed, my lips are bruised, and we are both perspiring."

"How can I help it with you looking so ravishing and throwing off all that warmth?"

"Enough of that blarney. You'd better eat your supper."

"Smells good."

"It's all ready to eat. Let's get it on the table."

Karol and Dus ate a hearty supper. They were engrossed with one another across a small supper table, lighted only by candles, and talked over the day's events and plans for the days to come. When they finished, Karol took the dishes to the kitchen while Dus poked new life into the fire. They returned to the table.

"Would you pour us some chardonnay, please, Dus? Then let's talk about us—not the church, not the hospital, not the dead guy, not Ox, not the children, nor the shootings. I want us just to talk about you and me, and about our life together, now and later."

He poured the wine, handed her a glass, and settled himself in his chair across the table, gazing at her through the candle's glow. He was bewitched by her beauty and sincerity. "Here's to us," he said, raising his glass, "for now and all the tomorrows. May every night be like this one, and may our talk be happy planning. May God's blessings and all of life be as beautiful, for everyone, as the woman I am privileged to be with tonight."

"That was sweet. Thank you."

"Thank you for the delicious supper and for inviting me to be here."

"You really do say nice things to me. Are they really true? Do you really love me so? Sometimes I get frightened about words. Sometimes when life is going so well for me with people, I get scared that the words they speak are not really what they feel down deep in their hearts. I guess it is part of the Native American's psyche to be wary of words. You've heard of the 'white man speaks with a forked tongue' axiom that goes with our suspicious nature. And there's a lot of good historical justification for our feeling that way."

"I know that history, Kara, and it has nothing to do with us. I would not tell you I loved you if I did not."

"I know, Dus. I'm just trying to explain why it is the nature of Indians to question almost everything good that happens to us. Of course, I believe you, but American history attests to the fact that the 'white eyes' have told us lies, broke the promises made to us, massacred our women and children, stole our land, and forced us to live on worthless, unproductive reservation lands."

He was somewhat taken aback by her review of Indian history at a time like the present. He was just as serious with her. "That's history with a lot of truth, but it has no relevance to the here and now. Anyway, your dad is a 'white eyes.' Your mom thought he was OK."

"That's true, and I do trust you, Dus. Please know that."

"I do, sweetheart. The words we speak should be as sacramental as Holy Communion and the marriage sexual union. They should be the indisputable, truthful outward and audible signs of what folk truly feel and think in their hearts and minds. Mankind has violated that maxim, and trusting people have been betrayed by deceit and broken promises since the beginning of time. That is, unfortunately, the historical shady side of man's character. But Kara, no one, no matter how he has been hurt, should paint everyone with the same wide brush of skepticism."

"I'm sorry. I just get scared about love."

"I love you, beyond my ability to find the right words to express it. I don't think I will ever find adequate words to describe how I feel about your having come into my life. There are not enough words, synonyms, nor definitions in the English language that would have you understand the depth of my love, nor my desire to fill up your life with joy. Because I can't find them does not mean I would tell you lies."

"I believe that the words you speak to me are true, Dus."

"I thank you for that, sweetheart. Now, speaking of Indians and true words, I think I ought to tell you some truths about my family, so you do not think that this 'white eyes' tells fibs to you Indians."

"I ant to hear about your family, about you. Sometimes I feel I don't really know all I want to know about the man who may be my husband someday. I love you, and want to be with you all the time, but you are secretive about your life. You've never told me much about your heritage."

"My heritage, eh? Well, now, I have a deep, dark secret about that," he chuckled, "that may or may not please you."

Karol looked at him in surprise, and was not laughing. "What won't please me?" she asked brusquely.

"I think you should know that Ellen is part Indian, too."

Her eyes lit up, but showed immediate Indian wariness. "We have just been through this 'white eyes telling fibs' stuff, Dus. Please don't joke about it."

"It's true. I promise you."

"Yeah, paleface's tales again! Well, that is interesting. I thought there was something very special about her. Was Ginnie part Indian?"

"No."

Karol was confused. She showed it. This revelation was not amusing her. She was afraid to ask. He had said that no other woman had been in his bed. Was Elly adopted? She tried to think of something to say. She had a feeling that whatever she asked would sound foolish. "Well, that makes three of us who are part Indian. If we marry and have kids, they're gonna be Indian, too. Maybe we'll all rub a little red on you." She wasn't liking her own jesting.

"You don't really want me to tell you about my life, do you, Kara?"

"I do so, but you're being comical about something important to me. I'm confused, and I don't know what you're talking about when you say that Elly is part Indian and Ginnie wasn't, and you never slept with any other woman but her. What am I supposed to think? Sometimes I think my being a Native American is a big joke to you," she sniffed. "Are you making fun of me?"

"No."

"Then quit speaking with a forked tongue. I thought I was going to get true words from you."

"Well, if I am honest, maybe we can't get married."

"What?"

"It's against the law for relatives to get married! I'm the one who is part American Indian, cousin," he smiled.

Karol straightened up in her seat and stared at him. "How can you sit there and tell me a big fib like that, after reflecting on my heritage all the time? You told me you would not fib to me."

"I've never made fun of your heritage, and what I'm telling you is true. Honest! My grandmother on my dad's side claimed she had Susquehonnock blood in her—only a smidgen, mind you, but enough that it should make you happy that I'm one of your kind."

Karol didn't know whether to smile or frown. "I'm not sure I want you to be one of my kind. Who the heck were the Susquehinnos, or whatever you call 'em? I never heard of such a tribe, and I doubt if anyone else ever did, either."

"Then you western cousins ought to catch up on your American history. The Susquehonnocks were an eastern woodland tribe that were chased out of New York by the Iroquois in the sixteenth century. They settled along the river that flows from New York south through the Central Pennsylvania corridor to the Chesapeake Bay in Maryland. The famed John Smith of Jamestown, Virginia, even wrote about them. Anyway, they were a pretty noble and powerful tribe until they were ravaged by war and disease. They lost their identity as a tribe after they were nearly annihilated by the Seneca Indians and white settlers in Maryland in 1675. The Susquehanna River, which was named after my kin, is the widest, if the shallowest, big river in America, and runs very close to my ancestral home in Pennsylvania."

"The shallowest, eh! That figures! It almost describes a certain Indian priest I'm beginning to learn about."

"Be disparaging, if you like, but you ought to learn about us Susquehonnocks if our tribal bloods are going to be mixed in marriage."

"I'm not sure I want to mix with your blood and have papooses that are part Susquahinny."

"Susquehonnocks, smart alec! Anyway, both my dad's and my mom's white descendants settled in Pennsylvania in the 1700s long before yours did in Oregon. My dad said some of his ancestors were German Hessians who fought with the British in the Revolutionary War. My mom, whose ancestors were English, claimed her folk were American Revolutionary patriots. Doesn't matter! I suspect there was as much ancestral white and

Indian blood-mixing and carnal hanky-panky along the river and backwoods of Pennsylvania as there was in Oregon. But you don't have to fear my tribal dominance, Nez Perce Princess, because if you were to prick my heinie again, as you like to do, I suspect all the Indian blood I have in my veins would drain out in one small bubble. Unlike yourself, I don't have enough Indian in me to warrant wearing a hummingbird-feather bonnet, let alone an eagle one. Nevertheless, I thought you'd like to know I was a real Indian, and one of your kinfolk. You don't seem to be too impressed with that revelation." He was chortling and enjoying his story.

"You are not humorous, Dus Habak, and you are really full of mare's marbles! I'll have you know, Chief Itty Bitty Indian, my ancestors never hanky-pankied along the river like yours did, I do not like to prick your pale heinie, and I don't care a twit if you have a milligram or a barrel full of Indian blood in your veins. I've heard enough of your bizarre Indian tales for one night."

"Well, I am deeply hurt with your lack of interest in my people, after I saved that information as a surprise gift for you. I can see you Nez Perce Indians, with your best horses and choice 'mare's marbles,' are a pretty snooty tribe. I guess you think you'd be contaminated by my Susquehonnock bloodline. Maybe we'd better rethink this blood mixing."

"Why don't you go jump in your shallow Susquehanna River," she chuckled, "take a bath, and wash that Indian nonsense out of your system. Let's get back to the 'truth' subject." Then her face turned more serene as she stared at Dus across the table. She was ready to talk about some serious things with the man she adored.

Dus, perceiving that the woman who had stolen his heart was done with the banter and seemed to want a more philosophical discussion and more serious attention paid to the subject of love, spoke to her in earnest. "Love is not only expressed in words, Kara. It's expressed by action, too. Remember when we were talking about all this stuff that night when we were with Tooter on the mountain, and I said sacramental love is outward actions expressing inward feelings and thoughts? That hugs, kisses, smiles, and handshakes are outward expressions of inward affection? Added to that is the beautiful outward sign of love between a husband and wife, which is called sexual intercourse. It is the ultimate outward physical expression of their inward spiritual oneness."

"I remember what you said when we talked about lovemaking, but don't you think life and love are oftentimes made too complicated with a lot of theological jargon? Why does a man's and woman's love for one another have to be defined by theology, medicine, engineering, law, economics, and all that cerebral stuff? It just confuses and frustrates loving men and women, and lures them away from their beautiful natural instincts. Why does there have to be a rationale for everything? Why can't love and life just be the simple carrying out of what we feel down deep in our minds, our souls, and our bodies? Why can't love just be unvarnished appreciation, and an expression of total spiritual and physical bonding, without so many restrictive human laws that inhibit natural law, when fulfilling natural law is loving someone and hurting neither God nor neighbor?"

Dus responded, empathizing with her. "It's because we have to discipline natural law so it doesn't get out of control, run amok, and hurt the society in which we live. Order has to be maintained lest some folk do a lot of harm to others, even in the name of love. Some emotions are suspect and misdirected. An example: A sixteen-year-old male village idiot tells me that he 'loves' Elly and therefore is going to marry her and get her pregnant, and they'll live happily together as missionaries to the poor pagans of Lower Sablovia, no matter what I, her father, think of that noble 'love'! I sired her, fed her, protected her, educated her, and loved her for thirteen years, and this pimple-faced squirt, who's known her for a month, says he loves her and says they ought to be one. A lot of dumb and cruel things have been done in the name of love!"

"I wouldn't want that to happen to Shawn, either, and I understand the need for order, but if we are decent people and are motivated rightly, why can't we just live freely, as the trees, animals, rivers, and mountains, disciplined by innate goodness, in harmony with our environment? Why can't you and I feel love and make love, and share it within the context of nature? Mountain folk and Native Americans live and breathe the forests, the wind, the rain, the snow, birds, animals, and beautiful sunrises and sunsets, and feel the love of God manifested in them; and they make love as naturally as the birds, bees, and bears. Why can't love between a man and a woman just be natural and complete, without the complication of moral casuistry? Why aren't we human beings allowed to express it as we feel it at the moment of its deepest passion, commitment, and conviction, allowing, of course, that we are responsible adults? Where do we so-called intellectuals and moralists get off telling everyone how God wants us to love, down to the minute details, as if he kept a big, long checklist of 'do's and don'ts' on our every movement?"

"Those questions are far too searching for my suspect theological expertise, sweetheart. I don't know. Yes, it would appear that we human beings have tampered a lot with God's mind and his creation. We have probably talked too much, written too much, invented too much, wanted too much, lied too much, pontificated too much, pumped up our egos and greed too much, and put our neighbors down too much. The only thing we don't do too much, I suspect, is love; and as you suggest, it seems like there are a lot of rules restricting love in all its many-splendored ramifications. But God, himself, gave us the basic moral and ethical commandments to govern our lives. Jesus interpreted them for us so we could love God and our neighbors, but it would appear that we English, Europeans, Asians, Catholics, Protestants, and Jews, not to mention Buddhists, Hindus, and Moslems, have translated them into thousands of laws that have reduced the natural law of love to confusion, frustration, and resentment. And, Kara, I am not the least of those in my profession who have done that."

"That's exactly what I mean, Dus. The theologians, politicians, lawyers, and even we physicians have so interfered with and complicated natural law with legislation and dissection that love is more obedience and erudition than natural outpouring."

"You're right about that in a way, honey, and I don't think God intended that it should be that way. I do think, however, and I believe as a priest, that he wants us to discern his will and discipline our emotions so they are not hurtful to society. Nature, as you know, in your experience with your profession, has its mean and seamy side. Some is just natural aging and physical deterioration, but a lot of it is just plain, old-fashioned sin, and while we, perhaps, have overdefined sin, placed unmerciful guilt trips on God's people, and wallowed in it to the point of our own destruction, the rule of moral and ethical law does discipline the bad side of our nature."

"I know that," Karol continued to argue, "nature does run amok and needs discipline, redemption, and healing. That's why I'm a physician and you're a priest. But is it the bad side of nature when the outward sign of the inner love between two people, what you call 'sacrament,' that serves to enhance their own and other people's lives, too, yearns for outward and complete expression as God has ordained it, without the trappings of license, ceremony, and witnesses?"

"What do you mean by that, Kara? You're trying to say something about our love relationship, aren't you?"

"Yes, because this all gets down to you and me, male and female human beings in love. I believe that in your serving God as a loving, compassionate pastor and spiritual healer, and my serving him as a loving and compassionate medic and physical healer, both of whom have great regard, through respect and love for him and all his natural creation, humanity will be greatly served and enhanced by the love we have for each other. And that love, if totally unselfish, should be totally natural, uninhibited, and completely fulfilling to us, without civil and religious zealots calling us into account."

"I understand what you're saying, sweetheart."

"Why, then, do God and society say 'No' to you and me, when we love each other so much and ache for the expression of human love between a woman and a man, knowing, even while doing it and savoring it, we can better serve God and humanity together?"

"That's what marriage is, darling—the spiritual union that makes that possible. Remember how we talked about that while we were walking down the mountain with Tooter, and we said we wanted our physical union to be right with God, free of guilt and consequence?"

"So are you telling me that the physical expression of love between a man and a woman in love is only right if it's sanctioned and licensed by the state and church, duly recorded in their registers, fulfilling civil law and denominational canons? So it's getting a bridal gown, calling the people to witness and feast, standing before an altar, making vows, and getting a priestly blessing that make it right? Is that what makes consummated love morally OK with God and society? Mare's marbles and turtle turds, Father Habak. I wonder if it occurs to anyone that there are men and women who love each other, who just can't get married according to the white man's law, for all sorts of reasons. Commitments and responsibilities often inhibit that for them, at least for a time. People who want to consummate their love can't always get officially hitched, even if they would like to do it as a civil and ecclesiastical commitment."

"Aw, sweetheart, state wedding ceremonies are just the legal frou-frou. They're not what makes marriage between a man and woman. State laws are designed for the welfare of the society. Marriage licensing is just how the wife and husband are legally protected. Matrimony is the sacramental rite that reassures a woman and a man that God blesses their union as husband and wife and the procreation of their children. But the vows are made between the two people. They are made to each other and to God. I guess this is going to sound trite to you, but a man and woman marry each other.

The church does not marry them, nor does the state marry them. They make their commitments to each other. The church just assures them of God's love and blessing for their union, and witnesses their commitment to live together in a holy marriage. Common-law marriage, without either the blessing of the church or the legalization of the state, is still a marriage. Civil-law marriage is marriage. To love, live together, have sex, and procreate children, a man and wife don't have to have the sanction of the state nor the church if they don't choose to, but then they cannot expect to be protected by the laws of those institutions. Every culture, religion, and nationality may have its own way of carrying out and recognizing marriage. Christians believe it should be legalized by the state and performed under the rules of Christian doctrine. I admit that it has become complicated and ostentatious, but that's the way it is for Christians."

Karol, her elbows resting on the table and her hands toying with her wine glass, glanced sporadically at the fire and then at Dus. She was listening intently. Her face had lost a bit of its previous luster. She was solemn. "Are American Indians, who marry according to their customs and beliefs, really married in God's eyes, Father?" she asked.

Dus was beginning to feel Karol's intensity. "Aside from my kidding about my Indian heritage, you certainly know more about Indian customs than I do, but even Indians have elaborate ceremonials and rites according to their laws when they marry. I'm a Christian priest, dear heart. I follow, to the best of my ability, the doctrine, worship, and discipline of the Christian church I serve as I understand them. This is God's world, not mine. I serve only one expression and understanding of how we should love and serve him and his people in this world. It isn't perfect, by any means. No religion is wholly right or wrong. I don't have any right to impose the Anglican understanding of God's will on others. I see it as my duty to share the wonderful gift made possible by the birth, ministry, death, and Resurrection of Jesus Christ, not to impose it on anyone. People can freely accept it or reject it as the Spirit moves them. I have not been chosen to sit in judgment and condemnation of American Indian's, or any other group's, customs and religious traditions. I am asked only to share Christ's love with them and pray they will enjoy, as I do, his love. Nor do I tell God whom to love and judge. He's perfectly able to do that without any advice from me. He'll take who he will, according to his own plan, into his arms and Kingdom. I just have to be sure that what I am doing with my life pleases him, and that I do as he wants me to do for others. He will ultimately decide whether I did that rightly or wrongly, and whether I really have done my best."

"You're very interesting, darling. Are you instructing me?"

"No, but if American Indians do what they do and believe they are doing God's will, that is for them and God to work out. Don't ask me to make judgments on people's relationships with God, when they are worshipping him, and being loving, compassionate, and Christ-like in their culture."

Dus paused. Kara's face was sad and little dribbles of moisture rolled down her cheeks. "Do you want me to go on with this stuff? It may be getting boring, with that fire and wine calling us to better things. I'm a sinful man, Kara, and I shouldn't pontificate about anything."

"Please, go on with your thought, Dus. It's helpful to me even if it is a bit confusing. Honest!"

"Just for a moment, then let's talk about our life together." He continued, "I do sincerely believe as a Christian minister, aside from the complications of doctrine, liturgy, canon laws, and all that, that Christ is the manifestation of God on this earth; to follow his life, his word, and his love as it is translated and revealed in the Bible is a great gift to all his people, everywhere, and if we could live in him fully and quit fouling up who he is with so much talk, writing, arguments, bias, prejudice, judgment, and condemnation, God's people would be happier and more loving—no matter what race, nationality, or religious culture we are of. Jesus is the best example of love, peace, and fulfillment we human beings have. He is the essence of the truth about what is good in God's creation. He is what makes us value other humans and appreciate all those natural things on earth you just reflected upon. And as a very natural, beautiful, and caring woman, Kara, you do reflect them wondrously in your life."

"How do I do that with all my doubt and uncertainty?"

"Because you are so intrinsically a part of his natural creation, and are such an indigenous, pure, and human manifestation of all that is good in this world. Perhaps with your understanding of God in your vocational-healing way and with my understanding of God in my sacramental-pastoral way, maybe our love, one day bonded in spirit and flesh, will serve God and humanity pretty well. Maybe we won't reach a lot of people in our time together, but if only ten or twenty lives are made better for our having loved and sojourned their way, what we will have done in just little ways may very well please God and help those twenty people a whole lot. Who knows? They just might be ten or twenty people who would not have been healed nor known him, had we not tried. And you, my Indian love, are a better pastor than I shall ever be, for you understand God and his creation better than I ever have. Your endemic experience allows you to get to the heart of the matter, so much better than my theology and liturgy. You must take me to your mountain home sometime and teach me more, 'Thunder Rolling In The Mountain.'"

"I can only say I love and adore you, Father Habak. I want you to come to my home now, your home in me. I want you to marry me now. I'm sure of that, and I don't want to wait anymore to be one with you. My whole being—my mind, my soul, my body, to their very depths—cries out for you this very minute. Call it love, call it sensuality, call it sacramental or what you will, but I believe God wants us to be one, and the only way that is truly possible is through the joining of our bodies as well as our souls, with or without the benefit of clergy, state, and witnesses. I will concede that the civil and religious ceremony in our society is a good idea for legal reasons, and we'll do that someday, with all the fluff, but I cannot believe that to love as we do, to be as committed as we are to one another, to God, and to our need to rightly serve him and humanity, we are wrong in fulfilling our love at any given moment we choose. God has asked me to love you, and has asked you to love me, hasn't he?"

"Yes, he has, Kara," Dus answered. "Yes, he has."

"Then why aren't we making love, Dus?"

Dus did not answer. Feeling they both needed a break from the intensity of the conversation, he arose from the table, took Karol by the hand, and sauntered into the kitchen. She allowed him the change, and they playfully washed and dried the dishes, cleaned up the kitchen, and refreshed themselves, then wandered around the house on a Karol-guided tour.

Dus loved the construction and the motif, and he was proud of the talented woman who had built it in her own image. "It seems like a fun place, Kara; you have done a beautiful job. I am happy you have it, and I thank you for asking me to come here and share it with you tonight."

"Thank you. I want you to enjoy it. It is your home when you're in Staunton. Now, throw some more wood on the fire and let's sit in front of it."

He sat down on the huge couch and she stretched out on it, laying her head in his lap. She looked up at him through tearful eyes, trying to smile. Beads of perspiration had developed on her forehead. She started to weep. Dus wiped her head and smoothed her hair. She was beautiful even in her solemnity. He lifted her head to him, and he kissed away the tears around her eyes and cheeks.

"Why are you weeping, Kara?" he asked.

"If you were a real Indian, you'd know that Indian girls not only cry when they are confused and hurt, but when they are happy, too. It's hard to believe we are here like this, together, in love, with so many questions about man and woman, their union with each other, and with God and humanity, all unanswered. It is almost too much, Dus, and when you think you know the answers, they don't ever seem complete. There are so many feelings for people who want to be good and decent, who want to do the right thing, to have to deal with when they are in love. There is so much emotion, and there is so much need down deep in us that screams out for expression and fulfillment. Life is so glorious, Father, but it can also be sad and confusing."

He felt a need to reassure her, but he was certainly empathetic with her. He has often felt as she did. He tried to answer her previous question about whether God approved of their love—and, if so, why not express it at any given moment? He looked down at her beautiful face and said, "God has told me to love you, Kara, forever. I do, and I always will. How could I deny such a gift as you? I will always want to be wholly one with you."

Fire burned brightly in the hearth as it began to come alive in the loins of the man and woman trying to understand and discipline the depth and potency of their love.

Kara sniffed. "Then love me completely tonight, Dus, and believe that God will discern our good intent and understand. Let me love you without reservation, and know I do it because God's love and your love have led me to this moment of our lives."

Dus was entranced with this beautiful, intellectual, contemplative, innocent, guileless Native American woman who had claimed his heart and wanted all of him. He adored, respected, and honored her for all that she manifested in her mind, soul, and body. She was now generously and spiritually inviting him into her whole being, believing God intended it so. He was deeply honored. He was, however, a priest, and the paradoxes vexed him. He had just finished a trying Lent dealing with the vagaries of love between a man and a woman. He was sure what God wanted and expected of him morally, but as a man, he found it difficult to resist Karol's candid logic and invitation to fulfill their love. He spoke softly and kindly to her. "Are you sure you love me that much, and want to do this after all we said and hoped for on the mountain? We decided then to wait until marriage. We wanted it right with God. What has changed, Kara?"

Her demeanor changed with his provocative question. "What has changed? I'll tell you what has changed. Need has changed. Love makes demands on the human soul and body. The heart calls out for fulfillment and, God forgive me, if he must, he made and gave us this wondrous thing; I see no harm nor sin in our possessing the joyful gifts of love given us. What has changed, Dus? Me. You. We have changed. I am sure of your love for me now, and am sure of mine for you. I did not know that on the mountain. I know it now, and so do you."

"Kara, if we do what our hearts and emotions are asking us to do tonight, there may be terrible guilt and anger with each other, with ourselves, tomorrow and after."

"There will be none of that with me. I have thought about what I said up there on the mountain a thousand times. We are grown-up, responsible, educated adults with our years passing by. We know what we want, and how to work out our lives to accommodate the problems ahead of us. Our future will be better revealed to us as you and I are better revealed to one another, and when we know who we are completely. Our lives, our children's lives, and the lives of folk we are committed to will be better served when we are wholly one. I believe that, Dus. Don't you?"

"I believe you, Kara, and you are very convincing."

Karol raised her voice. She was somewhat piqued now, and relaxed her body from his. "I am not trying to convince you of anything, Father Habak," she railed. "I am no sex-starved concubine trying to talk you into an orgy. I love you with my whole being, but I have waited a long time for the man I love to love me physically, and I can wait longer if I must. I love you and want you, but it has to come from you and be right with you. Your conscience, your morality, and what you feel and do are very important to me. I don't want to hurt you, and I shall certainly not lead you astray from your convictions. You must love me on your own terms."

Dus was surprised by her retort. He was struggling with the needs of the spirit and the needs of the flesh, using her as his conscience. He was repentant. "I did not mean that to sound the way it did. What I do, I do of my own volition; and, whether right or wrong in the eyes of God or society, I take full responsibility for my actions. I do not love you because of your sexual appetite, nor mine. I love you because you are a woman of great quality who loves me. I want to marry you soon and share our oneness with the creation God has called us both to serve. I do not know how to completely love you without eventual physical union. I shall deem it a great privilege when you invite me into your body to consummate our love and become truly one as God intends."

"Thank you for saying that," she whispered, her eyes moist. She wiped them with the back of her hand. "I have invited you."

Dus thought about that unsubtle statement and kissed her gently, but did not respond to her anymore emotionally than that. They talked, planned, and petted on through the evening, just enjoying one another, and relishing the warmth of the fire.

The telephone rang. Karol arose and crossed the room to answer it. Dus overheard her talking to Shawn. "Thank you for calling, honey. Glad your practice went well. Have a good night with Bill. . . . Yes, dear, I am quite sure you don't need to come home tonight. Yes, Father will understand. . . . Yes, I'm fine, and yes, Father is still here. . . . Yes, I am sure. . . . No, Shawn, you are not to come home. That would be rude to Bill and his parents. . . . You will see Father soon again on the mountain. . . . Yes, he is very nice, and I like him, too. . . . Shawn, you do not need to say that to me again. I will be good. Good night, Son. Sleep well. . . . See you tomorrow. . . . Thank you. . . . I love you, too." She hung up the phone. Dus chuckled to himself as he listened in on the one-sided conversation.

"The little snooper wanted to come home to see you," Karol snickered.

"Why didn't you let him?"

"You know, Father Habak, I think your naïveté is greater than Shawn's. You don't understand much about romance, do you? I love and adore that boy, but I don't particularly want him butting in and usurping me with you tonight. Has it occurred to you that this grown-up woman might like someone other than her kid, as cute and cuddly as he might be, in her life, from time to time? Is it all right if I just want to be with you without my son nosing about, dippy Cleric?"

"Gee, you're a touchy Injun. I was just kidding."

"And you're a dense Injun!" Then she frowned and spoke seriously. "Dus, I'm scared about what happened at your cabin today. I'd die if anything happened to you. Please be careful. Scott has got to find the guy doing this stuff, and must stop it."

"He will. Don't worry about it, Kara. Everything will work out. Let's not talk about bad things tonight. We can look at it in a new light tomorrow. Tonight, I just want to be with you and make plans for the future. I like what is happening here and now."

"What's happening here and now, Father?"

"Kara, do I really have to explain the facts of . . . "

"Nah, darling. Do you remember all of our conversation on the mountain that night, and the things you said about Tooter staring, and it made you feel sexy?"

"I remember. What about it?"

"Are you feeling that sorta thing now?"

"What kind of a question is that, you vixen?"

"Well, you're a grown-up boy and I'm a grown-up girl in love. You afraid to deal with that, Parson?"

"No and yes," he joshed.

"What's that mean?" she whimpered.

"No, I am not afraid to deal with it; and yes, I am feeling that sort of thing. Are you?"

"Dus, I don't mean to be earthy, but my body is very warm and is aching all over for your touch. Why don't you quit talking so much and just hold me closer?" she whispered, snuggling up to him.

Both man and woman, whether voluntarily or instinctively, were distancing themselves from what seemed to be, at one time, their mutually agreed upon premarital restraints. They were rapidly straying into what the Bible called "concupiscence." Their former resolve and chaste disciplines were rapidly deteriorating, and they began to lose themselves in a maze of libidinous journeys, unimpeded by moral deliberations nor consequence. They pressed their bodies together, arms encircling one another. Their mouths touched, and Dus felt the pyramids of her chest pressing on his. She sighed, unable to contain her growing fervor. Only the garments between their flesh prevented them from carnal communion. It appeared as though nothing but full consummation would satiate their mounting amatory hunger.

"I love you. My body has been celibate long enough, and I can no longer deny its need," Karol panted.

"I know, Kara," he breathed, and because her passion demanded a response, he embraced her more intensely. His hand, already resting on her knee, moved up under her skirt, over the smooth flesh of her thighs. Karol purred as Dus' fingers moved farther up her flat, perspiring stomach to her breasts. He smiled at the absence of a bra, as a finger gently touched one, having already surmised that her aboriginal disposition would not have allowed her endowments to be so encumbered. He was enchanted with the ambiance of her bosom. Having not touched it before, he had fantasized about her breasts' proportions. Neither enormous nor petite, they were bountifully convex enough to fill up his large hand. Yes, he thought, in spite of her natural inclinations for freedom, she would have to wear a brassiere when she went into her professional world. He caressed them gently and found their texture soft, yet substantially robust, and nicely embellished. They were more voluptuous than he had imagined, and he massaged them with appreciative care. She sighed as she pulled his mouth tighter to her own. They glided into a state of ecstasy that would not be appeased with just amiable foreplay.

Suddenly, in what was a dramatic shift to self-control or conscience, Dus abandoned his foraging into the exotic, rolled away from her, and sat up. Tears welled in his eyes. Before he was able to utter a word, Kara cried out in deep pain and confusion, "Oh, God, no Dus! What's happening? Oh no, darling, don't do this to me! Don't do it to us. No, please!"

He looked at her with compassion. Speaking quietly and gently, but resolutely, he said, "I can't do this to you, Karol. I want to, but I can't. I promised God and you I would not. You will loathe me in the morning. I have just finished a long and frustrating Lent coming to terms with my lust for you. I'm a priest, my darling; I cannot seduce the woman I love. I cannot allow this to happen to us. Our sexual consummation must wait until God allows you to be my wife. I am sorry I have gone this far with you. I love you so much."

Her face flushed and grew ashen. She pushed away from him and, without speaking, stood up, pulled her pinafore skirt down over her legs, and brushed out her hair with her fingers. Wiping her face with the back of her hand, she went to the fireplace and sobbed. He tried to console her. She rebuffed him. Her voice was vitriolic. "Get away from me, white Priest; take your moral platitudes away from this strumpet and be off to your confessional," she wailed into her hands.

"I am sorry, Kara; I did not mean to hurt you," he apologized, trying to brush her hair down over her shoulders.

She shook him off. 'Don't touch me. I don't want neither your sympathy nor your hands on me. I have listened to your sermons on morality, and I have no need to have them imposed on me anymore. I have made a fool of myself tonight. I came to you with my love, and you have said 'No' to the most priceless treasure I have to offer you. I'm just not in your moral league, theologian. I feel dirty and whorish. We women are like that. We store up our emotions, our dreams, our passion, sacrifice our chastity and virtue for the men we adore, and stupidly let it all hang out for them to seize upon or spurn as the Spirit moves them. We're fools, and I, an intelligent, educated woman, have been the worst of foolish women tonight, wouldn't you say, Preacher?"

Her words stung like a cat-o'-nine-tails across his back. Gall and acid laced her voice, as she again wiped her cheeks and eyes.

Dus responded. "No! No! Kara. It's not true. Don't say these things! Please, listen to me. Let me explain!"

"To hell with your explanations. I have heard more of those than I ever want to hear in a lifetime. I listened to you on the mountain and tonight in my house. I tried to understand, and I tried to have you understand me. I allowed myself to think as an Indian squaw and prostrated myself at the altar of a white priest's frailty. Go away from me, Father Habak, so that I won't undo your virtue. You owe me nothing. The room and board are free. I know you have no place to go tonight, otherwise I'd ask you to leave my house. So please, just go to your room. I don't want to see, hear, nor have you touch me again. I felt so desirable, unsoiled, and wholesome just a few minutes ago, and now I feel smutty and vulgar," she sobbed. "Go away, Father, and leave me alone!"

He felt helpless. He could not believe what had happened to them in such a few harsh moments—from hours of superb visages of love and affectionate conversation, to furor, resentment, and rejection. The pain was excruciating, and there was no consoling her with either his words or his hands.

"All right, Kara. Thank you for the beautiful evening. I did not mean to hurt you, and I am very sorry. Good night. I love you, and I always shall," he said softly, as he turned and went to his bedroom. He heard her sobbing even more profusely as he closed the bedroom door. Without removing his clothing, he lay down on the bed, and wept, himself. He knew he would not sleep.

Karol continued to look into the fire for a long time, tears running down her cheeks. She threw another log into the flames and then shuffled around the house turning off lights, and went to the bathroom. She put on a flannel nightie and returned to the living room. Nestling on the couch, she watched the big, bright yellow and red flames sparkle in the shadows. Tears flowed again. She had not cried so much in years. It was like a floodgate had been released in a great reservoir spillway. She sniffed and wiped her eyes. Sleep would not come.

She castigated herself. "I'm a stupid, self-pitying bitch," she moaned. "Oh, God, if you love me, take this fury and pride from me. What have I done to have offended you that I must ache like this? Please don't take Dus away from me. He was almost killed today, and I nearly lost him. I'll die if he dies. I love him. Talk to me, Lord. Please tell me what to do."

There seemed to be no answer. She sobbed and trembled. "Mare's marbles!" she cussed. "Donkey dung, turtle turds, and bull shit!" Cussing didn't help, either.

Dus was faring no better. He tossed and turned in his bed for what seemed hours. He could not sleep, and he was angry with himself. He prayed, too, contrite and penitent. He was confused by his commitments and promises, and the last thing he ever wanted in this world was to hurt neither God nor the woman he wanted for his wife. He had lusted after her body, but his years of priestly moralizing would not allow him that luxury. He had wanted it for them both, but had only managed to make her feel like a tramp. She could never be that, he thought to himself. She is a decent and magnificent woman. She only wanted our love to be fulfilled, as did I. I led her on, and then cowered at the whole idea of making love now.

His thoughts, unknowingly, were running parallel to Karol's. "Lord, there is no health in me," he prayed. "I nearly got killed up there on the mountain today. You saved me again for something. I don't know what it is, but give me the courage to go away from here and hurt the wondrous woman no more."

He didn't hear any answer from God, either. He thought that maybe he didn't want to. He couldn't rest any longer, and wanted to find out if Kara was all right. It was dark in the house, but he saw embers in the fireplace; he tiptoed into the living room. He found her sleeping fitfully on the couch. He looked at her lovingly. Her gorgeous face was tear-smudged; her unbanded, long, soft hair, in disarray; her sublime flanneled shivering body pulled into a fetal position, with arms embracing her knees. He gently brushed her hair with his fingers, took the couch afghan, and tucked it gently around her body. He bent down and kissed her lightly on the cheek.

"You can't hear me, my darling," he whispered. "You are so beautiful lying there. I want you to know that I love you and will never hurt you again. I am so very sorry. Any fault or sin here tonight was of my doing, not yours. I hope someday you will forgive me. I am leaving now to hitchhike back to the mountain where I belong. Find peace in your life, dearest lady. I will not upset your life again. Thank you for all the love and joy you have given me."

He turned from her, ashamed and sad. He went to his room, and bundled his clothes and gear under his arm. He threw her a kiss as he passed by her on the couch, and reached for the knob of the front door.

"Oh, Dus, please don't leave me!" she called out to him. "Come back and hold me. Please, come to the couch, lie quietly with me, and keep me warm and secure from my muddled world. I love you."

"Oh, Kara," he cried, throwing down his bundle and crawling in under the blanket with her. "Forgive me."

She cuddled to him. "Shhh, my darling, I am sorry, too. Let our misunderstandings and anger pass with the smoke from this lodge. No more anger, no more regrets, no more words, only love and forgiveness between us. No sun shall rise in the morning on our harmful words nor memories. Tomorrow is a new day, and nothing can separate thee from me. Our time for consummation will come when God allows, some wondrous day, and if he must test our resolve and failings from time to time in the meantime, so be it. I love him and you. I am a woman who loves too strongly. My emotions and my need for you will not subside. You, Dus Habak, and I, Ollikut Karol Thunder Rolling In The Mountain Christianson Marson, will weather this momentary storm; and in the interim between now and the day of our marriage, we will live in expectation, pleasing God and knowing our sacramental oneness will be the most stupendous experience in our lives. You wait and see, my love. I am your woman, and I promise you that. I cannot guarantee my native passion will never cause you anxiety, but I will not ask anything but love and patience from you."

"Thank you, Kara; thank you for forgiving and loving me. You are the most extraordinary woman in this world. How could I be so blessed? I shall wait forever for you if I have to. I could no longer live without you."

"Kiss me good night, then, Dus; put your arms around me and hold me close. Don't ever let me go again. And please, please, never go away from me, no matter how angry I am. I cannot live without you, either."

"I will never go away from you, Kara. Good night. I love you," he whispered, as they both lay down on the rug on the floor in front of the fire. He pulled the blanket over them and snuggled close to her back. She took his hand, gently planted it on the soft breast closest to him, and held it firmly. He squeezed it tenderly. She smiled to herself, and both fell asleep.

# 26

Morning came quickly to the Marson house in Staunton. Karol and Dus, who slept all night in front of the hearth, arose, kissed, readied themselves for the day, ate a hearty breakfast, and left the house. Dus drove Karol's car. She was happy and vivacious, showing no sign of their evening rift in her demeanor. Both her Danish and Indian disposition had decreed that "what was yesterday, was yesterday's conundrum. This is today, and life starts afresh!"

"Drop me off at the hospital, my love," she said, "and use the car for any errands you have in Staunton. I have surgery until noon. Pick me up a little after that, and I'll drive you back to Joshuatown. I have to get right back here for a board meeting and then pick up Shawn, so I can't tarry on the mountain for more than a minute or two."

"Thanks, honey, that'll be fine. Scott and I have some important work to do this afternoon, anyway. I love you," he called to her as he pulled up to the hospital and let her out of the car.

"I love you, Father. Thanks for last night. It was nice. I really mean that. See you later!" she yelled, as she hurried up to the building and disappeared.

Dus found a mall, shopped all morning rounding up some tools and items he needed for his work on the vicarage, and then picked up Karol at the appointed time. They got a bucket of fried chicken and picnicked in the car on the way up the mountain. "How was your morning?" he asked.

"Oh, a few slices here, a little sewing there, and everyone seems OK. I was a little weary. Can you give me a little pastoral insight about why that should have been, Father?"

"I could, but I won't. Anyway, I'm hungry. One of those thighs, legs, or breasts should satisfy me for a while."

"Mine or the chicken's?" Karol giggled.

"Do I have a choice?"

"No, not here. You got it, but it won't be as good as my crabcakes."

"I believe that, too, and certainly not better than your endowments."

"Stop that kind of talk. You make a gal blush!"

They laughed, talked, and sang going up the mountain. They were a happy couple, having put their misunderstanding behind them. They did not mention it and acted as though it had never happened. She snuggled up to him as he drove, and kissed his neck.

"It's a beautiful day," he said. "Kinda nice view coming up this mountain, isn't it?"

"Yes, it is, and life is beautiful up here. All those good people. Can't wait to see Nancy, Ox, Patty, and Bessie again. I will soon, Dus. I'll be up again soon."

"Hope so!"

"Dus, you and Scott be careful. There is a nut running around up there trying to hurt people I love. I came up with an idea this morning while I was working. May I make an observation—well, maybe a suggestion—without you and Scott thinking I'm being a prying female detective again?"

"Sure, why not."

"While you and that grouchy sheriff are burying the old fellow's bones, why don't you just act like you know someone is watching you, and make a big thing of putting him back in the grave. If he was upset with you digging up the guy, perhaps he'll cool off some if he happens to see you and Scott putting it back in the grave."

"Sounds like a good idea, but we can't put him back in that grave. I'm digging my trench there."

"Still, wherever you bury him, make a big thing of it, just in case he's looking. Just so he knows you aren't robbing the grave of some loved one he is close to. You don't need to even tell Scott. Just act like you're doing a good thing for the guy."

"You are very wise and clever, sweetheart. How did you think that up?"

"Easy. I'm an Indian. That's the way we do things. We're good at getting people to think we are doing something one way, while we are thinking another way."

"Sounds a bit tacky after all that 'white-eyed, forked-tongue' talk you don't like."

"There's a difference when it's for a good cause."

"I guess so, but it won't hurt to try your idea. Who knows what goodness lurks in the hearts of men? God knows."

She laughed and continued to do that all the way up the mountain. Her laughter was like tonic to Dus. She lifted his spirits as high as the mountain they climbed. Before they knew it, they arrived in Joshuatown and pulled up to Sheriff Kirsh's office. Dus' jeep was sitting where he had left it the day before. Scott saw them pull up and came out to greet them.

"Hi, lovers," he laughed. "Glad to see that you survived the night, and the trip down and up the mountain. How was your evening?"

"Hi, Scott," Karol said. "Got him back safe and sound for your dirty work. He's no worse for wear!"

"Were you two good?" he quipped.

"We had a wonderful evening together, and yes, we were good. Better than we wanted to be, but that is none of your business, snoopy. Were you good?" Dus asked.

"Well, that depends on what you mean by 'good.' It was a very good evening, but then I am married to a pretty, compassionate practical nurse with a very practical and super bedside manner!"

"Bedside, eh," Kara snickered. "I'm going to tell Patty that you were talking like that."

"Don't do that, Karol. You know how private she is about family matters. She'll drub me so bad it'll take you a week to patch me up. She doesn't like husband and wife private things talked about outside the house. You know her. If it comes from her, OK, but otherwise, nix! Don't get me in trouble."

"Then wash out your mouth with soap, copper."

"I will; I will. Gosh, Dus, what did you do to that feisty woman last night to make her so ornery? I told you it was a mistake to get her involved with old Buck."

"Had nothing to do with Buck, that droll body carver. Dus did nothing, you dirty old man. I just love my nurse, and don't know why she puts up with a sourball like you," she remarked, getting out of the car then giving Scott a kiss on the cheek. "Listen, guys. I gotta get back. I leave you two to your own devices with the old geezer. Don't get hurt. You take care of him, Scott. I'll hold you responsible."

"I will, Karol. Not to worry. I'll save him for another night for you."

She kissed Dus and climbed back in her car. "Watch your mouth! So long! Say 'Hi' to Patty, Nancy, Ox, and all the kids. I'll see you soon. Thanks, Dus, for a great time. I love you!" she yelled, as she drove away.

"Love you, Kara! I'll miss you!" he yelled back.

"Now, there goes some kind of woman," the sheriff said to his priest friend.

"Yeah, you have that right," Dus responded sadly. "She has become a very big part of my heart, Scott. I love her more each day."

"I can see that, Dus. You're a lucky man."

"I truly am, Scott. It was wonderful being with her last night."

"That's none of my business, Parson."

"It's OK. Just food and talk at her place, like a great big wonderful high school date. She's a great cook, a great hostess, and a lot of fun."

"Yeah," Scott agreed. "Sorta hard to believe of a brainy gal like Karol, but you can see the love of life in her eyes. Don't know about the Indian part, but the Scandinavian part of her personality just flows out all over the place. Patty says that beyond the professional exterior, she is soft, kind, compassionate, loves people a lot, and is an excellent physician. We need her here in this village, Dus, and I must reluctantly admit we need you, too. You two make a fine team of caregivers. Patty and I are happy you have fallen in love, and we wish you the same kind of happiness we've found on this mountain, even with its bad side."

"Thanks, Scott. She is a beautiful person, and I am blessed with her love. Gosh, I hate to see her go away again."

"I know, friend. I feel for you. Guess you wouldn't be interested in burying those old bones at a gloomy time like this, would you?"

"Sure I would, ghoul. It'll cheer me up."

"Well, maybe it will. The old fellow still has a smile on his face. Hey, I want to ask an informed theologian like you about that. Don't you think it is sort of weird how skeletons are always smiling, no matter how they met their fate? Do you think maybe they saw a little bit of heaven or something before they died? Maybe we're just made that way from the beginning, and it's all this skin and stuff on our face that make us look so melancholy. I don't know. What do you think?"

"I think a farcical sheriff is pulling my leg. Ask Karol or Patty. They know all about anatomy. But laughing or crying, we gotta get that old dude who's in the back of your truck into a grave up there at the church before someone in town sees us carrying a corpse around. I'll dig another hole in the cemetery with the backhoe, and we'll shove him in it with a blanket around that body bag, and have a prayer."

"I don't want to see him smile when we do that. The way dead folk smile, Dus, is creepy!"

"If we can't stand dead people smiling, we are both in the wrong business."

They laughed together and went to Scott's pickup to get about the chore of burying the dead. They moved the backhoe high in the top section of the graveyard, dug a hole to accommodate the body, wrapped the oilcloth around the body bag, and laid the decayed cadaver to rest, again. They put a large unmarked mountain stone and a wooden cross at the head of the grave, and then scattered leaves and debris over the dirt so no person nor animal would disturb it. Dus said some Burial Office prayers, and the two men left to continue their chores for the day. Dus had made a big affair of it without Scott realizing it. He thought that his friend Ollikut would approve.

"I don't know whether he was a minister or just some poor soul of another vocation, but isn't it sad the way people die, and are buried unknown, uncared for, and unlamented?" Scott mourned.

"Yeah, it is, Scott. But let's try to think on the positive side. Even though there was no coffin, and no grave marker, he apparently was laid to rest with some care. He was positioned well, face up, his hands as in prayer, and was covered with an oilcloth. Maybe somebody did care. Maybe that old preacher who no one knew, who went away at one time, took pity on a wandering and dying soul, and gave him some final last rites. Who knows? But I believe that you and I have now done the right thing, even if we don't know who it was that I made very angry for digging the skeleton up. But then, as you have said to Karol and me many times, the solution of that mystery is your job. I just did my job of burying one of God's children, no matter the degree of his celebrity, sin, or virtue."

"Yeah, you're lucky. You say the prayers, and I still have to do the work. Mare's marbles! Jeez, Dus, now you got me using that colorless expression of yours. You know, Father, sometime when you have a free moment, I'd like to talk to you about some of your cuss words. They're really bizarre."

# 27

Spring had enveloped the Cutty and Blue Mountains, and they were aglow with flowers, tree buds, and bush blossoms. Newly born animals were frolicking with their mothers, learning to feed and run. Birds were chirping and singing, and Dus' heart, soul, and body swelled with contentment and love. Things were going well with his mission and with his beloved. The folk at the church and throughout the countryside looked revitalized with the passage of winter. You could see them all over hill and dale, beginning to plow the fields and leading cows to pasture.

Ox was doing very well with his new "wooden" leg. Nancy was happy with his progress, and patient with his grumbling. The tireless "titan" was anxious to get into the woods again to do some hunting, but until that happened, he bided his time helping with the vicarage. Weeks had passed, and a lot of progress had been made on the house. Lou Casalano had come down to help Dus and Ox. Cyrus, Jed, Scott, and some neighboring men volunteered with the heavy work when their time allowed. Patty and many of the female parishioners painted and cleaned up after the men, and provided sandwiches and cold refreshments. It reminded Dus of the Amish barn raisings in Pennsylvania when all the neighbors turned out to help. The diocese was true to its word by providing money and materials, and HUDSON & SON COMPANY was very good in seeing that everything Dus needed from the store was available.

Terry had not come down with Lou, an illness of a friend having prevented her, but Dus knew she wanted Lou to be with him alone, so they could talk. Dus was pretty upset with Lou's declining appearance. The once-husky man was now gaunt and tired, but that did not keep him from working hard, laughing, joking, and enjoying his time with his old friend. Lou did the cooking for the two of them during his stay. Being a cook, he relished the opportunity to impose his talents on Dus. They ate well while he was there, and work kept them both happy and robust. Lou began to tire toward the end of his stay, and it was obvious that his energy was waning from his disease. Damnable cancer, Dus cursed to himself. It's a killer. I wish it had not happened to this good man.

The day finally arrived when Lou had to return home. They had done a lot of carpentry, masonry, and electrical and plumbing work together, and the house looked good. It was bigger, sturdier, and modern, but kept its rustic appearance. It was amazing what they had accomplished in such a short time. Karol will love it, they both thought, and so will the people of the church. It was good that Karol stayed away while the building was going on. She will be happily surprised.

"Well, I gotta get up the road to Terry," Lou said. "I promised her a week's vacation with just the two of us when I get back. It was great being with you and doing this, Paesano. Looks pretty good, if I must say so, myself."

"It was really nice of you to come, Lou. It was good to be working beside you again. I appreciate it. I've learned a lot from you through the years. Thanks for all the good meals, too."

"Anytime. You and that lady of yours come on up to Pennsylvania soon to see us, and I'll cook a real Italian meal for you. I mean it. Tell Karol I'm sorry we didn't get to meet. Terry will want to meet the lovely lady and put her sign of approval on her. You know how these Italian women are about other women."

"She'll approve of my Indian princess, believe me."

"Just be sure she takes good care of you."

"She will! Lou, you didn't talk much about how you're feeling. You OK? Would you like to talk about it with me?"

"This stuff is really a literal pain in the butt, Father, but I can handle it. I won't allow it to get me down. I got too much to do and live for. Anyway, God, Terry, the kids, and friends are there, and they take good care of me. Don't you worry none. I'll still be around to watch the Chicago Bears kick the tar out of the Washington Redskins. Shucks, everybody's got something to contend with as he gets older, ain't that so, Father?"

"Yeah, we all do, Lou, but you're very special, and if I can help you in any way over the bumps, let me know. Speaking of our favorite football teams, watch what you say about the Redskins. Don't forget, I am going to marry one."

"Gosh, that's right. I'd better start watching my mouth. But when I think of it, ain't it interesting, historically, how Indians and bears always seemed to get along together in the forest until we screwed it up by making them into football teams? It's just a game, but I sure don't want any Bear beating up on your pretty Indian wife. Tell her it's not our fault what they call the teams. I wish they would change the names. I don't like the idea of hurting anyone's feelings. You'll assure her of that, won't you? Howsoever, I still gotta cheer for Chicago to beat up on Washington," he grinned.

"She's going to love you and Terry. Anyway, it was great having you here; I appreciate everything you've done for us."

"You're surely welcome. You have helped me a lot by asking me to come. It's been a pleasure building a house that will serve the Lord and make a home for my friend, his wife, their children, and the Lord's people. Thank you, Father."

Lou Casalano had called Dus "Father" ever since the latter was ordained to the priesthood. Dus had told him that it was OK for a friend to call him by his first name, but Lou had declined. It was Lou's simple way, as a good Catholic, of respecting Dus' priestly profession.

They had prayed together before Lou left, and Dus gave him a blessing. They embraced each other with an old country kiss on the cheeks, like they had always done, and Lou drove away in his old Ford station wagon full of tools, waving and smiling. "I love you, Amico. Arrevederci! Thank the sheriff for taking me down to mass at Staunton on Saturday. I enjoyed your mass on Sunday, too. You haven't lost your touch. Bye!" he yelled as he departed.

"Ciao, Paesano; I love you. My best to Terry! Please take care of yourself." Tears had again formed in Dus' eyes. "Oh God, take care of him, please. He is such a good man, and loves you so much."

Four more weeks passed as neighbors helped with the finishing touches on the outside of the vicarage. He was proud of what they all had accomplished. Karol, as Lou had agreed, would love it. Her work had kept her in Staunton for six weeks. They had talked on the telephone every day, and he had kept her informed of the progress. Though he had sorely missed her, he was glad that he was going to be able to surprise her with her new house. She was coming home that Friday and he would bring her up the hill to see the renovated cabin, but he would not let her see inside until it was completely finished. She was going to be nosy and cranky about that, but he was determined to control her access into the inside until the right time. Dus was from a family who loved surprises.

Friday came, and Dus dropped in on the Conleys at dusk to pick up his pretty girlfriend for their date. After making salutations to Nancy and Ox, they strolled up the hill with arms around waists. It was a beautiful, cool spring afternoon with a gorgeous red sun slowly setting behind the summit of the Blue.

"Oh, darling, I am so excited to see what you and Lou have done to the house," she said.

"It wasn't just us. A lot of other people helped, too. But you have to know, you're not going to see a stick of that house until you give me a kiss and tell me how much you missed and love me. I've missed you!"

"Me too; me too," Karol cooed.

They stopped on the dirt road, and hugged and kissed away the days and time they had been apart. "I do love you, Dus, so very much. I hate being away from you for so long. I wanted to be here, too, to help, but you know the needs at the hospital. I just couldn't get away. Surgery seemed to pile up. I guess folk saved up over the winter to have their bodies tidied up. I'm sorry, too, that I haven't been able to get up to the clinic, but Nancy said people have been pretty healthy, and Patty took care of the few who had the dropsies. Mostly minor stuff."

"It's OK. Anyway, you'll see the house in a few minutes, but you can't go inside."

"Wadda ya mean I can't go inside? How am I gonna see it, if I can't go inside? Has the springtime affected your senses, Parson?"

"The springtime has only turned my senses to what you've been thinking about all winter."

"I see," she laughed, hugging him tightly. "And what is that?"

"You know! What we promised each other we wouldn't do until we're married."

"Uh-huh. Well then, you'd better turn me loose, show me the house, and help me plan a wedding."

"Are you serious, sweetheart? Do you want to do that soon?"

"Yeah, I'm tired of all this distance, time, and mortified flesh between us. But we'll discuss wedding details after I see what kind of wigwam you're gonna lodge and board your bride in."

They came around a familiar bend in the road, and looked up from where they had stood to view their Christmas crèche. "Well, what do you think?"

Karol could not believe her eyes. "Oh, Dus, it's beautiful!" she yelled, as they walked up to and around the cabin, hand in hand. Dus pointed out various facets of its construction and new additions. The well had been rebuilt in stone, with a little roof, and a hand-turned wooden wench with a rope and bucket. A covered water pump along the side of it was ready to do its work of providing water to the house. The outhouse, still standing, was now painted brilliant red, and was surrounded by new plants and shrubbery.

"Well, farmer boy, why is that outhouse still standing there in all its glory?"

"Shame on you, Indian gal, for not appreciating the finer utilitarian antiquities of the farm and reservation of our youth. I kept it so you and the kids could have your private moments. I shall, I'm afraid, have to contend with the new plumbing inside," he kidded.

"Then I shall not marry you. If I wanted one of those crude things in my life, I would not have left the wigwam!"

"Well, then, I guess I will have to let you use the facilities in the house. I surely don't want to be married to a malcontent. Really, I did keep it because Ox told us many people pass this way on the trail; they may have a need for it, and won't want to bother us. Course, we may too, if my plumbing system doesn't work."

"It had better work! OK, you can keep your outside potty monument. It is kinda cute." She was excited about everything she saw, and listened intently to his explanations, fascinated and pleased. She was very proud of him for what he had done with the vicarage. There was little semblance to the old structure she had visited before, but it maintained its rustic appearance. The building was reconstructed in stained vertical cedar and stone, and had cottage windows and doors, trimmed with white shutters. A split cedar shake roof jutted out over two gables, with a massive mountain-stone chimney running up through the eaves of the front one. A big porch, off the living room, faced the woods, as did a cantilevered small porch jutting out from the second floor of the rear gable. A one-car garage was attached to the kitchen side. The whole area was surrounded by a rail fence, hemlocks, blooming mountain laurel, azaleas, and dogwood. It was cozy and pretty.

Dus had made her laugh when he called it her "chalanty"—part chalet and part shanty, as he described it while building it. He had made it rustic because he had wanted the transition back and forth to their two respective houses to be easy for her. The outside of his house had the character of hers, and she was pleased. When he was finished with the interior, it would be equally decorous and comfortable.

"It's gorgeous, Dus, and so much bigger than I'd imagined it would be. I can hardly wait to see the inside."

"I'm glad you like it, honey. I made it for you. But as I told you on the road, and I am going to be firm about this, you're not seeing the inside until it's done and we're married."

"Come on, sweetheart! You were kidding, weren't you?"
"No, I wasn't!"
"Can't I just peek in the windows?"
"Nope! It's not done in there yet."
"You're very knavish, and you're gonna pay for this, Dus Habak!"
"Yeah, I know, but you're not going inside no matter what you call me. Come on, Indian Princess, we're going back down the trail before you talk me out of my resolve."

They stopped at the road again and looked back up at the cabin. The sun had set, and stars and a quarter moon were beginning to appear. Karol's face glowed with satisfaction, and she beamed at Dus. He looked into her face. "You said something about a wedding. What did you have in mind? It was right at this spot at Christmastime that I knew I loved you, so it seems like a good place to talk about marriage."

"That's right. It is a good place and time. What I had in mind was a proper marriage proposal from you. We aren't even engaged."

"Didn't I already do that? I thought that was understood?"

"Understood, baloney! I want a genuine proposal."

"You don't want me, woman; you just lust after the inside of my house."

"Not true! I do want to marry you, Dus Habak, and a proper marriage proposal from you might very well hurry me up to make the proper arrangements for that auspicious occasion."

"Do I have to take you out to a restaurant with wine, candlelight, and a black-tied waiter to pop that question?"

"That's be nice, but I don't want to wait that long."

"How long will you wait?"

"Mmm, about five more minutes!"

"Doesn't give a guy much time to ponder whether this is what he wants to do with the rest of his life!"

"You just had six weeks all by your lonesome at night up here with old Tooter to make decisions relative to the matter at hand. Come on, big brave, quit stalling and get down on your knees."

"Here on this old gravel road in the dark? My pants will get dirty."

"I'm serious. I'm just as resolute about this as you are about not letting me inside the house. Forget the pants! I'll wash 'em for you when we're married. Don't forget, you're the one who wanted all the formal nuptial froufrou so we can sleep together. Well, this is part of it."

"OK, but you have to close your eyes for a moment while I prepare for this," he laughed, "and don't open them until I tell you."

She closed her eyes. Dus got down on his one knee, fumbled with his jacket pocket, and tugged at her jacket. "OK. Open your eyes!"

She did that. He took her hand in his and spoke very softly to her. "Ollikut Karolina Thunder Rolling In The Mountain Christianson Marson, will you marry me and be my lawful wedding wife till death do us part? I want you to know, it's a great privilege for me to ask. Now, will you please say 'Yes' so I can get off of my aching knees?"

Karol smiled at Dus and helped him to stand up. She put her hands on his shoulders and looked straight into his eyes. "Yes, Dus Habak, I will marry you and be your wife. It is a great honor to be asked, and to accept your proposal."

"Will you kiss your betrothed?"

"Oh, Dus, stop this farcical stuff. Hold and kiss me."

They stood in the middle of the dirt road again and exhausted their pent-up emotions. She was the first to break away. "Gosh, Dus, we're really engaged!"

"Not yet. I still have something for you to make it official."

Excitement grew in her eyes. "You do? What?"

"I had a piece of mountain stone from the fireplace mounted on a ring for you."

Her face registered disappointment, but she fibbed and whispered an appreciative, "Mountain stone—that is really sweet and sentimental."

"Close your eyes and hold out your left hand."

She was not exactly euphoric about mountain stone on any of her fingers, but did as he had requested. He slipped a ring on the third finger of her left hand. She opened her eyes and looked disconsolately down at the ring on her finger. The moonlight made it glisten. Big tears rolled down Karol's face. She had difficulty speaking. She could see from the reflecting light that it was not a mountain stone, but a very elegant diamond, sided by two exquisitely polished green-and-gray turquoise pips mounted on an Indian silver ring. She lifted her finger to her face and stared at it. She was overcome with love and joy.

"It's beautiful. I don't know what to say. You dear, dear man. I never expected this," she cried, rubbing it, putting it to her lips, and kissing it. "Did you plan this all along for tonight?"

"I did, indeed, my betrothed," he smiled, "because I knew you were going to try to make an honest man of me. Besides, I want to marry you so you can see the inside of my house and make your home there with me."

"When did you get it?"

"Well, the diamond is from my mother's engagement ring that she gave me before she died. She thought it was silly to have such a beautiful thing buried in a casket. I have kept it with me from that day. I ordered the turquoise stones from the Wallowa Reservation through a friend of mine in Kamiah. I had them grind, polish, and set the diamond in the ring at a jewelry store in Staunton. I picked it up the morning you were doing surgery, and had it in my pocket when we drove up here from your house. It has been waiting for your finger ever since. I'm glad you like it."

"Oh, Dus, it's beautiful. Thank you. I feel so close to your mom and dad now, even though I will never know them."

"They were good people, Kara, and they would have loved you. My mother was very beautiful, both physically and spiritually, and was very special to me. We were very close. You will see what she looks like when you meet my sister, Margaret."

"You're so sweet darling, and I thank you, too, for the stones that came from my valley at home. What a wonderful sentimental gesture. I love you so much."

"And I love you. So now what do you think of tradition, rings and things, and getting married in church?"

"You've convinced me, theologian. Can't wait," she said, beginning to weep. Pushing her hand out from her, she gazed at her newest possession with tears running down her cheeks and added, "It's so beautiful. I have been so wrong about tradition. It's going to be wonderful getting ready for our big day at the church."

They fell into each other's arms again. He looked into her eyes. "And furthermore, my bride-to-be, I'm tired of resisting temptation!"

"Oh, me too, and bribery will get you everything of me," she declared, sniffing and wiping her face.

"And the day you go over the threshold into that house up there on that hill, in my arms as my wife, there will be no more resisting temptation. Right?"

"Oh, right, my love; yes, yes. I will wait impatiently for you to act upon that conviction. In the meantime, I have a lot to do. We gotta start right away now, my fiancé. Doesn't that sound nice?"

"Yes, fiancée. So when are we gonna do this wedding thing?"

"Hmmm, let's see. Let me do some quick figuring. How about June twenty-eight?"

"That soon?"

"Yeah. That OK with you?"

"Sure, but why that particular date?"

"Well, for a few reasons. It's a Saturday, when people can be off work and can come to a wedding. I have a week of vacation coming up about then, and for other reasons I will explain to my Indian brave someday. Do you think you can find us a preacher to tie the knot?"

"Sure; I'll ask the bishop."

"Great. So it's all settled. You think you can handle your new Indian bride in that new lodge?" she laughed, taking his hand and pulling him down the road to Nancy and Ox's house. They ran all the way, and breathlessly entered the house, where Nancy, Ox, and their children were waiting for them.

"Wal, 'bout time ya showed up fer some vittles, younguns," Ox grumbled. "Whar en tarnations ya be'n?"

"Dat's none a yer bus'ness, Ox," Nancy admonished him. 'Donna ya know da young folk in love has things deys hafta set'le?"

"Guess what?" Karol asked them.

"What?" Ox and Nancy asked simultaneously.

"Dus just asked me to marry him. I said 'Yes.' Look what's on my finger," she said, running to them with her finger held out.

"I'll be dinged," Nancy laughed, hugging them both. "I know'd it. I know'd it. Din't I, Ox?"

"She sho did, en war happy fer ya. We loves ya so," Ox sniffed, pecking Karol on the cheek and shaking Dus' hand.

"It's a bootiful ring fer a bootiful gal," Nancy said.

"Yeah," Karol smiled. "From a beautiful guy! Well, we have a lot of work to do getting ready for the big day on June twenty-eighth, and we don't have much time."

"Well, ya donna have ta worry none 'bout de food fer da wedding pauty, 'cause Bessie en me will take car' a dat fer ya. Wold ya like dat, sweet thing?"

"Oh, yes. Thank you, Nancy. And will you be my bridesmaid?"

"I sholy would be mos' honored, I would, dear gal," she said, and went into Karol's outstretched arms. They both wept, and Nancy nodded her head on Karol's bosom. Ox put his huge arms around Dus, and they smiled at the elegant women who filled up their lives with love and happiness. Cyrus and Jenny congratulated them, and everyone in the house, including the children, laughed, hugged, and cried. Tooter, whose happy countenance had been virtually ignored by everyone, and who did not understand about rings and things, jumped up and put her paws on Dus and Karol. She wagged her tail, and seemed genuinely happy for her master and mistress.

# 28

Dus looked over the pulpit on Ascension Sunday, trying with some difficulty, to explain the significance of that religious celebration.

"During the forty days that Jesus spent on earth with his disciples after his Resurrection, he worked very hard trying to prepare them to start building his church, which we now call the Christian Church. It was so long ago that it is difficult for us to realize that Jesus was a real human being like us, and, like for us, his life on earth had come to an end. His rising from the dead at Easter after his death was the fulfillment of his promise that he would come back from death; and with that, it is possible for every human being to have life in heaven with God forever. But, as a human being, he, too, had to leave this earth and go to heaven to be with the Father. He always told his followers that he had to go away from them eventually, but he said, 'in my Father's house are many mansions, and I go to prepare a place for you. Where I go, you will go, too.' He promised we would be with him in heaven with God forever."

"What a mess," Dus said to himself, as he looked out on confused faces. "I don't think they understand a thing I'm saying, and I don't blame them." He was frustrated trying to explain this part of Jesus' life. Getting these simple people to understand a part of historical Christian theology that didn't make much difference to their relationship to God just wasn't happening for him. He could not recall even when the so-called intelligentsia could understand that theology, nor be spiritually enraptured with it! We clergy may think it is essential and important to the laity, but the laity don't think so. It doesn't put food in their stomachs and clothes on their backs. Nevertheless, it was important that Jesus did it for us, and I have tried to explain the best I can.

"Let me put it this way. The only reason we have the church today is because Jesus went away from this earth to heaven. He did that so he could get around in his Spirit to all the people in the world. God couldn't just leave his Son walking and sitting around in a little country like Israel forever like some old mountain guru, telling people to be good, and if they were, they'd have a place after death where everything would be OK. So, while he was once a human being on earth, he is now in heaven with God the Father, just as we will be someday. He is now, because of going up to heaven on Ascension Day, accessible to all people in the world. Because he is in heaven, every person can know him as his Savior. So it doesn't matter, as I told you before, whether you're an Asian, African, European, American, Islander, or a mountaineer of any sort; nor do your color and nationality matter. People everywhere can know about Jesus. They can know that God loves them. He promised, in returning to heaven, he would send the Holy Spirit, who would come to us. We call that day, Pentecost. It comes next Sunday, when we will celebrate and talk about it, too."

He looked at the folk, and surmised they had no earthly or heavenly idea what he was talking about. They're sitting there trying hard to understand. God bless them! They want to respect me and listen to what I'm saying about Jesus and his word. "Well, Lord," Dus said to God, "if you think all this is important, I guess you will have them understand. I'm not so sure that a flunked-out cathedral dean can make the gospel easy for them. They just want to know that you love them, will take care of them while they're here on earth, and will take them to heaven with you when they die. Lord, help me to learn to talk to these people about you and Jesus in a language they can understand. On the other hand, they may understand a lot more than I think they do. I leave it in your hands, God."

Dus quit preaching and went on to finish the service. Many of the villagers who greeted him at the door had heard about his engagement to Dr. Marson, and seemed more interested in that little piece of village gossip than about the mystery of the Ascension. Not that they were not religious; it was just that they better understood a man falling in love with a pretty lady, getting "hitched," and having "younguns." They might not know much about theology, but they sure knew about moonlight, holding hands, "smoochin'," building a house, and making babies. They also knew about working hard, getting "vittles" on the table, trying to keep warm and well, and finding happiness in life. If God could help them with all that by sending Jesus and having him go back to heaven to sit at his right hand, that was "jist" fine with them. "Dey 'preciated it, en dey woulda git ta chu'ch ta thunk da Lo'd fer dat!"

Whatever they thought about the way Dus put it in a sermon, they were nice to tell him, "Sho did enjo' yo' message." Many of them had said that as they left the service—perhaps sparing Dus the pain of the truth was part of their compassion. God love 'em! Aside from that, they told him that Dr.

Marson was a "go'geous lady, en youse is lucky, Preacha, ketchin such a beauty." Then they urged him to "be good ta 'er 'cause she was a wunnerful docta, too, en we needs 'er!" A slap on his back and hearty guffaws from many of the people reassured Dus that they approved of their forthcoming nuptial, and would rejoice in it;. They also kidded him about the vicarage being turned into a "honeymoon house," and about how nice the old outhouse looked, all shiny with flowers around it. Some of them were not aware of the new plumbing in the house. Most of the people had none of that in their own, and would not even think of it. He laughed with them throughout their comments, but he knew that Karol and Elly were going to love the new inside commode and bathing facilities. He could not help but think that Ox was a very wise person in suggesting that he keep the outhouse in the yard, aside from the need of trail people. If it was there and visible, there would be no need for the people to postulate about him living better than they, though they were glad to have him provide for the lady doctor the best he could, having done it with the sweat of his brow, the muscles of his back, and the talents of his own hands.

Time sped on as he divided his time between visiting the folk around the area and finishing up the interior of the house. He worked long hours into the night, each day, taking time out on occasion to call Karol. Her days were full, too, doing surgery and preparing for their wedding day.

"I called J.K. and Julie," he told her, "and told them we'd love to put off the spelunking until late summer for the best of reasons, and they agreed. Said they'd make it to the wedding. J.K. thought you might like to go spelunking on our honeymoon."

"Yeah, I know," she said. "J.K. was here for a couple of days, and the old sarge gave me a hard time about that and for marrying you. He said I could have done better, should have picked Army instead of Marines, and a professor instead of a preacher, but allowed that I would do OK with a Penn Stater. You know what else he said?"

"I can imagine a lot of things, but what?"

"He said you were a very lucky man to get me as a wife. Is that true, Penn Stater?"

"Yeah, it is! I think I'm lucky. What did he say about your luck in getting me?"

"I told him I thought I was lucky, too. He said that was because I was a bit silly in love, and couldn't make good judgments. He's right!"

"I'm in love, too, and J.K. understands that kind of thing. Wait till you meet Julie."

"Looking forward to it. Did you call the bishop yet and ask him about the wedding day we chose?"

"Yep; he said he wanted to do it, but we have to go in to see him for marriage counseling."

"What? An old widower like you and an old widow like me have to go to marriage counseling? You're kidding?"

"No, I'm not. He's a stickler on the canons, but I really think he just wanted an excuse to meet you and see if you're as beautiful and intelligent as I have described you."

"Bless his heart! Will he let us come some Saturday?"

"I'll check and see. He knows about your working hours, and I'm sure he'll do his best to accommodate us."

"Good. Let me know. Love ya. Won't be long before I'll be your pretty little wife inside your pretty, new lodge. Bye!"

\* \* \*

The marriage counseling session with Bishop Mueller lasted about two hours, and was, for Karol, more fun than spiritual. The bishop understood, of course, that both she and Dus had been married before, and that they probably did not need much counseling. But knowing how difficult a husband's priesthood can be for wives, he wanted Karol to be aware of the thorns in that rose patch. It was not any easier working full time for God and his holy church and tending people's souls, than it was fixing up their bodies. God simply did not always keep you from stumbling in the pitfalls of humanity, no matter how close you felt to him. Being a clergy wife might sound very ethereal, but many a clergy wife have lived to tear out her hair over their "pie in the sky when you die, orators," and would have like to have seen their husbands "ushered into the Kingdom" sooner rather than later. While the priesthood was a holy sacrament, as, perhaps, was medicine, he reminded the couple that marriage was, too; and if they didn't understand the considerable responsibility it would take to do both, they had better kiss good-bye, shake hands, and go their separate ways. "Dus is not in the Roman Catholic Church, Karol. A priest in this church has got to find a way to devote time to one vocation without neglecting the other. He already knows the pitfalls of that."

Karol listened intently to the bishop's wise admonitions. Nodding her head, she allowed that she would be asking more of God's help with her new life than she had in the past.

Having gotten some of the thorny issues out of the way, the bishop turned to the lighter side of the meeting. He was enthralled with Karol's personality, and conversed at length with her about her family and her life in general. He questioned her and Dus about how they planned to manage their respective vocations between Staunton and Joshuatown, and fulfill the needs of their children. "How are Shawn and Elly taking to this idea of you two getting married?" he asked.

"They knew it was coming, and were not very surprised," Karol answered him. "Shawn loves Dus, Bishop; and Elly, I believe, approves of me."

"She loves Karol, Bishop," Dus interjected, "and has a pretty keen eye for her new brother, too."

"That's fine. I already knew about Elly. I hope you don't mind that she came to me to talk about this."

"She did?"

"Well, don't be so surprised. That little girl and I have become pretty good friends over the last several months. When she gets tired of the cranky old sisters and the discipline of the priory school, she sometimes comes over here to my office, and we talk. Mrs. Mueller and I have taken her out to supper on occasion, and we've had some good times. I must say, the young lady has done exceptionally well, considering what she's been through with her mother's death and her separation from you, Dus. You can be very proud of her. From what I can ascertain from our conversations, she's supportive of your marriage. She is happy for her father and for you, Karol. She not only approves of you, but I noted with a degree of happiness that she has been calling you her new mom."

"That's sweet of her," Karol replied, "and we get along well. I think that with Shawn, too, the four of us will make a happy family. Anyway, it's nice she has you to talk to. I look forward to your meeting Shawn. You'll like him, too."

"I'm sure I will if he's anything like his mom."

"Well, that might not be all that encouraging, but that he is. I know, being the little acolyte he is, he'll think it's cool, as do I, that his bishop approves of his mom's marriage to this neat priest."

"Well now, young lady, before you and your son get carried away with my benevolence, is his mom sure she really wants to live' out in the mountains with this bucolic missionary of mine? You're an awfully sophisticated lady to leave medical academia and live in the sticks with this recalcitrant mountain man."

"You aren't exactly reassuring my bride-to-be about my potentialities as a husband," Dus laughed, reproaching his bishop.

"Well, he's just become a mountain man, and I'm dealing well with his recalcitranced," Karol interceded. "I adore him with all his eccentricities. Anyway, Bishop, we reservation women have had a lot of experience with the kind of person you have described. My mother married one, and she taught me how to handle the type. Furthermore, being a mountain gal, myself, and having been up there with those folk in Joshuatown for some time, I think I can tame this wild priest and be helpful to him in his ministry. Don't worry about me. I'm looking forward to living with this missionary, and learning about God, the birds, and the bees."

Dus grinned, thinking, That's telling him, Ollikut!

The bishop smiled, too. "Well, Father, I'd say this fiancée of yours is pretty well set on going to the woods with you to learn about whatever she doesn't already know about the birds and the bees. It appears like you have found yourself a wise, free-spirited, candid, and lovely woman to take care of your heinie in the future."

"Take care of what?" Karol wailed.

"Didn't I hear, somewhere, Karl, that when you two first met, you asked my priest to drop his pants and show you his heinie?" the bishop chuckled.

Karol's face turned red, and she glared at Dus. "Did you tell him that embellished yarn, Father Habak?"

"I don't remember telling it that way," Dus hedged.

"How do you remember telling it, Preacher?"

"I just told him that you and I first met when I went to the clinic and you treated a little wound on my rear end."

"Oh. And did you tell him how you got that wound?"

"No. That is privileged communication between a doctor and her priest."

"You be careful, Father, or I may have to come to my new bishop with some true confessions. I think you're right, Bishop Mueller—maybe I am taking a big chance marrying this mountain man, whose veracity is somewhat wanting."

"Now, now, you two," Bishop Mueller interjected. "He's pretty nice,

Karol, when you get to know him. I'm sure you'll straighten him out. And you have my permission to work on his heinie all you want. Anyway, I am happy about your marriage plans, and I think you're both very fortunate to have found each other to love and care for. I believe, Karol, that you will be a tremendous help to Dus."

"Thank you, Bishop," Karol answered. "And I do want you to know that I do love this preacher of yours, and will carefully tend all of his wounds."

"I'm sure of that. Well now, it's time to find Mrs. Mueller and have some lunch. Dus is one of her favorite priests, and I'm pretty sure she's going to think he is getting a super wife in you."

"I am anxious to meet her."

"She'll be interested in your Indian heritage. She was a history professor, and knows a lot about Native Americans. You and she will have some good things to talk about. Since I have spoken to her about you, you'll be interested in knowing that she is one of those historians who thinks the Nez Perce and your great-grandfather Joseph got a lousy deal from the Blue Coats, and should have whipped the pants off the Yankee cavalry. But then, she's also one of those misled southern ladies who still wishes that her granddaddy had whipped the blue pants off of my Yankee granddaddy."

"Sounds like a very discerning woman," Karol smiled.

"By the way, you two, don't forget that as your bishop and counselor, I expect a continuing report about the progress of your relationship, even after your marriage."

"We'll do that, Bishop. Thank you so much for caring," Karol reassured him.

After enjoying a nice lunch with the Muellers, Karol and Dus drove up the mountain, happy and content. "Well, what do you think?" Dus asked.

"They're awfully nice people, darling. I enjoyed our lunch with them, but I especially liked our talk with the bishop. He's fun."

"You made me very proud, sweetheart. It was a great honor for me to introduce you to him."

"Thank you. He seemed to like me, and Mrs. Mueller is really a neat woman. When we were alone in the bathroom, she told me all about you and gave me some pointers on being a clergy wife. She said that my Indian skills will help."

"Tell me the pointers."

"She said you are the priest, and I am the wife, mother, and doctor. She said there will be plenty of work in those vocations. She said that it will be my job to take care of my patients, my kids, and you, and that you will take care of the people in the church. She said I only need to do the things in the church I want to volunteer for. The priesthood is not a dual ministry, and I should only become as involved as I want to, and not allow you nor parishioners to give me a guilty conscience about church work. And I am to remember that our kids are kids, and that we are not supposed to make them into little pocket-book editions of Jesus and insist they be examples to other kids."

"Sounds like good advice. How did you respond to all that?"

"I told her that I would take care of you, and you would take care of the parishioners and me. Oh, yes, she told me that while you were her pet priest and I should take care of you, you were a very fortunate priest in finding such a comely and intelligent gentlewoman for a wife. She also said I would make a good priest, myself."

"Oh, my Lord, I didn't know she was into that touchy issue."

"She's not a feminist. She just disagrees with her husband. She thinks, though, I'd be a better surgeon than a priestess."

"That's true enough. Why did she think your Indian skills would be helpful to our marriage?"

"Because Indian women know when to pick up the lodge, family, and belongings when the chief says they have to move. And Episcopal chiefs ask clergy braves to move a lot."

"Well, Indian wife, we ain't moving for a long, long time from the mountain, no matter what the Episcopal chief says. And you are always going to be the physician and the mama, and I, the priest and the daddy."

"Oh, yes, boss. I told her that, and that the arrangement sounds just fine to me. I never did like moving wigwams. You want to know something else I told her?"

"I'm not sure I want to know. I need to have her on my good side."

"I told her that her husband, the bishop, had now become my priest, because her favorite priest, Father Habak, had given up that arduous chore to become my amorous husband—that I would not be baring my soul anymore to Father Habak, just my body!"

"Good heavens, Kara, you said that to the bishop's wife? How did she respond to that?"

"She laughed and said that she loved my feistiness and humor. She said I am exactly who you needed as a mate in the sometimes droll business of saving souls. I think she and the bishop like me. I will be very proud to be your wife, Dus, even though it's going to be hard work. And I am happy the Muellers love you, and will help me to help you."

"The bishop's been a fine friend for many years. Were it not for him, I would never have survived this vocation and would not have found you. He sent me up here on the mountain to save my life, and I have come down from it with the woman who saved it. He always believed I would find my way back from chaos to happiness; and sweetheart, you made that possible."

"You're sweet to say that. I don't mean to be selfish, but I will always love Bishop Mueller, if for no other reason than for having sent you to the mountain for me. I can hardly wait for our wedding day, to see your heinie again and learn more about the Habak bird—and for you to learn more about the Thunder bee."

"Have you no shame, Nez Perce?"

"I have, but you started it by telling your bishop that I asked you to drop your pants when we first met, so I could see your heinie!"

"All right, Doc, I concede! May I help you with anything to prepare for the wedding?"

"I have things pretty well in hand, but it would be really helpful if you could give me the names of friends and family you would like to invite. And, darling, I do want us to have an open invitation for all folk around the village and mountain to come if they want to, done in such a way that they don't feel obligated to give us presents. I want them all there to celebrate. To be our guests. Everyone has been so good to us. Nancy and Bessie have the reception all taken care of. How's the 'chalanty' coming along?"

"It will be ready for us by the time we are finished with our honeymoon."

"Oh, Dus, I can hardly wait!"

"Wait for what?"

"To see the inside of the house," she giggled.

"Oh," he frowned, and drove on up the mountain with his bride-to-be, hoping she might have had a more ardent answer in mind, but he was happy contemplating being her groom. Anyway, he had learned to love being baited by his beautiful, coquettish, and shrewd Indian fiancée. It put zest in his life and taught him how to laugh again. He thought back to how angry he used to get with her bantering. Now he understood what she meant when she said that "laughter takes the cutting edge off the sharp realities of life.

Laughter is very, very good medicine," she had taught him, and a doctor ought to know.

* * *

Following Karol's and his visit with Bishop and Mrs. Mueller, Dus had another discussion about the shooting and the discovery of the corpse at the vicarage. Scott insisted that Dus just work on the vicarage, carry on with his pastoral duties, and leave the detective chores to him. He had found no further evidence in the woods to help identify the shooter. He had found no shell casings nor blood in the area up behind Dus' cabin, and was somewhat content that, with the reinterment of the cadaver, the situation would cool a bit. The suggestion of Karol's, that if they made a quiet, respectful, and open thing of the reburial, may have worked. Both he and Dus had discussed that possibility and did what they could with her idea. Only time would tell. But Scott was a policeman, a crime had been committed, Dus had been nearly killed, and Ox had been sorely wounded. He was determined to find and prosecute the perpetrator.

The wedding was approaching. Dus had finished all that needed to be done on the house, and he looked toward the day when he and Karol would abide there. The arrangements had been made, and all was well, except for the message from Terry Casalano. Lou's condition had worsened following his return from the mountain and their week's vacation, and Lou was in the hospital for more chemotherapy. They would not, she had said, be able to come to the wedding.

"We're sorry, Terry, that Lou is so sick again. I hope it wasn't too hard on him being here. Don't worry about the wedding. We understand. Is there anything I can do now, Terry? I'll come if you need me."

"Thanks, Father, but we'll be OK. We are disappointed that we can't come. Give Karol our love and blessing, and we will meet her another time. Perhaps you both can come see us after the wedding sometime. Lou would not want you to come now. He sends his love and prays for your happiness. Please forgive us." She was weeping.

"Don't cry, Terry. We will come see you soon. I promise. We love you both, and are praying for you, too."

"I know that, Father. Tell Karol to have a wonderful and beautiful wedding day, and to have a happy life with you. Bye." She hung up the phone.

Dus had called Karol to tell her the sad news. She was equally disquieted by it, and asked Dus if he wanted to postpone things so he could go to Lou now.

"That's generous of you, sweetheart," he had told her, "but those Italian friends would have none of that. It would embarrass them. We will go forth with our plans and try to swing by their house on the way back from our honeymoon."

"Good idea. That should be easy enough. We'll just take the time. I know how much you love that man, and I want to meet Terry. I will always love him and be grateful for the work he did to make our house so beautiful."

After that, Dus busied himself with services and pastoral visits. He had gone from house to house around the mountain and village, inviting everyone he saw to the wedding. He had called his family members. Some could come; some could not. No matter; it would be a happy time, Lou's sickness notwithstanding. Perhaps it would be best if the wedding were to be small and simple. The church was confined, and he didn't want to impose too much of a burden on Nancy and Bessie, who were busy, as they had promised, preparing all the food for the occasion.

The evening before they were to be married, Dus returned home to find a crudely written note tacked to his door. It read:

> Youse a giten hitched, Precha, en gonna 'ave our nice docta fer yer wife, en 'ave da sweet younguns roun' dis purty house ya done built. Ya wodent wanna have dem hurt ner anythung ta happen ta dem. Be betta iffen ya jist take 'em off a da mou'ta'n wid yer pre'chin' en snoopin' in our bus'ness up har. We thank da lady docta fer watta she done fer our sickness, en we donna wanta er or anybody 'ave en accident ner nuffin. Dis har is a warnin' ta ya. Jist take her en da younguns en git outta har en git to war ya come from.
>
> A frien'

"You sorry, cowardly dirtball, whoever the hell you are!" Dus cussed. He decided right there on the spot to say nothing to Scott nor Karol about the threatening note. He would try to dismiss it from his mind until after their honeymoon. "No one is going to ruin Karol's wedding day. Not you illiterate note-writing weasel, nor myself! That is a fact of life. To hell with you. You hurt my wife and kids, and I'll find you and bury your sorry carcass so deep in that graveyard over there it will take anthropologists a thousand years to find your broken bones!" He looked up to heaven. "Oh, Lord, forgive me for what I just said. I get so angry! Please make a beautiful day for Karol, the kids, our friends who come to our wedding, and for me. Thank you. Amen."

He heard some birds singing and a calf mooing, and decided that God had used those tones of nature to answer in the affirmative and to calm his spirit. He smiled and knew that the morrow would be a beautiful day of blessings and consummation for two middle-aged American Indians—Ollikut Karolina Thunder Rolling In The Mountain Christianson Marson and Dus Byrd Habak.

# 29

A midsummer breeze swept over the Blue and Cutty Mountains and down the valley on Karolina Christianson's and Dus Habak's wedding day. It was almost eight months to the day when they had first met in the Joshuatown clinic. The little mission church overflowed with guests who came to share their joy. Ox Conley served as Dus' best man, and Nancy Conley attended Karol as her matron of honor. Their pleasure in having been asked to do that made the limp in Ox's leg much better and the smile on Nancy's face, wider.

Dus was saddened that Teresa and Lou could not be there. And, of course, the threatening note left on his door bothered him, but it was a beautiful day, anyway. He was in love with God and Karol.

Bishop Mueller performed the ceremony in his most precise ecclesiastical manner, and everyone could tell that he was delighted to be, as he put it, "locking the theologian and scientist in wedlock." Having developed a fatherly affection for Karol, too, he would not have allowed any other priest to do the honors, no matter the diocesan emergency.

Karol's wedding apparel was dramatically different than most brides'. Atypical of her heritage, she wore a figure-fitting, white doeskin sheath, bedecked with Indian beads and tan thongs, that reached just below her knees. Matching, soft, calf-high white leather moccasins covered her legs, and a handsome, beaded-leather headband was pulled taut across the top of her brow to the back of her head. Long brown braids, interwoven with thin strips of white rabbit fur and "angel-breath" flowers, and tied with white ribbons, flowed down over her shoulders and bosoms, nearly to her waist. Etched Indian silver earrings and a necklace, studded with turquoise stones, reflecting very light touches of pink lipstick and rouge from her face, accented her patrician Scandinavian and noble Native American features.

Her flawless tan skin glistened with light beads of perspiration as she walked up the aisle of the church on her father's arm to meet her fiancé at the altar. She carried white roses in her hand and was, Dus thought, the most superbly beautiful woman he had ever seen in his lifetime.

Dus wore clerical black pants and shirt with his white clerical collar, over which he wore a thonged albino buckskin jacket, tanned and given to him by Ox Conley, friend, hunter, and best man, as a wedding gift. The meat from the same deer was roasted and served at the reception.

Everyone thought Karol and Dus were a handsome couple as they faced each other, held hands in front of Bishop Mueller, and gave him their undivided attention. They repeated their vows, following his whispered direction, and Karol, smiling longingly into Dus' happy eyes, was the first to make the pledge. "I, Ollikut Karolina Thunder Rolling In The Mountain, take thee, Dus Byrd Habak, to be my lawful husband, to have and to hold, from this day forward, for better, for worse, for richer, for poorer, in sickness and in health, to love and to cherish, till death us do part, and thereto, I plight thee my troth." She then coquettishly added her own impromptu declaration, with no prompting from a surprised bishop. "And I also solemnly pledge, before my bishop, this assembly, and you, beloved brave, Dus Byrd, to obey my Susquehonnock husband."

There were suppressed chuckles in the congregation, though few understood the private humor between the couple. Some people thought that Mrs. Mueller would have the vapors, but she smiled at the couple and said in her heart, Thatta way, Nez Perce Princess!

Dus' grinning mouth and smiling eyes gazed directly into hers. He wanted to laugh with her, but he knew her audacious spirit now, and he was truly overwhelmed with the sincerity of her words and the depth of her commitment to him. Looking devotedly into her wet eyes and anticipating face, he made his vow. "I, Dus Byrd Habak, take thee, Ollikut Karolina Thunder Rolling in the Mountain, to be my lawful wife, to have and to hold, from this day forward, for better, for worse, for richer, for poorer, in sickness and in health, to love and to cherish, till death us to part, and thereto, I plight thee my troth." Then, borrowing from her lead, he also added, "And as we spiritually blend our distinctive heritages here, before our bishop and this assembly, my beloved Ollikut Karolina, I solemnly vow that if it is within my power to inhibit, you will obey no one but God and your own native and natural Nez Perce personage."

Karol held his hands tighter, nodded serenely, and smiled at the bishop. He nodded at both of his charming charges who he dearly loved, and continued with the ceremony. Many of the witnesses wiped their eyes as the couple exchanged simple engraved silver and turquoise stone rings that matched her engagement ring, earrings, and necklace, after which the bishop pronounced them husband and wife. They then had the Eucharist, took Communion together, sharing it with their friends, and received the church's blessing.

Bishop Mueller's face turned a shade of red as Karol and Dus kissed longer and deeper than church propriety usually counsels. After a loud clearing of his ecclesiastical throat, the newlyweds marched down the aisle hand in hand, smiling at everyone, while Julie Stewart tried heroically to play Purcell's "Trumpet Voluntary" on the old and groaning reed pump organ.

A half hour later, the wedding party flowed into Bessie's for the wedding reception, where Karol and Dus kissed and hugged the guests and received congratulations. They then sat down and ate a sumptuous wedding feast served very stylishly by the café employees. Karol's father, Ox, J.K., the bishop, Scott, Patty, and Julie made some short plaudits and offered toasts of cider and champagne for the happy life of the bride and groom. A well-respected orthopedic surgeon, Dus' brother-in-law by virtue of his marriage to Dus' beautiful, sagacious physician sister, not only gave Dus his new black shirt and pants as a wedding gift, but provided the mandatory nuptial toasting of the bridegroom. He put on a good, if embellished, show, and had the wedding crowd in hysterics about Dus' something-less-than-spiritual past. Dus took it all in good humor, but responded with one of Karol's favorite idioms, "I don't get mad; I get even"—and Dus did, many times, beginning with the cutting and sharing of a chocolate wedding cake. It was serendipitous from Dus' point of view that his brother-in-law was deathly allergic to chocolate, caused by his overindulgence of a novel and special ten-pound Hershey's chocolate bar that Dus had given him for his birthday. "Gluttony will get you every time," Dus, who was, in reality, a very close friend of his sister's husband, had told them.

Then, Dus ceremoniously slipped a blue garter from Karol's thigh, to the "oohs and ahs" of the crowd, and threw it to some anxious bachelors. Karol, following another tradition, threw her wedding bouquet over her shoulder to a gathering of maidens, laughing with all the others as it fell into the hands of a giggling and astonished Elly.

Elly and Shawn had remained quiet through the wedding, but with the Conley and Stewart kids, they managed to have a good time at the reception. They had approved of the marriage of their respective parents. Shawn thought Dus would make a super dad, and looked forward to Dus being a father figure in his life—something that his friends so enjoyed in their families. Elly, after her talk with "Grampa" Bishop, had more and more looked to Karol for the mother's love and caring so necessary to her young life. She had, several times, since she learned of her dad's intended marriage, told Karol on the phone that she loved her and thought she would be a good mom. The new parents were extremely relieved that both kids reacted as they had to their marriage. Their family home life and schooling would have to be worked out, but they would all sit down and discuss their future in Staunton, Joshuatown, and at the priory school in the late summer. Big decisions would have to be made, and the children's input about their own needs would be respected and honored, as long as they were not selfish and meanspirited. They did not fear that from their children, both of whom had grown to like each other a lot. Elly had told her new mom, however, that she didn't particularly like the idea of Shawn being her brother because "it would complicate her growing affection for the handsomely cool guy in the future." Karol knew that Shawn shared that view. Even as very young teenagers, Shawn and Elly were aware of each other's sexuality, though it appeared healthy and innocent. How much longer that would last, Karol and Dus had no idea, but they would keep close watch on that "puppy love" as they grew older, especially on the occasions when they would all be living together under the same roof.

  Karol's parents had come from Oregon for the nuptial, and had stayed in Staunton with her for two weeks before the wedding. Her dad was a huge, gray-headed outdoorsman with a merry demeanor; her mother, a little more reserved, was indeed the attractive and stately pure Nez Perce Indian, about whom Karol had so often boasted. Dus, though having been introduced to and befriended by them over many telephone conversations, finally met them at Karol's house shortly before the wedding. They were fine people, and Dus was awfully grateful that they consented to his marriage to their daughter. They felt all along that it was time for Karol to marry again, and an Episcopal priest would be just fine as long as he took good care of her and Shawn, and did not completely remove her from her heritage. They also thought Elly was a lovely adoptive sister for Shawn. They had already planned to take their newly acquired granddaughter and grandson out to Oregon for the rest of the summer, following the wedding, while the newlyweds enjoyed their honeymoon and private weeks thereafter together for bonding their marriage. Dus and Karol agreed that it was going to be nice to have the first weeks of their marriage alone, discovering one another in all of love's various manifestations, some of which they, of course, did not plan to share with their kids. "Yah, we know when and why we aren't wanted around," the little smart alecs had snickered.

As dusk approached, Dus and Karol left the wedding reception, saying fond farewells and thanks to everyone. They drove off on their honeymoon in "Iodine," with traditional graffiti, old shoes, and tin cans decorating their automobile. Within minutes, they stopped along the road, cleaned and divested the car of all the telltale nuptial trappings, and drove on.

"Well, Mrs. Habak, what do you think of all that traditional marriage stuff now?" Dus kidded her, driving with one hand on the steering wheel, the other on her knee.

"I had a feeling you were going to bring that up. Anyway, we Indian ladies have a built-in prerogative of changing our minds when it serves our purpose. You are one up on me, my smug and mighty brave, but don't forget what you said of me at the wedding feast—'I don't get mad; I get even.' I have some very bewitching plans on how to do that the next few days." She smiled demurely, kissing his hand and twisting her new set of rings. Unknown to her, Dus had found an old logging road that bypassed Joshuatown and went back up the side of the Blue and came out near the church. Dus drove only a few miles from the reception before reversing direction and driving to the renovated vicarage that was to be their mountain home. He had not allowed her, as he had insisted, to see the inside of it until they were married. She had respected his wishes. The days since their engagement had been long and frustrating for her, but she was content knowing that the house was his wedding present to her, bought and paid for with both his own and diocesan funds. He had wanted it rustic, reflecting her heritage and geography, yet suitably blended with modern conveniences and utilities for their own and their children's needs. He had done that.

As they pulled up the hill and into the driveway, Karol noted his wedding surprise right away. She sighed and hugged him. "Oh, darling, you've brought me home. I thought we were going to stay in some motel on the road tonight."

"A musty and worn motel room is for the unimaginative bridegroom. You and I, my wife, are going to honeymoon in our new home tonight."

"Great idea. But won't people know we are here when they come to church tomorrow?"

"Nobody knows where we are going on our honeymoon, and we will be long gone when Bishop Mueller has a delayed Eucharist for the people next door tomorrow."

"How did you talk him into that?"

"I didn't. He whispered around to the guests the time of services, that he would be having them, and that he expected them to be dutifully there in the absence of their regular priest."

"Bless his sweet heart," Karol beamed.

They sat for a moment looking at the house. Dus was pleased with his handiwork. Karol squeezed his hand. She had tears in her eyes. "Oh, darling, you are so thoughtful. Thank you for bringing me here. It has gotten even more beautiful since you first showed it to me. The flowers and trees set it off so perfectly. I appreciate all that you have done. You have made it so special."

"My pleasure. Tell me, Mrs. Habak, would you like to see the inside of our lodge?"

"Indeed, Father Habak. Are you going to carry me over the threshold?"

"Of course," he said, climbing out of the Jeep, lifting her up, and carrying her in his arms to the door. Kissing her fully on the mouth, he walked through the threshold to the living room, and sat her gently on the couch. "Look around while I get your suitcase from the car," he said, and left.

Karol gazed around the room, examining the structure that so pleased her. She was impressed with how Dus, Lou, and their friends had transformed the dank old cabin into a bright chalet that so epitomized the very heart of her heritage. Tears welled in her eyes as she mused how hard Dus had worked with his hands to please her. It was a dream house, indeed. She felt at home, and wiped her eyes.

"How do you like it, lovely bride?" he asked, as he returned to her.

She turned around, kissed him with fervor, and said with joyful, if teary, eyes, "It is so beautiful and perfect, darling. I thank you from the bottom of my heart."

"It was my pleasure, but I had a lot of help from Lou and the parishioners."

"I'll thank them, too, when I get a chance. Now take me on a tour."

Dus took his excited bride by the hand through their new home. She savored every inch of the journey. After their downstairs tour, they went up the steps to the bedroom loft, where they were greeted by a haven replete with a log-beamed ceiling, a colonial king-sized bed with matching dressers, large closets, western wallpaper, a wall-length mirror next to the bed, a large bathroom, and a sliding patio door opening out on a rear cantilevered porch, where they could sit unnoticed, gaze into the woods, and watch the birds and animals.

Karol's face gleamed with approval; she then eyed the provocative mirror mounted on the wall, with amusing suspicion. Dus noticed her smile and asked, "So, what do you have to say about our honeymoon boudoir, my wide-eyed bride?"

She kissed him. "Wow! The bed is certainly big enough for sleeping and stuff," she grinned, staring at the mirror, "but don't you think that mirror is somewhat risqué for a demure, religious reservation gal like me, if not for a pious and reverent gentleman of the cloth such as you?"

"Nah." Dus smiled. "Seems just about right for a natural Indian gal and mountain guy on their honeymoon!"

Eyeing the mirror again, she quipped, "Well, mountain guy, we shall see what we shall see. Your handiwork is very innovative and, shall I say, picturesque. You have made me blushingly elated."

"Well, I did it for the church, too, but making you happy is what a husband ought to do for his bride. A honeymoon requires a very special place for a gorgeous wife and an appreciative husband."

"It's very special, and I love the stone fireplace and that massive cozy rug in front of the hearth. It is so like being home in Oregon."

"I'm glad. Of course, it belongs to the diocese, but it is all ours while we are in the mountain. We'll work out something to spend time between here and your house in Staunton."

"It is our house in Staunton, now, Dus."

"Thank you. That's generous of you, Kara, and we will have our special times in that special place, too. We are blessed, thanks to you, that we have two places to share our love. Tonight, however, this is our first-night honeymoon lodge."

Dus and Karol returned to the living room and relaxed with each other, conversing, sipping wine, and listening to music. An evening cool had crept into the room, and Dus built a fire in the hearth. They sat in front of it, gazing into it and into each other's eyes. They were not rushing, however, into that wondrous culminating milestone that was to make them one. They were not intimidated by the urgency of time nor hormones. Perhaps it was the nature of their maturity and appreciation for the gifts of God that had been bestowed in the months past and on this day, that allowed them to savor the time and each other. "It has been a wonderful day with a beautiful lady, whom I am now privileged to call my wife," Dus remarked.

"It has been a wonderful day, a lovely marriage service, and joyful wedding reception. I am grateful to all those special people for doing what they did for us to make it such a happy time. I've felt nothing but joy since I arose from my bed this morning to take you as my husband, but I am sorry about Lou and Terry. I know how much you wanted them here."

"It's all right, honey. You're going to love them. Lou will be out of the hospital by the end of our trip. Maybe we could spend a day or two with them on the way home."

"Of course, darling. But for now, I think good Italians like them would understand 'amora,' and that honeymoons are meant for frolicking, not for visiting."

"And so, my bride, do you have some thoughts about how we might 'amora' and 'frolick'?"

"One or two," she kidded. "For a starter, I think if frolicking is in order, we frolickers should get out of these wedding togs, do some refreshing laving, and get into some suitable frolicking accouterments. May I use the loft bedroom and bath?"

"Sure. I'll use the one downstairs. Take your time and enjoy our playground up there."

"Playground! Wal, Preacha," she jested, lapsing into mountain vernacular, "ya oughta be 'shamed ta tea talkin' ta me lack dat. I declare, a virtuous, bashful, en innosant lady lack me wal sholy have da vapors listenin' ta sech naughty talk from a holy man!"

"Well, your innocence, I have a few thoughts that might very well test the veracity of your virtue. Get on with your laving and primping, and enjoy," he said, slapping her rump.

"How do you like that solid heinie, Preacher?"

"I'll check it out later, Doctor, for my report to the bishop."

"You're nuttier than a fruitcake, Susqueheinie," she giggled, happily climbing the stairs to the loft. Dus waited for Karol to finish her bath before showering, himself, not trusting that the new plumbing would not drain the cold water from her hot bath, thus hurting her flesh. He heard the water in her shower and envisioned his wife bathing, and wished he were with her. He put that thought to rest, knowing there would be many nuptial opportunities ahead for fulfilling fantasies.

Karol sang in the shower, soaping the mounds and vales of her body, while steady and invigorating jets of water pounded her body, cleansing it and her soul. She left her bath and went into the bedroom to dry herself, rotating her body in the mirror, searching for defects and reflecting upon the fitness of her body. She gave it tacit approval, and allowed that it was a fertile field for her missionary husband. She arrayed herself in seductive Indian attire, and then, hearing Dus in the downstairs shower, descended to the living room, warmed herself at the hearth, and waited for her husband to come, refreshed and ready for her.

Dus showered with care, wanting to be unsullied for his comely wife. The most of her flesh that he had ever seen was when she was in a bathing suit, but given her fetishes for cleanliness, he knew her body would be immaculately prepared for him. He finished his bath, shaved and lotioned, dressed in casual pajamas, and entered the room to meet his awaiting bride.

The fireplace burned brightly in the large room where Karol was standing, lighting it up in haunting shadows, reminiscent of a scene from a western epic. A beautiful barefooted Indian woman stood before him, covered from her shoulders to her calves with an elegant cloak, open at the sides, partially revealing curvaceous hips and buttocks. The beaded headband that she wore at the wedding was still in place above her brow, securing the long fur-and-flower-entwined braids that flowed over the mounds of her breasts. She was, to Dus, breathtakingly gorgeous.

"Ollikut Karolina Thunder Rolling In The Mountain Habak," he beamed, "I believe I am beholding the most beautiful woman I have ever seen in my life. I thought today, as you came up the aisle of the church on your father's arm, no woman in this world could look more lovely, but now I have discovered a reality more phenomenal than the best dream I have ever had of you. Do you have any idea what an astonishingly gorgeous woman you are? God has greatly blessed me."

"Thank you for the accolades, hubby," she beamed. "I took a peek in the mirror a little while ago and decided, myself, that this middle-aged Indian gal was not too frumpy for her brand-new brave. If I am pretty, it must be because God blessed me with a handsome prince who came along and kissed this ol' Ollikut into a princess. Do you think this red skin is pretty?"

"I think it is incredible—your pierced nose, ears, dark eyes, luscious lips, lovely hair, and fantastic body, enchantingly accented by that stunning attire you're wearing. What is it?"

"It's called a 'summer serape' by the Mexicans, and is Spanish in origin, but American Indian women have been wearing variations of serapes for hundreds of years. They're warm, cover the body completely, give freedom to the limbs, and are very utilitarian for a gal's plumbing. My mother was once a loom supervisor at the Pendleton woolen mills, and a talented weaver in her own right. She made this lightweight cotton version for me as a 'going-away' present when I came out east. I have never worn it, saving it for the handsome Indian prince who would someday carry me away, make me his wife, bed me down, and sire our children."

"It is beautiful, as is the wonder who fills it so gorgeously. Now that I have carried you away and made you my wife, may I bed you down and sire your children?"

"You may, my Prince."

"Then come and sit with me in front of the hearth."

Dus sat down on the thick rug, and Karol lay down, putting her head in his lap. Looking up to his face, she whispered, "Thank you for becoming my prince of all the love fables of the ages."

"And thank you, most elegant Princess of them all," he responded, "for taking a gloomy, rancorous old clergyman and turning him into a happy man."

"I'm happy, too, darling. Being a mother and a physician has its rewards, but I always knew in my heart that someday my prince would come along and carry me away to his castle; and this chalet, dear plumber, carpenter, electrician, and Priest, is really a very nifty castle."

"God has greatly blessed us, Kara."

"Yes, he has," she whispered.

The sun disappeared across the horizon as eventide settled in the mountain on Karolina and Dus Habak's wedding day. Moonbeams drifting through the chalet windows mated with the flames of the hearth to cast soft shadows across the living room, transforming the newlyweds into animated silhouettes. Their chatting, banter, and courting in their honeymoon abode were slowly leading them toward the inevitable culmination of their marriage. In the months since their passionate misadventure in Staunton, they had become more temperate and subtle with their sexual conversation and behavior. It had been, indeed, a frustrating romance for the ardent couple, loaded, as they were, with churning hormones. Though their kisses were ardent and their eager hands roved over enkindled bodies, their religious convictions and promises compelled them to keep their vows not to go "all the way." Though sexual behavior and virtuous pledges may only be in the mind of the beholder, and while tepid physical endowments of males and females are exceedingly difficult to supervise, the middle-aged lovers kept their physical contact disciplined and did not engage in coitus.

All that tempered desire and firm discipline notwithstanding, the moonlight, fireplace, and the dynamics of amatory necessity blended together were now moving the aroused husband and his sensuous wife toward the obvious climax of the honeymoon adventure. Their love and marriage had brought them to his quickening moment, and in the natural order of passion there was now, for the wedded couple, no turning back. The stage had been set during their courtship and wedding, and it was now ready for the last act of the conjugal drama. Only the opening of the curtain and commencement of the first scene, with the appropriate words and movements, remained. Dus, concluding that the initiative was traditionally the bridegroom's, gently took Karol's hands into his own, gazed in her eyes, and avowed, "It's been many weeks since that happy day in the clinic when we acknowledged our love, Kara. We have been sorely tempted and tested, and have longed for this day and time for a very long time. We promised we would keep our vows to wait to consummate our love, and we have. The time has arrived, now, to do that. We have bantered and laughed about this moment, but please believe that I love you with my whole person and everything I have. I am sure you want no homily here, but you must know that this is now a compelling and beautiful venture for me. You are almost too beautiful and precious a woman for me to even contemplate making love to. You are almost too exquisite for me to ask you to give over to me your most valuable and sacred oasis for the quenching of a man's love for his wife."

Karol looked into his eyes with a self-effacing countenance. She spoke to him in unassuming agreement. "It has been a long wait, darling, and I, too, through all our discipline, wanted almost desperately for you to make love to me. Now my body is warm, anxious, and ready for yours." But then, with curious reticence, she added, "But I would like you to do something very special for us before we begin this wondrous and passionate lifelong journey."

Dus, a bit bewildered, asked tentatively, "What is it, sweetheart?"

"I'd like you to bless our bodies for their union."

He ogled her in surprise. "But the bishop did that at our wedding this morning," he said.

"I know that he blessed our marriage, Dus, but I want my priest husband to bless the union of our bodies." She beamed demurely. "You told me that consummation is the most important symbol of the marriage sacrament. You said the physical union of a man and woman's bodies was the outward and visible sign of their inward and spiritual love. Do you remember that lesson you gave me, dearest theologian?"

Dus shook his head and smiled at his sagacious wife. He adored her for her remembering the pastoral things he had said to her. "I do, my love," he declared. Solemnly taking her hand in one of his, he made the sign of the cross on her forehead with the other and intoned, "With my body, I thee wed, Karolina Habak, in the name of the Father, Son, and Holy Spirit."

Karol happily responded, "And with my body, I thee wed, Dus Habak, in the name of the Father, Son, and Holy Spirit, and I give it completely over to you for your joy and the procreation of our children. Now, would you hold out your hand for me?"

Father Habak, now the amenable husband, dutifully did as he was asked. Karol took a pin from her serape and pricked the palm of his hand, and then her own. Little beads of blood oozed. She pressed her palm very tightly into his, and spoke, "Now, my brave, the great Nez Perce and the amiable, if obscure, Susquehonnock tribes are forever bonded in blood and are one in wedlock. Thank you, my fine warrior. That was important to me."

"Why so, sweetheart?" he asked, wiping the blood from both of their palms.

"Because a holy man's benediction and the mixing of tribal blood means good fortune in the union of a wife and husband's bodies. Now that we have taken care of the things of the spirit, it is time for us to take care of the things of the flesh."

He was moved by that symbolism, then asked, "That was an interesting thing that you added to your vow at the wedding. Why did you do that?"

"Oh, it was just a sign to let God, you, the whole company of heaven, and those wedding witnesses know that we Indian wives are delighted to surrender our bodies to our braves, whether we believe in that Ephesians 'wives, obey your husband' chauvinism or not. And, Dus, lest you think I didn't hear, I adored you when, before that same company, you gave me that marvelous reprieve. You are a grand, if funny, groom, big brave. But I want no reprieve. Now, please take this panting bride off yours off to our nuptial nirvana."

He put his arms around her and started to kiss her. She pushed him away, stretched her sensuous body out on the rug, and rested her head in his lap. Tiny tears trickled down her cheeks. He smoothed her hair and kissed her wet face. "Why are you weeping, Kara?" he asked. "Shouldn't this be a happy time?"

"I am very happy, darling. Remember when I told you I get weepy when I am happy? Then again, maybe I am a bit anxious. I'm a novice at this amatory stuff, you know, not having had much practice at it," she sighed.

"Nor have I, but I guess I know what you mean about getting misty about all this 'amora,' " he sniffed, and wetness appeared on his own cheeks.

She put her soft fingers to them, wiped them, and put them to her lips. "Your tears are sweet, my love, and so are you. Thank you for being gentle and understanding with your funny Ollikut."

"You are a gift from God to me, Kara. He has asked me to love and take care of you. Please know, this first night of our marriage, that I'm going to do that for the rest of my life."

"I know you will," she whispered, "so love me tonight, as a prelude to all of the tomorrows, my darling, and make us one forever."

Dus was captivated by the wistful woman who was now his wife. He not only adored her, but appreciated all that she embodied in mind, body, and spirit. "I will love you tonight and always."

Her face was now bright, all the tears gone. "And I, you, my husband," she whispered, as she sat up, rotated her body, and turned her back to him. Lifting the serape from her body and setting it aside, she exposed a lustrous, tan, bare back to him, which began at her pristine neck and ended at the top of her buttocks. She slipped the headband from her brow and threw her hair back over her shoulders.

"Would you unbraid it and comb it out for me with your fingers, please?" she asked.

He unwound the long, soft hair, removed the leather strips and flowers, ran it through his fingers a number of times, and allowed it to flow to her waist. He was enchanted by its silken texture, and brought it to his face. It smelled like fresh clover. "Your hair is fine and fragrant," he lauded.

"Thank you. I'm afraid it has been, for too long, a naughty vanity of mine. I now give it to you this night, my love, with all my bodily endowments, as my wedding gift, for you to have and to hold, forever," she proffered, rotating around and facing him again.

Dus ogled his wife with adoring awe. Her tan, moist body, reflecting flames of the fireplace, created an illusionary portrait of a gorgeous nude American Indian maiden, painted by some nineteenth-century artist—supple, unblemished, voluptuous breasts; graceful, regal neck and shoulders; slender waist; shapely thighs and calves. Her lovely face, framed by the silky hair, radiant, natural lips and cheeks and ardent eyes, looked confidently into Dus' face.

"Well, handsome brave, are you just going to sit there and stare at me? Tell me, quickly, lest I swoon from suspense, whether you fancy your Indian wife," she beamed.

Dus, sitting before her, smiled, his eyes transfixed on his bride's glowing nude body and demeanor. "Fancy? Kara, you are an incredibly exquisite woman," he whispered.

She did not answer, but her mouth and eyes told him that she savored his approval. Her naked loveliness, as spectral as it was in the shadows, immediately enkindled Dus' loins. Karol, observant of his growing fervor and alive to her own, leaned over to him and adeptly helped him out of his pajamas, leaving him as naked as herself.

They sat together in their nudity, appraising, touching, and appreciating each other's flesh. They lovingly put wine glasses to each other's lips, sipped and swallowed the sweet liquid, and breathed deeply. They gazed at one another. "I thirst for all of you, Kara," Dus confessed.

"And I for you," she whispered. "So love me tonight, Dus, and always, to the depths that a husband can love his wife."

Putting the glasses aside, Dus lay down on the rug and pulled her down beside him. He assayed his wife. "Ever since I met you, I have been entranced with your intellect, humor, and free spirit, but the quality of your flesh is more marvelous than my best dreams of it. You are a magnificent specimen of womanhood, Kara, and I thank God for you. I am hardly worthy of such a gift."

"Of course you are! And I tell you that within this body of mine is a gold mine of passion awaiting discovery by you. Come into my quarry, my love. Dig tenderly for its nuggets, and you will find treasures you have never known before."

Her prose further enraptured him. He held her close to him. "I believe that, Kara. Your body is more elegant and perfect than the most precious of stones."

"How do you know that before you have searched for and found the gems? What will you say, loving prospector, when you find all of Ollikut's bumps, warts, and scars?"

"If I find them, I will kiss them and appreciate them as part of your uniqueness."

"Your kisses have been magic ever since we first touched lips, so I am persuaded you will. And, if I may say so, my brave, I note with great appreciation that you have a very nice white masculine body that appears as though it might configure very compatibly with this red female one, with which you seem to be so captivated," she bantered, plausibly as a way of relaxing and readying herself for her most sacrosanct personal experience as a woman.

If any other bride and groom or married couple were to be privy to the comportment and colloquy of this man and woman, this husband and wife, with desire and passion erupting within their nakedness, who had waited for months for this moment of nuptial bliss and fulfillment, they would hardly believe the time that they were taking in sexually consummating their marriage. But these disciplined, middle-aged, previously married newlyweds were obviously not going to rush into orgasmic detonations. They were grown adults who, having waited a long time for these moments, now feasted on their nudity, bantering, play, and fun. It would be unnatural for Ollikut Karolina Thunder Rolling In The Mountain to behave otherwise, and just as unnatural for Father Dus Habak, who now understood, enjoyed, and enjoined his beloved wife's persona, to do anything other than play her game lovingly and indulgently with her. If bantering is what this splendid lady, who has given herself to me today, wants, in order to prepare herself for this drama, Dus thought to himself, then that is what she will have. She has motive in her jest, and I shall find out what it is soon. It shall be an intriguing and extraordinary night with this lovely woman. "Well, doctor," he smiled, "I am not as learned about the human anatomy as are you, but isn't that the way it is supposed to be with us girls and boys?"

"Yes it is, Parson! Furthermore, while we are discussing anatomical nomenclature, I feel compelled, before you push too far, so to speak, ah, ah hmn, ahem," she stammered, blushing a little, "into this nuptial encounter, to dispel some folklore that you, 'white eyes' might have heard and perceived about us Indian brides."

Dus looked quizzically at his facetious bride and countered, "I am no longer a 'white eyes,' and am now joined to you by blood; I can hear and perceive only what I see here tonight. Now, is this going to be some sort of feminist declaration I am going to have to deal with right now, when my mind, heart, and soul are already focused on ah, ah, hmn, ahem, another area of interest?"

She smiled coyly. "It is not a feminist declaration, my love, but a marvelous truth that you need to know so you won't be too surprised while you're roving around this red bod you've been hankering after for so long."

"That sounds a bit more positive, but tell me, quickly, what it is, lest you frighten me away."

"Well, in case you have been hearing a lot of tacky tales about us Indian ladies being passive sexual chattels to our braves, you should know that we are, in reality, rather lusty wenches who love to make love. So beware, Preacher! This body has not been designed just for husband merry-making, birthing, and suckling papooses!"

He humored her. "That's just what I needed to know at this ethereal moment. So, tell me, Doctor, for what other purpose has it been fashioned and consecrated?"

"Well, to your surprise, no doubt, for wifely delectation, fun and ecstasy," Karol giggled, "and plain old sensual luxuriating! What do you think of that enlightenment, Preacher?"

"I am not surprised in the least that that may be true of you, exotic sawbones, as I will no doubt find out in due course. As to what I think, I think you are using synonyms for just plain old female passion."

"You are quite correct in that assessment, my Priest, so how long do you think it is going to take you to put more wood on the fire of passion you have already enkindled in this plain old female?"

Now done with the jesting, he drew her naked body close to him. "Whenever you quit chattering so much about the mundane while passion is leaping around in my loins," he chortled. Her flesh exuded an alabaster scent. He pressed his face to it. His excitement grew, as did hers. So with no further bantering, the lovers began their journey into the culmination of their nuptial. Their hands very slowly and gingerly entered and tested the waters of eroticism, and frenzied emotion enabled them to instinctively enmesh their fully naked bodies. As sexually unseasoned as they were, nature directed their sensuality, and their bodies responded spontaneously to each other's amatory signals. The long seasons of chastity sent them reeling into innovative and robust foreplay. Karol's receptive flesh encouraged Dus to move his hands over her whole body. He plied and nuzzled it, enchanted by the smoothness of its rises and hollows.

Confident in the feminine gift she was offering her husband, Karol stretched out her pristine body in naked splendor. He was entranced with the unclad beauty who reposed in unadorned innocence before him. He stood up, and lifted her lithe body up into his arms.

"What are you doing?" she lamented.

"I am taking you to our wedding bed in the loft."

"No, no, darling, please," she protested. "I want you to make love to me on the rug here in front of the fire. Please, lay with me here to consummate our marriage."

Questioning her no further, he lowered her to the rug and lay beside her. Conversation between them subsided. Love directed their movements. Hands and mouths moved to where they found their pleasures, not daring to rush the moment. She cherished the rough, callused, bruised hands that had built her this house, now filled with love, tenderly roving over her flesh. He adored the slender, soft fingers that salved and healed human bodies, now holding his close to hers. Sighs and moans communicated the ambiences they felt throughout their whole beings, as passions drifted toward the finality of their consummation. Congenital ululations flowed with every fresh nuance of pleasure. They now had no control over their emotions. Eyes and lips locked in hungry communion. Karol lay there, her blinking, tearful, yet joyful, eyes urging her husband into her. Her tongue glided over teeth and lips, and her beautiful, dark hair flowed like rivulets of volcano lava down over her shoulders, breasts, and pillow. Dus was riveted to her countenance.

With all modesty, all inhibitions, all emotional barriers scattered to the wind, the priest and physician, the husband and wife of eight hours, made unrelenting and earthshaking love. No longer able to suppress the very long, sensual temptations of waiting, nor the overwhelming potency of their erupting loins, they shared the most phenomenal God-given experience ever known between male and female when exhilarating orgasms gushed through the depths of their beings. Rapturous spasms inundated their bodies as they sighed words of love and fulfillment, and held it together in rigorous ecstasy, basking in the pleasures of their first sacramental consummation.

They stayed enmeshed as long as they could, trying almost desperately to maintain the sweet elixir that had just united them. They looked with beaming eyes and loquacious smiles into each other's faces, as their passions gently forced the last few spasms of pleasure from them. For several breathless and submissive moments, they pressed their bodies together in an instinctive effort to not loosen the mystical tribal blood infusion that had bound them together.

They did not speak, relaxing in the pleasures of their coitus. Their journey into the nuances of marital copulation had been an ecstatically satisfying adventure, and they were contented and gratified. Finally, Dus whispered into her ear, "Thank you, Kara. That was an incredible adventure with a lovely and enchanting wife. I love you."

"And I, you. It was superb, darling," she whispered in return. "We are wholly one now, and I love you beyond the ability to explain it." She smiled, still breathing and pressing her body into his, refusing retreat. "It was wonderfully satisfying. You have shown me the epitome of a husband's love for his wife. I hope that I showed you that, too, with my body."

"You were wonderful, and are a fantastic gift. You must be the most sensual woman in the world. I am again without words to describe the beauty of you. I don't believe there can be a more perfect consummation of marriage than what we just experienced."

"I guess it was a matter of husbands and wives doing what comes naturally with their love, and it appears to have come out pretty special. It was so exhilarating and fun. I felt like I was floating in air. It was so mystifying."

"It was that, indeed. May I ask you something about that, sweetheart?"

"Of course, hubby."

"Why were you so intent on consummating our marriage on the floor in front of the fireplace?"

"You will have to forgive me that, Dus. I guess that it was the nostalgia and sentiment within me. I just wanted you to make love to me for the first time in front of the fire here in this chalet that so reminds me of the environs of an Indian lodge. I guess there is much about me, my husband, that is still very Indian. I hope you will someday understand. I am very attached to my culture. Someday I hope you will return with me to Oregon, visit my home, and then know why I feel and am the way I am, about so many things."

"I love you the way you are, Kara." Sensing a weariness in Karol, Dus moved away from her. They sat on the floor, touching and conversing about the future for a while. Then Karol, responding to one of nature's basic necessities, excused herself. "I have to go to the potty," she acknowledged, and walked majestically up the steps to the bathroom.

Dus watched her go, captivated by her nudity. She was statuesque, as though she had, like Venus, been carved out of rich Italian marble. The configuration of her lithe body, shed of exterior wrappings, defied the casual countenance she carried when attired. She was very handsome in clothing, but a naturally patrician person in her nudity. I do not think, Dus noted to himself, as poised a woman as she is, that she really appreciates her own splendor. But then, observing that she ambulated as she climbed the stairs, sneaking glances in at him, he reassessed that thought. Yes, he smiled, changing his mind, she is quite aware that I am sitting here admiring her.

He smiled at his wife's natural and unpretentious management of intrinsic need. He pondered her heartfelt and sincere invitation. "Someday I hope that you will return to Oregon, visit my home, and then know why I feel and am the way I am, about so many things." He believed now that it was not just because she was a physician that his guileless wife was so open about the human body, whether it was sex or physical necessity. It was true that her vocation was all about the anatomy, its function, its complicated machinery, its well-being. It had mostly to do, he now believed, with her heritage; her affinity with nature, through her love of the forest, the animals, the birds, the trees, the skies, the weather; and her spiritual attachment. Everything God made was wholesome, pristine, and naked until man became licentious and dirty-minded and put clothes on it. She was not being immodest nor whimsical when she went up those stairs just now, Dus thought to himself, nor trying to shock her clergy spouse. She was simply sharing natural practicalities with her new husband. She has already become less shy about her body, and he began to realize she was not going to be too introspective around him. With Kara being Scandinavian and Native American, he believed that the realities of life in their marriage would be an open book between them.

He knew she was earthy from the day he had met her, and that perception of her only served to make her more complete as a woman. He was impressed with her insight and honesty, recalling her prose as they made love. He felt a real affinity with her psyche and personality, as well as with her body. He believed that life was going to be wonderfully exciting with her. He would adore her in her best and worst moments. He would love, cherish, respect, and take care of her, as he vowed at their marriage ceremony, in sickness and in health, naked or clothed, in all her natural, spiritual, and unconventional manifestations, until death parted them from each other.

Karol came out of the bathroom, her naked body glowing, her fingers combing and arranging her hair. Any diffidence to her body around her husband she might ever have had was gone. She was unblushing as she completed her grooming, and rejoined him with bewitching smiles. He thanked God again that she was his wife.

They cuddled in the afterglow, and relaxed in the coolness and tone of the evening, talking about their love and future. Then, looking at his wife, whose eyelids were beginning to close, Dus said, "We should get some sleep, sweetheart, so we can get an early start in the morning. It will take a few hours to get where we are going."

"Yes," she replied sleepily, "it is time. Thank you for a wonderful day and night. I love you."

Dus lifted his wife in his arms, and she snuggled into his neck. He carried her upstairs to the loft and gently laid her on the big bed. He lay down beside her, pulled a light sheet over them, kissed her softly, and said, "Thank you, too, beautiful wife, for a beautiful wedding day and night of consummating it. I love you, Princess. Good night."

"Sleep well, my love," Karol whispered, as she began to hum a love song, lullabying Dus to sleep. They snuggled their bodies together on the bed, his thighs and chest pressed into the configuration of her back, rump, and legs. She clutched the rough masculine hand that had reached over her shoulder and embraced one of her supple breasts, and listened to him fall asleep. Love's fruition had finally been fulfilled after years of waiting. The day and the experience of nuptial bliss had not only been gloriously rewarding, but it had been novel, fun, humorous, inquisitive, and edifying. There was no turning back now. There was only tomorrow, a dawning frontier for the man and woman, deeply in love, who had exhausted themselves expressing it, ultimately, in the only completely satisfying fashion there is for a wife and her husband.

The moonlight through the windows cast shadows across the room, silhouetting a quiet and unevenly configured mound on the bed, shrouded by a pastel sheet that seemed to stir in rhythm with the ticking of the Seth Thomas mantle clock. Peace was in that house and in the hearts of those who abided there. To the west, thunder rolled in the mountain. Dus did not stir, but Ollikut Karolina Thunder Rolling In The Mountain Habak, with her Indian wife's and mother's ear cocked, heard the rumble, beamed a great Nez Perce smile, snuggled again into the body of the husband she adored, and fell asleep.

## 30

The newlyweds got an early start the next morning and drove north to a lodge in the Pocono Mountains, where they had reserved a special haven for their honeymoon. Looking for a place along the way to do their Sunday worshipping, they vied for a quaint Roman Catholic Church nestled in the hills of Pennsylvania. As Episcopalians, they knew they would not be invited to receive the Eucharist, but were uplifted, anyway, by joining in the liturgy and making a spiritual Communion. Karol snickered in her hanky and wiped tearing eyes, meriting a gentle elbow poke in the ribs from a chagrined husband sitting properly next to her in the pew, when the Irish priest preached a uniquely colorful homily from Solomon's Song of Songs. It seemed apropos, if serendipitous, to her and Dus' circumstance, and her mirth was only exacerbated by Dus' nudging. The cheery pastor quoted selected poems from that elegant Old Testament scripture. She was especially intrigued with:

> Let him kiss me with the kisses of his mouth, for his love is better than wine.
> Our bed is green. The beams of our house are cedar and our rafts of fir.
> My beloved cometh leaping upon the mountains and skipping upon the hills.
> He is like a young stag on the mountain.
> On my bed at night, I sought him whom my heart loves.
> My beloved said, Rise up my love, my fair one and come away.
> Let me see your pretty countenance, and let me hear your sweet voice.
> Your eyes are like doves.
> Your lips are scarlet red.
> Your two breasts are two fawns, twins of the gazelle, feeding on the lilies.

She had never read the "Song" before, but liking what she was hearing from it, she was sure to find a Gideon Bible at the lodge, read, and ponder that whole text.

The audacious priest preached a poignant and witty message on the subtleties, duties, and joys of marriage from those several verses. After the mass ended, Dus and Carol complimented him on his homily, then introduced themselves as a visiting Episcopal minister and his wife.

The jovial priest welcomed them in his best brogue. "We 'ad a maurage har yestaday, we did, of a lass en a lad what grew up in this wee church tagather," he said. "Though I'm sure, t'was a bit risqué fer the likings of a few of the codgers, I give it again this moanin 'cause they surely needs ta har the word now and again about ta nature and joys of maurage, as well as the duties."

"They do, indeed, Father. I loved it, and so did my wife, even though she giggled all the way through it. Hope you didn't notice."

"Oh, indeed I did, good lad," he smiled. "I notice most everything in my teeny flock when I'ma preaching! And what did I say, now, that occasioned the giggles, lassie?"

Karol blushed. "I'm sorry, Father. Your quotes were so befitting. My husband and I were just married yesterday, too."

"Ah, begone wid ye, lass. Be gory, may the good Lord forgive me, darlin', as ye and yer hubby must," he blurted out, his own grinning face turning red. "'Tis a clown I've become, not knowing the circumstance of me visitors. I'm a truly sorry if I embarrassed ye."

"You didn't embarrass me, and you made my very earthy spouse's day. She'll be joining your church here if we stay too long, Father."

"'Twould be a gladness ta my soul, ta 'ave ye both, Father. Come again on yer anniversary," he invited, "en I'll preach on the 'Songs' ag'in, en maybe even sing one er two for the likes of ye." Then, to the disdain of some nettled onlookers, the two priests and doctor laughed hysterically.

The irony of the morning was funny, Dus and Karol both agreed, and they left the little mountain church with renewed souls, minds, and bodies, delighted with the bubbly priest who had retroactively confirmed and blessed their wedding night of love, fun, and repartee.

Later in the afternoon, they settled into the lodge for their five-day honeymoon. It was a time of eating, hiking, horseback riding in the lush forest trails, and enjoying the cool lakes and waterfalls. They reveled in the freedom to exercise and relax together, to be away from other people, their vocations and the troubles that had so immersed their lives since they first met. They played, they danced, they swam, and they made love over and over again, basking in the frontier of their newly achieved union. When the time came for them to return to the reality of work and children, they lamented leaving their transitory paradise with its unique oneness with God and each other. They vowed they would return again on a second honeymoon, stopping again, too, at the little Roman Catholic parish in the hills, with the funny and friendly Irish pastor.

They arose early for their trip home, with an intentional stop to visit Lou and Terry Casalano. They had packed a picnic lunch, and were now driving over back roads of pristine hills and vales covered with summer green, wild berries, and flowers. Taped romantic music echoed quietly throughout the car, as Karol napped with her head in Dus' lap. With one hand on the steering wheel, his free hand, always aware of the fine, rounded flesh nestled close to him, roved over her head, unable to resist the temptation to caress.

Karol yawned, awakened, and grasped fingers that were kneading her. "Good morning again, rover boy. Are you paying attention to the road?" she asked.

"Good morning, sleepy wife," he answered. "What makes you so weary this lovely day? I haven't worn you out with all the girl and boy exercise, have I?"

"Don't be silly. I just feel the exquisite pangs of fulfilled love. My body rejoices for having known both the fury and tenderness of your passion. I suspect there will be many twinges in my bones and muscles for a few days that will speak to me of your passion, but it will be an affliction I will cherish and savor," she reassured him.

"It has been a wonderful honeymoon. I was wondering why it is that you and I, not having made love before, could experience such overwhelming joy in our first coitus. Whatever the reason for the rhythmic magic between us, it is a mystery that cannot be explained, but I can tell you for sure, Rolling Thunder, I am glad we waited for our marriage to experience it."

"I am, too. I really am. The discipline is hard when two people are so in love, but the reward is so thrilling and so worth the wait. The consummation that comes with the oneness of marriage is truly sensational. But isn't that the way it is supposed to be? Isn't that, as you have said, the sacramental nature of marriage?"

"It is, indeed, my love. You are superbly beautiful in your whole being, body, soul, and mind, but I must say, whoever invented honeymoons for the discovery of husband and wife bodies ought to be canonized."

"It's funny that a theologian would propose such a weird thing."

"Why do you say that?"

Karol giggled. "Even a physician knows that God invented honeymoons, Father. Isn't it a bit irreverent and paradoxical to suggest that God ought to be canonized?"

Dus blushed. "So it is; so it is. I'm so infatuated with what I have discovered in you, I am saying silly things. You are so beautiful that I'm getting goofy, if not ungodly."

"I love it when you are silly, Preacher. It gives me a lot of hope for the priesthood. It's time that you church workers got a little goofy and earthy like the rest of us. And, Father, if you like my body as much as you say you like my soul and mind, our marriage may be very busy."

"Why is that, philosopher?"

"Because, as a surgeon, my specialty is bodies, and I think your body is every bit as nice as your mind and soul. I really like it. And, by the way, as I adventured around it, I glanced at that wound that first brought us together at the clinic. I must say, I did a pretty classic job of patching it. Of course, I have reasons to cherish it, because it was my first peek at your heinie. But, Dus," she said, with a noticeable change in her demeanor, "the very thought of how it happened still frightens me. When is Scott going to find that scoundrel who hurt you and Ox?"

"Come on, sweetheart, this is our honeymoon. Let's not waste all this beauty and loving time talking about bad things," he admonished her. He then thought about the threatening note he found on his door the day before his marriage. He squeezed his wife's midriff, and swore under his breath, "You hurt this beautiful woman, you loathsome coyote, whoever you are, and I'll cut out your gizzard." His hand grasped her tighter. "Now, let's stop and have some lunch," he suggested, changing the subject.

"I'm ready," she agreed, looking for a picnic ground along the road. "Look; there's a waterfall and grassy knoll down there by the woods where we can eat."

They stopped, ate lunch, and rested. "It's a little sad leaving our honeymoon nest, darling, but I look forward to getting back to our new house," Karol mused. "I can hardly wait to tell Nancy, Patty, and Bessie about our trip. I was thinking what a wonderful thing it would be if Bessie could take another chance with a guy and go honeymooning with him in these Poconos."

"Why do you think of her now, sweetheart?"

"Oh, she is just one in the paranorama of people I love, whose lives I wish could be as happy as mine is. She is one of those sweet people at home who I thank for my being on this journey with you. She wooed you into asking me to that dance that made me realize how much I really did love you. She sure didn't have a very happy life of her own, losing her husband and having no children. She adores children. She must have really loved her hubby, to have been so faithful to his memory all these years."

"Yeah. It's kinda interesting to think what sort of a life she would have had if she'd married Jed Hudson. He was sweet on her as a teenager, and he's sweet on her now. I'm sure he is faithful to Helen, but those two old sweethearts still do like and admire one another. And Helen doesn't seem to mind. Old friendships like that are few and far between. I think the folk in Joshuatown not only respect those two, but understand their relationship."

"Yes, they do. I'm glad all those people are in our lives. Anyway, Padre, this place is awesomely gorgeous. It reminds me so much of the hills in Oregon, and the Blue and Cutty."

"Would you like to know some trivia about these rolling Appalachian Mountains? I know you westerners are proud of your Rockies, and you should be. They are spectacular. These mountains aren't as tall nor as rugged as they are, but they're older, smoother, and greener. As a matter of fact, the geologists say that the Appalachians that we see now are supposed to be the second growth of mountains in this area since the Ice Age. There are seven distinct mountains separated by valleys, that make up the Appalachians. They start in Maine and go all the way to Georgia."

He pointed his finger above the falls. "Up there atop that ridge is an ancient Indian passageway called the 'Horseshoe Trail,' where people have hiked or ridden horseback the whole one thousand, five hundred miles, for many years. That trail is usable even to this day. In my youth, my friends and I used to pack and ride our horses on it for days, camping and exploring. If you and I were to go up there right now and start walking on that trail, we could walk from here to within a few miles of my hometown, and farther down, to our house in Joshuatown. Would you be up to that, Indian?"

"That's fascinating. We oughta do some of that trail walking at home someday, but for reasons probably known only to brides, and frequently caused by grooms, I am not going to hike anyplace today," she giggled.

He smiled at his loquacious wife. "I accept your excuse, my dear. You know, J.K. says there are a lot of caves in these mountains that he's explored. Would you like to walk up near the falls and see if we can find one?"

"No, spelunker, we are not going spelunking on our honeymoon. As a matter of fact, I am not going caving at all without J.K., Scott, and Tooter. There are just too many bullets and bears around you when you go traipsing around mountains. By the way, where is Tooter staying while we're gone?"

"He's staying with Scott and Patty."

"I've been missing her."

"Well, I don't miss her on our honeymoon."

"I don't miss her that much either, but sitting here reminds me of that hike we took last winter, when we were tempted to make love in the snow and Tooter sat spying on us. That was so much fun. The scenery and the conditions are a bit different here, but we don't have to resist temptation on hikes anymore, do we, Parson?"

"No, Kara, we don't. Why do you ask?"

"I don't know. I was thinking about the 'Song of Songs.' Old Solomon was quite a writer, wasn't he? Things like, 'Let him kiss me with the kisses of his mouth; my beloved cometh leaping upon the mountain; he is like a young stag; your lips are scarlet; your two breasts are two fawns; on my bed at night I sought whom my heart loves.' Pretty sexy stuff coming out of the Bible on a Sunday morning, don't you think, Parson?"

"I think it is beautiful scripture."

"I read the whole thing the other night. Wow! It is so true of us. Our honeymoon has been so gorgeous."

He kissed her and said, "Yes it has, Kara."

They sat and lounged by the woods. Karol lay on the grass with her head in Dus' lap, gazing at the waterfalls. She was fascinated by their flowing grandeur. She challenged Dus, "I'm not up to a lot of hiking, my love, but I'd like to go up there and see if we can walk under those falls."

"Sounds fun! Let's go!"

"Why don't you say, 'Arise up my love, my fair one, and come away'?"

"Come on; I'm just old Dus, not old Solomon." They walked over to the edge of the stream, where the water cascaded from the high rocks down into what looked like a boiling cauldron. The heavy falling water hit the bottom rocks of the stream, and created a great noise and mist. Holding tightly to Karol's hand, Dus climbed up near the top of the falls. There, they discovered a rock ledge under the cascading water. It was damp, but well behind the flow. They could see a jutting rock about halfway in on the ledge where they could rest, and they wandered in. They then sat with their backs against the rock and gazed out through the back side of the pouring water.

"It's beautiful, isn't it?" Kara mused. "I have never been on the inside of a waterfall before. Look at the colors of the mist. Like a million rainbows! It really is fantastic!"

"Yes, it is, my love. It's sort of like being inside a cave. Dark and no one around but us."

"It's not like a cave, but I like the idea of it being private."

They sat there for a long time holding hands. Karol queried Dus, "So, Chief of the Susquehonnocks, do you think at one time a Susquehonnock brave and his demure bride ventured in here on their honeymoon, like we have today, made love, and consummated their marriage? Maybe they did it on this very ledge. It sure is a romantic place for such things."

"Yes, it is. I don't knows what those Indians did here, but it looks pretty hazardous for an inexperienced half paleface, and half Nez Perce and Susquehonnock to be mating. What are you thinking about, squaw?"

"What are you thinking, big brave? As you said, this slippery ledge is no place for either of us to get passionate. We might go over the edge."

"I am already over the edge with you, my pretty wife."

"And what do you presume to do about it, paleface?"

"Well, how about, 'Our bed is wet, not green, my love; I am like a young stag on the mountain; your countenance is pretty; your voice is sweet; and I can wait for you no longer'?"

Dus took her in his arms, and they gazed through the falling water at the animals of the forest, the birds of the air, and the road above the grassy knoll for peering humankind. Not seeing any of that species, they made, like the birds, bees, and critters, instinctive and precipitous coitus. But, like the birds, bees, and critters, and very much like Indian and paleface humankind, they were deeply in love, and their lovemaking on the wet ledge behind the misty waterfall was very tender, very passionate, and sweeter than the finest wine.

\* \* \*

They arrived in the evening in Dus' hometown, and took overnight refuge in the local lodge that Dus knew well. They called the Casalanos and made arrangements to visit them the next day. Terry had assured them that Lou was up to a visit, and they would be glad to see them.

"You look good, Paesano," Dus lied to his old friend, after they all had greeted one another with hugs and tears. Karol had not shared that view of Lou's condition, either, and, being a physician, knew exactly the depth of his illness.

"Thanks, Father. I'm pretty good. Chemo seems to take its toll, but let's talk about this beautiful bride of yours. You did well, Amico; you did well."

"You sure did, Father," Terry added. Then, turning to Karol, "Dus is very blessed in having you. We are happy to meet you and to see that this guy has a pretty and good wife to take care of him. He told us all about you, and every word was true."

"Thank you. He has told me much about you, too. I am terribly sorry you couldn't get to the wedding."

"We are, too, but this old man of mine wasn't feeling too good. You must have worn him out doing all that work on your house."

"He didn't wear me out, Terry. That'll be the day when a priest can out-work this carpenter."

"Lou, I owe you a special kiss," Karol said, putting her arms around him and planting her lips on his cheek.

"What was that for?" Lou wiped his cheek and smiled.

"For helping my preacher man build the most beautiful and romantic honeymoon nook in this whole world. I love it! Thank you, and thank you, Terry, for allowing him to come. I'm sorry if it was too tiring for him, but I would not have wanted anyone else to do it for us."

"I was just kidding," Terry said. "He loved every minute of it. To be with Dus—to reminisce about the old days, pound a hammer, and cut with a saw—was the best medicine for him. Someday, when he is feeling better, we're going to come down and see that chalet."

"Please come soon."

The happy couples sipped red wine, ate a hearty pasta dinner prepared by Terry's expert Italian hands, and talked into the late hours. Karol and Dus finally said it was time to go the lodge for the night.

"Are you going to stay and visit for a few days in your old hometown, Dus, and take this lovely woman around to meet some of our buddies?" Lou asked.

"I'd like to, Lou, but I have to be back to the church on Sunday, and Karol has to do surgery on Monday. I'm going to take her on a short tour of our hometown tomorrow, put some flowers on Mom and Dad's grave, and then head back to the mountains. We'll be back here another time to see you and the buddies."

A great sadness came over Lou's face, as it did Terry's. Dus and Karol knew what they were thinking. They did not pursue it. "You two take care. Get well, Lou, and we'll be back and have some fun together. Get in that kitchen and cook up some stuff like I have been bragging about to Karol. And, remember, we are counting on both of you to come to visit our mountain soon."

"Ciao, Brother," Lou said, hugging him. "I love you!"

Karol and Terry watched the exchange, and tears welled in their eyes. "Love you, too, Karol," Lou said. "You sure have made that old priest a happy man. You're pretty, and just what the recalcitrant old goat needs."

"I sure do second that," Terry said. "I wish you both all the happiness in the world!"

"Thank you, again," Karol sniffed, hugging them both. Lou and Terry could feel the new wetness on their necks. They all kissed and said their good-byes. The Casalanos stood at the door, waving at the Habaks as they drove away.

Dus smiled, waved back, and then vehemently jammed the car into gear and raced away. Karol did not speak. She knew Dus was angry and crying.

"He's dying, isn't he? I won't see him again, will I, Kara?"

Karol moved beside Dus and affectionately rested her head on her husband's shoulder. She was silent, trying to control her own tears. She didn't want to add any more anguish to his aching heart by answering his question.

"Tell me the damned truth, Doctor. My lifelong buddy is dying, isn't he?"

Karol cringed, but accepted the epithet. "I know you're hurting, darling, and I am, too—for you, for Terry and Lou. I understand."

"You doctors can't do a thing for cancer-ridden people, and God doesn't give a damn. Isn't that true?"

Karol's patience with Dus suddenly came to an abrupt halt. "Stop this car right now, Dus Habak," she scolded.

Dus pulled the car to the street curve and stopped it. He knew his bride was angry at him, and was not going to sanction his outburst. He was immediately penitent. Gee whiz, I have tried so hard with my anger and language, he thought to himself.

Karol sent a barrage of harsh words at him. "This is our honeymoon, Dus Habak, and you have no cause to heap abuse on, nor curse around, God nor me. I'm sure Terry and Lou would not appreciate it, either. If you need to know that unhappy answer tonight, then yes, Lou is dying. I don't know how long he has to live. Maybe three months, maybe six, but he is dying. I know it, he knows it, Terry knows it, and now, you know it. Now, if you want to get out of this car and shake your fist and swear at God, go ahead, but you are not going to sit here with me and indulge in a lot of bitterness and self-pity—which Lou does not have for himself, nor want from you—and wreck our honeymoon and our visit with those good people! I'm sorry about the painful truths of life. You and I know them well. I am sorry about Lou. I'm sorry science hasn't found a cure for cancer. I'm sorry Ginnie, Dusty, and Doug were killed. I'm sorry we docs can't save precious people like them from pain and dying. I'm sorry you priests, with all your miracles, supplications, and votive candles, can't, either. I am even more sorry that God doesn't, for whatever reason, but those are facts—nasty, hurtful, terrible facts—and your cursing and pointing accusing fingers at God and me are not going to save Lou. Now sit in this car for an hour on this dark street all ticked off if you want to, but you're going to have to make the decision about whether I'm going to get out of this car and walk down the street to the lodge by myself, while you curse God, or you're going to come to me, cry with me, say a little prayer with me, and ask God, who cares for Lou and Terry an awful lot, to take care of them and relieve their pain. They are at peace with their knowledge, Dus, and they know Lou is headed for a better life, where there is no more pain and tears. If there is any person in this world more ready and more deserving, it is Lou. You taught me that, Father, and I believe it now. Don't take it away from me. When his time comes, we will go and be with him and Terry to say goodbye."

Dus leaned over the steering wheel and cried, "Gosh, I'm sorry, Kara. I'm such a jerk! I'm so ashamed!"

"You are not a jerk! You are a very good and caring man, darling. Lou, Terry, and God know that, and we all love you very much, but you need to control your temper."

"Gee, Kara, when am I ever going to learn that?" He turned to her and took her into his arms. They wept and prayed together. Karol pushed him away, and he started the car and drove. She spoke cautiously. "Now wasn't that better than swearing, my love?"

"Whatever am I to do with all your love for me, Ollikut?"

"Take me to our mountain cabin and love me. And, might I suggest, hubby, when bad things happen to good people, don't swear at God and me. Just say, 'Mare's marbles.' And if that doesn't help, remember what you used to say down on the farm, and what I used to say in the wigwam, sometimes when I got mad about something?"

"What's that?"

She blushed. "I'm a little embarrassed to say that in my bad moments, I say, 'Oh, shit!'"

He laughed. "Isn't that a bit uncouth, coming from a refined lady like yourself?"

She smiled as tears leaked from her eyes. Kissing him gently, she whispered, "I want to be refined for you, precious white eyes, but sometimes we aboriginal ladies are pretty pragmatic and basic when the folk we love are hurting. And in case you have not yet learned in the last several days when you have been fooling around with this concubine, I really do love you."

"I know that, Kara."

They returned to the lodge where they were staying, showered, and went to bed. Dus looked down on his wife and said, "Thank you, Kara, for helping me with my anger tonight. I am sorry. Lou's dying is very difficult, but I have no excuse for lashing out at you or God. I'll try harder; I promise. And thank you for our honeymoon. It's been beautiful. Someday I will write a book about your love, your passion, and understanding."

"Will it be beautiful prose and poetry?"

"Yes."

"Will our sexuality be shown to be sweet, wholesome, and sometimes funny?"

"Yes, because our life will be wholesome, and our sex beautiful and refined, as it has been on this honeymoon."

"I appreciate that, darling. I am so grateful that we can love sex, talk about it, and have fun with it without making it crude. I don't like dirty words about sex and body parts. I don't think God does, either."

"I love you, and revere your body and our relationship too much to ever use dirty language, Kara. We are one now, and we will have fun with our sex life. We will laugh, and we will kid, but I promise you, there will be no bad words from me with or about my exquisite wife."

"I know that. Then write of love, if you wish, and start with us, so the whole world will know the beauty of a husband and wife's true oneness."

She kissed him and said, "Good night. Thank you, Father, for your pastoral care to this heretofore lonely maiden and now happy wife."

"You're a nut, but a very beautiful one."

"Dus?"

"What, Kara?"

"When you were roving around my heinie, did you find it as nice as I found yours to be?"

"Good heavens, Ollikut, what a thing to ask. But yes, I did. It is very nice."

"Then tell the bishop that when he asks us how our honeymoon went. I think he'll want to know," she giggled.

"You tell him. Good night. I love you." He held her close and began to drift off to sleep.

"Has all the vigorous honeymoon exercise made you tired and sleepy, big brave?" she asked.

"Mmm, yeah," he mumbled.

"Then have a good night's rest from it. I'll wait until tomorrow to ask if you think we made a baby on this honeymoon."

Dus opened his eyes, pushed her away from him, and stared at her. "You shouldn't jest about a thing like that, Kara."

"I'm not kidding." She smiled coyly. "I know that you don't know much about medicine, husband, but you do know about birth control, don't you?"

"Yes. What about it?"

"You should know, then, I haven't been using any. Maybe I should have pretended naïveté, but I noticed, unless you have something very scientific this doctor has not yet discovered, you haven't been, either."

"Uh-oh! I guess I was so enraptured by your beauty, I didn't think of it. We never discussed it, did we?"

"I guess we should have discussed it before we got married, but it's too late now, I would think. So don't be too surprised if some little squiggly sperm of yours has met up with some little egg down there at my womb and is already begetting a little Habak. We will know in a fortnight."

"Two weeks?"

"Yes, Father, because that's when I will have one of those natural, if sometimes pesky, girl things called a period. In the vernacular, it's called menstruation."

"I know what it is called, Doc. How do you know it will be then?"

"I'm a woman, for pete's sake. Women know. Why do you think I told you 'June twenty-eighth' when we were discussing when we should marry? Wedding days are not exactly the most decorous time to have a period!"

"Then I guess you are in a fertile time now."

"Yep, that's right. I am very fertile, and am probably ovulating all over the place. But, to be truthful, Father Habak, I don't care if I am pregnant. I guess it isn't the right time, with so much ahead of us, but we could manage if it happens, couldn't we? Wouldn't you like us to have our baby, Dus?"

"Having babies with you would be one of the most wondrous things in the world. I hope she or he has the beauty and spirit of her or his mother."

"Thank you. Then you're not worried that you might have made me pregnant with all this boy and girl frolicking we've been doing on rugs, beds, and waterfall rocks on this honeymoon?"

"Well, let's see—if you get pregnant on our honeymoon and you have our husky baby in eight months after our wedding day, instead of nine, what do you think the bishop, our families, and friends will be thinking and saying about our moral certitudes?"

"I guess they will be thinking that the priest and his physician concubine were making whoopee under the church steps. 'Tis a shame when we tried so hard to be good. Ah, let them think what they will. I'd love to have your baby, anytime, and have a sibling for Shawn and Elly."

"If God wants you to be pregnant, it will happen. I'll be greatly blessed to be the father of your baby."

"You're sweet, and I love you so much. Anyway, my womb will let us know soon. What if I am pregnant?"

"I will take you in my arms and thank the Lord."

"And what if I am not?"

"I will take you in my arms in thanksgiving, take you to some convenient rug, bed, or waterfall rock, and make love to you. I cannot imagine making papooses with you as being anything but fun, Ollikut, and I will love them as I do their mom."

"Thank you. I think you will be a good father."

"And you will be a good mother. I'll put my order in for one. Girl or boy?"

"How about a girl and a boy at the same time, like 'the twins of a gazelle eating lilies'?" It has happened before in the Thunder Rolling family!"

"Twins? Sure, Why not? Whatever you want. Anyway, since we have settled that, good night again, sweetheart. We have a lot to do tomorrow, and a long trip home. I love you. Thank you again for marrying me, and for all the fun we've had, or are going to have, making babies, whether they get here sooner or later." Dus smiled, nodding off to sleep, adding, "Thank you, too, Lord."

"I'll let you know, darling, whether you are going to be a new daddy or not in a few more weeks, when the Lord lets me know." Cuddling her body into her husband's, she prayed, "Thank you, too, Lord. Amen," closed her eyes, and dreamed of being a new mother again.

# 31

The summer weeks, following Karol and Dus' honeymoon, rushed by. Dus returned to his mission work on the mountain and Karol, to her surgery at the hospital in Staunton. Shawn and Elly stayed in Oregon, spending the summer with Karol's family in the Wallowa Valley. Karol was delighted that her son was having an opportunity to reestablish his roots in her birthplace, and that Elly was getting attached to her new grandparents.

Dus missed Elly, but he was glad that his daughter was being drawn back into a wholesome and full family life. Having no grandparents on either her father's nor mother's side, he believed that Karol's parents would be good grandparents for her. Her letters and phone calls over the summer seemed to reassure him of that assessment.

Karol, surrendering to the practicalities of marriage and her cherished medical work at the Joshuatown clinic, decided to close her private practice in Staunton and limit her weekday labor to surgery at the hospital. She had made the proper arrangements for a four-day surgery schedule there so that she could spend long weekends with the mountain clinic and her husband. She and Dus realized that such a working schedule would be difficult for them, but they had resolved the issue with renewed dedication, knowing that they would make the most of the time between Thursday evenings and Monday mornings.

They also knew that their friends, Karol's associates at Staunton, and the village folk of Joshuatown would understand that not all of their time over the weekends would be devoted to the perusal of religion and medicine. Given the nature of love, the Joshuatown folk would just have to envision what the character of love for newlyweds was about—mostly, that not all weekend hours of the priest and physician would be available to them for the resolution of their spiritual and medical well-being.

Their separation made their time together full and intimately precious. It was. However, less than three weeks had gone by, when Karol called from Staunton. "I'm very sorry, hubby, but you're not going to be an earthy kind of father just yet. The 'begetting' has yet to begin. That's OK for now, isn't it?"

"Sure, sweetheart. Like we said, it is always fun to keep trying. We have to be the 'begetters,' but God will bless us with a child when the time is ready. I believe that, and I love you, with or without a new baby right now, and always."

Nancy, Ox, Patty, and Scott, who seemed to have grown to be closer friends with Dus and Karol over the months of their blooming romance, during the adversity of Ox's injuries, and through the ordeal with the dead man, understood that Karol and Dus would not have a lot of time available for socializing for the first few weeks of their marriage. They knew how precious time was for them, and did all they could not to be intrusive.

Tooter was glad to have his master and mistress back, and aside from her being sent to the nether lands at particular times, she occupied a very special place in the Habak's togetherness. She spent a lot of time walking in the forest and lying in front of the fireplace with them, and did her best to help nurture their time together. Patty, with some degree of canine acumen, had regulated Tooter's diet during her time at the Kirshes', so that her bad habit of tooting no longer caused tears to form in the eyes of the newlyweds nor drove them out of the house for fresh air.

After a few Sundays of services and pastoral visits among his charges, Dus felt reconnected with his parishioners and the townspeople. Most of them seemed genuinely happy for the couple, and wished them well. Dus' visits to Bessie's to eat were always greeted with good conversation and laughter. The respect that the townsfolk held for Karol and him was a source of pride and joy. He tried to be a good pastor and friend who listened, and Karol's heart as well as her medical skills were a great source of comfort to the people. Just knowing that the husband and wife, minister and doctor, with their gospel and medical talents, were home and among them again seemed to make their lives happier and hopeful. And 'happier' and 'hopeful' were words that did not always portray and describe real life in the Appalachian Mountains of Virginia.

"So you had a lot of fun up there in those romantic hills of Pennsylvania, did you, Father Habak," asked a jealous and complaining friend, Sheriff Kirsh, "while I was down here taking care of your smelly dog? By gosh, I'm greatly appreciative that my smart wife, Patty, cured that mutt of that awful malady of hers, and you and Karol should be, too. I'd a sooner had a skunk in my kitchen."

"Quit bellyaching. You wanted her for the kids to play with while we were gone, didn't you?"

"Yeah, I did and I have to admit, she was fun. Glad you two had a good honeymoon. Were you able to see your friend Lou up there? You had said you might stop off to see them on your trip, since they were not able to get to the wedding. Sure was nice of him to help you with the house. It was a pleasure to meet him. He really did a great job for the church. We enjoyed riding with him to mass. We learned a lot about you. You were something of a scalawag when you were growing up, weren't you?"

"Takes one to recognize one, Scott. We did get to see him and Terry, but I'm sorry to say that his condition has worsened. Cancer is an awful thing."

"Yeah, it killed my dad. It was awful for him, my mom, and the whole family. I'm sorry. Patty and I have been lighting candles for Lou at mass and praying for his recovery."

"Thanks. That will help. We'll see what the days ahead will be like for him."

"Anyway, Dus, I've been snooping around during your absence, trying to find out some more stuff on Ox and your cadaver friend. It's a dead end, so far. I talked to some police friends of mine about the spike in the tree that caused Ox's chain saw to fly apart and cut him up. They're inclined to believe it was an accident. It was a rail spike, but only God and the guy who drove it into the trees know why. I've asked Ox where he cut the tree down, and he doesn't remember. That thing might have been embedded in it for some years. Somebody might have, at one time, used it just to hold some other timbers to the tree. It's not solid evidence yet, but some radical weirdos have been known to spike trees out in the northwest to stop timber cutting. Some really terrible things have happened to lumberjacks when their chain saws hit those spikes—far worse than Ox's injuries. I am not, however, ready to concede that what happened to him was an accident."

"Maybe it wasn't, but I'm sure skeptical. Anything more on the shooting up at my house?"

"No, the trail is kinda cold. I did go up to that group of trees in back of your house where you said the shooter was hiding, and took a look again. I have some things figured, but I'm not sure of them yet. I want to tell you, Dus, whether you're offended or not, I'm going to keep some evidential things I find to myself for a while. I have some thoughts I am not ready to share with anyone but the FBI and the state police. I need their help. I will be as candid with you as I am able; I promise you that. It's for your own good. Your roaming up on the Cutty and digging into graves has ticked some folk off. I suspect they might be watching us. I need to divert their attention away from me so I can do my chores in private. Some misguided people in these parts are trying to keep some secrets from me, and I'm determined to find out what they are. According to Dr. Buck Underpine, the statute of limitations has run out on the corpse we found, but there is no doubt you have gotten close to something sticky that upsets some people. I am going to find out what it is, but I must insist, again, that you and Karol not to bug me about things."

"We aren't going to bug you, Scott. We understand you are trying hard to help us, and we appreciate it. I'm scared for Karol and the kids. You're really going to be peeved at me for not telling you about this, but I found this note tacked on my front door the night before our wedding," Dus admitted, pulling the wrinkled note from his breast pocket and handing it to the sheriff. "I didn't tell you nor Karol, 'cause I didn't want to upset her before our wedding. It would have frightened her and spoiled our honeymoon."

"You know, Father, you are a royal pain in my butt. Give me that," he said irritably, taking the note and examining it.

"It really made me angry when I thought about it during our honeymoon," Dus continued. "The guy threatened my wife and kids, Scott. Priest or not, I am not going to turn my other cheek to this."

"Hold on till I read it."

Scott read it aloud and said, "I'll be a son of a gun. That's not a very nice wedding congratulations, is it? I don't blame you for being mad, but you should have given this to me before. It's police evidence, and if I'd a had it, I could have sent it up to the FBI lab for analysis while you were gone. Does Karol know about it yet?"

"No. I told you I didn't want to mess up Karol's wedding day, and I sure didn't want any Feds coming around here when I was getting married."

"Whether Feds get in on this or not is up to me, Dus, not you."

"OK, but what do you make of it?"

"It's crude and ominous."

"It is that. There are sure to be prints on the paper that can be lifted, aren't there?"

"They would be pretty hard to lift off an old piece of paper like this. Then, too, how would you compare them with prints of the local folk? I doubt if many of them have ever been fingerprinted."

"Well, surely some bank people have."

"Come on, Dus, I know you don't like old Brush, but you really are going far afield there. I can't believe he had anything to do with this nor with the potshots taken at you at your house. Let me see what I can do. I have some FBI and smart police lab friends who will help us and keep it quiet."

"OK. Let me know. I gotta go up to the office and do some work. See you around, Sheriff. Tell Patty I said 'Hi.'"

"No use in you eating by yourself all the time while Karol's out of town. Come up to the house and have some supper with us. Bring Tooter with you. The kids miss her. Tell Karol we send our love."

Dus returned to his office and switched on his telephone recorder. One message was from Karol, who reminded him that she loved him and he should call her in the evening. The other was from J.K. Stewart. "Hey, gyrene. Sorry you're out! How's the old married man? Just wanted to tell you and your bride that our kids are going to summer camp for two weeks in August. Julie and I would like to take a long weekend and come down to visit the newlyweds, and maybe take a look at that cave you've been talking about. Give us a call! Bye!"

Dus was ecstatic with that news. "Hot dog!" he muttered. "Maybe we can find out what's up there. Better check with Karol and see if it's OK with her." He called Karol that evening.

"Hi, hubby," she gushed. "I have been missing you. Four days away from my brave is pretty hard on this brand-new bride. Who's been making your corn bread, jerky, and buffalo stew, and tanning your hide? I have really missed patting your hide. I love you," she told him.

"Love you, sweetheart. I've missed your hide, too, and this being alone is for the birds. Tooter is no substitute for you. Can hardly wait for the weekend. Have something to tell you. J.K. called on the recorder."

"That sweet thing—what did he want?"

"Didn't want to call him back until I'd checked with you. He and Julie would like to come to our house for a long weekend in August, to visit and to check out the cave I found."

"I should have known he'd have another motive besides just coming to visit. He hasn't been here all summer. I'd sure like to tell him what I think about his spelunking stuff. Sure, they can come. Love to have Julie, but I am not going caving with a sawed-off-at-the-knees computer nerd and a preacher. I hate the idea of wet, dark places, bears, bats, and crawly critters. You, J.K., and Scott go. Julie, Patty, and I will fool around at our house, or take an outing down here to go shopping. Be nice to get together with the girls for a change."

"Tired of me already, eh? What about tanning my hide?"

"I'll tan your hide, Preacher, good and proper, if you make me go into any caves. Waterfalls, fine, but no caves! Tell J.K. that any weekend will be all right, but to let us know so we can pack in some food and so I don't have an emergency weekend here. And don't you dare tell him I'll be going caving, because I won't."

"But Julie is a caver, honey, and she'll want to go."

"She won't want to go when I talk to her about other alternatives. Maybe she'd like a break from hobbling around rocks and stalagmites with that old, gimpy coot. He's going to get himself killed with those peg legs of his."

"OK. I'll call him back and tell him what you said. Boy, you are a grouch today."

"I'm not a grouch. I'll run around in the woods, climb rocks, and ford streams, day or night, as naked as a jaybird with you, if you want, but I am not ever going inside a cave. You can call me a grouch, sourpuss, crab, and say I'm paranoid, but I am not going caving!"

"How about all that courageous talk about wanting to be in on the solution of the mystery that's been plaguing us."

"I had a feeling you would bring that up. You said you were going caving, not sleuthing. I don't care. Nose into whatever you want, but I am not going, Dus. That's final. You, J.K., Scott, and Ox can do all the snooping into dark places you want, but if I have a vote, the girls will stay at home, or go shopping or something."

"Ox, you said. That's an idea. He knows the mountain and can be helpful to us."

"Thought you told me Ox didn't believe you found a cave up there on the Cutty."

"I love Ox, but I'm not sure he's being candid about a lot of things."

Karol sounded peeved. "Shame on you! Ox Conley is one of the most honest men there is, and the best friend you have on the mountain, except me."

"I know that, honey. Maybe he is just trying to protect us from something."

"Like what?"

"I don't know. I had no interest in that cave until Ox, who knows the Cutty like the back of his hand, denied its existence. There is something about that cave. Anyway, I'm going to ask him and Scott to go with us."

"Oh, sure. Sounds like a really savvy, stalwart posse is going to be assisting Sheriff Kirsh. There's ol' J.K. Stewart, with no real legs; Ox Conley, with just one; and a megalopolis cleric by the name of Father Habak—all slipping and sliding around underground rocks and rivers, fighting off bats and bears, gouging their butts with stalagmites, and cracking the bones they have left. Yep, gonna be a really fun expedition for ol' Copper Kirsh. I'd better be prepared to use my medical skills when the posse returns."

Dus was not laughing. "Being scornful doesn't become you, Kara. Look, J.K. and I are going up to that cave to see what's in it, whether you, Ox, or Scott goes with us or not. Now, you can be supportive or a spoilsport. J.K. is an expert spelunker with or without legs, Ox is a seasoned woodsman, and Scott is an excellent policeman. It is true I'm a novice at caving, but I'm ex-military, with terrain, hunting, and probing skills. So, you have no cause to put us down."

Karol was repentant. "I'm sorry, darling. I just love you all so much and don't want you to get hurt. Dus, don't be too harsh with me. I'm scared of all the weird stuff that's been happening to Ox and you, and being an Indian doesn't make me brave about everything. I really am terrified of dark places with bears, bats, and crawling things. Just let me be hostess, cook, and social organizer for the girls. You guys spelunk all you want, but please be careful. Call J.K. and Julie and tell 'em we'll be glad to have them. You can talk to Scott and Ox, too, if you want. I do love you, you know."

Dus was repentant, too. "I know you do, honey, and I'm sorry I snapped at you. I just want to get this thing ended so you and the kids will be safe up here. I don't want any bad stuff hanging over our marriage. You understand that?"

"Yeah, I do. Good night, my love. I gotta get some sleep for early morning surgery. I really miss you. Thank you for wanting to keep me and our kids safe. I love you," she assured him, ending their conversation.

"I love and miss you too, sweetheart. Good night!" More than you'll ever know, he said inwardly, hanging up the phone and thinking again of the threatening note. "I don't know who you are, but if you ever hurt anyone I care about again, I'll find your rotten hide. Don't count on this forbearing priest to 'turn the other cheek.'" Dus had talked a lot under his breath to his unknown "shooter," and had threatened him with pain as many times. He tried to dismiss the threatening bullets and note from his mind.

He made arrangements with Julie and J.K. to spend a long weekend in a fortnight hence, and Scott reluctantly agreed he'd go along to look at the cave. He also said that it would be a good idea to take Tooter to scare the critters away. No one was concerned about the bears this time of the year. They would mind their own business if no one messed with a sow's cub. Patty was delighted that she, Julie, and Karol were going to do some things together, and allowed that maybe even Nancy Conley might like to socialize with the three younger girlfriends. Ox's reception of Dus' idea was less than cordial.

"Damnation, Pawson. I done tol' ya dat thar ain't no cav' up thar on da Cutty, en I ain't gonna go a crawlin' 'roun 'dem hills wid on'y one leg. Yousa looney as a possum ta go up thar, messin' 'roun 'dem high rocks en stuff. Ya jesta precha man what don't knows nuffin 'bout da woods, en takin' J.K. wid no legs is jes wacky. Youse is gonna git yo'self hart bad. Look at dis leg amine. I donna wanna it ta happen ta ya!"

"Ox Conley," Nancy chimed in, "I agrees wid ya hundert pacent, butta I'll no' 'ave ya talkin' to de fadder lak dat. Now, ya watch yo' mouf en talk like da genalman yo' is." Turning then to Dus, she admonished him, "Ox is ri't 'bout da hills, Fadder. He knows dem good. Iffen he says thar no cav's up thar, thar's no cav's. He en me an our families be'n har fereva, en we know da moun'an. No one is betta than Ox. En he tells da truf."

"I know that, Nancy," Dus conceded, taken aback by the couple's contentiousness, "but I really was in a cave or some burrow in the side of a rock up there, when I believed a bear was after me. I want to go back and see what it is. J.K. is a skilled caver, and we will be fine. Scott will protect us well. Because Ox knows that terrain, we want him to lead us around it."

"I donna wanna go, 'specially wid des bad leg, en I donna wanna ya ta go, e'ther. Ya gonna git inta somethun ya donna know nuthin 'bout."

"Ida lisen ta 'im, Fadder; I sholy wou'd," Nancy urged.

"Nancy, I love you and Ox with all my heart, and I respect everything you say. You have been so good to Karol, Shawn, Elly, and me. The last thing that I ever want to do is go against you. I know you care for us, but there are things I must find out for myself. I hope you'll forgive me for rejecting your advice, but I am going up to that cave with or without you, Ox. Now, you've been tramping around in the mountains with that bad leg, and you're as good as new, but if you don't want to chance it way up on that hill, I understand. I know, too, you doubt me about the cave, but you know the mountains better than any of us, and we could use your help. If you won't go, I'll still love you."

Ox and Nancy sat still with their heads bent, shaking them. They appeared hurt that Dus had been so strong-willed with them. Dus was ashamed he had hurt them.

"Ya betta go wid em, Ox, cus da lad is stubbo'n 'bout dis har 'ting. He does need ya, fer sur, iffen he's gonna do it. I ken only pray fer ya'al," Nancy said, looking up at Dus with a tear in her eye. "Ya ken go wid my blessin', Fadder, cause ya is like a son ta me."

Ox nodded his head. "Ma Nan wan's me ta go wid ya, Dus, en so I will. I ain't 'appy 'bout it, but iffen ya gonna go anyways, best I take ya, les ya gits yersef in a bad fix. I loves ya, too, ya knows, en I donna wan anythung ta happen ta ol' J.K. en Scotty, nethar. Ya all done a lot fer me 'bout des ol' leg amin'. Sorry we had dis spat 'bout it. Yesir, I'll help wheneva ya git it in yo' mine ta go."

Dus went over to where the endearing man and woman sat, and hugged both of them. "I'm sorry, too. I love you and thank you for all you have done for us. Karol will be very pleased that we won't be going up there without you. We'll be safe in your hands, Ox."

Ox shook the priest's hand, and Nancy bonded their hands with hers. "Yeah, ya'll be saffer wid ol' Ox, Fadder," she smiled. "Ya shurly will. Butta, ya gotta take care of 'im, too, fer me. He's all I got. Donna ya let anythung happen to 'im wid dem funny wooden legs."

"We'll take care of each other, Nancy, and Tooter will watch out for all of us."

"Dat dog's da Lo'd's blessin'," Nancy smiled.

"She stink worsen a polecat, but b'ars stink, too," Ox grumbled. "One t'ing 'bout stinkin' b'ars, ya sholy knows war dey is when dey 'round ya, and dat's good, 'cause ya donna want ta meet no bar, Son!"

## 32

Karol and the Stewarts arrived on a late Thursday afternoon at the Habak house. Dus had invited Patty and Scott Kirsh, and Nancy and Ox Conley to join them on the porch for a barbecued venison and trimmings supper from the grill. They spent the evening eating, reminiscing, and exchanging tales of the honeymoon and summer doings, then made plans for the cave expedition up the Cutty in the morning.

Though she had just driven up the mountain, Karol invited the women folk on a trip back to Staunton the following day to tour the sites there, visit her house, and do some shopping. She did not have to persuade a cheery and amenable Nancy Conley to accompany them.

"Ya knod I staid et Karol's place when Ox was in da hospial thar. 'Tis a lovely home. En I know da hospital well, a corse, butta neva 'ave I be'n on a real shoppin' trip ta da city. Had no chance wid Ox so sick down thar, so t'will be fun en a new sperience fer me ta go wid ya ladies. Thank ye!"

"Ya take good car' of er, en donna let 'er spen' da li'l bit a money I 'as," Ox joked. "En donna let 'er come back 'ere dressed wid al dem newfangled city clothes lookin' like one a dem women a da night."

"Ox Conley, yo' shut yo' mouf 'bout sech silly things," Nancy scolded.

"What do you know about 'women of the night,' Ox?" Scott asked, grinning from ear to ear. "I was a city cop for years, and I don't know anything about them."

"You big fibber," Patty jabbed. "When you were on the vice squad graveyard shift in Toledo, you knew those professional girls by name."

"I'm sure learning a lot about these Joshuatown folk, Julie," J.K. said. "We don't have those kind of folk in our 'happy valley!'"

"The heck we don't! My husband is certainly not as naive a professor a she lets on," Julie responded. "Enough of his nonsense. Don't worry, Ox; we'll take good care of Nancy, and she'll come back to you dressed just as pretty as when she left here."

"So we'll all meet her for breakfast at eight tomorrow morning, and then be off on our excursions," Karol proffered. "Julie and I will pack some knapsack lunches for these guys here. You and Nancy can take care of your men, Patty. We gals will lunch at some swank restaurant in Staunton."

"Talk about wasting the Lord's tithe," Dus quipped.

"I brought all the flashlights, rope, and spelunking gear we'll need," J.K. said, "and I have an extra pair of arm-clamp walking sticks if you want them, Ox. They'd be helpful on the rough terrain."

"Be obliged, Prof," Ox smiled.

"Looks like we're ready for tomorrow, then, so let's call it a night," Dus urged, noticing the anxious 'come-hither' countenance on the face of his wife. Her eyes were nodding, signaling her readiness to go to bed. "The radio says the weather will be good. Let's meet back here no later than six tomorrow night. We oughta be able to see what we are looking for up there, and you gals should accomplish your town spree by then, won't you, honey?"

"No problem, spelunkers!" Karol smiled gratefully and beguilingly at Dus, and added, "So now, let's all get a good night's sleep!"

The others looked at each other, smiled at the newlyweds, and agreed. The Conleys and Kirshs went home together. The Stewarts were tired from their long trip, and went to bed almost immediately thereafter in the Habak's guest bedroom. Dus and Karol retired to continue their oft-interrupted honeymoon. Tooter, the dog, having been relegated to the porch on a short leash, snored and waited for the morrow.

\* \* \*

In the morning, after a hearty breakfast, the friends were on their way. Julie, Karol, and Patty, with a cheerful Nancy in tow, took off down the mountain in Dus' Jeep to Staunton. Ox, J.K., and Dus, carrying backpacks filled with food and caving stuff, climbed aboard Scott's pickup. Tooter jumped in with them. They rode as far as they could up along Cedar Creek, then climbed the Cutty on foot. Ox, with his shotgun and axe strapped to his chest, took the point, with J.K., binoculars and climbing rope hanging around his shoulders, following. Both of them trekked stalwartly, if slowly, on their impaired legs. Dus followed, a machete belted on his side. Scott, armed with his police revolver and rifle, took the rear sentinel position. Tooter sniffed the ground and ran after critters.

About two hours into the climb, Scott yelled up to the limping leader. "How's it going, Ox?"

"Me en da prof ain't doon bad fer a cuppa cripples, ain't we, J.K.? Even if we is lookin' fer Dus' big pipe dream!"

"We're fine. I'm used to this. It's good for what ails couch potatoes and classroom types. You fellows keeping up, back there?" J.K. asked, buoyantly.

"They's jest followers, Prof. Be betta iffen I know'd were ya thunk ya seen dat cave!" he yelled at Dus. "I see dem three ceda's above us."

"I think we're getting close, Ox. Let's stop at that dogwood patch on that knoll right above you and rest. Maybe I can recognize the outcropping from there."

They stopped on the knoll, and Dus pointed toward a high rock with sturdy green brush at its base. "Let me borrow your binoculars, J.K." He ogled the magnified area he had recognized. "That's it, not more than three hundred meters away."

"I be'n ova nar der before, en I neva in my life seen a cave," Ox insisted.

"Were you ever there in the winter, Ox?" Scott asked the protesting woodsman.

"Kent say dat fer sur. Maybe I on'y be'n up dis fa ta dat place in da summertime."

"Maybe the cave entrance is covered with foliage in the summer," Dus suggested.

"Well, let's go see," Scott said, equally assertive.

"Dus and I'll lead and clear the trail, Ox, and make it easier for you and J.K. Dus is right about the growth. There may be no trail with so much brush in the woods this time of year."

"Wah, do as ya ple'se, en wal see iffen Dus es right."

Scott and Dus hacked a trail with the machete and axe. J.K. and Ox followed, and within an hour, the dog and trekkers arrived at the stone wall. The cavity in the rock was well-hidden behind the foliage, but it was there. Dus and Scott quickly cut away the growth and pulled it aside. The four men gaped at an aperture and tunnel the size of a huge concrete water culvert, large enough for a man to walk through.

Dus was ecstatic, but kept his calm. "Well, what do you think, guys?"

"I'll be dinged," Ox bawled, sitting down on a nearby rock, his eyes as big as saucers. 'Ya were right all da time, Dus. I sholy owes ya en apol'gy. I is shamed I done doubted yo' word, Son, butta I be'n in des hills all ma life huntin', en neva seen dat big hole. I gus I neva be'n roun' dat rock in da winnatime. I gus da brush jest had me fo'ld. Ma Nan be glad ta know I was wrong 'bout dis, 'cause she truss ya so much, Fadder."

"Forget it, Ox. It's OK. You led us here, and we are grateful to you. Now we know!"

"Let's have some lunch and get our stuff together before we go in there," J.K. suggested.

The climbers ate, threw Tooter the scraps, put their gear together, and made their plans to explore the cave.

"It may go nowhere," J.K. said, putting on a miner's helmet with a flashlight attached to its visor. "I'll go first." He wound the rope around his hand and held it tightly against his walking sticks, and handed the line to each of his friends. "You fellas hold tightly onto that, but don't tie it to your bodies. We don't want to be encumbered by it if we have to run."

"That sounds ominous," Dus stated. "Why would we have to run?"

"I tol' ya, Dus, if ya smell a big stink, der's a b'ar right atop ya, en ya betta skidaddle fast," Ox grumbled.

"He's right," J.K. said. "Anyway, you all follow me, with your flashlights on. Scott, you follow with your guns, just in case we have trouble. Ox, you follow Dus, so that his feet can test the trail for you. Tooter will no doubt sniff where she wants to. Maybe she'll help us find something."

They entered the cave. It was wet with the odor of animals, but the rock floor was relatively easy to traverse. The cave became more spacious in places, and as they trekked on, they noted smaller tunnels along the walls. It was dark, but their powerful lights gave them good vision, leaving them unafraid. The floor was strewn here and there with small animal bones, none of which interested the men or the dog. It was devoid of human remains and live animals. They heard the chattering of bats hanging from the ceiling, but none flew about them. There were no streams, big stones, nor stalagmites to impede their progress.

After exploring for a hundred meters or so inside the cave, Dus, sounding disappointed, said, "It's roomy, but not very long, so far. Maybe if we peered into some of those smaller apertures back there with our lights, we'd see something. What do you think, J.K.?"

"Well, it's been easy walking in here for Ox and me, and it doesn't seem fraught with danger. I've been in caverns and caves a heck of a lot more challenging than this. We can look into those depressions on our way out, if you want."

"I'm not a spelunker and have no knowledge of places like this," Scott interjected, "but I don't see any mystery here to be solved. Easy or not, it's not the kind of place I'd like to do my recreating. Now that we found it and studied it, I suggest we go home!"

"Come on, Scott," Dus admonished. "This is fun. Let's go a little farther. Who knows what we'll find?"

"I don't want to find anything, Dus. It's just a cave, and I don't have a big hankering for caves, like you and J.K. do. We came to look. We have looked. Let's admit there is no mystery here, and go back to our warm houses and wives."

"I agrees wid da sheriff," Ox joined in the discussion. "Der's nuffin h'ar, my leg is bodderin me, en we still needa ta walk down da hill."

"It's up to you fellows," J.K. said. "I'll go along with whatever you decide. You rest here for a minute, and let me go up that way a little farther. I see Tooter standing at a lighted spot, and I'd like to know if she has sniffed out anything."

"How far do you think it is?" Scott asked.

"Maybe forty meters or so."

"Then I'll go with you."

"Wah, I wal too, den," Ox crowed.

"I will, too," an elated Dus agreed.

The men plodded upward and around a curve toward the light. It got bigger and brighter. Tooter was jumping about, waiting for them. It was a large opening to the outside of the cave. They approached it cautiously.

"Come here, Tooter. Here, girl," Dus called the dog. She came to him and he snapped on her leash to keep her from moving toward the ledge.

"We need to go slowly. There might be a sheer drop off a cliff beyond that opening," J.K. warned.

"Let Dus and me go out there first, J.K. We can't be sure how slippery it might be," Scott insisted.

They arrived and then crowded together at the opening, peering at the bright sun and landscape. They stood on a wide rock ledge with a trail leading down from it into a patch of trees in a deep ravine, hidden from view from every angle except from the heights where the men were standing.

"Let me have your binoculars, J.K.," Scott said. He scanned the lay of the land, muttering "I'll be damned; gosh; hmmnn," then turned to the other men. "Back away from here a little bit, then follow my hand where I'm pointing."

They did as he ordered. "First, look down at that clump of trees in that deep ravine, with the wisp of smoke rising from it. Now, if you look hard, you'll see a path winding up and out of there into the woods. Note that it then goes out of the woods, crosses a cornfield, heads through some more woods for about two miles, widens a bit, and egresses onto that highway curving down the mountain. Do you see all that I'm pointing to?"

The others agreed that they did. "Well, that highway is what we all travel when we go back and forth between Joshuatown and Staunton."

"Son of a gun," Dus muttered.

"Now, look at the narrow trail coming out of that clump of trees, where you see the smoke on this side," Scott continued. "Notice it is leading along the side of this cliff, right up here to this ledge?"

J.K. retrieved his binoculars and scanned the terrain. "I see everything you're alluding to, Scott."

Dus and Ox borrowed the glasses and said the same. "Wah, I be dinged," Ox scratched his head. " 'Cept fer goan up en down dat road ta Staunton, en seein' des stone wall on des side a da Cutty from da road, I neva tracked down in dat canyon en woods. Neva had da need, en der war no way to it, anyhow. Dat's a big gulch en struch a woods en field, en it do looks like nuffin butta mules ken git in en outta on dose paths."

"You got that right for sure, Ox," Scott agreed. "Nothing but plodding men and packed mules can get in and out of there from the highway, and up to this cave. We'll take a look at those tunnels back there, J.K., and see if those mules are bringing anything up here. I think the people working down there can probably drive a vehicle far enough in from the highway at that wide spot in the path so no one could see it from the highway. I can't even see one from here, but I'd bet there are some pickup trucks and horse trailers hiding in there. I'd bet, too, that that access to the highway is where Karol stopped and saw those men pushing logs and branches off the road and into the trail to cover it. I sent a deputy down there after you talked to me about it. He found nothing along the highway, but I can see it from here."

"What do you make of it all?" J.K. queried Scott.

"Well, my curious spelunkers, it doesn't take a CIA agent to figure out that where there is smoke, there is fire. Where there is a fire in a clump of woods in a ravine near a cornfield, in these hills, there are likely a lot of vats, copper coils, wooden barrels, and glass jugs. I think there might be a lot of those barrels and glass jugs stashed away up in some of these little tunnels in this cave, too. No wonder people were shooting at you, Dus! There's a moonshine still down there, my friends, that's distilling the best, premier, Virginia one-hundred-and-thirty-proof 'white lightning' corn whiskey in America. It's sixty-five percent pure grain alcohol, fifty percent better than any state-approved booze, and selling for fifty percent less. Now that we know all of this, I strongly recommend that we turn around and rapidly move our butts back through this cave to where we came in, and get off this mountain. If those 'moonies' down there see us, they're going to come up here with their guns firing."

The four men, with one accord, turned to leave. Tooter, still held by her leash, wagged her stumpy tail in excitement over the movement of a frightened chipmunk, and let out the loudest bark a Labrador bitch ever bellowed, its sound ricocheting against every rock wall in the mountain and down through the canyon.

"Jeez, Tooter," Scott swore, as he saw a bunch of men come out of the clump of woods and start firing rifles at the cave entrance. Bullets cracked off the boulders, spraying hard fragments of rock all around the men and dog. Tooter yelped and stumbled to the ground. Dus pulled her by the leash out of harm's way. "Tooter's been hit!" he yelled.

"Anyone else hurt?" Scott asked.

"A chip of rock hit my cheek. It's bleeding, but I don't think it's very deep," Dus answered, dabbing it with his sleeve. "Tooter's bleeding on her rump, but I think she's OK, too." He patted his whimpering dog. "You'll be all right, girl."

Scott crept to the ledge and peered out of the cave. Bullets racked against the boulders again, and he ducked back. "There are three of those goons starting up the path to this ledge. We've got to get out of here, right now. They could be here in less than twenty minutes! J.K., you and Ox take your rope and flashlights and work yourselves as fast as you can back through the cave to one of those small tunnels, and hide. Don't stop until you're hidden, and be careful not to fall. Can you do that?"

"Sure, can't we, Ox?" J.K. assured him.

"Sho ken, Prof, butta I hates ta leave Scott en Dus 'ere by demselves wid dem pack a polecats. Got me da doubba barrel, en I'ma good shot."

"I'm not going to argue with you, Ox. This is no time to be stubborn. I'm the law, and you have to do as I tell you. Give Dus your shotgun and some shells; get going with J.K. and help him, like right now."

"I'm good with a gun, too, Sheriff," J.K. offered. "I got an expert shooting medal in basic."

"I know you are, Prof, and I'm not questioning your and Ox's marksmanship, but right now, with those legs of yours, you two need all the time you can get to hide from the firepower those guys are bringing up here. Dus and I will try to hold them off, and then run down there and join you at the tunnels. Now, please go, and Dus and I will take care of this mess."

J.K. and Ox grumbled a few choice words, but did as they were told, turned on their lights, and hobbled back through the cave. Dus loaded Ox's shotgun and stood with Scott just inside the entrance. Scott had his police revolver already in his hand. Tooter lay in a small depression in the path, breathing softly. Though wounded, she did not complain. Her bleeding had stopped, and she licked at her tail end. Dus calmed her with hushed tones.

"What now, Chief?" he asked his detective friend.

"Well, Father, you'd better use your clerical skills and pray, then use your old Marine skills and help us out of this little war we got ourselves into. It looks like the mystery of Ox getting hurt and your getting blasted at is coming to a screeching halt."

"This is no time to jest, Scott!"

"I'm not joking! We are in big trouble here. That's why I wanted our disabled friends out of here. I have been in these kinds of scrapes as a cop, and I know what you have experienced in Korea, so if you can help me with the firepower, I think we'll be OK. We have the high ground, and they have to come up that narrow trail one at a time with very little cover. So they're going to have to keep shooting at us. They won't be able to see us too well, and in this cave, we have a good defensive position."

"You're right. What do you want me to do?"

"Just aim Ox's shotgun out and around this entrance and down the path, and pop off both barrels, one right after the other. You won't hit them because they're too far away, but they will know we're armed. Moonies are deathly afraid of shotguns. I am going to yell some big lies at them, and then I'm going to make them jump for cover with some pistol rounds, before they get up too far. I won't try to hit them, just scare 'em enough so they know they are in a confrontation with the law. Are you ready?"

"I'm ready, but I must say this is a terrible way to spend my honeymoon. If those guys don't kill me, my bride will when she sees Tooter's bloody butt."

"Quit beefing! It's about time you quit honeymooning, you old geezer. I warned you about trying to be a detective and messing with 'moonies.' Ya oughta listen to a lawman! Now pop off those barrels and make those varmints wet their pants with some of that horse pee they drink."

"You are poetic, Sheriff," Dus scoffed, firing both barrels of the shotgun, the recoil of the twelve-gauge nearly knocking him off his feet.

Scott peered out the aperture to check the results. The men jumped off the path and took cover behind some trees and bushes, as he had predicted. He yelled at them. "This is Sheriff Kirsh, you moonshining turkeys. My deputies and I are heavily armed up here. We have rifles, shotguns, and a bazooka!" he lied. "We're gonna blow your still to hell, and put enough buckshot in your asses that you won't be able to sit down the whole twenty years you're gonna spend in jail!"

Just as his echo died in the forest, some more slugs hit the rock. He returned fire with three pistol shots at the bottom of the tree trunks, quickly took the shotgun from Dus, loaded both barrels, and blasted at the bushes. He hollered as loud as he could, to be sure the outlaws could hear him. "Load that bazooka, Deputy, and hand it up here; I am gonna blow that booze joint and those varmints to Kingdom come!"

The moonies emerged from the bushes and ran helter-skelter down through the woods to the clump of trees in the gorge, where the smoke already was turning to steam. Some of the moonshiners were dousing the fire. Scott gave Dus his rifle, and together they fired a fuselage of lead at the tops of the trees, cutting away branches and leaves that fell down to the ground. They heard men screaming and mules braying, and stopped firing to watch a half dozen culprits chasing three mules up and out of the ravine, into the woods, and across the cornfield, leaving their whiskey still behind.

"Reload the rifle, Dus," Scott commanded, as he reloaded his pistol. "Follow that steam down to the ground, and blow away whatever is sitting in there. You can't see it, but believe me, we will put some holes in the equipment."

They sent another barrage of bullets into the clump of trees, and heard metal being punctured, glass breaking, and steam hissing.

"Well, that's that; they won't be back for a long time. I'll call the Feds tonight and go in there with them tomorrow. Thanks for your help, trooper. You did a good job."

"Whew! That was something. Aren't you going to chase after them and put 'em in jail?"

"Nope."

"Why not, for God's sake?"

"If I see them around town, recognize them, and believe they were involved with shooting at us today, I'll have a talk with them."

"Is that all?"

"If they were, I'll shackle them and turn them over to the Feds. Will that suit you?"

"My God, Scott. Those goons nearly killed Ox and me."

"Maybe they did, and maybe they didn't."

"You're not sure?" Dus shouted angrily at his friend.

"No, Dus, I'm not. And don't shout at me. Come on," he calmly said, holstering his pistol and shouldering his rifle. "Get Tooter up and let's go find Ox and J.K. Is she able to walk?"

"I think so." He pulled on Tooter's leash, and she got up. "Come, good girl; time to go home and get some Band-Aids from the doc."

Dus, Scott, and the dog went back through the cave, calling for the other two men.

"We're in here!" J.K. shouted. "Everything OK now? Come see what we have here."

"Everything's fine," Scott answered, as he and Dus squeezed into a crowded tunnel, where flashlights were shining. They found Ox and J.K. scanning the room with their lights. They could hardly make out all the stuff stored in the small room. A dozen unlighted lanterns hung around the walls.

"Anybody have a match?"

"I carry ban burnas al de time in ma pockat, jist in case," Ox offered.

"Good. Let's light up the lanterns and see what we got here."

They lighted up the room. A multitude of wooden kegs and hundreds of glass gallon bottles full of whiskey met their eyes. Scott whistled.

"Holy smoke!" Dus wailed.

"Well, my friends, we have found the moonshine."

"Dem varmints be'n havin' a good time up here, ain't dey, Sheriff?"

"Yeah, Ox. They have thousands and thousands of dollars worth of booze here. Let's take the lanterns and look around these other holes."

They did, and found many filled with the whiskey.

"I oughta blast all this stuff with the shotgun, but the Feds wouldn't like that. It's evidence, and they'll want to look at it before they taste it and get crocked."

"Shame on you, Scott," J.K. bantered. "That's not a nice thing to say about our noble government employees."

"'Tis truf," Ox affirmed. "Des is jest as bad as da polecats, sometimes. I donna know why ya wanna go afta des varmints, anyways. Dey donna hurt nabudy wid der lika."

"They hurt you, Ox, tried to hurt Dus, and tried to kill all of us today.

But you are right. There are hundreds of moonshiners around the country who aren't hurting anyone. But the licensed distillers are hurting the folk who like to drink that horse pee with labeled stuff. It's just that the Feds want to regulate them, make 'em have permits so they have to pay taxes, and, of course, licensed distillers don't want the competition. But, it doesn't matter what I think. I am the law and I have to enforce it, even though I sometimes think it is a waste of time. It is not likely we lawmen of any stripe are ever going to stop the moonshiners from setting up their stills someplace. But we have stopped this operation here, at least for a while."

"What do we do now, Scott?" Dus asked.

"Let's fill the lanterns with the kerosene they have in those rooms and put them at both entrances of the cave. The moonshiners, wherever they have run to, and everyone else in the mountain, will see the light tonight and think the law is up here in force. They won't come near here tonight, and tomorrow morning I'll have the Feds up here."

"What will they do, Scott?" Dus asked.

"If they do what they have done in the past, they'll probably take a few kegs and jugs out of here as evidence, blow up the cave, and seal it with the stuff in it, with nitro. They'll also blow up the still, cut down timbers to screw up the road in from the highway, and give our new groom and his brand-new bride a lot of peace of mind."

"Big joke, Sheriff," Dus quipped.

"Wah, theta be a relaf fo' shur ta al our ladies, en me, too," Ox agreed.

"I am sure it will be, Ox, so let's get our chores done and get down the mountain to those ladies. They aren't going to be happy about these developments!"

"Julie's used to my getting bumps and stuff crawling around caves, but she's going to be a mite unhappy with this story," J.K. mumbled.

"Do we have to tell them the details?" Dus argued.

"You know damn well, Father Habak, that the last time you tried to cover up things, you got into trouble with that Indian woman of yours. How in the hell are you going to hide your and Tooter's bloody flesh? She's not going to like what has happened to you and that dog, but she's going to scalp you if she finds out you lied to her. I thought you clergy types were into honesty and stuff. Better practice what you preach, Preacher."

"Yeah, P.F.C.," the old Army sergeant admonished.

"Come on, Tooter, let's go tell the gospel truth to our gal, and see if she's in enough of a forgiving mood to mend our wounds. Mare's marbles!"

the former Marine P.F.C. and present vicar of Moonshine Mountain growled.

* * *

"What in the name of all that is holy have you old coots been up to?" Julie Stewart asked, as J.K. led the disheveled and weary group into the vicarage.

"Yeah, it's a way pas' seven, en we be'n a waitin' en have suppa r'ady here fer ya," Nancy joined in. "Wadda ya be'n doin' thata took so long?"

"Oh, my God!" Karol screeched, as she looked at Dus' gory face and Tooter's bloody rump. "What happened to you and Tooter?"

"I'll check Tooter's wound. Karol, you see to Dus," Patty said.

The women were visibly upset, and showed it. Karol ran into the kitchen to get some swabs and disinfectant for both her husband and dog, and ordered her husband to sit down and let her tend to his wound. Patty soothed Tooter and gently washed her cut.

"Now, don't you gals get all upset. We are all OK," Scott admonished, trying to calm the women with lighthearted banter. "We found the cave, entered it, and found no bears, no wildcats, nor gold. You would not have liked it, Karol. It was dark, creepy, and full of bats. Sorry we are a little late, but we got delayed with a little problem. The wounds on Scott and Tooter were made by flying rock fragments, and are superficial. J.K., Ox, and I are fine, but weary. J.K. and Ox did great with their gimpy legs. When we get cleaned up and sit down to eat, you can tell us about your day shopping and we'll tell you about our spelunking. Let's wash up, guys, while Dus and Tooter get patched up."

"Superficial, eh?" Karol grimaced. "This cut on Dus' cheek is deep, and will need some stitches. How's Tooter, Patty?"

"Her cut's not bad. She's licked it pretty clean, and I swabbed it with some peroxide. She's OK."

"I don't need stitches," Dus whimpered. "Just tape it together and let's eat. I'm hungry!"

"This is the second time you've thought you knew better than the doctor about your wounds, Preacher, and you were wrong the first time, too. Now, don't embarrass me by getting me angry around our nice guests. Julie, would you, Nancy, and Patty see that these guys of yours get cleaned up and get something to eat while I take my guy down to the clinic? Come on, big brave! Let's go and get you sewed up."

While the women agreed and took care of their chores with their respective husbands, Karol loaded hers in the Jeep and took him to the clinic.

"Well, Father Habak, we meet again in the place of our first powwow," Karol teased, as she gathered together her suturing supplies in the clinic and began to tend to Dus' cut. "You don't have to take your pants off this time and show me your heinie, Father, but you must sit very still so I can sew up your Cupid face without leaving it disfigured. That's a nasty wound, and I don't want you talking, because if you use any facial muscles while I'm doing this, I can't guarantee you won't have a noticeable scar on your cheek. Course it might make you look a bit more ruggedly handsome."

"I don't want to look rugged. Just sew me up. I love you, and I'm sorry about Tooter."

"I love you, too, darling, and I'm glad none of you guys got hurt too badly. We'll talk about that expedition another time," she sniffed, a tear rolling down her own cheek. "I hate to see you hurt, and this is going to hurt a little. Now, grit your teeth and think about nice things, like how I'm going to heal your wounded body, give it a soothing bath, and fix it with love when we get home."

She began her work. He just stared at her eyes as she sprayed a substance on his wound to anesthetize it. She then expertly threaded the curved needle and, with forceps, pushed it through the outside of the skin on one side of the cut, then through the inside of the other. She then drew the ends of the thread tight and tied them. 'I want you to be happy that I am not mad at you, nor will I ask you about what happened up in that cave until tomorrow. And, I promise, because I am so thankful to God you were not killed, and because anger is such a waste of time for a bride and groom who only have short weekends together, I won't be angry tomorrow, no matter what you tell me about how you and Tooter got hurt today." He smiled. 'Don't do that," she scolded, and neatly sewed in two more sutures. She swabbed his face with peroxide. "Now," she quipped, "give me a big smile and kiss your doctor wife in appreciation for the job she did on your pale face, paleface."

He did that, and they embraced. "Ouch! Not so hard, Doc. That hurts," he complained.

"You need to feel the strength of my kisses. They're part of my healing techniques."

"You're a weird doctor, but thank you, sweetheart." He looked in the mirror. "Boy, that is ugly, isn't it? How long do the stitches have to stay in?"

"Let's see—tomorrow is Saturday. I'll yank 'em out a week from Sunday. That will give Mrs. Quidmire, who is as blind as a bat and can't hear your sermons, who sits in the second-row pew in front of the pulpit, two Sundays to check out your fresh facial features."

"What are you talking about?"

"I'm talking about old, sunburned, craggily, pruneface Bertha Quidmire, who likes to notice pimples and other blemishes on people's faces. She asks them if they know that they are there, then asks how they got them."

"You're pulling my leg, Ollikut!"

"I am not! She always does that! You can stand in front of a mirror for hours trying to cover a pimple or blemish on your nose, forehead, or cheek with some kind of cosmetic, and then if you run into her, she'll ask if you know you have a pimple. It's downright embarrassing when a person has worked so hard to get rid of it. She's a scourge to the local teenagers." Dus chuckled at her statement.

"It's not funny, Preacher. Wait until she sees your mug for two Sunday mornings. I'll bet you wampum to donuts that when she sees those stitches, she's gonna meet you in the aisle after service and say to you in front of everybody, 'Did ya know, Pawson, ya 'ave t'ree flies buzzing 'round yer nose and mouf while ya was preachin'? Why'd dey do dat?'" Karol warned him, putting a hand over her mouth to stifle her own developing giggle.

"It's not funny. You put a Band-Aid on this cut right now and yank these stitches by next Saturday," he commanded.

"Then she's gonna ask you what you're covering up under the bandage. What are you going to tell her?"

"I'm going to tell her that my wife bit me on the face while I was making love to her!"

"You do, and I'll put those stitches out of your face before they're ready." Karol laughed at her husband, put a Band-Aid over the stitches, and kissed him again. "You wouldn't dare tell her that, but maybe I will bite you tonight and add some zest to Mrs. Quidmire's dull life and fascinating fantasies."

"You're loony! Come on, medicine woman, clean up the mess here and let's get home to our guests and supper."

"Dus, I want to tell you something." Karol's face was full of concern.

"What is it, sweetheart? You don't look happy."

"I'm sorry, you're still not going to be a brand-new father just yet. I had my period again, so there was no 'begetting' this time. I hate to disappoint you again."

"It's OK, sweetheart. Don't worry. As I told you before, I will always love you, with or without anew baby. We have two beautiful kids to take care of now. If they are to have a brother or sister, it will happen when it will happen."

"Maybe it is going to be harder because of my age and the long time between Shawn and now. I guess I'll have to be patient."

"That's right. I don't know much about these things, but as they say, 'Anxiety doesn't help the process.' Don't worry about me, Kara. I will be patient, too. God will take care of a lot of it, and I shall be very happy to continue to do my part."

A big smile came over Karol's face. "Yeah, me too! Thank you for understanding. Now let's go eat, and then get those folk out of our house. The 'begetting' needs to get started again."

They arrived home to anxious friends who had not yet eaten. They were glad Dus was OK. They ate supper, then sat around the table as the men told about their adventure in the mountain. Their wives were upset with what they heard, but their husbands calmed them down with assurances that the dangers were past, and that the problems they had encountered in the cave would be resolved by the Feds in the morning.

The women also shared their day in the city, and they all ended the evening with laughter and prayers of Thanksgiving for their safety. They agreed among themselves that they would not talk to anyone about the incident, allowing Scott to handle the necessary police advisory with the Feds. They said their "good-byes," and the Habaks and Stewarts went to bed. The Kirshs dropped the Conleys off at their house, and then drove slowly to their own house.

"Quite a day, sweetheart," Patty said to Scott. "I know that it was just police work for you, but I hate it when you're in danger. I am so glad you were with the guys. They needed you, and I am sure Karol, Nancy, and Julie are very grateful. You're a good policeman, and I am so very proud of you. It's all over, thank God, but you still seem rather pensive."

"We pretty nearly got killed up there today, honey. There's a lot we didn't elaborate on because Karol has been so frightened about Dus. Nancy is just getting over Ox's injury, and J.K. and Julie, for crying out loud, are just on a short vacation. The fact is, that while we all agreed not to discuss the happenings today, the moonies will be. They will be discussing this among themselves all over the mountains. I don't think that they will engage me anymore, nor show their faces, lest they think I'll recognize them, but it won't be long before they'll be building a still someplace else."

"It's the nature of the beast in these parts, isn't it, dear? Are they really any worse than the rumrunners in Toledo?"

"No, they're not, but they broke the law here and hurt people, and my job is to stop them."

"Nobody knows that better than I, and I know you will work out the bad stuff, as you usually do."

"The Treasury guys and I are going to nail some of those goons sooner or later, Patty. I am sure of that. But this is far from over. This old expert cop husband of yours you are so proud of knows in his bones that the mystery about the cadaver that Dus dug up at the church, and the subsequent shooting at him up there, hasn't been resolved by anything that happened today. I don't mean to frighten you, and you are not to say anything to anybody. Karol and Dus are still in serious danger in their beautiful chalet."

"Oh, my God," Patty cried, reaching for her husband's strong hand and squeezing it. "Oh, no. Please, Scott, no. Please be wrong about that. Please, God, don't let anything happen to those two happy friends of ours who just found each other!"

# 33

It was now mid-September in Joshuatown. The rest of the summer had flown rapidly. Elly and Shawn returned from Oregon and spent the last few weeks before school in Joshuatown with Dus. They had become very close as sister and brother during their stay with Karol's folks in the Wallowa Valley. Elly had learned a lot about the Nez Perce Indians, and asserted that they were an American Indian tribe, "a heck of a lot more important than the Susquehonnocks ever were, Dad!" Karol teased Dus about Elly's laudable perception, but had acknowledged that her Susquehonnock bloodline had given Elly a fine sense of history. Dus didn't care one way or the other who was the best Indian tribe. He loved his Nez Perce wife far beyond the whimsy of history. Karol's son, Shawn, thought that if his new sister was a descendent of the Susquehonnock, then they had procreated, through the generations, one of "the most neat and cool Indian princesses in the Americas," with, of course, the inclusion of his mother.

Dus and Karol's marriage, and Elly's growing affection for her new mother and brother had made her more covetous of family togetherness. She told her father that she really would miss her friends, the nuns, and the bishop and Mrs. Mueller at the priory school, but she now wanted very much to live in the house in Staunton with Karol during the weekdays. She wanted to go to a "regular girls' and boys'" school with Shawn, and to be with her daddy, her new mom, and new brother up in the mountain on the weekends and during vacation times.

Karol, naturally, was jubilant about Elly wanting to do that, but knew it was up to Dus concerning what was best for his daughter. The whole family sat down together at dinner one evening, discussed and prayed over Elly's wishes, and the decision was made that her being with Karol and Shawn at Staunton would strengthen the new family's ties. Shawn, Elly, and Karol were ecstatic about the arrangement, but "cautious old Dad" took a more "try, then wait and see what happens with the experiment" stance. He instinctively thought of Ginnie and the bishop, and wondered what they would think. He called his bishop.

"Well, Mrs. Mueller and the nuns will miss her, Dus, and you know how much she has meant to me. We love her and have become very close. Did she say anything to you about that?"

"She did, and you will always be an important grandfather figure in her life. She'll come to visit you and the nuns often, but she wants to make this change and needs the stability of living within a family. I believe that Karol and Shawn can provide that in Staunton."

"I do, too, Dus. You can't blame me for being a bit selfish. It's been a joy to us to have her here. Go ahead with your plans. You have my blessing. Ask Elly to call us from time to time, and keep me abreast of her progress. I will reassure her that her decision is right, that we will be here for her if she needs us, and that I love her. She sure is gaining a wonderful mother in Karol. You are a lucky man, Father Habak. Oh, by the way, Dus, how was the honeymoon and your summer?"

"They were both wonderful," he fibbed. "I would, however, appreciate your adding my friend Lou Casalano to your prayer list. We stopped to see him on our way home from the Poconos in June. Even then, nearly three months ago, Karol's prognosis of his condition was that he probably wouldn't live another three months. We have known each other since we were kids, Bishop, and have grown very close over the last several years. His death will be a very great loss to me, as well as to his family and the church. Mrs. Casalano is doing pretty good, but she knows in her heart that Lou's death is in sight."

Bishop Mueller knew his priest was weeping as he responded, "Of course, Dus. I will have special intentions for him at services at the cathedral on Sunday. I am very sorry, and I hope his wife is doing well under the circumstances. Give them both my best wishes. I noted what a extraordinary job he did on your vicarage. His craftsmanship certainly demonstrates his skills and his esteem for you. It is a fine memorial to him. I believe you will find peace and comfort living there with Karol, remembering Mr. Casalano's caring for you in such a visible and special way, even in the last few months of his life. I shall write a note to him to thank him for that good offering to the church and diocese."

"Thanks for doing that, and for understanding about him and Elly. I'll be around soon to talk to you about the summer." He had no intention of talking to his bishop about the confrontation that he and his friends had with the "moonies" in the cave. That had been more or less resolved to some people's satisfaction, if not to Dus', but he felt it was best that the details be left in the hands and hearts of those who had been involved.

Dus had clearly not been one of those happy with the resolution. The FBI had had an investigation, questioned Dus and his spelunking friends for all the details, had the ATF blow up the cave and whiskey still, plowed the corn underground, and let the incident die. They had rounded up some of the "moonies," asked them a lot of questions. They let most of them go. As for the rest, the state district judge fined them for "operating a spirits production business without a state license," and sent them packing back to the woods and cornfields, with a warning not to make whiskey again.

The whole incident seemed to have become a joke to almost everyone except Scott and Dus. The FBI had not found any evidence that connected the "moonies" to Ox's injury, and concluded that it was just an accidental wound that Ox had inflicted on himself. As for someone shooting at Dus, that was the local sheriff's problem. Not much public notice ensued from the incident, but there was a lot of quiet gossip around the area, some of which was critical of Scott and supportive of the outlaws. The general attitude of most of the townsfolk and hillfolk was that "the sh'riff en his depyhaties had foun' da moonies up on da Cutty, shot 'em up a mite, and brung in da 'Revenooers' to shut da po' debils down fer a spell. So watta erse is new in des pawts? Ya hear 'bout dat stuf all da time!"

Mrs. Quidmire, as Karol had predicted, asked Dus about the Band-Aid on his face after services on Sunday. "Dad ya try ta squiz a pimple outta ya cheek der, Pawson? Dem is buggas ta git out, ain't dey? Ma grankiddies git 'em a lot, en I tell 'em neva ta squiz 'em, er dey mak' 'em worsa. Ya oughta natta do dat, Fadder," she had challenged him.

"It isn't a pimple, Bertha," Dus had indignantly answered the old woman, almost yelling at her so she could hear. "Tooter and I were cavorting a little too roughly, and I accidentally hurt her. She didn't mean to, but she bit me." That was a "white lie," and it seemed to Dus he was telling too many of those these days. But he excused himself, because, as a priest, he did not feel candor was always the best policy. He had told a lot of "white lies" in his ministry to spare people some honest truth that would have either hurt them or was none of their business. What he used to say to people who could not help being "truthful," when not even asked, was, "Spare me and the world your honesty."

"Wah, I do declar. Ya ne'ds ta be mo' car'ful wid dem bitches, Pawson. Da gits en a bad mod w'en des in heat. Sho glad ya has da good doctor fer yer wife, sose she ken take car' a ya," she finished, ambling out of the church with a smug look on her face—a face, which Dus now noted with an unholy kind of glee, that had the countenance of a crone.

Karol, standing back in the aisle with Nancy, overheard the confrontation and giggled into her open palm.

"What is ya laffin 'bout, girl?" Nancy asked.

"Oh, something silly, Nancy," she told her friend, tears running down her face. "I just think my husband is very funny sometimes."

"Wah, dat may be, butte he's a good preacha en has a lotta good samuns 'bout God en Jesus, en sho says nice thungs 'bout folk."

"He sure does," Karol said proudly of her husband. "But still, he is one of the funniest preachers I have ever known. He brings zest to my life, and I am glad he's my husband. I wonder if Mrs. Quidmire is glad he is her pastor, and thinks he brings zest into her life."

"Wah, dat nosy biddy donna see ner har a thung, anyways."

"Dus is comical, but is a very sweet and loving pastor. Course, I am prejudiced."

"Two peas en a pod, iffen ya asks me." Nancy smiled.

\* \* \*

Fall came, the children were happy in school, family life was getting ordered in the Habak's two households, and Karol and Dus were giving more attention to their vocations and marriage. Dus could not get the cave encounter, Ox's injury, and the cadaver at the cabin out of his mind. He had become a bit derisive about the machinations of the law. Scott had assured him that the decisions were final, and that is the way it was. Dus knew he would have to, for his and Karol's peace of mind, put the whole episode behind him and be more pragmatic about life in the Appalachians. He was, he also knew, being too judgmental and suspicious again, and that was not good for his family, his friends, nor his ministry to the people who were his godly charge. That being a condition that needed immediate correction, he decided to preach a sermon on those sins, aimed directly at himself. He thought of the old adage, "It's impossible to point your finger at someone else, without pointing three fingers at yourself." Giving such a sermon, he had told Karol, might not only cleanse his own mind and soul, but might be a helpful admonition to his flock. She agreed, for as his new wife and the physician to the people they both loved, she longed for peace of mind for all of them. She reminded him, however, that their pact with their friends about the cave incident was not to be compromised. He assured her that it would not be.

It was a clear, tranquil September Sunday when he preached his "penitential" sermon. Following his reading of the gospel narrative where Jesus talked of "forgiveness" and "self-righteousness," Dus spoke to his congregation about the loose talk around the village and mountain about the occurrence on the Cutty, the sheriff, and the "moonies." He had listened to the complaints of the so-called leaders and business people, regarding how "the criminal element was beginning to infiltrate their lovely town" and then, from plebeian folk regarding how "the moonshiners had always made whiskey, and always would, and as long as it didn't hurt anybody but themselves, why bother them and destroy their only means of making a living and taking care of their families?" He was glad that Jed Hudson, probably the leading businessman in town, was not one of Sheriff Kirsh's critics. He was very supportive of Scott, and appreciated the work he did to protect the people of his town.

"I want to tell you a story," Dus said, as he began his sermon. "A very beautiful friend told it to me some years ago.

"There was a man who was very scornful about life. He was always grumpy, and never said anything nice about anyone or anything. He never believed that much of anything could happen in the world, people being what they are. Life was just lousy, he would say, and believing in God and miracles was just plain crazy. Things like faith, hope, charity, Santa Claus, and angels were just fables, and probably only good for children.

"One day, he was shuffling down a dirt road, cursing the world, when he heard a voice calling from the forest. 'Kiss me,' the voice yelled out to him, 'and change me into a beautiful princess!' He stopped and walked into the woods to see who was speaking to him. He heard the voice again, saying, 'Kiss me and change me into a beautiful princess.' He went farther into the woods, where he found a pond with a log floating on it. Upon the log was a forlorn, bumpy, warty, bulgy-eyed, fat, female frog, who looked longingly into the man's eyes and appealed to him again. 'Sir, please kiss me and change me into a beautiful princess.' Whereupon, the grouchy man reached down, grabbed the frog from the log, stuffed her in his pocket, left the woods and continued to shuffle on down the road, still grumbling about how lousy life is. The lady frog, struggling and protesting from his pocket, cried, 'Sir, the fable says you are supposed to kiss me and change me into a beautiful princess. If you will do that for me, it says, I will love you and serve you all the days of your life.'

"'No,' said the cynical young man, 'I'd rather have a talking frog the rest of the days of my life.'"

There were some scattered muffled laughs in the congregation, and a big smile from Karol, who remembered how many times she and Dus had identified themselves with that famous fable when they courted.

"There is a very valid point to the story," Dus continued. "When we get upset with life, and things don't turn out our way, we are often like that man. Rather than seeing the joyful side of life, believing that good things can happen, that solutions to our problems are available, we look very cynically at life. We think no one can love us and change our lives. We blame others for our problems, we make judgments on others, we are unforgiving about their sins, and we become very negative about everything. We are unwilling to see the light at the end of a dark tunnel." He saw Karol frowning, and realized his metaphor was too close for her comfort.

"We have to allow God to change that attitude in our lives. We need to recognize that good often comes out of the bad happening in our lives. By allowing God to change us into being hopeful and trustful in him, and into being good people, we can help him make a change in others. We can change people by being open to them and by performing random acts of kindness.

"Maybe you won't approve of this analogy, but I think Jesus was a genuine frog kisser. God sent his Son down dusty roads and into the back woods and swamps of this world to pick up us sinners, with all our warts, scars, bumps, and sins, to kiss us into beautiful princesses and princes, so we can find peace and happiness here on earth, and then in the palace of the King.

"The bad side of our human nature too often compels us to look at people as novelties, as the man did, as playthings to make us feel good. We too often think other people are here around us to enhance our egos, to serve us, and to make us feel good, like some kind of psychic pill or a bottle of moonshine, and then we discard them when they have served our purpose. Like in the fable, we often view people just as talking frogs—curios—rather than potentially beautiful persons, changed and redeemed into children of God.

"We don't really expect that God can do such miracles, and we don't believe we can, either. But Jesus is the person who God sent to do miracles with us, to turn us from frogs into loving, giving, forgiving people who, in turn, because he loved us, become frog kissers, ourselves. Having been changed, ourselves, by the miracle of God's love and his willingness to bring us back to him 'while we were yet sinners' bogged down in our individual swamps, we, in turn, can reach out into the muck and mire of people's lives, lift them up, and be so positive about the good things in life and in people, such that they will be changed and will want to go out and change others.

"Instead of making judgments of people and situations based on our limited knowledge, merely looking at the outward appearances of people—the warts on their faces, the pimples on their noses, and the scars on their minds, souls, and bodies—we should reach out to them, hug them, and kiss them, if we must, as Jesus did the lepers, and share our own miraculous changes, made by Jesus, with them. Sure, it's chance taking, but most things in life are risks. Yes, we could get hurt by taking chances, but think of the miracles that could be wrought by our trying!"

Dus wasn't sure that his metaphor was working with the people in the pews, but his conscience forced him to detour for a moment from his meditation process, to ask God to forgive him for thinking nasty things about Mrs. Quidmire's face and character flaws and, specifically, to forgive him for his unabated hate for the moonies.

Karol was engrossed in his words. She listened more closely to her husband, who was saying, "Several weeks ago, we had a nasty incident up on the Cutty that affected our community." He looked at Karol. She was shaking her head as though warning him not to reveal that secret. He gave her a look of reassurance. "Because our good Sheriff Kirsh and some people we know, even friends of ours, were involved, it has become a topic of gossip and rumors. It was exciting for a time, and folk have differing opinions about it.

"No one was hurt, thank God, and our sheriff, the federal agents, and the courts ended the matter. We may not all be satisfied with the outcome, but it's now over, and we can put to bed our speculations, our judgments about how well the sheriff did his job, how criminalized our neighborhood is becoming, and what people perceive to be the inalienable right of some folk to continue their long-held custom of making whiskey and selling it to anyone they choose, no matter who it hurts.

"I must remind you, as a priest and pastor, that it is the sheriff's—and our—duty to uphold the laws, whether we agree with them or not. It is also our duty to support our sheriff by having confidence that he is doing his job as best he can to keep our community free of criminal activity. Christians support the law. On the other hand, we are asked to love people who have made mistakes in their lives, those who have paid the consequences for those mistakes, and who are making amends. It is God's business to make final judgments on the right and/or the wrong of people's customs. We are not to become vigilantes and take the law into our own hands against our neighbors, no matter the grievance. We are to support the sheriff and the decisions of the courts in matters of law, and if our friends are breaking the law out of custom, let's try to change them and help them find jobs whereby they can use their talents legally, do good, be at peace, and stay out of jail."

The people were listening intently to Dus, but looked confused. He didn't blame them. He went on trying to build on the theme of trust, forgiveness, judgment, and loving people enough to help God change them, but he was not sure he was doing it. He ended his homily by saying, "Many of you are sitting there thinking that I am just a preacher, just preaching what I have to. Let me tell you something about us preachers. We are very human, too, and make many mistakes. Big ones! The man in the fable was me, too. When I came to this mountain, I was very cynical about life, like the young man on the road. My wife and son had been killed, I was mad at God; I let grief almost destroy me. The frogs who wanted to change their lives came to me, their priest, for help. They called to me for help, and I sorta put them in my pocket as though to play with them. I lost my friends, my job, and my self-respect. I was a prince who allowed the fabled witch to kiss me into a frog. I was carrying a load of rotten baggage on my soul and a lot of warts and scars in my heart when I came to this mountain. I had become a frog, myself, who desperately needed to be kissed. I was bogged down into a swamp of self-pity. You might not have known what I was until now. But you took me in as a stranger and friend, and gave me love. Less than a year ago, all of you folk and a wonderful lady doctor, who came to this mountain, out of sheer love, from her own duties in Staunton to tend your illnesses, kissed this frog and changed him—if not yet into a prince, at least into a priest who can listen and learn from you good things and hear the voice of God once again. I have had some things happen here that you may nor may not know about, that still make me angry and suspicious. I did not like what happened on the other side of the Cutty with the sheriff, because he is our friend and protector, and was nearly killed in that shooting. I did not like, as you know, what happened to Ox, because he is a good neighbor and friend to all of us, and has given to this community all his life. I believe the people who make whiskey, whether or not they are hometown folk and your friends, tried to hurt Ox. I still do, but I do not want to judge people falsely. I'll leave that up to the sheriff and the courts.

"Some people feel that moonshining in this mountain is a business that harms no one. I think the manufacture of spirits ought to be regulated, whether we drink them or not, because booze can be a demon, even when it is regulated. It kills innocent children and adults, and God doesn't want them—nor the guilty, nor anyone—killed. Maybe I feel that way because I am a priest. Maybe I feel that way because I came up here and you made a man out of a frog, and I love you deeply, and don't want anyone to hurt you in any way. Moonshining hurts the moonshiners, eventually, too; it hurts the people who drink it; and it hurts our good sheriff, who has the responsibility of keeping us, all of whom are children of God and are valuable to him, safe from people who could destroy us.

"Now, I'm going to end this sermon. I have talked too long, but it was important that you know how I feel. I am sorry for my impatience with, and my judgments of, the law and people. I am also sorry for my refusal to kiss frogs who have asked me to help change them into princes and princesses, and lead them back to their Creator. So I end by saying to you today, my friends, that I, a big wart-covered frog from the swamps of life, whom you took a chance on and kissed into your priest and pastor, wish you a good day, a good life, and God's blessings. Thank you for loving me, being patient with me, and listening to me today."

Dus stopped his homily, celebrated the Eucharist, gave brief greetings to the congregation, who gave him unexpected accolades, put his arms around Mrs. Quidmire, planted a kiss on her forehead and smiled into her face, thinking it looked beautiful, and went to his "chalanty," with tears running down his own. A beautiful princess, holding tightly to his arm, smiled at him, kissed him hard on his healing wound, and took him home to the vicarage, vowing she would never eat frog legs again.

# 34

"Hey, Dus, how about meeting me over at Bessie's for a bite of lunch?" Sheriff Kirsh asked Father Habak over the telephone.

"Sure, Scott. I'm ready for something to eat. What's up?"

"Not a whole lot, but I wanted to share some thoughts with you. I promised you I'd keep you posted if I came up with anything related to the shooting up at your house. I've been pretty busy with a lot of other things besides your concerns, but I've drawn a couple of conclusions that might interest you. I can use your help in developing my thoughts."

"So you think a public restaurant is the best place to be talking about this subject?"

"Well, I wouldn't be asking you if I thought it wasn't. It's OK. Bessie will give us a private table where we can talk without being overheard."

Dus arrived at Bessie's within ten minutes. Jed Hudson was talking to her at the cashier's desk when he came in. They both inquired of Karol and the kids. "Glad to hear all is well with the bridegroom and his family," Jed Hudson said. "Come over to the store sometime, Father, when Karol is away. I have a lot of new stuff that might interest an old farmer and mechanic like you. How'd you like to have a new Harley-Davidson to run around up and down these hills when making your pastoral calls?"

"I'd love it, Jed, but I don't think the bishop would approve!"

"I woul'n't etha," Bessie said. "Des old Jed jist loves dem high-powered noisy thungs. Ya en 'im get yerselfs kilt, iffen ya ain't kerful. Ya donna wanna ask Helen Hudson watta she thunks a dis old man ridin' one a dose thungs."

"Lady, you are a pure spoilsport," Jed complained.

"Don't you worry, Bessie. Karol is not going to allow me to be riding any motorcycle, but I do love to look around hardware stores. I'll be over after I finish eating, Jed." Dus then went over to join Scott Kirsh, who had already ordered him a tuna on rye. Dus sat down to his meal.

"I see that Jed and Bessie cornered you. They're a real twosome, aren't they?"

"Yeah, they sure are nice people. Jed told me one time he and Bessie were childhood sweethearts, but he went off to the Navy and they married different spouses afterward. They have remained close friends ever since. Jed wanted to know if I wanted a motorcycle for my pastoral work."

"Yeah, I overheard that. I think you'd better stay off of those nasty things in these mountains. Your brand-new pretty doctor wife wouldn't appreciate your body being all busted up at this stage of your marriage. Eat the tuna. Patty says tuna is good for keeping you from getting fat. Anyway, you're my guest today, and it is all I can afford on the salary that you local folk pay a cop in these sticks."

"Sounds fine, cheapskate! I'd buy some of Bessie's ham loaf for you if I were paying, and I make a heck of a lot less pay than you."

"Well, I work harder than you do keeping people from sin!"

"Maybe you do, at that. Anyhow, I'm not buying any motorcycle. They're fun, but, as you say, dangerous. I used to have one in seminary and have gone to the ground many times. They'd really be a hazard up on these twisting roads. And you're right about Karol, too. Surgeons hate what motorcycles do to people's bodies. Well, what do you have for me that brings me in for tuna?"

"Lower your voice; let's talk a bit quietly. I don't know how much detective work you did while you and Lou were tearing up your house, but did you happen to look around for or find any rifle slugs embedded in the floor or beams?"

"No. I just assumed you'd already done that."

"I do have some shell casings from up in the clump of pines behind your cabin, and some lead slugs from inside your house."

Dus was excited. "Where did you find them?"

"I didn't find them. Someone else did, but I am not at liberty to tell you who, nor any of the circumstances until later. The police lab is doing some work on them."

"Come on, Scott. You can tell me."

"No, I can't, so let it go for now. I've nearly come to the conclusion that the shooting at your house had nothing to do with the moonshiners we had the fracas with in the cave up on the Cutty."

"You're kidding."

"No, I'm not. To be sure, the moonies took shots at you last fall when you got too close to their cave with all that whiskey stored in it. Knowing what we know now, you can hardly blame them. I'm sure that Ox was sincere when he said that he never knew about the cave, even though he probably walked close by it a number of times. I'm not so sure he lost his leg because he got too close to that whiskey cache on one of his hunting safaris, either. The spike in the tree seemed pretty new, with no rust on it. I talked to a railroad detective friend of mine, and he thought that spike would have had to have been driven in that oak with a heavy sledge or axe. It might have been driven into an already cut log in Ox's back yard when none of the family were around. It seems logical to me that the person who did such a thing only meant to hurt Ox just enough so he wouldn't be walking around up there anymore. It worked, but I don't think it was meant for Ox to be hurt so badly that he lost his leg. Of course, I could be awfully wrong about all of this speculation. I'll keep on it. If some folk hurt Ox and are trying to hurt you, too, they're in real trouble if I catch them. I'll lock 'em up and throw away the key."

"Well, I should think so!"

"It's not always easy to resolve these things when folk are not forthcoming with information. I'd like to know, Father, why you didn't tell me that someone had sliced into your brake lines when you were going down the mountain to visit your bishop."

"Who told you that?" Dus fumed. "The bishop? I never told him about that incident!"

"The bishop doesn't know anything about that, but a certain car mechanic and good citizen, by the name of Hosea, does. I'm a former detective, Dus. I know from experience; I don't always have to ask people for information. There are sometimes good citizens who care enough about others, who come to me with helpful stuff. Hosea is one of them. He was upset enough about you nearly getting killed in your car that he came up here to tell me, and no one else. He's a very reliable person, and did a good deed. I'll not have you chastising him nor even pursuing the matter with him. He wants no trouble, but people who cut brake lines on cars that travel around mountains are premeditating murder. However, I think the moonies probably cut your brake lines just enough to scare you, and you can thank God they were clever enough to do it in such a way that you got down the mountain safely. But they could have killed you, and I'm going to get them for that. I don't think they want to do anything more than scare you away. Now they know, after that episode at the cave, that you and I want to put them out of business. That raid on the cave only slowed them down. They'll be back in business very soon, somewhere. It's a way of life for some folk around here, and a lot of people don't think it's a sin. It's against the law, but not necessarily a sin. I heard about your sermon, and I appreciate both your accolades and your concern for me. Sin or not, the Feds and I are going to nail the goons if they deliberately tried to hurt anyone. They are wrong to be making that bad juice, but most of them are more or less harmless people who don't need prosecuting. It's a living for them—in a very poor place to make a living. But I don't think they really wanted to hurt you."

"That sounds well and good, Scott, but what about the goon who shot up my house and put that threatening note on my door the night before my marriage to Karol? What about the dead preacher I dug up, who we took down to the morgue?"

"We don't know whether or not he was a preacher, nor whether that is related to any of this. Anyway, I think that shooting at your place is unrelated to the moonie incident. I feel pretty certain there was a murder or an accident up there many years ago, which someone or some people around this area want to keep a secret. Whoever that corpse was, your digging up his grave while renovating the vicarage has surely put someone in a snit."

"What about the threatening note?"

"The FBI couldn't tell me anything about that. The fingerprints weren't there, and they wouldn't have any prints to match, even if they were. The paper is too old, and a smart person might have worn gloves. Who knows? But the experts think, even as crude as the writing was, a literate person may very well be trying to make you believe differently. Any number of people in the village or in the hills, or even some old enemies of yours, are suspect."

"Enemies of mine, for God's sake?"

"Sure. Maybe someone from out of town is trying to get you to think that the moonies are after you for snooping around their whiskey operation. Now, I am just speculating, but I will find out; trust me. Do you have enemies, Dus? Somebody you ticked off with one of your sermons?"

"Not funny, Sheriff. I'm sure there are some folk who don't particularly agree with my stance on things, but they aren't enemies—at least none who would want me dead!"

"Well, what I have told you is strictly between you and me. There is to be no pillow talk with your bride about the stuff I'm telling you. You are both in danger. I don't have a lot of deputies to protect you, but I have some plainclothes friends who have volunteered to mingle around the area enough to watch after you. Just go about your business, and make your visits around town and all that. Don't go near the new grave we put the bones in, and don't look suspicious or be suspicious of people. Now, people know that we are friends, and it is better that they see us talking like this in the open, rather than as some detective co-conspirators. Please, Dus, leave the detective work to me, and keep that lovely wife of yours completely—and I mean completely—out of this stuff. When I want your help, I'll ask for it. And Dus, quit talking and eyeing Mr. Brush as though he were out to get you. If he had anything to do with this, we will find out, but I doubt the man would sacrifice his standing among his peers or his associates by doing anything nutty. He is what he is—just a pompous, lecherous, old rich man who loves to have people think he is a very important leader in the community. He wouldn't know a rifle from a witch's broomstick. And unless he thought you found a pot of gold up there in the side of that graveyard he could make twelve percent on, he doesn't care what goes on up at your church, or any church for that matter."

"OK, Scott. I'll just do my work, lay low, and cooperate with you. Thanks for all your help. I know that you are doing the best you can for us, but please understand why I am frightened for Karol and the kids. I'll try not to be accusatory about Mr. Brush anymore. It's just that he's always leering at my wife."

"You wouldn't like the way anyone looks at Karol. She's a fine-looking lady, and people around here love and appreciate her. If it will help your psyche, Brush leers at Patty in the same way, and he knows I carry a gun!"

"Then I give permission for you to part that dumb toupee he wears!"

"Boy, you sure are paranoid for a priest. Maybe tuna isn't good for you. Dus, we are going to resolve all this moonie business in court, and Ox's injury soon. The note and the shooting at your house will take a little longer. I have a lot of querying of people to do, and a little studying of the history of this neighborhood. I really do want to find a resolution to all of this for you and Karol so that you can enjoy some peace in your marriage soon. It almost seems that trouble brought you together, and has been following you ever since. Patty is really upset about it all. She loves you and Karol, and hoped for less stress for us when we left Toledo. She and the kids are happy here, and she loves the people, but now she is scared for you two. But we will figure it all out and be done with it soon. Hang in there, friend. I'll do my best."

"I believe you," Dus reassured Scott. "I'll do as you ask, and will help in any way I can without getting in your way. I'll watch after Karol and the kids. I only ask you one thing. If you find anything or anyone, and we have to deal with the mountain folk, please let me know. You're the law, but I am the pastor of a lot of them who have no church affiliation. Whatever you heard about my sermon, I care for you and I care for them. It will be best if you tell me what is developing as we go along, so we can resolve the bad and the good, and be gentle and kind with our actions. God would want that of us both."

"That's a deal, Father. Among the lady physician, the lady teacher, a good cop, and a patient pastor, maybe we can bring peace and concord back into our community. I know my little ol' wife is sure looking forward to it. And, Dus, when I promise her something good, she expects to get it. It's nice to have a partner like that in life. It's a heck of a chore being married to a cop. Worse than to a pastor. Like you have become to feel about that beautiful Indian of yours, I don't know how I'd get along without Patty. She's a wonderful mother, too. Sometimes she gets a little itchy to have another little one, but I'm stubborn about that. I'd like to raise the ones we have to be healthy and wise, and to get them an affordable, good education. Hope she doesn't get too itchy, 'cause I'm pretty firm about that. Like I said, I don't get paid a lot, and I do want some good things for my family. Anyway, who knows? Maybe the four of us will soon get all the 'mare's marbles' out of your life, and Karol and Patty will kiss us two frogs into princes."

"So you did hear my sermon."

"Nah, but the story got around. Patty has been kissing me ever since she heard it so the moonies and the bad guys don't make me into a cynical cop here on this beautiful mountain she loves so much."

"Well, she has a heck of a long way to go to make you into a prince, with all those warts, bumps, and scars you carry around on your soul and hide. Nonetheless, Scott, you're a good friend, and I thank you for all you do for this community."

"Ah, shucks, pardner," Scott drawled, giving his favorite Gary Cooper imitation.

# 35

Long before dawn the following day after Scott and Dus met, a weeping Teresa Casalano whispered over Dus' bedroom telephone, "Lou's nearly gone, Father. Please come before he goes. He wants to see you. He's in the hospital and his condition is very bad; the doctor says he doesn't have much time. Monsignor Leon is with him every day now, Dus, but he wants you, too. I know that it's the middle of the night, but I just had to call you."

"It's OK, Terry. The time doesn't matter. I am so sorry. I'll get there as soon as I can. Tell Monsignor Leon that if there is anything that Karol and I can do, we will. We know you have lots of friends and family to look after you. Are the kids OK?"

"They're doing pretty good, but you know how much they love their daddy. Oh, Dus, what am I going to do? He has been my life, ever since we were in high school. Please, Dus; come soon."

"I'll call Karol right away, and we'll be there sometime before noon. Remember, we love you. We have been praying for you both."

"Thank you. We love you, too. Ciao, Father," Terry said, hanging up the phone, leaving Dus with tears rolling down his cheeks. He dialed Karol.

"Darling, what's the matter? I'm half asleep. It's the middle of the night. What's wrong?" a frightened Karol implored.

"Terry called, honey. Lou's dying."

"Oh, Dus, I am so terribly sorry. How's she doing?"

"She is devastated and wants me to come right away. I hate to ask you when you are so busy there, but could you go with me?"

"Of course I'll go with you, sweetheart."

"Can you get away from the hospital?"

"Sure; I have nothing going on that I can't get a substitute for. The kids will be OK. I'll get a friend to stay overnight with them for a few days."

"I would sure appreciate it, Kara. I promise I'll be good. I won't get mad."

"I know that, Dus, and I feel very sad for you, Terry, and their family. When will you pick me up?"

"As soon as I shower, shave, and throw a few pieces of clothing together. Can you be ready in an hour or so?"

"Sure, sweetheart. I'll tell the kids and will call my friend. Please be careful coming down the mountain."

"Yes, Kara."

"I love you. Thank you for asking me to go with you."

"I love you, too. I just don't know what I'd do in this life anymore without you. Gosh, honey, there sure is a lot of pain in people's lives. It stinks."

"I know, darling. Please, please, my love, don't get angry about Lou. You know God loves him, and Lou knows it, too. He's ready to go, and I am so happy he wants you there when he does."

"I love him, Kara. It hurts."

"Come down to me, dearest husband, and let's cry together."

Karol and Dus arrived in mid-morning at the Casalano house, where they found Terry surrounded by friends and family. They hugged, kissed, and commiserated with her. Monsignor Leon was there also, and greeted Dus as an old friend. They spoke in hushed tones about Lou's impending death, and about what would be done for a requiem mass for him. Monsignor thought it best that Dus go directly to Lou at the hospital, and he did. He took Karol with him.

Lou was lying flat in his bed, all the life-support paraphernalia disconnected from him. He was very drawn and weak, a mere shadow of his former self, but he smiled as Dus entered his room.

"Tonti saluti, Amico. I'm so glad you came. I've been waiting for you. Where is that beautiful wife of yours?" Lou whispered, holding out his weak arms to him.

"Hi, Lou," Dus answered, going over and giving his old friend a hug and a kiss on the cheek. "We came as soon as we could. Karol's in the hall outside."

"Well, bring her in. I want to see the lovely lady."

Dus did that, and Karol came in. She kissed Lou on the forehead and said, "I love you."

"Now that is what I call a greeting," he smiled. "How are you old married folk getting along, and how is your honeymoon castle? Did we build it good enough to stand all that loving, Karol?"

"Shame on you, talking like that," Karol smiled, a tear still lingering in her eye. "You built it strong, Lou, and it will always be loved and full of love."

"She's a beauty, Father. You are a very lucky man. But then, I think I told you that several times before, didn't I?"

"Yes, I am, and you did, Paesano. How are you doing?"

"You know how I am doing, Amico. That's why you're here, isn't it? I've waited for you. I am dying, old friend, and it won't be very long now. Before I go, I want to thank you for being my friend all these years. I am a very happy man. God has graced me with a good life, a good wife and children, and many friends, and I am ready to be ushered into his Kingdom to be with him."

He breathed haltingly as he spoke. It was difficult for him, but he went on, "I just hope that I have been good and faithful enough for him, and that he knows how thankful I am for all he has given me. I know, Dus, that you and I have followed him in our separate church ways, but I want you to know that I have always believed you to be a priest as well as my friend, and I love you for never allowing our varying ways to interfere with that. I won't live long enough for us to take Communion together. I had hoped that would happen someday, and I regret that the differences between our churches have not allowed it. But you and I have been in spiritual Communion for a long time as friends, and whatever happens here on earth, we shall meet again in heaven and have Communion there together."

"I know that, too, Paesano. Thank you for being my friend, and for teaching me so much about life and carpentry."

Karol stood watching the old friends conversing, then turned to the window so they would not see her cry.

"Come here, Karol," Lou called to her. "I am tired now, and have to sleep a little. It is so beautiful to have such a pretty lady shedding a few tears for me. It's OK. Will you take care of Terry for me? This is going to be very hard for her. Call her from time to time. Drop by when you are able. You know how fond she is of you both. She is a lovely lady, too."

"Yes, she is, Lou, and we will do whatever we are able. But rest now, and we will come back again to see you later."

"No. Don't come back again, Amicos. I won't be here. Will you and Dus hold my hand and have a prayer for me before you go?"

They had a prayer, with Lou gripping their hands with his very weak hands, very tightly. "Now, Father, it is time to bless me," he said.

Father Dus Habak, an Episcopal priest, and a Roman Catholic layman, Lou Casalano, closed their eyes; Dus made the sign of the cross with the church's blessing over Lou, as Lou, in turn, made a very weak sign of the cross, placing his thin finger to his forehead, then to his heart, over to his right breast and then to his left, finally kissing his fingers. Karol sniffed, and tears poured from both of the men's eyes.

"Thank you, Father. Good-bye, my friend, Dus." Dus choked as Lou said his first name for the first time in their friendship since he had become a priest. "When we meet in heaven, there will be no priest or layman—just an old Amico and Paesano. Good-bye, Karol. Arrivederci, beloved. Have a wonderful life in that house beside the little church in your mountain, and remember this old man who left his mark of love there for you. Take your hand and feel above the rafters in the loft over your bed sometime, and see what you will find on this side of heaven," he said. "Please tell Terry and the monsignor to come to me. I am very tired. I will see you again in another place at another time. Take your time in getting there, and have a happy life together. I love you. Ciao, Paesanos." He closed his eyes.

"We love you. Ciao, Amico," Dus said, as he, then Karol, kissed Lou on his thin, blue lips and then left, holding tightly onto each other and wiping their eyes with their sleeves. They called Terry. She and Monsignor Leon went to the hospital right away to keep the vigil with Lou.

Dus and Karol were eating dinner in the hotel dining room, when the dining room hostess told Dus there was a telephone call for him. Karol stared at him, and took her hanky and put it to her eye as he left. He returned in a minute, with wetness on his cheeks, and spoke to her.

"That was Terry. Lou died an hour ago."

"Yes, darling. I thought that was probably what the call was about. I am so sorry. He was a fine man, and a good friend. I know you will miss him," she said, wiping her eyes again.

Dus sat down, reached across the table, and took her hands in his. "Yeah, he was, and I will miss him, but I am glad that he will suffer no more. Terry is at peace, and I told her we would see her tomorrow after she gets some rest tonight. The burial service will take place Friday morning. Terry and Monsignor Leon have asked me to preach the homily, and say some prayers at mass and at the grave site. I said I would do that. There will be a simple reception at the Italian Club afterward for friends and family, and we will attend that before we go home."

"I will see if there is anything I can do to help Terry tomorrow. I am so pleased that you were asked to help."

"Terry told me that Lou had asked Monsignor Leon a long time ago if I could have a part in his burial service. Monsignor Leon asked me to."

"Bless all of their hearts. What now, darling?"

He called to the waiter, who then came and asked what he could do for them. "Bring the lady the finest and oldest bottle of Italian red wine you have in the place."

"Yes, sir," the waiter said, and left. He returned in minutes, showed it to Dus, who nodded, popped the cork, and poured a little in Dus' glass. He tasted it and said, "Very good. Please serve the lady, then fill my glass." The waiter did as he was asked, and left.

"Now, my very pretty and very healing wife, Doctor Ollikut Karolina Thunder Rolling In The Mountain Habak, would you join me as I raise my glass to Louis Casalano, the finest friend a man could ever have—excepting, of course, the beautiful lady who sits across from me—and drink to the arrival into heaven of the most decent, loving, faithful, and hardworking carpenter, friend, husband, father, and churchman this town and country has ever had the privilege of passing their way?"

"I will, indeed, my love. Here is to my husband's best friend, Louis Casalano, who I had the great privilege of knowing, even if only for a short time. May the soul of the faithfully departed rest in peace, and may God's face forever shine upon Louis Casalano," she saluted, as they both made the sign of the cross.

People watched them as they crossed themselves, sipped the wine, rested, and sipped again, finishing their drink and meal. They didn't care. They were celebrating a life; and if they could have had their way, they would have told everyone in the room about the life and times of Lou Casalano, who, like Jesus, was a very good carpenter and a very good friend.

Dus signed the check, took the rest of the bottle with him, and they retired to their bedroom. They talked a long time, finished the bottle of wine, undressed, took showers, and, as had become their habit when they were at home alone in Joshuatown together, went to bed naked.

"Dus," Karol whispered gently to him, "you have suffered a great loss today. I know it will be very difficult for you when you bury Lou on Friday, but I will be very proud of you. You have lost many loved ones in recent years, and it has been terrible for you. I know you so well now, and I understand and appreciate how very much people mean to you. I just want to thank you right now before you go to sleep, and tell you how much I love you for not getting angry about Lou's death. My heart aches for you, but I am also very pleased that in the midst of your pain and sorrow, you are not railing at nor blaming anyone. I am proud of you for your love for God, and for being so strong and so sustaining to all of us."

Dus sniffed. "I have really been praying hard that my recalcitrant farm boy, mechanic, Marine temper and bad language won't keep trying to resolve my feelings about life. I don't know why, after all these years as a priest, I still allow that dumb and irreligious junk to erupt out of me. Thank God his patience—and yours—is helping with that lousy character flaw. I hate it. I hate my cursing and lack of faith, when I am angry. Thank you for helping me, Kara. You have been so good for and patient with me."

"Well, you have been even better to me. It's because of you that I have become less the cynical scientist and, I hope, a better person and Christian. Now, darling, rest your weary head on my bosom, and know it is all right for us to cry about Lou and Terry."

She took his head and pulled it to her naked chest. He wept almost uncontrollably. She felt the liquid of his tears run down her bosom and the side of her body. Her tears, falling down her own cheek and neck, drained onto her pillow.

He sniffed. "If I have no anger now, if I now accept God's will in these things, and know the immensity of his love and compassion, it is because my wife has led me very gently along this stony path. My friend has died and gone to heaven, and I will see him no more; but in the house that he built for God and for us, I will feel his love, his friendship, and his talent. And in that house I will have you, the loveliest princess to ever kiss the most pitiful of frogs into a better, if sometimes mean-spirited and brokenhearted, prince. I love you, Kara, and I thank you for being here with me today."

"I wanted to be with you, Dus. I love you more than I can explain. I have been a testy and haughty person with you sometimes, too, and I am going to do better. But please always know that I respect you as a very devoted priest, friend, pastor, father, husband, and lover. If sometimes my native, earthy, bantering spirit gets out of hand and needs to be disciplined, you tell me, and I will try harder. But even with those particular scars, bumps, and warts on my disposition, which always need to be healed with kisses and patience, every part of me—all that I am— loves and adores you more than I will ever have the sacramental words to tell you."

"Thank you, Kara. Thank you, my sweetheart, for telling me that." She felt wetness on her breasts again.

"Dus?"

"Yes, Kara?"

"Let's make the tears go away now. Make love to me tonight. Make love to me now, my husband, on this day when you are giving up the life of your friend here on earth to a life with God in heaven. Make love to me tonight. It will be very special."

"Tonight? Is it right to make love when we are mourning a fallen friend?"

"You are the theologian, dear heart; I cannot argue that question with you. But I do not believe Lou would permit us to mourn his death nor would God judge us for finding peace, solace, and comfort in our oneness. Life goes on for us. What we do with our love is good and wholesome, and a gift of God. Neither Lou nor God would fault us. So let's offer our tears and oneness to God, and celebrate Lou's entrance into his Kingdom. It would be a very special occasion and observance; I promise you."

"Yes, Kara, yes," Dus murmured, and took her into his arms. They made love, wiped their tears, and fell asleep in each other's arms.

\* \* \*

Lou's funeral was simple but beautiful. So many friends crowded the church and cemetery, and the parish hall, for brunch. Their presence was a great tribute to the simple carpenter who knew the Great Carpenter so well. Terry did fine, while knowing the lonely days were ahead. She said she would manage, and Karol promised her she would call often. She and Dus also said that they would have her down soon, just so she could have some time to herself away from friends and family. Having remembered Lou's secret in a hiding place at their house, they promised that they would not look for it until Terry was there with them.

That time came about six weeks after the funeral, when another friend of Terry's had to make a trip to southern Virginia for a few days, and would bring Terry as far as Staunton. Karol picked her up at a mutually agreed upon waiting place, and took her to her home there. They visited together overnight, where Terry got to meet and enjoy Elly and Shawn. They did some shopping and lady things together the next morning. Karol showed Terry the hospital and, by coincidence, ran into J.K. Stewart, who had been doing some work on the computers. J.K. and Terry took to each other immediately, and he promised that he and Julie would soon steal away from Penn State, visit Terry, and eat Italiano. Terry said she'd really like that.

The two women laughed, cried, and bonded as they drove to the mountain, to find Dus waiting for them at the door of the chalet. They all hugged, and Terry entered the house that Lou had built. She walked through it, scrutinizing it very closely.

"Oh, it is a beautiful place. You and Lou did a fine job, Father. You must be very happy here. I can feel and see that old carpenter of mine in this place. He was a good carpenter, you know. He built our house, too. It shows here, doesn't it?"

"It does, indeed," Dus said. "Come to our loft and see the bedroom he built for us."

They went upstairs. Terry looked about, and smiled demurely. "Quite a place to sleep and make love. Lou might frown a little hearing me saying that kinda thing around a priest, but then he'd grin from ear to ear. He was such a lover. It is very nice, isn't it, Karol?"

"As my preacher hubby would say, 'indeed, indeed.'"

Dus grew solemn. He took Terry's hand and said to her, "Just before we left Lou for the last time at the hospital, he asked us to reach up in these rafters and search for something he left for us. Karol and I decided we would not do that until you could come here."

"Oh, I don't know, Father," she said, beginning to weep. "Perhaps it is better that I not intrude on that special thing of his for you."

"It's OK, Terry," Dus reassured her, as he ran his hand over the rafter above the bed. He felt something. It was a little wooden corpus of Jesus on a cross. "It's a crucifix. There's a note with it. You read it, Kara."

"All right," she said, unfolding the paper. Her hands were trembling and her mouth was dry. Her eyes welled up and her mouth quivered as she read:

To my dear old friend Dus and Karolina, his betrothed:
What a privilege it has been for me to build this house for those priests who will serve God in this beautiful mountain for years to come. I wish that I had the strength to renovate the church, too.
What a special ceremonial it has been for me to have been able to build it with and for my friend of so many years. I built it for both you and God, Dus. I have no better way to serve him nor honor you than with the talent he has put in my head, heart, and hands. Love will surely abide in this place. Love for God, love for humanity, and the love between a good man and his

lovely wife, who will share it with each other and their children. God's love and mine will abide here as long as you live here and love here. This is Terry's and my wedding gift to you.

I am ill, Amicos, very sick. I am going to die soon. Terry knows this, and she still wanted me to come. There will be no more time left for me to take up my tools and build when I return home, so I expend my last efforts, and the last of my body and my skills, here. It is the last of my carpentry work for the Great Carpenter, whom I have loved and has loved me. I am so grateful to God that he has allowed me the strength to do this one more time for him and for my friends. Please think of me from time to time. Know how much I have loved you. Look to Terry's comfort when you are able. She is the essence of my life, as Karol will be of yours, Dus. She has honored me with her unselfishness. Her allowing me to come here, to expend my body for the last time in creating something good, was typical of her Italian graciousness and the criteria of the fine woman she is. To allow me to lift my pain up to God and give him, and you, for the last time, my talent and my strength—these hands to hammer, to saw, to plane, to nail, to raise the formed and bonded wood and metal to his glory—was a blessed act of kindness on my beloved wife's part. Honor her, not me, for what I have done here so you can share your love and protect your loved ones from the elements. For without her, I am nothing.

I made this crucifix as a little memento for you to hang somewhere in this house. It is the symbol of how much Jesus, a better Carpenter than I could ever be, loves you. It is to remind you who will lament my pain and death that it is nothing compared to what Christ has done for humanity. To leave you with this symbol of his giving, in this house of love that has so absorbed my pain and brought me joy these last few days, is my gift to you. Be happy here. Let Christ abide here with you.

When you celebrate his Eucharist next door in the little church, remember Terry and me in prayer, the Italian carpenter and his wife, whose love has raised and dedicated this building to God and to Karol and Dus, our friends, whose friendship and love for us have been a blessing. We return that blessing to you, praying it will translate into God's blessing through both of you, the husband and wife, the priest and physician, the healers, to his people on this breathtaking mountain, so they will be healed over and over again by Christ's suffering and love. I don't mean to sound like a priest, though I aspired to be that, myself, at one time. But, you see, God arranged a better life for me. He made me a simple carpenter like his Son, and gave me Terry, my children, and many good friends, like you. He has blessed me a hundredfold.

I love you both, Amicos. Ciao and Arrivederci, beloved Paesanos.

Karol finished. She wept without shame, as did Terry and Dus. None of them could speak for several minutes.

"You knew, didn't you, Terry? You knew he was dying when he came. You let him come, knowing that. Why, Terry? Why?" Dus pleaded.

She was sobbing, but murmured through the fountain of tears, "Because he wanted to, Dus. He wanted to, and I would not have stopped him. I wanted him to finish his craftsmanship in the way he loved best. He was a wonderful carpenter, and he wanted to build one more time for God and for his friend. You gave him the opportunity, and he loved you for it. Yes, he came home weak and tired and never put a tool in his hand again, but I never saw him more happy in his life, except when he made love to me, when I gave him his children, and when I cooked his favorite food. Yes, I knew he was dying when he came here, but I didn't know about the note nor the crucifix. But he was Lou Casalano, a lover of God and a carpenter like, as he said, God's Son. I could have expected such a thing of him. But Karol, Dus, this is our secret. This is our gift to you; it is his gift to all of us. Perhaps one day, years from now, you may share it with your loved ones if you choose, but let it just be ours for now. Please."

She started crying again. Karol took Terry's hand and sat with her on the big bed. "Of course, Terry, just our secret. You had a long day. We will eat in a little while. Rest now. Sleep a little in this beautiful house made by Lou's hands, and dream nice dreams of the man who brought you and all of us so much joy and happiness in his life of giving."

Terry continued to sob in the pillow. Karol patted her back and said, "Shh, shh, Amico; sleep now."

Finally, Terry let out a big sigh and fell asleep. Dus and Karol tiptoed out of the loft, holding Lou's note and the crucifix in their hands. They could not talk for a long time.

Terry's visit lasted only a few days. Dus said his farewell to Terry, and sent her with Karol back down the mountain to Staunton, a renewed and smiling, if lonely, widow. Because she was a lady of great faith, deeply in love with her departed husband and God, they decided not to worry too much about her. She would be fine, they believed, now knowing she had known of Lou's pending death and both of them had prepared themselves for it for a longer time than Dus and Karol had first thought. Terry had journeyed courageously with Lou through all his pain until his demise, then thanked God he suffered no more.

Karol and Terry connected with Terry's friend coming up from the

South to take her home within a couple of hours. Parting was hard for them, and they vowed they would keep in touch. The regal Indian, physician, and wife, and the comely Italian widow, who had bonded and fallen in love with one another through the comradeship of their respective husbands, would be friends the rest of their lives.

"Ciao, Karolina Habak," Terry said from the window as the car pulled away. "Take care of yourself, and remember to keep our secret. I love you."

"Ciao, Teresa Casalano. Yes, and you remember to keep our secret. Thank you for coming my way. I love you, too." Karol waved, then turned away to wipe her eyes. "Oh, God," she said, "I'm getting as bad as Dus with all this bawling. Won't I ever stop wiping this redskin nose that keeps getting redder and redder? Well," she shook her head and started home, "all I can say about all this is what my handsome preacher would say at a time like this—'Mare's marbles!'"

# 36

Thanksgiving Day was just a week away. A light powdering of snow lay on the ground. It was a cold day outside, and Father Habak was keeping warm in his clinic office by reminiscing about his first Thanksgiving on the mountain with the Conleys and Karol. It was the day that she offered him an office and a telephone there. A lot had happened since then. He smiled and looked forward to the following week, when his whole family would be home for a four-day vacation; they would gather again for Thanksgiving dinner at the Conleys. Dus had wanted to eat at home, but given the living arrangements, it would be too difficult for Karol to prepare it, and he couldn't cook worth a hoot. All that mattered was that she would be coming home with Elly and Shawn the coming weekend, to take care of him and the host of people in need of her at the clinic. He was anxious to see his bride and their children. He had been very lonesome for them since Lou Casalano's death. Dus was also reflecting on that morbid occasion.

Everyone in Joshuatown, it seemed, had learned of Lou's death. Many were sympathetic and tried to comfort him. His congregation, of course, knew that Lou had worked hard with Dus on the vicarage renovations, and some had met him. They expressed their appreciation of his fine carpentry skills and the work he had done for the mission. They, of course, had no knowledge of the note that Lou had left at the cabin, so they were unaware of his total commitment to the little church family.

Lou's death had provided the opportunity for Dus to preach to his congregation about death, and he had, but now he was thinking that the way he had talked about the church's theology on that ancient subject might have fairly well gone over their heads. They were mountain people, he mused, who already had a running acquaintance with the reality of death. What they already understood, he thought, is that being sad and upset about the death of a beloved person is not a reflection on one's faith in God. They and Karol are right when they allow that it is OK to mourn the loss and final departure from this earthly life of someone we have loved and cared for. The ones we love are alive, real, and touchable, and we know them in the flesh, not as wisps of smoke. They are here, then one day they are gone forever, and we know we won't ever see them in the flesh, again. That's a pain that lasts a long time. I know that, myself, with Ginnie and Dusty. We miss people when they are dead; and if God is who the Bible tells us he is, he is big enough to understand our pain, and will be patient with us until we work all that out of our broken hearts and fragile souls. I don't need to burden these good people with great big platitudes about "pie in the sky when we die" stuff. I just need to reassure them, as I need to reassure myself, that God does promise life after death for our loved ones, but he does understand our grief and loves us in the midst of our sorrow. And, as Karol says, only that love; the love of family and friends, with their comforting words and arms; good memories; and time—not pious platitudes—will eventually fill up those awful voids left by the death of someone you have desperately cared for and miss so much. I wish I had thought this way when I was a high and narcissistic dean of a cathedral, especially when Ginnie and Dusty died. Why did I have to go through all that debilitating breast-beating and self-pitying garbage, and come to this mountain to learn all this simple stuff from spiritually guileless country folk and a beautiful physician? Well, God has his ways of teaching, and I am surely the benefactor of their and her simple understanding about life and love.

The telephone rang. It was Scott again. He was dead serious and in a hurry. "Father, I don't want to interject negatives into our lofty Thanksgiving sermon preparation, but I want you to come down here to the courthouse right away."

"What's up, Scott?"

"Something important that I should share with you. Come now," he ordered.

Dus arrived at the courthouse, and was in his friend's office within minutes. Scott appeared upset, but Dus needled him anyway. "Well, Sheriff, what is so interesting that I have to tear myself away from my favorite work, telling people how to run their lives, to answer your beck and call?"

"This is not funny, Dus," Scott answered gruffly, handing him a piece of paper. "Look at this, and then I'll tell you about it."

Dus read the note. It was very much like the threatening note that had been tacked on his door the night before his marriage. The paper and the crude language were pretty much the same, except it was directed at Scott and alluded to the moonshining operation on the Cutty. It was basically a warning that he was no longer wanted in the county nosing into people's business, and that if he cared for his family, he would leave the mountain soon and find police work elsewhere.

"That's appalling, Scott, and I'm sorry," Dus empathized.

"It's worse than that. That SOB threatened a law officer and his family."

"Now you know how I felt! Where did you find this?"

"Yes, I do know how you feel." Scott showed him another piece of paper. "There were two of them, both alike. One was shoved under my door at this office, and the other, Patty found thumbtacked on our front door at home. She nearly got hysterical."

"I'll bet. What happened? Why are you here instead of at home with her?"

"I am here because I caught the little creep, and he's locked up in the jail downstairs!"

Dus' excitement was now uncontainable. "What happened? Tell me!"

"Patty just happened to see the guy running off the side of the front porch. She went to the door, found the note, and called me immediately. She was crying. I drove home as fast as I could. After I calmed her down, she described him and said that he had headed up to the woods behind the house. I thought he might be going up to a high place to take some potshots at the house to scare her, like the 'shooter' did to you. But the dummy didn't think about leaving tracks in the snow, so I just followed them around the side of the hill for about an hour, and then I found him, huddled behind a tree, nearly frozen to death. He wasn't armed and didn't resist arrest, so I yanked him up by the collar and dragged him down here. Gave him a warm cell and a cup of coffee. He's as snug as a bug, happy to be out of the cold."

"Who is he? Do you know him? Do you think he might be the same guy who put the note on my door and shot at me?"

"I don't know all of that yet. But I have the feeling he's just a poor ridge runner who the moonies have been using as a courier, and a poor, dumb gofer. He can't even write his name, let alone pen a letter. He's a frightened little turkey who is about to sing like a canary. I am going to bring him up here with Edna Shoney, our court stenographer, in a few moments, and you and I are going to have a heart-to-heart talk with him."

"You sure I ought to be here to listen? Shouldn't there be a public defender here to represent him? What about the Miranda law?"

"I read him his rights. He knows that he can have a lawyer anytime he wants one. After I talk with him a little, he might not want one. Right now, I want you to see him, and for him to see you, and find out if he is the same guy who tacked the note to your door. I'm not too sure I want to book the poor guy. Probably has a common-law wife and a bunch of kids, and is just looking for some means to house and feed them. But he will have some helpful information. Let me do the questioning, and, Father, when you see the poor guy and start feeling sorry for him, like a good pastor might, don't interfere with the interrogation with a lot of sympathy. Renewal and forgiveness will come later, if you get my meaning."

"I understand, Scott. I'm a bit peeved at him, myself, you know."

Scott called out to the front offices of the courthouse, and a uniformed deputy and a middle-aged woman entered the room with a shabbily dressed and forlorn-looking man.

"Father, this is Deputy Bud Carson, the acting bailiff here, and Edna Shoney, our court stenographer. You know Edna's husband, Si, our barber who makes us look so good."

"Hello, Bud. Hello, Mrs. Shoney," Dus greeted them.

"They will witness our conversation with our friend here, and Edna will record it. I have a tape recorder for my own use."

Dus nodded and gazed at the accused man, and in spite of his anger over the note, he could not, as Scott had foretold, help feeling sorry for him. He was very thin, with long, black greasy hair and an unkempt beard. He had eyes sunken in his head, a runny nose, and a mouth full of fragmented, black-and-brown teeth. He was nervous, and could not stop shaking. He looked pitifully at Dus.

"Yo' is da precha, ain't cha? I so is sorry iffen I scairt ya en da lady a da house. I din't mean ta hurt nobody. I jist did watta da man ask me ta do."

Scott turned on the tape recorder. "You talk to me, Mister, and no one else in here," he scowled, and began his interrogation. "What's your name?"

"I'ma Jakey Peesy, Sher'ff, en I'ma sorry too 'bout scaren yo' missus en runnin' away in da woos. En I thanks ya fer finin me an a makin' me warm heah."

"It's OK, Jakey. Where do you live?"

"Downa da mountain tawad Staunton."

"Do ya live close to the road that goes up to the still on the other side of the Cutty?"

"Yaser."

"Did you help to make moonshine up here before they blew up the still a while ago?"

"Noser; I donna know how ta do dat. Jist some a doz folk give me a bit a money ta run favas fer 'em. I jist does as da ask, butta I ain't eva been up to dem smoke pots en kettles."

"Did you tack those writings on the preacher's house, and my office and house?"

"I's alr'ady said I done dat en I's sorry, Sher'ff."

"Did you write those notes?"

"Noser. I donna know how ta writ', not even my name. I jist uses da X when I needs ta sign somethung lagel like."

"How do you get around?"

"I have a mule en I trudges."

"Do you use your mule to haul moonshine?"

"Noser, Sher'ff, butta da man, he gives me money ta borry my ol' Jenny sometimes."

"Do you have a pickup truck, Jakey?"

"Noser. I kent driv', en I'dda 'ave no money ta buy one anyways. I'sa too po' fer dat."

"Could you fix one if you had one?"

"Noser, Sher'ff; I donna know nuffin 'bout caws."

"Then you don't know how to cut a car brake line?"

"Watta dat, Sher'ff? I donna know watta ya mean."

Dus looked at Scott. The sheriff was good at interrogating. Jakey didn't know a thing about cars and didn't cut his brake lines.

"Do you have a family, Jakey?"

"Yaser; I has a wife en seven younguns."

"Do ya try to take good care of them, Jakey?"

"I tries, Sher'ff, butta der's neva a nuff food en togs fer 'em. Itta be hard on des mountain fer us. It sholy is."

"Can't you find a job at the mine or the mill?"

"Noser. I tried dat butta doz folk tol' me I ain't no good worka. Dey said I wern't sma't enuf ta work in doz places."

"So you try to take care of your family by running errands for people?"

"Da's 'bout it, Sher'ff. Ma misses washes some close en reds up der houses fer folk, en gits some money fer dat. It sho helps a lot butta she's so tired. She's a good woman."

"I'll bet she is, Jakey. Ya said a man borrowed your mule. Did he pay you to tack up the notes on the houses?"

"Yeser!"

"Who was he, Jakey?"

"I donna knows, Sher'ff. Des fella jist give 'em ta me en tol' me ta hammer dem on da preacha's door, en give me five twenta dolla bills ta do it. He tol' me not ta let anybody see me, so I run fast away soon as I done it. Das alota money fer me, en I sholy needs it fer my fam'ly."

"So let me get this right, Jakey. The man asked you to hammer the notes on the door three times? Once last summer on the preacher's house, then twice today—on my house and office—and both times he paid you a hundred dollars?"

"Noser. He paid me da first time, butta ya got me in da poky, en I donna thunk he'll pay me anymo' fer da secon' time. He mighta be a bit snited 'bout me gittin caught by ya, Sher'ff."

"Have you ever been in the poky before, Jakey?"

"Yeser! Long time ago, when I's a youngun. I got sosed up on lika en got en a fight. I donna like da poky, Sher'ff. I sholy don't. I git beatin up purty bad by fellas in der dat time. I ain't been back since den."

"Yeah, Jakey, it's bad in jail when ya have to spend your life there. You wouldn't want to go back there, would you?"

A very worried Jakey asked the sheriff, "Emma I gonna be a locked up in da pokey fer my lifetime?"

"I don't know, Jakey. It depends on whether you meant to do the preacher and me and our families harm."

"I din't mean no harm ta nobody. Sher'ff. I jist done watta I was asked by da man fer some money ta help my fam'ily."

Dus winked and smiled at Scott.

"Well, Jakey, maybe the preacher and I will believe you about that if you are telling us the truth. You say you don't know the man. Have you seen him around town?"

"Maybe once er, so, butta I ken't be sho, 'cause I neva seen his face so good."

"Where did he bring the money to you if you don't know him?"

"Ta my house at night on da porch."

"Did your wife or your children ever seen him?"

"Noser; I donna thunk so. I hopes not! He mighta hurt her en da younguns."

"No he won't. Will he bring you the money tonight at your house, Jakey?"

"Spose to, butta he won't iffen he done seen me come in heah wid ya.

He may jist bre'k my neck fer lettin' somebody see me git caught by yo', Sher'ff."

"Jakey, I'm going to ask you two more questions, and you'd better tell me the truth, or you might spend the rest of your life in jail. Were you one of the shooters at the still in the woods when we were in the cave?"

"Noser; I wern't thar. Neva been thar."

"Did you shoot at the preacher last year up near the three cedars on the barren?"

"Noser; I 'erd 'bout dat, butta I ain't neva been ta da smokehouse, en I neva been up ta dem trees, netha. I has a twelve-gauge, butta I neva shot anybody ner nuffin but deer, rabbit, bards, en squarel. I swear on da Bible 'bout dat, Sher'ff."

"Then if you have only a twelve-gauge, you didn't shoot at the preacher's house last spring with a rifle upon the Blue behind the church, when he was digging with a machine up there, and you had no intention of shooting at my house today, did you, Jakey?"

"Aw, God no, I din't Sher'ff. I wount done a thing like dat! I said I din't shoot at nobody in my lifetime. I be scared outta my pants ta do dat ta a preacha en sher'ff. Anyway, I gotta nuffa ta answer ta da Lawd 'bout widout da shootin' a dem on my soul." He looked right at Dus. "Ya gotta b'lieve me, Preacha, 'cause da Lawd knows I din't do dat ta ya ner da sher'ff. Pond my soul en da soul a my missus en my younguns, I'd neva do dat ta a preacha, ner a sher'ff, ner anybody. Ya jist gotta b'lieve me on dat!" Jakey Peesy looked up to the ceiling and pleaded, "Oh Lawdy, please have da preacha en da sher'ff b'lieve dat ol' Jakey coulda neva done a thing like dat!"

Scott shook his head at Dus, a warning not to say anything. Dus took the silent message to read, "This is no time for pity and understanding, and the offering of forgiveness, Father. Pity this man later and let me do my business now."

The sheriff turned to the secretary. "Edna, you can stop writing now. Please type that all up for the court in case it is needed someday. Thank you for your help. As you know, none of this is to be spoken of outside this office. You go now and have your lunch."

"You're welcome, Sheriff. Nice to meet ya, Father. I've seen ya 'round town, en I know that Si cuts yer hair fer ya," Mrs. Shoney said as she left the room, smiling at Dus.

"Nice lady, Scott."

"She is. Self-educated and very competent. Helps Si out at the shop.

They're in that business together." Then, turning to Jakey, he said, "Now, Jakey, you go with the bailiff, get your hat and coat, pull your hat down over your head, and walk home to your wife and kids. Don't talk to her or anyone about what we did here. Ride your mule around home if you must, and do the work you have to do, but keep your mouth shut. Stay put until you hear from me. Do you want to talk to a lawyer?"

"Noser; I donna need one a doz, en I got no money no how."

"We'll give you one for free, Jakey. You understand what I am saying?"

"Yeser. Do you mean I ken jist go, Sher'ff? Ya ain't gonna put me in da poky tonight?"

"That's what I said, Jakey. Go now. And sometime soon the preacher here will help you and Mrs. Peesy with food and clothing," Scott said, turning to Dus. "You'd like to do that for Jakey's family, wouldn't you, Father, seeing what need they have?"

Dus scowled at Scott. He knew the sheriff was fleecing the clothing shop at the Episcopal Diocese and the Bishop's Discretionary Fund to help a poor family in the mountain. Scott grinned.

Dus nodded. "Of course, Sheriff. We can help Jakey and Mrs. Peesy with some clothing and food. I'll get some for them soon. Your parish will be glad to help, too, won't they?"

Scott scowled, but nodded his head as the bailiff watched both of them.

"Thunk ya; thunk ya, Preacha. Thunk ya, Sher'ff. I'ma obliged. I'll does as ya ask, en keep my mouf shut. Donna ya worry none. Be as close mouf as Jenny, my mule. Bye now." Jakey left with the bailiff.

"Well, schemer, did you get all that bribery stuff on the tape, too?"

"Nope. I turned it off for that, but I got everything else. Don't you think it was nice that a lawman got a little pastoral before the priest jumped in with his righteous compassion? I'm a caring cop, you know. You priests need to let us layfolk do some charitable things from time to time. Enjoy your trip to the diocese for the clothes and money for the Peesys. Karol told Patty what a sweet and generous person your bishop is. He likes you a lot, so maybe he'll give you what you want and need for old Jakey. Give him my regards."

"Pastoral caring guy, eh? Bribery, I call it. Oh well, our diocese has plenty, and I'm gonna see that my bishop talks to yours about your church kicking in, too. The Peesys do appear to need it."

"He's a victim and a witness, Dus. We've got to let him help us without his getting hurt. If he realizes that we are the good guys, he's going to help us nab the real bad guys. I just hope none of them saw him coming in here with me. Anyway, I'll try to take care of him."

"What do we do now?"

"Don't do anything but your pastoral work, Dus. Don't tell Karol any of this. I told Patty to keep quiet about it, too. I'll let you know when I need your help. I have been trying to keep you up to date, haven't I?"

"Yes you have, Scott, and I appreciate it."

"It is important that I do my work, Dus, without your and Karol's active participation. Please understand that I can't allow you two to get hurt. Thanks a lot for coming. You're a real friend, and I appreciate it. Go out the back door and go work on your Thanksgiving sermon. Patty and I will be coming up to your church on Thanksgiving, so it had better be good. You have a lot to be thankful for. We are getting close to resolving this thing."

"We still don't know who did the threatening notes nor the shooting up at my house."

"Does not the Bible say that 'Patience is a virtue,' Father? You clergy should practice what you preach."

"Mare's marbles," Dus scowled.

"Gee, Father, I know that you are a priest, but can't you find a better cuss word than that?"

Dus appeared a bit indignant. "I hadn't meant to offend the village police psychologist with my lack of gusto for cuss words, Sheriff, but I don't think it is within your expertise to advise a priest how to effectively cuss. I'm trying to do better with the quality of my language since I am a priest, even though I slip a lot. It might make you happy to know that my wife has already instructed me on the same subject. When she feels really angry and decides to vent with appropriate vernacular, she yells out an epithet that would make a real macho cop like you proud."

"What does your beautiful, pristine, and decent squaw say when she's mad?"

"I'm not telling you. Ask her sometime."

"I will. I believe that reservation bride of yours is teaching you a few things about the realities of life."

"Yeah, she's very earthy, and I have a lot to learn from her, but I still like ladies to talk like ladies. By the way, Scott, are you a racist?"

Scott turned red. "Why do you ask that? Of course I'm no racist. I fought against that stuff my whole career on the police force in Toledo."

"Oh, yeah, well, when I tell my Indian wife that her friend's husband, the Sheriff of Nothingham, referred to her as a 'squaw,' she and Patty are going to have a scalping party at one bad-mouthed sheriff's office."

"Gosh, Dus, I didn't mean that. Come on, that just slipped out. I was only kidding. Please don't tell her or Patty I said that. They both hate that ethnic stuff, and you know very well I'd never do or say anything racially denigrating about those two ladies, or anyone. If Patty hears I said anything bad about Karol, even in jest, she'll give me the silent treatment for a week. Have a heart, Dus. Priests are supposed to be forgiving."

"Sure, Sheriff," Dus laughed. "I'm in the habit of hearing confessions and keeping the content to myself. But that's in a confessional, not a sheriff's office. Now, when was it I heard you say you were going down to Staunton to your church, getting in the food pantry and clothing bins, and bringing your pickup truck full of that stuff up to the Peesys?"

Scott sighed. "Next week, you blackmailer."

"That's what I thought I heard you say, penitent," Dus cackled as he left his friend's office.

Back at his own cold office, Dus was shivering and not thinking about the sheriff, the Peesys, nor his Thanksgiving sermon. He was thinking about his pristine Indian wife, who was coming back that night with their beautiful children to his teepee to make him warm with family love.

\* \* \*

Karol and the children arrived home at 7:00 P.M. to enjoy a hearty, talkative, and humorous supper and evening with Dus, and then went to bed. But the stuff of professional life does prevail on physicians, ministers, and police, and so the telephone rang at a late hour. Dus moved away from a warm Karol to answer it. "Oh no," she crabbed. "Please, Dus, come back to bed, and don't let that ringing wake up Elly and Shawn, so I can enjoy some loving time with my husband for a change. Tell whoever that is to call back later."

Dus didn't say that to the caller. He said, "Hello, Scott."

"Dus," Scott Kirsh begged, "I need you and Karol here at the clinic right away!"

"This is very bad timing, Sheriff. What was it you called my wife? A pristine, decent squaw or something?" Dus said, hoping Karol would hear him.

"Shush, Dus; she'll hear you," a dismayed sheriff whispered over the telephone. "I know it's awfully late, but Jakey Peesy is here with a broken head. Patty's here, too. She opened the door for us, and is trying to do something with his bleeding skull."

"Just a minute, Scott," he said, turning to his miffed wife. "Sweetheart, Scott has a wounded man at the clinic, and needs both of us right now."

"Tell him it's a very inopportune time, but we're coming. Someday I'm going to teach that cop some manners," she carped, getting out of bed and into some clothes.

"We will be there in ten minutes, Scott, but my wife is not very happy with you."

"I'm sorry, and I can understand that. It's happened to Patty lots of times. Thanks, guys!"

Karol and Dus arrived at the clinic to find Jakey Peesy lying on an examination table, moaning. Patty was wiping blood from his head, while Scott tried to calm him.

"Let me see, Patty," Karol said, slipping on rubber gloves. "What happened here, Scott Kirsh, that you had to interrupt my conjugal visit home?"

"I'm sorry, Karol, but this is the guy who tacked the note to the vicarage door."

"What note?" Karol screeched.

"Didn't Dus tell you about the note?"

"You told me not to, for gosh sakes, Scott," Dus retorted.

"You'll tell me in a minute, won't you, Father Habak?" the piqued physician said to her husband. "What happened to this guy, who hasn't bathed in a month and smells like a bear? What have you been doing for him, Patty?"

"I've just been swabbing his wound with some peroxide until you could get here. The wound looks long and deep."

"It is, and it's going to take a dozen or so stitches. Get me my stuff, and we will see what we can do for him. He'll need a tetanus shot, and we will squirt some painkiller right into that wound to make it easier for him as we sew him up," Karol said as she filled up a hypodermic needle and injected the liquid into the wound. "This is going to sting, Jakey."

"Ooh, thatta do hurt, Docta," Jakey complained.

"Good. That's what you get for writing notes and scaring preachers' and sheriffs' wives."

"I'ma sorry, Mum."

"You'd better be, you stinking goat. Now shut up and be still, or I'll sew up your mouth, too," she fumed as she waited for the skin on his skull to become numb.

Turning to Scott, she said, "So, Village Crime Stopper, what spellbinding mystery is going on here that you dragged me away on this cold night from my cozy husband and sleeping kids. What about a note this dip tacked to our house?"

"You really didn't tell her, did you, Dus?" Scott queried.

"I told you; I didn't want to ruin our wedding day and honeymoon."

"That's nice, but you two secret agents didn't mind ruining my biweekly visit tonight, did you?" Karol scolded. "So tell me, what great crisis has come about with this bloody creature, that I have to mend his smelly body? Couldn't it wait until morning?"

Patty Kirsh, clearly amused by her irate friend, covered her mouth to stifle a laugh.

Dus, who was not amused, answered, "This guy tacked a note on my door at the vicarage the night before we were married, warning me to leave the mountain with you and the kids, or you would all be hurt. He did the same to Scott and Patty today."

"Why, you smelly pony turd," she castigated Jakey, "it's a good thing I took an oath to take care of the wounded, or I'd tack a note to your nose!" She was very angry at Jakey.

"Please donna do dat, Mum. I'sa sorry. Tell 'er da whole story, Sher'ff," Jakey stuttered.

"Shut up, you polecat! Patty, shave that mucky hair off around his wound and let's sew him up. I'm not all that dedicated to fixing him after what I've heard, but it's gotta be done. He has a billion cooties crawling over his scalp, but at least we can keep the wound aseptic."

"Go easy on him, Karol," Scott said. "He's a victim and a witness, not the bad guy!"

" 'Scuse my reservation language, Mr. Detective! You tell me this obnoxious piece of buffalo poop threatened my kids on our wedding day, that my husband has kept that obscenity in his heart for five months, and then you say he's not a bad guy. Please enlighten this ticked-off Indian wife before I hatchet his damned scrawny neck like a chicken's!"

Jakey's forehead sweated, his eyes bulged, and Karol threatened to punch them out. A chastened Scott stared at Dus as if to remind him what he had said about his "pristine" Indian wife's anger threshold. Patty snickered, and Scott glared at both women. "Tend to your business, Patty, and watch your language, Karol. Profanity coming from an attractive and decent lady like yourself, I hear, is unladylike!"

"I'm not a nice lady when I've been rustled out of bed with two children home alone, to be told that this paleface weasel has threatened my family. Perhaps my demeanor and language will improve when someone tells me in some intelligible words what the hell is going on in my life!"

Scott and Dus, feeling ashamed, told her about the courthouse interview with Jakey.

"What happened after I left, Scott?" a fidgety Dus asked his beleaguered friend.

"I drove down to Jakey's house after dark, hid my truck, and waited around the side of his porch to see if anyone would show up to pay him the money he was owed. Someone did, and brought a whiskey bottle with him. When Jakey came to the door, and before I could get over the porch rail, the man cracked him over the head with the bottle."

"Holy cow!" Dus exclaimed.

"I arrested the attacker, took the hundred dollars in twenty bills and gave them to Jakey's wife, put Jakey in the cab of my pickup, handcuffed the basher onto the truck bed, and brought him up to jail. I've had a busy night."

"Sound like it. What then?"

"While the guys at the jail cleaned up Jakey a bit, I asked Patty to take him up to the clinic and try to patch him. It was a little much for her, so that's why I called you two. In the meantime, I had a little talk with the payoff guy and rounded up some folk. Now I have three people locked up here at the courthouse. One of them knows the place well."

"Who, Scott? Aren't you going to tell us?" Karol urged.

"I'm not sure you'll want to know. They might be friends of yours. Two of them are friends of mine, and it is a sorry mess. When you hear who they are, you're gonna rub your hands over your ears and hair, and feel bad, Dus."

"Come on, Scott. This is not funny. This is serious stuff to Karol and me. Who are they?" Dus berated him.

"Two of them are Mr. and Mrs. Simon Shoney, your favorite barber and my favorite court stenographer!"

Dus shook his head and rubbed his hands over his hair and ears. Karol and Patty stopped their work of suturing Jakey, and stared at Scott in wide-eyed disbelief, then said, together, "You're kidding!"

"I'm not kidding. Get Jakey sewed up as soon as you can, so we can get him home to his family. His wife and kids saw it all, and are really scared."

"Sure, Scott; we're nearly done. He's going to have about fifteen sutures in his head, but he'll be OK," Karol assured him.

"Good. Take care of old Jakey, because if it weren't for him, we'd know nothing about this. We are closing down on this ongoing drama. About time, I'd say!"

Karol looked down on the unmoving patient with more respect. "I'm sorry I judged you so harshly and said those nasty things about you, Jakey. Don't worry; we'll take good care of you and your family."

"Thunk ya, Docta," Jakey groaned.

"Go on with the rest of the story," Dus beseeched Scott.

"Well, my good friend Edna walked out of the courthouse at lunch time, went straight to her husband, Simon Shoney, one of the partners in the moonshine operation, and told him about our private talk with Jakey. Si, planning to save himself some money, went down after work tonight to Jakey's house and smashed in Jakey's head for his loose talk. Now Si and Edna are sitting in jail, wanting to do some loose talking of their own. They are a very frightened man and wife. Si confessed that he was the one who buggered the brake line on your jeep, that he was one of the shooters at the still, and that he was the guy who shot at you up near the cave last fall when you first came to the mountain. He said he never tried to hit you. He just wanted to scare you so you wouldn't mess around that area anymore. But," Scott added, looking at Dus' somewhat hypnotized wife, "that wasn't all bad, was it?"

"What do you mean? He pretty near killed Dus!" Karol sizzled, as she tied off the last suture in Jakey's skull.

"Well, he didn't hurt him, and provided a most advantageous and romantic opportunity for you to meet Father Dus Habak and his paleface heinie. You could say that Simon, the barber of Joshuatown, was sort of the Cupid responsible for you two falling in love and getting married. Sounds like an opera, doesn't it?" Scott kidded the master kidder.

Karol didn't laugh. "You're not very funny, you loony spook. I have a lot of sympathy for Patty, being married to a weird Sherlock Holmes like you."

"Actually, Karol," Patty, who had been stifling laughter nearly the whole time in the clinic, said, "it's not all that unpleasant living with a spook. Given your revitalized devotion to the topic of anatomy since your meeting of and marrying Father Habak, and your blooming fascination with romance, ministry, and mystery, you might hope that your priest's expertise in investigating, probing for, and uncovering the *corpus delicti* would be as accomplished and sensational as are those of my snoopy detective husband. You'd be surprised what that man finds when he is snooping around in the dark."

"Ah ha! Sounds interesting," Karol began to grin a bit. "So he is good in the dark, eh?"

"Beware, Patricia; you are getting near the brink of our private life," her husband warned her. "Remember how you always told the kids and me that we are not to discuss family matters outside the house."

"Oh, poo! We're among friends here. You'd better learn to laugh, snoopy, 'cause your demure wife is learning a lot about life from her Indian medicine woman friend!"

"OK, sweetheart; I'm not gonna argue with two medics. Anyway," Scott continued, "our usually quiet and sweet, if now sorry, Edna admitted to me that she wrote the colloquial notes that Jakey tacked on our doors, claiming that she composed them under pressure from her husband and his partner in crime, our third guest in the slammer, who dictated them to her, word for word. I believe she is simply another victim. They have been bullying her into telling them what was going on in the courthouse, for years. She is a very scared lady who wants to talk. So, friends, what do you think of my sleuthing?"

"I'll be darned," Dus breathed. "And who is the third sinner in this nasty troika?"

"You may not want to know. He's one of your favorite people in Joshuatown. This may hurt?"

Karol said to Patty, "I'm done here with Jakey. Clean him up, give him a tetanus shot, and get him up on his feet. I want to hear this. I am afraid I won't like it." She pulled a chair next to Dus and held his hand. "Who is it, Scott?" she frowned, peering longingly into his face, feeling that her worst fears were about to be realized. "Please, not Jed, Ox, nor Cyrus. Please, Scott, not any of those we love!"

"No, none of them," he chuckled. "It's your old admirer, Banker Raymond Brush, the nice, leering, 'money-changer' gentleman who thinks that you're sexy and that Dus is something of a dunderhead. You know, the little bald-headed guy with the oily hands and ready lips your green-eyed hubby has suspected from the first day he met him. You know, the Brush that ogles you and Patty, and has exacerbated Dus' sin of jealousy a mite. I must confess, however, that your perceptive husband suspected the old coot all along, and I wouldn't believe him."

"Scott Kirsh, I'm gonna take a tomahawk to you for scaring us like that. Patty, where in the world did you find this sadistic creature? He had me thinking it was one of our friends who was involved," Karol sighed in relief.

"I don't know where I found him! Come to think of it, I was wondering if he had learned some of his newly found banter artistry from a certain Indian woman!"

"I knew it! I knew it!" yelled Dus, who had been waiting to do that. "That scoundrel with the slimy hands and dollar-sign eyes roving all over my wife's body like some pervert, was guilty all the time. I'm gonna kick the bastard's ass!"

"You'll do nothing of the sort, Dus, and stop that swearing," a now-composed wife calmed her angry husband. "Mr. Brush will pay dearly for his iniquities, won't he, Sheriff?"

"He will, indeed, Doctor. Let's see—conspiracy to murder, bankrolling the illegal production of a controlled substance and profiting from the same, threatening minors with mayhem, and numerous other misdemeanors. He is sitting in my jail right now thinking about how all those charges against him are going to cramp his opulent lifestyle for a few years to come. Of course, he is in denial and has called a bunch of lawyers, but I believe that Simon, Edna, and their moonie friends are thinking about saving their own skins and blowing the lid off of Mr. Brush's innocence."

"I'll be darned," Karol sighed. "I guess there is going to be a lot of talking in this town this weekend. I'd like to hear all the gossip about the lecherous money changer. I wish I had a microphone in this clinic's waiting room."

"You and your clergy husband listening to village gossip does not sound very spiritual to me. Anyway, the prosecutors will want to question us all as witnesses. We'll have to testify. So will Jakey, here. It will be very interesting."

"So old Si, who could have cut my throat anytime he wanted to when he was cutting my hair, shot at me up in the mountain and then at my house."

"Yeah, and they tried to kill Ox, too, the snakes in the grass," Karol bristled.

"No, Karol. We have all been wrong about that. I've asked all three of them about the Ox incident; they deny having had anything to do with that and the shooting up at your house. I believe them. With all the charges against them, they couldn't hide those happenings."

"Why do you believe them?"

"Just doesn't fit. Shells and bullets are different, and no one person would be fool enough to go into Ox's back yard and drive a rail spike into a single oak log, hoping Ox would hit it with an axe or chain saw. No, the lab people just think the spike was driven into that tree for some other reason a long time before Ox cut it down, and Ox missed seeing it when he unloaded it from his truck. He hit it accidentally with his chain saw while cutting logs for fireplaces that Sunday afternoon when you two were having lunch with him and Nancy."

"You're sure?" Karol asked.

"I am only as sure as the lab guys are, and they're pretty good at what they do. Lots of railroad people used spikes in the old days to make ladders on trees. They used them to climb up high so they could tell what the landscape was like ahead of them. Who knows? I've been wrong all the time about Ox's accident. He did it to himself, and I think the reason that he and Nancy have not been too angry about it nor blamed anyone, is that, in their hearts, they feel that way, too. You haven't heard them blame anyone, have you?"

"No, Scott; as a matter of fact, we haven't."

"We just made assumptions because of all this other stuff. You can't outfox an old fox like Ox. If it would have been somebody else who had done that to him, he would have found the guy in short order. His prowess, strength, and wisdom are well-known in these parts, and I doubt if anyone would ever mess with him for any reason. I talked to him and questioned him at length. He never mentioned that nor tried to make any of the people he knows believe that there was someone out to get him for anything. It's only suspicious Yankees like us who think that way. All the folk in this mountain are Ox's friends, and none of them would hurt him. That incident is over, even with Ox and Nancy. They and the kids have come to terms with the injury, and I am sure they will be fine. There is a philosophy around these parts about letting old dogs lie."

"Are you saying, then, Scott, that none of this is connected in any way to the cadaver we found and reburied, nor to the shooting at our house?"

"That's right, and I am about ready to concede that episode was over and done with when we put it back in the grave. Take away the note on our doors, the moonie fracas, the Jakey incident, and the people repenting in the jail; what do you have left?"

"Nothing but peace and loving," Karol admitted, with a coy smile on her face. "And I shall be glad, quite frankly, to get back to that at my house with a warm husband."

"Patty and I will take Jakey back to his family now, and you two can go home," Scott said.

"When am I gonna git home, Sher'ff? My fam'ly needs me," Jakey began to complain.

"You're going home now, Jakey," Karol told him. "You'll be OK. Leave the bandage on for a while, and come back and Mrs. Kirsh will take the stitches out. Keep it clean, now."

"Thunk you, Mum! I 'preciates it."

"Can you walk all right?" Scott asked.

"Mite goofy, Sher'ff, butta I ken make it."

"Well, I still want to know who shot at me when I was digging at the vicarage, Scott," Dus complained. "That is something important that is unresolved for Karol and me."

"It will be resolved soon; I promise. As for me, I'm going home. I suggest that you do the same."

"He's going, too. Come on, hubby," Karol said. "We have some unfinished business to attend to while the kids are asleep."

"Sounds like wrapping Christmas presents," Patty giggled.

"No," Karol smiled. "What I have in mind is more like unwrapping a honeymoon present."

"Sounds like a great idea," Patty agreed. "Come on, Detective. Let's go home, too, snoop in the dark, and unwrap some honeymoon presents."

Scott's face turned red. Damned Indian sawbones, with her sexy chatter, has made my heretofore demure wife into a shameless coquette! The girlfriends giggled and the two couples left the clinic, reassuring Jakey that life would be better for his family. Karol and Dus drove back home, promising God they would personally help that to become a reality for the Peesys. Scott and Patty Kirsh made the same promise before they started "unwrapping honeymoon presents."

# 37

Time in the mountain flowed gently toward Christmas. The short Thanksgiving vacation had been for Dus, Karol, Shawn, and Elly a phenomenal time of family bonding. The four days of living, eating, laughing, joking, sleeping together, and physically embracing each other, with affection, under the same roof, confirmed the ultimate and final fusion of the widow and her son, with the widower and his daughter. Two families, once divided and alone by tragedy and circumstance, through the power of God's grace and the commitment of vocation and love, had now become one family. A man and his wife, their son and daughter, sister and brother, through the inexplicable mystery of adoptive love and grace, were a family as solid as any natural love could have consummated. Their solidarity and kinsmanship were a joy to behold among friends and strangers alike, on the mountain.

The Habaks and the Conleys had eaten another sumptuous Thanksgiving dinner together, this time, at the vicarage. Karol and Nancy had had a grand time of preparing the meal, while Dus and Ox kept the hearth fire glowing and the children played in the snow. Neither the men nor the children intruded into Nancy and Karol's time together, nor their quiet dialogue, smiles, and activity that seemed to safeguard the secrets of life known only to womankind. They were joyful wives and mothers—fulfilled with their men and broods, pleasing those admiring and satisfied human treasures, not only with their culinary talents, but with their feminine mystique and happy demeanor. There was an aura of peace and tranquillity in that house Thanksgiving Day with the families, who had a lot to be thankful for.

Banker Brush and the Shoneys, who had been released on bail while awaiting indictment and trial, were able to spend the holidays with their families—somewhere, it was thought, off the mountain, because no one had seen them in the village since their release. Banker Brush had been suspended from his banking position pending the outcome of his trial. Si Shoney had hired a barber to take care of his business until his future, too, was resolved. His wife, Edna, had resigned from her job at the county courthouse.

The attending gossip surrounding the whole affair, none of which had rubbed off on the good names of Dus and Karol, had a rather short day in the sun, and died a quick and unlamented death. The county judge, a friend of both Banker Brush and Sheriff Kirsh, had very judiciously arranged that nothing would be done about the incident in his court until after the first of the year. Everybody was happy about that, because no one in the county wanted the black spectrum of scandal hovering over his holiday merriment.

Karol and the children had returned to school and surgery after Thanksgiving, but visited on weekends in Joshuatown as Christmas approached. Dus went about this pastoral chores of visiting the sick and having church services.

Advent, the season for the preparation of Christ's coming, was a spiritual time that he thoroughly enjoyed. He reveled in the joy of people, the music, and the biblical lessons, intrinsic to the time of year. He had long ago given up his "Scrooge" insistence that Santa Claus had no place in Advent, having subscribed to the theory that "If you can't lick 'em; join 'em." So he shopped at HUDSON & SON COMPANY and the other hometown stores, put up decorations, and waited anxiously for Karol to come home to help him put up the big crêche at the church. The crêche had not only enchanted the people the year before, but had brought Dus and Karol tenderly together for the first time.

It was not only a happy season of "coming" for Christians, but a happy time of ",becoming" for a now-happy priest, who had suffered the tragic loss of his cherished first wife and only son, and endured debilitating grief, and the destruction of dignity and vocation that followed it. But renewal had come to him in the person of Ollikut Karolina Habak, and through the mountain people. As he sat in his office, pondering the past and present, he thought of Ginnie and Dusty in endearing recall. The memory of the good life they had given him was, and would always be, a significant part of his mortality. He talked to them in prayer and hoped that, one day, if he rejoined them in heaven, God would allow him the pleasure of hugging and talking to them, however the immortal configuration of his and their ethereal bodies and souls might be fashioned by the promises of eternity. He often discussed his past and present life, especially his marriages to two fine women, with God, prayerfully seeking his counsel and blessings on the comportment of his life, hoping he had been a reasonably good man, husband, and father to his family of his past life, and praying mightily that he would be all of that in the present and future to his new family. His alive and loving daughter, Elly, of course, was his connection to both sides of the grave.

He was not ready just yet to discuss those inner abstractions with Karol, and it was no reflection on his deep, compelling, and abiding love for her that he, on occasion, when he was alone, sojourned down the mountain to the cemetery where Ginnie and Dusty rested, laid fresh flowers on their graves, and spent a few moments in prayer with them. Those meditative chats were generally about the ambiences and rightness of the life and love that he now shared with Karol, Elly, and Shawn, and the pastoral vocation he had among the people on the mountain, in spite of the nettlesome events that shook his faith from time to time. He knew Karol would understand, as he would understand her link with her western heritage and past life, and vowed, when the time was right for her and their children, he would bring them to Ginnie and Dusty's graves for an introduction and visit, and then take them to Oregon to visit her family and friends, and the grave of her former husband and Shawn's father. He anticipated, too, now that he knew and appreciated the extraordinary and deep native spirituality of his aboriginal spouse, that she would instinctively bond the allusive love of their former lives to the passion of their new life. She would somehow, in some mythical, loving way, take his and their children's hands in her own and lead them across that legendary bridge of time that joins the quality of the past life to the beauty of the present, and the wondrous expectations of the future. Dus knew in his heart that his elegant, coquettish, and sometimes mysterious Indian wife, mother of their children, and physician, so steeped in Native American tradition and the natural verities of life, would do that over time, without even knowing nor thinking about it. It would just be her way of living life as only an Indian lady can.

But now it was late Saturday afternoon, just ten days before Christmas Day. Dus was in his office, and that elegant Indian wife and lady of his was in hers, next door, tending to her last patient before closing down the Joshuatown clinic for the day. The telephone rang, and Scott Kirsh asked if the two of them were busy.

"No, Scott. Karol is closing the office, and I'm just getting some crêche things together for us to put it up at the church tonight."

"Do you need some help?"

"Sure; we'd love it!"

"Well, tell Karol I have some people here who'd like to come by the clinic to see you two, and help you put up the crêche."

"Come on by. We'll be ready. We are going to load up the jeep with all the Nativity structures now."

Dus and Karol waited for their guests. Ox, Nancy, Jed Hudson, his wife, Helen, Scott, Patty, and Bessie Clayton arrived, bearing Christmas gifts and treats. They entered the clinic waiting room, greeting the priest and his wife with hugs and kisses. The couple were overwhelmed with the affection.

"Oh, this is so wonderful," Karol sniffed. "You should not have done this."

"No, you shouldn't have," Dus agreed with his tearful wife.

"Sure we should have," the visitors seemed to say in one accord. "Butta, dees boxes 'ave ta go unner da tree en yer house, en ya ain'ta open dem till Chrismus," Nancy interjected.

"Da's right," Ox added.

"Butta," Bessie said, "we're a gonna visit yer house, en da soup en goodies is fer tonight der, when we raze up da crêche. Jed, Helen, en me is gonna take 'em up ta yer house soon as we leave heah."

"So what do you think of the plan for the evening? Neat, huh?" a happy Scott asked.

"Beautiful! We love you all for it," Karol said.

"Could Shawn and Elly come down to Ox and Nancy's place to play while we are up at the church?" Patty asked. "Our kids are over there now. We thought it would be nice for us adults to eat, talk, and do our thing with the crêche without the kids. Jenny and Cyrus will watch the youngsters."

"Sure; come on up to the house and sit by the fire. We'll have some of Bessie's goodies and then do the crêche," Karol invited.

The group of friends met at the house within the hour. Dus, Ox, Jed, and Scott laid crêche paraphernalia out to be erected later, while the ladies prepared the food. Then, they all sat in the living room before a blazing fire, nibbling and talking. Karol and Dus were happy that their friends were in their home during the holy season amid Karol's attractive Christmas decoration of wreaths and candles. It was a solemn as well as a happy occasion.

Jed Hudson popped a wine bottle cork and went about filling everyone's glasses. Even Ox and Nancy, who seldom imbibed, conceded to a taste. Jed, apparently the designated toastmaster and orator, stood up in front of the little group. "I want to propose a toast to our priest and doctor, who have brought so much love and caring to our community. Their presence here has made us a better village and a better people."

"Hear! Hear!" everyone joined in, as Karol and Dus acknowledged the praises with thank-yous and tears.

"This is a happy occasion," Jed smiled, then turned serious, "but also a somber one. I have some serious stuff to say to you, Dus and Karol, even if our Advent and Christmas observance must endure it. Only Scott, Bessie, and I know the whole story I am going to tell. Helen, Ox, and Nancy know only part of it, and Patty knows none. But first let me say first, Dus, that you have taught us a lot about God this past year. You have opened our minds to truths we might have known at one time, but have somewhat forgotten, here in these hills. You have taught us about forgiveness and love and about caring. And you, Karol, before Dus, came unselfishly to us to heal our bodies and souls with your medical skills and love. With your native and natural beauty, you have also given us a new appreciation for the animals, birds, the forest, and the loveliness of God's creation, which we had almost taken for granted and forgotten to enjoy here.

"Your marriage has taught us how love brings together ethnic cultures and vocation, and how victory is wrestled out of tragedy. Your commitments to God, and your pastoral and medical care and love toward us have made us a strengthened and more dedicated people. We would hope that you will never leave us, and I speak for hundreds in our community who are not here, but who would tell all that I am saying to you, if they were. You have taught us about sacrifice and healing. Your friend Lou came to help us with his love to make our vicarage worthy of any clergy family, and we love him for it. Scott and I have been around, Father, and we could see that Lou was not well when he came to help us. That he did that while in pain before his death was a great tribute to you, though we know how sorrowful it was for you both. But it is the criterion of the man, and says so much about you. And the fact that this beautiful physician would love you and marry you says even more about your worthiness as a person. That your bishop would trust you with us, God's people, here is a recognition of your pastoral ability, and we, your friends, hope our being here tonight—and feeling as we do—is an indication of our love and admiration for you both.

"We heard your frog story; we know what you suffered before you came to us. We have felt your anguish; we know what you have overcome; we honor your courage; and we are grateful for your strength and ability to put the past behind you, and serve us with zeal and fervor.

"There are, however, some among us in our village who have not always and fully appreciated everything you have tried to do for us since you came to the mountain, and have not been worthy of your love and efforts. Not all of us have been happy with the questions you have asked, nor your interest and curiosity concerning us. We have been wrong about that, and we have made some terrible mistakes."

"Jed, you don't have to tell us all this. This is Christmas, and what is done is done. Let's not spoil this beautiful evening," Dus said.

"Let him talk, Dus, please," Scott urged.

"It's gotta be said, Son," Ox joined in.

"Yeah, it sholly do, en Jed's da best one ta tell it fer usins," Nancy joined in.

Karol's eyes scanned the room and looked into every face. The happiness she had seen in them before was gone, and their solemnity bothered her. Patty looked frightened. Dus' demeanor changed drastically, and now he looked worried. Something ominous was occurring, and she had no idea what it could be. Nancy, Ox, and Bessie looked like robots.

Jed went on. "Father Dus, we have brought you gifts and kind accolades this day out of love and respect for you and Karol, but on this joyful night, I must confess, we have also returned to you, in the past, evil for good."

"Please don't say that, Jed," Karol pleaded. "You people have been wonderful to Dus and me. We love you! Bessie, please; don't let him say any more. Helen, Ox, Nancy, Scott? No. No, please."

"Letta Jed go on, deary, please," Bessie pleaded.

"Karol, you hold Dus' hand on the couch and listen closely," Scott urged.

She grabbed Dus' hand. Tears were welling in anticipation of Jed's revelation.

"Dus, God and you forgive me. I was the one who shot at you when you were digging up the body you believed to be the body of the Reverend Tucker Benson."

There was stony silence in the room for a full minute. When the impact of Jed's words hit Dus, his face turned red, his forehead broke out in a sweat, and his body stiffened. He started to rise up from the couch, but Karol held his arm, and Scott, who had moved in back of the couch, held Dus' shoulders down in his seat. He glared at Jed. "Oh, God! No, Jed. Not you! Why, you bastard? Why, for Christ's sake? How could you? You're my friend. You're supposed to be my damned friend. How could you try to kill me? Do you know how much and how long I have despised the person who frightened my wife and children?" His fury turned to Scott. "Why, Scott? You knew all the time, didn't you? You're supposed to be my friend, too. What a fool I've been! What a hell of a Christmas this turned out to be."

Scott held his friend tightly. Karol, hanging on to her husband's neck, sobbed, "Please, Dus, though you hurt, don't swear, particularly here with these friends. Please hear Jed out before you vent your anger. The people around you here love you. Look at Jed; look at Helen, Nancy, Ox, Bessie, and Patty. Look at them all, and see that they care about and love you. Don't rail on them and hurt them with words you'll regret. They are as frightened as you are angry." She was shaking with her own inner fear and anger.

Dus slumped on the couch. His eyes were wet, his face hostile, his nerves cutting into every crevice of his being. Haven't I been here before, goddam it? he swore to himself. Wasn't it just a year ago when I had to listen to this bullshit in the bishop's office? God, at least then it wasn't Christmastime, when we are all supposed to be friendly and happy about life. He jerked his shoulders away from Scott's hands and Karol's body, refusing their solicitations and comfort. Karol was visibly hurt, but did not pursue it. She was just as confused and hurt with Jed as was Dus, but refused to show it. How could he have tried to kill her husband?

"Yes, I shot at you, Father. But I am an excellent marksman with a .22 rifle. I could have wounded you or killed you, if I had wanted to, but I never came close to hitting you. I never intended to physically harm you."

"The hell you didn't. You nearly killed Tooter, too, you lousy friend! That was a goddamn 30.06 you were plugging into my house."

"Please, Dus, you promised me and God not to curse," Karol scolded him.

"Not it wasn't, Dus, and he didn't try to hit you," Scott said, taking three marred and bent lead slugs and seven brass shell casings out of an envelope and placing them on the coffee table. Dus picked them up.

"Where did you get these?" Dus scowled.

"I got them from your good friend Lou Casalano. He dug them out of the heavy rafters in the house and found the casings nearly buried by pine needles up in the pine clump behind this house. He sent them to me in a package from his home."

"You mean Lou knew about all this, too?"

"Only about me, those casings and slugs, and another thing I will tell you about later. He was afraid that your knowing about them would upset you and Karol, and ruin your wedding plans. He was a great friend to you both, and wanted to spare you worry and fear."

"God love his soul," Karol sniffed.

Scott continued, "I was about to take this evidence that Lou sent me right to the police lab to match the shells and slugs with someone's rifle. Instead, I decided to go to see Jed, because I knew he is the only one I know in these parts who uses a .22 rifle. But Jed, at the persuasion of his conscience and these friends, anticipated me, and came to me with his confession and story. I decided, before I did anything legal, I would like them all to talk to you and Karol. What happens next depends pretty much on you both."

"Why us, for God's sake?"

"Git on en tell 'em, Jed, sos we ken git this all right wid 'im en Karol," Bessie encouraged him.

"All right, Bessie. No, Father, I didn't come near hitting you when I tried to scare you. You came nearer to hitting me with your pistol when you shot back at me. I would never have hurt you. I don't know how I will ever get you to believe that, nor have you understand why. I am sorry about the shooting; I don't expect you to forgive me. But I have to tell you the whole story. As Scott said, God, Bessie, Helen, Ox, Nancy, and my own conscience told me I had to tell you now, before Christmas, so you and your family can celebrate this holy season with no lingering questions and fears, and get on with your happy life."

Dus lowered his head and held it in his hands, shaking it. Karol looked up at Jed. "Why did you do that to him, Jed? He's your friend; you're one of the first people he met in Joshuatown. And you, Nancy, Ox, and Bessie, how could you be a part of this? We have loved you, and have broken bread with you! Dus would give his life for every one of you, even at this moment. So would I! Can you blame him for being angry? I'm angry, too! I have been angry a long time at the person who tried to kill my man, and, God, he turns out to be our friend. Can you blame us? The Shoneys, and Banker Brush, maybe; but you?" They all looked at her in shame.

"No," Jed said. "I can't blame either of you for being angry at me, but the rest of these folk had nothing to do with it. They knew why I did it, but would have never agreed nor allowed me to do it, if I had told them I planned to scare Dus this way. They are part of the old story about the preacher, but were not aware that I shot at you until I told them just a few days ago. They were just as appalled at me as you are. I knew that Scott would find out it was me, sooner or later. I had to tell them and the sheriff the truth before I told you. It was an awful thing I did, and I am prepared to pay for it. Scott knows that, and will have to make that decision soon."

"No, Jed, no; ya tain't gonna go ta jail. Ya done it fer me. Ya done it fer me; tell 'em! He done it fer me, Sher'ff," Bessie wailed, and then sobbed.

Helen and Nancy moved over to comfort her. "Der, der, sweety. Itta gonna be allright. Fadder and Karol is good folk, en des gonna unnerstan in time. Donna ya cry now," Nancy said, looking pleadingly into the faces of Karol and Dus. Karol's heart was breaking.

"Tell them the whole story, Jed. They'll listen," Scott encouraged.

Dus got up from the couch. "The hell we will. I'm not going to listen to one more damned word of this. I'm sorry I am angry, I am sorry about my language, and I am sorrier still, that I ever came up to this mountain. When I think of all the bullshit you told me about what a good guy I am, just an hour ago, how great Lou was, how Karol and I changed your lives, I could throw up. You bring us gifts and food, stand in our house, and say you love us. Softening me up for the big hit, eh? Bullshit! Now, before I really get mad, I want all of you to leave my house and let us alone. I have a lot of packing to do, and must make some plans for my family and vocation!"

"No, Dus," Karol cried. "Whatever has happened in all this confusion, these people are our friends. Whatever they've done or haven't done, they came here tonight because they care for us. I am not going to let you leave our home here, nor your church, nor my clinic, and we are not going to order our friends out of our house. I am a doctor and you are a priest, and the nature of our business is listening and healing. I'm angry and hurt, too, darling, but the bigger hurt would be if we just walked away from friends without listening to them. Please, Dus. You heard the things Jed said about our ministry here. I believe he sincerely meant it, and we know deep in our hearts how hard it is for him to be in our home telling us the terrible thing that he did."

"Yeah, this home he shot the windows and doors out of! Yeah, and there is my friend the sheriff, with all his damned evidence, knowing tons of stuff, lying to me every damned minute. Shit! He even knew about Lou's part in it! How could you do this to me, Scott?"

Patty began to cry, too. Scott and Jed recoiled from Dus' verbal onslaught upon them, but stood firmly in place, determined to resolve the issue.

"Darling, all these people sitting here know that I adore you. Now, please, don't push me aside in the midst of this pain and make me leave you alone with it. I cannot allow you nor my hurt to destroy us. It almost did before. Don't you remember? I am not going to allow it to happen again!"

Dus shrugged his shoulders, sighed, and sat down again beside her.

"Thanks, Karol," Scott said. "You're my friend, Dus. I am a law officer, and it is my responsibility to solve crimes. I'm not going to apologize to you for that. I did what I had to do to protect you and Karol, Jed and Bessie, before this became public knowledge and hurt a lot of people. I have to do things a cop's way in spite of your injured feelings and anger. Now, please be quiet and let Jed tell his story," a frustrated Scott ordered his friend.

"Dus, please hear me out. I don't blame you for being angry nor even hating me, but please let me finish. When I am finished, Helen, Bessie, and I will leave your home if you wish, but please don't leave the mountain. The people need you and Karol here. Don't neglect them because of my stupidity. Stay, Dus; stay and judge me, and me alone."

"I'll listen, shooter, but that's all I promise," Dus carped.

Jed stiffened at that designation, but went on. "You know about the preacher who came here about twenty or so years ago. He was a loner, but tended the graves for us, and had prayers for the people who asked. We never knew where he came from nor what denomination he represented. We didn't even know if he was properly ordained. He called himself the Reverend Tucker Benson, and we had no reason not to believe him. He worked hard, and built the church and this vicarage with no help. He stayed to himself. He seldom came into HUDSON & SON COMPANY. He bought his supplies from the local lumber company and down in Staunton."

"'Twas a funny one, he was," Ox offered.

"Yes, he was peculiar. And an awful thing happened concerning him that only Bessie, Helen, Ox, I, and now, Scott, are privy to."

Bessie began to wail again. Nancy and Helen continued to soothe her.

"What?" Dus asked, a little more civilly.

"I don't really know how to tell this without hurting Bessie more, but perhaps, if it all finally comes out, it will heal everyone's wounds. Bessie and I were teenage sweethearts, but I had to go off to war in the Navy. While I was away, Bessie met Lee Clayton; they fell in love and were married. I never resented that, and found my Helen while in college at Charlottesville, where we married. Helen always understood that Bessie and I were old friends, and she became her close friend, too. Anyway, Lee and Bessie were a happy couple, fun-loving and well-liked in town. When Bessie got pregnant, she and Lee were ecstatic, and everyone in town who knew them was very happy for them, too."

Bessie's sobbing continued; her groaning was almost unbearable for everyone in the room, even for Dus. "But Lee got hurt in the mine," Jed continued, "and couldn't go into the military service during the war. He was embarrassed that he was 4-F, and some guys made fun of him. Even though he and Bessie were happy in their marriage, with the new baby coming, he was not happy in his work; he wanted to leave it and move off the mountain. Bessie didn't want to. She loved Lee and he was crazy about her. But this was their home that she loved, and she could not bear to leave it, even for him. Bessie didn't care what people said about Lee. She would not allow them to drive her from their home.

"But one day, a local bully who was headed for the Army called Lee a draft dodger, and Lee beat him up. Though Lee was a minor boss himself, the company suspended him for a week without pay. That's when it all happened."

"Do ya have to tell it all, Jed?" Bessie cried.

"Bessie, you, Helen, Ox, and Nancy asked me to tell the sheriff, Father Dus, and Karol, and that is what I must do, no matter how it hurts. You know, Bess, I wouldn't hurt you for anything in the world, if I could avoid it. You know how much I have always cared for you."

"I knows Jed; I knows; but da rembance do pain."

"You're gonna be all right, Bessie," Helen tried to reassure her friend. "Let Jed talk."

Jed went on, "Lee got drunk after work and then went home. He told Bessie he was leaving, and when she tried to stop him, he hit her hard."

"He din't mean ta do dat, Fadder," Bessie said. "Lee was a ver' good man watta loved me, en neva meant me no harm. Hitting me was jist an accidont, en my fault, too. I tugged on 'im too hard, en he poshed me away in his anga, en I got hurt! I knows he neva meant ta hurt me!"

Jed continued, "Lee left, never telling Bessie where he was going nor for how long he'd be gone. Bessie was beside herself. She was five months pregnant, and had no one to talk to. She wouldn't come to Helen nor me with her marriage problems, because we were all so close and she didn't want us to know of her troubles. She was ashamed.

"She had heard that ministers listen to people's problems. Believing she had no one else to ask for help, she went to Reverend Benson to ask for advice. He was half drunk when she told him about Lee leaving. He told her that wives were always driving men to drink and were the cause of bad marriages. He said that Bessie must have done something very wrong to drive her husband away and cause him to drink. He called her a whore. Imagine—a minister calling our beloved Bessie a whore."

"My God! That terrible man! I'm so sorry, Bessie," Karol said. "I am so sorry!"

"Ever'body but da Reve'nd Benson knowd I wern't no whore," Bessie cried. "I'da neva be a whore, Fadder. No man neva teched my person 'cept Lee en dat reve'nd!"

"I sure never did, and I believe her," Jed said. "The reverend told her that she was going to hell if she did not confess her sin and wash that sin from herself in the church. He ordered her in there. She went and prayed for a long time. He came in with a very cold bucket of cold water and told her he was going to cleanse and rebaptize her. He ordered her to take off all of her clothes, and he would personally wash the evil from her body. She believed him. She was, and is, a wholesome and good Christian woman, but, unfortunately, at that moment she believed in him. It was humiliating and horrible for her, but she stood naked in the church and allowed him to wash her body. In the middle of the washing, that almighty functionary of God's wrath to the wicked, the Reverend Tucker Ben . . ."

"No, no, Jed. Pl'ase!" Bessie screamed. "Donna sey it!"

"I'm sorry, Bessie. You know that I have always loved you, as does Helen, as do Ox and Nancy. We will always be your friends and take care of you, but this has to be known to the good priest and physician. They needed to know the 'why' and 'how' of all this."

Karol and Patty were shuddering and crying.

Jed went on, "As I was about to say, Father Dus, a minister of God, the so-called Reverend Tucker Benson, told Bessie that the real cleansing came when a minister took a woman's body and blessed it with his own."

"That's disgusting!" Karol irrupted.

"She said 'No' to him many times and resisted, but he brutally beat and raped Bessie right there in the aisle of your little church across the way, where you are having services, Father. He told her he was administering God's retribution for her being a bad wife, but it would cleanse her soul. He then warned her, of course, that God would send her straight to hell if she told anyone else about her sin and the mode of cleansing. No one else, he told her, was to know the content of a private confession and penance."

"Oh, my God, Bessie; I am so sorry," Dus sympathized, getting up and going over to the woman, who was sobbing uncontrollably. Karol joined him. Helen and Nancy stepped away to allow them to move close to the crying woman.

"You have borne so terribly much over all these years, Bessie," Karol said with an aching heart.

"So Bessie crawled and stumbled down the hill to her house," Jed said, "bloody and bruised. She lay on the bed for several days with her dead little baby boy she had miscarried that very night she was raped."

"Oh, no! That beast! Oh, Bessie, a little boy. How awful," Karol empathized. "The man was guilty of not only rape, but murder!"

"We had been missing her at the restaurant and in town, so I went looking for her at her house. She had told people she would be out of town with Lee, looking for a job, but I didn't believe that. I went to her house and found her beaten to a pulp, dried blood all over her emaciated body, thin from the lack of food, and putrid from the lack of a bath, with her dead baby rotting on the bed with her, his umbilical cord wrapped around his neck. The stench of death was so bad, I threw up. I thought at first Lee had done this to her, and I wanted to kill him. But she told me the truth and swore me to secrecy."

Everybody was weeping. Dus blew his nose. "I'm sorry, Jed. It must have been awful for you both. What happened then?"

"Bessie said it would be all right to tell Helen, so I asked her to help me with Bessie. We bathed and fed Bessie, tended her wounds, buried the baby in a little grave behind the house, burned Bessie's clothes and bed linens, cleaned up the house, and alternately stayed with her for three days. The store had to be minded, and we took turns at Bessie's house caring for her.

"Lee came home a week later and found me with her. He threatened me at first, and then Bessie told him what had happened. He apologized for his first thoughts, hugged and thanked me, and took over Bessie's care. He was livid and threatened to kill the preacher. I didn't blame the poor guy, but Bessie persuaded him to let the law handle it. When I finally left them to themselves, Lee and Bessie were sweet talking each other again." Jed paused.

"Tell the rest, Jed," Scott ordered.

"Lee and Bessie felt the shame to be too much to go to the law about Reverend Benson's attack on Bessie. Lee thought everybody would believe the preacher, and accuse him of hurting Bessie and causing the baby to abort. So Lee kept all that in his heart and really tried to reorder his life.

But he seethed with hate and, according to Bessie, finally went berserk. Not being able to suffer any longer what the minister did to his beautiful wife and his little son, he decided to kill him. Bessie told Ox and me that she tried to stop him, and told us what Lee had related to her before he died, himself.

"Lee climbed the hill with his shotgun to this vicarage one night, and screamed to Reverend Benson to come out on the porch and face him.

"Lee said the preacher yelled out, 'No, Lee, I won't come out! Tell Bessie she must forgive me! You must forgive me, Lee! Oh, God, please forgive me!'

"Lee said the man was screaming like a maniac about sin and forgiveness, and then he heard a gunshot blast and there was quiet. He broke down the door and found the Reverend Tucker Benson lying wounded on the floor from a self-inflicted gunshot wound to his chest. He was moaning and asking Lee and God for forgiveness. Lee told Bessie the man was so mortally wounded, he could not help him. But, then again, he didn't try nor want to help him. He simply stood over him and watched the reverend agonizingly die, coughing up blood and gurgling prayers."

"Oh my, oh my; ta relive des ag'in, 'tis awful. But what Jed seys is da truf, as Lee tol' me," Bessie whimpered. Everyone else was stone quiet, listening. Dus and Karol squeezed Bessie tighter, and they shook their heads. "Lee buried him in a plot up on the top side of the cemetery that very night. Then he cleaned up the preacher's house, loaded all his possessions, trash, and liquor bottles in the preacher's pickup truck, and drove it up through the trees and brush to the top of the Blue. He set it afire and pushed it off a cliff into a huge ravine, where probably no one has seen nor been before, until Scott found it a few days ago after I told him this story."

"I didn't go down there and find it, Jed. I searched the canyon with my binoculars and spied the burnt-out skeleton frame of a pickup hidden deep in a gully. I have decided there is no point now in disturbing it after all these years, since no one else knows about its location."

"How terrible," was about all a shaking Karol could say.

"Lee was never the same. He was morose and bitter, and couldn't come to terms with what happened to his wife, his son, and Reverend Benson. Bessie never knew whether he blamed her or not, but she knew that he loved her, and she loved him. She was afraid he'd go to jail for the Reverend Benson's murder if the law ever found out. They lived in abject fear until the end of Lee's life.

"The law and everyone around these parts thought that the nomad-like minister just up and drove away. Ox, Nancy, Helen, and I thought so for a long time until Lee died.

"Lee took good care of Bessie, but she took a long time to recover. Lee went further and further into depression. We could see that. There was no joy in their lives anymore; they became recluses, and few of us saw them around town. There was nothing we could say nor do for him. Bessie tried to help Lee with her own fortitude and courage, but Lee sank deeper into craziness."

"Den, Fadder, Lee done killed hiself," Bessie moaned and sobbed. The remembrance was difficult for her.

"People believed he fell into a deep mine shaft and couldn't be found," Jed said. "His body was never discovered by the company nor the law, so the sheriff ended the search and investigation."

"I don't understand, Jed," Dus questioned him. "Lee buried the preacher on the top side of the graveyard, then committed suicide by jumping into a mine shaft, and his body just sank down in there so deep that nobody could find it?"

"Yes; Lee killed himself, long after he had buried the preacher. Did I tell the story right, so far, Bessie?"

"Ya did, Jed! Ya tol' da tale right, en it is all da truff, but ya got ta tell it all, Jed," Bessie whimpered.

"Why didn't the folk who worked in the restaurant come to your house, Bessie, to see if you were ill?" Karol asked.

"Like Jed, seyd, I 'ad tol' ever'body dat I was goin' 'way ta be wid Lee while he hunted fer a job, butta I raly was goin' up ta sees da preacha 'bout my problem wid Lee. I thunk him, bein' a holy man, he cou'd help me. And then afta dat, I was so 'shamed what da Reverend Benson done to me, I din't wanna anyone ta knows ner see me. So I stayed in da bed wid my li'l daid baby till Jed foun' me."

"Didn't anyone miss the preacher?" a less angered and more compassionate Dus asked the storekeeper.

"The village people, who always thought Reverend Benson was odd, just accepted that he was a loner and a wanderer, who just left the mountain when he felt like it. I wanted everyone to believe that. We did not want anyone to know any of this, so we encouraged that story. Because Helen and I thought Bessie needed the companionship of her close friends and some shoulders to cry on, we told Ox and Nancy, and all of us together vowed to keep the secret forever. That is what we have done all these years until now. Nobody in the village, nor on the Cutty or Blue, knows about any of this. It is a sorry thing that you, Father, Karol, Patty, and Scott have to know it. You share a very dark secret with us, and it will be up to Scott to decide about my fate and where we go from here."

"You shot at me, then, hoping to stop me from digging up the minister's body? I thought you said that Lee buried the minister's body on the hill."

"Come on, Jed. Get on with the whole truth now, please," Scott admonished him.

"What whole truth?" Karol asked.

"Yes, Dus, I did shoot at you, God help me, and I am ready to take my punishment. I wanted to protect Bessie and her awful secret."

"Why? How?"

"Wh, Wh, why, Dus," Jed stammered. "Be . . . be . . . because, my friend, you we . . . you were digging up Lee's body, not the minister's, and, for Bessie's sake, I couldn't let you do that."

Everybody but Bessie was stone-cold quiet, and she was softly weeping.

"What, Jed? Lee's body was the body that Scott and I lifted out of the trench, took to the coroner, and reburied?"

"Yes, Dus, it was. Lee never jumped into any shaft at the mine. We let people believe that. He hanged himself. He hanged himself from one of the beams from this house. Bessie found him, after days of looking for him. So two people died here of their own hand, Father."

"Oh, my God." Karol shivered as she looked around the renovated home that Dus and Lou had built, with a bit less appreciation.

"There was no note, no explanation, no nothing. His shotgun stood against the wall. Lee had kicked a chair from under him, with the noose around his neck. Bessie believes with what happened to her, Lee's hate, his allowing the preacher to die, his rejection from the service, his hate for his job, and his depression, all put together, were just too much for him, and he killed himself."

"I'm so very sorry, Bessie." Dus quieted her with a strong arm around her.

Jed went on again, "Bessie came to Ox and me and asked for our help. The three of us, without Helen, Nancy, nor anyone else knowing about it, took Lee's body down and buried him with his shotgun in the grave, where you dug him up."

"Why didn't you bury him in the graveyard with the other people over there?"

"Do you want to tell him, Bessie?"

"Yeah, Jed, I will. I b'lieves I ken do dat now," Bessie said, her tears subsiding. She seemed to have regained her composure, and her face was serene as she spoke. "Ya sees, Fadder, many a usins in des pawts does b'lieve dat it be a ho'rible sin ta take yer own life. Das what da Reve'nd Benson, what hurt me so bad, tol' all us folk. Den he done it ta 'imself. All da preachas who eva we knowd told usins dat suside be sinful, en it be wrong ta bury a pawson in consocratd groun'. So I donna let Lee be buried in da church graveyaud. Ain't suside a sin, Fadder Habak? Tain't it wron' ta bury a body in da graveyaud effen dey do demselfs in like de Reve'nd Lee done?"

"It is wrong for a person to kill himself, Bessie, but God forgives that, too. We can talk about that some other time. We folk have no business deciding so many things for God all the time. Lee should be buried in the church graveyard. I'm sorry you decided that he could not be."

"We is too now, Fadder. We sho be sorry 'bout a lotta thungs now. Anyway, we buried Lee down in da front der thar war ya digged 'im up. We cove'd 'im nice wid da oilclof, put da groun' on 'im, seyd the praws, en dat's war he's be'n for twen'y y'ars er so, until ya foun' 'im. We jist taught it betta dat fo'k din't knows he done hissef in, en led dem think he died in da mine shaft war he work, and dat's all thar is to it. Butta I'ma glad yo' en Scott buried Lee in da chu'ch graveyaud now, en he have a nice place ta rest, now."

"Bessie, you have been through so much. I am so sorry we had to put you through this again," Karol said.

Dus followed her words. "Ox," he said, turning to the big man who sat in silence, his head bowed, rubbing his hands, "you and Nancy knew about Bessie and Lee, how the preacher disappeared, and Jed's involvement all along when you first met me at this house last year my first day here, didn't you? And you knew about the preacher when Karol and I discussed it with you and Nancy when we were eating at your house last fall, didn't you?"

"Yeah, we did, Dus, boy, butta we 'ad no right ta brak Bessie's ol' secrut. Ya war a stranga har, en a preacha, en we had no cause ta truss ya wid a secrut what was none a yer bus'ness den. Me en Nancy is good people, Dus, en we donna go 'bout tellin' lies 'bout 'tings. We is powaful sorry dat des happen ta ya, butta we weren't gonna have Bessie hurt no more afta al des time. She's a bless'd lady, she is, en a fren fer many yars, en we done plaged amongst oursalves, she neva gonna be hurt ag'in, but by you ner nobody erse. Nancy en me donna know nuffin 'bout Jed shootin' a tya till da udder day fer da firs' time, en we sorry he done dat to ya. We wash he haden't, butta he's our longtime frien', too, en we knows he din't mean ta hurt ya. En he din't. He jest loves Bessie lak we all does, en he dinna wanna have anyone knows 'bout dis story, eva."

"Das da truff, Fadder," Nancy said. "Me en Bessie en Jed go afar back tagather. We been frien's sunce we was li'l tikes, en des secrut was ours ta keep fereva. All usins har, Bessie, Jed, Ox, en all us, loves ya en Karol mo' den ya ken eva knows, butta we had ta see ta Bessie's need. She loved Lee so much, en as hurt sa mush ova da y'ars 'bout dat preacha en what he done ta her en his enself, we jist din't wanna have dis sorry thing brung up ag'in, fer ta hurt her. Wal, it is now, en we is so sorry, en I be'n cryin' eva sunce." She put her hanky to her nose and eyes. Karol laid Nancy's head on her shoulder and hugged her.

"Jed, you could have come to me and told me."

"I realize that now, Father, but I had promised Bessie that no one would know about Lee, ever, if I could prevent it. I have had no trust of clergy until you came along, and I never went to church again after Bessie's experience. I have been going ever since I shot at you, for good reason. And I have had a lot to talk to God about since Easter, and a lot of penance to do. Over and above that, I have learned a lot about God, Jesus, and the church from you, and I'm grateful. I have learned to love you, Father, and I am truly sorry."

"Wasn't it enough just to warn me with just a few shots at me at the backhoe, Jed? Why did you have to keep shooting at me in the house when Tooter and I were in there, and take a chance on hitting me, or me shooting you?"

"I should have known better, but I thought if I scared you enough, you would cover up Lee's body and think just some irate mountaineer didn't want you messing with a loved one's burial grounds. But you and Tooter drove off to get the sheriff. From a distance up in the woods, I watched you go and watched you come back, and I grieved over the whole mess. I was so afraid Bessie's story would get out from an investigation, and the law would accuse her of Lee's murder—maybe even the preacher's death. I watched you and Scott rebury Lee the next day over in the cemetery. I was awfully glad to see you do that, and I really believed it was all over and Bessie would be OK. None of them knew what I had done until I told them a few days ago. You might as well know, Father, I hated Reverend Benson with a passion. I wanted to kill him, myself, when I stayed with Bessie and watched over her until Lee came back. I hated that minister, his bones, his grave, his memory, and for his betrayal of those of us who trusted him, because he did such good work with the graves and built the nice church. But he abused and sorely hurt someone I cared for. He killed Lee and Bessie's baby. But he did what he did. Lee did what he did. Ox, Bessie, and I had to do what we thought was right at the time for her, Lee, and the community, right or wrong, and I live in peace with that.

"It's been twenty-some years, and Bessie has recovered. Yes, she has, but I have never had any faith in, nor fondness for, clergy after that, until you came into our lives and showed me a better side of the vocation. Anyway, after you and Scott buried Lee again, I just hoped that the affair would die— let old bones lie, so to speak—and hoped you would soon forget it and leave the whole incident alone. I really thought you had, but with Ox's accident, the moonie shoot-out, and Ox telling me that they might have tried to shoot you last fall when you first came, I was afraid you and Scott would blame the moonies for what I did, and I couldn't have that on my conscience too. Then, I also knew in my heart that Scott, being the good detective he is, would figure out that it was not the moonies. So it was time to tell the truth to Nancy, Ox, Bessie, and Helen. They love you and Karol, as I do, and they urged me to come clean with the sheriff and then with you, and then count on Scott's wisdom, and on your forgiveness. You can't know how sorry I am, Father. I betrayed our friendship, and took a chance with your life, and that's an unforgivable sin. I understand if you hate me."

"Dus Habak is not capable of hating anyone, for anything, Jed," Karol assured the storekeeper.

"I don't hate you, Jed. I was just terribly angry with you a while ago when you told me that it was you all along who shot at me. Karol and I have been so afraid for so long. We didn't know any of this. We were scared for the children, and we thought the moonies were going to hurt them. I am sorry about my anger and for swearing around these ladies I love so much. Sometimes my anger causes me to say things I hate to say as a decent man and priest. I am trying, thanks to my lovely wife, to do better with my attitude and words. I have no excuse, except that ever since I came to this mountain, and fell in love with it, you people, and Karol, all these terrible things have been happening to shake my love, efforts, and confidence."

"I know that, Father. It was stupid of me to try to dissuade you from digging up Lee by shooting at you. I just wanted to protect Bessie so much that I would have done most anything. She has recovered and done so well over these years, made Lee an honored memory in this community, is a very happy lady now, has made such a success of her restaurant, is most everyone's sweetheart, and is the grand matriarch of our town. I just couldn't, Father. I just couldn't have let her be hurt again by you or anybody; I just coul . . . coul . . . coul . . . " he stuttered.

And then big Jed Hudson, high school football star and Navy hero, Joshuatown's only homegrown college graduate, the generous and fair-minded storekeeper of his great-grandfather's HUDSON & SON COMPANY, manager of the Joshuatown food bank for the poor, bank board member, churchman, friend to everyone in the county, and lifelong protector of Bessie Clayton, sat down on the hearth of the Habak's home, put his head in his hands, and wept for the first time since he found his teenage sweetheart, Bessie Clayton, bloody, bruised, and dying in her bed with her dead baby.

Dus went to him, sat down beside him on the hearthstones, and put his arms around him. "I'm sorry, Jed," he said. "I didn't understand. If you'd only come to me. But it is over now. It's over for me, for Karol, and our children. It's over for you, Bessie, Helen, Nancy, Ox, and the community. Scott will have to make the decisions about the law, but I forgive you, and in my power as a priest, I can assure you and all our friends here, that God loves and forgives you, too. I won't press any charges against anyone, and will let this whole story and episode die right here. Your confession, Jed, and the love of all of you, our friends, have cleansed this house of Tucker Benson's life and his death. The celebration of Christ's life and death in the Eucharist in the little church beside it, where we have gathered so often, in his name, has already cleansed that terrible effrontery to Bessie's personage. That a minister could do that to a good woman—to any woman—is a tragedy, but God will judge him accordingly," Dus said, going over to Bessie. "God, Bessie, I am sure, will have already taken account of Lee's broken heart, spirit, and mind that caused him to do what he did with his life. It was not the right thing for him to do, but he was in terrible despair, and God makes his judgment by his standards, not ours. Lee thought he was doing it for you, and paid with his life. We will all go to his grave again, where Scott and I buried him, mark it properly, say the Burial Office prayers, and commend him to God for his mercy and comfort. We will also go to his and your son's grave, Bessie, dig up his little body, and bury him with Lee."

"Thank you. My son wouda have be'n a gro'n man now, Fadder," Bessie whimpered, "and wou'da be'n a fine one, runnin' da café r'al good. He's daddy wou'd a be'n proud a 'im. Butta I'm r'ady to let 'im en Lee go, now, en I knows God will forgive Lee en love 'im even mo' dan I done."

They all looked at her. Everybody in the room let his tears flow. Even Scott Kirsh, the hard-nosed city cop, but good pastoral mountain sheriff, wiped his eyes and said, "I have but one more thing to show you. It is a note that came with the shells that Lou sent me. He found it under some floorboards in this house. He added no comment of his own, except that he felt I might want the note and the shells to help solve the mystery. He also hoped that it would help his friend, Dus Habak."

"God love him," Dus added.

Scott took an old piece of paper out of his pocket, and unfolded it. "This note was written by Reverend Benson. The paper has not deteriorated much through the years. Reverend Benson appears to have been well-educated, and his penmanship is excellent. He wrote it in ink. It reads:

To whomever finds my body and this confessional letter:

I am Tucker Benson, the former owner of a building construction business. I was called many years ago by God to become a minister in his church. It does not matter where I lived nor in which denomination I was ordained.

I and many people felt I was a good minister, with a big church and large congregation. My beautiful wife was unable to bear me children because of my impotence as a husband. I cherished and loved her deeply, but she was used to our other more social and opulent kind of life, and found no joy in my ministry. She grew less fond of it, and me, as an inadequate man, and I put more and more of my time and life into my work. I could hardly blame her at the beginning, but she finally left me for another man. Our divorce was an embarrassment to me, my congregation and, of course, my church and superiors. Nobody was very happy about it. Most believed it was my fault, and never let me forget that a minister ought to be a better example to people.

I hated my wife for that, and my bitterness destroyed not only my heart and soul, but my ministry, as well. I said and did many loathsome things, and I was eventually defrocked and deposed from my church.

I was not poor, having invested the money from the sale of my former business, and had plenty of resources to support me for a very long time. I could afford to do as I wanted. So I wandered all over the world and country, doing nothing except living a riotous, self-indulgent, self-pitying, drunken, whore-filled, prodigal life. As the Bible says, "I would fain to have eaten the husks that the pigs did eat," but I had no loving father, not even God to rise up and go home to.

One night in a barroom, far from here, I met a very pretty woman, with a character not unlike my own, who was also embittered and disconsolate. We became friends, with our mutual empathy and pity, over a jigger and a bottle of good whiskey. I fell in love with her. She did not fall in love with me. One night when we were both very drunk, we made love in an expensive hotel. I wanted nothing but the best for my newest true love. It was consensual sex, but I was awakened in the morning by the police knocking on my hotel door. My true love had told them I had gotten her drunk and raped her. Maybe I did! The ensuing experience needs no telling. Suffice it to say, for my sin, I paid the lady a lot of money and spent seven long, hard, never-to-be-repeated years in jail. Where? That does not matter, either.

Thereafter, I found it easy to hate women, to become a drunk and a recluse. I had no friends, and one day I woke up in a hospital, where I spent many days recovering from the D.T.s. When I left the hospital, I swore I would never drink again, and work on becoming a better man. I became a dedicated teetotaler and celibate, bought a pickup truck, and traveled all over the country, trying to repent, reacquaint myself with humanity, and make a new start with God.

Along the way, I found this hill above Joshuatown. Because I had the experience and the knowledge, I thought I could find forgiveness from and favor with God, by using my God-given craftsman talents and all the money I had left to my soul. I decided I wanted to build this vicarage and the little church to his glory. Mr. Conley was generous in giving me this land on the condition that I would keep the adjacent cemetery in good order. I did that and, I think, very well. I bought the material for the house and church at the local mill, and other building supplies in Staunton. I brought them up here in my truck and constructed the buildings by myself. No one helped me, and I did not ask for help. From time to time, I offered religious services. I had no takers. I did not make friends easily, and I found none here. I have been a recluse here for three years now, and I have taken up the bottle again to soothe my loneliness.

Tonight, a Mrs. Clayton wandered up here seeking help about her husband. I have never seen the very alluring and pretty woman before. I had been drinking and was somewhat inebriated when she told me that her husband had left her. She was distraught, and needed someone to talk to about it. She had heard that I was a minister, and thought that a holy man would help her. She didn't know that I was no longer a holy man. Though I had been repenting my former sins for many years and built the church here to abate God's judgment upon me, I had not known a woman for years. I cannot explain nor justify it, but at that moment I did not care about Mrs. Clayton's sin, her husband, God, or the church. Her sex, her beauty, and pure innocence drove me into a frenzy of sexual insanity. I loved and hated her at the same time. My manhood had been taken away from me by my former wife and a host of cruel women. I wanted to prove I was still a man, and so I deceived the lovely creature with my spiritual counsel into washing the sin from her body in church. I cannot explain why, but I brutally beat and raped that pristine, flawless, pregnant body.

As I write this, she has crawled away from here in despair, gone to the police and her home. I am a despicable person, and there is no health in me. I have no God nor father of any kind to go home to and love me—none who would kill the fatted calf and celebrate my homecoming. I am nothing. I am not a man, but a beast. I am the prodigal son who can never return nor go anywhere but to hell. I have no right to even hope for anything—but if I could, I would hope that, perhaps, someday someone will come, consecrate these buildings to God, and, in some way, use them for the purpose for which all church buildings are intended. There is, to be sure, no salvation for me, but perhaps he will be helpful, someday, in helping others to know God and be saved. That is my only and final prayer.

Sometime, very soon, they will find Mrs. Clayton, and the sheriff will come to take me to jail. I will never go to jail again, as I have no desire to live in this world any longer, where life, at one time, was good to me, but now is lost. When they come for me, I will be dead, by my own hand. That is wrong, too, but it is the story of my life.

Whoever should find this letter, do as you please with it. I wanted someone to know. Tell Mr. Clayton I know the hate he feels for me. Tell Mrs. Clayton in my dying moments, if God will hear any prayer of mine, I will pray for her recovery of body, mind, and soul. I despise myself for the contemptible thing I did to her. It will cleanse her soul and body to hate me. Good-bye. I shall soon pass out of this wicked life into hell.

      Sincerely, Reverend Tucker O. Benson, BS, BD, DD

Scott finished reading, folded up the paper, walked to the hearth, and threw it into the fire. Everyone was quiet and watched it burn. Bessie spoke. "I donna hate Reverend Benson ner anyone. I done fineshd hating a long time ago, lest I los' ma own soul. En, Fadder, I gu'ss it is haud fer Jed en me, en ma'be fer all us here, afta ya knowin' en hearin' da secrut en da preacha's own letta, butta cou'd we go by da Reverend Benson's grave too, en say a prawr fer 'im? We mus' n't hate 'im anymo', en mus' clean our souls of da bad mem'ries. We mus' let 'im rest in peace wid on'y God's judgment, if we er gonna ta have any peace fer ourselfs."

Scott spoke again, "I want to say one more thing, my friends. And please listen closely. Patty and I have come to love this mountain and you people on it. I represent the law here, and I do the best I can to keep order.

That is my job. I hope you know that I do it with no meanness in my heart. I am a religious person, myself, and try to live my faith in my home and vocation. You are all my friends. Jed, you and Bessie are my friends, and I know that you did what you did with Dus because of your longtime friendship with Bessie. It was wrong, but you know that, and have confessed it. Dus and Karol forgive you. And so, as far as I am concerned, this whole affair is ended now, right here. We have talked, we have listened; there is no more to be done. My work on this episode is finished, and the book concerning this whole affair is, of this minute, closed. The story remains only with us, and the judgment only to God. The rest of the world will never hear it, and we shall put it to rest here; none of us will speak of it again outside this house. That shall be God's Christmas gift to us, and our gift to one another."

Dus arose and asked his friends to stand. "Please, take each other's hands and bow your heads and pray with me," Dus asked, and his friends did just that in the hue of the flaming hearth.

"Lord," Dus intoned, "hear our prayer. Forgive Lee and Tucker, and all of us, for the sins that we have committed. Fill our emptiness with love and compassion. Forgive Jed for his mistaken way of trying to help our friend Bessie, and forgive me for my anger and bad language. We thank you for the friendship of Ox, Nancy, Jed, Helen, Patty, my beautiful wife and our great physician, Karol, and for Scott, our sheriff, whose compassion and willingness to forget these bad affairs of life and circumstances is the finest of Christmas gifts to us, his friends. Thank you, too, for Lou, whose love kept a secret in his heart to his death to spare us anguish on our wedding day. Keep him in your loving arms forever. Take away our pain, frustration, and misunderstandings. Restore to us any love we may have lost for each other. Always comfort us and all the people who turn to you for mercy. With your loving arms, lift us up now that we might rejoice in the birth of your Son, stand tall and strong, go forward with smiles instead of tears, and raise up the crèche that symbolizes the coming of your Son, who came to earth at this time many years ago to show your love and forgiveness to all of us frail people, who have to keep coming back and back again seeking your understanding and forgiveness. Bless our village and all the people on this mountain, and make your love known to them. Let them see the light of that love in the torches we light on this hill tonight. And before I forget, Lord," Dus continued, "though it's hard for me to ask, help old Simon, Edna, and that grizzled turkey, Banker Brush, through their time of trial. Mend and change their souls and hearts, and give their families a new start in life. Bless the Peesys and help us to make a better life for them. In Jesus' name, we ask. Amen."

"Amen," everyone else in the room echoed.

Dus' friends were half sniffing and half laughing when he, starting with Jed, went to each one of them, where he sat or stood, helped him to his feet, hugged him, kissed him, and told him he loved him. When he came to Karol, he whispered that hugging her just now wasn't enough, and he had a special message for her later in the evening. She told him she had one for him, too. "Now," he said, "all of you, my friends, sip your last glass of hot cider, put on your coats, and let's go out and put up the crêche so this whole mountain will be reminded that Christ is coming."

They proceeded to do that by raising the walls of the crêche, spreading straw, propping up the Nativity figures, and lighting all the tiki torches. Having finished, admiring their work, they all said good night and thank you to one another, and went back to their homes.

"So, my husband, what is that special message you have for me?" Karol asked as their friends left them in the quiet and peace of the night.

"Well, it is not so much a message as it is a nice reminiscence of last year when we stood here in this very place, not knowing what to do with our budding love. So, now, we Indians, sometimes homesick for our mountains, reservations, farms, and Christmases of the past, are going to walk hand in hand down to the curve of the road, where we were last year, turn around, hold each other tightly, look up here, and thank God for this mountain, these people, and their love. My soul has been cleansed tonight, my dearest wife, and I am a happy man again. I see no more clouds hanging over our love. For the first time since I have known you, there is no more mystery, there is no more threat to us and our children, and there is nothing but romance and the good life ahead."

As they looked up at the crêche that lighted up the whole sky, they kissed and thanked God. Karol spoke, "I love you, Father Habak, for what you said and did up in that house tonight. It was terribly painful for you. It was painful for all of us. I think it took a lot of courage for Jed to stand there in front of us and tell us that horrible story. It is unbelievable what he and Bessie went through so long ago, as is the secret they've kept in their hearts and souls all these years. But notwithstanding your anger and cussing, your prayer, your compassion, your willingness to forgive, your hugging and kissing us all, and your leading us out to build the crêche not only purified the vicarage and drove away whatever evil that was committed or remaining there, but consecrated it as our home to the glory of God. It was the most wonderful Christmas present you could have given me."

She soundly kissed him on the mouth. "Well, that's certainly better than the little platonic peck on the cheek you gave me last year," he kidded. "I felt, at the time, like the boy whose girlfriend invited him into her bedroom for a glass of ginger ale!"

Karol giggled. "You are so funny sometimes, Father Habak. Anyway, a lot has transpired since then, so why don't we go up there to the crêche with the baby Jesus, Mary and Joseph, kings, camels, donkeys, and sheep, and I will give you the Christmas gift I told you about in the house."

"I don't like to open gifts before Christmas. I am old-fashioned that way."

"I am too, but this can't wait. You can't open it, anyway. I just want you to take a peek. The old Scrooge in you is going to have to make an exception just for the night."

They walked up the hill and stood before the crêche.

"Now show me your gift in the light of these torches, so I can see if it as lovely as the diamond ring I gave you last summer."

"It is more beautiful than all the diamonds, gold, frankincense, and myrrh in the world."

"Show me then."

"Are you sure now that you want to peek at it before Christmas?"

"Yes; you convinced me now, so don't keep me in suspense."

"OK, but first let me tell you that Terry, Patty, and Nancy helped me with it."

"That's nice. They are good friends. Now quit stalling and show me."

"Well, I can show you only a little of it now, and tell you about the rest of the package that will come later."

"What, for goodness sake?"

She smiled into his eyes. "Give me your hand. I know that you can hardly notice, but feel!" She took his hand and pressed one into her blossoming breasts and one to her bulging midriff. "You shall, by the grace of God and good health, become the fine father of Louis Oxford or Teresa Nancy Habak, or both at the same time, close to our wedding anniversary on June twenty-eighth next year!"

"You're kidding? Oh, gosh, gosh—you mean you're pregnant? I'm going to be a father? You're going to be a mother? Elly and Shawn are going to have a brother or a sister, or both? Oh, my gosh, Kara! Are you all right? How do you know? Terry, Patty, and Nancy know, don't they?"

"Yes to all the above, Father, who is a father-to-be. Terry went with me to see my doctor in Staunton the first time. Nancy and Patty went with me to see her the second time. The third time, I went by myself. On the fifth time, my obstetrician, Dr. Margaret Champion, thought she could hear two heartbeats, and said we might have twins. It is too early to tell. I am sure God will let us know in due time, and we will love whatever baby or babies he gives us."

"Oh, sweetheart. Thank you. Thank you for the greatest of Christmas gifts. Do the kids know?"

"You're welcome; and no, they don't know. Elly asked me once why I have been so icky in the morning and getting hefty. Maybe she suspects. I'm going to give you the pleasure of telling them both on Christmas Day. Oh, yes, Father, I think I ought to thank you for this gift, too. You had a lot to do with it, you know. But I was surprised that you didn't know I was icky in the morning and getting hefty."

"Because you always look beautiful and healthy to me. I'm so happy, Kara. I thank you, I thank me, and I thank God. Wonderful! Wonderful!" He looked at the wood images in the crèche of Mary, Joseph, and Baby, through the flickering light, and added, "Thank you, Jesus!"

"Dus?" she said, looking solemnly at her husband.

"Yes, Kara?"

"You should know, as we stand here, that our baby or babies were conceived on the night of Lou's death, in the lodge of your hometown. That is why I wanted you to make love to me in the midst of our sorrow. I knew that I was ovulating then. When Lou left this earthly life, I wanted very much to replace his life with a new life for you. It was in my arms you found your comfort that night. It was while you were in my arms that your life poured into me; and together, we gave Lou to God for all eternity and replaced him with one or two new lives here on earth. I believe in my heart that Lou would have approved of that. Terry believes that too, and we both believe that God will love the exchange."

"I love you for that, Kara," Dus whispered to her.

She looked at the images of Mary gazing at her Baby and husband in the crèche, and said, "I love you, my husband, for making me a mother again. I would not be so presumptuous as to compare it with the greatness, majesty, beauty, and significance of what happened to the world on that perfect night two thousand years ago, depicted in the symbolism and imagery we see and feel here, but I can certainly feel, this night, as Mary did. I, too, am 'blessed among women.'"

They sat there in the straw for half an hour or so until they heard a chorus of voices coming up the path singing, "Angels we have heard on high, singing sweetly o'er the plains . . ."

They stood up and turned around. It looked as though everyone on the mountain—Jed, Helen, Bessie, Ox, Nancy, Scott, and Patty, leading them—had seen the light of the crêche and was coming to pay tribute. They smiled at each other and walked down the hill to join the singing, then returned with the people to the crêche to watch. Then everyone, with no leadership, no instruments, burst into carols, and the melodic voices thundered and rolled over the mountains. Two American Indians, a man and his wife, in those mountains wept for joy; a baby in the womb of the woman leaped for joy; and God, Ginnie, Dusty, and Lou, looking down from heaven, smiled.

# Epilogue: The Dust File

1. On Christmas Day, Shawn and Elly, along with their other Christmas gifts, learned that Santa Claus and the Stork would be coming down the chimney sometime in June to drop off a baby sister or brother, or both. They were thrilled with the present, but definitely thought it was time to tell their parents that their teenage kids already knew how babies were made, carried, and delivered. But if their parents wanted to continue believing in the Santa Claus and Stork myths, it was OK by them.
2. On January 6, the Feast of the Epiphany, Dus had a church service celebrating the coming of the Magi, the wise men and/or kings, bringing gifts from the East to the manger of the Christ Child. Not many folk had come to the service, but among those who did were Karol and Patty, who snuggled together in the cold church. Karol went to Communion. When she returned, she found Patty in prayer and tears. After the "Amens," Patty hugged her best girl buddy and asked her if she could talk to her about something very special.

    "Of course, Patty, but if this is a confession, maybe it is something that you should talk to your Catholic priest about."

    "It's not a confession. It is something between wives and mothers for now. These are tears of joy, not woe. I just want to tell you that as we celebrate the Epiphany, a very wise man, a sweet cop, husband, and father, gave me the most priceless of all Christmas gifts."

    "Well, hurry up and tell me before my caring hubby comes out of the sacristy and sees you in tears," Karol nearly shouted at her cherished friend.

    "A baby, Karol. We're going to have a baby, too. I will be following you into the maternity floor at Staunton Memorial around July twentieth."

    Karol wiped the tears from Patty's cheek, and her own baby seemed to again leap in her womb for joy.
3. By January 15, the new bank manager who succeeded Mr. Brush was a retired Navy finance officer and a friend of Jed Hudson. Obvious nepotism aside, an old sitting member of the Staunton National Bank Board,

the same Jed Hudson, nominated Bessie Clayton, a respected Joshuatown businesswoman, as a sitting member of that same bank board. She accepted the nomination with humility and was elected unanimously.

4. By January 30, Scott Kirsh suggested to Father Habak that it would be practical, convenient, pastoral, and even prudent if he opened a checking and saving's account at the Joshuatown subsidiary of the Staunton National Bank for his wife, children, and himself. Father Habak did that, and Bessie Clayton and Jed Hudson seemed to be pleased with that wise decision.

5. By February 3, Simon Shoney, his wife, Edna, Banker Raymond Brush, and other fellow conspirators were tried and found guilty of manufacturing federally controlled substances without a license. Sheriff Scott Kirsh and Father Habak refused to press charges of endangerment, and appealed to the court on their behalf, to just heavily fine the offenders, put them on five years' probation, and exact a pledge from them that they would never again build a moonshine still in the county—under the certain penalty that if they did, they would go to jail for a minimum of five years.

6. By February 11, Simon Shoney, a repentant former moonie and bootlegger, returned to his barbershop to cut Dus' and Scott's hair with considerable precision and aplomb. Edna, his retired and long-suffering wife, became his business partner, and the shop was suddenly cleaner and more decorous than it had been in many years.

7. By February 10, Mr. Raymond Brush, former manager of the Joshuatown subsidiary of the Staunton National Bank, was gainfully employed as the new groundskeeper and treasurer at the compassionate and humanitarian First Universalist Church of Staunton, where he worked out some of the conditions of his probation. He did that work with considerable zeal in his heart and joy in his soul, knowing he would not be cutting poison ivy and trimming sumac bushes on the Virginia Interstate Highway median strips under the watchful eye of a Virginia State Prison guard.

8. By Ash Wednesday and Lent, a goodly number of people attended services. Dus spent every day in church, repenting his anger and bad language over the past year, and thanking God for his wife, children, and friends, and for the joy he was now finding in his mountain ministry.

9. By Palm Sunday, the tiny bones of little Lee Clayton, Jr., were exhumed and laid to rest with his father's remains in a single grave.

10. On Easter, after almost 100 people came to church to celebrate Christ's

Resurrection, a very small assembly of intimate friends with a heavy secret in their hearts went to the cemetery by the church. There, Father Habak consecrated the graves of Lee Clayton and his son, and the Reverend Tucker Benson with appropriate prayers for each, and then set upon them appropriately inscribed memorials made of mountain limestone.
11. By April 1, Mrs. Jakey Peesy was gainfully employed as a kitchen aide at Bessie's Café. She, her husband, and children were now neatly attired in new clothes and looking healthy. Her children were in school under the wise supervision of Patty Kirsh. Jakey Peesy, who had a new shelter for Jenny, was gainfully employed by HUDSON & SON COMPANY as a mule skinner and gofer, working very hard under the strict work ethic of big Oxford Conley, the new lumberyard manager for HUDSON & SON COMPANY.
12. On May 18, Dr. Habak requested a six-month leave of absence from Staunton Memorial Hospital, and was granted it with best wishes and love from the administrators, doctors, and staff.
13. By May 30, under the auspices and hard work of Oxford Conley, Father Habak, Dr. Habak, Sheriff Kirsh, Patty Kirsh, Jed Hudson, Helen Hudson, Bessie Clayton, Cyrus Gruber, Jenny Gruber, Jakey Peesy, and Tooter, Mrs. Nancy Conley had a new bathroom and kitchen with running water and electricity. On that same day, with grateful smiles and joyful utterances, she hugged and kissed all the workers, then demurely announced that Jenny and Cyrus Gruber were going to make her and Ox grandparents again, sometime between the delivery time of Karol and Patty. The new facilities in the house "jist come in time, en itta be nice fer da younguns wid da new li'l one." No one told her that most everybody could tell that Jenny was going to have a baby, and that was the very reason that all of them had quickly pitched in to be sure the new facilities were in place for the occasion. Nancy added, "Wal be nice fer me en Ox en da chil'ren, too, donna ya knows, en I thanks ya en da Lo'd so mush fer it." While all wiped their eyes, Ox said, "I thanks ya, too! We be'n needin' dis fer alon time fer my Nan!" Tooter sniffed around the kitchen and slurped a drink out of the new commode.
14. On June 4, Ellen Habak was invited to her first school prom by her classmate, Shawn Marson. She was thrilled. She got a new dress, and he got a new suit, provided by the same parents. They left the same house together for the prom and returned to the same house together after it,

and their parents gave both Shawn and Elly permission for one kiss before they went to bed in separate rooms in the same house. The teenage brother and sister thought that their kind of dating was fun, convenient, economical, and "cool." They also thought it would be cool to do it again sometime, but it would also be, as it was in their in-house living arrangements, under the very close observation and supervision of a priest and physician. Elly and Shawn had already become accustomed to that, but conspired that sometime in the future they would have to find a way around snoopy parents. In the meantime, they could always babysit together.

15. On June 28, on the very day, if not the very hour of their first wedding anniversary, the Reverend and Mrs. Dus Habak announced the healthy arrival of Teresa Nancy Habak, who was preceded, by three minutes and twenty seconds, by the arrival of her little brother, Louis Oxford Habak. Both were sixteen inches long and weighed five pounds, fifteen ounces. Mother, daughter, and son were all doing fine. Father Habak, the priest, was smiling, bragging, and handing out Hershey's chocolate bars with blue and pink boy/girl wrappers—as an alternative to cigars—like a clever and earthy father should, so that "Proud Daddy" largess could be handed out to women and children, as well as to men.

16. On July 23, Nancy Jennifer Gruber, the granddaughter of Oxford and Nancy Conley, was born very suddenly, during Father Habak's Sunday sermon, to Jenny and Cyrus Gruber at the Joshuatown clinic, under the expert medical supervision of a very pregnant nurse, Patty Kirsh, and a forlorn, worn mother, Dr. Habak. Dr. Habak, suffering from postpartum blues, a protruding tummy, and weary, grandiose bosoms, which she blamed on a set of voracious twins, sat on a chair, holding Jenny's hand and saying, "Hold your breath and push, honey, and be glad it won't be twins you have to feed and diaper!"

17. On August 17, Karol Lynn Kirsh was born to Sheriff and Mrs. Scott Kirsh at the Joshuatown clinic instead of Staunton Memorial, because her parents believed that Dr. Habak could provide immediate obstetric and delivery expertise. In that way, they could also have their baby close to their friends. The baby, mother, sibling, and detective all did well. The sheriff, without much class in Dus' estimation, didn't hand out Hershey bars. He handed our McGruff Crime Stopper and Smoky Bear badges. The new little Kirsh was baptized six weeks later in Saint Paul's Catholic Church in Staunton, with all the Kirsh's mountain friends wit-

nessing the event and snapping photos.
18. On September 1, at the little church on the Blue, Nancy Conley, Bessie Clayton, Teresa Casalano, Jed and Helen Hudson, Patty and Scott Kirsh, and Julie and J.K. Stewart all became the godparents of the new Christian babies named Terry, Lou, and Nancy, and the baptismal sponsors of one huge-bewhiskered, one-legged, newly baptized adult by the name of Oxford Conley, who grumbled when the holy water ran down into his beard. Tooter, who tooted no more, became the new babies' assigned protector.
19. By September 8, Bishop and Mrs. Mueller, and as many invited people who could come, joined in to consecrate the new church that he named "The Church of the Mediator on the Mountain," with Father Habak instituted as its new vicar. It was at the reception that the good bishop announced that the Standing Committee of the Diocese had approved of and appropriated the funds for the complete renovation of the old mission church, and the project would begin in the spring.

At 2:00 P.M. of the same day, Bishop Mueller told Father Habak that Canon Burkey had resigned his position as assistant to the bishop to accept a call as rector of a parish church. Then, in the presence of the new vicar's wife, Father Habak was offered Canon Burkey's former position in the diocese.

At 2:05 P.M. of the same day, Ollikut Habak glared at the bishop and her husband, and was about to growl an expletive, when Dus, anticipating her, said, "Thank you, Bishop, for the nice offer, but I am staying as vicar here until the day I am 'ushered into the Kingdom,' laid to rest in that cemetery next door, and my wife does her war dance around my grave during the burial office." Karol smiled at them both, and the bishop said, "I understand your decision, Father Habak, and I don't blame you, with a hostile Indian lady throwing buffalo knives at us with her eyes."
20. On October 1, Dr. Habak resigned from Staunton Memorial Hospital and became a full-time Federal Physician employee of HEW and the administrator/physician in charge of the Joshuatown HEW clinic. On that same day, Patty Kirsh became a part-time nurse employee of HEW, working for Dr. Habak.
21. On October 15, Jed Hudson, Helen Hudson, and Bessie Clayton, the new partners and underwriters of the Lee Clayton Memorial Child Care Center (a pay-only-if-you're-able service), moved a monstrous mobile home

right in beside the clinic, and hired Nancy Conley and Jenny Gruber to manage it. Patty's and Karol's babies were the first full-time paying attendees, with Jenny's two children attending as one of her employment perks.

22. By October 20, at the end of his two years of being a mountain man, priest, pastor, husband, and dad, Father Habak renewed his commitment as a priest. He vowed he was done with his past life of pain, grief, anger, and bitterness, and would walk faithfully with the Lord and his dog, Tooter, in the valleys and hills of his parish, serving God and shepherding his sheep in the very best way that his modest priestly abilities would allow.

23. By Advent of that same year, just before Christmas, for ten evenings, several hundreds of people of all denominations came by the Mediator Christmas Crêche to sing carols, pray, and just watch the glory of it all. Some of the mountain people brought a couple of live sheep, goats, calves, chickens, and a real donkey, to give the scene a more realistic quality. It was beautiful!

24. On Christmas Eve, Father and Mrs. Habak looked out of the vicarage window at the crowd at the crêche and noticed some familiar adult faces with their children, standing together but apart from the rest of the people, holding small wrapped packages in their hands. He asked Karol to go with him to greet them. They put on their coats and rushed out to the little band. Dus smiled. Karol grinned tentatively.

"Hello, Father and Dr. Habak," said Raymond and Mrs. Brush, Simon and Edna Shoney, and Jakey and Mrs. Peesy, almost in unison.

"Welcome, friends," Dus said, greeting them.

Mr. Brush spoke for them all. "We have come to bring you Christmas presents, to thank you, and to ask you to forgive us. We are sorry for the pain we caused you, and any insults that may have embarrassed you, and we want you to know that we believe you to be very good and caring people. You have been more than fair and kind to us, considering our transgression against you. Si and I stopped by Jakey's place to apologize to him and to bring him and his family up here to see this scene. He and his wife have forgiven us, and they wanted to come. The crêche was beautiful, as we saw it from afar last year, but we were afraid to come by. It seems even more beautiful tonight as we approached it, and as we now stand here. It is a new light of hope and forgiveness for us, and while we do not expect friendship from either of you for the terrible distress we have brought upon you, we hope that perhaps the Christmas Spirit of the Almighty will allow you to accept our offerings of friendship and prayers for your peace and happiness. Thank you."

"He speaks for us all, Father," Edna said. With no further words, they gave their little gifts to the priest and doctor, turned, and went to stand before the crèche.

Karol looked lovingly into her husband's eyes and winked, and Dus called to them. "Wait; please come back!"

They returned to where he and Karol stood, and Dus spoke, "My wife and I thank you for the gifts, for coming here tonight, and for the things you said. Our hearts are full, so our words will be few. We do forgive you for what has happened in the past. We accept you no longer as our antagonists, but as our friends, and we wish all of you and your children a very blessed, merry Christmas, and a very healthy and happy New Year."

Then he and Karol went from one person to another in the group, including the children, and hugged every one of them. Tears flowed, of course, but happy faces indicated peace and reconciliation. It was probably exactly what God wanted on Christmas Eve.

25. On Christmas Day, the church was full of people who prayed mightily, sang lustily, and talked happily. Having wished each a merry Christmas, they all returned to their homes for Christmas dinner and an afternoon of special family times. The Habaks, with their children, had opened their presents before services, but Karol and Dus had waited to open the small gifts from Mr. Brush and friends. The Peesys had made them a little hand-carved cross, accompanied by a very primitive handwritten note from Mrs. Peesy indicating that the little cross was just a replica of the big one that he wanted to hand-aze for the renovated church. Dus smiled, nodded his head, and said, "Yes, Jakey; thank you!" The other was from Simon and Edna Shoney. It was a note that offered their services, to come up to the church every night after the carpenters did the work on the church, and clean it up for the next day. Again, Dus nodded his head and said, "Yes, Simon and Edna, thank you!" He would deliver his gratitude and acceptance later in the week. The third gift, from Mr. and Mrs. Brush, contained a bank check for 3,000 dollars, with a note that Father Habak could use it at his own discretion for anything he needed in refurbishing the sanctuary. He was encouraged by his wife to spend it on much-needed organ repair. Included in the note was a rather long letter of repentance, contrition, and amendment of life. It

was a sincere letter, and both he and Karol rejoiced in its content. He also wanted to thank them for not destroying his life, and wanted to tell them that the bank, also out of compassion, had taken him back, and he was now working as a consultant and teller in the main bank in Staunton. Not much pay, but he rejoiced in the opportunity to start his life over again. His wife wanted to also convey her thanks and best wishes. They hoped the Habaks would have a very nice Christmas and a prosperous New Year in the church. Mr. Brush also told Dus that he realized the "Clergy only work on Sunday" joke was inane, that Dus did "seem to be getting a lot of action for his efforts," and that he should not be surprised if a "Universalist" took a fresh look at the traditional Anglican Church on the mountain. He added that never again will he make fun of doctors and priests talking together for the betterment of the society and world, and never again would he be ill-mannered around ladies, especially a very distinguished, beloved, and respected professional lady like Dr. Habak. He ended by saying that he knew they appreciated the donation to the church, but he would be pleased if they neither thanked him nor made mention of it to anyone else. Karol and Dus smiled at each other and, together said, "Thank you, Mr. Brush; and thank you, too, Lord!"

26. On New Year's Day, Dus made no resolutions, saving them for his Lenten intent. He did, however, take Karol and the children to Ginnie and Dusty's graves to introduce them all. Standing together in that quiet place, the family prayed, wept, laughed, and made plans to go to Oregon in the summer to visit Karol's family, friends, and her deceased husband's and Shawn's father's graves.

Seven weeks after New Years, on the first day of Lent, Dus made the following resolutions and vows, that:

1. He would pray and read his Bible more, do more acts of charity, and be more loving toward, and patient with, all God's children, including himself.
2. He would try harder not to tell bishops, when they complained about how hard the work of the Episcopacy is, that "He or she who seeks the office, deserves it!"
3. He would no longer allow himself to be drawn into any further arguments about women's ordination to the priesthood. He just didn't

believe anymore, in the heated arena of the "equality" debates, that he could convince anyone in or outside the holy church that, though he loved, admired, and respected women beyond measure and believed them to be the crowning achievement of God's handiwork, the whole subject of ordination was an issue of historical theology, not equality. Anyway, in reality, since women won the vote to be ordained priests at the summer General Convention of the Episcopal Church, it was now only an academic question. They were now being ordained, and Bishop Mueller, having cast his vote in a "politically incorrect" way, was being reminded by the priory sisters that "they had won over his 'live' body, and not his dead one." The trade-off with Karol was that if she did not bring up the subject anymore, he would never again refer to her as a "squaw," "Injun" nor "redskin" if she promised, in return, to quit calling him "preacha," "pawson," "fadder," "rev," and "Pastor Dust!" He also resolved, since he and his wife had done enough osculating to guarantee their status as prince and princess, rather than frogs, he would abstain from calling her "Ollikut" except when he was sorely exhausted with her protracted Indian bantering.

4. He'd put $50.00 in the "money can" at the Joshuatown clinic for the Clayton Child Care Center and go to confession every time he took the Lord's name in vain, no matter the provocation. He would put $100.00 in the money can if he ever put a cigarette in his mouth again, and Karol would put $50.00 in the money can if she ever again called him "a fifteen-karat, gold-plated, weed-sucking dipstick."
5. He would never do detective work again without Scott Kirsh's request, nor mess with animals of the forest without Ox Conley's instruction, nor go into any caves without J.K. Stewart's companionship. He would humbly consider himself, in recognition of those three friends' expertise, a mere neophyte in criminal investigation, forestry, and spelunking. In return, they would never argue with him about theological matters about which they knew nothing.
6. He would again never say "mare's marbles" anywhere near the cocked and critical ears of the "know-how-to-cuss-more-effectively" experts, Dr. Karolina Habak and Sheriff Scott Kirsh, if they promised not to say "pony turds" and "horse shit" around him. If he was going to clean up his act, they had to clean up theirs.
7. He never again would drink any spirits but a beer when he was hot or vintage wine when he was supping with Karol and/or a friend. He

would tell Scott Kirsh to quit annoying him with that worn-out expression, "Where there are three or four Episcopal priests gathered together, there was generally a fifth."
8. He would try harder this year than all the previous years to keep all these New Year's and Lenten resolutions and vows, and not to succumb to his heretofore favorite vow, to "Never say never." If, however, he caught himself backsliding, he would be most diligent about resolution number one.
9. He would remember, with fond affection, his father's favorite adages and institute them in his mountain ministry. To wit:

- "One's ignorance is seconded only by his/her unwillingness to learn."
- "Be a good listener. Always consider what other people have to say to you. If it is true, it is interesting. If it's not true, it is still interesting."
- "If you make a mistake, don't submit an Excuse for a Reason."
- "Remember that the 'green grass on the other side of the fence' that so tantalizes the envious is fertilized with the same old B.S. that fertilizes the grass on this side of the fence."
- "Trying to keep up with the Joneses is a sojourn in futility. It's chore enough to keep up with the relatives with your same name."
- "Being married, birthing, rearing children, getting along with one's family and peers, and appreciating the 'Golden Years' ain't for the fainthearted!"
- "You're neither as good nor as bad as you think you are, nor as your critics think you are."
- "Other people will seldom believe you're much smarter than the last stupid thing they heard you utter."
- "It is gospel truth that God loves a cheerful giver, but he really appreciates a gracious and grateful receiver."
- "Don't be a Christian who lives one hundred and sixty-eight hours a week receiving from God and thinks     it is a big sacrifice to give him back an hour a week of worship in his church."
- "It is easy to give God back ten percent of what he gives you, if you take it off the top!"
- "Don't get mad at God. He's the best friend you'll ever have, who will never harm you and who will love you after you make your worst mistakes."

And remember this old truth about bigotry:

- "If you hate me because I'm ignorant, I have a duty to educate myself. If you hate me because I'm dirty, I have a duty to take a bath. If you hate me because I'm ill-behaved, I have a duty to correct my manners. If you hate me because I'm unloving, then I have a duty to take needed lessons on how to love. BUT, if you hate me because of my nationality, my gender, the length of my body, the size of my feet, my homely face, my birth infirmities, or the color of my skin, hair, or eyes, then I can only refer you to my ancestors and Almighty God who made me this way."

10. He would pray to God daily, "Accept my thanks, Lord, for all of your many blessings on me and mine, and for sending this unworthy shepherd to these gorgeous mountains, where I was able to expel the goblins of the past, find a new life and good wife in my vocation, and find friendly folk to share them with. Please help me to be truthful, courageous, and loving to all of your people. Help me to be a good example to your flock, and to work very hard for them, my family, and you. Help me to be patient, control my temper, and keep my language pure, that I may not be an offense to anyone. Please, Lord, keep my precious wife, children, friends, and all of your people here in this 'little acre' of yours, and everywhere in your Kingdom, safe and faithful to you. Help us here to help feed the hungry, clothe the poor, shelter the homeless of the world, and bring your sheep back into your Fold. And, Lord, please don't ever allow me to go down this mountain, seeking to go up higher in your church. Finally, Lord, please, I humbly beg you, never ask me again to, nor ever let me, 'SHAKE OFF THE DUST' and move on to another place. Amen."